"Today's dreams are the stories of tomorrow."

Worlds of the Crystal Moon: The Tear of Gramal
View high-def maps of the Worlds of the Crystal Moon
www.WorldsoftheCrystalMoon.com

Phillip "Big Dog" Jones' Facebook fan page:
www.facebook.com/worldsofthecrystalmoon

The language of the Elves acquired on the web from English to Elvish translators.

Author: Phillip E. Jones
The author has dedicated this novel to his sons: Christopher and Chase Jones

Principal Editor: William Zavatchin - **William@worldsofthecrystalmoon.com**
Assistant Editor: Christopher Salisbury - **Christopher@worldsofthecrystalmoon.com**

Library of Congress Control Number: 2012951863
Library of Congress Cataloging-in-Publication Data
First published in 2010 under ISBN — 978-1-939116-03-1

Appropriate for readers
of advanced seasons
13 and older.
Parental Guidance Suggested
Violence
Mild Language
Mild Suggestive Content

Printed in the United States of America
10 9 8 7 6 5 4 3 2

Project funded by NWQ Ventures-Bryant Hayward
Published by:
WOTCM Media, LLC, Las Vegas, Nevada

Printed by: Worzalla Publishing Co., Stevens Point, WI
866.523.7737

From the day I was introduced to the "Worlds of the Crystal Moon" I was enthralled. When you've been in the business as long as I have, it doesn't take long to recognize real talent and a writer gifted with that rare ability to create a compelling world that not only entertains, but profoundly touches the heart, mind and soul. The Worlds of The Crystal Moon is such a story. I implore all of you to enter and explore this powerful and magical story which will stir and inspire your imagination for generations to come.

Richard Hatch (Apollo – Battlestar Galactica)
Actor, Writer, Director and Producer

Thanks to the Worlds of the Crystal Moon Artists

Todd Sheridan - Cover
sheridan.todd@gmail.com

Cindy Fletcher - Ultorian King
cinfl37@yahoo.com

Kathleen Stone - Inside Color and Black and White Illustrations
www.kastone-illustrations.com

Aaron Bristow- Coin Designer
aaronshardwork@gmail.com

Shamand (Bumps)
The Leader of the Isorian Army

Clandestiny and **Medolas**

Shiver

Sagar (Slips)

Gablysin [Gab-ly-**sin**]
The Ruby Eyed Man

Thoomar [Thoo-**mar**]
The Leader of the Isorian Counsel

Blandina [Blan-**dee**-na]

Fosalia [Fo-sa-**lia**]
The High Priestess of Harvestom

Kepler and **George**

Mosley

The United Kingdoms of Southern

Temple of the Gods

Springs of Grayham

Griffin Cliffs

Temple Platform

Griffin Falls

Latsky Divide

Siren's Song

Lake Blood

Blood River

War

Dark Forest

Pool of Sorrow

Angel

Angel's Crossing

River of Death

Enchanted Forest

Ocean of Mall089

Neutral Territory

Minotaur Hills

Champion

Latsky River

Bear Clan

Zandra

Scorpion Island

Zander River

Lake Zandra

Cottle

Lake Cottle

Poison River

Serpent City

Snake River

Carlosam

Territory of Serpents

Grayham

Blood Sea

BLOODVAIN

Blood Sea

Isthmus of Change

Territory of Bloodvain

Cat Plains

Change

Bloodvain River

Lake Latasef

Latasef

Cave of Sorrow

Gessler Village

Skeleton Pass

City View

Pass of Tears

Sorrow's Release

Mts. of Latasef

The Iron Chains

Lethwitch

Mountain View

East Utopia

Lethwitch Platform

Cliffs of Latasef

Territory of Brandor

Ocean of Utopia

West Utopia

Brandor River

Empire

Lake Brandor

Merchant Island

Cripple River

Penninsula of Prosperity

Cottle River

Brandor Platform

Haven

South Utopia

N

W   E

S

BRANDOR

Ocean of Utopia

Northern Grayham

Toldes

Dyan

Malla

Shedris

GESPER

Sea of Gesper

The Kingdoms of the Ice Kings

Home of the Ko-dess

Pass of Nayala

Esliep

Lake Nea

Nivrat

The Caves of Carne

Nestie

Polid

Meslan

Mols

Colath

Jene

Ged

HYDROTH

Ocean of Utopia

Mountains of Tedfer

Cave of No Return

Edsmar

Ibble

Auacia

Blood Sea

Isthmus of Change

Village of Crossing

N
W E
S

Western Luvelles
Lands of Kerkinn

Grogger's Swamp

City of Loss

Folon

Lake Bright

Kingdom of Hyperia

Lake Teza

Ocean of Volfon

Lake Colop

Hyperia

Lake Id

City of Froland

The Void Maze

Bestep

Lake Cull

Petrified Forest

Lake Iple

Mountains of Vesper

Lake Kallif

Lake Floren

Floren

Shade Hollow

Fairy Kingdom

Eastern Luvelles
Doridelven

Merchant
Island

The Hills of
Matba

Lake
Hedrog

*Forest of
Arolc*

Plains of
Morrell

Island of
Tarian

Ocean of Ayregan

Big Malpon River

Lake Jespon

Mountains of
Oodaran

Gulf of
Larlac

• Specks

Little Malpon River

Big Malpon River

Lake
Goldawn

Merchant
Island

Kingdom of
Tagdrendlia

Woods of
Tagdrendlia

Solain
Sea

Ancients Sovereign

Plains of
Bounty

Hosseff's Garden

Sylvan
Spirits

Allistar's
Home

Calla's
Home

Lake
Dimshore

Plains of
Redemption

Yaloom's
Home

The
Barren
Lands

Meionus's
Home

Lectina's
Home

Falls of
Divinity

Peaks of Angels

Valley of
Tunasia

Lake
Divinity

Jervaise's
Home

Lake
Gavel

Bassorine's
Cabin

Lash
Valley

Catalyst
Mountain
Range

Mountains
of Leandra

Bailem's
Aubade

Orchard of
Nasha

Lake
Fairdale

Owain's
Cave

Falls of
Faith

The Book's
Hall of
Judgement

Verm Forest

Keylom's
Home

Sea of
Bragondesh

Mountains
of Niyesh

Forest of
Tradaine

Helmep's Home

N
W   E
S

Dragon World,

Cliffs of Saybless

Feeding
Grounds

Falls of
Drazule

Home of the tiny
Ice Dragons

Mountains of
Grosingdan

Merchant
Island

Island of the
Source

Feeding
Grounds

Dragonto
Reef

Shaymlezman

Feeding
Grounds

Tewtalon
Forest

Mountains of
Dedlion

Mountains of
Farrowmore

Mountains of
Bargesstain

Mountains of
Shovaneer

Lake
Scaleion

Feeding
Grounds

Mountains of
Carondawn

Temple of
the Gods

Mountains of
Sheplestawn

N
W • E
S

Dragonia
The New Hell

Marshlands of
Gilladia

Plains of Errod

White Demon
Territory

Red Demon
Territory

Dragon Tears
Tar Pools

Island of Sajor

Dragon's Backbone

Ocean of
Karamoore

Green Demon
Territory

Mountains
of Gannesh

Home of the Vampire
King and Queen

Mainland
Dragonia

Merchant
Island

Criminal
Stronghold

Forest of
Pordrilian

Temple of
the Gods

N
W   E
S

Glossary

Dawn
The moment when the sun rises just above the horizon.

Morning
Period of the day between Dawn and Early Bailem.

Early Bailem
When the sun has reached the halfway point between the horizon and its highest point in the sky, the Peak of Bailem.

Peak of Bailem
The moment when the sun has reached its highest point.

Late Bailem
The moment when the sun has passed the Peak of Bailem and taken a position halfway between the Peak of Bailem and when the sun disappears behind the horizon.

Evening
The moments between Late Bailem and when the sun is about to disappear behind the horizon.

Night
The moments after the sun has disappeared behind the horizon until it once again rises and becomes Dawn.

Midnight
An estimated series of moments that is said to be in the middle of the night.

———————————————— SEASON or SEASONS ————————————————
There are different uses for the words *season* and *seasons*.

Season
The common meaning referring to winter, spring, summer, and fall.

Seasons
People can refer to their ages by using the term *season* or *seasons*. For example: if someone was born during a winter season, he or she would become another season older once they reach the following winter. They are said to be so many winter seasons old.

TABLE OF CONTENTS

CHAPTER 1
TRAVELING COMPANIONS

The peak of the most treacherous mountain on Northern Grayham was just ahead, and beyond, the frigid lands of the Isorian King covered a vast territory.

Mosley stopped his ascent. He took a moment to admire his surroundings. The valley below the path he was standing on was an undulating sea of white that extended as far as the eye could see. The snowfall from the night before had become another hardened layer and added to the daunting task of climbing to the summit.

The night terror wolf took a deep breath. Though his magic was protecting him, the bite in the air was becoming more severe as he approached the peak. A shiver followed as he muttered, "My coat was not meant for these temperatures."

After commanding the warming effect of his magic to increase, he lowered his snout to the base of the boulder that was next in line to climb. "Hmmm ... must be my lucky Peak," he assessed while he lifted his hind leg to give the rock a squirt. "I must claim as much of this territory as I can. I may not be fortunate enough to pass this way again."

Grinning, Mosley sniffed the yellow ice before he took a step back. He crouched, dug his claws into the snow that covered the boulder he was standing on and then sprang to the top of the next rock. With his climb far from over, he sang to pass his moments.

> One big wolf just climbin' up a mountain.
> Don't mess with me ... don't mess with me.
>
> Who has territorial dominance and breath to make you slumber.
> Don't mess with me ... don't mess with me.
> I will hunt for George and make him tremble.
> Don't mess with me ... don't mess with me.
> This night terror wolf is comin' for...

Suddenly, Mosley's footing slipped. He was forced to stop his tune. He had to fight to pull himself back onto the rock. Once his footing was again secure, he smirked as he looked down at the rocks that would have greeted him if he had fallen. "Perhaps I should pay attention."

The morning passed, and so did the Peak of Bailem before the wolf reached the summit. With the change in terrain, the ice was now working against the curve of his claws as he began his descent. The moments it took to find a secure grip made his destination seem that much farther away.

It was just before Late Bailem when Mosley was forced to stop climbing. A path lay ahead, but to get to it, he had to jump down a small cliff.

The path was covered with a crusty layer of ice just as the boulders behind him had been. Mosley sighed. "I'm beginning to wonder if revenge is worth the hassle." A moment later, he grinned. "Of course, it is. George must perish"

Though the landing would be smooth, and the path was nearly two paces wide, Mosley was unsure if he would be able to stop himself from plummeting off the edge before he secured his grip. "There must be a better way."

Lifting his head to study his surroundings, his eyes scanned the area.

Only a short series of moments passed before he grumbled, "There aren't any other options. My father could have made this jump. So can I."

With his front paws dangling over the edge as far as they could, Mosley crouched to reduce the distance he would need to fall. He pushed off with his hind legs and extended his claws to prepare for impact, but his landing was not what he had expected. Instead of sliding toward the edge of the cliff, the top layer of snow broke and his paws sunk. "Whew!" he exhaled.

Mosley's next 11 steps were relaxing. With the placement of each paw, the snow continued to break apart and provide a welcomed traction. But his enjoyment of the moment would be short-lived. His twelfth step was not relaxing. As his paw broke through the snow, a defensive growl penetrated the evening air, and a number of barks and snarls followed.

Mosley redirected his gaze down the face of the cliff. What he saw caused him great concern. Five large hounds with white coats were stalking a much smaller wolf whose fur was as dark as his own.

The black-coated wolf yelped as she collapsed to the ice. She was weak and bleeding, and her right front leg was bent in an awkward position. Helpless, she growled to ward off her attackers, but her threat was ignored.

Mosley recognized the growl. "It can't be!" he proclaimed. He focused harder on the injured wolf's form. "My Luvera passed. This is impossible."

The snowhounds were closing in on Luvera.

Mosley had only a moment to act. He lifted his head and howled.

The snowhounds halted their approach. Their heads snapped back over their shoulders as they looked up the face of the cliff.

Mosley lowered his head, exposed his fangs and shouted, "If it's prey you seek, then choose me!"

The pack leader responded, "Get him, boys! She's not going anywhere! We'll finish her off later!"

As the snowhounds ran toward the path, Luvera looked up the icy face of the cliff. "Run, Mosley! You must run!"

Mosley kept his gaze fixed on his wife. "I won't abandon you! I can't lose you again!"

Luvera fought to stand. As she hobbled across the snow toward the daunting pass, her haunches trembled beneath her dark fur while she kept her injured limb tucked to her body. "I'm coming, my love! You can't defeat them alone!"

Mosley's green eyes narrowed. "Stay where you are!"

As Luvera continued to limp across the snow, Mosley shook his head and whispered, "She never listens." A moment later, he redirected his gaze toward his attackers. The snowhounds ascent had been quick. They were accustomed to prowling the territories of the north, and as the placement of each paw broke through the snow covering the path, their dark eyes gleamed with anticipation of their next meal.

Mosley backed up, his eyes searching for the best moment to attack. The chunks of packed snow that were being dislodged by his paws were rolling off the ledge and plummeting to a hazardous end. It was now or never. The cliff he had jumped from was directly behind him, and he was running out of path.

Crouching, Mosley sized up his foes for one final moment. The hounds were nearly twice his size, and the white fur covering their rippling muscles had been stained with Luvera's blood.

Mosley's lips curled, exposing his fangs. The steam from his snarl rose past his determined eyes as he watched the pack leader's drool fall to the snow. Mosley's legs extended, launching him head-on into the first of his five attackers.

◦⟨⟨•⟩⟩◦

Yelping, Mosley's eyes snapped open—allowing him to escape his nightmare. It took a moment, but he eventually realized that he had been dreaming. The snowhounds that were attacking his Luvera were not real, and the spirit of his lost love was still waiting inside the Book of Immortality for her chance to live again.

The night terror wolf's eyes searched the darkness. The truth of his surroundings was equally as depressing as the fiction of his dream. He was still lying on a prison floor made of ice. Every muscle ached, and no matter how he struggled, it was hard to hold his eyes open. They were swollen, and the pain—oh the pain—was agonizing. He sighed. "Revenge is not worth my suffering. What was I thinking?"

◦⟨⟨•⟩⟩◦

Fellow Soul … allow me to bring you up to speed. The last 5 Peaks for Mosley had been filled with suffering during his waking moments. The night terror wolf had been beaten, tortured, and questioned for answers the wolf was unable to disclose. Yet, somehow, Mosley found the strength to rise again and again as another enemy—a real enemy—threatened to end his existence.

◦⟨⟨•⟩⟩◦

The Frigid Commander of Hydroth grabbed the bars of the wolf's cell, pulled the door open and then stepped inside. After ensuring the lock was secure, his blue hands that were covered with gloves made from the hide of a slagone, released the ice.

Mosley squinted to protect his eyes as the commander passed his club above an orb that was attached to the wall of the cell. The orb illuminated, and the light reflected off the commander's milky-gray eyes while thousands of crystallizations embedded in the Isorian's skin glimmered.

The light from the orb was strong, yet no heat was cast from it—the magic it was filled with allowed the ice to remain solid. Hundreds of thousands of these orbs had been scattered throughout Hydroth over the seasons. And just like this orb, they remained hidden far beneath the frozen tundra of Northern Grayham with the rest of the city.

The commander's body was mostly uncovered, except for a hooded cloak, a dangling hide covering his groin, two tribal bands that encircled the width of his biceps, a chest piece made of bone and beads, and guards to cover his shins and the top of his feet.

As the powerful warrior turned to face Mosley, he moved to stand over the wolf and then motioned for his guards to turn away. A cruel smile stretched across his face as he looked down to watch Mosley hobble into the corner furthest from him.

The wrinkles around the commander's eyes tightened as he crossed his arms. "It pleases me that you're up, wolf. You're resilient. I'm going to relish this Peak's trobleting."

Mosley snarled as best he could. He was barely able to expose his fangs. "As I have said during many other moments, Darosen, I will not speak with you."

The Frigid Commander grinned, exposing a perfect set of teeth. "You have discovered my name. A friend within these walls you must know … or a fool. Perhaps you would satisfy my curiosity, and share this friend's name."

Mosley growled again. "I'm not in the mood for sharing. I wish to speak with Clandestiny."

The Frigid Commander knelt next to the fallen God of War and punched the night terror wolf on his right shoulder. As the pain filled Mosley's front legs, he collapsed, but the wolf refused to allow a whimper to escape.

The commander chuckled. The sound of his laughter echoed throughout the dungeon. "If you refuse to speak, then you shall continue to suffer. But the heaven your soul longs to see shall have to wait. The moments for your eyes to remain closed shall only come once I have the answers I seek."

The commander's eyes softened. "Wolf … do you truly wish to suffer the pain of a continual torment?"

Mosley fought to lift himself off the ice. As he stood, his stare turned dark and his brows deepened. "I shall only speak with Clandestiny."

The softness in the commander's eyes disappeared. Darosen slugged Mosley again and then watched the wolf fall back to the ice. The commander sneered, "So be it!" Darosen stood and backed off. "I shall troblet you until you call for your passing. You have my word on this, wolf." The warrior lifted his hand and clenched his fist. "You shall only receive an immediate end once I know the reasons you seek Clandestiny."

The commander's face softened again. He sighed, "Why not spare yourself the torture?"

Mosley struggled to lift his head. Icicles of drool hung from the end of the matted fur covering his snout as his frosty breath drifted toward the ceiling. Once his vision cleared, the wolf found the commander's form. The warrior's muscles were rippling beneath his bright-blue skin as he waited for Mosley's response.

Mosley's strength failed. The weight of his head was too much to bear as it thumped against the floor. With a sickly voice, the wolf fought to control the chattering of his teeth. "I … I…" Mosley clinched his jaws and sighed. "I refuse to speak with you. My reasons are my own."

The commander pounded his right fist into his left palm as his expression hardened. "Your attempted subterfuge shall not go unpunished!"

With his last ounce of strength, Mosley once again managed to lift his head off the ice. "If … If … If you'd just allow me to speak with Clandestiny. I am sh … sure this can be resolved."

The Frigid Commander planted his bare feet on the floor beside Mosley's head. The muscles in his right forearm bulged as he reached down and grabbed a handful of frosty fur on the back of the wolf's neck. He yanked upward and held all of Mosley's weight with his arm outstretched, parallel to the floor. "I won't allow Clandestiny to speak with an overgrown sudwal. I know you query to understand the power of the Tear's secret, yet you do not possess the nobility to do so. You know more than your words suggest."

Mosley searched his soul for strength. A glint of defiance lit his eyes as his chest expanded. "What I know … only Clandestiny will hear." He growled again.

The left hand of the commander balled up. "We shall see, mutt! We shall see!"

Howls filled the depths of the icy dungeon as a new day's pummeling began.

My soulful friends … allow me to take you back to an extended series of moments that happened 290 seasons before Shalee's entrapment in the Eye of Magic on Western Luvelles.

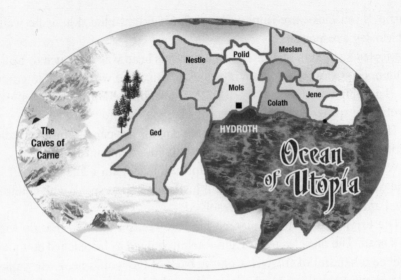

THE NORTHEASTERN TERRITORIES—THE CONTINENT OF NORTHERN GRAYHAM
THE UNDER ICE CITY OF HYDROTH

Fellow soul … before I begin this tale, I should tell you a few things about Northern Grayham and the beings who occupy its territories. First, I shall focus on a race that was known as Isorians. These miraculous beings had the ability to live in the extreme cold. Their unique blood flowed through their veins and acted like antifreeze, though it functioned on a more efficient level than the chemical that those of us from old Earth would have put into our cars.

Now ... for those souls who lived on some other world prior to the Great Destruction, I apologize for the comparison. I ask that you bear with me.

Isorian skin was impervious to the cold until the temperature dropped somewhere around 45 below zero, and even then, it adapted. It allowed their bodies to crystallize into an advanced, icy form that still allowed them to move.

One special Isorian was named Shamand. Shamand was the leader of one of seven clans to survive the Great Heat. He was also one of the few men with the bloodline necessary to become king. Yet, despite his lineage, the Isorian populace had not chosen a new monarch since the end of the Great Heat.

The Great Heat—also known as The Great Thaw—was devastating. Each clan occupying the territories in the eastern half of Northern Grayham suffered many losses when the warming began just more than 400 seasons before the birth of Shamand's daughter. With temperatures that reached unbearable levels of almost 39 degrees above zero, every Isorian was forced to seek refuge inside their homes that existed beneath the ice to stay cool. The people only surfaced to hunt for food, and they covered up as best they could to keep the scorching heat from stinging their skin.

Five seasons after the Great Heat began, the Isorian's homes became their undoing. Their structures failed to offer the safe haven they had come to rely on, and the remaining elders who sat on the council were at a loss as to how to compensate for the melting ice.

The ice that formed the walls of the Isorians' chiseled homes gave way. Cracks appeared, and the saltwater from the ocean rushed through them. Those inside were trapped beneath the ice with no way to escape before they drowned. Their gargled screams had been heard only by those who suffered the same fate.

This horrid way of dying was given the name Liquid End. Yet despite this threat, the people had no other place to go. To live above the ice would deliver a similar fate, and this way of perishing would hurt far worse. The heat would slowly cook their flesh, and at 39 degrees, it would not take long before they were covered with boils.

It was not until after the Great Thaw took nearly 50,000 Isorian lives that the climate changed. The ice solidified, and the people were able to rebuild. But the stability of the weather created a new instability for a race of beings called the Tormal who lived beyond the Mountains of Tedfer to the west.

THE SOUTHEASTERN TERRITORIES—THE CONTINENT OF NORTHERN GRAYHAM
THE UNDER ICE CITY OF GESPER

Fellow soul ... there were a few differences between the Tormal and the Isor. Living across the territories surrounding the city of Gesper, Tormalians had gills, one on each side of their spine near their shoulder blade. This unique attribute allowed them to survive beneath the water, as well as atop the ice. They also had the ability to survive in a warmer climate, as well as in the intense cold. These unique advantages had, over the seasons, given them the ability to hunt beneath the frigid waters of the ocean as well as atop the frozen shelves covering the tundra.

During the Great Thaw, the Tormal took advantage of their unique ability to survive in higher temperatures. They built a city on the surface of the ice to avoid the instability of life below it. The materials to do this were imported from Luvelles, and the Head Master during those moments, Hedron Id, used his magic to protect the goods. In short, they were sealed from the elements. Precious metals, exotic gems, woods and other forms of exquisite materials were delivered by the Merchant Angels and left for the army of Brandor to transport north.

The Tormal would later call their city above the ice, Gesper, and the architecture was grand, but not in the way the Tormal originally intended. The Tormalian architects made a critical error in judgment when designing the city. This decision would eventually change the lives of their people. But fellow soul ... this is not the moment to show you how the architects' decision affected the Tormal. I shall do this later on during this tale.

NORTHERN GRAYHAM
THE UNDER ICE CITY OF HYDROTH

A young Isorian crawled out of a hole leading down into the ice. Since long before his birth, this hole had been the entrance to Medolas' family's, glacial home, and the debt owed to the Isorian government for the chiseling of the structure had been paid in full many seasons ago.

Medolas stood, stretched his arms and took a deep breath of fresh air. Once again, he admired the way the sun defined the breaks in the rolling shelves covering the lands of his clan. It was this frozen wonderland, located within the territory of Mols, where his father had taught him to hunt, and do so with proficiency.

"Another glorious Peak," Medolas proclaimed. Dropping his arms to his side, he bent his right knee and grabbed his foot to stretch his thigh. After scratching at the numerous suction cups spanning the width of his foot to soothe an itch, he released his leg and then bolted across the ice toward a familiar destination.

With each footstep, the top of Medolas' blue feet contrasted against a fresh layer of snow. The blue of his skin had recently gained its intensity and the crystallizations symbolizing the completion of puberty had finally matured. He was thankful that his skin was now as intense as his father's.

Medolas' smile grew as he hopped over the neighbor's hole that led down into their home. This was his kind of Peak. And despite the temperature being cold enough to freeze a megrastle whale's carcass in a single night, he still wore no shirt, pants or shoes as he navigated the terrain covered with more than a hundred paces of ice.

Medolas sang as he made a hard right at the hole leading down to the home of the City Treasurer. He then headed due south toward the home of Shamand, climbing over the undulating shelves and leaping over countless holes that led into the homes of other members of his clan. It was not long before he stopped and ducked behind a drift that had accumulated not more than six paces away from Shamand's hole.

Visiting Shamand was not the reason why Medolas sought the elder's abode. His reason was similar to that of any boy of 15 seasons. He desired the company of a young Isorian female. And this young lady was not just any ordinary girl. She was a challenge, and a great deal fairer than other females her age—and she was off limits.

Also 15 seasons, Clandestiny's skin was soft blue, and it would remain that color even after her body finished maturing. Because of her intoxicating beauty, Medolas was always anxious during the moments just prior to seeing her. To settle his anxiety, he often whistled to calm his nerves.

A mischievous grin appeared on Medolas' face as he grabbed a knife tied to his ankle and used it to chip away at the shelf under which Shamand's home had been chiseled. After dislodging a few chunks, he tossed them into another hole not far from the main entrance that spiraled downward into Clandestiny's bedroom.

After a moment or two, Medolas crawled on his belly toward the hole and lowered his head into the opening. He called out in the only language known to the inhabitants of Northern Grayham, a language that I, your spirited storyteller, still fail to comprehend without proper translation to this very Peak. *"Tee-gres meé feéje seéde creé dence seéde meé feéje! Dee moonét er peeréet crés keenégiins!"* When translated, Medolas said, "Hey, wake up,

Clanny! Come on, Clanny, wake up! The moments are perfect to play with the kenaguins!"

A sharp voice responded, but it did not come from inside the hole. Medolas whirled around. To his surprise, Clandestiny had snuck up behind him. "My father is going to learn of us. You must stop this silliness," she scolded.

Medolas' grin widened. "Ah, come now, Clanny, I've missed you."

Clandestiny's brows furrowed. "If you insist on throwing things into my hole, my father is going to troblet our backsides. I told you I'd meet you. Why must you insist on being so eager? You're determined to see that we sit in suffering."

Medolas closed his eyes as he stood. He pretended to walk around as if he was blind. As he stopped near the hole, he chuckled. "How will your father learn of us? The old man cannot see."

Clanny crossed her arms. "You jest, but his ears have eyes. Now stop! You're talking about my father. I'll not hear another ill word."

Reaching out with his foot, Medolas pushed what was left of the chunks into the hole.

Clanny frowned as she watched them disappear. "Now look at what you've done. I shall have to clean upon my return. You could've kicked them elsewhere."

Medolas sported his most innocent grin, and as if the ice had never been an issue, Clanny soon returned a smile of her own. She cared deeply for Medolas, and she was unable to stay mad whenever he gave her his cutest, sudwal look—a sudwal being Northern Grayham's version of a hairy dog.

Every moment spent with Clanny made Medolas joyful. Feeling excited was the norm when she was close. He loved her beautiful blue skin and the way her white hair cascaded over her shoulders. Even at 15 seasons, he admired her every curve, and as I came to know so well after spending so many moments learning the ways of the new worlds, male teenagers, no matter what world they were from, were all the same—they were afflicted by hormones.

Medolas fidgeted as he scratched the ice with the toenail of his right big toe. "Perhaps I want your father to know of us. I should inform him that you're mine, and that we'll be running off together."

With a smooth gait, Clanny moved in to take his hand. "Your boldness is adorable, but my father would have you fed to the gashtion if he discovers us. I request that you not throw anything else into my hole. I couldn't bear the thought of seeing you torn apart. We'll be able to determine our course with enough thought being put into our moments. You shall see."

Medolas sighed, his jovial self fading for the moment. "I know you're right. It vexes me that we cannot tell the elders how we feel."

Clanny's long, white hair fell forward, forming a cover of intimacy as she put her forehead against Medolas'. Once her eyes commanded his, she whispered, "Let us venture to find some fun. I shall fetch a bucket of fish."

As Medolas watched Clanny bound across the shelf, he smiled as she dove into another hole.

THE SWIMMING HOLE
EAST OF THE UNDER ICE CITY OF HYDROTH
LATER THAT SAME PEAK

As Medolas and Clandestiny tread within the frigid water, the kenaguins darted about them. Every now and then, one of their black flippers splashed saltwater into the children's mouths as they laughed at the eagerness in which these penguin-looking creatures fought for fish.

This was the one swimming hole that never froze. The elders of the kingdom said it was because of a current of warm water that somehow worked its way up from the south and through this very spot—but swimming in this territory was forbidden, and the children knew it.

It was not long before a third swimmer appeared and joined the fun. Gablysin was a clever boy. He was well known for his ability to entertain nobles, and it was said that even at the young age of 14 seasons, Gablysin was going to be the best actor/singer in all the land.

The boy possessed charm beyond his seasons and his wit topped off his charismatic appeal. He was, by far, one of the most handsome children by Isorian standards and was also one of the few who had been blessed with the ruby colored eyes—a trait that blessed only one special Isorian every 3,000 seasons.

To say Gablysin was considered esteemed would be an understatement. As fate would have it, Clanny and Medolas were two of the few children with bloodlines noble enough to associate with this remarkable youngster.

"Gabs, your arrival pleases me," Clandestiny said as she tossed a fish up the embankment for the ruby eyed child to catch. "Jump in. The water is lovely, and the kenaguins are spirited."

"Were you able to bring Gesple with you?" Medolas added while gazing at the woven pouch Gabs had tied to his waist.

With a slap to his forehead, the ruby eyed child responded. "Ohhh, drat!" He frowned. "My mind misplaced the responsibility. My forgetfulness shall haunt me."

"No, no, no, no, no! You must go back to retrieve it!" Medolas admonished. "I've been waiting for Peaks to lay my hands on your father's sour ale." Medolas pointed to the sky. "Your father's ale is the drink of the gods. Praise Helmep for allowing such perfection to subsist."

"Don't you dare bring Helmep into this!" Clanny chastised.

Gabs grinned as he watched Clandestiny push Medolas under the water. Once he had resurfaced, Clanny splashed the salty liquid in his face and continued scolding. "Our lord should strike you down! You shall not make Gabs leave us to fetch such wickedness. I won't love a drunkard, Medolas. Mark my words."

"Ahhhhh, come now, Clanny," Gabs responded as he patted his chest and then pointed at Medolas. "It isn't like our eyes look upon each other every Peak. I vigorously doubt we shall become drunkards by stealing my father's ale now and again. Besides, we are thankful to Helmep. Our god would appreciate our eagerness to show our gratefulness."

"Well said," Medolas responded. "You see, Clanny? Everything is delightful."

"Hmph! I still disapprove!"

Medolas tried to capture Clanny's eyes as he swam to her. After a few moments of resistance, he was able to pull her close. Despite her vexed mood, she gave in and allowed his milky-gray eyes to find hers, and as always, Medolas gave Clandestiny his most innocent of looks. "Come on, Clanny," he said, stroking her cheek on the right side of her face. "You know my mind. I'm canny. I know when enough is enough. I'd never drink beyond my ability to stay sane." He puckered. "Be sweet, and give up a kiss."

Gabs shook his head as he watched the pair close in on one another. The ruby eyed child dropped the pouch that was holding the sour ale to the ice and then jumped into the air from the side of the embankment. Grabbing his knees, he pulled them to his chest and shouted on his way down to the water's surface. "No kissing, you guys!"

Both Clandestiny and Medolas were greeted with a wall of saltwater that found its way into their mouths. To pay Gabs back for ruining their moment, they waited until the ruby eyed child resurfaced, and then they pushed Gabs back under the water before he could take a breath.

The three continued to frolic, thrashing about while feeding the fish to the kenaguins. It was a great series of moments, but little did they know—they were being watched.

From the depths of the swimming hole, five eyes lined the forehead of a slimy predator as it looked up at the children's feet while they played. The sensors on its tentacles glided through the water collecting their scents, savoring each smell as it decided which child to feast on first.

Back and forth the bled swam while sizing up its prey from the shadows that were cast by the icy walls descending hundreds of feet into the darkness. It was not long before the predator chose a target. Four of its five eyes closed, leaving its large center eye open to calculate the final distance of its strike.

Gabs cleared his throat as Medolas surfaced. "Tonight, I have been requested to perform at the celebration to announce our new sovereign. Word
has reached my ears ... the council insisted that I perform. What should I
sing?"

Medolas and Clandestiny looked at each other and then shrugged. "What do you want to sing?" Clandestiny queried.

Gablysin returned a shrug of his own. "I don't know. Do either of you know who has been chosen to be our new sovereign? Perhaps having this knowledge would help me decide."

"I possess this knowledge," another voice answered from atop the bank. "The Council of the Seven has chosen my father, though I've been ordered to hold my tongue."

Clanny continued to tread water as she looked up the embankment and stared at their unexpected visitor. "Shiver, I failed to notice your arrival. Are you truly bound with this information?"

Shiver nodded. "I am."

Clandestiny frowned. "Then why speak of it?"

"Yeah," Medolas added, "then why speak of it? And when was the moment of your arrival?"

"I have only just set foot on this post. I wanted to swim with you." Shiver focused is gaze on Clanny. "My father was the one chosen. I speak of it only because we are friends. Why the grand inquisition?"

Clanny frowned again. Her last encounter with Shiver had made her uncomfortable. He had made an advance for her affections—affections that Shiver knew belonged to Medolas—and she had put Shiver in his place. She had made it clear on that Peak, and on a number of others since, that her love was for Medolas and Medolas only.

"Hmpf! You may stay!" Clanny sneered. She dunked Medolas beneath the water and held him in place to keep his blue ears from hearing her as she continued. "But if you dare make my moments intolerable, I shall dispose of what's left of our friendship."

Shiver nodded. "You have clearly spoken this intent more than once, and as I have said, I comprehend your message. I understand your fixation with your hidden love. Besides, you've kept your secret well, and I don't want to hurt you." He bowed, "Again, I'm sorry."

Clanny scowled. "Hmpf! You best hold steadfast to your promise."

"What are you two speaking about?" Medolas inquired after fighting his way back to the surface and hearing the words, "steadfast to your promise." "What promise?" He grabbed a handful of fish from the bucket that was sitting next to the swimming hole and tossed Shiver a fish.

Clanny put her hand on top of Medolas' head. "It's nothing to concern yourself with." She playfully dunked him again as three kenaguins dove in to steal the rest of the fish from Medolas' hands.

At 16 seasons, Shiver possessed a natural strength. His father's bloodline had always been stronger and larger than most Isorians. With short, white hair and flawless blue skin, Shiver's features were well suited for a crown—a crown that would pass to him if what he had said about his father was the truth.

Medolas resurfaced and motioned for Shiver to join them. "The water is pleasant. Jump!"

Shiver was about to comply when he spotted the beast. He could see the bled swimming toward Gabs. "Get out!" he shouted. "You must get out! Gabs, protect your blindside!"

Before another word could be spoken, Gabs' shoulders were surrounded by two, large tentacles. The ruby eyed child was yanked beneath the surface and carried into the depths of the swimming hole.

Medolas pulled Clandestiny toward the embankment and shoved her up and out of the water while Shiver removed a large knife from a sheath he had tied to his ankle. To save further moments, Shiver cut the rope that secured his cape around his neck and allowed the garment to fall to the ice as he dove into the water.

Clanny and Medolas climbed to the top of the embankment and stood in silence as they watched the water settle. Their hearts pounded as their eyes scanned the depths for signs of life, but they could see none.

"What do we do?" Clandestiny pleaded. Yellow, blood-filled tears rolled down her cheeks and fell to the ice as she continued. "It's taking too many moments. What if they've perished?"

Without saying a word, Medolas dove in and disappeared. Clanny shifted her weight from one foot to the other. The tiny suction cups on the bottom of her feet suckled the ice for traction as she muttered, "Careful, Medolas, careful."

Eventually Medolas resurfaced empty handed.

"Did your eyes bear witness?" Clanny questioned, her voice filled with despair.

Medolas climbed to the top of the embankment. "I saw nothing. They're deeper than I'm capable of swimming. I could go no further. The pressure punished my ears."

Deep beneath the surface, Shiver maneuvered through the icy caverns as his eyes adjusted to the darkness of his surroundings. Turn after turn, he kept his knife ready in case the bled struck. It seemed as if the cavern walls continued forever. He knew the bled had come this way since he had seen the beast enter while dragging Gabs with its tentacles.

With each stroke to propel him through the water, the urgency of the situation compounded. He knew Gabs' air had long since been exhausted, and as he pulled himself around yet another corner, all he could do was hope for the best.

After many, many, long moments, Shiver's eyes located the shadowy forms of Gabs and the bled. Gabs' body lay limp in the cephalopod's tentacles, and the beast's backside was turned in his direction. There were no moments to waste. The bled's teeth became visible as it adjusted to a more comfortable position from which to feast. A moment later, a long tongue with flesh ripping hooks at its end extended toward the ruby eyed child's belly.

With all of his might, Shiver pushed off the icy wall behind him. With a slicing blow, he attacked the bled with his knife. The weapon severed the tentacle closest to him, and its blood flowed as the first of the beast's nine, slimy limbs fell to the cavern floor.

Shiver's knife quickly found a second target. The blade penetrated one of the beast's outer eyes before another of the bled's tentacles was able to seize his hand. With three large suction cups attached to his skin, the pressure built. It felt like Shiver's flesh was going to be ripped off the bone while the rest of the tentacle rolled up his arm. With the beast tightening its grip, the blue of Shiver's skin on his right arm faded from lack of circulation as his knife fell to the cavern floor. A moment later, three more powerful tentacles enveloped his waist and latched on.

Shiver screamed. The bubbles produced by his cry rose from his mouth and rolled along the ceiling of the cavern before they popped.

THE CITY OF HYDROTH
THE GREAT UNDERHALL OF ICE

Fellow soul ... a quick note ... the Great Underhall was located deep beneath the surface of the Isorian people's frigid lands at the center of Hydroth, not far from the late king's undercastle.

With this known, allow me to tell you more about Shamand. A strong, elderly male, Shamand's short, white hair was often covered by the hood of his cloak. His face carried the scars of a seasoned warrior and the wrinkles of an overprotective father. He was the type of Isorian who worried about preserving the innocence of his daughter—a daughter who, unbeknownst to her, was to have her hand offered to the future prince of the Isorian people—Shiver—if the boy so desired.

Shamand's nose bore the remains of a scar, compliments of a nasty break he suffered while saving his wife from drowning. You see, it was during the Great Thaw when the water broke through the walls of Shamand's home and threatened to end his mate. It was on that Peak that Shamand's mettle was tested. He shielded his wife from harm as a large piece of ice fell from the ceiling of his abode and crushed the bridge of his nose, nearly knocking him unconscious. But Shamand's resilience was stronger than the ice and the raging water that poured into his home. As a result of his heroics, Herlesda, his devoted wife of 527 seasons, was pulled to safety, and many seasons later, she was able to give birth to Clandestiny before losing her life during childbirth.

The effect of the break to Shamand's nose became his Achilles Heel. His vision deteriorated since that Peak, and with his eyes becoming useless, his role within the Isorian army was forced to change. He would assume the position of advisor to the future king, a duty that was scheduled to commence once the coronation of the new sovereign occurred.

Despite Shamand's desire to command the army as its Frigid Commander, he planned to step down to embrace his new position with humility, all the while running into walls as the further progression of his blindness continued to take what was left of his sight.

Shamand entered the Great Underhall with his guide, Doejess. The future advisor hummed a familiar beat that helped him mark the perfect moments in which to lower his feet onto the steps that descended toward the stage.

Doejess whispered into Shamand's ear. "My Liege, the steps leading up to the stage begin in 20 paces. Lord Thoomar stands waiting beyond, not far to your left."

Shamand returned a whisper of his own. "Thank you, Doejess." The elderly warrior lifted his eyes in the general direction of his friend. "Thoomar!" he called out. "My eyes find joy in seeing you, old friend. You appear fit and ready to fulfill your duties as sovereign of our great kingdom."

Thoomar rolled his eyes that were hooded by thick, milky brows. "Who are you jesting, Shamand? Your eyes fail to see the glory of a face that rests upon a body that was sculpted by the gods." Thoomar allowed his grin to go uncovered as he moved his powerful frame across the stage to adjust the chairs spanning its width.

Shamand pulled his arm free of Doejess' grip and then ascended the stairs of the stage while he rebutted. "Even in blindness, my eyes are incapable of forgetting the tragedy the gods placed upon your shoulders. I still see you, old friend. "

Thoomar could only smile as Shamand crested the final step, but as Shamand approached the first chair, a look of concern appeared on the future king's face. "Bumps! Bumps, beware! The chair blocks your path."

Shamand's shin caught the edge of the icy seat, stained red to define its shape. He groaned as he lowered to rub away the pain, only to bump his head on the chair's arm that had been covered with a thin padding.

With his friend groaning in pain, Thoomar rushed across the stage and assisted Bumps into a seated position.

Shamand cursed his eyes. "Frejet! I would've missed this treachery if you hadn't called me that ludicrous name." Turning his head in Doejess' general direction, he shouted at his guide. "What good are you if you cannot keep an old man from hitting inane objects?"

Doejess' arms extended, seeking forgiveness. "But, My Liege! I—"

Thoomar spoke overtop of Doejess' nervous response to save the frail-looking Isorian with pale, yellowish-white hair further chastisement. "Ahhh, come on, Bumps. Your blind backside would have hit it anyhow. Many of your moments are spent walking into motionless decor. Besides, we should be celebrating our good fortune, not berating servants. Let us grab a drink. Our nerves beg to be calmed."

Shamand's lips pursed. "Perhaps two ales would suffice."

Thoomar grinned. "Perhaps. But we shouldn't consume too much. I'd hate to get snocked before the ceremony begins. It wouldn't be wise to fall like a drunkard on my first Peak as king. It wouldn't bode well with the clans, agreed?"

"Agreed," Shamand responded. He stood and fumbled to find the width of Thoomar's shoulders. "You shall guide me to the dining hall." Again he turned his head in the direction of Doejess. "It appears my guide is incapable of such transit."

Doejess cringed.

Squeezing Thoomar's shoulder, Shamand continued. "I, too, would prefer to stay sober, especially if our ears are to listen to the ruby eyed child sing. I've spoken with his father. The blessed one shall most certainly be lifting his voice to the heavens for you tonight."

Thoomar's admiration could be heard in his sigh. He often spoke of hearing the ruby eyed child's songs. "We shall indeed be blessed to savor the boy's melodies. Thank you for this gift, Bumps. To have the sacred one sing for only me is a dream come true."

Shamand growled. "Must you always call me that ludicrous name?"

Thoomar reached behind Shamand and squeezed his shoulder. "You know I must, old friend."

BACK AT THE SWIMMING HOLE

Medolas paced as Clanny stood near the edge of the embankment. With the placement of each foot, the tiny suction cups on the bottom of his feet gripped the ice. They made popping noises as he twisted to walk in the opposite direction. The despair in his voice could be heard as he stopped next to Clandestiny and looked toward the horizon. "I fear the sun is fast becoming our enemy. The Peak will betray us soon." He looked into the depths of the swimming hole. "We can do nothing. They are lost to us."

Clanny reached out and grabbed Medolas' arm. "We should run to the city and find my father." Her head lowered as she thought of what Shamand's reaction would be. "My father warned of the danger. Even the council commanded that we not swim in this hole. Why did we fail to obey?"

Medolas spit in frustration. He watched the brown, mucus-filled saliva fall onto the water and begin to sink. "Your father is going to rip our limbs off our bodies before the council gets the chance to feed us to the gashtion."

Clanny crouched and grabbed the top of her head. "How do we deliver the news?" She lowered her chin onto her chest. Two blood-filled, yellow tears, one from each cheek, rolled down her face and fell to the ice beside her feet. Upon contact, the droplets froze and left behind two shimmering crystallizations that possessed the brilliance of diamonds.

"I fail to know this answer," Medolas responded while pulling Clandestiny up to his side. "But if we fail to find your father, the council won't be able to initiate a search for Shiver and Gabs' empty vessels."

Replaying the sound of his words in his head, Medolas swallowed. "Your father is going to be …" He swallowed again. "We best hurry. Evening will be lost to us before our arrival."

As they ran, the sun abandoned the sky, disappearing below the horizon in the west. What was left of the world of Luvelles to the north and Harvestom to the south also vanished below their respective horizons as the last bit of light across the terrain faded.

Despite the darkness, the children did not slow their sprint toward the city. Their eyes adjusted to the blackness of night, another amazing ability of Isorian people. This ability allowed them to navigate terrain that would have been deadly to any normal man during the estimated series of moments that were known as midnight.

THE ISORIAN THEATRE
LATER THAT SAME NIGHT

Fellow soul ... the Isorian theatre was also known as the Great Underhall. It was a massive place, and everything that would have normally been made out of various building materials had, instead, been chiseled by hand and sculpted into the shelves of ice that covered the Isorians' lands.

The balconies high above the stage were shaved to a perfect finish, and a dark-brown stain was applied to the ice to define their curves, much in the same manner that stain would have been applied to a piece of wood on old Earth. Even the seats inside the balconies and on the main floor had been stained bright-red and numbered more than 15,000.

There were only two parts of the structure that were not made of ice. A large, black curtain that draped from one side of a 60 pace long stage to the other, and thick black cushions that were secured to each seat. The cushions were made out of seal hides and stuffed with vestle chick feathers that were imported from Luvelles and Southern Grayham.

The Isorian people filed into the theatre as Shamand stood next to Thoomar behind the heavy curtain that spanned the width of the stage. Bumps was peeking out, despite the fact that he could not see. "Midnight draws near, old friend. Have you seen the children? Their presence should be known to us by now."

"To my knowledge, the children aren't present," Thoomar responded.

Shamand grumbled, "I told Clandestiny that tonight was important. Before she left on her gallivanting this morning, I instructed her not to be late. I should've quizzed her for her intended destination."

The future king put a hand on his future advisor's shoulder. "I imagine the children will wait until the last possible moment to announce their arrival. You know Shiver loves to try my patience."

Shamand allowed himself to smile, and then a frown followed. "What of the ruby eyed child? Where is he? I have yet to receive word of his presence from the guards."

"Figures!" Thoomar grunted. The future king could see the ruby eyed child's father sitting in the front row next to the stage. "At least the child's father is here." After a deep breath, Thoomar pushed his chest forward and forced a smile. "The moment has come, Bumps. We must proceed with the ceremony. Let's hope the children arrive prior to its completion."

Thoomar's dark-blue skin and short, white hair complemented his white robe that was trimmed in yellow. His strong, gray eyes showed his irritation as he made his next statement. "For their sakes, they best make themselves known before I finish addressing the crowd." The future thumped his fists together to symbolize his desire to troblet the children.

Despite his inability to see Thoomar's actions, he could feel the intensity of his friend's frustration. The advisor smiled and then snapped his fingers. Two Isorian boys entered from the wings of the stage carrying his ceremonial garb. After donning his robe that was made of a thin, green material that allowed the chill of the theatre to penetrate to his skin, the future king motioned that he was ready.

As the curtain parted, the people stopped visiting and rushed to take their seats. Shamand, also the leader of the Ged Clan, took center stage with Doejess' assistance to ensure his lack of sight would not cause him to accidentally stumble and fall off the stage into the crowd.

The podium the advisor stood behind had been stained red. Shamand placed his hands on either side of it and waited for the people to settle. When they did, he lifted his hands toward the ceiling and opened the ceremony with a prayer. "Lord Helmep ... hear us ... your loyal followers who serve you with unyielding faith!"

The prayer continued for many long moments before Shamand ended it with the following. "...My Lord ... the Peak has come to announce our new sovereign! I ask that you guide this Isorian, a man who has been chosen by the Council of the Seven ... a man who steps forward to lead the Isor! We ask that your wisdom be bestowed upon him as our kingdom moves into unexplored Peaks!"

Shamand lowered his hands and allowed his blind eyes to pass across the crowd as if he could see. A broad smile followed as he continued to address them. "I know those present have gathered because we have longed for this Peak! For most, the decision made by the Council of the Seven will come as no surprise! To delay the revelation of our new sovereign would be cruel, so I shall deliver him unto you now! Our new king ... shall be—"

Before the future advisor could speak Thoomar's name, the door at the back of the theatre burst open. Its handle, stained black, shattered as it hit the wall. Medolas scanned the crowd as the chunks of ice rolled beneath the door and stopped next to his left foot. The boy looked down the steps toward the stage and shouted, "Shiver and the ruby eyed child have been lost in the depths of the swimming hole! They've been slain by the bled!"

The theatre erupted with a thousand questions as Thoomar stood from his chair. He rushed past Shamand, leapt from the stage and then ran up the long flight of stairs. Grabbing Medolas by the back of his arm, the future king motioned for the guards to follow and then tossed Medolas over his right shoulder. As they ascended to the surface, the future king shouted over his opposite shoulder in the direction of the Frigid Commander of the Isorian army! "See to it that my wife follows!"

After exiting the hole that led up and out of the undertheatre, Thoomar dropped Medolas from his shoulder. To ensure the younger Isorian did not fall behind, Thoomar drug Medolas across the ice toward another hole and threw him in, head first. Listening to the boy's cries, Thoomar dove in and followed Medolas as they dropped back into the depths of the shelf. Their descent stopped only after they slid into the understables that housed the mounts of the army.

Before Medolas had the chance to survey his surroundings, he found himself being thrown up and onto the back of Thoomar's harugen, an abominable giant, white, fur-covered, centipede-looking creature. Medolas' legs split as his backside came to rest on a padded saddle that was made of leather and conformed to the length of the first seven segments of the beast's back.

Without wasting another moment, Thoomar removed his ceremonial garb, tossed it to the ice and then backed away from the harugen. After a quick whistle, the beast extended one of its legs and formed a step. Since mounting the beast required a running start, three large strides were taken before Thoomar jumped into the air. His right foot grabbed hold of a fur-covered bone that protruded from the creature's leg. The future king's muscles rippled as his leg uncoiled to launch himself toward a familiar spot near the head of the beast.

Medolas watched in amazement as Thoomar landed on the harugen's saddle in front of him. But before he could say anything, the future king looked over his shoulder. "Tie yourself in! Make haste, Medolas!"

Grabbing the harugen's reins, Thoomar barked an order. The creature began to skitter toward a large opening that led up and out of the understables. The mammoth's legs scurried back and forth with great velocity as the point at the ends of its legs dug into the ice and sent chunks sliding back into the depths toward the stables.

Medolas had never been this close to one of the army's mounts before, and since this was his first experience sitting on the back of one, Thoomar's shouting about how much trouble he and Clandestiny were in went in one of his blue ears and out the other. Despite the trouble ahead, Medolas could only marvel as the speed of the harugen increased. The terrain became a blur beneath them as Medolas thought, *How can so many legs move without tripping over one another?*

Fellow soul … as with most harugens, this creature's body had 25 segments and a pair of legs that protruded from each segment on either side. Medolas knew from his studies in gedwesh, or if you prefer an easier name—school—most adult harugens stopped growing once they reached 22 paces in length. They were not considered aggressive creatures, yet despite their gentle nature, Medolas also knew that there had been many incidents in which harugen riders were squashed beneath the creature's weight—a punishment for not paying attention while tending to the beast.

It was not long before Thoomar commanded the beast to stop. He dismounted, using one of the harugen's legs on the opposite side, and then hurried toward the banks of the swimming hole. With eyes filled with stress, the future king looked into the depths of the water. "Medolas! Is this the proper hole?"

"Yes, My Lord," Medolas responded. The tension in the boy's voice returned now that the newness of his experience riding the harugen had worn off.

Thoomar directed his attention toward two other harugens as they skittered across the terrain toward them. Shamand was sitting atop the larger of the two. The future advisor shouted from the top of his mount with Clandestiny tucked in front of him. "Do your eyes bear witness, old friend?"

Thoomar pushed his hands through his hair as he responded. "No, Bumps! My eyes fail me as yours do! There is no way for me to swim into such depths! We must wait for Blandina! Only she is capable of searching so deep!"

After commanding his harugen to halt, Shamand snapped his fingers and sent the other harugen carrying the army's new second in command back to the undercity. "See to it that Thoomar's wife is on her way!"

Once his ears had heard that his order had been obeyed, the future advisor turned back toward Thoomar and sought to calm his friend. "Shiver benefits from your wife's bloodline. I'd wager that he has taken shelter somewhere beneath the ice to avoid the bled. The gills your wife has blessed the boy with will give him the advantage. He shall see other Peaks."

"But he is only a boy, Bumps," Thoomar rebutted.

"He's not just any boy. He's your boy," Shamand argued. "Don't worry, my friend. Shiver is alive. If I know the boy, he's sharing his air with the ruby eyed child as we speak. They are most likely waiting for us to retrieve them. Garesh ... I'd even wager that they're enjoying the irritation they've caused us to suffer."

Thoomar shook his head as he stared back into the water. "Let's hope you're right, Bumps. Let's hope you're right."

CHAPTER 2
BREATH FOR A BREATH

Shiver's search for the ruby eyed child had been frantic, and though his eyes had adjusted to the darkness, he had become lost and had made too many wrong turns.

The brisk air of the cavern greeted Shiver's face as he pulled himself out of the water and onto an icy shelf. With both hands, he reached back in and yanked Gablysin out. Once the ruby eyed child had been rolled onto his back, Shiver took a deep breath to silence his own breathing and then placed his right ear to Gabs' mouth. Despite the air he had forced into Gabs' lungs, his attempt to save the chosen one had failed. The ruby eyed child's chest was empty, and as Shiver pulled back, he realized the color of Gabs' skin was almost solid white.

Taking another deep breath, Shiver leaned down, secured his lips to make a seal and then blew. During the next series of moments, Gabs' chest would lift and fall on 26 occasions before Shiver would concede that the ruby eyed child's life's source had been extinguished.

Exhausted, the future prince of the Isor fell against the wall of the cavern to look around. Though spacious, the cavern was unwelcoming and lifeless. The sound of his breathing echoed off the walls, and the realization that he was alone caused his thoughts to overflow with despair. Shiver wept.

BACK ON THE BANK OF THE SWIMMING HOLE

The harugen carrying Thoomar's wife came to a stop next to the embankment. Without wasting a moment, Blandina rose into a standing position and used the suction cups on the bottom of her feet to grip the surface of the saddle. She ripped off her yellow shawl and dove from the creature's back without saying a word. She entered the water and slid into its depths with ease.

Thoomar looked at Shamand. "Bumps, did you see that?" The future king frowned. "Bahhhh! Of course you didn't. Blandina dove into the water from the back of her harugen."

Shamand grunted. "My eyes fail me at the worst moments. But I heard the disturbance. I swear to you, old friend, I despise blindness."

Thoomar nodded as he turned toward the water. "All we can do now is wait."

The gills on Blandina's back harvested the oxygen she needed as she searched for her son and the ruby eyed child. Her long, white hair floated back and forth as her head snapped in one direction and then another. Her brow furrowed as she saw four entrances that led into separate caves beneath the ice.

Entering the first, her movements were silky smooth. Her Tormalian heritage allowed her to move effortlessly beneath the water while she marked a trail behind her. The future queen systematically searched every nook and cranny of the first cave before she returned to the entrances of the other three. Entering the second cave, she swam next to the walls and peeked around each corner, scanning the shadows for evidence of the bled.

Many, many moments passed before Blandina found the shaft that led up to the cavern where Shiver sat weeping inside the third cave. To her surprise, the body of the bled was lying around the final corner at the base of the shaft. Four of its five eyes were missing and pieces of the bled's brain had been pulled clear of its eye sockets and discarded to the floor. Tiny plasons—small fish that those of us from Earth would have referred to as minnows—were picking at the bled's remains. Blandina knew the corpse's smell would eventually attract larger predators. Her moments to find the boys were limited, and she would need to hurry before she, too, would become a feast.

Blandina swam past the bled and planted her feet on the floor of the cave. With all her strength, she pushed off and shot up into the darkness of the shaft, unable to see its end. Twenty-seven heartbeats passed before her nose found the air of the cavern where Shiver sat.

When Blandina's eyes located her son, Shiver was still sitting next to Gabs' body. The future queen recognized the despair of the situation. Pulling herself onto the shelf, she took no moments to console her son. "Shiver, you must swim to the surface. Tell your father that he will need to use the Tear of Gramal to save the ruby eyed child. Go now!"

Shiver wiped the yellow, blood tears from his chin. "Why Mother? Gabs has expired."

"I said go!" Blandina reiterated.

"But the way out has been lost to me."

Blandina frowned. "I taught you to leave a trail. Follow my markings to the surface. Go, boy!"

Shiver wanted to object, but to do so would be a waste of his moments. He stood on the shelf, dove in and disappeared.

Blandina jumped off the shelf and then pulled Gabs' body back into the water. With a few sudden movements, she dragged the chosen one back into the depths.

When Shiver broke the surface of the swimming hole, torches had been lit with their ends holstered into the ice. His eyes stung as they adjusted to their glow.

With the light flickering off Thoomar's silhouette, the future king reached down the embankment and offered his son a hand. Once Shiver stood beside him, Thoomar dropped to his knees, enclosed his large arms around his boy and pulled him close. "Thank Helmep you have been spared an early termination. Do you fair well, boy?"

"Yes, Father," Shiver responded while looking over Thoomar's left shoulder into the blackness of the swimming hole. "Gabs failed to hold onto his life's source. He suffered the liquid end before I could retrieve him. Mother required that I inform you to be ready with the Tear of Gramal."

Thoomar released his grasp on Shiver and stood to take a step back. He knew the severity of what the Tear's use would be on his being if he had to use it to restore the ruby eyed child's life's source. His gaze found the water as he moved to the edge of the embankment. Without looking at his son, Thoomar spoke. "Shiver, I want you to return to the city. See to it that a place is waiting for the expired."

"But, Father, I can help you get Gabs home."

Thoomar moved away from the water. Again, he pulled Shiver close. "I know you can." He placed his forehead against Shiver's. With his right hand on the back of his son's head, he held it in place so he could kiss the top of it. "I recognize your skills, but I need you to run ahead and do that which I cannot from here. I love you, boy."

"But, Father—"

Thoomar gave Shiver a look.

"Yes, Father."

Thoomar watched Shiver grab a torch from the harugen's pack, light it, and then run across the tundra. He admired his son's strength for a few moments before he turned to face Shamand. "He's a fine boy, old friend. But if what he says is the truth, I shall never see him again. If the ruby eyed child has expired, the chosen one's passing will require that I surrender my life's source to retrieve his. There are things that must be spoken before sacrificing all that I am."

Clandestiny sat in silence on the back of her father's harugen as Shamand reached out in search of his old friend's hand. Once secured, Shamand cleared his throat as if it had suddenly gone dry. "I don't wish this burden to befall you. Perhaps saving the ruby eyed child isn't what Helmep would ask of you. You're to become this kingdom's sovereign. This shouldn't be your burden to bear."

Medolas looked up from the embankment and watched as Clandestiny buried her face in her hands. The torchlight reflected off the tears that rolled between her fingers and then froze to the back of her hands as she listened to the conversation.

"Bumps," Thoomar responded, "we both understand the importance of the child. The prophecy was clear. Only a child with the ruby eyes can save the races of Northern Grayham."

Shamand thought a moment. "I agree that this was foretold, but what's he to save us from? There's no conflict within the territories. Your marriage to the Tormalian princess saw to that. Perhaps a different child with the ruby eyes is the chosen one. Perhaps we're wrong."

Thoomar cupped his left hand around his old friend's neck and extended his right arm. Turning his palm over, he stared at the lines crossing its width as he responded. "What kind of king would I be if I failed to do everything within my power to protect this kingdom before my coronation? I won't wager against fate. This isn't a risk I'm willing to take."

Thoomar grabbed Shamand's free shoulder with his right hand and faced him. "I've shared with you the stresses that haunt my union with Blandina. No matter how stable our alliance with the Tormal may appear, I cannot risk the safety of our people by failing to heed the words written in the prophecy."

Shamand reached forward and placed his hands on Thoomar's face. A moment of silence passed as he viewed his friend through touch before he pulled Thoomar's forehead to his own. "You do realize this is your life's source you're surrendering, do you not?"

A smile crossed Thoomar's face as he squeezed Shamand's shoulders. "To give my life's source for the child with the ruby eyes is a blessing to my being ... and to the Isor. Please see to my affairs once I've expired, old friend."

Resigned, Shamand's heart was heavy as he responded. "What do you wish of me?"

"You're a true companion, Bumps. See to it that my son wears the crown with honor. I want him to be the leader that I would've been. See that he leads our people without taking the will of others. It is my wish that you be his advisor, just as you were to be mine."

"I swear to you, I'll do as you've commanded."

Thoomar moved his right hand and then squeezed the back of Shamand's neck. "Shiver's mother has an affection for swaying from what's right and honorable. With your guidance, my boy shall become a great king. Don't allow Blandina's influence to threaten Shiver's ability to employ good judgment."

Shamand sighed and then forced a smile. "I'll serve your son with the same dedication I've given you."

A wide smile appeared on Thoomar's face as he turned to look at Clandestiny. With his right hand, he reached down and grabbed a large, tear-shaped crystal that hung around his neck by a leather strand. Once he was sure Clandestiny's eyes were fixated on the object, he spoke. "Young lady, the Tear of Gramal was bestowed upon me by the High Priestess of Harvestom. Helmep, himself, gave the Tear to her so that it may be delivered unto our people. It was the priestess who taught me to understand the crystal's abilities. The power within the Tear protects us from certain doom.

"The High Priestess commanded: if the Peak was to ever arrive that I was unable to bear the responsibilities of the Tear's burden, another would need to take my place. You, Clandestiny, were given this responsibility. A blessing by the High Priestess was bestowed upon you when you were delivered. You will need to help the chosen one save our people."

Thoomar allowed Clanny a moment to think. "You must bear the Tear's burden once I've expired. The crystal must always rest above a pure heart."

Clanny had no idea what to say or how to act as Thoomar lowered the crystal back to his chest. She also had no idea what Thoomar was talking about. She nodded her head and hoped that clarity would come while she waited for Thoomar to continue.

Thoomar motioned for Clandestiny to climb down from the back of Shamand's harugen. "I understand your trepidation, child, but alas, the moments are unavailable for me to prepare you for this burden." Thoomar held Clanny's gaze as he patted Shamand on the chest. "You'll need to speak with your father, for he is the only one with whom I've shared the knowledge of the Tear's abilities. But this knowledge won't be enough. There is another whom you must seek."

"Who is this other?" Clanny questioned, her voice trembling.

Thoomar's facial expression changed to something far more serious. "The Ko-dess."

Clandestiny gasped. The harugen beside her shifted as if the beast knew the sacredness of the Ko-dess' name. Clanny pulled her hand away from her mouth. "The Ko-dess is an abomination. Why must I seek that monstrosity?"

"Make no mistake, girl, your journey to find the Ko-dess will change you forever. Your father will ensure the High Priestess visits to prepare you for this task."

Before another word could be uttered, Blandina's hand broke the surface of the swimming hole. Thoomar turned and outstretched his arms. He snagged Gablysin by the wrists and pulled the ruby eyed child up the embankment and lowered him onto his back.

Once Blandina had also been pulled clear of the water, Thoomar knelt on both knees next to Gabs. He lifted the Tear of Gramal from his chest, and a moment later, it began to illuminate. As if it was Thoomar's first moment ever laying his eyes upon it, he marveled at the way the Tear's blood-red facets caused the crystallizations embedded in the palm of his right hand to reflect a soft purple while he wrapped the leather strap around his wrist.

The Tear was flawless, and the leather strand passed through a small hole at its narrowest point. The crystal was shaped like its name and was almost the size of Thoomar's thumb.

Staring intently at his palm, it seemed like an eternity before Thoomar was able to refocus. Looking up, he watched as a harugen scurried toward them with the Frigid Commander of the Isorian Army on its back. Once its appendages had stopped skittering, the commander climbed down.

Thoomar waited patiently on his knees as the commander walked toward him, dressed head to toe in crafted armor made of ice. The crest of the Isorian race had been chiseled into his breastplate, an image of the most powerful creature the Isorian people respected, also the one they most feared—the gashtion—a symbol chosen by the council. No stronger representation of power was known to exist.

Thoomar motioned for the Frigid Commander to stop a few paces away from Gablysin's body. "Darosen, your moment of arrival is perfect."

"I came as soon as I could, Lord Veelion." The Frigid Commander's eyes widened once he realized the lifeless form lying on the ice was that of the ruby eyed child. Darosen took a knee and bowed his head. "How may I be of service?"

Shamand was the one to answer. "You can listen to the wishes of a man who shall soon pass."

With a brave smile, Thoomar added, "Well said, Bumps, well said."

It was clear by the look in Darosen's eyes, he had questions. But before he could speak, Thoomar spoke again. "Commander, you must bear witness. Tonight ... I was to be named king over the Isor. But Helmep has other plans for me now, and I must surrender to this calling. The ruby eyed child has perished, and I am the only being who can save him so that he may fulfill the prophecy."

Thoomar brushed his forearm across his forehead to remove the frozen beads of sweat and then continued. "I must call forth the power of the Tear to return the child's spirit. This will require me to surrender my life's source. My soul will ascend to find its place with Helmep."

The Frigid Commander's face remained unwavering. "Word of your sacrifice will be spread throughout the territories of the seven clans. The men under my command shall know of your greatness."

Thoomar smiled again. "I'm sure they will, Commander. It appears your promotion could not have come at a finer moment. The Council of the Seven can rest knowing that you're capable of keeping the army prepared until my son has acquired the skills of command."

Thoomar adjusted his gaze to find his wife's eyes. Blandina had moved close to one of the harugens, and she was using the beast's fur to stay warm enough to allow the water from the swimming hole to drip off her skin instead of allowing it to freeze as a thin sheet of ice. "It's my wish that our son become king," Thoomar decreed.

Pulling the harugen's hair away from her face, Blandina nodded. Her candor expressed her sorrow, but her mind contradicted her theatrical show of concern. "It shall be done, my love."

Thoomar continued. "It is also my wish that our son be counseled by Shamand."

No sooner did the word Shamand leave Thoomar's lips before Blandina objected. "I should be the one to advise Shiver. Shamand doesn't need to bear the burden. I shall—"

"Nonsense!" Shamand objected in a strong voice to ensure he cut Blandina off. "To advise the king is not a burden. I shall instruct the boy as if he was my own, and you shall do as a mother should. You shall not interfere with the governing of this kingdom. Am I understood?"

Blandina glared at Shamand, but the nasty message within her stare was not received as it fell on clouded eyes.

Knowing the hate in his wife's heart, Thoomar shook his head. "As I have said, Shiver is to become king, and Bumps shall be his advisor. There shall be no further discussion on the matter."

Once again, Thoomar looked at Darosen. "Do you understand my orders, Commander?"

Darosen bowed his head. "Indeed, My Lord. To what else am I to bear witness?"

Thoomar motioned for Clandestiny to come to him. Without haste, the child rushed to stand before him. Despite being on his knees, Thoomar's size was more than double Clandestiny's. The powerful Isorian reached up and pulled the girl into a seated position on his lap while he leaned back on the calves of his legs.

With Clandestiny's hands in his palms, Thoomar looked up at the Frigid Commander. "Darosen, this child, the daughter of Shamand, shall be given the Tear of Gramal to hold and guard as sacred. She shall keep the Tear safe as the High Priestess commanded in the event that I was to leave this world. Clandestiny shall be provided a proper place of solitude to prepare for her journey beyond the Pass of Nayala, and you, Commander, shall ensure the priestess is summoned from Harvestom. It may take many seasons before the child can learn to communicate with the Ko-dess in its own tongue."

It was clear to see that Clandestiny had a question, but Blandina ignored the child's desire and snapped out a question of her own. "And who is to advise the girl? Am I to be kept from helping this child as well?"

Thoomar took a deep breath. "You may help Bumps with the girl's training."

With another nasty glare, Blandina responded, "I suppose I should be thankful that you've found a use for me."

Thoomar sighed, his heart heavy. "For a woman who is about to lose her husband, you seem to be overly concerned with matters pertaining to your own desires. Perhaps you could find it in your heart to console a man who desperately wants to feel the love of his wife during his moments of need. Garesh, woman! Have you no heart?"

Blandina forced her beautiful face to soften and then feigned another look of caring. She moved to pull Clanny off of Thoomar's knees and then helped her husband to his feet. She pressed her bosom against his stomach and then looked up. "You're right. I've been selfish. Please forgive me. I shall fall to pieces once you've expired."

Though Thoomar knew his wife was lying, he still embraced Blandina for a short series of moments before he redirected his attention to the Frigid Commander. "Leave now, Darosen, and go into the city. Tell the council that I've given all that I am to save the ruby eyed child. Tell your men to spread word that Shiver shall be their new king, and Clandestiny is to become the protector of the Tear. Ensure that all Isor know that Shamand is to be their advisor."

The Frigid Commander jumped to his feet. "Shall I speak of your wife's role regarding the girl?"

Thoomar shook his head. "That won't be necessary."

The Frigid Commander nodded. "By your leave, My Lord."

"Be swift," Thoomar replied. "Go."

Blandina watched the Frigid Commander run past Medolas and mount his harugen. As Darosen's beast skittered into the night, Blandina waited until the commander was out of sight before she turned to walk to the edge of the swimming hole. As she stared into the water, she rolled her eyes while she thought. *Just hurry and give your life's source so the chosen one may live, fool. Advisor to our son or not, Shiver shall listen to his mother, and I shall find a way to control the lives of the Isor.*

Blandina grinned inside. She turned to look through the darkness in the direction that Darosen had traveled and further thought, *Shiver is not of your loins, Thoomar. The boy's roots have been well planted.*

Thoomar motioned for Blandina to come to him. As she strolled across the ice, she forced a tear to roll down her cheek and then lowered her head against his chest. "I fail to see how to carry on with what is left of my existence without you."

"Hmpf!" Shamand growled without hesitating. "No doubt that you shall find a way."

Yet again, Blandina's nasty glare was shot in Shamand's direction while Thoomar rebutted, "Bumps! Perhaps this is not the moment to pick a fight, old friend."

Despite his disdain for Blandina, Shamand reluctantly nodded and crossed his arms.

Lifting Blandina's chin with his right hand, the blood-red light of the

Tear of Gramal lit the Tormalian's face as Thoomar spoke ever so softly to her. "Would you allow me one last kiss before I say goodbye?"

Blandina forced a smile and then placed her lips against Thoomar's. The exchange was far from passionate. Her lips remained hard and failed to offer the tenderness that Thoomar was seeking. She quickly pulled away and pretended to be overwhelmed as she rushed back to her harugen and pulled its fur around her for comfort.

A deep sadness and regret of so many seasons spent with a wife who failed to love him appeared on Thoomar's face before he dropped to his knees next to Gablysin's body. Many moments passed before he was able to gather his thoughts. He looked at Clandestiny. "Once I pass, you must seize the Tear. See to it that no other touches it. It's to be immediately placed around your neck. You must allow it to dangle above your heart, and don't remove it until your training is complete. Do you understand?"

"Yes," Clanny replied in a shallow voice. She turned to bury her tear-covered face into her father's robe.

Medolas wanted to comfort Clandestiny, but to do so would not have been considered acceptable, so he remained steadfast while the conversation around him continued.

Shamand reached down and rubbed Clanny's back while he spoke to Thoomar. "I shall miss you, old friend."

"And I you, Bumps."

Shamand gently pushed Clandestiny aside and then moved to embrace Thoomar. Both men held each other for a long series of moments, each knowing their lifelong friendship, since the age of three seasons, was about to end. "Your name and bravery shall become eternal on the Scrolls of Old," Shamand professed.

Thoomar cupped the back of his friend's neck and grinned. "You're the finest companion a man could have. Please turn my son into the king I know he can become. Troblet him thoroughly if you must."

Shamand allowed a sly grin to appear. "I give you my word. If I can find his backside, I shall undoubtedly kick it. Now quit stalling. You act like you're about to end yourself. I'd wager that you have some sort of foolish notion that your passing shall, somehow, benefit this kingdom."

Both men pulled each other close and chuckled while Blandina stood within the draping fur of her harugen, tapping her right foot.

Hearing the suction cups on the bottom of his wife's foot suckle the ice, Thoomar released Shamand. His eyes welled as he once again took his knees beside the ruby eyed child's corpse.

Clandestiny began to sob. She knew this was it.

Seeing her pain, Medolas broke protocol and moved to take her into his arms.

Taking solace that Shamand's eyes were unable to see Medolas' actions, Thoomar ignored the boy and lifted the Tear of Gramal skyward. He shouted, "Helmep, bless your loyal servant with your healing power! A soul for a soul, a breath for a breath, an eye for an eye and an end for a rebirth! I give freely what is mine to give so the chosen one may exist again!"

Suddenly, the night sky filled with the brightest of light. Blandina, Medolas and Clandestiny were forced to cover their eyes to shield them from harm, but Shamand did not bother to cover his. Instead, the old warrior smiled. The light was strong enough to allow his eyes to see the powerful silhouette of his friend's last moments. As the light faded, so did what was left of Shamand's sight as Thoomar's body fell limp across Gablysin's body. Shamand would enjoy the fact that he, too, had sacrificed something on this night.

As the last bit of life escaped Thoomar's body, the blue of his skin began to fade. A quiet series of moments passed before the ruby eyed child's chest began to heave.

Medolas ran to help. He pulled Gabs out from under Thoomar's dead weight.

The look in Gablysin's eyes was one of confusion as he watched Clandestiny kneel over Thoomar's body. "What happened, Clanny?" Gabs asked as she retrieved the Tear of Gramal and draped it around her neck.

As the light inside the Tear faded, Clanny tried to explain, but Blandina commanded her silence. "Enough of this foolishness! Hold your tongue, girl!"

The children moved to stand next to Shamand and watched as Thoomar's widow rushed toward her harugen and mounted it. Grabbing hold of the mammoth's reins with her right hand, she pointed at Thoomar's body with her left index finger. "See that this fool's body is brought to the city! I want him prepared for the ceremony to light the pyre of his passing! His memory will blow away with his ashes!"

As Blandina's harugen skittered across the frozen tundra, Shamand grunted, "What a shanavel!"

"Father!" Clanny chastised, her voice filled with disgust. "No one deserves to be called such illness."

Shamand shrugged. "No one, but her."

Chapter 3
Into the Darkness

The Next Peak
The Peak of Bailem

Now, fellow soul … before I continue this tale, allow me to tell you about the legislative chamber of the Council of the Seven. This expansive room was where the wisest of all Isorians gathered to create law. The chamber was located beneath the undercastle, the same castle that would become Shiver Veelion's new home.

A domed ceiling rested above a large, arena-style, circular room with a diameter of nearly 70 paces. There were hundreds of benches, dyed a golden hue, that sat in arching rows on 13 tiered levels. The floor of each level had been polished to a high sheen and the ice was dyed burgundy while black cushions had been attached to the surface of every bench. These benches were used to seat the members of the Isorian populace who wished to attend while the council convened.

The esteemed Isorians who held positions on the council gathered around a circular table that was placed at the center of the chamber. Nearly eight paces in diameter, the table was not made of ice. It was predominantly black with a thick marble surface and veins of gold that branched in every direction.

The floor where the table rested had been left white, the same color as the ice from which the structure had been chiseled. Its surface was polished, leveled and smoothed, and no visible imperfections could be seen.

Though the chamber was grand, there was a focal point that no Isorian could overlook when entering. The symbol of the Isorian army, a metal image of the gashtion, had been plated with gold and hung above the council's table since the end of the Great Thaw. This likeness of the gashtion was a gift that had been created by a community of dwarves on Trollcom. It was then transported by the Merchant Angels to Grayham before being delivered by Keldwin Brandor's great, great, great, great, great grandfather, Nayton Brandor, who accompanied his army while sailing the statue to the western shores of Northern Grayham.

There were also seven large, red tapestries that hung from the ceiling to symbolize the seven remaining clans. The tapestries were made of the finest silk spun by the kedgles on Luvelles. To add the final touch of perfection, black thrones were spaced evenly around the circumference of the table. They were covered with burgundy cushions that complemented the council's white robes.

Five of the six remaining members of the Council of the Seven had gathered in the Isorian's legislative chamber.

"Thoomar's sacrifice brings need of another vote," Poemas said through stained teeth while taking a seat on his cushioned throne. "This council cannot allow Thoomar's son to rule. Shiver is not of pure blood. The Jene shall require us to vote anew." Sitting back, Poemas rubbed his fat belly that protruded from his open robe and then continued. "Of course, we must wait for Shamand before we begin a discussion of this magnitude. But I think it's fair to say that we all know who among us is best suited for a crown. I fail to see how this could be anything less than an expeditious vote."

A husky-looking female stood from her throne on the far side of the table. Her hair was short like a man's, and her shoulders were broad. She was taller than the tallest male by nearly a hand, and with her weight behind her, she was an imposing force. Her milky eyes glared defiantly at Poemas as she spoke from beneath wavy hair. "I would wager that you think you're the one this council should vote into this esteemed position. I laugh at the thought. Perhaps a strong queen is what our people need. I, alone, saw to it that the Polid survived the Great Thaw. I needed no husband for that. I have proven that the blood to rule courses through my body."

Despite Arath's dominant posture, the others surrounding the table laughed. Many moments passed before Ohedri, the strongest of the four men, also the leader of the Meslan clan—the wealthiest clan behind Shamand's—stood and responded with a voice to match his female counterpart. "Do continue to spoil us with your humor, Arath. Your boldness has created a pain in my belly. I can't remember the last series of moments in which I've laughed so hard."

"I'm not your jester, Ohedri!" Arath shouted. Her brows lowered to deepen her scowl.

Ohedri stopped laughing. "Please! Do this council good service, and shut up. There's not a soul sitting at this table who would dare vote a woman into kingship. Your best and only chance at the throne perished along with your dejected representation of a father during the Great Thaw. Besides, we all know the opinions of the Polid are worth shallow consideration at best. Your people thrive at the bottom of the barrel, and this is where you and your clan shall remain. That is, if this council can find the means to fit your roundness into the barrel."

Without a response, Arath reached into her robe and pulled a knife. She began to circle the table toward Ohedri.

Seeing her intent, Ohedri retreated toward one of two sets of double doors that rested on opposite sides of the room. As he did, he pulled a blade of his own, but his experience with the weapon was not as proficient as his tongue. All he could do was wait for Arath to close the distance.

Arath's bosom bounced as she chased the backpedaling Ohedri. The fear on the councilman's face was evident as the burly, blue woman's smile widened. Preparing her first strike, the older Isorian dropped to his knees and balled up like a beaten sudwal. As her blade made its first slicing descent, it did not find its target. Instead, a much larger hand grabbed Arath's wrist and yanked. The next thing Arath knew, she was lying flat on the floor with the Frigid Commander's blade pressed against her throat.

Darosen's voice was calm as he spoke. "Arath, your eagerness to slay could be easily matched by my own. Need I remind you of your position? There are laws that govern this kingdom … laws that this council created. I'd hate to see your dispute end with your last breath."

Arath growled. "You'd be stripped of your rank for taking my life's source. Do I look like a fool, Commander? Allow me to stand, or I shall—"

Before Arath could finish her sentence, the tip of the Frigid Commander's dagger pierced the skin on the left side of her neck, but stopped just before a mortal wound was suffered. Darosen watched Arath squirm, enjoying the pain as it filled her milky eyes. "Or you shall what, Arath? You shall what? Who commands the army? Do you believe a passing as insignificant as yours would cause the men to change their allegiance? Are you truly so vain?"

"That's enough, Commander!" Shamand ordered as he held Doejess' arm while entering the room. "Everyone … please … take your seats. There shall be no further commotion in my presence."

The Frigid Commander released his grip and allowed Arath the freedom to stand. Despite Shamand's inability to see the gesture, the commander bowed. "Yes, My Liege."

Rolling to her feet, Arath shouted, "Are you going to do nothing, Shamand? His blade has been stained by my life's source!" Arath reached up to wipe away the yellow blood that rolled down her neck and moved back to her seat while she waited for a response.

Shamand shook his head. "If the Commander's blade was at your throat, I assume he had good reason for it being in such an undesirable place."

"I didn't say it was at my throat, old man. Perhaps you can see better than you claim. How else would you know its location?"

Shamand barked, "Woman, sit, and don't speak another word! The army also serves me … just as it does the commander. Don't make this blind, old man force this counsel into proper conduct."

The Frigid Commander gave Arath a half-cocked smile as she sat with a plop, her throne creaking beneath her weight as she did. Darosen moved to take his place next to Shamand as the most respected of all Isorians assumed control of the meeting.

The voice of the kingdom's advisor was strong as he spoke. "There shall be no other vote made by this council. The decision has been made as to who the clans' sovereign will be."

Shamand paused, waiting for objections, but when none came, he continued as they all sat waiting for his explanation. "This council made a choice to put the crown on Thoomar's head. It was his passing wish that his son be extended the benefit of this honor."

Grumbling came from all angles around the table, but now a new voice spoke. "Great One, I mean no disrespect, but I must object." Drydeth was a slender Isorian male with a blotchy, blue face. He was completely bald, yet handsome, despite one of his blue ears sticking out farther than the other. He reached beneath his robe and removed a scroll. "This council was created to make these decisions. The decision of who is to be king was not for Thoomar to decide. His ceremony was not yet complete. Again, with all due respect, Lord Shamand, further thought on this matter is necessary … just as a vote is necessary. Please! Allow me to explain my point of view."

Drydeth cleared his throat before he continued. "My head is also well suited for a crown. And as you all know, it was my son who pulled Thoomar clear of danger when the ice fell from beneath his feet during the Great Thaw. Without my bloodline, Thoomar would not have survived. Nor would he have received the vote this council honored him with. Therefore, it is only logical that I become king."

Everyone in the room, except Shamand and the Frigid Commander be-gan to argue. As they shouted amongst each other, now all holding scrolls of their own and pointing them around the large, circular table, the Frigid Commander leaned over and whispered into Shamand's ear. "This is point-less, My Liege. You should settle this matter quickly so that we can prepare the undercity for Thoomar's passing. The army has already received word that Shiver shall be their king, and they are passing this word to the popu-lace. This squabble gets us nowhere."

Shamand smiled and adjusted to a position where he could return the whisper. "Such is politics, my friend. Go now, and prepare to light the fire. See to it that Thoomar's pyre is the tallest any Isorian shall ever behold. I want his memory to be burned into the minds of all Isor. I'll stay behind and ensure that this council settles on a proper outcome. I dare say the wit at this table is not the strongest in our kingdom ... well, excluding the two of us, of course."

The Frigid Commander smiled and then turned to leave.

Shamand sat in silence for a long series of moments and allowed the council's angry shouts to fill the expanse of the room. When he had enough, he held up his hand and commanded their silence. "I have heard all I intend to hear! Now ... I shall tell you my point of view!"

Before another word could be uttered, three of the five minds Shamand would address already knew they would agree with Shamand out of respect. Only Arath and Drydeth would need a strong political hand to mold their points of view. This was a hand Shamand wielded with ease.

THAT SAME PEAK
LATE BAILEM

Now, fellow soul ... allow me to interject again. Ever since the end of the Great Thaw, wizards, warlocks and witches traveled from Luvelles once every five seasons. They were allowed passage by the King of Brandor, and their magic was used to help the Isor rebuild. In doing so, many special items were manipulated by their magic to better serve the people.

An example of this exceptional use of magic was Clandestiny's bed, spe-cifically her mattress and pillow. They had been altered and felt like she was lying on a real mattress and a real pillow that had been stuffed with vestle chick feathers. These magical adjustments were everywhere throughout the city, and as long as another Great Thaw never happened, the ice that shaped Clanny's mattress and pillow would never need to be replaced.

Clandestiny also received many other gifts because of her bloodline. Her room was filled with soft touches—most of them handcrafted. Her bed was covered with her most prized possession, a blanket that was made of cotton grown on Harvestom, and the magic cast upon it allowed the cover to radiate a soothing chill. The blanket was hand stitched, and its colors were bright. The reds, blues, and yellows—oh, those golden yellows—were her favorite. With all the stuffed dolls and animals scattered about Clanny's room, it looked like any child's from Earth ... except for the walls of ice that felt cave-like.

Medolas slid into Clanny's room through the same hole he had thrown chunks of ice down the Peak before. As always, he landed on his feet and sprang forward to catch his balance. Once settled, he looked to find his heart's desire and then frowned once he did.

Clandestiny sat crying in front of a fair-sized desk that had been stained brown. She was holding her fluffy, white, overweight sudwal that she had named Sajeen. The fat, little dog was licking her cheeks and nuzzling her with its nose while trying to cheer her up.

Medolas looked into the large mirror above the desk and found Clanny's reflection. The oval frame surrounding the mirror was made of ice, and it had been stained red.

Seeing Clanny's crystallized tears lying on the floor, Medolas moved to put his arms around her from behind, but Sajeen growled to stop him from comforting her.

Medolas ignored the dog's threat. "Ohhh, Clanny," he said softly. "I hate seeing you like this."

Clandestiny lowered the sudwal to the floor and watched as the dog lumbered across the room. It barely manage to jump onto the bed before she turned and buried her head into Medolas' shoulder. "I cannot believe Thoomar is gone. It's our fault. We should've honored our fathers' wishes and failed to swim in restricted waters."

Stroking the top of Clanny's head, Medolas looked for a way to justify their actions within his own mind, but when no justification could be found, tears of his own began to escape while he responded with as much confidence as he could muster. "I know this is hard for you. You're right. The responsibility of Thoomar's passing lies with us. What can I do to make it better?"

Clanny leaned back and found his milky-gray eyes. "You cannot fix this, Meddy. The greatest of Isorians is gone because of our transgression. This isn't some chip in a piece of furniture that we can simply patch. What's wrong with you?"

Medolas backed up to give Clandestiny some space. "Since there's nothing I can do..." He shrugged. "What now?"

"I'm scared, Meddy." Clanny moved across the room and took a seat on the bed. Her form sank into the magically altered ice as she wiped a large tear off her face. As the yellow blood smeared across the top of her hand, the small, blue crystallizations in her skin altered their color and temporarily created a shade of green. A moment later, Sajeen waddled across the bed and licked at the discoloration until Clanny's hand returned to its normal color.

Shaking his head at the dog's heft, Medolas waited for Clanny to continue. Eventually, she was able to collect her thoughts. "With the Tear hanging from my neck, something within me is changing. I feel peculiar ... as if an unknown emptiness that exists within my being has begun to fill."

Rather than respond, Medolas continued to listen.

"Will I also be required to end myself as Thoomar did for Gabs? Am I truly special, or am I just another sacrifice when the moment comes that I'm needed? I don't even understand what the Tear does or how I should act. How does this responsibility change our lives?"

The sudwal backed up to the head of the bed and growled as Medolas took a seat beside Clanny. He reached across the bed, snagged the chubby pooch and then pulled it into his arms. "It's only been a short while, Clanny. Things will come into focus. Thoomar would not have left you with the responsibility if you weren't capable of bearing it. He was a wise leader, and he would've been a great king."

When Clanny just sat in silence, Medolas added, "Besides, it's not your lack of understanding about the Tear that bothers me. I'm more worried about your health."

Clanny's eyes found Medolas'. "Do I look sickly, Meddy?"

"No ... not sickly, but since you took possession of the Tear, your skin feels warmer to the touch. It's as if you have a fever. Are you feeling alright?"

"I feel healthy ... yet strange. But the words to explain this strangeness and what my body is going through escapes my lips. I feel as if I'm becoming powerful ... growing somehow. I'm so confused."

Clanny stood and returned to the mirror. She reached across the desktop and pulled a small, silver, tin case in front of her. She removed the lid, opened the desk drawer and then grabbed the handle of a small brush. "My understanding of the training I'm to receive is lacking. All I know is that I must work with my father and Shiver's mother to become whatever it is I'm to become."

Medolas tossed the sudwal onto the bed behind him. "What of the Kodess? Do you have any knowledge of the beast?"

Clanny sighed, "None, other than I know the beast is said to be an abomination."

Crossing his left leg over his right, Medolas scratched at the pysples on the bottom of his foot. "How are you going to handle Shiver's mother?"

The thought of Blandina made Clandestiny clinch her hand around the handle of the brush. She looked into the mirror and found Medolas' reflection. "I dislike her, Meddy. Wickedness permeates her every pore and surrounds her like a fog. Though I've seen no ill doing, I know her heart is wrong. Do you think I should tell Shiver that she seemed happy about Thoomar's demise?"

Medolas stood from the bed. "Have you gone nordel? Do you truly think it's best to bring such an accusation to your future sovereign? Telling him wouldn't accomplish anything."

Clanny dabbed the brush into the tin and began to apply the soft blue powder to her face. "It appears that I shouldn't have asked you for your opinion," she responded with a half-hearted smile and eyes filled with irritation. "My mind is still intact … I think." She pondered. "I'm stressed. Perhaps it's possible that I have gone nordel. Do I seem off, my love?"

"No more than usual." Medolas knelt on the floor and began picking up Clandestiny's frozen tears.

Before Clanny could turn away from the mirror to scold Medolas, another figure slid into the room through Clanny's hole. Gabs bounced a bit to try to keep his balance, but since the ruby eyed child had been running when he began his slide, his momentum forced him to tumble across the room. He rolled over the bed, squishing Sajeen as he did and then fell off the other side, hitting the nightstand covered with stuffed toys.

The sudwal yelped as the stuffed animals fell, the largest bonking Gabs on the head as the ruby eyed child came to a stop with his bare feet resting atop the bed and his back on the floor.

Frightened, Clanny's sudwal darted out of the room while she shouted, "Gabs, what has become of your mind? Do you wish to perish again?

Phillip E. Jones | 49

Thoomar has already sacrificed himself, yet you treat this gift as if it isn't something you cherish! You should be fed to the gashtion!"

Before another word could be uttered, another young man slid out of the hole. His attempt to catch himself was far worse than Gabs'. He not only rolled across the top of Clanny's bed, but he also managed to roll to his feet and slide out the door and down the hallway.

Now Clanny was more than furious. She stood, stomped through the doorway, and without saying a word, she grabbed Slips by his arm. As she pulled him back into the room, he lost his balance and fell to his backside on three occasions before Clanny could force him into a seated position on the edge of her bed.

Fellow soul … when referred to by his given name, Slips was called Sagar. He was the son of Ohedri, the leader of the Meslan Clan, the same Isorian Arath intended to end before she was stopped by the Frigid Commander. Slips was born with an irritating birth defect. It was this deformity that had given Thoomar the idea to assign Slips his nickname.

Though other Isorians were unable to see Sagar's flaw when he was standing still, his birth defect became evident as soon as he started walking. Slips was born without pysples, the small suction cups that all Isorians and Tormalians were born with. Without pysples, traction on smooth ice was practically impossible.

"Have you all lost your intellect?" Clanny scolded. "What if my father saw the lot of you in my room? He'd troblet us for sure!"

Slips was the first to speak. "Stop being dramatic, Clanny. Gabs and I felt it necessary to check on you. We're here to show our devotion as friends. We wanted to ensure your wellbeing."

As Gablysin picked himself up off the floor, he added, "Besides … I couldn't stand another moment with my father. He has been scolding me in counsel for far too many moments. My backside is sore from the strap that hangs behind his bedroom door." The ruby eyed child flopped onto the bed and tucked Clanny's pillow behind his head. After resting his feet on the wall above the headboard, he continued. "Did you guys get trobleted?"

"I have failed to return home," Medolas responded. "I fear my grandmother's reaction. I don't want to have my hair pulled when she decides to drag me through the home. The last series of moments in which she reacted so harshly, I almost spent what was left of my youth ugly and bald."

Slips and Gabs began to laugh, but Clanny did not see the humor in the situation. She was about to scold the lot of them further, but Shamand's voice echoed from down the hallway. "Clandestiny! I'd like to speak with you, child!"

Slips was the first to his feet. "We must flee," he whispered. "He'll tear our limbs off if he sees us."

"Shhhhhhh," Medolas commanded. "Just go up the hole."

All three boys hurried to the hole, keeping Slips upright as they bickered about who would go up first.

Seeing their moments were short, Gabs grunted and lowered onto his knees. Slips stepped onto the ruby eyed child's back and then reached up into the hole. He grabbed chiseled hand-holds and began his ascent. Once Medolas was in, he reached back and pulled Gabs up. The three disappeared from sight just as Shamand entered the room, holding Doejess' arm.

Clandestiny took a deep breath, wiped the sweat from her brow and exhaled as her father's large frame cleared the icy archway. She knew Doejess had seen the boys and could only hope he would say nothing.

Understanding her anxiety, Doejess smiled, nodded and then waited for Shamand to speak.

"Clanny, come to me," Shamand commanded as he extended his arms.

Clandestiny did as she was told. "Father, I had no expectation of your return. Is everything as it should be?"

Shamand took a deep breath. "I've come to request that you dress elegantly for the lighting of Thoomar's pyre. I'd like you to stand at my side when the celebration begins. The fire will be large enough to warm the hands of Helmep, and since your mother will be looking down on us, it is my desire that she marvel at your beauty from the heavens."

Clandestiny wrapped her arms around her father and squeezed. "It'll be my joy to make you proud."

Shamand smiled and then turned to leave the room. Just before he passed the arch, he lifted his head into the air and sniffed.

"What is it, Father?"

Shamand grinned and waited. He knew something was amiss. His ears could hear the shallow sounds of the boys' struggles as they worked to push Slips up and out of the hole. Sure enough, Slips lost his hand-holds and all three boys came sliding back into the room and piled on top of one another.

Medolas' breath was knocked from his lungs as Slips landed on his chest, and Gabs was the first to speak as he stood to brush himself off. "Ohhhh-hhh! We must have slid down the wrong hole," he announced. "Medolas, I thought you said this was the spot."

"Yeah, Medolas," Slips added while looking down through his legs at Medolas' face. "How could you have failed to choose the proper hole?"

"Enough!" Shamand said sternly. "Don't mistake my blindness for ignorance. I could smell your stench when I entered the room. The night is filled with a breeze, and it carried the smell of your fear to my nostrils. Stand before me. Now! Clanny, you move to your bed and sit!"

All the children did as instructed. Once the boys were standing at attention, Shamand continued. "Gabs, your father needs your help. His wheeled chair has broken, and his legs are not strong enough to ensure his arrival at Thoomar's passing. I shall decide what action to take for breaking the sacredness of my daughter's room after I've had the moments to think of a proper punishment. Now go, and bring your father to the pyre!

"Slips, you shall return home. See that your family knows of your trespass. If your father fails to troblet you thoroughly, I shall do it myself. You best make sure the beating is severe. Do you understand me, boy?"

With a nod, Slips responded. "Yes, sir."

"Go!" Shamand snapped.

Shamand asked Doejess to leave and return when the moment arrived to depart for Thoomar's passing. Once the skinny assistant was gone, Shamand addressed Medolas. Unexpectedly, his voice was soft and far from angry. "I know of your affections for my Clandestiny, Medolas. I'm no fool. I know your love for her is genuine, and under other circumstances, I would've blessed your relationship. But I fear a union between the two of you will be impossible. You must protect your heart and pull back."

Clandestiny stood from the bed and moved to take a spot beside Medolas. "Father, Meddy is the other half of my life's source. How dare you say our love is an impossibility."

"I agree," Medolas added. "I love Clandestiny. Great One, I complete her."

Shamand sighed and forced a fatherly smile. He knew that what he was about to say would rip out the hearts of both children, and his face displayed his dread. After clearing his throat more than once, he spoke. "Clanny, with the blessing that has been bestowed upon you by the High Priestess, you have many responsibilities that will command your attention."

Clanny's face appeared confident as she responded. "I can handle them, Father. You'll see. I can handle anything with Meddy at my side."

"I can be there for her," Medolas added.

Shamand smiled. "I love you both. But your romance must end."

"No!" Clanny grabbed Medolas' hand in defiance. "I won't do anything without my Meddy!"

Shamand's heart broke at the thought of what he had to say next. "Clandestiny … I have no control over fate. Our laws force me … force you … into this position, and I regret it as much as you. I'd love nothing more than to see your hand fall lovingly into Medolas' on the Peak of your union. But I fear that this Peak will never come."

"But why?" Clanny queried. "What law would prevent us from bonding eternally?"

Medolas remained quiet while he waited for Shamand to respond.

"Only a direct descendant to the throne can bear the responsibility of the Tear. This is why Thoomar was chosen to be king. Now that he has passed, and you bear the responsibility, you are to be bound to Shiver and become queen over the Isor."

"Shiver?" Clandestiny protested. "You must be mad. Then I won't bear the Tear. Medolas is the only one who can complete me." Clandestiny grabbed the Tear of Gramal and began to remove it from her neck. "Here, Father, take it from me."

Before she could finish taking it off, Shamand's voice rose to a level that Clanny had never heard directed toward her. "Do not remove the Tear from around your neck! To do so, would cause all Isorians harm!" His voice softened. "You must be selfless and serve. This is larger than you ... larger than us."

Medolas and Clandestiny looked at each other. Confused, Medolas shrugged and then responded, "Great One, what would become of our people?"

Shamand reached out. "Clanny, show me to your bed." Medolas followed. Once Shamand was seated, the children plopped onto the bed and crossed their legs.

Shamand removed the hood of his cape and scratched the top of his head. After a long silence, he answered. "If the Tear was removed from above Clanny's heart for an extended period of moments, our people would suffer. The Tear can only rest above the heart of one who wishes no ill will. If it was to rest above the heart of a wicked being, the result of this abuse could take many forms."

Medolas could only watch as the magnitude of Shamand's revelation burdened Clandestiny's face. The understanding that she was the only reason her people could maintain their way of life was unbearable.

Clanny's voice trembled as she uttered a response. "W ... wh ... why must I suffer this injustice? Why must I give up all I desire? I don't want to bear this burden."

"Nor did I want this burden to befall you," Shamand responded.

"Then take the Tear from me and place it above your heart, Father. You're a good man."

"I cannot." Shamand reached out and took hold of Clandestiny's hand. "Without a blessing by the priestess, my shortcomings would effect the crystal's ability to protect our people. Unknown wickedness would befall us."

"I don't believe you!" Clanny snapped.

"It matters not!" Shamand snapped back.

Clanny crossed her arms in a huff. "I'm listening!"

Shamand took a few deep breaths. "As I have said, I cannot bear your burden. The removal of the crystal from your skin for an extended series of moments would deliver an end to your own life's source. You cannot run from this responsibility. You must live a life of service to the Isor now that the Tear has been placed about your neck."

Clandestiny took a moment to gather her thoughts. She stood from the bed and moved to take a perceived position of power in front of Shamand. "Father, how dare you allow me to put the crystal above my heart. How could the one who claims to love me most allow me to accept this responsibility? If I were to remove the Tear, how long would it be before I pass?"

Shamand's scarred face fought back the sadness that threatened to escape his eyes and sat in silence for a short series of moments before he responded. "To do so, would bring your end within 10 seasons."

"Father ... clearly, my faith in you was misplaced! What else have you failed to disclose?"

Medolas cringed, hearing Clanny's tone. He knew what was coming and moved to the far corner of the bed as he watched Shamand stand. The strong Isorian towered over Clandestiny's petite frame. Shamand's tone was harsh. "Young lady, silence your tongue! You will show me the respect the wisdom of my 684 seasons commands! Now sit! And never question my love for you again!"

As Clanny moved to take a seat near Medolas, Shamand moved toward the desk and turned around once his hand touched the table top. "When the

High Priestess blessed Thoomar nearly 20 seasons ago, it was agreed upon by the Council of the Seven that when the moment was right, Thoomar would become our new king. The council passed a law that the Tear of Gramal must be worn by someone sitting on the throne or someone who was to ascend to the throne.

"The council believed the Tear's power, and the responsibility the Tear commanded, should only be worn by someone with this esteemed position. It was not until after this law had been in effect that you were born, Clanny. Try to imagine my consternation when the High Priestess arrived, only to announce your heart was the only one pure enough to accept her blessing. She said, 'Only this child may bear the responsibility of the Tear's endowment when Thoomar passes.'"

Shamand moved his hand around until he found the chair. After taking a seat, he continued. "Burdens often find us when we are least prepared. I have also carried many burdens for our people. You're my daughter. You're proud, strong, and possess a gift that should be cherished, not mourned. As the seasons pass, you shall become one with the Tear and be loved by our people."

As Shamand continued to speak, he would divulge many secrets of the Tear—secrets the children refused to hear as they prepared to run. Clanny silently folded the blanket from her bed and handed Medolas her pillow. She tucked the blanket under her arm and then grabbed his hand. Without a word, both children tiptoed from the room. The moment had come for them to flee, just as Medolas had requested for nearly a season. Exiting the home through the main hole, they darted across the tundra.

Moments later, Shamand realized he was alone. He began to call out for their return.

The children could hear Shamand shouting as they leapt over the hole leading down into Clanny's room. It was not long before they disappeared into the darkness.

CHAPTER 4
RING OF FIRE

Now … fellow soul … I'm sure you can imagine the anger Shamand felt as he sat in the confines of his home waiting for his assistant, Doejess, to retrieve him for Thoomar's passing. The whole way to the platform where Thoomar had been laid to light the fire, Shamand vented his frustration, commanding Doejess to guide him faster.

Doejess had always been nervous while leading Shamand under normal circumstances, but sprinting with an angry, old, blind man across the rough shelves of ice covering the city was the guide's definition of insanity. Shamand tripped and fell on six occasions before they arrived at the platform, and on each, he cursed Doejess.

I should tell you, only those Isorians with royal bloodlines received a passing ceremony by fire. Since wood was scarce, it was expensive, and had to be imported from Southern Grayham. Because of this, common Isorians were thrown into the ocean from atop the icy cliffs south of Hydroth. Their bodies were weighted so they sunk, and though it was never discussed, the people knew their loved ones were devoured by predators that lived within the waters of Utopia.

For those Isorians who did burn, their bodies were placed on a platform nearly 20 paces above the ice. There were two sub-platforms directly below the main level that reinforced the structure. This was to ensure their bodies were fully consumed by fire before the towers collapsed onto the ice. The council did not want the ice to melt and create an early end to their ceremonies.

Since the Isorian people were affected by heat, they had to sit in special grandstands that were chiseled more than 100 paces away from the platform. Just as you would have seen in the arenas of Southern Grayham, the nobles sat in boxes tended by servants until the ceremonies were over.

Fellow soul ... let us return to the story when Shamand and Doejess arrived at the royal box where Blandina, Shiver, the Frigid Commander, and the ruby eyed child were waiting.

As soon as Shamand and Doejess stepped through the archway, Shamand listened to the voices of those present to get a sense of where everyone was. He pulled his arm free of Doejess' grip. "Release me, fool ... unless you intend to trip me again!"

Doejess tried to object, but Shamand sent him away. "Be gone with you!"

Satisfied that his irritation had left, Shamand called for the Frigid Commander to guide him to his chair. Once seated, he patted the cushion of the seat next to him. "Sit, Commander. We have business to discuss."

Darosen nodded. "As you wish, My Liege."

Seeing Shamand's distress, Blandina leaned forward in her chair. "What angers you, Shamand?"

The advisor cringed at the sound of Blandina's voice and then pulled the hood of his cape back. "I told Clandestiny her hand was to be given to Shiver, but I fear this news has fallen on rebellious ears. My daughter has run away with Medolas. My neighbors search for them now."

Blandina rolled her eyes. "Did you expect your daughter to be pleased, Shamand? No young woman wants a union she doesn't choose."

The embarrassment Shiver felt could be seen as his mother continued. "I wouldn't worry about Clandestiny. Your neighbors will find her, and if they don't, the commander can organize a search."

Seeing the stone cold look on Shamand's face, Blandina offered further encouragement. "Clandestiny is a brilliant girl. I'm sure she'll come to understand the wisdom behind a union with my son. She'll accept her responsibility to the people. I wouldn't fret over her disappearance. Besides, where could they go?"

Ignoring Blandina, Shamand called for Shiver. The future king stood from his seat and moved to stand in front of his advisor. "I want you to go, boy. Wait for me at the platform. We'll light the fire of your father's passing together."

"I want him with me," Blandina objected. "I should be the one to light the fire with my son."

Shamand reached forward and secured Shiver's arm. With his other hand, he reached up and grabbed the back of the boy's neck and squeezed. "I said go!"

Without looking in his mother's direction, Shiver did as he was told. Once the child was gone, Shamand turned his head in Blandina's direction. "Because of your hatred for Thoomar, I won't allow you the pleasure of lighting his pyre."

"This isn't for you to decide," Blandina rebutted.

Shamand stood from his chair and snapped his fingers.

The Frigid Commander moved to his side.

Once his hand rested on Darosen's shoulder, Shamand responded. "Your son is to be king, but don't doubt my position. Your influence over Shiver stops with me."

Blandina stood from her chair and crossed her arms. "We shall see about that."

Seeing that Shamand's resolve would not bend, Blandina softened her voice. "Perhaps we should search for a way to find peace between us. After all … our children are to be united. Fighting gets us nowhere."

Shamand shook his head, "How can Clandestiny be expected to see wisdom in a marriage she'll despise. I also fail to see wisdom in this union. My daughter can bear the burden of the Tear without marrying your son. I won't take her happiness from her and also watch her suffer the Tear's curse. Shiver will be an unwed king until he takes another bride from some other clan."

Blandina's face tightened. "There's no other with Clandestiny's beauty. You don't have the authority to override the council. Law is law, and as mother of this kingdom's future sovereign, you'll conform. Clandestiny will marry my son, and you can't do anything to stop it."

Chuckling, Shamand responded. "Woman … I am the council."

"Is that so?" Blandina looked at Darosen. "Do you agree, Commander?"

Darosen nodded. "Shamand's voice falls heavily upon the council's ears, My Lady. They'll listen to him."

Grinning, Shamand added, "The only man who had a voice more powerful than mine passed while saving the ruby eyed child." The advisor's voice turned cold. "I assure you, the law governing the Tear will change. I won't offer Clandestiny to your son."

Without listening for Blandina's response, the advisor turned his head in Gablysin's direction. "After the commander guides me to the platform, I want you to sing a song fit for the departure of my old friend. Once complete, Shiver and I shall light the fire to free Thoomar's soul."

Gablysin nodded and then lowered his burgundy eyes to the floor, "I understand, Great One."

Shamand motioned for the Frigid Commander to take him away.

Once he was out of earshot, Blandina scoffed, "I hope you fall off the platform!"

MEANWHILE,
A GREAT DISTANCE WEST OF HYDROTH

Dropping her blanket, Clandestiny fell onto the ice, her chest heaving. "Medolas, wait! I can go no further!"

Medolas stopped running and returned to Clandestiny's side. He put the pillow on the ice and sat on top of it. After catching his breath, he responded. "We must keep moving. They'll be searching for us. We need to hide where they'll fail to search."

Clandestiny reached forward and pulled Medolas' knife free of its sheath. She chipped the ice and then placed the chunks in her mouth. She responded only after her thirst was quenched. "Where should we go? I can think of no place my father wouldn't seek for us."

Medolas lowered to his back and pulled the pillow beneath his head. After pondering a moment, he rolled to his side and propped his head up with his right arm. "Thoomar mentioned the Ko-dess. They'd never think to look for us there. We can learn to avoid the abomination and exist in its territory."

Clandestiny gasped. "You'd have us run toward greater danger? The Ko-dess would steal our life's sources. I don't want to be eaten by an abomination, Medolas."

"Spoken like a girl," Medolas chuckled as he rolled onto his back. "Do you think your father would allow you to stand before the Ko-dess if the creature intended to feast on your flesh?" He bent his right leg and then placed his left foot on his knee so he could scratch the bottom of it. "Helmep has granted you the gift of exaggeration."

"Leave Helmep out of this!" she snapped.

Before Medolas could respond, a noise filled their ears. The children quieted and stared into the darkness. Two glowing eyes were headed in their direction at a rapid pace. Medolas jumped to his feet and retrieved his knife out of Clandestiny's hand. He took a stance and prepared to strike.

A moment later, the creature's mass came into view. Clandestiny's sudwal was panting. His tiny legs were nearly worn out from chasing them this far. Clanny smiled. "Medolas, look. It's Sajeen. How adorable."

After watching the sudwal flop down at Clanny's feet, Medolas responded. "Sajeen, you frightened us." He lifted the blade and pointed it at the dog. "You nearly met your end."

Stroking the sudwal's head, Clandestiny added, "It appears we'll have other companionship now. A little something from home will be pleasant. I must remember to thank Helmep for his gift in my prayers."

Medolas reached out and patted Sajeen's fluffy back. "I wouldn't call Sajeen little. I can't believe his roundness allowed him to run this far. Helmep must have sent him to us for a reason."

No sooner did Medolas finish his statement when another noise was heard. Once again, the children stared into the darkness. "Who do you think it is?" Clanny whispered.

"Shhh," Medolas ordered. "Be quiet."

Two forms materialized. They were large, imposing, and possessed mouths filled with razor-sharp fangs. The snowhounds were gnashing their teeth as they crept toward their prey.

"We cannot outrun them," Medolas whispered. "They'll surely end us."

Clandestiny grabbed the back of Medolas' arm. "Meddy, what do we do? They must have followed Sajeen's scent."

Without another word, Medolas grabbed the sudwal out of Clandestiny's arms. He stabbed Sajeen with his knife, just deep enough to allow blood to flow. Clandestiny screamed as Medolas tossed the sudwal onto the ice. The dog slid toward the snowhounds and passed between them. As expected, Sajeen panicked and started to run.

Smelling the blood on the dog's fur, the snowhounds gave chase.

Medolas grabbed Clandestiny's hand and shouted, "Run!"

The children fled. It was not long before they heard the yelp of Sajeen's demise.

KING SHIVER VEELION'S THRONE ROOM
5 PEAKS OF BAILEM HAVE PASSED

The Frigid Commander entered the undercastle and made his way to the throne room. Upon entering, he removed the hood of his cape and bowed to his new sovereign. "My King, last night's coronation was a grand celebration. Be assured, I will serve you well. How does it feel to sit at the head of this kingdom?"

Standing to the right of the throne, Shamand spoke before Shiver could. "Do you bring word of Clandestiny, Commander?" Familiar with his surroundings, Shamand's blindness was not an impediment in this part of the undercastle. The advisor walked down seven of the twelve steps leading away from the throne as he continued. "She isn't safe with only Medolas to protect her. Tell me you have word."

Darosen lowered to one knee and bowed his head. "My Liege, there are 11 search parties with more than 30 heads in each. The wilderness is vast. Finding her will take more moments than have transpired since her departure. If only I was authorized to assemble additional parties."

Turning on the step, Shamand bowed in Shiver's direction. "My King, with your permission, I'd like to double the search."

Darosen looked up to see Shiver's reaction. The look on Shiver's face was exactly what the commander expected. He knew this was Shiver's first opportunity as king to give a command. Darosen lowered his head to hide his smile and enjoyed the child's awkwardness.

Shiver pondered for many moments. Instead of answering, he stood from his throne and walked down the steps. He stopped next to Shamand. The king whispered in his advisor's ear, "What would you have me say, and how should I say it?"

Shamand smiled and whispered his reply. "Go back to your throne and say this: I think doubling the search is a fine idea, Lord Shamand. The return of Clandestiny is this kingdom's highest priority. Carry on." As Shiver turned to reclaim his throne, Shamand tapped him on the shoulder. The child stopped and listened. "Say these things with authority, boy."

Though Shamand could not see it, Shiver nodded. The boy walked up the steps with his chest pushed forward. Upon reaching the throne, he turned and saw his mother as she crept into the room. The young king gave Blandina a smile and then looked past Shamand toward Darosen whose head remained bowed. "Rise, Commander," Shiver ordered in the most authoritative voice a boy of 16 seasons could muster. "The return of Clandestiny is this kingdom's priority. Double the search, and..." The child thought a moment, then added. "I shall accompany you."

Proud of his delivery, Shiver enjoyed the look on both men's faces as he watched his mother stop behind the commander. He could see the pride in her expression as Darosen questioned, "My King, with respect, the wilderness is no place for a boy. Perhaps it's best for you to stay behind and govern the city."

"Agreed," Shamand added. The advisor turned his head in Shiver's direction. "We have much work to do, Your Grace. You have many lessons to master before you can become the king your father wanted you to be."

Before Shiver could argue, Blandina placed her hand on the commander's shoulder and spoke in rebuttal. "Lord Shamand, the clans have not had a king for many seasons. A few Peaks in the wilderness will not cause this kingdom distress. It would do Shiver well to know the lands under his rule." She placed her hand on the commander's left elbow and squeezed. "I shall also accompany you, Darosen."

Any relief Shiver should have felt because of his mother's defense was overshadowed by Shamand's reaction as the boy watched his advisor clench his teeth. Shamand walked down the remaining steps and stopped where the scent of Blandina's perfume emanated. He scoffed, "Woman, you don't decide what's good for this kingdom. Mind your place."

Blandina rolled her eyes as she reached out and patted Shamand on the chest. She leaned in and allowed her weight to rest against him. Shamand could feel the sting of her words and the chill of her breath on his face as she hissed. "Blind men are in no position to object to a king's orders."

With two fingers, one on each of Shamand's pecs, Blandina pushed clear. She then brushed past the advisor and ascended the steps to the throne. Sitting on Shiver's chair, she pulled the boy onto her lap. "Do you wish for adventure, my son? If so, you have only to voice your desire. You have the power to do that which other boys cannot. Command Shamand to show you your kingdom. See for yourself what he cannot." She gave Shiver a squeeze, kissed his cheek and whispered in his ear. "Do it now, my son."

Before Shiver could do as his mother instructed, Shamand stormed up the steps. He reached forward, "Take my hand, boy!" After Shiver did as he was told, Shamand pulled the king down to the step below him and then grabbed the child by his left ear. After dragging Shiver to the lower level of the throne room, Shamand turned his head in Blandina's direction. "Shiver won't be leaving the city! Take your accursed tongue, and see that it finds some other soul to torment!"

Before another word could be uttered, Shamand felt around and placed his hand on the commander's shoulder. "Take us away from here, Commander ... perhaps to the stables. I'd imagine they have a better stench at the moment."

As the commander led Shamand and Shiver out of the room, Darosen turned his head in Blandina's direction. With his free hand, he lifted his palm as if to say, "What would you have me do?"

As the throne room door slammed shut, the ice it was made of cracked. Blandina sat back on the throne, threw her legs over the right armrest and chuckled.

The Harugen Understables
Early Bailem, the Next Peak

"Everyone to the surface!" the Frigid Commander shouted from atop his harugen. "I shall assign each group a territory once there! If you haven't said your morning prayers to Helmep, do so before we disburse."

Fifty-five harugen-mammoths, with seven men on each, skittered up and out of the understables, leaving the commander and his mount behind. The ice of the hole leading to the surface crumbled beneath the weight of 5,500 legs as the beasts used their sharp ends to assure a quick ascent. In awe of the repairs the stable hands would need to make to the tunnel, the commander watched as the last chunk of ice slid back into the understables and stopped at the front legs of his harugen.

After dismissing the stable hands, Darosen dismounted and walked into an empty stable. He looked toward the back wall and whistled. A moment later, Blandina stepped from behind a large watering trough.

"My moments will not be the same during your absence," Blandina said as she walked toward the commander and placed her arms around his waist. After a passionate kiss, she continued, "It won't be long before you and our son will venture into the wilderness. Soon, you'll be able to teach him to be a man. Shiver needs the company of his father."

The commander frowned. "How can I create such a relationship when Shamand commands the boy's attention?"

Blandina placed her hands on each of the commander's cheeks. "Do not fret, my love. Everything is as it should be. Soon, the Tormal will rule Hydroth, and you shall have the freedom to become a proud father."

The commander pulled Blandina's hands from his cheeks and pinned them between his own. "What of Shamand? He's a mighty warrior, despite his affliction. I worry for your safety."

Blandina removed her hands and reached inside a small pouch that had been tied about her waist under a thin, lacy, pink shawl. She produced a small, silver pin that had been cast in the form of a beetle and secured it to the commander's cape. "This trinket shall animate and return to the city when the moment comes to call for Shamand. All you must do is speak Shamand's name and lower the beetle to the ice. After the fool leaves Hydroth, see that Shamand makes his way into the southernmost entrance of the Caves of Carne. I shall do the rest."

"What of Shiver? Shamand will bring the boy with him."

"Worry not, for at that moment, Shiver won't be of good health and will need to rest. Shamand shall be forced to journey without him."

"And you'll follow?"

"No. I'll depart before Shamand."

"Again, what of your safety? Perhaps my blade should be the one to take Shamand's life's source, though I don't see how I can ignore my bond with him. He has been like a father to me."

With a seductive smile, Blandina responded. "You needn't worry. I wouldn't ask that of you, nor is the betrayal of your friendship necessary." She took the commander's right hand and kissed the top of it. "You must go."

After a long embrace, the commander ran toward his harugen. He mounted the beast with ease, grabbed its reins and commanded the mammoth-centipede to skitter up and out of the understables.

60 Peaks of Bailem have Passed
Medolas and Clandestiny are
10 Peaks North of the Pass of Nayala

This was Medolas and Clandestiny's first journey into the Mountains of Tedfer. Tired, and with sore muscles, compliments of the harsh terrain, Clandestiny lowered to her back on a snow covered rock. This flat boulder was at the top of a mound that had piled with others during a recent landslide. The slide happened only Peaks earlier, leaving the mound sitting atop the edge of a cliff, and the boulders that failed to stop, plummeted to a crumbling end.

Clandestiny covered herself with her colorful blanket and allowed the snow beneath her to act as her cushion. The snow conformed to her curves as she reached back to fluff her pillow. Once satisfied, she rolled onto her side and closed her eyes, leaving Medolas standing on the rock next to her with his mouth open.

Medolas' milky-gray stare tightened. Turning away, he bit his lip and looked toward the horizon. After a moment, he began to trace the peak of each mountain in the distance with his eyes while a frown pursed his lips. Shaking his head, he turned back to Clanny and thought, *How dare she sleep.*

Medolas squatted next to Clanny, took a deep breath and then pushed her off the rock. He enjoyed her squeal and smirked as she landed with a thud on the boulder below.

Clandestiny jumped to her feet. Once she understood what happened, her eyes spoke for her as they looked up and burned into Medolas'. "What in Helmep's name?" she barked as she threw her hands up in disgust. Grabbing a handful of snow off the stone she had been pushed from, Clanny pitched the packed wad at Medolas.

"Whaaaat?" Medolas said as he swatted the snowball aside.

Clanny pulled herself back onto the rock and stopped only a hand in front of Medolas' face. "Have you lost your ability to employ clear thought?" She slapped his chest. "I could've been wounded. Must you attack me to win conversation?"

Medolas kicked Clanny's blanket down onto the stone where she had fallen. Then he reached for the pillow. After fighting her for it, he pulled it free and tossed the pillow down the ledge. Both children could only watch as the cushion caught on a branch that protruded from the ledge and ripped. The magic filling the pillow poured out of the opening, and as a result, the softness the magic offered to the cushion vanished. All that was left was a pillow-shaped mass of ice that fell to the base of the cliff and burst into hundreds of pieces.

Clanny slapped Medolas' arm. "Look at what you've done. Now our heads will suffer. You've gone nordel."

"Nordel? Our heads? Only your head has enjoyed the comfort!" Medolas hollered. "You've ignored me for more Peaks than I can remember!"

"Did you expect any less?" Clanny snapped back.

Medolas crossed his arms in defiance. "I've done nothing wrong! If you want me to leave you to your own accord, then say so. I can suffer in silence without you, and you can find the Ko-dess on your own."

Clanny sat on the rock and let her legs hang over its edge before she responded. "Don't feign to misunderstand my anger. You know my mind, Meddy."

"Your mind?" Medolas rebuffed. "How could any sane Isorian understand?"

With that, Clandestiny jumped to the rock below and grabbed her blanket. "If I have become tedious, I will continue on my own."

"You wouldn't last."

"I can handle my own affairs!" Clanny defended. She jumped down onto the next rock and then hopped forward across a small gap before she jumped down to another stone.

Medolas scoffed.

"Do you doubt me, Medolas?"

"I doubt nothing. Go ahead. Leave if you want."

With that, Clandestiny leapt from the final stone onto the ledge. She dropped her blanket to the ground, grabbed a handful of snow, balled it up tight and chucked it at Medolas.

Again, Medolas swatted the snowball away. "What angers you?"

"If you must know … Sajeen is the cause of my distemper."

Medolas' face showed his confusion. "Still? On how many occasions must we discuss this? Sajeen saved our life's sources. Why does this loss continue to make me suffer your malice?"

Clandestiny shook her head. "Men!" She turned and began to walk up the ledge toward the top of the mountain.

Without hesitation, Medolas hopped from rock to rock and then ran to catch up. He grabbed Clanny by the back of the arm. "Stop! You do realize that you're angry with me for saving us, don't you? You must realize that the sudwal was an acceptable loss."

"Sajeen was my friend, Meddy!" Tears began to flow down Clanny's cheeks, causing her skin to discolor.

Medolas took a step back and thought for a short series of moments. He knew there was no way to soften the pain. Instead of trying to fix it, he pulled Clanny close. "I'm sorry," was all he said.

Clandestiny would cry on his shoulder for a long series of moments before she finally accepted the loss of her pet. Since they were not far from the summit, Medolas led Clandestiny to the far side of the mountain before they lowered to the ground and fell asleep cuddled beneath Clanny's blanket.

MEANWHILE, THE SOUTHERNMOST ENTRANCE INTO THE CAVES OF CARNE

Now, fellow soul … in case you don't remember, the Caves of Carne acted as a safe haven for the Tormal during the Great Freeze. When the Tormalians abandoned the caves to return to their city, they left behind a great deal of history in the process. Culinary vessels, weaponry, books, and various hieroglyphics were scattered throughout thousands of rooms that existed off the main veins of the caves. The southernmost entrance was called *Feéjeseéde*—a name given by the Tormalian Council. The symbols were chiseled into the stone above the entrance, and their meaning was hidden from the Isor.

The Isorian Frigid Commander, Darosen, the Isorian army's second in command, Shefrome, and three of Darosen's Orland Lieutenants, Severen, Ograss, and Polomayne, had gathered around a seal's carcass just outside the mouth of the cave's southernmost entrance.

With his dagger, the Frigid Commander cut out the seal's lungs, sliced them into chunks and then tossed each of his men a piece. "My mind is tortured," the commander said with a half-chewed mouthful.

Shefrome, a strong, long-haired warrior with dreads, was the one to respond. "Tell us of your anguish."

After swallowing another mouthful, the commander buried his dagger into the side of the seal. "Shamand will be here tomorrow."

Shefrome's head tilted to one side. "Why would Shamand's presence cause you anguish?"

Darosen stood and walked to the opening of the cave. He peered inside to ensure hidden ears were not listening in on their conversation. "The king's mother waits inside. I have been commanded to bring Shamand to her upon his arrival. She intends to deliver an end to the Great One's life's source."

The men were speechless. After a long series of moments, Severen, a short, muscular male with a braided beard, leaned forward toward the seal and grabbed the knife. After cutting a fresh piece, he leaned back. "We cannot allow this. Shamand has become like a father to us all."

Darosen nodded. "I agree, but the king has ordered his demise."

"Why?" Severen questioned. "Shamand is the best advisor Shiver could have."

The Frigid Commander shrugged. "The king wants what his mother wants. Her influence over the boy is growing, and once Shamand passes, there won't be any stopping her."

"Are we going to try to stop this?" Ograss, a plain looking warrior with short hair, interjected.

"No," Shefrome responded. "It's not our place."

Darosen cut in. "The boy doesn't understand the consequences of his ruling … yet I can see no recourse. Despite my affections for Shamand, I must do as our sovereign commands."

Another long series of moments passed before Shefrome stood and moved next to Darosen. He placed his hand on the Frigid Commander's shoulder. "Your commission was given to you because of your loyalty to the Isor. There will be many moments in which you must choose to do something against your conscience."

"We always have a choice," Darosen replied. "How can I be expected to follow an order that demands I be a part of ending a great man?" The Frigid Commander redirected his gave and stopped on Severen. "Like you said … Shamand has become like a father to us."

Shefrome placed a hand on the Frigid Commander's shoulder. "A life of service is no easy task. If the king has ordered Shamand's demise, then it's our duty to ensure the Great One is delivered into the trap that awaits him."

Shefrome removed his hand and looked toward the others. "Shamand, himself, would expect us to obey our king. He would hold no ill will toward us. I would further say that he would be angry with us for not obeying."

The Frigid Commander patted Shefrome on the arm and then took a seat on one of four blocks of ice that had been placed around the seal's carcass. Darosen reached out and grabbed a pouch filled with ale that he had tucked next to his block and poured each man a goblet full. He then lifted his goblet skyward and proclaimed, "To king and clans."

The men lifted theirs in kind. "To king and clans."

The Caves of Carne
The Peak of Bailem, the Next Peak

Doejess pulled back on the reins to stop Shamand's harugen next to where three other harugens had been tethered.

Upon seeing their visitors, the Frigid Commander exited the cave, walked around what was left of the seal's carcass and strode another 50 paces across the ice to greet them. Seeing the souls who straddled the harugen's back, the expression on Darosen's face did not show his surprise as he waved for Doejess to toss him the harugen's reins. Once tethered, Darosen bowed. "Your arrival pleases me."

Shamand looked toward the ground in the general direction of Darosen's voice. "Good Peak, Commander."

Darosen looked past the advisor toward Shiver who sat on the saddle behind Shamand two segments back. "My King, I was told you were ill. Your presence is unexpected. I assumed that you would've remained in the city."

Shamand responded before Shiver had the chance. "The boy fairs well, Commander … without gratitude to his mother, of course." Shamand reached forward and grabbed three bags that had been secured to the harugen's saddle in front of him. He tossed them toward the commander without waiting for Doejess to complete the task. "Catch!"

Shamand then reached into a small pouch that was attached to his belt. He retrieved the pin that Blandina gave to Darosen before the commander left Hydroth. "I came as soon as I received your summons, Commander."

The advisor tossed the silver beetle to the ice. The pin animated and scurried toward Darosen before it solidified at his feet. The commander picked the beetle up off the ice and pinned it to his cape while Shamand dismounted.

Shamand's tone sounded irritated when next he spoke. "Blandina has been missing for over 20 Peaks now. When the boy's mother could not be located, I was forced to drag the boy with me. I tended to his fever during the first 2 Peaks of our journey."

Darosen lifted his arms and motioned for Shiver to jump. The boy-king brought his right leg over the saddle and pushed clear of the top of the harugen's back. The commander caught Shiver and then lowered him to the ground. As soon as Shiver had his balance, the commander dropped to one knee. "My King … how may I be of service?"

Again, Shamand spoke before Shiver had the chance. "Grab our bags and take them inside the cave, boy."

"I can do that for him," Darosen objected.

"Nonsense," Shamand rebutted. "What good is a king if he isn't strong enough to carry bags." Before the commander had the chance to argue, Shamand redirected the conversation. "Doejess, mount an orb to one of the walls inside the cave, and see to it the king begins his studies." Again, Shamand redirected the conversation. "Shiver, tonight, you'll read the story of Klidess the Mighty and recount the tale to me when you're finished."

The Frigid Commander looked at Shiver. "Ahhh … that's a wonderful story, My King. If only one man in your army was as mighty, what a fine army you'd command. Perhaps after you complete your studies, you would allow me to show you some of Klidess' movements with a blade."

Shiver smiled and then looked up at his advisor. "Would this be acceptable, Lord Shamand?"

Shamand grinned and motioned for Shiver to come close. He rummaged his powerful, weathered hand through the child-king's hair. "Of course you may train. You have your father's spirit."

Darosen cringed at the sound of Shiver being referred to as Thoomar's son, but he said nothing of his irritation. "You will make a fine warrior, Your Grace."

"Agreed. May Helmep be praised," Shamand added. "But remember … you may train with Darosen only after your studies are complete."

The Frigid Commander cleared his throat. "Lord Shamand, there are matters that we must discuss. Perhaps our sovereign's studies would be best accomplished from the back of your harugen until our meeting is complete."

Concern appeared on Shamand's face. "Does this pertain to my daughter, Commander? If so … I see no reason why the king should not be present."

Darosen reached out and placed his left hand on Shamand's left shoulder. "My Liege, I only ask you trust my judgment."

Shamand paused a moment before turning to Shiver. "Boy, you heard the commander. See that your backside returns to the saddle. Go." Again, Shamand redirected the conversation. "Doejess, see that the king is fed."

Shiver grabbed a large, leather-bound book out of Shamand's bag and backed up to get a running start toward his harugen. Shamand waited for the child-king to settle into the saddle and begin reading aloud before he put his arm across Darosen's shoulders to allow the commander to lead him away from the harugens.

"Commander, what is it? Does this matter pertain to my daughter?"

Darosen looked toward the cave. The officers with whom he had dined the night before were standing outside the entrance waiting for his signal. He sighed.

"What is it, Commander?" Shamand questioned again, sensing the commander's anxiety. Though he could not see the stress on Darosen's face, the tension in the commander's shoulders was speaking for him. "Your mind troubles you, doesn't it? Your silence begs to tell a story." Shamand used his powerful hand to rub out the tension in the commander's neck. "Speak to me. You have my ear."

Darosen stepped out of Shamand's grip and walked a few steps toward the cave. Pulling at the top of his hood, he signaled his men and then turned back toward Shamand as they disappeared inside the cave.

Shamand only waited a short series of moments before he commanded, "Darosen … return to me. Why are you so troubled?"

Darosen did as instructed. He took hold of the back of Shamand's arm. "Walk with me, My Liege." Shamand could feel the hesitation in Darosen's gait as the commander sought isolation. They would take 41 paces before the commander would speak again. "The way before us remains flat for as far as my eyes can see. There are no obstacles to betray your footing."

Shamand walked for another 30 paces before he stopped them both from venturing further. "Darosen, enough. Clearly, you're not yourself. Trust an old man, and speak your mind."

The Frigid Commander took a deep breath. "I fear that I've failed you, My Lord. Blandina is waiting inside the cave. She has had you summoned to a trap. She desires to end your life's source."

Shamand's expression did not change as he remained silent and motioned for the commander to continue.

"The men believe their king has ordered your demise." The Frigid Commander fondled the handle of his sword as he chose his next words. "If it was not for our bond, I would not be telling you now, but I cannot betray you in good conscience. What are your orders, My Liege?"

Shamand remained silent while he thought through the seriousness of the situation. Eventually he cleared his throat. "Do nothing other than return to my harugen. Keep watch over the king, and … well … watch Doejess, if you must."

Shamand's candor turned serious. "Are there others assisting Blandina? If so, how many have been commanded to spring the trap?"

"Four men, My Liege—Shefrome, Severen, Ograss, and Polomayne. They follow orders only."

Shamand chuckled. "That shanavel certainly understands the strategies of a trap, does she not?"

"Indeed," the commander responded. "I was to tell you that your daughter lies wounded inside, but I cannot fulfill this deception. Though my agendas are not your own, I cannot allow your betrayal. I regret that my decisions over the last 17 seasons have led us to a place where you stand in harm's way."

"Why participate in this ruse, Commander?" Shamand patiently questioned.

Darosen bit his bottom lip and then confessed, "Shiver is of my loins. I am also Tormal. Shiver is not a king."

Shamand's brow furrowed. "Why tell me this now? You've always had my trust."

The commander looked toward the clouds as if he was too embarrassed to look at Shamand. "I only want to be a father to my son, not destroy a kingdom of innocents in the process."

Another long silence filled their moments. Eventually, Shamand chuckled. "Somehow … I knew the boy wasn't Thoomar's."

Darosen pulled his eyes away from the sky and found Shamand's. "How could you have known, My Liege?"

"When Shiver was born, I felt the child favored neither his mother nor his father. As he grew, this never changed. Eventually, my eyes failed me further, and by his tenth season, I was no longer able to clearly witness the changes to his face."

Shamand stepped forward, placed a hand on each of Darosen's shoulders and then squeezed. "Blandina's treachery runs deep into the heart of this kingdom. Please don't fret over where your choices have led us. Most men succumb to the will of a seasoned seductress."

The commander's eyes dropped. "I fear the wonder between her legs has been my weakness. What will you do with me?"

Shamand took a step back and extended his hand. "Give me your blade, Commander. I shall determine your fate upon my return. For now, shall we see if a blind man can dispose of four men and the shanavel they protect?"

The commander unsheathed his long sword and extended the weapon, lowering the handle into Shamand's palm. "May Helmep be with you, My Liege. The men are scattered throughout the cave, and you will only need to face one man before you reach Blandina. This man is also Tormal."

Shamand twirled the blade in his hand. "Tormal?"

"Yes. He is Tormal, though he doesn't know I am also Tormal."

"How is this possible? Are you saying he's unaware of your lineage?"

The Frigid Commander smiled. "Yes, but 'how' is a conversation that would encompass many of our moments. I pray to Helmep that your blade will free me from the burdens of my choices. All I wanted was to be a good father."

Shamand extended his free arm. "Care to guide a blind man to a fight, Commander? It appears that I fight an unexpected enemy on this Peak."

A large smile appeared on Darosen's face as he grabbed hold of Shamand's forearm to shake it before leading him to the cave. "You have nerve that matches the gashtion's, My Liege."

Upon entering the cave, the Frigid Commander whispered, "The tunnel branches in three directions. Each branch will return to the main vein. Blandina hides in waiting just beyond where they merge. Shefrome is the Tormalian who will stand between you and victory."

Shamand nodded. "And the others?"

Darosen reached down and unsheathed a knife that he had tied to his right thigh. "I cannot allow you to hunt alone. I'll dispose of them myself."

Shamand placed his left hand on Darosen's chest. "There's no need to end their life's sources, Commander. Show mercy. Send the men home to their families."

"What of Shefrome?" Darosen questioned.

Shamand spun the long sword in his right hand. "I'll ensure that he sees the value of his departure. Don't fret. This blind man can still see in other ways."

The Frigid Commander placed a hand on Shamand's shoulders and turned him in the right direction. "The width of the cave at its narrowest point is 10 paces. Use your blade to determine the location of the walls. The room where Blandina hides is 313 paces from where we stand. She waits in the first room on the right after the tunnels merge."

Shamand nodded. "What are the dimensions of the room? Does it remain open or confined with obstacles?"

The Frigid Commander thought a moment. "From the entrance, the width of the room is 20 paces to either side, and its depth is just over 51. All obstacles sit against the left wall. They consume four paces. Beyond that, the room remains open with smaller objects scattered throughout. If you were to keep your feet low to the floor, these obstacles could be kicked aside with ease."

Again, Shamand nodded and motioned for Darosen to come close. "Thank you."

The commander did as instructed, placing his forehead against Shamand's. "You treated me like a father while I was under your command. I deeply regret that I'm not Isor. The deceptions my heritage have required of me are inexcusable. You, Shamand…" Darosen patted the advisor on the sides of both arms and then squeezed "You're a great man. You deserved better from me."

Shamand reached up and grabbed the back of the commander's neck with his left hand. "You only wanted to serve your kingdom. I can respect that. I also cannot find fault in a father who wishes to do what is right by his son. Every father must make impossible choices. You're forgiven, Darosen."

Though Shamand was unable to see it, Darosen smiled as he backed away. "May Helmep be with you, My Liege."

Without responding, Shamand entered the tunnel. The placement of each footstep was calculated. He controlled the pysples on the bottom of his feet and lowered them to the surface without making a sound. One hundred thirty paces and two bends in the cave would pass before he stopped.

Shamand stood still, his breathing quiet. After a short series of moments, he spoke. "Shefrome, your heartbeat gives away your location. I can smell the scent of your fear."

Directly to Shamand's right, Shefrome stood with the blade of his short sword lifted above his head. Shefrome wanted to respond, but to do so would truly give away his location. Over the next five heartbeats, he took in a slow breath and held it to soothe his anxiety. Lifting his right foot, he allowed his body to fall forward and brought down his blade in the direction of Shamand's head.

Sensing Shefrome's movement, Shamand grinned as he spun to defend. The weapons seared against one another as Shamand continued to spin out of the block and into the offensive. The advisor used the backside of his foot in a sweeping motion to knock Shefrome's legs out from under him. Hearing Shefrome land with a thud, the Tormalian's blade clanked against the cave floor. Shamand used the noise to calculate the placement of where his enemy's arm would be. A split moment later, Shefrome's blade laid useless after his right hand was severed above the wrist.

Ignoring the warrior's scream, Shamand kicked away the appendage that was still grasping the blade. Before Shefrome could move, Shamand mounted him with his long sword pressed against Shefrome's neck. "Be still!"

"Please, Great One! Spare my life's source!" Shefrome begged.

Shamand pressed his blade a little harder against the Tormalian's throat. "Begging doesn't become you, Shefrome."

"Then what would you have me do?"

Shamand pulled back his blade and stood. He turned and walked in the direction of where he kicked his attacker's severed hand. Prying the blade out of its rigid fingers, Shamand tossed the weapon onto the floor next to Shefrome. "I will offer you a choice. You may stay and fight, or you may flee and return to Gesper."

Though Shamand could not see the look on Shefrome's face, he enjoyed the warrior's surprise as he listened to the break in the Tormalian's breathing.

"Yes … I know you're Tormal. Choose your fate."

Shefrome moaned as he crawled up the wall of the cave and into a standing position. Groaning, he pushed clear of the rock so he could remove his belt from his waist. The leather straps covering his manhood fell to the floor as the belt pulled free of the loops that kept them in place. He cringed as he tightened the belt around the stub of his right arm to stem the flow of blood.

"I said, choose your fate," Shamand demanded.

Shefrome bent over and grabbed his sword. He pointed the blade in Shamand's direction. Upon seeing a large grin appear on Shamand's face, he allowed the blade to fall back to his side. "I choose Gesper."

"A wise choice, Tormalian. Perhaps your people are wiser than I've given them credit for over my seasons. Leave your blade on the floor and abandon your post. Upon exiting the cave, speak with Doejess. He'll see to it that you're covered and that your wound is sealed."

Shefrome looked down at his nakedness and then back at Shamand. "How did you...?"

Shamand frowned. "Just go!"

The advisor listened as Shefrome made his way past him toward the mouth of the cave. Once satisfied the Tormalian was no longer a threat, Shamand worked his way beyond where the caves merged and found the door that led into the room where Blandina was said to be hiding. He rubbed his hand across its wooden surface until he found an iron ring that served as a doorknob.

Before pulling the door open, Shamand thought back to what Darosen had said. *"From the entrance, the width of the room is 20 paces to either side, and its depth is just over 51. All obstacles sit against the left wall. They consume four paces. Beyond that, the room remains open with smaller objects scattered throughout. If you were to keep your feet low to the floor, these obstacles could be kicked aside with ease."*

Pulling on the ring, the hinges of the door squealed as if the weight of the wood burdened them. Shamand quickly lifted his sword and pointed its tip in the direction of the opening. He listened. Ten controlled breaths passed before he felt confident enough to step inside.

Every movement he made was silent and calculated as Shamand's feet passed above the smooth floor. He kept his feet turned inward to avoid stubbing his toes against one of the smaller objects.

At the back of the room, sitting in the far left corner, Blandina waited on an old crate the Tormal had left behind. Well lit, the rectangular room had six orbs secured to the rock walls. To her right, another crate sat with a pile of eight plates sitting atop it. With her feet crossed beneath her yellow shawl, she quietly removed four pieces of pottery from the top of the stack. As Shamand worked his way toward the center of the room while kicking various sized relics to the side, her excitement grew.

With a sinister smile, Blandina tossed the first plate, angling it toward the far side of the room. The piece of pottery landed not more than five paces to the right of Shamand. Blandina grinned as she watched the blind man react.

With lightning reflexes, Shamand took a quarter turn to face the noise, lifted his sword and took a defensive stance.

Before the advisor could gather his wits, Blandina tossed another plate. During this series of moments, the plate passed over the top of Shamand's head and shattered 10 paces directly to his right. Again, the advisor reacted, taking another quarter turn and remained ready to defend.

An instant later, a third plate landed behind Shamand. Blandina had to cover her mouth to muffle her laughter as Shamand spun with an arching blade intended to kill.

Once her laughter settled, Blandina pitched the fourth plate. As the plate flew across the room, she sneered, "You fool." The plate shattered to Shamand's left as her last word was completed.

The advisor did not react to the noise the pottery made. Instead, he reached down to the inside of his right ankle. With one swift movement, he pulled a small knife and threw the dagger in the direction of Blandina's voice.

Blandina was forced to abandon her crate. She rolled forward onto the floor near the back wall as the point of the projectile penetrated the air her head had occupied. The butt end of the weapon slammed into the rock and fell behind the crate.

Blandina exited her roll and grabbed a heavy, wooden pitcher by its handle and slung it at Shamand. The bottom of the vessel struck the advisor on the bridge of his nose, re-injuring the wound he had suffered while saving Clandestiny's mother so many seasons ago.

Stumbling to catch his balance, Shamand lowered his long sword to his side and grabbed the bridge of his nose with his free hand. Blandina seized the advantage of the advisor's weakness. She sprinted toward Shamand, carefully placing her feet to avoid making a noise. As she ran through the debris, she reached beneath her shawl and pulled a knife of her own. Seeing the left side of Shamand's neck was exposed, she lifted the blade and started its descent.

Sensing the threat, Shamand reached up with his free arm and snatched Blandina by her wrist. He dropped his sword to the floor, grabbed Blandina by the front of her neck, and with one fluid motion, began pushing her backward. As he shoved, he squeezed her wrist until she dropped her knife. Shamand did not stop pushing until the flat of Blandina's back collided with the wall opposite the door.

Shamand's hand tightened around Blandina's neck as he lifted the Tormalian while keeping her weight pressed against the rock. The blood running from his nose sprayed onto Blandina's face as he shouted. "I have often dreamed of choking you! You didn't deserve Thoomar!"

With her eyes blinking to clear away her attacker's blood, Blandina tried to respond, but Shamand's grip was too tight. The air she needed to speak was unable to pass through his grip.

"I shall enjoy ending your life's source," Shamand continued, but during this series of moments, his speech was calculated and calm. "But your soul may rest easy. Your son shall become a great man under my tutelage. I won't destroy Thoomar's dream."

As Shamand's speech continued to spray blood onto Blandina's face, the Tormalian woman reached under her shawl and pulled a second knife that she had tied to her left hip.

Blandina closed her eyes. The next thing Shamand knew, his enemy vanished and reappeared behind him. A split moment later, Blandina's dagger had been buried deep into the small of his back.

The advisor reacted, spinning with his left elbow extended. The force of his spin caused the blade in Blandina's hand to be ripped out of his back, shredding the muscle and opening the wound wider. But Blandina was not without injury. Shamand's elbow had smashed into left side of her head. The blow was severe enough to cause the Tormalian to stumble and fall against the wall on the right side of the room.

From the floor, Blandina struggled to gather her wit while Shamand fought equally as hard to gather his. The Tormalian princess teleported to the door and reappeared in a standing position, gasping for air.

As Blandina glared across the room at Shamand, she rubbed the side of her head to ease the pain. She knew her blade had opened a mortal wound, and it would be only a matter of moments before the Isorian would be overcome. Through her agony, she smiled as Shamand stumbled toward her while his blood poured down his back, over his buttocks and then down the length of his leg before it dripped off of his heel and stained the floor.

Just as the advisor was about to lay his hands upon Blandina to continue his assault, the Tormalian princess teleported again and reappeared near the back wall. She continued to search for the oxygen she needed to recover while Shamand tried to follow the sound of her breathing.

With his blood flowing fast, the advisor's footing was becoming more unsure with every step. The pysples on the bottom of his feet were popping loudly as he stumbled to his right and then to his left. But before he was able to reach Blandina, he lost all sense of balance and stumbled toward the wall on the right side of the room and had to use his calloused hands to catch himself.

Many moments passed while Blandina stared down the Great One as he fought the dizziness that was consuming him from the loss of blood. Shamand was doing everything he could to remain erect, but the longer he stood against the wall, the more his balance became his second enemy. Eventually, he worked his way into the corner at the back of the room and dropped to the floor, his blood smearing along the way.

Blandina approached, though she stopped beyond the Great One's reach. After studying Shamand's condition, the Tormalian princess moved a little closer. "You should say your prayers, Shamand. You'll be seeing Helmep soon."

Shamand spit on the floor, his brows furrowing in pain. "How…?"

Blandina grinned. "Have you not heard the stories of my witchery?"

"Witchery?" he winced and then groaned. "I've heard nothing."

Feeling more confident in Shamand's demise, Blandina lowered into a seated position directly in front of him. She brought her knees up to her chest and surrounded them with both arms. With her chin resting on top of her left kneecap, she responded, "It appears my journey to Luvelles has remained a secret from Isorian ears."

"What journey?" Shamand slurred.

"Have you become witless? I am witch, Shamand."

Blood spewed from the Great One's mouth as he scoffed. "You are no more witch than I am god. The Eye of Magic on that world would not have accepted a being like you."

Blandina shook her head. She knew that she had been rejected by the Head Master of Luvelles and was not given the opportunity to stand before the Source, but she was not about to admit her flaws to Shamand. Her voice remained calm as she responded. "Enough talk. Bear witness to the extent of my power." The self-proclaimed witch lifted her hand and made an arching motion through the air as if she was tracing a line onto the floor around Shamand. A low-burning ring of fire appeared. Though the flames never touched the advisor, the heat cast from the fire was enough to cause the Isorian's skin to be effected. Boils surfaced and filled with fluid, and one by one, they popped. The fluid oozed down Shamand's body and dripped onto the floor.

Blandina savored the Great One's agony while the heat continued to dwindle his life's source. Once she was sure that Shamand had taken his final breath, and the torture would no longer offer her solace, she lifted her hands in the direction of the flames. With an inward roll of her wrists, she commanded the fire to close in on Shamand's body while she backed away to the far side of the room. Further, her thoughts commanded the magic to spare her skin the heat as the flames intensified. To ensure the stench of Shamand's flesh would not fill the cave, she also ordered the fire to consume the aroma. Finally, with her last thought, she commanded the fire to burn long enough to incinerate Shamand's body without releasing its toxic smoke. There was to be no evidence of the advisor's destruction. As she shut the door of the room behind her, she enjoyed knowing her sins would never be revealed.

CHAPTER 5
A SMEARED MEMORY

It was Late Bailem when Shiver closed the tale of Klidess the Mighty and tossed the book down to Doejess who was standing at the head of the harugen. After working his way to the front of the harugen's saddle, Shiver climbed down one of the mammoth-centipede's legs and then bounded across the ice toward a small camp that Doejess had established. Five large blocks of ice, chiseled from the shelf covering the tundra, sat placed in a circle around the bags that held their belongings.

After grabbing Shamand's bag, the king pulled it next to one of the blocks and took a seat. He reached in and pulled out a good sized tub that had been filled with the blubber of a megrastle whale and started eating. As the fat dissolved in the boy's mouth, Shiver savored the way it melted on his tongue and covered his palate with oil.

Upon seeing Doejess lower the tale of Klidess the Mighty onto his bag, the assistant looked at the blubber inside the pail and licked his lips. Shiver took pity and tossed the frail looking assistant a hefty piece. Doejess bowed and crammed the handful into his mouth. "Thank you, My King," he slobbered while in the midst of chewing. The assistant then took a seat two blocks to Shiver's right.

It was not long after when the Frigid Commander exited the cave. Shiver swallowed his bite and then cupped his hands around his mouth to shout in the commander's direction. "Your return pleases me, Darosen!"

The commander lifted his hand and waved to signal his receipt of the boy's message. Rather than shout a response, Darosen finished making his way to the camp and then took a seat on the block to Shiver's left before he spoke, "Did you enjoy your studies, Young King?"

Shiver's excitement grew upon hearing the question. "Oh yes, Commander. I especially enjoyed the part where Klidess tore himself free of his mother's womb as she fell lifeless at the paws of the bearogon. To know the bearogon were frightened at the sight of Klidess' tiny, bloody, screaming face as he pushed clear of her belly, brought pain to my stomach as I rolled with laughter atop the harugen. I suppose it was destiny that wandering travelers found him on that Peak. For without them, Klidess would not have been brought home to Hydroth."

Darosen smiled. "As I said, if only you had one man within your army as mighty." The commander unsheathed his knife and used it to chip a piece of ice off the block beneath him. He put the chunk in his mouth and sucked on it to quench his thirst. "What else did you learn?"

The commander motioned for Shiver to toss him a piece of whale blubber as he listened to the child king respond. "I learned that Klidess was blessed with the ruby eyes. I also found another point of intrigue. The picture that was scribed onto one of the pages resembles Gablysin."

The commander nodded. "Yes. Klidess' blood flows through your friend."

Awe struck, Shiver replied, "That's amazing. Does Gabs have knowledge of his potential greatness?"

"No. The boy's ears have remained uninformed."

"Why? I know Gabs would love to have this knowledge."

"I agree, but Thoomar felt that Gablysin needed to mature before he was told. News of this nature can go to one's head. Perhaps it's best to maintain the secret until I determine when the right moment will be to reveal this truth."

As Shiver nodded his understanding, he caught a glimpse of his mother exiting the cave. Again, he cupped his hands around his mouth. "Mother! What are you doing here?"

Blandina smiled, but she did not shout a reply. Instead, she did as the commander had done and made her way across the ice toward the camp. After bending down and kissing the top of Shiver's head, she took a seat on the block of ice next to the commander. Without wasting a moment, she looked directly to her left toward the block where Doejess was sitting. "Since when has it become accepted for a servant to occupy his moments by sitting with royalty? Get up, fool!" She pointed at the pail sitting in front of Shiver's feet. "Fetch it. I'm famished."

The joy in Doejess' face vanished as he jumped to his feet to retrieve the pail. As he did, Blandina looked at the commander and smiled. "My dearest, Darosen, perhaps you'd be willing to quench a lady's thirst."

Before the commander could respond, Doejess extended the pail.

Blandina's eyes turned cold as she looked up at the assistant and snatched the bucket out of his hand. "Prepare the harugens!" she barked. "We leave shortly!"

Blandina enjoyed watching Doejess scamper away after he gathered the bags and slung them over his shoulder. In his haste, he left the tale of Klidess the Mighty sitting on the ice at the center of the camp.

The self-proclaimed witch turned her head back in the direction of the Frigid Commander and put another smile on her face. "Now ... about my thirst, my love." She lowered the pail to her feet and extended her hands to caress the top of Darosen's as the commander handed her a piece of ice.

Upon hearing the words, "my love" and seeing the object of his mother's affection, Shiver stood from his block. "What madness is this?" The child-king pointed to the commander as he stared at his mother. "How could you love him? Enough moments haven't been lived since my father's passing. Your actions speak against his legacy!"

After hearing Shiver shout at his mother, Doejess dropped the bags next to Shamand's old harugen and hurried back to the camp. Shiver was still yelling at Blandina when he stopped just outside the circle of blocks. When the king paused, Doejess spoke out. "My King, is everything alright?"

Blandina did not wait for Shiver to respond. Her eyes were filled with hatred as she whipped the backside of her hand through the air in the direction of the assistant. Doejess lifted off the ice and flew backward 30 paces toward the tethered group of harugens. He landed with so much momentum that he slid the remaining eight paces and stopped beneath the mammoth-centipedes only after he collided into their legs. Startled, two of the four beasts shifted, the smallest throwing its weight into the largest which had been Shamand's. As a result, six different legs, five from the largest beast and one from the smallest, speared various areas of Doejess' body as they battled for position. The worst of the damage came from the smallest haru-gen's leg as it entered through the Isorian's mouth and out the back of his head.

As Shiver and Darosen stood in silence, Blandina sighed, "Thank Helmep he can no longer interfere." She turned her attention back to Shiver. "You were saying?"

Shiver backed away. He stepped over his block to create distance between him and the stranger who was standing before him. The young king pointed at Blandina. "Stay back! I know you not!" He adjusted his retreat and moved in the direction of the harugens. "Commander, come with me! I want to return to the city!"

Darosen stood from his block. Before he could take a step, Blandina commanded in a calm voice, "Sit, my love. The boy is going nowhere."

Shiver shouted, "I said, come with me, Commander!"

Blandina stood and moved in front of Darosen, kicking the tale of Klidess the Mighty to the side. She placed her hands on the Frigid Commander's shoulders and spoke loud enough for Shiver to hear as the king continued to back away. "Perhaps the moment has come for our son to know the truth."

Shiver stopped his retreat. "'Our son?' What madness do you spew?"

Blandina looked at Shiver. A look of love appeared on her face. "My dear boy … there is so much you don't know. Nevertheless, you are loved..."

Meanwhile, the Mountains of Tedfer
8 Peaks from the Entrance to the Pass of Nayala
Late Bailem Approaches

X Marks Medolas and Clandestiny's Position

Howls filled the evening air. Upon hearing them, Medolas walked to the edge of the cliff and looked down. He spotted three large snowhounds running through the valley. He and Clandestiny were being tracked, and the beasts were working their way to the beginning of the ledge that they had been ascending for most of the afternoon. Judging by the wolves' speed, their moments were short. The base of the cliff began only 19,000 paces north of their position, and they needed to act quickly.

"Clanny, the snow has failed to mask our scent!" Medolas shouted as he motioned for Clandestiny to take a look. He pointed down the cliff. "They're coming for us. Our moments to prepare must be filled with haste."

Squeezing Medolas' hand, Clandestiny responded, "We cannot overpower them. We must run, Meddy."

As Clanny turned to go, Medolas stopped her. "No. Our strides would be overtaken." Without further explanation, Medolas pulled Clanny toward a circular group of stones that sat 11 paces from the edge of the cliff.

Medolas jumped over the rocks and landed inside their camp next to a pile of skinned carcasses that he had killed the night before. Grabbing the rope he had secured to the icejacks' legs, he climbed back over the stones. Once his feet found the snow, he extended his arm above his head and allowed the meat to dangle in front of him. "I knew these would serve a purpose."

Medolas led Clanny away from their camp and ascended the trail to a tree that had grown horizontally out of the side of the cliff some 20 paces away. As they went, he dragged the icejacks behind him to mark the trail with their scent. Stopping at the edge of the cliff, he looked down to where the tree emerged. Its trunk sat more than the length of his body below where they stood, and the snow atop the trunk looked threatening and seemed as if it would make sure footing impossible.

Shaking his head, Medolas sighed. "I pray to Helmep that this works."

Clanny's brows furrowed. "You pray to Helmep? What's your intent, Meddy?"

Medolas smirked. "I'm saving us." He swallowed and added. "I hope."

"What do you mean, you hope?"

Without responding, Medolas took a seat. He put the rope holding the icejacks in his mouth and then tossed the meat over his shoulder before he rolled onto his stomach. Using his arms, he pushed himself backward until his legs dangled off the edge of the cliff, and then he lowered onto the tree. With his feet on the trunk and his hands above his head, grasping the edge of the trail, the young Isorian ensured his footing was solid before he turned around.

With his back against the cliff, this new position caused Medolas' heart to pound as he looked from branch to branch toward the last limb that grew out of the end of the trunk. With the tree looming above a 330 pace drop, falling would be a sure end to his life's source.

Setting his fear aside, Medolas lowered onto the trunk and straddled it.

Clandestiny took a seat on the edge of the cliff and prepared to follow. "Make room for me."

Medolas shook his head. "No! Stay where you are!"

A look of confusion appeared on Clanny's face. "Why?"

"There aren't the moments to explain! I said stay where you are. I'll be right back." Without further discussion, Medolas brushed the snow off the top of the trunk in front of him and then lowered onto his belly.

As he began to slide his way toward the end, Clanny chastised, "What are you doing, Meddy? Have you gone nordel? Return to me at once!"

Medolas rolled his eyes and continued to crawl. Eighty-seven heartbeats passed before he was able to hang the meat from the last limb that protruded from the end of the branch. Ensuring the knot was tight, he released the rope and allowed the icejacks to fall into a dangling position.

Satisfied that everything was as it should be, Medolas crawled back to the edge of the ledge. After pulling himself up, he grabbed Clandestiny's hand and led her back to their camp behind the rocks. "What are you doing, Meddy?" Clanny asked over and over as he scooped her off the ground and tossed her over the stones, causing her to land on her backside on top of her blanket.

Rubbing her tailbone, Clanny shouted, "Meddy, you will answer me! Now!"

Medolas snapped back, "Hold your tongue! The moments are unavailable to explain! Do as I say! Stay inside and hide behind the stones!"

Ignoring Clanny's spiteful glare, Medolas pulled himself over the rocks. He retrieved a pouch filled with the blood of the icejacks and nine pelts. He tossed them over the stones and then retrieved a spear that he had created out of a long stick. His knife had been tied to one end.

Climbing back over the rocks, Medolas worked his way down the path 20 paces in the direction the snowhounds would approach. He dropped the first of the pelts and began to walk along the path while pouring the blood of the icejacks onto the snow. Further, he dropped the other pelts every few paces near the edge of the ledge as he returned to the tree.

The last of the pelts and the pouch with the remainder of the icejacks' blood was tossed off of the ledge where they landed four paces onto the trunk. As Medolas sprinted back to their hidden camp, he bounded over the stones. Landing inside, all he could do was hope that the pelts and the blood of the icejacks would be enough to keep the snowhounds from following his and Clanny's scent.

Lowering the spear to his side, the young Isorian quieted his breathing and pulled Clanny close. He made sure she was tucked into the stones as he whispered, "You must quiet your breathing. They'll hear you. They're upon us."

With his eyes peeking through a crack, Medolas held onto his spear and watched as the three snowhounds finished their climb and stopped at the first pelt. He could hear their heavy panting as the largest sniffed at the first pelt before he continued beyond it to sniff the impressions that had been left behind by Medolas' feet.

Exhausted, the beast's drool fell freely to the snow as its snout found the trail of blood. The wolf looked up and scanned the area as if it was deciding which trail to follow. His growl amplified before he snorted and lowered his snout back to the ground. The other hounds followed as their leader made his decision as to which scent to pursue.

Medolas' eyes widened as the beasts started to walk toward their camp. The pack leader kept his snout next to the ground as he sniffed one footprint and then the next. It was not long before all three wolves were examining the base of the stones of their camp.

Medolas was forced to roll quietly to the side of the crack as the pack leader's snout penetrated the hole from the other side and sniffed. He could hear the beasts' growls intensify. A moment later, a large paw started to scratch at the crack.

Sensing the danger, Clandestiny grabbed a large pebble that sat on the ground between her legs and then tossed the rock up and over the boulders. The stone landed behind the beasts, near the trail of blood. It worked. All three hounds whirled around and rushed to sniff the pebble as it rolled to a stop.

Medolas peered through the crack. His heart sunk as the pack leader lifted his snout from the pebble and looked in the direction of the boulders surrounding their camp. The wolf sniffed the air and then snorted again. A moment later, the beast lowered his nostrils to the ground. It was not long before the hound's snarls amplified.

The young Isorian closed his eyes and quietly thanked Helmep as the hounds began to follow the icejacks' blood toward the second pelt. It was not long before the trail led the pack to the point of the ledge where the tree protruded not far below. The head wolf licked his chops and snarled at the vision of the meat hanging from the branch at the end of the tree.

The trail of blood Medolas had left behind stopped on the trunk where the last of the pelts and the pouch sat waiting. The lead wolf jumped off the ledge and landed on the trunk. Upon reaching the final pelt, he snatched it from under the pouch and discarded it, causing both objects to plummet to the ground. As the pack leader moved further onto the branch, the others grew anxious as their desire to devour the meat intensified.

The next largest of the three jumped onto the tree. His weight shook the trunk and caused the pack leader to crouch to secure his balance. The lead wolf twisted his head back over his shoulder and growled a warning. The second hound snarled in defiance and took three steps forward as the third wolf leaned over and pressed his front paws against the face of the ledge to size up the jump.

Seeing that the third wolf's rear haunches were raised and pushed back to maintain his balance, Medolas grabbed his spear and quietly started to creep over the rocks. Clanny tried to stop him, touching his free arm, but Medolas ignored her, and put his finger to his mouth, ordering Clanny to remain silent. It was now or never. The offensive had to be taken.

Lowering to the ground, Medolas ensured his steps were silent as he crept toward the rear of the final hound. He was counting on the pack's snarls to mask any sound that his approach might make, and with the distance almost closed, the final wolf was about to jump when the young Isorian lunged the remaining four paces and kicked the beast in the rear.

The third wolf fell forward, its weight landing on the trunk in an awkward position. Its paws were spread too wide and with each falling to opposite sides of the tree, it made it impossible for the beast to soften the impact. The hound's head turned to the side as the rest of its body rolled over the top of its mass and stopped only after it collided into the back of the second hound. With a broken neck, the third hound rolled off of the trunk and began its descent toward a crunching end.

Because of the impact, the second hound's back legs had been knocked off of the tree. The beast tried to claw his way back onto the trunk, but his best efforts to save his life's source failed. He, too, would tumble end over end toward a terminal impact as the pack leader used the girth of the final branch near the end of the tree to turn around and face Medolas.

Seeing Medolas raise his spear, Clandestiny shouted from behind the stones. "Be strong, Meddy! Be strong!"

Medolas did not respond. Instead, he taunted the pack leader with his spear as the beast approached the ledge. The blue in his palms faded as his grip tightened. A moment later, the wolf crouched and then launched into the air.

Closing his eyes, Medolas thrust the spear forward. The snowhound howled as it was impaled by the end of the weapon. The weight of the impact caused Medolas to step back with his right foot to reclaim his balance, but before the young Isorian could react, the mass of the hound fell below the edge of the cliff. Medolas' failure to release the spear would be his undoing. The weight of the hound pulled the Isorian off of the ledge.

"Nooooo!" Clandestiny screamed.

Bounding over the rocks, Clanny ran to the edge of the cliff and looked over. Medolas was gone. "Meddy! Meddy! No, no, no, no, no! Meddy!"

Moments Earlier,
Shiver, Blandina and Darosen's Camp
The Southernmost Entrance to
The Caves of Carne

"It matters not how you feel, Shiver," Blandina argued as she reclaimed her seat to the right of the Frigid Commander. She looked at the child-king who stood outside the circle of ice-blocks that surrounded the camp. "Your birth was commanded by my father. Like you…" she paused and pointed to Darosen, "…and like your father … I was born to fulfill a calling. The three of us live to bring about the fruition of my father's dream to conquer the Isor."

A look of determination appeared on Shiver's face. "I won't betray my friends." The young king's voice was calm and solid as he reiterated. "I won't wrong them."

Blandina shook her head. "You'll do as you're told. You cannot stop what has begun."

"You lie!" Shiver shouted. "I'm King of the Isor. I can do as I wish. I can even surrender my throne. This would stop what you've begun."

Before Blandina could respond, the Frigid Commander cut in. "Perhaps the boy is right. The wilderness is vast. We could live out our Peaks as a family. Happiness would find us. Your father doesn't need to know our location."

Blandina's eyes turned cold as she turned to face the Frigid Commander. "Your words are treasonous against the Tormal, Darosen. Do you wish to suffer the same fate as the last traitor who stood before my father?"

Darosen remembered how the Tormalian king's sudwals had feasted on the pieces of the elderly impostor. The dogs hid below an altar while Blandina's father methodically dismembered the retired officer during a scream-filled series of moments comprised of 2,000 cuts.

"My apologies, my love," Darosen conceded. "I exist only to ensure your happiness."

Shiver crossed his arms. "As for myself, Mother, I cannot say the same. I have no knowledge of this Tormalian king you claim as a father. I've never laid my eyes upon him. My loyalties shall forever remain with the ones I love and know as my own."

Blandina stood and stepped outside the circle of blocks. She walked around their circumference and took a few paces toward the harugens. Stopping next to Shiver, she turned to reclaim his eyes. "My son ... you're destined to lead the Tormal into the uprising of the ages. Your children's children shall speak of your greatness, because you will be the one to unite the kingdoms."

Blandina pointed at the book that sat at the center of the circle. "Do you not desire to be studied as Klidess is studied? Scholars 4,000 seasons from this Peak shall speak of you as they read from the Scrolls of Old." She extended her right hand to touch Shiver's left cheek and then smiled within at the way the child-king flinched. "Don't fret, my boy. I don't wish harm to befall you."

Shiver walked back to the circle and claimed a seat two places to the right of Darosen. "You said your king—"

Blandina stopped him mid-sentence. "Our king," she corrected.

Scoffing, Shiver continued. "You said *your* king wants to conquer the Isor. You also said that I was destined to unite the kingdoms. I fail to understand how conquering any being can be called unification. Please, Mother ... enlighten me. How can a conquered people stand unified with those who enslave them?"

Realizing Shiver's logic was sound, Blandina took a new approach. "How dare you defy me!" The sorceress whirled in the direction of the harugens and lifted her hands. She commanded her thoughts to invoke her magic. Fire erupted from the ends of her fingertips and engulfed three of the four harugens. The heat seared the ice beneath the beasts, and the pain inflicted by the flames caused them to cry out as they thrashed about.

Breaking free of the ice-totems they were tethered to, the injured harugens skittered north not more than a few paces before they collapsed to the ice. As each perished, the nerves within their bodies convulsed. The pointed tips of their 100 legs tore at the ice, sending chunks flying in all directions.

Frightened, the fourth mammoth-centipede also broke free from its totem. As he scurried away, Blandina was forced to snare its large, undulating body with her magic until she could settle the harugen down.

With the harugen's cries filling the evening air, Blandina spun around to face Shiver. The power she had invoked caused blood to drip from her nose while she hissed, "You've been given a gift, Shiver. You will use it to unite the kingdoms."

Blandina wiped the blood away and continued to speak in a firm but softer tone. "You will play the part of the Isorian King. And you will not fail me ... or your true king ... my king ... Darosen's king." The sorceress pointed to the deceased harugens. "For if you do, your Peaks upon the ice will be shortened as theirs were."

Darosen stood from his block. "You speak to our son as if he's a slave. Has your love for the boy vanished?"

Hearing the concern in the commander's voice, Blandina's face softened again. She walked back to the circle and reclaimed her seat before she responded in a normal tone. "You're not witless, Darosen. I treat you and the boy as I must. If slaves you must become to fulfill the will of my father, then slaves you shall be."

Tears rolled down Shiver's cheeks as he stood from his block. "I know you not, Mother. If I must, I will choose to end my life's source before I betray the Isor. I won't serve a king who wants those I love to be enslaved."

Laughing, Blandina stood from her block and sauntered across the ice toward her harugen. Before she finished her fourth stride, she vanished and reappeared atop the mammoth's saddle. With a wave of her hand, the reins lifted off the ice and settled into her palms. After releasing the beast from her magic, she turned the abominable centipede back in the direction of the camp and commanded it to charge. Shiver and Darosen were forced to dive clear of the circle as the mammoth's sharp legs smashed the camp into hundreds of pieces.

The sorceress stopped her harugen and turned at the waist to face both Tormalians as they lay looking up at her. "You have 60 Peaks to return to Hydroth. If you fail to concede to my father's will upon your arrival, your lives will be forfeit ... just as Shamand's life was forfeit." Without waiting for a response, Blandina turned toward the front of her harugen. The beast would skitter 75 paces toward the setting sun before they vanished.

Shaking his head in disgust, Shiver looked at Darosen. "She ended Shamand? Did you know this?"

The Frigid Commander walked back to the destroyed camp and kicked at the chunks. "I told Shamand of your mother's trap before he went into the cave. It appears my warning did not save him."

A look of despair appeared on Shiver's face as his eyes dropped. Amidst the ice, the tale of Klidess the Mighty laid torn apart from the weight of the harugen. The beast's underbelly had shredded the book as it scraped across its binding.

The young king looked up at Darosen again. "If only Klidess was with us. What greater counsel could an impostor king seek?"

Darosen put his hand on top of his son's head and rummaged his fingers through the boy's hair. "We should leave. Our journey back to Hydroth will be treacherous."

MEANWHILE, BACK AT THE MOUNTAIN PASS OF TEDFER

Sitting on the path directly above the trunk, Clandestiny hung her legs over the edge of the cliff. With the sun tucked behind the mountains that sat beyond the valley below, the crystallizations in her skin were unable to activate. This lack of light would not allow the color of her cheeks to turn green beneath the streams of yellow blood-tears as they strolled down her face. Between sobs, she babbled Medolas' name again and again. At one point, the force of her exhale caused a bubble of snot to escape from her nose and pop.

It was not much longer before Clanny's ears perked up. "Meddy … is that you?"

From beneath the trunk, Medolas hung by his left arm from a branch that grew out of the bottom of the tree before it curled to the side to join the other branches on the left side of the trunk. "When you've finished sniveling, perhaps you'd be gracious enough to offer me some assistance. My grip weakens, and I can wait no longer."

Clanny stood on the ledge and moved to her left. With this new angle, she could now see Medolas. His grip was fastened to the end of the branch, and his free arm was dangling toward the ground with the spear in his hand. "How…?" was all she said.

Medolas frowned. "Perhaps you would allow me to offer an explanation once you've ensured my safety?"

Without hesitation, Clanny jumped down onto the trunk. After lowering to her belly, she extended her left arm while holding onto a branch that protruded from the right side of the tree.

Medolas lifted the spear. "Pull."

Clanny did as instructed. It was not long before Medolas' right hand managed to grab onto another branch. He used this new handle to swing his right leg up and over the trunk while his left leg pressed for leverage against yet another branch. Releasing the limb he had used to stop himself from falling, the branch snapped back in line with the others. Eighty-seven heartbeats later, Medolas and Clanny were once again standing on the ledge embracing for a long series of moments with their eyes closed.

Clanny's ears snapped to attention as another growl penetrated the night air. Medolas pulled his arms free and snatched his spear off the ground. He reared back and was about to hurl the weapon at the approaching snow-hound when a smile appeared on his face.

Seeing the threat was no larger than her old sudwal, Clandestiny sighed, "Oh, Meddy, it's a pup." She walked over to the snarling cub and lifted it off the ground. Frightened, the baby snowhound tried to nip his way free as she rolled it onto its back to check between its legs. "It's a boy. He must have fallen behind when the others gave chase." She grabbed hold of the beast's snout and kept it closed so she could snuggle it. "Oh, Meddy, he's adorable. Helmep has sent me a replacement for Sajeen."

Medolas rolled his eyes. "Perhaps he can be trained to bite you since I cannot."

Ignoring Medolas' snide comment, Clanny moved to the edge of the cliff and looked in the direction of the three splattered masses that stained the rocks below. "I wonder which one was its mother." Clanny lifted the snapping cub above her head. "Strange," she said as she stared into its eyes, "I wonder why one so young would fail to stay in its den." She secured the hound's snout again and pulled the pup to her bosom. "Perhaps you were hungry and could no longer wait for the return of your mother."

Medolas grinned. "Or perhaps he could smell your scent, Clanny, and determined you were a morsel of choice."

"Bah!" Clanny huffed. "Become productive, Medolas. Retrieve the meat. I want to feed him."

Medolas stood with his mouth open as Clanny walked back to the camp and climbed over the stones before she lowered the cub to the ground. A moment later, another grin crossed Medolas' face as he heard Clanny yelp.

Medolas shouted, "You deserved that!"

Peeking her head back over the rock, Clanny chastised, "Meddy! I said, retrieve the meat! Make haste!"

After watching Clanny lower back behind the stone, Medolas turned toward the ledge. He shook his head and whispered, "'Make haste, Meddy. I said, retrieve the meat.'" He put his hand over his heart. "Why, Meddy, thank you for saving my life's source ... AGAIN. I thank Helmep for the gift that is you." Medolas continued to grumble as he lowered onto the trunk. "No one can replace you Meddy ... no one."

ABOVE THE UNDER ICE CITY OF GESPER
THAT SAME NIGHT

Now, fellow soul ... if you don't remember, I told you at the beginning of this tale that the architecture of Gesper was grand, though in a different way than originally planned. The Tormalian architects made a critical error in judgment when they surveyed for the perfect spot to build their city. They convinced their sovereign, King Meerum Bosand, to allow the city that was to be filled with beautiful spires and elegant cathedrals, to be constructed on the floor of an enormous crater.

This decision would later alter their lifestyle as the Great Thaw weakened the walls of the crater. Fissures appeared in the ice—fissures that extended south toward the Sea of Gesper. As a result, saltwater worked its way north toward the crater and filled it to the rim, which in itself was not a problem since the Tormal had the ability to breathe through their gills while they lived beneath the water.

The real problem began when the Great Thaw gave way to the Great Freeze, a storm that moved in after the gods changed the climate. The Tormal had no other choice but to abandon their homes and seek safety inside the Caves of Carne until the devastating cold ended. When the Tormal returned eight seasons later, their homes were frozen beneath an expansive block of ice. They would spend the next 10 seasons creating a series of tunnels to hollow out each structure in an effort to make the city habitable once again.

Since those Peaks, a man or beast could pass above the city and look down through the ice to see the peaks of the spires in key spots where the ice remained transparent. At night, the orbs lighting the city illuminated the ice above it, and the location of the city could be seen from a distance. Over 80,000 Tormalians moved throughout those well-preserved structures on a Peakly basis.

Blandina appeared on the back of her harugen and stopped the beast next to a series of totems that had been implanted in the ice above the city of Gesper. After dismounting, she tethered the mammoth and walked 150 paces north before she looked down through the ice. Below her feet, the peak of her father's tallest spire, marking the southernmost boundary of his castle, glowed as the orbs surrounding the structure cast light upon its golden tower and its crystal apex.

The sorceress lifted her nose in the direction of the starless sky and followed the rays of light as they shot up into the darkness. She took a deep breath and then exhaled. "Ahhh … home." A moment later, she vanished, only to reappear outside the door of her father's bedroom chamber 90 paces below.

With her right hand, she tapped the iron ring against the oak door and waited. Thirty heartbeats later, a gruff Tormalian with a balding head and a beard that hung to his waist opened the door. The king's grin was illuminated by an orb that had been secured to the stacked, stone wall of the hallway behind Blandina. "Daughter, the moments could not be more perfect for your return. Please … enter … and delight your father's ears with words of your progress."

"Hello, Father," Blandina said as she stepped across the threshold.

"Did the bled seize the child as planned, and has Shiver donned the crown?" the king urged.

Blandina reached out and caressed her father's cheek and then kissed his forehead. "There's much to tell, Father." The sorceress walked across the polished, wooden floor past a burning fireplace that emanated no heat and lowered onto a mattress that was laden with wool from the Plains of Errod on Dragonia. She rubbed her hand across the mattress and smiled. She remembered her studies. As a child, she had been taught how the wool was shaved from the backs of weresheep during their season of transformation. She remembered that, when out of season, these cursed humans remained slaves to the white demons who occupied the plains. She smirked, enjoying the knowledge that these demons often made their humans wear clothing spun from the same wool they shaved from their backs.

Looking up to find her father's anxious gaze, Blandina responded to his questions. "The children journeyed to the swimming hole as you prophesied. The bled attacked the ruby eyed child as you commanded it to, and Thoomar was forced to surrender his life's source to save the Isorians' belief in their foolish prophecy."

The king rubbed his hands together. "Also as I foretold."

"Your visions are always correct, Father."

Meerum basked in his own glory for a moment and then questioned, "Does Shiver wear the crown?"

"He does."

"Wonderful! And has word reached his ears that Darosen is his father?"

"It has."

"And does the boy know that I'm his true king?"

Blandina sighed, "Yes, My Lord. But his acceptance of the truth was less than encouraging. I was forced to leave him with his father in the wilderness before I returned to Gesper. They'll walk for many Peaks before Shiver accepts his calling."

"What of Darosen? Was his performance genuine?"

"He reacted as you said he would. His love for Shiver will ensure the boy becomes loyal. He's a good father."

The king clapped his hands. "Just as I had also foreseen. My visions remain trustworthy." The king moved to the bed and took a seat next to Blandina. "Once Darosen convinces the child to wed Clandestiny, the blood exchanged upon their union will give the boy purity. Then, and only then, shall he be able to control the Tear." Meerum smiled and pushed Blandina's hair clear of her face. "And you, my princess, you shall harness the power of the gashtion through Shiver."

The king kissed Blandina on the cheek. His eyes gleamed as he pulled back to reclaim those that longed for a father's love. "Under your command, my lovely daughter, the dragon shall feast upon the Isor. The beast will rid us of this impure populace. Their lands will become mine, and you shall be the princess over all Northern Grayham. We shall wait for the High Priestess of Harvestom to return, and together, we will force her blessing upon me."

"Why do you need the blessing, Father? Your magic is strong."

Meerum frowned. "Have your studies taught you nothing, girl? With the Priestess' blessing, I can don the Tear without fear of its power consuming my being. With the gashtion under my control, I shall become a god. I shall rule without opposition."

Blandina leaned toward Meerum and then placed her arms around the king's neck. "But Father, my power grows stronger by the Peak. When the moment comes, perhaps I will be strong enough to bear the burden of the Tear without forcing impure blood to course through Shiver's veins. I could surrender the Tear to you once the priestess arrives."

Meerum's heavy brows furrowed. "Foolish child. Must I speak of this yet again?"

"But Father, you seek to abolish the Isor. What is to become of Shiver and Clandestiny once the priestess has fulfilled your will?"

The king stood from the bed and moved to the hearth of the fireplace. He stared at a hand drawn picture of his late wife. Upon seeing his daughter's face in the queen's, he grabbed the frame by its base and turned around. "Your mother questioned my authority until the moment her life's source was ended. As I released her neck and let her form fall to the ice, I stood back and watched a hungry pack of hounds devour her corpse. Shiver and Clandestiny are no less expendable."

Blandina gasped. The sorceress stood from the bed and lifted her right hand. A ball of energy appeared in her palm. "Shiver and the girl will not be harmed. For if they are, your corpse will meet a similar fate as Mother's."

Meerum chuckled as he casually strolled across the gap between himself and the self-proclaimed witch. As he approached, Blandina stepped backward until the bed stopped her retreat. With her magic ready to end, the king ignored the threat and backhanded his daughter with his free hand, sending her flopping onto the bed.

Meerum watched Blandina's magic fizzle. "Stupid girl! Do you think that I failed to foresee this Peak? You will never savor the joy of ending my life's source."

Holding the left side of her swollen face in the palm of her hand, Blandina pleaded. "Please! At least allow the boy to continue his existence. Take the girl, for I care not. Do with her as you must."

The king's face softened. "Perhaps I shall make her my plaything. I have needs that have gone unattended since your mother's demise." Meerum returned to the fireplace. "I will allow your request. As long as Shiver behaves, his eyes shall continue to see sunsets."

Meerum put his hand to his chin. "See that your mind remains free of foolish notions, daughter. Your power isn't strong enough to control the Tear without the blood." The king tossed the picture of Blandina's mother across the room and watched it land on the bed. Satisfied that his message had been delivered, he left the chamber and used his magic to slam the door behind him.

Blandina rolled over and placed her good cheek on the edge of the frame. A tear rolled from the corner of her left eye and dropped from the bridge of her nose onto the drawing just above her mother's head. With her right thumb, she wiped the tear away. The graphite used to create the illustration smeared, marring her mother's face. Upon seeing the ruin, the sorceress sat up and hurled the last remaining treasure of her mother into the fireplace. She would watch the flames consume the memory before she teleported out of the city.

8 Peaks of Bailem Later
The Entrance to the Pass of Nayala

Medolas and Clanny stopped walking once they reached the entrance to the pass. Clanny tugged on the rope the baby snowhound had been leashed to and commanded, "Keeba, sit." Reaching down, she rewarded the pup with a piece of meat she had cut from the leg of their final icejack. "Good Keeba. Good boy."

Medolas sighed as he dropped the blanket and his spear to the ground. He looked beyond the entrance toward a narrow ledge that spanned a gap more than 2,740 paces between two mountain peaks. To the right of the ledge, the fall was a sheer 1,100 pace drop. To the left, he estimated the fall to be an additional 800 paces. At the bottom of both drops, a violent end waited for those who were unable to cross without being blown off the ledge.

Listening to the whistling wind as it crested the walkway, Medolas rubbed the goose bumps on his arms. "This place doesn't offer peace to my being."

Clandestiny lifted Keeba off the ground and scratched the bottom of the pup's chin while she studied the entrance of the pass. Two stone skeletons, one Tormal and the other Isor, sat atop thick, circular pillars that rose above her head. The skeleton on the pillar to her right was sitting on his knees with one end of a large, rickety, wooden sign resting between them. His bony arms were extended toward the top of the sign to hold the arching placard upright. The skeleton to her left allowed his legs to fall over the side of his pillar. His side of the sign sat between his legs with his bony knees strad-dling both sides. He, too, had his arms outstretched to ensure the placard remained erect.

Clanny read the sign aloud:

Through a sea of wind one must pass
Should one not fall, madness one may suffer
For to see beyond this Peak
Does not promise a life worth living

"What should we do, Meddy?" Clanny said as she continued to study the sign. "Perhaps we should turn back."

Medolas bent down and grabbed a handful of snow and packed it tight. He chucked the snowball at the head of the skeleton sitting to his right and watched it hit his target. "Go back? What can they do? They don't appear capable of chasing us." He grabbed another snowball and chucked it at the skeleton with the sign between his knees and then laughed as the snowball caused its head to break free. The stone skull hit the ground and rolled out onto the ledge before the awkwardness of its shape caused it to plummet into the chasm. "See, Clanny? What are we to fear?"

Annoyed, Clanny stormed up to the edge of the walkway. She turned and glared at Medolas while she pointed toward the mountain peak at the opposite end of the ledge. "Do your eyes fail you, Meddy? Do you find me witless? I don't fear inanimate life forms made of stone!" She cupped her hand around her right ear. "I fear the spirits who guard the pass before us. I value what sanity I possess."

With a brush of his arm, Medolas dismissed Clanny's concern. He snatched his spear and Clanny's blanket off the ground. With the blanket beneath his left arm and the spear clenched tight in the same hand, he passed Clandestiny on her left and began to walk out onto the ledge.

Medolas grinned as Clandestiny shouted a familiar phrase. "Meddy, return to me at once!"

The young Isorian ignored the command and continued his trek. He was no more than 60 paces away from Clanny when a strong wind from the south collided with the left side of his body. Medolas was blown to his right across the width of the path that spanned only five paces. To stop himself from falling off the ledge, he allowed his knees to collapse under him while stabbing the point of his spear into a crack. With his heart pounding and his backside firmly planted next to what would have been his demise, Medolas' body started to tremble as he watched the blanket float up into the air before it dropped into the chasm.

Frantic, Clanny lowered the snowhound to her side and placed its leash beneath her foot. She cupped her hands around her mouth. "Medolas Armichael Loverum, you shall return to me at once! Don't make me speak it again!"

Despite Clandestiny's demand, Medolas was unable to move. Her voice, though strong, was muffled by a dense fog that filled his mind. His body would not stop shaking, and his eyes remained fixated on the blanket until it vanished from sight. He knew he needed to move toward the center of the path, but the command to make his muscles react failed him.

Clandestiny shouted at Medolas again and again during the long series of moments before she finally realized that he was unable to regain control of his movements. Looking down at the barking snowhound, an idea came to her. She lowered to her hands and knees. With the hound's leash clenched between her teeth, she crawled out onto the ledge toward Medolas. On two occasions, she was forced to battle gusts of her own, but the third gust was too much.

The wind lifted Keeba and threw the snowhound off the path. Clandestiny tried to catch him, but she was forced to drop to her belly to keep herself from being thrown. With her body flat against the path, she listened to Keeba's cries as he fell below the ledge.

Clandestiny's breathing was heavy behind clenched teeth as she listened to Keeba's whimpers. Grateful that her bite on the leash had remained strong, she pulled the snowhound back to safety. Keeba would not stop licking her face as Clanny tucked the snowhound between her arms in front of her and continued her journey to Medolas on her belly.

Once she was at Medolas' side, Clanny reached out and pulled him onto his back. With the snowhound against her left cheek, and Medolas' head against her right, she held them tight while she professed her love for both amongst a barrage of kisses.

It took a while before Clandestiny's coaxing found its way through the fog in Medolas' mind. The boy rolled to his stomach. After a short series of moments filled with the sweet sight of Clandestiny's smile, Medolas' confidence returned. It was on this pass—the most dangerous crossing on all the worlds governed by the Crystal Moon—where the young Isorian would steal his first passionate kiss.

As their lips separated and his eyes opened, something moved over Clanny's shoulder near the entrance of the pass. Medolas' enjoyment of the kiss would be stolen by the sight of a spotted lynx and her four cubs. The feline was growling as she stepped onto the walkway.

"Clanny, we need to press forward!" Medolas urged.

Unaware of the danger behind her, Clanny questioned, "Your boldness has returned. Was my kiss so great that it caused you to forget the danger lurking ahead?"

Medolas rolled his eyes. Rather than answer, he pointed over Clandestiny's shoulder.

Staying on her belly, Clanny turned her body around. Her eyes widened. The cat and her cubs had already traversed 20 paces, leaving only 40 between them.

Watching the foam drip from the feline's jowls, Clanny started to crawl backward away from the lynx. "She's rabid, Meddy."

"Agreed. My eyes bear witness. Get behind me and continue to retreat."

Clanny did as instructed. She pulled the snarling snowhound with the leash as she pinched the rope between her teeth. As Medolas slid toward the center of the ledge, he yanked his spear free of the crack and moved it to his right hand.

Now, fellow soul … this is one of those moments where I must intervene. I think we all know that neither Clandestiny nor Medolas—and yes, the stupid snowhound—were destined to perish on that Peak.

Allow me to say this: their journey to the far side of the pass was rough. I'm sure you can imagine what it would be like to scoot backward on your belly across the length of an 2,740 pace ledge while defending yourself from a bunch of rabid felines.

Medolas and Clanny were more than half way across before the wind blew the lynx and her cubs off the ledge. Needless to say, there was no point in turning back. Like I've said before during the telling of this tale, garesh happens. Now … allow me to say it again. Garesh really does happen. Do you think Clandestiny and Medolas suffered some seriously wicked pass rash on their bellies? I can assure you, they did.

Garesh so happens.

43 Peaks Later
The Mountains of the Ko-dess

Like the Mountains of Tedfer, the mountains of the Ko-dess were filled with predators. Because of this, restful sleep evaded the children since journeying beyond the Pass of Nayala. They had to navigate a series of canyons, hunting whatever they could while they worked to avoid being the hunted.

Clandestiny stopped walking. Lowering to a small boulder, she longed for her old blanket. "Meddy, please. I can't continue. We've walked for more Peaks than I can remember."

Medolas lowered the baby snowhound to the ground and then placed the end of its leash beneath his foot. After removing one of the small strips of meat he had tied to the belt of his loin cloth, he tossed it onto the ground and watched the hound snatch it up. "We cannot rest until we've found a safe haven for us to exist."

Clanny grumbled, "I miss home. What were we thinking? Only a sure end waits for us amongst these wretched peaks."

Sensing Clanny's sadness, Keeba trotted over to her feet and licked her toes.

Medolas smiled. "As I've said on many occasions, we've come too far to turn back. Please don't make me speak it again. If we must suffer an end to our life's source, then it's my desire that we suffer an end of our choosing. I won't return and hand your love to Shiver. You're mine." Medolas walked to Clanny and lifted her chin with his right hand. "Do you understand me? You're mine."

Before Clanny could respond, the walls of the mountains echoed with a sound they had never heard before. Clanny stood from the boulder and lifted the snowhound off the ground. Pulling the pup to her bosom, she whispered, "Must we run again so soon?"

Medolas did not answer. Instead, he left Clanny standing speechless and bolted further into the depths of the canyon. He darted 74 paces before he made a hard left and disappeared from sight.

Seeing what was before him, the young Isorian was forced to duck behind some bushes that grew amidst a cropping of rocks. He would need to settle his breathing and collect his nerve before he could poke his head over the top of the thicket.

Prancing in front of the mouth of a cave was a silver-backed beast with dark, spotted markings and a flowing mane that matched the color of Clandestiny's hair. Medolas had seen beasts of this nature when the wizards from Luvelles showed the Isorian people drawings of their homeworld during their last visit. Though the creatures on Luvelles looked similar in stature, their colors were brown, black, and in some cases, white, but none had markings like the one before him. They had called their beasts horses.

Medolas continued to stare at this new kind of horse as Clandestiny caught up. She lowered the snowhound next to her feet and slapped Medolas on the arm. "How dare you leave me behind!" she scolded.

Medolas turned and placed his hand over her mouth. "Shhhhh. Must you speak so often?" he whispered. "Danger lies ahead."

With his hand still across her mouth, Medolas lifted Clandestiny and turned her head in the direction of the silver-backed beast. He leaned in and placed his mouth next to her ear. "I'm going to let go now."

Medolas grinned as he pulled his hand away from Clandestiny's mouth. Clanny's heated glare was strong enough to burn a hole through everything in its path, but nothing could ruin Medolas' enjoyment of the moment until a gust of wind passed between them carrying the silver-backed beast's scent.

Keeba reacted. The snowhound bolted from behind the bushes and headed in the direction of the beast with his leash dragging behind him.

In the heat of the moment, Clanny's fear for the hound's safety caused her to call out. "Keeba, return to me at once!"

Medolas slapped the top of his forehead. "Clanny! Have you become dense? I said to shhhh!"

Clanny slapped Medolas on the arm again. "Don't you shush me, Meddy!" She pointed overtop the thicket toward the hound. "Now, fetch him!"

Medolas crossed his arms, smirked and then nodded his head in the direction of the silver-backed horse. "It's too late. Friends have been made."

Clanny pried her eyes away from Medolas' cocky stance. To her delight, Keeba's nose was nuzzling against the nose of the horse. Excited, Clanny stepped from behind the bushes and approached the beast with caution.

Upon seeing Clanny, the horse lifted its head. Its demeanor was peaceful while it trotted toward her. What happened next caused Clandestiny to stop and stand in silence. The silver-backed beast spoke in her native tongue as it circled her. "Thou art not the child I expected. Tragedy must have befallen the man who bore the burden before thee. I see thou doest possess the Tear."

Clandestiny placed her hand over her chest. A long moment of silence passed as she fondled the Tear of Gramal. Eventually, she turned around and found Medolas' eyes which were still peeking over the thicket. "Meddy ... our journey is complete! We must thank Helmep!"

The Ko-dess added, "Art thou not the protector of this girl, boy?"

Medolas stepped from behind the thicket. "I am."

The Ko-dess snorted. "Doest thou always do thy duty from a coward's position?"

Before Medolas could respond, the Ko-dess nudged Clanny with his nose and walked into his cave.

As she turned to follow, Clanny grinned. "You may want to hide again, Meddy. It's dangerous in there."

Medolas' jaw dropped as Clanny disappeared into the shadows with the snowhound on her heels. After a few moments, he began to mumble, "No, no, no … don't defend me, Clanny. It's not like I've ever saved your life's source or anything."

17 PEAKS LATER
THE UNDER CITY OF HYDROTH
THE PEAK OF BAILEM

Shiver and the Frigid Commander slid into the depths of the ice and landed on their feet at the entrance to the undercastle. Their journey to the city had given them the moments to bond and the child-king had accepted Darosen as his father.

Opening the massive, chiseled doors that arched toward one another at their tops, Darosen led Shiver through the castle and into the dining hall. Snapping his fingers, the Frigid Commander sent a middle-aged male servant to fetch a platter of blubber and a pouch filled with sour ale.

Taking a seat, it was not long before the servant returned with the pouch. "Commander, your meal will arrive momentarily." The servant turned and bowed to Shiver. "Your Majesty."

Nodding, the young king dismissed the Isorian.

After filling two goblets, Darosen handed Shiver a drink. "You've earned this, my son. Despite the trials laid before you, I watched you become a man in the wilderness. I'm proud of you."

Shiver was unable to respond as the sour ale tore at his taste buds. The Frigid Commander chuckled, only to have his amusement stolen as Blandina appeared out of thin air, standing beside them.

Both males jumped from their seats and took a step back.

The sorceress laughed. "Does my company frighten you so?"

Shiver frowned and reclaimed his seat without answering. He grabbed his goblet and took another drink before he motioned for his father to join him.

Upon watching the commander reclaim his seat and sit in silence, Blandina moved to the opposite side of the table and sat in the seat across from Darosen. "Did you not miss me, my love?" She looked at Shiver. "Your return pleases me. I trust your journey has strengthened your relationship with your father. Have the last 60 Peaks offered you the moments to make a wise decision? Do you now see the wisdom of fulfilling your grandfather's wishes?"

Shiver lowered his goblet to the banquet table of ice, stained auburn, and stared at the rim of his wooden glass for a short series of moments before he found his mother's eyes. "If I have failed to see the wisdom in your father's desires, what then? Would you end your own son?"

Blandina's face hardened as she leaned forward. Out of the corner of her left eye, she saw the servant carrying the platter of blubber toward the table. Keeping her gaze fixed on Shiver's, she reached out with her left arm and flung her wrist to the side. The servant lifted off the floor, dropping the platter as he flew across the room and smashed into one of the pillars that supported the ceiling. The middle aged Isorian's head cracked open on impact.

Shiver could only focus on the splatter of blood as the father to 11 Isorian boys fell lifeless to the floor.

50 Peaks of Bailem Have Passed
The Cave of the Ko-dess
Early Bailem

Sitting on a rock toward the back of the cave, Clandestiny lowered the Tear of Gramal and watched as the red glow emanating from within it faded. She sighed and allowed her eyes to fall to the floor. "I can't feel anything, Blazzin. It speaks not to me."

From the far side of the cave, the Ko-dess walked over to Clanny and nuzzled the right side of her face. "Didst thou truly believe thou wouldst command the power of the dragon before the end of thy first season? Sit not in sadness nor despair, for thy will is strong. Lift the Tear and start again."

Sitting against the wall at the back of the cave, Medolas scratched beneath the chin of the growing snowhound as he watched Clandestiny cup the Tear in the palm of her hand and lift it level with her eyes. Once again, the Tear began to glow, causing the crystallizations in Clanny's face and body to turn purple.

As Clanny focused, the Ko-dess moved behind her. The horse shut his eyes and lowered his head. A soft white light, one not powerful enough to overtake the glow of the Tear, appeared around Blazzin's form. A moment later, Clandestiny's arms flew to her sides. Her chest pushed forward and her muscles started to quake, causing the young Isorian to fall to the floor. Clanny's mouth opened and a treacherous sound erupted from it.

Keeba pulled away from Medolas' hand and darted for the gap between the small of Medolas' back and the cave wall. The snowhound's body shivered as he forced his head between them with his front paws placed over his ears.

Medolas had no choice but to cover his own ears. The noise was loud enough to cause the snow sitting on top of the mountain above the cave to fall. The rumbling of the avalanche was overshadowed by Clanny's roar as the snow settled into the canyon and sealed the mouth of the cave.

As Clanny's growl stopped, the white light encompassing the Ko-dess faded, yet the glow of the Tear remained strong and Clandestiny's eyes remained shut. Her body no longer trembled, but her eyes moved rapidly behind her eyelids.

Medolas stood, leaving Keeba behind. The snowhound refused to look up from beneath his paws as the Isorian walked over to the Ko-dess. Seeing the horse lift his head, Medolas uttered, "Blazzin, is her life's source in jeopardy?"

"No. The affection of thine heart hath not been lost."

Medolas sighed with relief. "In my 16 seasons, I have heard that sound before. My father had to comfort me on the first night. For upon telling me the sound was that of the gashtion, I cried tears of fear."

"Thy father was a wise man to comfort such a young lad. Twenty-nine more roars must our ears suffer before thy love hath the power to withstand the Tear's greatness. To master the gashtion's call is a path filled with memories of old. These memories must become one with her being. Only then, canst thou return to Hydroth."

Medolas pondered as he knelt next to Clanny to clear the hair from her face. "How long will she sleep?"

The Ko-dess lowered his head and sniffed Clanny's scent. "Perhaps beyond the Peak beyond the morrow."

"So ... 2 Peaks," Medolas confirmed. "And the Tear? Shall it remain as it is until her eyes open?"

The Ko-dess nodded. "The Tear shall emanate its glory until Clandestiny commands it once again."

Medolas thought in silence while he stroked Clandestiny's hair. "When will she roar again?"

The Ko-dess started walking toward the mouth of the cave. "Clandestiny shall not call out again for another 10 seasons."

Medolas stood and did the math. "Do you mean that we shall reside in the wilderness for 290 seasons before our eyes see home?"

The Ko-dess continued to walk toward the snow-covered entrance. "It is mine hope that our seasons together shall feel short-lived. Follow me, young one. There is work we must suffer before we shall see freedom beyond these walls."

Medolas nodded. As he walked with Blazzin toward the mouth of the cave, he noticed something from within the Ko-dess was glowing. "Blazzin, why does your belly illuminate?"

The Ko-dess stopped and dropped his head. "The Tear hath a kindred spirit that exists within mine being. If ever there was a Peak when thine love was to fall in battle while protecting thine existence, it is I who would bear the burden of the Kindred Tear."

Medolas stood in silence for a short series of moments as he pondered Blazzin's words. "What would happen to Clandestiny's Tear if she fell?"

The Ko-dess lifted his head and found Medolas' eyes. "The gashtion would ravage thine lands until the moment of mine arrival. Thou doest not want to know the suffering the Isor would face."

"Are you saying that only you could save the Isor?"

Blazzin whinnied. "One could only hope. It would be mine steadfast desire to do all that is within mine might..."

Fellow soul, those were the events that happened
just over 290 seasons ago.
Let us now return to the season from whence we last left the
Worlds of the Crystal Moon—the same
season when George trapped Shalee inside the Eye of Magic.
5 Peaks have passed since that event.

Welcome to the first edition of:

The Crystal Shard

When you want an update about your favorite characters

George Nailer—After the warlock trapped Shalee in the Eye of Magic, he returned to the family homes on the northern shore of the Head Master's island on Western Luvelles. The warlock spent the first few Peaks relaxing—but over the last 2 Peaks, he has been constantly looking for baby Garrin. The child keeps teleporting out of his crib.

With a new sun rising, another dose of Brayson's potion will be given to the toddler to bind his magic, but during this series of moments, they plan to administer a heftier dose.

Kepler is lying on top of the rocks at the center of the family homes. The demon-cat has a full belly, and he is waiting for George to finish breakfast with Athena, baby Joshua, Mary, Brayson, Susanne, Gregory, baby Garrin, and the fairy-demon-child, Payne. Kepler plans to travel with George to the city of Brandor. George needs to speak with the king of the newly named United Kingdom of Southern Grayham, Sam Goodrich.

Mosley—the night terror wolf, also the former God of War—After befriending Rash, the ormesh of the mightiest saber clan to occupy the Cat Plains on Southern Grayham, Mosley traveled with the saber lord to his lair. Rash then commanded four of his strongest subjects to accompany them across the Isthmus of Change. Over the last 135 Peaks, Mosley's feline escorts kept all threats at bay until Mosley entered the village of Edsmar on the southern shore of Northern Grayham, just north off the coast of the Blood Sea.

Mosley entered the village to question the locals about the frozen lands beyond the Cave of No Return. His queries regarding the Isorian people and the Tear of Gramal landed the wolf inside a frozen prison beneath the undercastle of Hydroth. He has been beaten over the last 11 Peaks by the Frigid Commander, Darosen.

As for Rash and his saber tooth subjects, they did not have the ability to protect themselves from the extreme cold. As a consequence, they froze to death during the journey to Hydroth after being separated from Mosley. The group was ambushed by Darosen, Blandina and 400 sentries when they exited the Cave of No Return. Mosley has survived only because he uses what little magic he commands to warm himself while he suffers in the depths of the Isorian icy dungeon.

Gage the badger and **Gallrum** the serwin—goswigs freed of their corrupt masters—have arrived on the Merchant Island of Grayham. They will journey to the frozen lands of Northern Grayham because of the dream the Book of Immortality planted in the badger's mind. They have no knowledge of the territories of Grayham, thus making teleportation an unacceptable risk.

Lasidious, God of Mischief, **Celestria,** Goddess of Beasts, and **Alistar,** God of the Harvest—Over the last 135 Peaks, the group has enjoyed success. The number of those who worship Lasidious continues to grow on Harvestom, Southern Grayham and Western Luvelles. The moment has come for the trio to implement the next part of their plan to take control of the Book of Immortality. A meeting of the gods has been called in Gabriel's Hall of Judgment on Ancients Sovereign.

Lord Boyafed, Chancellor of Dark Magic, and **Lord Dowd,** King of Lavan—Boyafed and Dowd are standing on the Battlegrounds of Olis that are located on Western Luvelles. They are monitoring the creation of the Protector of the Realm's new home. Kepler has requested that his palace be completed before his return from Dragonia. The jaguar has informed them that he will be seeking a mate.

Shalee, Queen of Brandor, **Helga,** Shalee's former teacher of the magical arts, **BJ,** Sam's former trainer of weaponry, and the unknown **Fourth Figure**—Upon announcing Shalee's quest to create a new Heaven, the fourth figure inside the Eye of Magic commanded Shalee to sleep. Helga and BJ have been waiting for the sorceress to wake. When this happens, a revelation will occur.

Medolas and **Clandestiny**—Both Isorians are now 305 seasons old. Clandestiny blossomed into a mesmerizing woman while studying under the Ko-dess to understand the power of the Tear. With her final roar complete, Medolas and Clandestiny have decided to return to Hydroth. They will travel without their pet snowhound, Keeba, since he passed of old age many, many seasons ago. Upon their arrival, Clandestiny has agreed to form a union with Medolas and surrender to him that which he has desired for so long.

Clanny and Medolas have no idea the turmoil Hydroth has seen since their departure. With the Tear resting on Clanny's chest so many Peaks from Hydroth, many lives have been lost to the belly of the gashtion.

Shiver, King of the Isor—Shiver lived in fear of his mother for more than 287 seasons before he decided to take a stand. For the last three seasons, he has stood in defiance of his mother—ever since he realized that she will not harm him and that her threats against him are empty. But no matter how empty his mother's threats are against the king, many of the men in Shiver's army are scared of Blandina. This has creating constant struggle while trying to create alliances within his own kingdom. Shiver is now 306 seasons old.

The king's relationship with Darosen never flourished. Though the pair bonded on their journey back from the Caves of Carne so many seasons ago, the Frigid Commander feared Shiver's mother. Because of this, Darosen chose to devote himself to Blandina rather than be a good father to Shiver. The result: Shiver despises Darosen and has had to confide in Gablysin for the last 290 seasons.

Though Gablysin does not know it, Blandina considers the ruby eyed man her enemy. She has never expressed any ill-will toward Gabs, yet she keeps Gablysin under Darosen's watchful eye in case the prophesy is true.

With the absence of the Tear of Gramal, Gablysin has fought with the army over the last 30 seasons to fend off the gashtion's attacks. The ruby eyed man now stands beside Darosen as the Frigid Commander's second in command. Because of the Frigid Commander's training, Gabs has become a powerful warrior and a mighty hunter. The commander has kept Gablysin occupied so the ruby eyed man would not be able to develop his talent as a singer—a talent that was mentioned in the prophecy.

Now, at the age of 305 seasons, the ruby eyed man is worried about Shiver—for tonight, at Late Bailem, Shiver will meet his grandfather, a withered, feeble-looking, King Meerum Bosand, for the first moment in his life.

Slips, the child born without pysples, the small suction cups on the bottom of his feet—Slips has spent the last 7 Peaks tunneling through the ice beneath the undercastle. He now wears special shoes that grip the ice to ensure his footing. What he is about to do could be considered heroic—or stupid.

Thank you for reading the Crystal Shard

CHAPTER 6
JUST ONE DROP

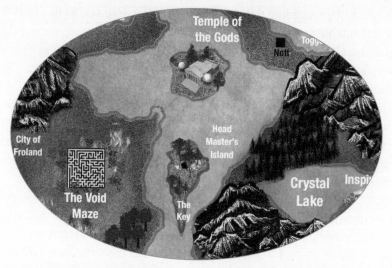

WESTERN LUVELLES—THE HEAD MASTER'S ISLAND

Now, fellow soul ... if you do not remember, the houses that Brayson Id, the Head Master of Luvelles, created for George and his family were based on George's memories of old Earth. These memories were divulged to the Head Master by Lasidious when the Mischievous One appeared to Brayson as Amar to ask the Head Master to take George as his Mystic Learner.

The homes sat in a circular subdivision, with the outside walls made of a combination of stone, brick and stucco. Of course, there were no streets or sidewalks, but the mound of stones sitting at the center of the clearing between the homes served as a playground for the older children in the family.

Much of the furniture inside the homes was also reminiscent of Earth. There were a few differences, however. Homes on Earth did not have circular platforms near the front door that teleported you wherever you wanted to go inside the house. They also did not have beds that made themselves, food closets where the temperature changed on each occasion the door opened or lights that illuminated from no apparent source. Finally, the homes on Earth were not alive. The walls did not carry a pulse from funneling magic throughout hidden veins that existed beneath their surfaces.

WESTERN LUVELLES
THE NORTHERN SHORE OF THE HEAD MASTER'S ISLAND
EARLY BAILEM

"Garesh! I'm dreading this damn meeting," George said as he stood from the kitchen table and walked to the food closet.

Hearing George swear, Payne hit the top of his high chair on either side of his plate and shouted. "Damn meeting! Garesh!"

Athena glared at George.

The warlock shrugged. "I know, I know. I'm sorry, babe." He looked at Payne. "Watch your mouth."

Turning back to the food closet, George opened the door and looked in. "Sam isn't going to take the news very well. Shalee's soul has obviously been swallowed. Five Peaks have passed since she entered the Eye."

Brayson lowered the vial filled with his potion to bind Garrin's power and watched as the toddler grimaced. After wiping the baby's chin, the Head Master returned to his chair and added, "The King of Brandor is strong. As tragic as this news is, I wouldn't worry about his reaction. Sam will accept the loss of his queen and lead his people with honor."

Athena wiped a piece of greggled hash from the corner of her mouth. "Still, Sam will be heartbroken." She looked at George as he shut the food closet and carried the corgan milk back to the table. "I can't imagine how I'd feel if you didn't come home to me."

"I agree with Athena," Mary added. She reached to her right and collected Payne's empty plate. As she stacked it on top of her own, she continued to speak while she reached for Garrin and Joshua's plates that were sitting on their high chairs behind her. "I'm sure Sam will present a strong face … but he'll mourn."

Susanne cut in, "I saw the way Sam looked at Shalee when we feasted with them in Brandor."

Swallowing his bite of scrambled vestle chick eggs, Gregory added, "At best, we're guessing as to the king's reaction." He looked at George. "Perhaps you should get it over with."

George nodded. "Yeah, yeah, yeah ... I know. I hate delivering bad news. It sucks ass."

Athena slapped George on the forearm. "Don't you dare speak another ill word. I told you to stop speaking like that around the children. Since you stood from this table, you've ignored my rules twice."

Mary reached out with her right arm and put her hand on Athena's shoulder. "You tell him, daughter."

Instead of reacting to Athena's chastisement, George looked across the table at Brayson. He rolled his eyes and then grinned before he lifted his mug to his mouth and swallowed his last drink of corgan milk. After lowering the cup to the table, the warlock shrugged. "Well ... the moment has come for me to get ready." He leaned to his right to kiss Athena.

After a quick peck, Athena grabbed the red collar of George's black tunic and looked him in the eye. A sly smile appeared on her face. "Don't think this conversation is over, Mr. Nailer. Make sure that mouth of yours remains clean around these children from now on. Do you understand me?"

George reached out with his left hand and cupped his wife's chin. "You're so hot when you're rough with me."

Before Athena could respond, the warlock vanished. She turned to her right and looked at Susanne who now held baby Garrin in her arms and was wiping his face. "I love it when he does that."

Mary reacted by grabbing Brayson by the collar of his red robe. She pulled him close. "I second that. You magic men are intoxicating." She then nibbled the Head Master's right ear lobe. "Mesolliff wine may be in order tonight, my love."

Watching his brother's eyes widen, Gregory looked toward Susanne to see what her response would be. Instead of receiving the playful response he desired, he watched as Garrin started to grunt. The White Chancellor's nose crinkled at the pungent smell that followed. "Somehow ... that's not what I expected."

Susanne grinned as she handed the baby to Gregory. "Let's see how sexy a magic man can be when he changes a messy diaper. Perhaps a kiss will follow."

Gregory snapped his fingers and a fresh diaper appeared on Garrin. "There. It's done."

Susanne smiled. "Now that deserves more than a kiss." She removed Garrin from Gregory's arms and handed the baby to Mary. "We'll be back." Grabbing Gregory by the hand, they walked into the next room.

MEANWHILE, WESTERN LUVELLES
THE KINGDOM OF LAVAN
THE GRASSY PLAINS OF THE
BATTLEGROUNDS OF OLIS

Now, fellow soul … the foundation of Kepler's palace was finished, but the materials to form the outer walls had only recently arrived from Troll-com. After speaking with Lasidious during yet another dream the night after Shalee's entrapment in the Eye, George spoke with Kepler about the design of the structure. The demon-cat had stopped its creation long enough to implement Lasidious' suggestions. The Mischievous One had told George about a special ore that was mined by enslaved dwarves on Trollcom. He said the metal possessed regenerative properties, and it had the ability to rejuvenate one's magical foundation over a shorter series of moments. As a result, Kepler and George would be able to recuperate much faster after a heavy Peak's use of power.

Boyafed pushed Lord Dowd's wheeled chair up the ramp to the top of a platform that overlooked the site of Kepler's unfinished palace. After setting the brake, the Dark Chancellor folded back the collar of a black trench coat that George that created for him. He remembered the young warlock saying, "Boyafed, you need a cooler look." He smiled at the memory and enjoyed the oddness of the statement.

Cupping his hands around his mouth, Boyafed looked down and shouted at the lead creator who was standing on the ground at the base of the platform he and Dowd were on. "Taugor ... you better get this right! The ore cannot be replaced. The council of neither kingdom can afford a mistake."

Taugor turned and looked up. He pushed his hair clear of his face and signaled his receipt of the message with a wave of his hand. After receiving the go-ahead from Lord Dowd, the lanky elf strolled across the clearing and climbed to the top of a circular pedestal that sat 25 paces above the ground. Removing his shoes, he placed his bare feet into a shallow pool of water at its center. Once confident in his footing, he removed his shirt and signaled Dowd and Boyafed that he was ready to begin. A moment later, he wrapped his shirt around his shoes and allowed them to fall to the ground.

Three elves, all without shirts and shoes walked up to the base of the pedestal and encircled it. They placed their hands on metal rods that ran up and through the pedestal to the pool.

Once Taugor had received a nod from each, he began swirling his arms in a circular motion. The elves on the ground began to chant, and a long series of moments passed before their hands began to glow. The energy from their magic ran up the metal rods to the pool of water and caused it to bubble. As a result, Taugor's magic was amplified three-fold.

The massive piles of ore that sat more than 100 paces to the right of the tower that Boyafed and Dowd were standing on began to stir. The top of the first mound segregated itself from the rest and floated across the grass toward the foundation of Kepler's palace. As it did, an infrastructure of beams with holes at their centers formed. Once above the foundation, they assembled and lowered into place.

Next, though still sizable, a much smaller mound of ore lifted from the pile and began its approach toward the framing. As it did, the metal reshaped into long strands of hollow wire and worked its way through the holes in the beams until the veining was complete.

Third, the rest of the mound lifted off the ground and molded into large sheets. One by one, they attached themselves to the outside of the framing until the structure was sealed on all sides.

With the outside covered, the network of veins doubled back along the inside of the structure and worked their way toward the rear of the palace. They slithered up the back wall and attached to a number of cylinders that would later be joined with an enormous heart that would be created out of more than 200 hearts harvested from slaughtered corgans.

Clapping his hands, Dowd shouted, "Remarkable work, Taugor!" The new King of Lavan extended his right arm and used his magic to lift the tired elf off the top of the platform. After setting the lead creator on the ground, Dowd released his magic and allowed the elves surrounding the pedestal to catch him when Taugor collapsed.

Dowd looked up at Boyafed. "When do the hides and muscle of the corgans arrive?"

"Six Peaks," the Dark Chancellor responded. "For now, they remain frozen in Froland."

The king cringed. "You could've chosen another name."

Boyafed released the brake of Dowd's wheeled chair with his foot and then patted his friend on his right shoulder. "I renamed the city to honor our friendship. Does this not please you, Henry Froland Dowd?"

"You jab at my expense, Boyafed. Perhaps, some Peak, we will need to have our fight after all."

Boyafed grinned. "You will have to learn to roll quickly if that's going to happen." The Dark Chancellor then directed Dowd's wheelchair to the top of the ramp. As they began their descent, he changed the subject. "The jaguar's taste is exotic, is it not? Materials continue to arrive on Merchant Island Peakly. I long to see the completion of the structure."

Dowd smirked. "I sense the cat's taste resembles that of the prophet's. Perhaps I should teach Kepler how to garden."

Boyafed chuckled. "Where did that come from? Ha! The sight of a predator gardening. How tragic."

Dowd's brows furrowed. "Gardening can be peaceful. I should take you to my old home in Inspiration. Cultivating is not just for women and servants, you know."

Boyafed patted Dowd on his shoulder again. "Sure, it isn't. You keep telling yourself that."

MEANWHILE, ANCIENTS SOVEREIGN GABRIEL'S HALL OF JUDGMENT

Lasidious stood from the heavy, stone table to address the gods. "How wonderful it is to see you all again. My influence continues to grow Peakly, and soon I shall have the power to control the Book." The Mischievous One stopped talking. He looked down the table at Gabriel who was hovering above it and grinned. "My apologies, Gabriel. I shouldn't have called you a book."

Without waiting for Gabriel to respond, Lasidious continued as he scanned the faces of the others. "Anyway, as I was saying..." He paused again and looked deeply into the eyes of Gabriel. "Soon, I shall control the Book, and this collective will be forced to live by my laws and not the laws written on its useless pages."

Mieonus stomped the lifted heel of her right shoe and leaned forward. "Your arrogance is thick enough to cut with a knife. There are those of us on this Collective who plot against you. Your Peaks as The Almighty will never come to pass."

Murmurs filled the room as Celestria stood and started to circle the table.

The Goddess of Beasts held the Goddess of Hate's eyes as she responded. "Yet, there are those of us, Mieonus, who desire an Almighty. I'd gladly sit at Lasidious' side and worship him for eternity." Stopping next to her lover, Celestria caressed Lasidious' face. "Is that not right, my pet?"

Feigning his irritation, Alistar slapped his right hand on the table. "Save your dramatics for the theatre, Celestria. You put too much faith in your pet prophet. George will only be able to spread Lasidious' supposed good word so far."

The God of the Harvest stood and circled the table as well. As he did, he touched each of the gods on the shoulder as he passed. "Soon, George will be faced with a dilemma … one that will consume his moments. He won't be able to deceive the worlds into misplaced worship." Alistar stopped on the other side of Lasidious. He reached up and caressed the Mischievous One's cheek just as Celestria had done. "How does this news make you feel, my pet … my cute, little devil-god?" He spit on the floor. "I may vomit."

As Celestria stormed back to her chair, Mieonus rolled with laughter and pounded her lifted heels against the floor to punctuate her enjoyment of the moment. "Oh, my dear Alistar, we must converse upon the completion of this meeting. I desperately desire to know your scheming."

Kesdelain looked across the table at Hosseff and then turned to his right to nudge Owain with his elbow. "Must every meeting exude such hatred?"

Hearing the troll-god's comment, Sharvesa spoke out. "Yes, do tell, Hosseff."

A hissing laughter emanated from the nothingness beneath Hosseff's hood. The sound caused all the gods to pause and look in his direction. The God of Death pulled back his hood and allowed his face to materialize. "The scheming of this collective, filled with ruthless, devious, malicious power seekers, should be cherished. What fun would immortality be without the games we play?"

Sharvesa sat back in her chair and lowered her head. "If I would've understood the truth of the gods prior to my ascension, I would've chosen to remain on Dragonia. I care not for the hate of my peers." The demon-goddess looked down the length of the table at Lasidious. "With respect, if I would've understood the depravity of your heart, the races of demons would not have served you when I was queen. My only consolation is that my people have now abandoned their service to you and have begun anew. My daughter has seen to it that all demons speak my name in their prayers."

Sharvesa moved behind her chair. Her yellow gown swayed and contrasted gloriously against the red of her skin as she pushed the chair under the table. She looked at the Book of Immortality. "Gabriel, I must excuse myself from this meeting. I'm feeling sick."

Before the Book could respond, Lasidious vanished and reappeared next to Sharvesa. He reached out and placed his hand on her forearm. "Aren't you the least bit curious as to why this meeting was called? After all, a decision was made seasons ago that will effect your homeworld."

Without moving her head, the orange surrounding the yellow irises of the demon's eyes filled her sockets as she looked to her left. "I'm listening."

Vanishing again, Lasidious appeared in his seat with his feet resting on top of the table. He leaned back and placed his hands behind his head. "I thought you'd say that. This collective has convened to announce the moments are right for Dragonia to become the new Hell. As per Gabriel's judgment, the darkest souls within his pages are to be released. They shall wander the territories of your old homeworld by the end of the Peak, 7 Peaks from now. They will survive inside temporary bodies that cannot perish. They'll feel pain, fear, sadness, anger and remorse for the sins they committed during their lives, and it won't matter what world they committed them on ... they will suffer."

The Mischievous One crossed his arms. "With the dragons removed, the criminals who were banished to live out the rest of their Peaks on Dragonia will be free to do as they please. Because of this, a new hierarchy will form, and the most ruthless of these degenerates will rule. They'll murder, slaughter, burn, rape and pillage not only those who occupy Dragonia but also those who will be cast upon it who cannot die. The souls released from Gabriel's pages will be forced to suffer. They may even fight back in an effort to avoid reliving the experience again and again. Everyone on your old homeworld will endure this living Hell until they, too, pass to join the ranks of the damned."

Sharvesa reached up and grabbed the horns that rolled over the top of her head. The red in her knuckles displaced as she squeezed. "And what of my people? Shall all demons suffer, or will they be moved to some other world?"

Lasidious chuckled. "Your people were created for a different calling. You have no memory of your past, but you were once used to administer pain and torment for the mightiest of all governors who ruled a Hades that no longer exists. You were—"

The demon-goddess cut Lasidious off. "My kind will do no such thing. They exist in harmony on Dragonia. They won't do the bidding of this collective or any being who is chosen to govern the Hell that Dragonia is to become. I'll see to that."

Lasidious chuckled again. "Your people will accept their fate, because if they don't, they'll perish as a result of their inability to adapt. Your kind will have no choice but to resume the true purpose for which they were created, or they will quickly join the ranks of the damned."

The demon-goddess scanned the faces of the others. Her eyes stopped on the Book of Immortality. "Is this wickedness true, Gabriel? Did my people once exist as foot soldiers for an ultimate evil? Were we once servants of a cause that we couldn't control?"

The Book floated across the room and stopped eye-level with Sharvesa. Remorse filled his expression. "What Lasidious said is the truth." The Book sighed. "When I was created, it was understood that all races of demons would once again resume their function once the dragons were given their new homeworld. Though you cannot remember the ways of old, you existed to torture and do the bidding of one who has long since perished. There are members of this collective who believe the demons should resume this charge."

Gabriel's eyes dropped to the floor as if embarrassed. "Your kind will torture the souls that I release from my pages. As a result, these beings will exist in suffering until the moment comes for them to be reborn on some other world."

Sharvesa took a step back as she scanned the faces of the others. "You all knew of this treachery?"

Kesdelain threw up his hands. "Don't look at me. I knew nothing of it." The troll-god elbowed Owain again. "I'm glad my kind is on Trollcom."

As Kesdelain mused over his comment, the others were expressionless. A long, awkward series of moments passed before the gods acknowledged the truth.

Seeing their nods, Sharvesa reclaimed the Book's eyes. "Where does this leave me, Gabriel? I was given godliness for nothing if this is what my homeworld is to become."

Sharvesa could see the Book did not have an answer. She placed her hands on top of her seat as she continued to ponder the consequences. Looking across the table, she spoke to Lasidious. "If the words you've uttered are true, chaos will ensue. The vampires will break their treaty with all races of demons. War will erupt as each race seeks to survive. There will be no harmony amongst my kind."

The demon-goddess paused again. Her eyes scanned the Collective again as she made her next statement. "Every being on Dragonia will fight for goods delivered to Merchant Island. Blood will flow freely." Sharvesa paused yet again and then added, "The criminals' numbers are too many. Over the seasons, they have found ways to survive. They'll be a formidable foe, and they'll not only fight for the goods delivered ... but for new territories as well."

"Goods?" Lasidious sneered. "There won't be any goods. The Merchant Angels will be instructed to abandon Dragonia. There will be no more deliveries." Lasidious lowered his feet to the floor and stood. He leaned forward and placed his hands on the table. "Now that you understand the fate of your kind, know this ... I can ease their suffering. I have a solution that will allow your people to continue to exist in harmony."

Bailem spoke out before the demon-goddess could respond. "You lie, Lasidious! There's nothing you can do to keep that world from eternal damnation! This collective voted on this over 10,000 seasons ago!"

Chuckling, Celestria nestled into Lasidious and pulled his right arm about her waist. With her head on his chest, she looked into his eyes and sought his approval. "Perhaps you'd allow me to tell Sharvesa your plan for sparing her kind, my sweet?"

The yellow irises of Sharvesa's eyes flashed. "Yes, Lasidious, allow your harlot to share with me."

Celestria quickly redirected her gaze. A sharpness filled her words as she delivered a cutting response. "I'm not a harlot. To think ... I would've had compassion for your loss. Well, no more. I was even going to tell you where you could find your son. But not now—"

Lasidious pinched the back of Celestria's arm, but Celestria's anger overrode the Mischievous One's warning. She pulled her arm away and continued to berate the demon. "Now you'll never know the joy of Payne's company."

The room became disgruntled as the gods' questions rolled off their tongues. None of them knew about the fairy-demon.

To cover Celestria's slip, Lasidious had to act fast. He lifted his voice to command everyone's attention. "Sharvesa's bastard is of no concern to this collective." The Mischievous One vanished and reappeared leaning against the table next to Sharvesa's chair. "You cannot change Dragonia's fate, but

I can offer the demons a peaceful existence … even while living on the Hell your world is to become."

Without waiting for Sharvesa's response, Lasidious turned to address the others. "None of us can change Dragonia's fate. The souls within Gabriel's pages will be released as per our laws, but nowhere does it state that I couldn't prepare for this Peak. When I'm finished, every being on Dragonia will worship me." He looked at the Book. "Even the souls released shall look to me for reprieve. The damned will call out my name to ease their suffering, and their prayers will also add to my power."

The room erupted as the gods cursed Lasidious, but Kesdelain remained quiet. The troll still feared Lasidious and would wait for a better opportunity to act.

Sharvesa pulled her chair out from under the table and then lowered onto it. The demon looked down the table at Celestria. The Goddess of Beasts had a smirk on her face, and she was clearly enjoying her suffering.

Eventually, the Book of Immortality called for order. The gods who had abandoned their chairs slowly returned to them as the Book spoke. "Yet again, the gods have failed to create complete laws. The consequences of this carelessness shall manifest once I fulfill the travesty that has been decreed." Before another word could be said, Gabriel vanished.

Lasidious clasped his hands, but before his enjoyment of the moment could escalate, Sharvesa spoke loud enough to command the attention of the room. "Lasidious, I'd like to speak with you in private!"

Alistar slapped the edge of the table with his right hand. "Yes, my pet! Why don't you leave, and let the rest of this collective cherish the moments of your absence. We will use this reprieve to conspire against you."

Lasidious held Alistar's cocky gaze for a short series of moments before he allowed a sinister smile to appear on his face. Without justifying the God of the Harvest's comment, the Mischievous One returned to Celestria and extended his arm. "Don't you have someplace to be, my love?"

Helping the goddess up, the Mischievous One stood between her and the Collective. He placed his lips next to Celestria's ear and whispered, "Don't ever allow your emotions to get the best of you again. You disappoint me."

Celestria's heart sunk. As she pulled back, she could see the coldness in Lasidious' eyes. She wanted to respond, but knew it was best to say nothing. With despair filling her mind, the goddess vanished.

Grinning, Lasidious faced the Collective and then walked around the table. Stopping next to Sharvesa, he touched the demon-goddess on the shoulder and then looked at the others. "We bid you good Peak." They vanished.

WESTERN LUVELLES

George teleported out of his kitchen after breakfast. He reappeared inside his bedroom, cleaned up and then put on a fresh tunic. After grabbing his staff, he closed his eyes. When the warlock reappeared, he was standing next to the mound of boulders that sat above Kepler's lair.

Instead of the cat sleeping in the darkness below, Kepler was lying on top of the rocks. His black, gem-lined saddle was secured to his back, and he was ready for the trip. The beast rose, jumped to the ground and then lowered to his belly.

After mounting, the warlock used his power to take them to a safe location outside of the city of Brandor.

As they approached the front gates, the guards standing on either side of the doors recognized the pair. "Prophet! It's good to see you again!" the guard on the right side of the gate shouted. He then turned and signaled to the men inside to open the massive, wooden doors since Kepler's body would not fit through the smaller opening to the left.

George smiled and reached down from the top of Kepler's back to take hold of the guard's forearm. "Hello, Cholis. How's your family?"

"They are well, Prophet. The coin you gave me helped tremendously. I have thanked Lasidious in my prayers on many occasions since."

George released Cholis' forearm and sat up. "I'm sure our lord is pleased with you." George turned his head in the direction of the other guard. "And you, Diayasis, have you been praying?"

Diayasis dropped his head. "I cannot lie, Prophet. I've prayed to no one since the Peak we met."

George reached inside his tunic and pulled out two Lasidious coins. He tossed one to Diayasis and the other to Cholis.

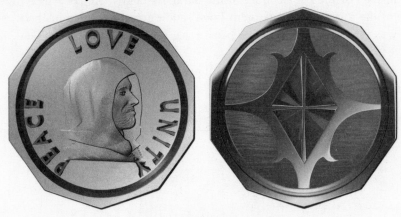

LASIDIOUS COIN

Diayasis looked up. "I don't understand. I said I haven't prayed."

The prophet smiled. "Lasidious said to reward you if you spoke the truth." George leaned down and took hold of Diayasis' forearm. "Perhaps you'll find it in your heart to avoid making this relationship one-sided. My lord wants to see your face in his Heaven some Peak."

Diayasis bit down on the coin and studied it before he responded. "Perhaps." He placed the coin in his pocket.

George smirked. "I'm not going to give up on you, Diayasis."

Passing through the gates, Cholis waited until the prophet was out of earshot. He slapped Diayasis on the back of his head. "What's wrong with you?"

The children running through the streets flocked to Kepler, knowing the demon-cat was safe to approach. Many of the children's faces were licked clean with one swipe of the giant cat's slobbery tongue. Though it took much longer to get to the castle than expected, this extended series of moments became the perfect opportunity to add to Lasidious' flock.

With the castle finally in sight, George and Kepler spoke telepathically to keep their conversation from being overheard.

"Kep ... I've been meaning to talk to you. Something has been bothering me. Can I dump on you for a bit?"

"One moment, George." The jaguar licked an annoying child with an extra slobbery tongue to get the youngster to back off. The demon's tongue was so large that it not only covered the boy's head, but the upper part of his body as well. With the child crying about how gross it was, the demon-cat enjoyed the boy's discomfort and then continued the conversation. *"If by dumping on me you mean seek my opinion ... then yes, you may dump."*

"Thanks, buddy. I'm sure you already know, but trapping Shalee in the Eye like I did has been bothering me. Ever since the Source said he saw something good in me, I can't seem to shake off his words. It's like every moment I do something wrong, I feel guilty about it. But for whatever reason, I do it anyway. Maybe I should stop being such a prick."

Kepler nudged a cute little girl with his nose. Though his gesture was gentle, the girl's brunette pigtails flopped forward as she took a step back to catch herself from falling. Giggling, the girl ran beneath the jaguar's chin.

Kepler stopped to make sure he did not step on the child.

With her arms encircling as much of the demon-cat's left leg as she could, she squeezed. "I love you, kitty!" she hollered.

The jaguar cringed and rolled his head back over his shoulder. *"Could you please do something about this, George?"*

From within an invisible veil, Celestria watched from the side of the cobblestone road as George patted the back of Kepler's neck. The goddess saw the prophet reach into his tunic to remove a pouch filled with Owain coins. She smirked as George shook the bag to capture the children's attention.

The children's eyes widened as the prophet spoke. "There are 300 Owain in this pouch. Who wants one?"

Hearing the children's exuberance, George opened the sack and poured out a handful. He tossed the coins as hard as he could over his shoulder and watched the children chase after them. Grabbing another handful, he tossed it to his right and then another to his left. Seeing the kids scatter, he placed his hands on Kepler's shoulders, and then the pair vanished.

Celestria watched the kids scramble. She enjoyed their excitement for a short series of moments. *I long for the day when I can see such joy on Garrin's face,* she thought. A moment later, she disappeared to catch up with George and Kepler in the courtyard of Sam's castle. The Goddess of Beasts maintained her invisible cover as she appeared at the center of the steps that led up to the door of the castle.

It was only a matter of moments before two guards recognized the prophet. The taller of the two men had a trimmed beard. He was stocky and walked with a limp. "Prophet, we weren't expecting you."

The sergeant lowered to one knee as George dropped to the ground from the top of Kepler's back. The prophet reached into his tunic and removed two Lasidious coins. He placed one in the sergeant's hand as he motioned for him to stand. "I'm here to see your king. What's your name, Sergeant?"

Before the guard could answer, Michael, the General Absolute, shouted from atop the steps of the castle. "As always, it's good to see you, Prophet." He began walking down the steps to greet them. "But where's the queen? Isn't she with you?"

Suddenly, the general reached up to rub the outside of his arms. "Brrrrrr! A chill just filled my bones."

A smile spread across the goddess' face as she enjoyed the sensation Michael felt as he passed through her.

The general stopped at the bottom of the steps and sneezed twice as George tossed the other Lasidious coin to the second guard. After enjoying the excitement on the man's clean shaven face, the Prophet responded. "Are you catching a cold, General?"

Michael wiped the snot from his nose. "I don't know what overcame me. I've never felt a chill like that."

George walked forward and placed his right arm around the general's shoulders. "Let's step inside and speak with the king. I only want to say what I need to once."

As the group entered the throne room, Celestria remained invisible. The goddess walked across the rough-hewn stones of the floor and leaned against the windowsill. Crossing her arms, she looked up the steps toward the throne. The king was sitting in his chair, playing with Sam, Jr. while the baby was lying in his lap. The sight of the child and the memory of the disappointment on Lasidious' face caused her longing for Garrin to increase.

Seeing George enter out of the corner of his eye, the king looked up. "Does your boy smile as much as mine? Better yet, does he poop as much as mine?"

Sam pinched his son's chin and then spoke in his best baby voice. "I swear, I think you're a pooping machine. Yes, Daddy does." The king tickled the bottom of the child's foot. "You're Daddy's little pooper."

Despite the news George had come to deliver, the prophet had to grin. "Yeah, man, I've got a crapping machine at home, too. I can always come back if you're too busy."

Sam looked up. "No. Don't worry about it. He needs a nap anyway."

The king placed his massive hands under Sam, Jr. and then lifted the baby off his lap. He stood from his throne and walked toward a female handmaiden who was waiting next to a bassinet. After kissing the baby on the forehead, Sam lowered the child onto his back and tucked a blanket around him. The king beamed with pride as the woman pushed the bassinet out of the room.

Facing George, Sam walked down the steps and stuck out his hand. "So, what can I do for you?" Seeing that George was by himself, he added, "Where's Shalee?"

George's face turned serious as he released Sam's forearm. "What I've got to say is going to piss you off, man. Perhaps you should take a seat."

Sam's demeanor changed. "She didn't make it, did she?" Sam looked away and snapped his fingers and pointed in the direction of an elderly man of 70 seasons. "Fetch me an ale, please!" He looked at George. "Want one?"

George shook his head.

Sam pointed to Michael. "What about you?"

The general also shook his head. "I'm fine, Sire."

As the old man hobbled out of the room, George continued. "I don't know what happened. I would've sworn that Shalee knew everything she needed to to look into the Eye. She should be standing with us right now. Hell, she should be as strong as I am."

From her invisible veil, Celestria pushed away from the windowsill and strolled across the room. She whispered to Sam and delivered a message to his subconscious. "The prophet lies, Sam! George always lies! Feel the hesitation when he speaks. You must question him. He knows what happened to Shalee. He deserves to be punished." Lowering to one knee, the goddess spoke directly to Sam's sword that hung from his hip. "The moment is right, Kael. You know what must be done."

George grew anxious as he watched the king stand in silence. "Are you okay, Sam?" He waved his right hand in front of the king's eyes. "You're checking out on me."

Another awkward series of moments passed before Sam finally responded. His glare was piercing when he did. "I think you know more than you're letting on. Tell me the truth, George. What happened to her?"

Stunned by the sudden change in the direction of the conversation, George placed both hands on his staff and held it close for support to avoid showing weakness. "Like I said, she never came out of the Eye. I didn't think this would happen, but we knew it was a risk."

Again, Celestria whispered to Sam's subconscious. "He lies. He knew she would fail. George wanted to take your child's mother away from you ... away from the baby. He was there when the Eye swallowed your queen's soul. The prophet deserves to suffer your wrath. You must end him!"

The goddess continued to whisper as George waved his hand in front of the king's face again. "Sam ... are you alright? You keep checking out on me. You're kind of freaking me out."

Sam snapped out of his trance. His brown eyes narrowed as he pulled them away from the window. A moment later, he ripped the staff out of George's hands and tossed it on the ground. He then grabbed the collar on either side of George's tunic and lifted the prophet off the floor. With the warlock's face within a hand of his own, the king's speech was deliberate. "Stop lying! I know you know what happened to her!"

George remained calm. "Look! I'm not messing with you. How am I supposed to know what happened inside the Eye?"

Again, Celestria whispered to the king, "Use your sword, Sam. Seek the truth. Only then will you know. Use the power of the gods to expose your enemy. Make the prophet an example. String him up at the center of your city, and cut him open in front of those who would fill the arena. Be merciless."

With his feet still off the ground, George waved his hand in front of Sam's face yet again. "What's wrong with you? Stop zoning out on me like that, and let's have a damn conversation."

Perplexed, Michael shifted his weight from one foot to the other as Sam returned to the conversation. The king lowered George to the floor. "Get on your knees. If you're telling the truth, Kael will confirm it."

Expecting the sword to lie for him just as it did during the first series of moments when Sam laid the blade on his shoulder, the warlock lowered to his knees. The king unsheathed the weapon, lifted the handle in front of his face and commanded Kael to seek the truth.

With the blade on his shoulder, George reiterated, "Shalee's soul has been lost to the Eye. I had nothing to do with it."

Sam removed the weapon and held it up. "Kael, does he speak the truth?"

A shallow light emanated from within the blade as Kael began to pulsate. "The prophet lies, Sam. His words are filled with deception."

Without waiting for George to respond, Sam grabbed the warlock with his left hand and placed the point of Kael against the center of George's chest with his right. He was about to push the blade through when George reacted.

With a flip of his wrist, the warlock forced Sam's arm back. With a second motion, the hand holding his collar released while the hand that was holding Kael dropped to Sam's side. With a third motion, the king was forced backward.

From within her invisible veil, Celestria applauded as the six-foot-two-inch, 250 pound monarch floated across the room until his back was pinned against the wall. The king's blade fell to the floor as a breeze entered through the open window and amplified her enjoyment of the moment as it carried the sweet smell of fresh bread from the kitchen below.

Though shaken, Michael stepped forward to assist his king, but his attempt was halted.

"Stay where you are, General!" George commanded. "There's nothing you can do."

Realizing he was powerless, Michael nodded as George turned his attention back to the king. "Think, Sam. Does it make any sense for me to save your son's life, save your life, and then turn around and end Shalee? Use that genius head of yours, and think this through for a moment. It doesn't compute, does it? I don't care what your sword says. I didn't do anything to her."

Unable to move, Sam responded. "Do you think holding me with your magic is going to convince me of that?"

George stormed across the room and stood on the tips of his toes to get into Sam's face. "Are you for real, man? You were going to end me. Did you expect me to wait and use my power after you skewered me? Are you an idiot?"

Sam did not back down. "I should've reacted quicker."

Michael stood in silence as George turned around, tossed his hands in the air and walked across the room. Whirling back around, the warlock argued, "I have the power to end you if I wanted to, and you know it."

The prophet released his hold on Sam and then pointed. "Just stay there, and let's talk this through."

Celestria moved to Sam's side and spoke to the king's subconscious yet again. "How can you lead a kingdom if you cannot dispose of one man?

Your life is worthless. You're worthless." Her whisper turned to a hiss. "Worthless. Worthless."

A moment later, the elderly servant that Sam had sent to retrieve his ale re-entered the room.

Celestria took the opportunity to whisper a command. "You must send a message to the prophet, and show him that you're strong. End the cupbearer. It'll make you feel better."

With Michael's attention focused on George, the general failed to stop the cupbearer as he strolled toward the angry monarch. "My King, your ale. Will there be—"

Before the old man knew what was happening, Sam knocked the mug out of his hand. The king grabbed the cupbearer's left wrist and then pulled him toward the window. With his right hand, Sam snatched the servant's belt and used it for leverage to throw his weight.

Before George could stop it, the 70 season old great-grandfather of two disappeared from sight and fell three stories to the ground below.

George heard the impact as he sprinted toward the window. The servant had landed in an awkward position. His arms and neck were broken and his chest was lying against the stone walkway of the empty courtyard with his right leg twisted beneath him.

The prophet turned away from the window. "What the hell did you do that for, psycho?"

Sam just stared at the window, his chest heaving.

George pointed at the corpse, but his eyes remained focused on Sam. "You just murdered him! What the hell's wrong with you?"

The General Absolute unsheathed his blade and pointed it at Sam. "My King, you must surrender."

As the demon in Sam's mind returned to its cage, the realization of what he had done appeared on his face.

Celestria laughed from within her invisible veil as she watched George move away from the window. The warlock looked down at Kael and then motioned to the general to retrieve the weapon from the floor, but before Michael could react, Sam dropped to one knee, grabbed Kael and then darted out of the room.

Michael started to give chase, but George held up his hand. "Let him go, General! You don't have the power to stop him. Too many lives would be ended before you could. Your king will cool off, and then he will return to face his punishment when he's ready."

The general's expression was stern. "Ready or not, he's a criminal. I've been sworn to protect this kingdom. I must pursue him."

Michael continued toward the exit, but George extended his arms toward the doors on each end of the room and flipped his wrists. They slammed shut. "He's not a killer, General. He made a stupid mistake. It could've happened to either of us."

The general's eyes narrowed as he whirled around to face the prophet. "Brandor's laws don't allow men to make mistakes that result in the murder of others." He lifted his blade and pointed it at George. "Allow me to go, or you'll be charged as well."

The warlock used his power to bind the general in place and then forced Michael to lower his blade. George closed the gap between them, removed the weapon from Michael's hand and then tossed it across the room. The handle of the sword thumped against the bottom step that led to the throne. "Don't forget with whom you speak, General. I may be here to do the bidding of our lord, but I'm still a man. Don't point your blade at me again, because if you do, you won't breathe another Peak."

Michael bathed in his frustration for a long series of moments before a massive sigh escaped his lips. "My apologies, Prophet. What would you have me do? I cannot allow a killer to run free. It's against our laws."

George nodded and then returned to the window. Other than the body, the courtyard was empty. After a quick flip of his wrist, the warlock turned to face the general. "It appears no one knows of the king's transgression but us. Knowledge of this tragedy will not leave this room."

The invisible goddess smirked as Michael joined George at the window and looked down.

"What about th…?" The General stopped speaking. "Where is—?"

"The body is behind you, General," George answered.

Spinning around, Michael's eyes widened. The body was laying against the far wall. "How?"

"Does 'how' really matter? Just protect your king."

Michael walked away from the window and stopped above his sword. After picking the blade up off the floor, he sheathed it and then pushed his hands through his hair. "What of the old man's family? What would you have me tell them?"

George crossed the room and then placed his right hand on Michael's left shoulder. "Tell them he fled the city. Tell them that he fell down a flight of steps. Tell them anything other than the truth."

The general moved away. "You would have me lie? To do so would be to dishonor the dead. How could I be expected to serve a god whose own prophet spews deception?"

The warlock sighed. "My service to Lasidious doesn't make me a perfect being, General. Haven't you ever done something you've regretted?"

"Of course, I have. But this is murder. It's not just some simple transgression."

George shrugged. "So what?"

"'So what?'" Michael snapped. "How could you speak that way? You're the prophet of the one true god. You're supposed to stand for all that's good. How can any man be expected to live in service to Lasidious if his own prophet doesn't hold dear to what is true and right?"

George nodded. "Your point is valid, but in your haste to react, you're not thinking clearly."

After a moment of watching Michael stand in silence, George commanded, "Come with me." The prophet walked up the steps and took a seat on Sam's throne. He then motioned for Michael to take a seat on the queen's chair next to him. "Michael, I'm going to tell you a story."

Seeing the general nod, George continued. "Many, many seasons ago, there was a man named David. Now David was a great king on a world that no longer exists, and he was considered a man after his god's own heart. Well … David screwed up, and he ended a man. And what's worse, he did it for selfish reasons."

"And what were his reasons?" Michael questioned.

George cleared his throat. "I hate to say it, but David's reasons were awful. He ended the man so he could have the man's wife. David was already having relations with her, but that wasn't enough for the king. He wanted her as his own … as his wife."

George reached out and placed his hand on Michael's forearm. "Now … if I am right … I think we both would consider that an awful wrongdoing, would we not?"

"We would," the general replied. "What happened to this David?"

George smiled. "As it turns out, David's god forgave him because he understood the kingdom needed its king, but not before he punished David in his own way."

"Explain," Michael demanded. "How did his god punish him?"

George's smile widened. "David's god told the king that he was going to take the life of his firstborn. Because of this, David pleaded with his god to spare the child and his wife the pain it would bring her. The king fasted for seven Peaks and lay upon the ground in a sackcloth that was covered with ash. But on the seventh Peak, the baby passed anyway, and David received the lesson that he needed to learn. After this, the king dusted himself off and became a much stronger, wiser leader."

Michael's brow furrowed. "Why do you tell me this, Prophet?"

The warlock stood from the throne and walked down the steps. "The reason I say this is because Sam's punishment will not be delivered by you or this kingdom's Senate. Lasidious will be the one to administer his punishment. I assure you ... our lord's punishment will be far worse than what you or I could deliver."

George motioned for Michael to join him at the bottom of the steps. With the general in front of him, the prophet placed his right hand on the general's left shoulder. "You should forgive your king and trust in your god to make things right."

Michael shook his head. "You ask a lot of me, Prophet."

"Of course, I do. I expect nothing short of greatness from a man of your stature."

Seeing the general nod and knowing that Michael's ego and sense of law had been appeased, George redirected the conversation. "You and I are the only men who know the sins of the king." George walked across the room and stopped above the old man's body. "This tragedy shall stay between us."

Michael questioned, "What will Lasidious do to Sam? What punishment will he face?"

George shook his head. "I don't know. I cannot pretend to know our lord's mind. But what I do know is this. This kingdom needs a great king, and Lasidious will do as he sees fit."

George motioned for Michael to follow him. "Walk with me." As they made their way toward the door, George passed his hand across the old man's body. They watched as the corpse shriveled, dried out and then crumbled to dust before they opened it. As they passed through the archway, George shouted, "Clean up, aisle seven!"

Celestria chuckled and then vanished.

When the goddess reappeared, she watched Sam burst through the door of his bedroom chamber with his arms loaded. The king's boots thumped heavily against the stones of the floor as he headed for the large, wooden chest that sat at the end of his bed. Remaining unseen, the goddess moved across the room and took a seat on the mattress.

Flipping the lid open, Sam dropped the supplies in his arms to the floor and then reached inside the chest. He retrieved a pile of clean clothes and tossed them onto the mattress.

The clothes landed where Celestria was sitting. The goddess looked down. From her point of view, the pile looked as if they were part of her body with the hems of various garments protruding from either side of her hips. She smirked, looked up at Sam and then spoke to the king, though he was unable to hear her. "At least your garments will not catch a chill from passing through my being," she jested.

At the bottom of the chest was a small vial that Sam had used to hold the other half of Yaloom's essence. The liquid contained what was left of the late God of Greed's power, and many of his memories were still glowing inside it.

The sight of the vial caused the king to pause. A moment later, Sam bent down, retrieved the bottle and then held it in front of his face. He turned toward the window and shook it. As the light-blue liquid sloshed inside, it shimmered in the sunlight that streamed through the cracks in the shutters.

Once again, Celestria spoke to Sam's subconscious. "Drink it, King of Brandor. No one is here to stop you. Everything you desire is in that liquid. The moments are right to begin your path toward ascension."

Sam removed the cork and sniffed its end. The smell was sweet and inviting. A long, quiet series of moments passed as the king stared at the contents of the vial. He placed the bottle to his lips and was about to drink when the memory of Shalee's reaction to the first half of the potion entered his thoughts. It had taken Peaks for the queen to recover, and Sam knew there was no guarantee that this half—the half he had promised to save for Yaloom—would not cause him to pass out just as Shalee had done, and since he did not want to wake up in the dungeon, he chose to re-cork the vial.

Tossing the potion next to the pile of clothes, Sam walked to the side of the bed and dropped to his knees. He pulled out a leather backpack, untied the strand that secured it shut and then pulled back the flap.

As the king reached out to grab his clothes, his hand passed through Celestria more than once. On each occasion, the goddess enjoyed the way Sam's body shivered as he fought through the sensation and continued to pack. At one point, Sam was forced to stop to wipe his nose. He used one of his clean shirts to wipe away the snot and then discarded it to the floor.

After tying the leather strand, Sam tossed the bag over his shoulder. He stood, looked at the vial he had left on the bed and then turned to leave, but he stopped before crossing the threshold. A heavy sigh followed as the king thought to himself, *What am I doing? Where would I go that they won't find me? I need to face the consequences of what I've done.*

Celestria pulled her eyes away from the potion. The goddess stood from the bed and moved behind Sam. She reached out and placed her hand on the king's shoulder. A soothing sensation filled Sam's body as the goddess spoke to his subconscious. "You must retrieve the vial, Sam. You mustn't leave it behind."

Though Sam could not hear the goddess' voice, the king responded as if he did. "Why? Why should I take it? What good would it do me?"

Taken aback by the king's response, Celestria had to collect her thoughts. "The liquid will strengthen your soul. You must put a drop under your tongue, Sam." She emphasized, "But only a drop." A smile appeared on the goddess' face as she removed her hand from the king's shoulder.

Sam just stood in the archway of the door looking across the room at the potion. The glow of Yaloom's memories illuminated the quilt around it as the goddess continued to speak. "A single drop will clear your mind. You will become more focused and have the strength to face the trials ahead." Again, she emphasized, "But only a drop, King of Brandor. Do it now."

Sam returned to the bed and lifted the bottle off the mattress. He removed the cork, unsheathed his dagger and then tilted the vial to one side. He allowed the liquid to roll toward the lip of the bottle before he dipped the end of his blade into the potion. As soon as this had been done, he lifted the point of the weapon above his mouth and allowed the drop to fall under his tongue.

Celestria's eyes sparkled with satisfaction as Sam closed his. The hair on the king's arms stood at attention above the goose bumps that covered his skin. She whispered again, "You're a king. You answer to no one. You are above the laws of this united kingdom." The goddess changed her tone. "But they won't understand that. They'll come for you. If you don't flee this world, they'll punish you ... and your child. You must run, King of Brandor. Run!"

As Sam's eyes opened, a fiendish gleam appeared. The cage at the back of his mind was now open, and the demon within was free to roam. Never again would the beast allow itself to be locked up. A new Sam spoke aloud as if he had heard the goddess speak. "Where would I go that they wouldn't find me?"

Celestria hissed, "Dragonia! You must flee to Dragonia. It's the only safe destination for you now. Go, Sam! Go!"

"Dragonia. Yes. It's the only safe place for me. No one would ever think to look for me there."

After rolling the potion into a sock, Sam put the remainder of Yaloom's essence into his backpack and then threw it over his shoulder. He then darted out of the room.

Chapter 7
A God that Spits

Western Luvelles
The Source's Cave
Inside the Cracked Eye of Magic

Fellow soul ... if you don't remember, Shalee wandered through the haze inside the Eye of Magic for 2 Peaks before three figures appeared who were surrounded by bright lights. After the glow surrounding each faded, the queen was able to see who was left behind, and the realization of who was standing before her gave her hope. Helga and BJ had not been lost to her after all.

The Queen of Brandor had gasped on that Peak. *"Oh my heavens,"* were the first words out of her mouth, and then she fell to her knees. She was quick to place her head on Helga's abdomen. *"Helga ... is it really you?"*

Helga's smile had been unmistakable as the older sorceress' lips widened. *"Hello, Child. Did you miss me?"*

And as if Helga's presence was not wonderful enough, another voice, a grumpier voice added, *"What about me? I'm also standing here."*

Shalee stood to face BJ, and then rushed into his arms. Her excitement was evident by her response. *"Of course, I missed you. Don't be silly, Grumpy Guss. Sam is going to have a corgan when he hears that you're alive. He hasn't been the same without you."*

But Shalee's excitement was short lived. A third figure had approached. This powerful being placed his right hand on Shalee's shoulder and turned her to face him. His voice was familiar, and he spoke with authority. *"The moments have come for you to create a Heaven for this plane of existence, Shalee. Only then can you return to the worlds."*

A moment later, Bassorine placed his hands on top of Shalee's head. She then slept for 3 Peaks.

Fellow soul … BJ and Helga's souls were left to wait inside a spacious, but rickety shack in an unknown location for Shalee, now a witch, to wake up. After their reunion, Bassorine removed BJ and Helga's spirits from their temporary bodies that he had restored for the purpose of their greeting. They were ghosts and would remain that way even after Shalee came around.

"BJ … come here. I think she's going to wake."

As BJ floated above the dirt floor of the shack, Helga admired Shalee's blonde hair. Helga's soul was sitting on a crate next to a shallow, mattress-covered cot the young witch was lying on.

"Wake up, Child. Wake up."

"Leave her alone," BJ growled. "She has gone through her share of awful moments. She doesn't need you hovering over her. The poor girl is going to experience even more of them once she sees us in this condition."

Helga looked up. "Hush! Her moments will not be awful."

BJ shrugged. "I disagree."

Helga's eyes narrowed. "I said hush! She'll be happy to see us."

A short series of moments passed before Helga sighed. "Three Peaks is more than enough sleep." The sorceress stood from the crate and moved close to BJ. Her ghostly face softened. "Just because we're no longer made of flesh … doesn't mean we should bark at one another. You know I still long for you."

BJ's eyes dropped. "I wish he would've allowed me to touch you again. I miss that." He looked at the dirt floor a few paces away. "If I could spit to show you my frustration, I would. I know Bassorine has his reasons for us being here, but I feel cursed. I don't feel whole. I wish he'd explain why he did this."

"Perhaps self-murder angers him," Helga reasoned. She paused. "But I've done nothing to anger Bassorine ... yet I suffer as you do."

BJ reached out to comfort his love, but his right hand passed through Helga's left shoulder. He growled, "This is frustrating. Only 3 Peaks ago, Shalee placed her head against your belly. Now we can no longer feel the joy of her embrace. Why does he punish us?"

"Stop it! You'll make me cry, and you know the tears won't come."

To change the subject, Helga pointed across the shack to a group of cabinets that started to the right of the door and ended against the far wall. "Since there's nothing we can do about it, perhaps you could help me." She looked back at Shalee. "At least he has allowed us to touch the objects in the room. Let's use this gift to make our child something to eat. She'll be famished."

Sitting in front of the cabinets against the far wall was a wooden barrel that had been filled with water. It was taller than BJ and had a diameter that spanned the width of the ex-trainer's shoulders, multiplied by three. To the right of the barrel, at a safe distance, was an iron stove. Beyond the stove, stacked to the ceiling, was a pile of wood that ran the length of the wall, some four paces to the back of the shack. This wall was mostly clear of objects, except for a tall dressing mirror that looked out of place. The mirror tilted on an ornate stand that sat on the dirt floor near the center of the wall. A pace or so to the right of the mirror, a square table had been shoved in the corner with one of its sides pressed against the shack.

The sorceress floated back to the crate while BJ hovered over to the cabinets that had been filled with non-perishables. After opening the door, he stood still for a long series of moments while he stared at its contents.

"Well?" Helga inquired. "Are you just going to stand there? They won't fix themselves."

"There's nothing worth fixing."

The former sorceress frowned. "Men are so helpless!"

Before Helga could say anything else, Shalee's arms lifted to rub the sleep out of her eyes. Helga cleared her throat to capture BJ's attention and then whispered, "Hurry up. She's stirring."

Shalee removed her hands. As she did, Helga's smiling face came into view. The witch tried to talk, but the dryness in her throat stopped her.

Helga lifted from the crate and floated over to the barrel. Grabbing a mug, she opened the tap near the bottom and filled it before she returned. "Drink, Child."

The witch sat up and did as she was told. After the fourth gulp, she exhaled, "Ahhhhh ... that's delicious." A moment later, a look of disbelief appeared on Shalee's face. "Is it really you, Helga?" She reached up to touch her old teacher, but her hand passed through Helga's face.

Shalee squealed, "Goodness-gracious! What's wrong with you? Am I dreaming? I can see you, but I can't feel you. You look pasty."

Helga giggled. "You're not dreaming, Child. I'm here ... or at least my soul is here." She pointed across the room. "BJ is here, too. We don't know much other than Bassorine has put us in this shack with you. We don't possess bodies anymore, and we've been instructed to watch over you and take care of you until he returns."

"Well, that sucks." Shalee threw her feet off the side of the cot and then rummaged her toes through the dirt. "Why am I not shocked? Leave it to Bassorine to not explain anything."

Shalee's belly growled. She grabbed it. "Goodness-gracious! Did you hear that? I think I'm fixin' to starve to death."

A clanking sound filled the room as BJ sat a pot of water on the stove to boil. "Your dinner will be ready soon enough."

Shalee's brows lifted. "How can he touch the pot if we can't touch each other? Doesn't that seem strange to you?"

BJ answered. "Don't ask us. Ask Bassorine."

Shalee sighed. "Well that just chaps my hide. This reminds me of when I arrived on Grayham. I was just as lost on that Peak. I guess it's no big shocker that Bassorine has something to do with this."

BJ grumbled, "Stop complaining." He pointed to the entrance of the shack. "There's a change of clothes hanging on the hooks next to the door. Perhaps you should clean up and then put them on. Though we cannot smell you, I'd wager you stink after sleeping so many Peaks."

Helga glared across the room. "She has only just woken. Leave her be, and show some compassion."

BJ shrugged. "What did I say?"

Shalee had to laugh. "Yep, y'all are here alright. Bodies or not, your arguments are still the same. I bet Sam would be happy as a lark if he saw the two of you poking at one another."

The witch stood from the bed and walked to the door. She unlatched the lock and then opened it. Beyond the threshold, there was nothing but darkness. Shalee stood at the edge of the frame, extended her hand and commanded the darkness to dissipate, but nothing happened.

"Interesting," Shalee remarked. "Helga, come over here for a moment."

The older sorceress floated across the room. As she did, Shalee's eyes widened. "That's just creepy. You're like a ghost or some kind of spirit."

"I know, Child. What's worse, we won't be able to high-five one another."

BJ grumbled. "It was a childish act anyway!"

Helga ignored the comment and looked out the door. A moment later, she looked over her shoulder toward BJ. "At least we know what's on the other side now." Helga looked back at Shalee. "We tried to open it, but we couldn't touch the lock. Bassorine must have had something to do with that as well." The older sorceress grabbed her chin in thought. "Perhaps if you had your staff, you'd be able to command the darkness to dissipate."

Shalee looked around the room. When she did not see Precious, she questioned. "Did Bassorine not leave it behind?" Helga shook her head. "No, Child. You didn't have it with you. I don't know where it is."

The witch frowned and then faced the darkness. She lifted her hand, and without thinking, she shouted in the language of the Ancient Mystics. Startled, Shalee allowed the light that burst from the palm of her hand to dissipate, and then she cupped her hands over her mouth. She held Helga's gaze for a brief series of moments before she said, "What in tarnation did I just say? I sounded like I was speaking in tongues."

Helga's face wrinkled. "Speaking in tongues, Child? What do you mean by that?"

"Must be another of her Earth expressions," BJ quipped.

Again, Helga ignored BJ. "I'm sure Bassorine will explain when he gets back." She looked toward the darkness. "Try it again, Child, but don't allow the power to fade."

Shalee extended her hand. She tried to remember the words, but they would no longer come to her. The witch dropped her arm to her side. "Samhill! I guess I don't know what to say. It's like my brain is all boggled up."

Before they could resolve Shalee's bewilderment, Bassorine appeared at the center of the shack. He was wearing a pure-white robe with a hood that cast a shadow over his face. Through openings in the back of his robe, a pair of glorious wings—the white wings of an angel—the powerful wings of his true self—lay folded against his back.

Without addressing those present, Bassorine opened the front of his robe and removed a large, thick, leather-bound tome. He walked to the back corner of the room and placed the ancient book on the table that sat in the corner some four paces beyond the end of the cot.

Turning from the table, Bassorine walked toward the witch. "You spoke in the language of the Ancient Mystics. For the last 3 Peaks, I've been teaching you through dreams while you slept. You're very powerful, though you do not understand your full potential right now."

The angel turned and pointed to the book. "That tome will be a source of reference until you're ready to return to the worlds."

Shalee queried, "What kind of power are you talking about?"

"You are witch, Shalee."

Shalee placed her hands on her hips. "Who do you think you're talking to, buddy? Don't you be calling me a witch. Just because you have wings doesn't mean I won't put my foot up your backside."

Bassorine smiled as he pulled back his hood. The scar that had run across his right eye and ended at the corner of his mouth was gone, and his skin was flawless. "I didn't call you a witch, Shalee. I said, you are witch."

"Hmpf, big difference," Shalee rebutted. "Sounds the same to me."

Bassorine frowned. "I assure you, there is a difference. You have surpassed the power of an ordinary sorceress." The angel looked at Helga. "Not that your moments as a sorceress were not put to good use while on Grayham, but Shalee's power has exceeded simple uses of magic."

Bassorine redirected his gaze. "Shalee, you have the ability to summon power even beyond witch. To do so, you must master the language of the Ancient Mystics, then the Swayne Enserad. Beyond that, you must become fluent in the language of the Titans."

Shalee's brows dropped between her eyes. "And how do you expect me to do all that?"

"As I have said, I taught you in your sleep. You've spoken in the language of the Ancient Mystics once already. You must learn to think it and then progress to the Swayne Enserad."

Shalee tapped her foot against the dirt floor. "I bet you think that sounds easy. What else are you going to throw at me?"

Bassorine scowled. "It has been more than a million seasons, and yet you never change. Even in this body, you still speak to me the way you did when we first met. But I suppose that matters not."

Crossing his arms, the angel changed the subject. "Before I allow you to return to the worlds, you must surpass the power of the Titans and then ascend without the help of those who claim to be gods."

Hearing Bassorine's mandate, Shalee looked at Helga. The older woman shrugged. "Don't look at me, Child."

Bassorine turned to walk back to the table.

Shalee was quick to follow. "Hold on just a cotton-pickin' moment, mister. You can't just say something like that and then act like you never said it. A million seasons is a long series of moments. You best start sharing some more info."

The angel pulled out a chair from the side of the table and motioned for Shalee to sit. Once the witch was comfortable, he pulled out a chair of his own, parted his wings and then took a seat. As he leaned forward, his expression became far more serious. "1,743,465 seasons, 243 Peaks, 7 hours and 14 minutes ago was when we first met, Shalee. Your real name … a name once glorified … was Anahita."

"'Anahita?'" Shalee reiterated. "Have you gone bonkers? I don't think you've got the right—"

Bassorine extended his hand and put a finger across Shalee's lips. "Be silent."

Shalee tried to argue, but she was no longer able to speak. A moment later, Bassorine continued. "As I have said, your name was Anahita. You were my wife."

Stunned by the angel's revelation, BJ and Helga floated toward the table while Shalee's eyes widened. BJ sat a hot bowl of porridge in front of Shalee, or rather, Anahita, as Bassorine continued. "My beautiful Anahita, you were once known throughout the heavens as the Angel of Fertility. You kept the Earth fruitful and multiplying as well as many other worlds.

"But what those who lived on these worlds did not know was that Lucifer wanted you for himself. He had already fallen from grace, and yet, he still pursued your affections. Sadly, he found a way to win your heart. You abandoned your love for me, and once you did, you, too, fell from grace and joined those who followed the Morning Star out of Heaven.

"It was not until after my father fulfilled his promise to create a new Heaven and a new Earth that you and I were reunited. Tragically, this reunion had to happen in the bowels of my brother's Lake of Fire. I convinced our father to allow me and two others to suffer an undeserved torment, and in doing so, we were commanded to provide an opportunity to those who would choose to be saved.

"As for the others who assisted me, those whom I will not disclose during these moments, they charged with me into the Lake of Fire, and we suffered for many seasons before we found an exit. This escape was hidden at the bottom of the lake's depths."

Struggling with the memories of their torment, Bassorine had to pause to collect himself. The angel used the left sleeve of his robe to wipe a tear out of the corner of his eye. Eventually, Bassorine calmed himself and refocused. "Everything you know, Anahita ... everything you were told inside the Temple of the Gods the Peak you awoke on Grayham, and beyond that Peak, has been a lie. You are not from Texas ... nor did you live on Earth. Your memories are false. They were bestowed upon you. You never lived as a human until the Peak your eyes opened on Grayham."

Bassorine stopped talking. Anahita tried to speak, but the angel lifted his hand to silence her as he looked up and closed his eyes. A long series of moments passed before he lowered them back to Anahita's. "I have been summoned. My father calls for me. I have found my way back to his plane of existence, and I must go for now.

"But before I leave, know this truth: BJ, Helga and you, Anahita, are one. Each of you is a piece of one soul that was split during a great battle that happened on this plane. Before I leave, your pieces will be rejoined, and your soul will become whole once again."

Bassorine leaned forward and caressed Anahita's cheek. "I've missed you so. There's a way for us to be together again ... if you'll have me. But first, you must create a Heaven for this plane. Once this has been accomplished, you must reclaim your former glory. For when you do, you shall become far more powerful than the mightiest being on Ancients Sovereign."

A deep longing appeared on Bassorine's face as he looked into the depths of Anahita's questioning eyes. BJ and Helga hung on his every word as they hovered closer. "My eternal love, you once called me by my true name. I desperately want it to be that way again. When next we meet, I ask you to consider calling me ... Michael."

Michael allowed Anahita a moment to process. "Remember ... you must find your way back to our father's house. For the love of our father is eternal ... even now. Even beyond my brother's Lake of Fire, our father has allowed those of us who would suffer needlessly to pass through the fire to this plane of existence. Our commission: do what we must to search for the good in those condemned, and provide them a place of reprieve. For if we do, we will be allowed to return home."

The archangel stood from the table and moved to the center of the room. He motioned for Anahita to come to him.

BJ and Helga remained silent as Anahita stood to fulfill Michael's wish.

Reaching out, Michael pulled Anahita close. With his left hand cupped beneath her chin, he lifted her head. Anahita melted into his arms as the archangel's soft lips took her breath away. The passion filling their moments far exceeded the deepest kiss she was capable of remembering.

With Anahita's eyes still closed, Michael lifted his head toward the ceiling and spread his resplendent wings. He commanded BJ and Helga's souls to join them. With the trio standing side-by-side, the archangel enclosed them within a shroud of feathers. As the brightest of lights filled the shack, he commanded, "Become whole once again."

A long series of moments passed before the glory filling the room faded. All that was left behind as Michael folded his wings to the flat of his back was a remade Anahita with wings of her own that protruded from openings on the back of a new, white gown.

Part human, part angel, the incoherent, un-ascended Anahita collapsed. Michael caught her, lifted her into his arms and then carried her across the room. After lowering her to the cot, he made sure the feathers of her wings were laying properly before he kissed her forehead. "Be strong, my love … for I long to be with you again."

Michael vanished.

Fellow soul … I feel the moment has arrived for me to apologize. By now, you must realize that I, your spirited storyteller, have misled you about a great many happenings. I ask you to forgive me. I did not want to spew deception, but as I said at the very beginning of this tale, the gods gave me no choice. I despise misdirection.

That said, there was a reason I was forced to unveil this story as the gods on Ancients Sovereign saw fit. If I had not agreed, they would not have allowed this series of tales to be told.

I ask that you hold steadfast … for I intend to share many more truths as we move forward. I can now share these truths because the balance of power is beginning to shift within the heavens. But to reveal the entire truth at this moment would be dangerous, and it would not provide good entertainment. Please allow me some leeway as I interject these truths when the proper moments arrive.

ANCIENTS SOVEREIGN
BENEATH THE PEAKS OF ANGELS
LASIDIOUS AND CELESTRIA'S HOME

After teleporting out of the Hall of Judgment, Lasidious appeared with Sharvesa inside his home. The Mischievous One waved his hand in front of the fireplace and smiled as the green flames erupted. Walking around the table, he took a seat and then motioned to an empty chair. "Please, sit."

Sharvesa refused. Instead, she walked around the table and stood in front of the fireplace with her hands extended toward the flames. "I haven't come for pleasantries or the enjoyment of your company. I want to know your terms for offering my kind a peaceful existence on Dragonia. I cannot allow my daughter and those she rules to suffer."

Lasidious took a seat at the end of the table. Leaning forward, a sincere look appeared on his face. "I'd like to apologize, Sharvesa. I hated speaking to you the way I did in front of the others. I often despise the games we play, but I cannot allow the others to see weakness. Your kind served me for more seasons than I can remember, and I harbor them no ill-will. When the vote was taken to turn Dragonia into the new Hell, I voted against it."

Sharvesa turned around and placed her hands on the back of the chair nearest her. "Why would I believe you?"

Lasidious' eyes filled with sorrow. "For thousands of seasons, I watched as your kind was forced to do the will of a fallen angel. Your people suffered because he pulled them into a hell that was created for him. Before that Peak, your kind thrived on a plane where happiness filled your moments."

The demon-goddess held up her hand to stop the Mischievous One from continuing. "Your manipulations won't work on me." Sharvesa scooted the chair aside and then leaned over the table toward Lasidious. The muscles beneath her red skin tightened as her hands pressed against the stone. "Though I do not remember your face, nor do I remember how my kind escaped the burning of an everlasting torment … I do remember the Peaks of old, and I know you were there."

The demon's yellow irises flashed. "My mind is not absent of those memories as you proclaimed it was inside the hall. I remember falling from grace, and I remember the screams that filled the depths of a Hell that was created for the Morning Star." The demon-goddess shook her head. "How could I have been so stupid?"

Though surprised, Lasidious shoved his shock at the demon's admission aside and responded without allowing a wasted moment to pass. "All was not lost. The gods saw to that." Lasidious rocked back in his chair. "We saved you. We pulled your kind from the fire and placed you on Dragonia. We did our best to erase the memories of the past. In your case, it appears we failed."

The demon-goddess returned to the fire and once again extended her arms toward the flames. "You didn't fail entirely. For many seasons, my mind functioned without ill effect. But those seasons were short lived. Eventually, my mind moved toward a state of confusion as my memories slowly returned. Soon, I was questioning my existence, but when I confided in my soul mate, Dogmay, he proclaimed me mad. For many seasons after his passing, I agreed with his declaration. I agreed that is … until *he* came to me."

Falling forward onto the front legs of his chair, Lasidious urged, "Who came to you? Who is *'he?'*"

"Gabriel," the demon responded.

Confused, Lasidious queried. "Gabriel? Do you mean the Book? Why would the Book come to you?"

Again, Sharvesa turned to face him. "I speak not of the Book."

"Then to which Gabriel do you refer, for I know of only one?"

Sharvesa paused. "You'd know him best as an archangel."

Lasidious shouted, "What?" The force in which he stood from his chair caused it to fall backward. "Gabriel is here? Where can I find him?"

Sharvesa laughed. "He said you would ask that. Gabriel also said that those who claim to be gods would one Peak try to steal the free will of my kind."

The demon-goddess pulled the chair back from the table and took a seat. After she crossed her arms, she continued while the Mischievous One paced on the far side of the room. "When the archangel came to me, I called him a liar and sent him away. After that, I never saw him again, but I didn't forget his words. I accepted my confusion and ruled my kind while showing strength. Now that I know Gabriel spoke the truth, I won't allow the races of demons to serve you."

The demon put her elbows on the table and allowed her chin to fall into the palms of her hands. "It was not until this moment that I truly believed you cared nothing for my kind. There's nothing you can offer that will ease the suffering they're about to face."

Lasidious stopped behind the chair on the side of the table opposing the demon. "If I harbored your kind any ill-will, I would not have voted against Dragonia becoming the new Hell. If you don't believe this claim, ask the Book. He'll confirm the truth."

Trying to reclaim his dominance, Lasidious pulled back the chair and took a seat. He pushed the vase filled with fresh flora to the right side of the table. "As for sparing your kind the injustice the Book will release upon your world, I can still offer you a solution. I've spent more than 1,000 seasons preparing for this. I don't need your kind to serve me to remain benevolent toward them."

The Mischievous One placed his chin in the palms of his hands just as Sharvesa had done. "Tell me … did I ever mistreat you or your kind at any moment during their seasons of service to me?"

Leaning back, the demon-goddess responded, "Never."

Lasidious could see the confusion return to Sharvesa's eyes. "Then why do you doubt me? Ask the Book. He'll tell you that I voted nay. You must allow me to help you save your world."

"And how do you intend to help?"

"By returning strength to your people. When the gods…" Lasidious paused. "When we, 'so-called' gods, placed your kind on Dragonia, the strongest of the demons were stripped of enough power to keep you under our control. I'd wager the archangel didn't tell you that, did he? I would further wager that he didn't tell you there's a way to return this power to you. Soon, I will command the power to control the Book, and with it, I will offer your kind a peaceful existence, and in doing so, return the power that you so rightly deserve."

"What of the moments prior to you receiving this control? Must my kind suffer until then?"

"No. As I said, I've prepared for the Peaks ahead for the last 1,000 seasons." Lasidious crossed his arms on top of the table. "Allow me to help you."

Sharvesa sat in silence for a long series of moments before she sighed. "I must think upon this." She vanished.

Lasidious grabbed the vase filled with flowers off the table and threw it against the wall. "Damn it!"

Southern Grayham
The Castle of Brandor
After Nightfall

After finishing dinner with Michael, George walked down the steps into the courtyard with the General Absolute. Seeing the giant cat sleeping at the bottom of the stairs, George tapped Michael on the shoulder and pointed.

Hearing the scuffing of their boots, Kepler opened his right eye. He did not bother to lift his head. "How did Sam react?"

Unsure how to respond, Michael looked at George. Seeing the general's hesitation, the warlock answered. "You know Sam. His growl is always bigger than his bite. I'm sure he'll settle down in a few Peaks."

Stopping next to Kepler, George patted the cat's neck. "Get up, and let's get out of here."

Once mounted, George looked down at the general. "Once Sam realizes the army isn't searching for him, that genius brain of his should figure things out. He'll come home soon enough. Until he returns, you will take over as king and take care of the prince."

Michael nodded. "And if Sam doesn't return?"

"Have the Senate summon me with Lasidious' Promise." With that, George placed his right hand on Kepler's shoulder. They vanished.

When the pair reappeared, they were on Luvelles standing next to the boulders above Kepler's lair. George hopped down from the back of the cat and looked toward the homes. Light poured through most every window of each structure, but his home was dark, except for one light that escaped from inside Payne's room.

"Athena must be reading to the children again. She's a good mother."

Kepler did not seem to care. Instead, he sat on his rear haunches. Lifting his right, front leg, he licked above his paw and started to clean behind his ears. "Are you going to make me read your mind, or are you going to tell me the truth of what happened in Brandor?"

For the next series of moments, George explained the details of what happened in the throne room. He further explained the reports delivered by the guards who saw the king leaving the city on his mist mare.

Kepler lowered to the ground. "Why did you stop Michael from throwing Sam in the dungeon?"

George took a seat on the ground and crossed his legs. "Aside from the fact that Sam could kill them all, I felt the need to protect him. I have screwed with the guy enough. This whole conscience thing is really kicking my ass. I'm starting to wonder if I'll be able to do what I need to when I get to Eastern Luvelles."

The demon-cat lowered his head on top of his legs after crossing them in front of him. "I suppose it won't be long before you'll find out. But you'll need to make that journey on your own. I leave for Dragonia in 4 Peaks to find a mate. Brayson has secured transport for me with the Merchant Angels."

The warlock's brow furrowed. "How will you know where to go once you're there?"

"Brayson showed me a map of that world. I have memorized the territories, and I know where to hunt for her."

George hopped up from the ground. "Why can't you just shack up with one of the cats from the plains on Southern Grayham? I'm sure one of those fine felines wouldn't mind coming to Luvelles to push out a few kittens for you."

Kepler snorted his disgust. "They aren't worthy of my company. I seek a mate with prowess equal to my own. She must be capable of hunting at my side."

George moved to Kepler and lay on top of the giant cat. He stretched out his arms and squeezed.

Kepler growled. "Must you always touch me? If you'll stop, perhaps I'll tell you I love you as well."

Laughing, George pushed himself off the cat. "I already know that, big guy."

The warlock started walking toward his home. Before reaching the steps, he stopped and turned around. "Hey, Kep! Before you get back, make sure you tell this new woman of yours about the family. Missing kids is probably not a good idea. Athena would garesh her pants."

Athena's voice emerged from the open window of Payne's room. "George Nailer!" she hollered. "What did I tell you about speaking so foul? Get up here and apologize to these kids!"

Kepler rolled his eyes as George rushed inside the house. After the door shut, the demon-cat went for a run. He ran across the clearing, jumped over the mound of boulders and then disappeared into the forest beyond the community of homes.

ANCIENTS SOVEREIGN
LASIDIOUS AND CELESTRIA'S HOME
THE NEXT MORNING

Alistar appeared beyond the far end of the table furthest from Lasidious. To his surprise, The Mischievous One and Celestria were shouting at one another.

"How could you be so careless?" Lasidious chastised.

Celestria crossed her arms and took a defensive stance. "I've already apologized on three occasions! I won't continue to beg for your forgiveness!"

Motioning for Alistar to take a seat, Lasidious continued berating Celestria. "Perhaps before you speak during any other series of moments, you should think first when the opportunity arises!" The Mischievous One slammed the side of his right fist against the table. "For all I know, you planted the seed that will cause Sharvesa to seek out her son!" Lasidious' eyes narrowed. "You're a fool!"

"'Fool?' You said she said nothing of Payne when you spoke to her."

"Sharvesa's silence makes you no less a fool! She may yet be the one to condemn us!" A long, awkward silence passed before Lasidious added, "How could you be so stupid? Perhaps you're usefulness is not what it once was."

Celestria took a step back from the table. Her jaw tightened as she walked to the side of the room furthest from Lasidious. Once there, she turned and glared in his direction. "How dare you speak to me that way! I've schemed with you for more than 10,000 seasons, and never have you lifted your voice to me!" Taking two steps in his direction, her voice softened. "I made a simple mistake, my love."

Standing from his chair, Lasidious leaned across the table. "My love? What a farce! There's nothing simple about losing our immortality! If Sharvesa seeks out Payne, the secret of Garrin's birth could surface!" The Mischievous One snatched up the new vase Celestria had filled with fresh flora and smashed it against the backside of the fireplace. The fire hissed, but the magic that caused it to burn would not allow the flames to extinguish. "I'm finished with this conversation!"

Celestria tried to object. "But—"

Lasidious lifted his voice to a level that caused the goddess to cover her ears. "Silence!"

A few moments later, the Mischievous One plopped down on his seat and looked across the table at Alistar. "What news shall we share on this Peak, brother?"

Feeling awkward, Alistar looked at Celestria. The goddess was crying with her hands covering her face. The God of the Harvest stood from his chair and assisted Celestria to the one closest to the fireplace. Once satisfied she was comfortable, he returned to his chair and resumed the conversation.

"I spoke with Keylom. Your hunch was right. Mosley did visit the Wisp of Song."

Lasidious slapped his right hand flat against the table. "I knew it. How did you get Keylom to talk?"

Alistar grinned. "You're not the only one with skills of manipulation, brother. I plan to keep the details of my success to myself."

"Bah! So be it." Seeing the redness of Celestria's face, Lasidious stood from his chair and moved behind her. He placed his hands on her shoulders and then caressed her arms. "I'm sorry for how I wielded my wicked tongue. Will you forgive me?"

The goddess did not respond.

Lasidious leaned over and whispered into her left ear. "You deserve better than me." He lowered to the nape of her neck and gently bit it. "My words were careless and hurtful."

Celestria pulled away and stood from her chair. She circled the table to the far side of the room. Leaning against the wall, she crossed her arms. "Continue your conversation with Alistar. I want no part of you."

Lasidious placed his hands on the back of the chair, dropped his head and sighed. A brief silence passed before he looked up at Alistar. "After speaking with the centaur, did you visit Cadromel?"

Alistar nodded. "I did."

"And?"

"The wisp divulged the wolf's destination." Alistar leaned back and smiled.

"Well? Are you going to share his location, or are you going to make me beg?"

Alistar chuckled. "You're no fun to toy with in this condition. The wolf is sitting in the frozen dungeons of Hydroth."

Confused, Lasidious confirmed, "Hydroth?"

"That's what I said."

"Why would the wolf go to Northern Grayham?"

Alistar fell forward and placed his arms on the table. "He seeks the Tear of Gramal. There are questions the wisp wants answered. In return, Cadromel promised to divulge the location of the gate. Mosley seeks to command the power of the Swayne Enserad."

"Really?" Lasidious grinned. "He's seeking the power to go after George, isn't he?"

"He is."

The Mischievous One clapped his hands, intertwined his fingers and then placed them on top of his head. "This is masterful. The moments have come to dispense with George anyway."

This announcement caused Celestria to break her silence. "Since when has George become disposable?"

Lasidious vanished and reappeared on the left side of his lover. He leaned in and whispered, "Ever since the moment you failed to control your tongue."

Seeing Celestria's irritation, the Mischievous One vanished again and reappeared next to the fire. He extended his hands toward the flames and continued to speak. "We cannot afford unsecured ends. George must perish." Pulling his hands back, he turned around and looked at Alistar. "We should just tell the wolf the location of the gate."

Alistar's brows furrowed. "What of Garrin? Who will parent the baby?"

Lasidious looked past his brother and found Celestria's eyes. "Perhaps the moments have come for our son to learn who his real mother is. Would this please you, my love?"

Celestria kept her arms folded. "Perhaps."

"And would you then forgive me once he's in your arms?"

A slight smile appeared on the goddess' face. "Perhaps."

"And if you were the one I sent to deliver the wolf the location of the gate? Would this be enough to allow me back into your good graces?"

Celestria uncrossed her arms and walked to the back of Alistar's chair. She pulled back the God of the Harvest's hood and started to run her fingers through his hair. "Perhaps."

Lasidious' eyes narrowed as he bit down on his bottom lip. A few moments went by before a smile found his face. "Then it's settled. You shall be the one to journey to Northern Grayham. Once there, take the wolf to the gate. From there, he can find his own way. Let's hope Mosley returns before Sharvesa learns about our secret."

The goddess stopped caressing the top of Alistar's head. She enjoyed Lasidious' jealousy as he watched her lean over and kiss the top of his brother's forehead. "Good-bye, dearest Alistar," she said in her most seductive voice. "I hope to see you again upon my return."

The Goddess of Beasts looked across the table. She held Lasidious' eyes for a brief moment and then said, "Mosley will ask why I'm helping him. As I look into your eyes, I imagine my response. Perhaps it's because I'm done with you." Celestria vanished.

Alistar rolled with laughter.

Lasidious frowned. "What's so funny?"

Grabbing his belly, the God of the Harvest answered. "I relish knowing that she'll never receive your forgiveness. I pity her." Alistar stood from the table and waved his hand across the top of it. A new vase filled with fresh daisies appeared. "Is everything in order, brother? Are you sure you want to pursue this next part of the plan?"

"If the Archangel Gabriel is, indeed, roaming the worlds, then I have no choice. I must employ new tactics. Besides, Celestria's mistake could very well bring about our demise."

Concern appeared in Alistar's eyes. "I agree. In your absence, I shall seek the archangel's location. He must be hiding amongst the beings on the worlds somewhere. If this is true, there are no laws on the Book's pages that protect his existence. Upon your return, we could capture Gabriel and steal his power."

Lasidious responded without hesitation. "No. I loved our brother. I won't conspire against him if he survived."

Alistar nodded. "I also loved our brother, but to leave him alive—?"

"It's not up for debate."

Alistar pondered Lasidious' demand and then changed the subject. "When will you leave for Dragonia to implement the next part of our plan?"

"Soon, dear brother. Soon."

The God of the Harvest smiled. "Are you sure you can make the switch without stopping either heart?"

"I am." Lasidious raised his hand and motioned for Alistar to give him a moment. The Mischievous One walked beyond the curtain, through the next room and then opened the door to his bedroom. Entering, he turned to his left and crossed to the bed. He lifted the mattress and pulled out a framed picture. On it, the Vampire Queen of Dragonia stood next to her king. He stroked the image of her beauty and thought back to the Peak when Celestria tried to force him to drink her potion of truth.

Now, fellow soul ... before I continue, I need to clarify a few points.

First—regarding the Peak when Celestria requested that Lasidious drink her potion of truth, they were standing in their newly created home beneath the Peaks of Angels. Pleased that Lasidious had consumed the liquid, Celestria then exited the home. It was then that the Mischievous One leaned close

to the fireplace and spit the liquid into the flames. On that Peak, the fire became very truthful. Ha, ha, just kidding. Fires can't talk. And if they could,
it would be just a bunch of snap, crackle and pop—fire gibberish if you will.

Anyway, Lasidious did spit it out. The Mischievous One never had to tell
Celestria a truth during their entire relationship. Though he did love her in
his own messed up way, he did not love her enough.

Second—a being's power resides within their heart. This is truth. As you
know, to steal the power of another, you must take the first bite of the heart
before it stops beating and continue eating until the heart is consumed. If
this is not accomplished, the power of the being will ascend to the Book
with its soul.

While we are divulging truths, I must correct yet another lie that I was
forced to tell. As I said before—I despise misdirection. I was commanded
to unveil this story as the gods on Ancients Sovereign saw fit. With this
reminder uttered, some of the conversations I led you to believe happened
between the beings in earlier parts of this story—never happened. Lasidious
and Alistar never went to Celestria's father's heavenly kingdom to recruit
him into the Farendrite Collective, nor was her father destroyed during the
supposed God Wars when they met. The truth is—Lasidious and Celestria
met while they suffered in the depths of Lucifer's Lake of Fire. It was not
until after they were pulled into this new plane of existence—a plane where
five worlds and a hidden ancient god world would later be created—that
Lasidious and Celestria had the opportunity to become close.

Also, the Collective was formed later than you were led to believe. It was
not until after a great battle began on this new plane of existence that the
so-called gods united. But I will explain more of the Farendrite Collective's
creation during some other series of moments.

Enough truths for now. Allow me to get back to the story. As I said, Lasidious stroked the image of the vampire queen.

Placing the frame back beneath the mattress, the Mischievous One returned to speak with Alistar. "Brother, upon my departure, keep Celestria
occupied until I depart from Luvelles. Once I'm on Dragonia, the magic of
that world should hide my location. It won't be long before this body will
not house the brother you know."

Alistar walked around the table and gave Lasidious a hug in front of the
fireplace. "I will miss you."

Lasidious broke the embrace, put his hands around the back of his brother's neck and then placed his forehead against Alistar's. "I will miss you, too. Let's hope I know what I'm doing."

Lasidious vanished.

CHAPTER 8
HEADS ROLL
NORTHERN GRAYHAM
THE UNDER ICE DUNGEON OF HYDROTH
LATER THAT EVENING

Darosen slammed the door to Mosley's cell as he exited. He looked back through the bars of ice and spit. The night terror wolf lay trembling at the back of the cell. This Peak's trobleting had been the most severe of all, and though the wolf's bleeding stopped only because the cold helped the blood coagulate, Mosley had refused to divulge the answers the Frigid Commander assumed he possessed.

Grabbing the bars, Darosen placed his face between them. "Sleep well, wolf, for Early Bailem will be upon us soon. If you refuse to expose your secrets then, tomorrow's trobleting will be your last. I'll enjoy casting your corpse into the ocean."

Before another word could be uttered, screams echoed through the tunnels that led into the dungeon. They carried with them a message. "The gashtion attacks!" The tunnel shook. Pieces of ice dislodged from the ceiling and fell to the floor.

The Frigid Commander swatted one of the chunks aside and rushed out of the dungeon toward the armory with his guards in tow. Again, the dungeon shook beneath the gashtion's weight.

A moment later, Celestria appeared inside Mosley's cell. Seeing the wolf's condition, the Goddess of Beasts knelt. She placed her hand on the night terror wolf's frost-covered coat. A soft glow emanated from her hand and penetrated Mosley's body. A lengthy series of moments passed before he began to stir.

The green of the wolf's eyes brought a smile to Celestria's face as they pried open. Her voice was soft. "Too many Peaks have passed, Mosley, since last my eyes were laid upon you."

Mosley lifted his head. His voice was shallow. "Celestria?"

"Yes, Mosley, it's me. Are you hungry?"

The strength of the night terror wolf's voice improved. "I'm famished."

The goddess nodded. A pile of rare corgan steaks and a bowl of warm water appeared on the floor in front of Mosley. Without waiting for an explanation as to why Celestria was there, the wolf tore into the meat. Once his belly was full and his thirst was quenched, his natural curiosity returned. "How many territories did you search before you found me?"

Celestria scratched behind Mosley's ears. "You hid well. I searched two worlds before I discovered your location. It appears my arrival could not have come at a better moment. You nearly passed."

Mosley's eyes filled with suspicion. "Your appearance vexes me." The wolf sat on his haunches and reached up with his left rear paw to scratch the back of his neck. "Why have you come?"

The goddess stood and motioned for Mosley to stand. After touching the wolf on the top of his head, they vanished.

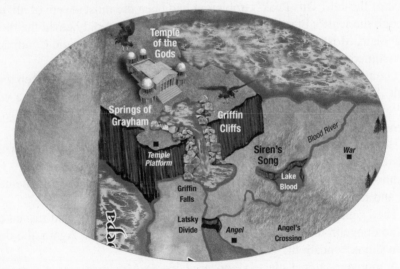

GRIFFIN CLIFFS
SOUTHERN GRAYHAM

When the pair reappeared, they were standing south of the Blood Sea on the shore beneath the northeast face of Griffin Cliffs on Southern Grayham. As Mosley sniffed around to gather his bearings, he made his way to the shoreline and waded into the water. Lifting his leg, he relieved himself as the goddess took a deep breath of the saltwater air.

"I trust this climate is more to your liking, Mosley?"

"It is, but why have you brought me here? This territory is not the one I want to prowl. I must return and continue my hunt."

"Do you mean your hunt for the Tear?" Celestria enjoyed the surprise on Mosley's face. "I know you seek answers for Cadromel."

Without waiting for the wolf's response, Celestria waved her hand in front of the cliffs. The rocks peeled back and revealed the way inside. "The cave ahead will lead you to the gate. You must pass through it. Beyond, a chalice will be waiting for you. Drink the liquid, and the power of the Swayne Enserad will be yours."

Celestria knelt and rubbed beneath Mosley's jaw. "The chalice sits in a chamber with five portals ... three to the left and two to the right. The portal farthest left will take you to the Merchant Island of Harvestom. Once there, you must make your way to the island of the High Priestess. She is capable of teaching you how to invoke the power filling the language of the Swayne Enserad, though she must teach you to invoke the power filling the language of the Ancient Mystics first."

Mosley walked down the beach, but kept his paws in the water. After a bit, he stopped, looked out across the Blood Sea and started to laugh.

"What's so funny, wolf?"

"You forget my service to Bassorine. I speak the languages of the Ancient Mystics and the Swayne Enserad fluently."

Celestria shook her head. "I didn't forget. Just because you speak the languages and possess the power ... that doesn't mean you can invoke it. The High Priestess can teach you how to speak the languages in such a way that you'll be able to employ the power."

Mosley walked clear of the water and plopped onto his haunches. "Why are you helping me?"

Celestria smiled. "I know you desire George's destruction."

"I may."

"Come now, Mosley. Be forthcoming. I'm here to offer my assistance. I also desire George's destruction."

"Why? George's service to Lasidious is devout. He poses no threat to your manipulations."

Celestria cupped her hands and placed them beneath her chin. "Why, Mosley ... you do remember me."

"Don't be too flattered. My memory is in pieces." The wolf's look turned stern. "I'll ask you again. Why are you helping me?"

Celestria pulled her hands away. Her smile vanished and a look of sorrow appeared. "I wouldn't be helping if it was not for my failed union with Lasidious."

A suspicious look returned to Mosley's face. "What trick is this that you would expect me to believe that?"

The goddess wiped the tears from her cheeks. "There's no trickery. Lasidious' love has abandoned me. For this, I want vengeance."

"How does helping me offer vengeance?"

Celestria playfully brushed the comment aside. "Come now, Mosley … must I truly explain?" The goddess waited for the wolf's response, but one never came. "Fine. You're as stubborn now as you were on Ancients Sovereign." She paused. "If George was to fall and a new prophet was to rise from his ashes, the numbers of those who worship Lasidious would dwindle. I will not stand aside while Lasidious seeks to control the Book ... especially without me at his side."

Mosley growled. "I have no desire to become your replacement prophet, Celestria. There may not be much that I can remember about the gods, but I do remember your untrustworthiness. I also remember Gabriel and his hall, though I don't remember his function. I also don't remember what consequences would arise if Lasidious was to gain control of the Book."

Again, the goddess scratched the back of the wolf's ears. "Lasidious seeks to control the worlds and those who created them. Lasidious' own, special vial of chaos will be uncorked. He will pour it upon the worlds and it will flow like a river. The pain and suffering of those who live will cause them to befriend their own demise, and they will seek the reaper's doorstep and knock willingly."

Mosley pondered Celestria's words as he looked out across the sea again. He took a moment to enjoy the peacefulness of twilight. Not looking at the goddess, he reiterated. "I may not remember everything about the gods, but I remember the deception at the core of your heart." The wolf turned around. Holding Celestria's gaze, he continued. "I won't accept your assistance. I must return to the ice, for it's within that territory I seek answers."

Celestria waved her hand across the pebble-covered beach in front of her. A heavily padded throne fit for a goddess appeared. Taking a seat, she responded, "You seek the secrets of what fuels the Tear, do you not?"

"Perhaps," Mosley shrugged. "A female named Clandestiny is the Isorian who is said to possess the Tear. I was searching for her when I was captured."

Seeing Celestria shake her head, Mosley queried. "Am I mistaken? Does she not possess the Tear?"

"She does. Why does it matter?"

"I have my reasons."

Celestria's brows furrowed. "Clandestiny has been with the Ko-dess for many seasons. To my knowledge, the Tear is still in her possession. Why were you seeking her in Hydroth? She abandoned the city nearly 300 seasons ago?"

Mosley walked up the beach until his paws were clear of the water. "How do you know this?"

"When the power of the Tear is invoked, Helmep feels this occurrence."

The wolf's eyes narrowed. "What else can you tell me?"

The goddess leaned forward. "The Tear was given to the Isor by Helmep. It's a divine object that works without flaw while laying above a pure heart. The Tear possesses the essence of a gashtion long since passed. This power was harnessed within the crystal to control its offspring."

The goddess placed her hand against her chin in thought. "If I was to wager a guess, the wisp told you that he desired to understand the Tear. Unlike the Tear's previous bearer, an Isorian named Thoomar, Clandestiny did not have the benefit of training with the High Priestess. She fled the city and sought the Ko-dess. Because of her lack of training, Clandestiny's moments with the Ko-dess were extended far beyond what they should've been.

"With the Tear missing from Hydroth for so many seasons, the gashtion's offspring have matured, and as all gashtions do, they fight for territorial dominance. The surviving male takes one of his sisters as his mate and then feasts on the rest. Once this sister has laid her eggs, she, too, is devoured, providing the male is strong enough. If he isn't, he becomes the consumed."

"Devoured? Consumed?" Mosley queried. "What does the Tear do to Clandestiny that would require her to train for so many seasons?"

The goddess pondered whether or not she should answer. After a few moments of staring into the wolf's eyes, she revealed the truth.

A fair series of moments later, Mosley responded. "Really?" he exclaimed. "No wonder the wisp wanted the details." The wolf stood in silence as his mind ran wild in thought. "Which of the gods would create a beast that would eat its brothers and sisters and then its mate?"

Celestria chuckled and removed her shoes before crossing her legs on the seat of her throne. "I did, of course. I created them for the amusement of Helmep."

"And why must they consume one another?"

"To have more than one mature gashtion would cause instability to the environment. Since a beast of that size eats an amount equal to its body weight every 5 Peaks, the eggs that have been left behind will not hatch until the beast perishes."

"How do the eggs know when to hatch?" Mosley interjected.

Celestria smiled. "Male or female, a mature gashtion must smother their eggs once per season with a natural secretion. This substance comes from a gland inside their mouth and mixes with their saliva. Since this particular water dragon's eggs float, a female gashtion must lay her eggs in a domed cavern beneath the water. Hundreds of eggs gather at the top of the dome and when the saliva is discharged into the water by the surviving parent, it floats to the top and covers the eggs. In short, the saliva keeps them from hatching. They remain dormant until the parent is no longer capable of performing this function."

Nodding his understanding, Mosley continued to question as he sniffed at the base of Celestria's throne. "You referred to how much the gashtion must consume. What does the gashtion weigh?" He lifted his leg and marked the back leg of the goddess' throne.

Shaking her head, Celestria leaned over the arm. "Must you?"

"I can't help myself. The wood calls to me," the wolf defended.

As Mosley returned to the front of the throne, the goddess studied his size. "To answer your question, the gashtion would eat 2,700 wolves of your size every 5 Peaks."

Seeing the surprise on the wolf's face, Celestria redirected the conversation as Mosley imagined the height of the mound of flesh that the gashtion would consume. "The Tear of Gramal has been around Clandestiny's neck, far, far away from Hydroth for too many seasons. The power of the Tear has been unable to ward off a new, recently matured gashtion. Therefore, the Isor remain on guard."

Celestria could see more questions behind Mosley's green eyes, so she remained quiet and waited for the wolf to speak.

"I heard the guards speak of a prophesied one when the Frigid Commander was away. They speak as if they know who he is. They talk of a descendent of a mighty warrior named Klidess. They speak of him as a savior, but not from just the gashtion. They whisper as if there is division amongst their ranks. It's as if they are waiting for this ruby eyed man to deliver them from Darosen's command."

The goddess could hardly control her laughter. "There is no prophecy. After Helmep convinced the Isor to worship him, Hosseff decided to undermine his campaign. He gave the Isor the story of Klidess and a ridiculous belief that a ruby eyed child was to be glorified as a savior from what was yet to come. Hosseff did this to create confusion amongst the Isor … to give them something else to believe in … something to keep Helmep from receiving the full devotion of their prayers.

"Since Hosseff gathers the souls of the deceased, he also gave the bearer of the Tear the belief that they could call upon Helmep's name to return life to another. In doing so, this chosen Isorian must surrender their soul. Hosseff did this to embarrass Helmep since he knew the soul of the one to be resurrected would not be returned."

"Are you saying two souls would be surrendered to the heavens?"

Celestria chuckled. "Mosley, you did forget much, didn't you? The souls would be surrendered to the Book, silly wolf."

"To the Book? Please explain."

Celestria waved off the question. "Move beyond that. I care not to take the moments to do so."

Annoyed, Mosley redirected his course of thought. "Did Helmep find out about Hosseff's betrayal?"

"He did. Helmep spoke with the Book. As a consequence for Hosseff's actions, the Book granted Helmep the ability to swap souls whenever the bearer of the Tear called upon his name. Further, Gabriel promised Helmep that a child with ruby eyes would be born once every 3,000 seasons. As a result, Hosseff realized that his efforts to undermine Helmep only added further glory to the God of Healing's campaign.

"This angered Hosseff, and in a last effort to cripple the number of those who served Helmep, Hosseff appeared to the beings of Gesper. He spread a rumor that the gashtion was the ultimate power on Northern Grayham. The Tormal believe that to have control of the dragon makes the Tormalian who possesses this control god-like. But this control of the dragon can only be accomplished through the use of the Tear, or perhaps even the Kindred Tear that exists inside the Ko-dess."

Mosley snorted his irritation. "If this is, indeed, the case, I must return to Hydroth. I must find Clandestiny and warn her about the commander's interest in the Tear. The commander's scent is different than the others. During my captivity, there was one other who smelled as he did. Her name was Blandina."

A dastardly grin appeared on Celestria's face. "Blandina is the daughter of the Tormalian King. They must be up to something. She is a sorceress. But beyond that, she can speak with and command the dead. The Tormalian Princess is powerful. She was wed to the last bearer of the Tear as an offering of peace between the Tormal and the Isor. Perhaps the Tormal seek to control the dragon, and Blandina's son is to be the vessel through which they plan to seize this control."

Mosley's ears cocked. "And how would this be accomplished?"

"If Clandestiny was to wed Shiver, a cut would be made across the palms of their hands. Clandestiny's blessed blood would pass to the king. If Shiver's mother was to employ her magic, she could command the king to use the gashtion against the Isor."

"Does she also possess magic that can control the living?"

"No, she doesn't." Another dastardly smile appeared on the goddess' face. "Blandina's heart is cold. Her son is capable of passing just like any other being. She would be able to take control of Shiver's corpse before the boy's life's source finished drying on her hands."

The goddess' smile was replaced with a matter-of-fact look. "Beyond the sorceress' control of the dead, I know of no other Tormalian who would have the power to control the gashtion ... except perhaps Blandina's father, King Meerum Bosand, but I'd wager he's too weak now."

Mosley snorted his disdain. "Are you saying she would slay her own cub to pursue this power?"

"I am. The sorceress and her father are ruthless. But their plotting is flawed."

"How so?"

"Without a blessing from the High Priestess, a Tormalian's best effort to control the gashtion would be catastrophic to everyone on Northern Grayham. The gashtion would break free of this control, and without the Tear resting above the heart of a truly blessed Isorian, the people of Northern Grayham would no longer be able to hold the gashtion at bay."

Mosley stood in thought for a short series of moments. "The queen's magic is powerful. I was unable to teleport out of captivity or melt the ice of my cell with my magic."

The goddess nodded. "Indeed, the sorceress' power is strong by this world's standards. It appears you now understand the depravity of the situation. You'll need power of your own if you're going to help the Isor."

The wolf's green eyes scanned the horizon in search of a plan before he redirected his gaze to capture Celestria's. "If I was to promise to drink from your chalice and go to Harvestom to train with the priestess, would you take me to Clandestiny first? I want to warn her of the queen's plotting before I go."

Celestria stood from her throne. She looked down at the wolf and winked. "Consider it done. But first ... you should rest for the night. Let me enjoy your company, and we'll leave in the morning."

The goddess waved her hand across the pebbles on the beach. The next thing Mosley knew, an oversized hide filled with vestle chick feathers appeared for him to lie on.

"See, Mosley. I can be pleasant." The goddess reached out and scratched the top of the wolf's head. "I've truly missed you."

THE UNDER DUNGEON OF HYDROTH
THE ESTIMATED SERIES OF MOMENTS CALLED MIDNIGHT

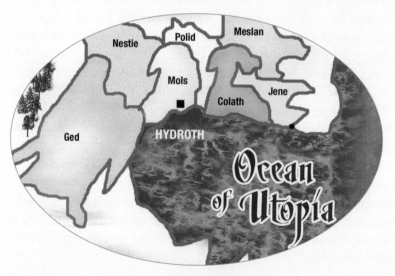

HYDROTH
NORTHERN GRAYHAM

The back wall of Mosley's old cell crumbled, bit by bit, as Slips finished tunneling his way into the under dungeon. Wearing his spiked shoes for balance, Sagar stepped through the hole and into the cell. He searched the darkness for the wolf, but what he found was a left fist that landed flush against the right side of his head.

As Slips fell to the floor, his ears heard the guard shout for the Frigid Commander before his vision darkened.

BACK ON SOUTHERN GRAYHAM
DAWN, THE NEXT MORNING

After a hearty breakfast with Mosley, Celestria touched the night terror wolf on the back of his neck. When they reappeared, they were standing on the west side of the Pass of Nayala looking toward the narrow ledge that spanned the gorge.

"Where are we?" Mosley questioned.

Celestria scratched the back of the wolf's ears. "You're within moments of meeting Clandestiny. To the west of our position is the home of the Kodess."

Before another word could be said, the goddess vanished, leaving Mosley standing by himself. Mosley did not have a chance to react before Medolas walked around a large boulder with Clandestiny's hand in his.

Mosley sat on his haunches, exuding a peaceful nature, and waited for the couple to cover the distance between them. He spoke in the Isor language as soon as they were within earshot—yet another language known to the wolf because of his service to Bassorine. "You must be Clandestiny!" Looking at Medolas, he added, "And who are you?"

Medolas grabbed Clandestiny's arm to stop their approach. "The beast. It speaks."

Mosley's keen ears heard the comment. Rolling his eyes, he shouted a response. "Of course, I can! I have come to speak with Clandestiny!"

Clanny stepped away from Medolas and toward Mosley. A fair number of moments passed before she looked back over her shoulder. "The beast's eyes look friendly. Perhaps Helmep has blessed us with the company of a gentle monstrosity."

"Monstrosity?" Mosley sneered. "I'm not a monster."

Intrigued by the wolf's response, Clandestiny moved even closer.

Mosley remained on his haunches as she knelt in front of him. He watched as her blue hand extended for him to smell it.

Instinctively, the wolf sniffed her fingertips and then abruptly stopped. Annoyed with his lack of control, Mosley spoke in a soft voice. "I'm not a common dog. I need not smell your scent to speak with you."

"Dog?" Clandestiny queried. "What a curious name." With the Tear of

Gramal dangling from her neck, she leaned forward and pulled at the fur on the top of Mosley's head. "You look like an overgrown sudwal with a darkened coat." She turned to look at Medolas. "Come here, Meddy! What do you make of the beast?"

Medolas shrugged. "Don't ask me. Why not ask it what it is?"

Before Clandestiny could pose the question, Mosley answered. "I'm a night terror wolf. I've come to deliver a message. Much has changed since you were last in Hydroth. Danger awaits your return."

Medolas' brows furrowed. "What do you mean? Our eyes have not fallen upon Hydroth for 300 seasons. We have no enemies there."

For the next long series of moments, Mosley explained everything he knew about the Tear of Gramal, Blandina, King Meerum Bosand, and the Tormalian King's desire to control the gashtion. He finished his revelation by saying, "You must protect one another. Your friends are few."

Clandestiny looked at Medolas. "Do you think Gablysin would betray us ... and Shiver?"

Again, Medolas shrugged. "The depth of their loyalty shall be learned upon our arrival, I suppose."

Clanny frowned. "Do you think Shiver's mother could've turned them against us?"

Yet again, Medolas shrugged. "I know not, Clanny. How could I speak of events that would've required my presence to acquire this knowledge? Must I remind you that I've been with you?"

A short silence passed as Mosley sniffed his surroundings while he waited for Clandestiny's response. It was not until after the wolf lifted his leg to mark a stone near the edge of the gorge that Clandestiny addressed him again. "What's your name, terror wolf?"

Mosley cringed. "I'm a night terror wolf, and my name is Mosley."

"My apologies, Mosley, I meant no offense. I must ask ... how do you know these things, and why does our fate concern you?"

Mosley lowered his leg and sniffed the rock. Satisfied with the scent, he responded. "I came to Northern Grayham seeking answers. Beyond that, I don't feel the need to say more. I've learned what I need to know."

As Clandestiny's glare burned into the wolf because of the abruptness of his answer, Medolas looked out across the gorge. The Isorian shuddered. "I remember this crossing." He turned to look at the wolf. "The way ahead is dangerous. We shall have to cross on our bellies. The wind is our enemy."

Mosley looked toward the far side of the ledge in hopes of seeing a place to teleport. Try as he might, his keen eyes could not focus on a target since the distance was too great. "I fear I cannot help … nor can I travel with you to Hydroth."

Before Medolas or Clandestiny could question, Celestria appeared. The goddess did not take the moments to enjoy the look of shock on the Isorians' faces. Instead, she waved her hand in front of them. The next thing Clandestiny knew, she was standing on the opposite side of the gorge with Medolas. They had reappeared not more than five paces east of the sign that arched above the entrance to the pass.

An owl was sitting on top of the sign. Its feathers were white with brown trim, and they were tucked tight to its body for warmth.

Hearing the pysples pop beneath Clanny's shifting weight, the owl's head spun in her direction. The bird's piercing, garnet eyes focused on the Isorian's face. Clanny looked confused. She was staring west back across the gorge with her mouth open.

The owl took flight.

Startled by the sound of the creature's wings, Medolas and Clandestiny looked up. Their eyes followed the bird until it was out of sight.

Back on the west side of the gorge, Celestria touched Mosley on the back of his neck. "Shall we go?"

When they reappeared, they were standing on the beach of the Blood Sea beneath the cliffs that ascended to the Temple of the Gods on Southern Grayham.

Celestria looked at the base of the cliffs and waved her hand. Once again, a way inside was revealed. "You see, Mosley, I kept my promise. You were able to warn Clandestiny of the danger that waits for her in Hydroth. Now the moment has come for you to keep your promise. The power of the Swayne Enserad waits inside." The goddess vanished.

Mosley looked toward the opening. "I hope my desire for revenge isn't consuming my ability to employ good judgment." The wolf trotted into the cave, singing.

One big wolf just entering a cave in a mountain.
Don't mess with me … don't mess with me…

The cliff shut behind him as he began the next verse.

WESTERN LUVELLES
THE FAMILY HOMES
EARLY BAILEM, THAT SAME MORNING

While sitting on a pair of rocking chairs on the front porch of George's home, Lasidious and Alistar watched from within an invisible veil as George opened the front door and stepped out onto the porch with Payne.

The fairy-demon pulled his hand out of the warlock's, rushed to the edge of the porch and then pointed at Kepler who was waiting not more than 12 paces beyond the bottom of the steps. Payne's face was beaming with excitement as he said, "Good morning, Kitty. Is Kitty here to say hi to Payne? Payne loves his Kitty."

The Mischievous One had to smile as Alistar commented in a voice that only he and his brother could hear. "I'm surprised that Kepler has accepted Payne the way he has."

Lasidious nodded. "I am, too."

The god's smirked as the demon-jaguar rolled his eyes. A moment later, Payne's wings began to flutter. The fairy-demon lifted off the porch, flew down the steps and wrapped his arms around the jaguar's front leg.

Kepler looked up at George and spoke telepathically. *"You could've told me the freak was awake."*

The warlock grinned and spoke aloud. "Ahhhhh. Come on, Kep. Just appease him for a bit, will ya?"

"If you insist."

Payne took a few steps back and then reached up to pull at the fabric of his new shirt. "You like Payne's shirt, Kitty? Mom say black make Payne look … umm … ummm..." The fairy-demon stopped talking and turned to address George. "What that word again?"

George smiled. "Dashing. Athena said you look dashing, Payne."

Both gods laughed as Payne whirled around to face the cat. A huge smile spread across the fairy-demon's face. "Payne look dashing, Kitty. You no have no shirt like Payne, so Kitty no look dashing."

Kepler lowered his head and whispered, "But you're still ugly to me, Freak." He nudged the fairy-demon in a playful manner.

Lasidious elbowed Alistar. "You've got to love that cat. Too bad he has to perish."

With wings flapping, Payne rushed under the jaguar's head and kicked Kepler on his right front shin. He then darted across the clearing toward the rocks above Kepler's lair, shouting, "Kitty fat! Kitty slow! Can't catch Payne!"

Kepler looked up at George. "He'll always be annoying. You know that, right?"

Before George could respond, the jaguar teleported across the clearing and reappeared in front of Payne, blocking the fairy-demon's path. He crouched and growled. "Gotcha, Freak!"

Startled, Payne changed course and headed for the woods. "Kitty slow! Can't catch Payne!"

Kepler allowed Payne to get close to the treeline before he vanished and appeared again in Payne's path while growling, "You can't escape the Protector of the Realm!" With a gentle thump of his paw against Payne's left shoulder, he knocked Payne to the ground. "I'm going to eat you."

The fairy-demon rolled to his feet and ran toward George. "No so fast, Kitty!"

Kepler chased Payne all the way back to the house, nipping at the air just behind the fairy-demon's wings to add to the youngster's excitement. The jaguar stopped at the bottom of the steps as Payne bounded up the flight and leapt into George's arms.

With his chest heaving, Payne looked over his shoulder and stuck out his tongue. "Kitty too slow. Must get gooder to catch Payne."

To appease the demon-child's pride, Kepler lowered his head and feigned defeat. "You'll always be faster than I am. Your dominance of this territory has been demonstrated. Perhaps one Peak, you could show me how to be as elusive as you."

Payne looked up at George. "What 'elusive' mean?"

The warlock chuckled. "It means no one can catch you, buddy." Lowering the fairy-demon to the porch, he added, "Run into the house, and tell Athena how elusive you've become."

Beaming, Payne ran inside. "Mom!"

George shut the door and then walked down the steps. "Are you ready to go?"

Kepler lowered to his knees. "I am. But I can only travel with you until Early Bailem tomorrow. Then I must leave for Merchant Island."

George climbed onto the saddle. "It was nice of Brayson to secure you a ride. Are you sure you want to go? Who knows what Dragonia will be like now that the dragons are gone?"

Rising to his feet, Kepler responded. "The condition of Dragonia matters not. The moments have come for me to find a mate. Only there can I find one worthy of my companionship."

George patted Kepler on the back of his neck. "I hope you know what you're doing, big guy." They vanished.

A moment later, Lasidious stood from his rocking chair and extended his hand to help his brother up. "I hope the cat perishes while he's on Dragonia. It's too bad George isn't going with him. I wouldn't have to plan his demise that way."

Nodding, Alistar changed the subject. "I hate to sound like George, but are you sure you know what you're doing? Once you journey down this path, there will be no return."

Lasidious put his left arm around Alistar's shoulders. "You worry too much." The God of Mischief led the God of the Harvest across the clearing to the steps that led up to the entrance of Susanne's home. Once there, Lasidious faced Alistar and placed his hands on the outside of the God of the Harvest's arms. "Hold steadfast, brother … for upon my return, the power to rule the gods will be ours."

"Let's hope you're right." A long embrace followed. "I love you."

Lasidious smiled. "I love you, too."

Alistar vanished.

The Mischievous One stared at the emptiness that Alistar had left behind for a moment before he redirected his thoughts. He walked across the porch and stepped through the wood of the front door without opening it. Once inside, he crossed the foyer and stood on the teleportation platform. When he reappeared, he was standing in the upstairs hallway not far from the door that led into Garrin's bedroom.

The door was cracked open, and Susanne's voice could be heard behind it. Once again, the Mischievous One passed through the door and stopped a few paces on the other side. From within his invisible veil, he smiled as he watched Susanne carry Garrin from the changing table to his crib. She lowered the boy onto his back and then rubbed the top of his head until the god-child was asleep.

Satisfied that all was as it should be, Susanne headed for the door. To get there, she had to pass through the unseen god. Instantly, she covered her mouth with both hands to muzzle her sneeze.

The Mischievous One enjoyed Susanne's discomfort as she fought to quiet her reaction to keep from waking Garrin. An ample series of moments passed before she shook off the chill and wiped the snot from her nose with the cuff of her sleeve. After ensuring the baby had remained asleep, she left the room.

Once the door shut, Lasidious stepped out of his invisible veil and walked to the crib. He bent over and lifted Garrin into his arms. The motion caused the toddler to stir, but the god was quick to react. With the child's head lying on his left shoulder, he rocked his son back to sleep while speaking in a fatherly whisper. "You have grown so. Your hair is changing. Soon it will be the color of your mother's. It appears the moments are ripe for us to become acquainted."

Reaching inside the crib, the Mischievous One grabbed a light-blue blanket and tossed it over his right shoulder. "This should come in handy." They vanished.

Not long after, Susanne reentered the room. Upon seeing Garrin's empty crib, she ran from the house, shouting for Brayson as she crossed the clearing to her mother's home. She burst through the door and ran to the kitchen where Mary was standing at the sink cleaning potatoes.

"Mother! Mother! Where's Brayson?" Susanne demanded. "Garrin has done it again! The potion Brayson gave him didn't work!"

"He did it again? Really? Brayson is with Boyafed and Dowd. They're discussing the details of Kepler's palace. He won't be home until morning."

"But … but, Garrin is gone! What do we do?"

Mary smiled. "First, you must stop shouting." Mary tossed the potato peeler into the sink. "That little guy is becoming quite the handful. Just relax. I'm sure he couldn't have gone far. Brayson did say he's only capable of teleporting to locations he's familiar with."

Mary grabbed a towel and dried her hands. "Call the rest of the family to the clearing. Garrin has to be around here somewhere."

When Lasidious and Garrin reappeared, they were standing inside an invisible veil next to the window of Sam, Jr.'s bedroom chamber. With the King of Southern Grayham abandoning the city, and the queen still trapped inside the Eye of Magic, the moments were perfect to implement yet another part of the Mischievous One's plan.

The baby prince was lying at the center of a heavy blanket that was spread across a thin padding placed on the stone floor. His caregiver was tickling the soles of his feet, and the prince was laughing so hard that he could hardly catch his breath.

Lasidious would have taken a moment to enjoy the baby's excitement, but the prince's laughter was causing Garrin to stir. The Mischievous One quickly lifted his hand toward the door at the far side of the room and motioned as if he was knocking.

The caregiver stopped tickling the prince. She stood from the floor and walked to the door. Grabbing the black, iron hasp, the young woman pulled the door open and revealed the empty hallway.

As she stepped beyond the threshold to investigate, Lasidious rushed across the room. He scooped up the Prince of Brandor and the blanket Sam, Jr. was lying on with his free hand just as the woman reentered.

All the caregiver saw was the prince hovering above the floor. A moment later, the baby vanished. The woman screamed as she ran out of the room calling for the guards.

MEANWHILE, NORTHERN GRAYHAM
ATOP THE ICE ABOVE
THE UNDER CITY OF HYDROTH

Slips squirmed within his bonds as the Frigid Commander tugged at the knot he had tied to bind Sagar's hands to one of the many totems the Isorian army used to tether their harugens. The top of the totem was nearly twice Slips' height, and it was equally as thick as his body. Almost 40 paces below his feet sat the undercastle.

Sagar's eyes scanned the crowd for familiar faces. Sixty officers of the Isorian army stared back at him. They knew nothing of the order he had been given by Gablysin to tunnel to the wolf, and in their mind, he was a traitor. There was no escape. The ruby eyed man was the only being who could clear up the mess he was in.

A moment later, a voice called out from behind the crowd, "Step aside!"

A pathway opened as the men scurried to allow the ruby eyed man to pass. Working his way through the crowd, the wind ruffled his hair as many of the officers touched his person. Their blue hands contrasted against the white tribal markings that spanned the width of Gablysin's chest and the girth of his upper arms. On his hip hung the short sword of the Frigid Omayne, the title of his commission.

Darosen greeted his second in command as the ruby eyed man emerged from the crowd and stopped near the totem that Slips was tied to. After shaking Gabs' forearm, the Frigid Commander stepped aside and pointed at his prisoner. "We have a traitor amongst us, Omayne. He was found tunneling into the dungeon. I was about to troblet him to learn of the wolf's destination, but alas, I haven't enjoyed the first punch yet."

Seeing Slips' frightened face, Gabs directed his attention toward the Frigid Commander. The ruby eyed man knew he was responsible for his friend's capture. He had been the one to ask Slips to accept the risk. He despised the way Mosley was treated, and he knew the wolf was not a threat because he had taken the moments to understand the wolf's mind when Darosen was not around to threaten him.

"Has the prisoner uttered an excuse, Commander?" Gablysin questioned.

"Not one. He refuses to talk."

Gablysin led Darosen across the ice 40 paces beyond the opposite side of the row of totems. Once sure they could speak freely, Gabs continued the conversation. "I know this Isorian. His name is Sagar. As a child, he was, and still is, my friend. Perhaps his intent has been misunderstood. Leave him to me. There's no call for his suffering to be made public. I shall gain an understanding of his trespass and punish him for you."

"And if he doesn't speak?"

"If necessary, I shall troblet him until he cries for mercy."

The Frigid Commander reached out and patted Gabs' right shoulder. "I bet you would. But friend or not, I cannot pass up an opportunity to inflict suffering. You know that about me."

Darosen grinned and then returned to the front of the totem where Slips was tied. Without wasting another moment, he lunged forward and buried his left knee into Sagar's abdomen.

Gablysin cringed as Slips cried out.

Again, the Frigid Commander struck, but during this series of moments, he slugged Slips on both shoulders. His knuckles sunk to the bone and caused Sagar to cry out again.

Gablysin closed the distance. He moved into a position between Slips and the commander. "Please, My Lord. Allow me to speak with the prisoner." The ruby eyed man stepped forward and whispered into Darosen's ear. "Please. This display is for naught. The prisoner is the son of Ohedri."

The Frigid Commander stepped back and spit on the ground. "This weakling is the councilman's offspring?"

Gabs' eyes narrowed. "This 'weakling' is my friend." He paused and allowed his voice to soften. "To punish the heir to the seat of the Meslan Clan without an understanding of his actions would bring disgrace to your commission." The ruby eyed man leaned in close yet again and spoke so that only Darosen could hear him. "Stand off, Commander. You'll accomplish nothing doing this."

Caught off-guard by Gablysin's stance, the Frigid Commander stood in silence. It was not long before he responded. "I lead this army, not you, Omayne." The Frigid Commander motioned for Gabs to step aside. "Get out of my way."

Gablysin took a step back and unsheathed his sword. He had no choice but to defend his friend. Pointing the tip of the blade at the Frigid Commander, he challenged, "I said, stand off!"

The gathering of officers surrounding the totem murmured, unsure what to do. On one hand, the ruby eyed man was said to be the prophesied one, and on the other, Darosen was their ultimate superior.

Recognizing the situation, Darosen addressed the crowd. "Stand back. I'll handle this." A moment later, the Frigid Commander unsheathed a blade of his own.

The murmurs of the crowd turned to cheers as Gablysin and Darosen started to circle. The Frigid Commander lunged with the tip of his blade aimed for the ruby eyed man's head, but Gablysin defended the strike. He pushed the blade to his left, and watched as the Frigid Commander spun out of his lunge to strike again with a slice to his mid-section.

Again, the ruby eyed man defended the attack, but during the next series of moments, he took the offensive. With his left foot, he kicked the commander in his groin. The blow was severe and sent Darosen to his knees where he vomited on the ice.

Gablysin pointed his blade at Darosen. "Yield, Commander. I don't want to hurt you."

The crowd went silent, except for two men who were standing at the front. They were encouraging the commander to stand and fight.

Darosen remained on his knees for a long series of moments before he was finally able to stand. After catching his breath, he lifted his sword. "You should've finished me."

The ruby eyed man shook his head. "As I have said, I don't want to hurt you." Gablysin pointed the tip of his sword at Slips. "Allow the council to determine his fate."

Everyone in the crowd agreed with the ruby eyed man's suggestion except the two officers who stood in support of the commander.

Darosen's eyes darkened. A few moments later, they softened, and then he lifted his arms horizontal to the ice and backed up toward the totem where Sagar was tied. "Perhaps you're right, Omayne. I'm being too hasty. The council is more than capable of determining his fate."

Gablysin exhaled and then lowered his blade. "Thank you, My Lord."

Seeing that the ruby eyed man had lowered his guard, Darosen spun. With a high slicing strike, he severed Slips' head and watched it fall from his shoulders and bounce across the ice.

While the ruby eyed man stood in shock, Darosen walked past the slumping body to retrieve the head. He snatched it by the hair and lifted it off the ice. Extending his arm in Gablysin's direction, he exclaimed, "I command the army, and I alone!" Tossing Slips' head to the ground, Darosen watched the yellow blood spew across the ice as it rolled to a stop near Gabs' feet.

Enraged, Gablysin kicked Slips' head aside before he rushed toward his enemy with his sword ready. A wicked series of searing, metal clashes filled the morning air before the ruby eyed man found the vengeance he was after. With a fluid spin, Gablysin's blade made a clean cut.

Just as Sagar's had, Darosen's head toppled off his shoulders and tumbled across the frozen terrain. His milky-gray eyes saw the ice up close as his head rolled to a stop, looking in the direction of his own corpse that still remained standing.

Darosen's fading brain processed the scene. The nerves inside the Frigid Commander's body caused his legs to take two steps forward before his corpse collapsed onto the ice toward his severed head. The final spurt of his life's source erupted from the gaping hole above his shoulders and landed on his forehead. The commander realized that he had been ended as his blood clouded his eyes before they went dark.

The two officers who had been cheering for the commander were now standing in silence while the rest of the crowd shouted praises for the ruby eyed man. Amidst the commotion, Gablysin leaned down and lifted the commander's cape to wipe Darosen's blood off his sword, but as he did, he discovered the gills on the inside of Darosen's shoulder blades next to his spine.

Gablysin dropped the cape and used the tip of his sword to lift the arch of each gill, exposing the filaments beneath.

Whispers emerged from the crowd. "He's Tormal," one Isorian said. "He is a traitor," another added. "How could this be?" a third questioned. From the back of the crowd, a fourth voice demanded, "Let me through. I want to see for myself."

Studying their faces as they moved in to get a closer look, the ruby eyed man's eyes stopped on the two men who had cheered for the commander.

They were working their way toward the back of the crowd. Gablysin lifted his blade, pointed its tip and shouted, "Seize them!"

Only a short series of moments passed before both men were on their knees in front of the ruby eyed man. The omayne reached down to his right ankle and unsheathed his dagger. He could see the fear in their eyes as he cut the strings of their capes and allowed them to fall to the ice. With their backs now exposed to the crowd, Gabs' suspicion was correct. They were Tormal.

Curses spewed from the crowd. A moment later, a large Isorian officer stepped forward. A heavy, milky-white growth of hair covered most of his chest, back, shoulders, arms and legs, and his eyebrows spanned the width of his forehead without a break in the middle. His commission was one rank beneath Gablysin's—Frigid Lamayne.

Lamayne Bridemoore, 597 seasons old, shouted, "A travesty has fallen upon the clans! Not only does the Isorian throne sit occupied by a half-blood, but there are Tormal hidden amongst our ranks. Check every man's back. Every traitor must be exposed. We must cleanse the undercastle. I say we slay the king and his shanavel of a mother."

The crowd roared in agreement. Gablysin was forced to think fast. The ruby eyed man held up his hands and shouted, "Hear me! Hear me! I say, hear me!"

As the crowd settled, they turned to face him and listened. "The king who sits upon the Isorian throne is the descendant of Thoomar."

A voice shouted from the back of the crowd. "But he's a half-blood! He isn't one of us!"

Remembering his conversations with the king, Gablysin threatened, "You will not challenge my command, for if you do, this Peak has not yet seen enough bloodshed! I won't say it again! Shiver is one of us!"

Scanning the crowd, the Frigid Omayne waited for an objection. When none came, he gave the crowd someone else to hate. "Shiver may be one of us, but I cannot say the same for his mother! She's a traitor!"

Absorbing the phrases, the ruby eyed man lifted his sword and pointed the tip of the blade in the direction of every man. "Heed my command! You will leave the king in peace, but Blandina is a welcomed hunt!" He lowered his sword to his side. "If my words have been spoken with clarity, confirm it now!"

Once again the crowd erupted, sensing their future enjoyment of Blandina's demise. Lamayne Bridemoore ripped his sword clear of his sheath and pointed the blade skyward. "Follow me to the undercastle! Let no Isorian harm King Shiver!"

As the frenzied group rushed across the undulating shelves covering the frozen tundra and dove into the hole that led down into the ice, Gablysin cut Slips' bonds and allowed his friend's headless corpse to fall. Taking his knees, Gabs lowered his forehead onto Slips' chest. The omayne's yellow blood-tears stained the pale white skin of his old friend who had lost his color.

MEANWHILE, INSIDE THE UNDERCASTLE OF HYDROTH SHIVER'S THRONE ROOM

Shiver was sitting on his throne. His left leg was bouncing in anticipation of his grandfather's entrance as Blandina ascended the steps to the throne and stopped to wait beside him.

Reaching out, Blandina passed the fingers of her left hand through Shiver's hair.

The king pulled away.

Smiling, the sorceress spoke. "One Peak, your love will return for me, my son."

Shiver looked away. "Never."

"Ahh, come now. Must you resent me until my life's source has expired? I've begged for your forgiveness for over two seasons now."

The king looked up at the sorceress. "Even your passing would not regain my favor. I will not lower myself to standards that were beneath my father's."

"Your father's? Darosen loves me dearly."

Shiver stood from his throne and moved to the backside of his chair. "Feign not, Mother, for you're not truly loved by Darosen, and you know of whom I speak." Removing the crown from his head, the king hung it on the edge of the throne. "Must we continue this ruse? You've failed to find Clandestiny. Your dreams of controlling the Isor shall never be realized, and I shall hold steadfast to my hatred of your existence until my life's source ends."

Holding Blandina's gaze, Shiver pointed to the exit. "You should return to Gesper. Your presence is unwanted here."

Though the king's words punctured the sorceress' heart, she did not allow Shiver to see the wound. Instead, Blandina responded with a grin. "Your tongue seeks to inflict pain on my being, my son. Perhaps you'll see things clearer after your grandfather arrives."

"He's not my grandfather. Never before have my eyes been laid upon him. Why do you allow your father's influence to harden your heart so?"

A weathered voice responded as Meerum Bosand entered the throne room. "It's only because I am her father that she obeys, young king. My blood courses through your veins as well, boy. You'll also learn to obey ... just as your mother does."

Shiver watched the feeble-looking Meerum Bosand cross the throne room and hobble up the steps toward his chair. Seeing the crown on top of his grandfather's head, the King of the Isor snatched his own crown off the back of his throne and then reclaimed his seat.

The King of Gesper laughed at Shiver's attempt to portray power. Meerum stopped in front of the throne. Using his magic to amplify his strength, the withered Seer of Gesper grabbed Shiver by the collar of his cape and tossed the youngster down the steps.

As Meerum lowered onto the throne, Blandina watched Shiver tumble and stop at the bottom. The princess boasted, "Your grandfather is powerful, Shiver. You must concede and obey."

Shiver reached up and used his hand to wipe away the blood that was dripping down his face. He had struck his forehead against the edge of the bottom step and was still woozy because of it.

Meerum enjoyed the pain on his grandson's face as Shiver struggled to stand. Eventually, the younger king looked up. "I've lived in fear of my mother's magic for too many seasons! I won't concede ... nor will I answer to a wretched Tormalian!"

Furious, Meerum extended his left arm and pointed. "You're Tormalian, boy! You will concede, or you will perish!" A split moment later, a wave of force emerged from the Tormalian King's fingertip and barreled down the steps toward Shiver. Upon impact, the younger king was knocked to the floor where he slid across the ice and stopped near the entrance.

As Shiver struggled to reclaim his feet yet again, the owl that had been sitting on the sign at the entrance to the Pass of Nayala flew through the door and headed up the steps toward Blandina. Seeing the bird, the sorceress reached beneath her yellow shawl, removed a piece of slagone hide and then placed it over her right forearm and then called for the owl to land.

With the owl now resting on her arm, the sorceress reached into a pouch that was tied to her waist and retrieved a small rodent. Seeing the creature dangling by its tail, the bird snatched the frightened mouse out of the Tormalian princess' fingertips and swallowed it whole.

"Gormad, my lovely goswig," Blandina said in a soothing tone. "I hope you've returned with pleasant news."

Though Shiver could not hear what the owl was saying, he could see the joy on his mother's face. He watched as Blandina bent over to whisper in Meerum's ear. Only a short series of moments passed before Meerum began to smile.

The King of Gesper struggled to stand from the throne. He shouted down the steps at Shiver. "It appears your future bride is making her way back to Hydroth! Summon your servants, boy ... for upon her arrival, you shall be united."

Before Shiver could respond, the officers of the Isorian army who were present when Gablysin slew the Frigid Commander barged into the room along with another 13 undercastle guards. They pushed Shiver aside to keep him out of harm's way, and then the crowd circled the throne.

In Gablysin's absence, Lamayne Bridemoore stepped forward. Recognizing the Tormalian King from previous diplomatic visits to Gesper, he unsheathed his sword and commanded, "King Bosand ... you'll surrender to captivity, or you shall perish!"

The mob shouted in agreement as Meerum lowered back onto the throne. Without responding, he motioned for Blandina to take a seat on his lap.

Placing the owl on the back of the throne, the goswig spun his head in the direction of every Isorian as Blandina obeyed. Once seated, her father estimated the distance to the closest Isorian and determined it to be nearly six paces.

Closing his eyes, Meerum began to chant. An awkward series of moments passed as the crowd looked to one another for direction.

Before the Tormalian king opened his eyes, he subtly patted Blandina on her outer thighs for twelve beats and then looked up at the Frigid Lamayne. "I have foreseen the outcome of this Peak. It's you who shall see captivity."

Most every officer started to laugh, including the lamayne. As they did, Blandina started to whisper in the language of the elves while she lowered her chin to her chest. Once the crowd settled, Meerum commanded, "Now, my daughter!"

The sorceress' head snapped toward the ceiling as she stood and flung her arms away from her sides. A powerful wave of force exploded from her person and barreled into the crowd. Every Isorian was lifted and thrown into the walls behind them. They collided with the ice, and like slices of bread on a cutting board, they stacked on top of one another as they fell limp to the floor.

Because the sorceress' thoughts were specific while she commanded her magic, Shiver was unaffected by the blast, along with Meerum and Blandina's goswig. The younger king stood motionless against the wall and stared at the bodies piled around him, and none were moving.

Meerum clapped his hands and started to chuckle. After using his power to help his weakened muscles elevate him off the throne, he hobbled down the steps toward Shiver. The elder Tormalian enjoyed the way the younger king cowered as he extended his left arm. Rolling his fingers toward his palm, Shiver lifted from the midst of the pile and floated across the room toward his grandfather.

Bosand used his magic to keep his grandson suspended as he stepped within a few hands of the boy to address Shiver. The Tormalian King's voice was filled with wickedness as he spoke. "Your men shall never be forgotten."

Leaving Shiver suspended, Meerum took a step back and turned to hobble to the top of the stairs. With a clear view from the throne room, he once again extended his hand and rotated in a circle while he passed his arm across the motionless pile of bodies.

The ice beneath the Isorians melted. Those who were dead, sank, and those who were still alive, awoke. The Tormalian King quickly adjusted his thoughts and commanded his power to push the living beneath the water. Bosand held them there until their last breaths surfaced as bubbles and popped.

With the last Isorian expired, Meerum commanded the water to solidify. As it crystallized, the ice remained clear, and Shiver could see into it. The faces of the officers who had drowned looked haunted.

The younger king could only hang in silence until Meerum released his hold on him. After falling to the floor, Shiver crawled over to the bodies and stared down into the ice. He reached for his dagger that was secured to his ankle, pulled it out of its sheath and then started to chip away at their frozen tomb.

Once again, Meerum laughed as he hobbled back down the stairs and stopped before he reached the bottom. "Boy!"

Shiver did not respond.

Bosand shouted again, "Boy!"

The younger king refused to respond and continued to chip at the ice.

Yet again, the Tormalian King shouted, "Look at me, boy! Or else!"

With a fluid motion, Shiver whipped around and flung his dagger with all his might. The blade traveled up the steps at a high rate of speed, aimed at Meerum's head.

Bosand lifted his right hand and used his power to deflect the knife. A moment later, a gurgling sound could be heard behind the withered king. The dagger had found an alternate target and had buried itself into Blandina's throat.

The Tormalian king spun around and watched helplessly as his daughter gasped for air. He could see the blue of her skin begin to fade as her eyelids grew heavy. She stumbled toward the edge of the steps and fell forward.

Bosand was forced to use his magic to catch the princess. As Meerum lowered Blandina to the ice, Shiver seized the opportunity to run. He stood and darted for the exit.

Hearing the younger king's pysples pop against the ice, Meerum lost his concentration. As a result, his magic failed and Blandina's body plummeted to the steps. Her head landed beyond the corner of the step beneath Bosand's feet, but the end of the dagger had a small point on its handle. It caught the edge of the step and did not budge. Because of this, the tip of the blade was pushed through Blandina's throat where it emerged from the back of the princess' neck.

Beyond enraged, Meerum's hand flew from his side in the direction of Shiver. Magical arrows erupted from his fingertips and hurled through the air in pursuit of his grandson.

As Shiver turned the corner, all the arrows, except one, buried into the ice. Shiver cried out as the arrow skewered the back of his right arm, but his fear overcame the pain, and he continued to run up and out of the undercastle.

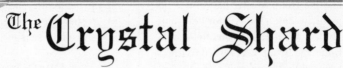

The Crystal Shard

When you want an update about your favorite characters

**4 Peaks Have Passed
Since Shiver Escaped from the
Undercastle of Hydroth**

NORTHERN GRAYHAM

Mosley, Medolas and **Clandestiny**—After Celestria left Mosley standing outside the cave beneath the Temple of the Gods on Southern Grayham, the night terror wolf ran inside. He rushed through the tunnels to the chamber the goddess had spoken about and drank from the chalice that held the power of the Swayne Enserad. On that Peak, a soothing surge passed through the wolf's body as he moved to the left side of the chamber and stopped in front of the portal that was said to take him to the Merchant Island of Harvestom.

The longer Mosley stood in front of the gate, the greater his guilt became for abandoning Medolas and Clandestiny. He dismissed his promise to Celestria and teleported back to the west side of the Pass of Nayala. From there, Mosley worked his way across the gorge. On each occasion he was blown off the crossing, the wolf teleported back onto the ledge where he continued to run until he was safely across.

Mosley later rejoined Medolas and Clandestiny, and Clandestiny was pleased with the wolf's companionship. Now she had another pet to love—and this one could speak.

Shiver and **Gablysin**—After running out of the throne room, Shiver encountered the ruby eyed man as he exited the undercastle. He explained that the moments were not available to have a proper Passing Ceremony for Slips. The young king then fled with Gabs to the understables where they mounted harugens and headed west into the wilderness to hide from the Tormalian King until they could devise a plan.

Gage, the badger, and **Gallrum,** the serwin—The pair has used their magic to expedite their journey to Northern Grayham. They are now passing through the Cave of No Return.

WESTERN LUVELLES

Chancellor Methelborn and **King Dowd**—After meeting up with the Brayson Id, Boyafed and Dowd continued to monitor the creation of Kepler's palace. Once the proper décor was added, the trio placed their hands on the pedestal to fuel the creator's power. They intended to give the structure life, but Taugor was unable to withstand the drain on his being. The elf doubled over and fell from the top of the column, and the Head Master had to use his magic to catch the creator before he landed. With Taugor unable to continue, the group was forced to find a replacement creator.

With the arrival of this new elf, the moments have come to reattempt the creation of a heart that will be strong enough to give life to the structure. They must fill the palace's veins with magically altered corgan blood and then shock the structure to life.

Mary and the **Family**—Since Brayson has not yet returned, Mary has asked the kedgles to help with the search for Garrin. Since the baby has not been found, Hepplesif has expanded the search. The leader of the kedgle army has called upon the students of Brayson's school of magic to assist.

With George traveling by boat to Eastern Luvelles, no one has a way of teleporting to the warlock to let him know that Garrin has disappeared. Worse yet, George's final destination is also unknown, which makes finding him at all nearly an impossibility.

Sharvesa—The goddess has appeared on the island of the Fairy King. She is sitting amidst the trees of the forest and is looking at an enormous mound of dirt that is covered with small cave-like entrances. She is trying to decide whether or not she will wake the Fairy King, Defondel, to speak with him. She

has not forgotten how the four inch tall fairy took advantage of her—raping her while she slumbered—leaving her impregnated with Payne four and a half seasons ago.

DRAGONIA
THE NEW HELL

Kepler—After the Merchant Angels left Dragonia, Kepler was forced to break free of his crate. With the docks abandoned, the demon-cat is now wandering the island.

Sam—The King of Brandor is still sitting in his crate. He is tired of waiting for someone to let him out.

Lasidious—After the God of Mischief left the castle of Brandor on Southern Grayham, he appeared with Garrin and Sam, Jr. on Dragonia. Lasidious has set up camp just south of the Mountains of Gannesh, home to the Vampire King and Queen.

The Mischievous One has been using milk from the Vampire Queen's bosom to keep the children fed. The queen's milk has special traits, one of them being the ability to suppress Garrin's magic. This is important because the god-child's power is strong enough to teleport between worlds and return to Susanne on Western Luvelles.

Over the last 4 Peaks, Lasidious has been working to build a trusting relationship with the boys. The milk of the Vampire Queen is addictive. The more the boys drink it, the more they want to stay with the Mischievous One. But there is a problem. Though only a toddler, Garrin doesn't trust Lasidious. The milk is the only thing that has kept the child from teleporting.

THE HIDDEN GOD WORLD
ANCIENTS SOVEREIGN

Celestria and **Alistar**—As planned, Alistar covered for Lasidious. He told Celestria that the Mischievous One sought solitude after their argument. The Goddess of Beasts has been waiting for her lover to return, and she refuses to leave their home.

The Book of Immortality—Gabriel has returned from Dragonia after leaving the most devious souls within his pages on that world.

The Book has called a meeting of the gods that will take place at Late Bailem.

A PLACE UNKNOWN

Anahita—Anahita has been asleep since her reunion with the Archangel Michael. Complications are about to arise.

Thank you for reading the Crystal Shard

CHAPTER 9
WHIMS OF THE MIGHTY ONE
WESTERN LUVELLES
THE FORMER BATTLEGROUNDS OF OLIS
KEPLER'S PALACE
EARLY BAILEM

Head Master Brayson placed his hands flat against the banister of the main staircase. Closing his eyes, he enjoyed the warmth of the structure and then smiled as the heart of the palace pumped the altered corgan blood throughout. Satisfied that the pulse was strong, Brayson removed his hands and then looked at Boyafed and Dowd. "Well done, gentlemen. Kepler will be pleased."

Dowd nodded in agreement, but Boyafed presented a look of concern.

"What is it, Chancellor?" the Head Master questioned. "Is something wrong?"

The Dark Chancellor looked to his left through the hallway that led to Kepler's new throne room. "This structure feels incomplete."

Dowd lifted his hands toward the ceiling and looked around. "I see no imperfections. The Protector of the Realm will be satisfied with our efforts."

"I agree," Brayson added. "No expense has been spared."

A few moments of silence passed before a grin appeared on Boyafed's face. "Perhaps a giant scratching post is in order."

King Dowd reached out and shoved Boyafed from his wheeled chair. "Yes, yes, yes, and a large saucer of milk."

Boyafed poked back. "And an enormous ball of string."

Brayson clapped his hands and chimed in on the fun. "And lest we forget a mouse hole. Kepler will need something to chase."

Dowd and Boyafed stopped laughing. Their demeanor turned serious as if they shared the same brain. "What about Lord Maldwin?"

"You're right," Brayson added. "We forgot."

A long, quiet series of moments passed while the trio looked for the perfect spot to add Maldwin's hole. Seeing the decision was going to be daunting, Brayson sighed. "Well ... this is a task the two of you can handle. Create well, gentlemen." the Head Master vanished.

"He must be jesting," Boyafed protested while he looked at the empty space that Brayson had left behind. "Can he just abandon us like that?"

Dowd shrugged. "It appears the position of Head Master comes with privileges."

Both men chuckled.

MEANWHILE, THE FAMILY HOMES
BACK ON THE ISLAND OF THE HEAD MASTER

When Brayson appeared, he was standing near the center of the clearing next to the rocks above Kepler's lair. Instead of the normal quiet he was accustomed to teleporting into, the forest beyond the homes was buzzing with voices.

"Head Master!" Hepplesif called out from the top of the rocks. "Your arrival has come at a moment of need." The kedgle's legs clicked against the boulder as he scurried across it before he used the wings on his spidery back to lift into the air.

As the kedgle approached, Brayson questioned, "Why are you here, Hepplesif?"

"A child has gone missing. Come with me."

Turning to follow the kedgle to Susanne's home, Brayson responded. "Are you referring to Garrin?"

"Yes. The potion you gave the child didn't work. The boy has been missing for 4 Peaks."

"Four Peaks?" Brayson snapped. "Why wasn't I summoned?"

"Perhaps you should speak with the child's grandmother. When I suggested your retrieval, she declined."

"Why?"

"Ask her. She's with the boy's mother."

Leaving the kedgle to rejoin the search, Brayson walked up the steps to Susanne's home. As he opened the door, he thought, *This isn't good. I have no way of finding George.* With the door closing, he shouted, "Mary, where are you?"

MEANWHILE, DRAGONIA
LASIDIOUS' CAMP AMIDST THE WOODS

THE NEW HELL
SOUTH OF THE MOUNTAINS OF GANNESH

Lasidious tossed three pieces of wood on the fire and then looked at Garrin. The god-child was sitting next to Sam Jr. on top of the prince's blanket not more than three paces away. Garrin was sucking on a bottle filled with milk from the Vampire Queen's bosom while Sam Jr.'s bottle was lying empty at the prince's side.

"Drink up, my son," Lasidious said in a soothing voice as he moved to sit next to Garrin on the blanket. "You'll need your strength. For soon, we'll begin our journey into the mountains."

The Mischievous One extended a hand and tried to touch Garrin on the head, but his hand was stopped when Garrin put up a wall of force. The barrier surrounded both children, and though Lasidious tried to pass his hand through it, he was unable to.

Acting as if it did not matter, Lasidious reached next to his foot and retrieved a stick. He poked at the fire. "Your power is strong. It appears we'll need to travel while you sleep." He looked at Garrin and smiled while he spoke in his best baby voice. "Only then will your guard be down."

The Mischievous One stood and took a few steps back. As he did, Garrin dropped the protective barrier. Lasidious smirked. "You'll learn to trust me. Don't you worry about that." The god looked at Sam Jr. "But why does he desire to protect you at such a young age, my little prince? Garrin is acting above his seasons."

Out of the corner of his eye, the Mischievous One saw a squirrel run up a nearby tree. Lasidious dropped to a knee and called to the beast. The rodent stopped its ascent, scurried back down the trunk and then rushed into the palm of Lasidious' hand. With a snap of his fingers, Lasidious fed the squirrel a nut and then scratched the top of the rodent's head.

Seeing Garrin's amusement, the Mischievous One moved back to the blanket, took a seat and then extended the squirrel toward the god-child. During this series of moments, Garrin did not put up a barrier. Instead, he allowed Lasidious to place the squirrel on his lap, but as soon as the Mischievous One pulled his hand away, Garrin reformed the barrier.

The God of Mischief smiled. "See? Now that wasn't so bad, was it? You trusted me, and now you have two friends to play with." Lasidious took a seat on the forest floor beyond the far side of the fire. He then lowered to his back and put his hands behind his head. "Being a father isn't so hard."

A moment later, Garrin's empty bottle thumped Lasidious on the head.

MEANWHILE, THE DOCKS OF HELL'S MERCHANT ISLAND

After the Merchant Angels left Dragonia, Kepler sat patiently in his crate and waited for someone to let him out. But when no one came, the jaguar decided to break out. Using his magic, he blew the doors off the container and sent them flying into a stack of crates that were more than 30 paces away. Since that moment, Kepler wandered about. The morning was hot and humid, and the docks appeared to be abandoned.

Strange, Kepler thought while he prowled his surroundings. *Something is amiss.*

Crates of all sizes were scattered everywhere. They had been dropped off and left disorganized, almost as if the Merchant Angels no longer cared. Some were tilted on their sides while others were leaning against one another with their opposite ends sloping toward the ground.

Kepler noticed that on each door of the crates, there was a large parchment about half a paw print wide and equally as tall. They were laying face up behind a thick, sealed sheet of glass. Taking a closer look, each page appeared to be a manifest of the cargo that was locked inside. Some contained lists of food supplies, while others contained various metals, precious gems, plants, brick, stone and wood for building.

After reading the manifest of a crate that spanned a distance of more than 15 paces, Kepler swiped at the lock with his paw. The force of the blow sent not only the lock but both hasps and the hoop the lock was attached to flying. Using one of his nails, the jaguar pried open the doors to look inside. A rush of cold air poured out of the container and provided a soothing relief from the humidity that blanketed the mainland of Dragonia as he stared at a line of slaughtered corgans that hung by their legs.

A giant smile appeared as the cat licked his chops. *Glorious! I shall have to hunt this territory often.*

Kepler had nearly polished off two hind quarters when he heard a faint noise. Stepping out of the crate, he calmed his breathing and lifted his ears. Again, he heard the noise. It sounded as if something was scratching at the inside of another crate.

Crouching, the jaguar stalked the origin of the disturbance. It was not long before he stopped at the base of a stack of containers and looked up. The noise was coming from inside a small crate that sat wedged between three others on top of four much larger crates that had been carelessly stacked on top of one another. He estimated the small, square box and those surrounding it to stand no taller than the distance from his paw to his knee.

Again, the scratching sound emanated from the smaller crate. Rearing back, Kepler launched himself skyward and landed on top of the highest crate. He lowered his ear next to the smallest container and waited. A long silence passed while he looked at the manifest on the door. It was written in a language he could not read. A moment later, the scratching began again.

Sure of his choice, the jaguar knocked the other three crates of similar size aside. As the remaining container toppled into an upright position, a muffled shout could be heard from inside.

Kepler took a step back. *Intriguing. What could it be?*

Reaching forward, he swatted the corner of the box, causing it to spin. As it did, a long series of muffled shouts in a language he could not understand could be heard as some sort of creature bounced around inside.

Sitting on his haunches, Kepler grinned as he pondered the situation. *Curious,* he thought. Again, he nudged the crate, and again, another series of muffled shouts emerged. Looking out across the docks, he sighed, "Lucky for you there's no one else around, or my curiosity would be fleeting."

Wedging one of his nails between the lock and the hasp, the jaguar pulled the door off the crate. What he found inside was not what he expected. A short, scruffy creature with long, hairy ears, big feet, a pot belly, a pointy head, wide cheeks and a mouth that spanned the width of its face stood shouting at him with a small dagger clenched in its right hand.

Not quite the size of Maldwin, the creature charged and used its tiny knife to stab the end of one of Kepler's toes.

The jaguar looked down and shook his head at the inconvenience. "So much for gratitude." With his left paw, Kepler pinned the creature to the top of the crate, leaving only its head exposed between two of the jaguar's claws. "Be calm, little one."

A long series of moments passed before the creature stopped its tirade and settled down. With its energy spent, Kepler released his hold and backed off. "Are you quite done?"

Rolling into a seated position, the creature sheathed its tiny knife and looked up. Its normal voice was far less irritating and sounded male. *"Pegon de-saw plutee. Pegon de-saw plutee."*

Kepler's right eye squinted. "I don't understand."

The creature motioned to the other crates Kepler had knocked to the side. *"Pegon de-saw plutee. Pegon de-saw plutee."*

Studying the creature's features, the jaguar noticed resemblances to two possible races. The first was grendle, a language he did not know, and the second was demon. He used this language and questioned, "Do you speak Demon?"

Stunned, the grendle-imp's eyes widened. "I do, I do," he responded in demon tongue. The imp pointed at the other crates. "Look at what you've done to my things."

Kepler rolled his eyes and thought, *Great. He doesn't appreciate being released.*

Watching the imp scurry across the top of the container to the other crates, the cat replied in the Demon language. "I've done nothing other than cast them aside. Your belongings are fine."

The imp pulled at the lock of one of the crates, his little muscles bulging as he placed both feet against the side of the container for leverage.

Kepler grinned as he watched the imp's face turn red. "Do you have a name?"

Lowering his feet back to the top of the container, the imp replied, "My name is Pydum."

Kepler snorted. "What kind of a name is that?"

Pydum released the lock and let it fall. "You sound irritated."

"I am. I released you, and you have failed to show your gratitude. I don't want to deal with the immaturity of another freak."

The imp moved next to Kepler and then placed his left hand on one of the cat's ankles. "I apologize for my brashness. Thank you."

"That's more like it," Kepler replied. Pushing the imp aside, the jaguar popped the locks on the other small containers that Pydum had claimed to be his and then jumped down to the ground. As the cat walked away, he shouted over his shoulder, "Good journeys, Pydum!"

After watching the jaguar walk around the next pile of containers, the grendle-imp walked into one of the containers and started to rummage through his belongings.

It was not long before Kepler strolled up to a collection of wagons that had been dropped on top of one another. *What happened here?* he thought. *No other Merchant Island I've seen has been in such disarray. Those who command this territory are unworthy of doing so.*

On the far side of the wagons, another sound caught the cat's attention. Leaping over the pile, the jaguar stopped and looked up toward its origin. He watched the tip of a blade puncture the side of a crate three levels up. The sword was white hot, and as it cut an opening into the side of the container, the metal directly around the weapon melted. A moment later, a heavy foot kicked the carved door open.

The King of Brandor watched as the metal plummeted to the ground and landed with a thud. Sam then sheathed Kael, retrieved his belongings and then jumped to the ground.

Since Kepler's last meeting with the King of Brandor was peaceful, the jaguar decided to approach. "What are you doing here?"

In disbelief of the cat's presence, Sam closed his eyes and then reopened them. "I should be asking you the same thing. You're a long way from home." The king paused. "Is George with you?"

"He isn't. Walk with me."

A long conversation ensued. They talked about the disarray of the island and about what happened in Sam's throne room. Hearing Kepler's opinion on the old man's demise, Sam convinced himself that he should go back to Brandor and face the consequences of his actions. The pair set out in hopes of finding Jehonas, the dock foreman, to see about getting the king a ride back to Grayham.

WESTERN LUVELLES
THE ISLAND OF THE FAIRY KING

It was just before dawn when Sharvesa appeared amidst the trees on the Fairy King's island. She took a seat on the trunk of a fallen tree and was staring at an enormous mound of dirt that was covered with small, cave-like entrances while she remained in an invisible veil. The demon-goddess had decided to confront the Fairy King, Defondel, and it was approaching the Peak of Bailem.

"Defondel!" Sharvesa shouted as she stood from the tree and allowed herself to be seen. Adjusting her dark, leather outfit, laced with veins of gold, she continued. "I want to speak with you, King of Fairies!"

Seeing the demon-goddess' size, over 40 fairies that were flying directly above the mound dove for cover. They disappeared inside the maze of tunnels that had been burrowed throughout the mound as countless other fairies flying amidst the treetops darted behind various branches and peered around the bark.

Again Sharvesa shouted. "Defondel! Make yourself known! I won't leave until we've spoken!"

When no answer came, the demon reclaimed her seat on the trunk. "Show yourself, rapist!"

Sensing that she would be there a while, Sharvesa lowered onto her back. She stretched out across the trunk and used a knot that protruded from the side of the tree as a pillow. After placing her hands behind her head, she looked toward the sky. "If I must ... I'll wait an eternity! You'll speak with me before I go!"

The demon watched the sun crawl across the treetops. It reached the midway point between the Peak of Bailem and Late Bailem before a tiny voice called out from inside the mound. "Have you come to smite me?"

The demon did not look away from a cloud that drifted past. "I mean you no harm! I seek only answers!"

"Just Answers?"

"Yes! Only answers!" She turned her head in the direction of the mound. "Show yourself! There's no need for us to shout!"

"If I come into the open … what guarantee do I have that you'll spare my existence?"

Sharvesa smiled. "Not one!"

"Then I choose to stay hidden!"

Sitting up, the demon smirked. "Do you truly believe your pile of dirt will protect you? Show yourself before I bury you within it!"

Defondel's tiny voice sounded confident. "My kingdom is protected! You have not the power to cause destruction! I am safe in here!"

"Ha! Your miserable mound is not a kingdom! It's an ant farm."

Sharvesa looked at the terrain surrounding the pile. Despite her irritation, she had to admit that the king's home was well maintained. Miniature fields extended away from the mound and spread throughout the base of the trees. Each field had been worked and planted like farmland. And though these areas of cultivated earth were miniscule in size to her, she knew that to Defondel's kind they had to feel as if they stretched forever.

When a response never came, the goddess softened her tone. "I swear it … I haven't come to inflict harm. I only want to speak with you about our son. I seek his location."

Defondel poked his tiny head out of one of the holes near the bottom of the mound. His face was still young, though his beard and short hair were gray. "Many Peaks have passed since you sent Payne to Luvelles. You cared not for him then, so why seek him now?"

"Circumstances have changed."

Defondel stepped out of the hole. Almost as if it had been planned, the clouds passing overhead opened up, and a ray of sunshine found its way through the trees to light his form. He was wearing a small suit of armor that allowed his wings to flutter in the back.

The Fairy King replied, "How have they changed? Does not the demon council still exist?"

"It does."

"Then why bother? Payne cannot return with you … so why torment his young mind?"

Sharvesa lowered from the tree and took a seat on the ground. Defondel took a step back toward the mound as the demon crossed her legs and leaned forward. "I simply want to look upon him," she sighed.

"Just look?" Defondel crossed his arms. "And nothing more?"

"Yes … nothing more."

The Fairy King studied Sharvesa's face for deception. "Payne is happy. Do you swear to the gods that you won't destroy his happiness?"

"I swear," she nodded.

Flapping his wings, Defondel lifted off the ground and hovered eye-level with the demon while still maintaining his distance. "If I tell you, will you promise to never return? Will you leave in peace?"

Again, the demon nodded. "I will."

Defondel held Sharvesa's gaze for a long while. "When last I heard, Payne had found happiness with a family of humans."

"Humans?" Sharvesa sneered. "Why would you allow that?"

"I allowed nothing. Payne's magic was too strong. I couldn't control him. I was forced to send him into exile."

"Exile?" the demon shouted. "First you rape me, and then you banish our son?"

Defondel lifted his right hand above his head and whistled. Thousands of fairies began to pour out of the holes in the mound and the treetops became alive as the sounds of their fluttering wings filled the air. They surrounded the demon-goddess and prepared for the worst.

Sharvesa laughed. "How brave of you, Defondel. But your threat is unnecessary and pointless."

Angered by the demon's response, Defondel snapped his fingers. "Now!" he ordered.

The air surrounding the goddess filled with thousands upon thousands of specks of light as the fairies unleashed miniature bolts of lightning that arced in her direction. Closing her eyes, Sharvesa absorbed the magic. Wave after wave, the fairies attacked. When the lightning bolts did not work, they hurled bolts of ice. And when the ice did not work, they sent tiny waves of force barreling into her.

With the final attack absorbed, the goddess opened her eyes and extended her right hand toward the Fairy King. Defondel protested as Sharvesa used her magic against him. The fairy army watched in horror as their king floated to Sharvesa and settled into her open palm.

With her fingers closed around his legs to avoid damaging his wings, the goddess spoke. "What is the name of the man who heads this family of humans? Speak now, and I'll release you."

Defondel stopped squirming. "I know not his name. I only know the humans live on the Head Master's island."

Releasing her grip, Sharvesa took a deep breath and then blew the fairy out of her palm. After watching him tumble through the air and catch himself with his wings, she smiled and then vanished.

A moment later, the embarrassed Fairy King looked around at all his subjects who were still staring at him. "What are you looking at? Get back to work!"

The New Hell
The Abandoned Docks of Merchant Island
Late Bailem is Approaching

Sam stepped out of the dock foreman's office and then walked down the plank-way back to where Kepler was waiting. "Jehonas isn't in there either," Sam announced. "His office is a mess ... just like everything else is around here. It looks like he left in a rush."

Sitting on his haunches, the jaguar stopped licking the back of his paw. "Perhaps he had better territories to prowl." Lowering his paw to the ground, the cat lowered his head between his legs and continued to lick himself.

Curling his nose, Sam replied, "Perhaps ... but why would he leave everything in disarray? There must be rules for how his island is to be maintained."

Kepler's reply was muffled since he was nibbling at his inner thigh. "Yes, there must."

Sam looked back toward the office. "When I looked through the papers on Jehonas' desk, there was a log. There are four containers filled with criminals that were scheduled to be dropped off last night. If that's the case, why would the dock foreman abandon his post ... especially when he needs to get them out? It doesn't make sense."

Kepler stopped cleaning himself and looked up. "Perhaps the criminals broke out of their crates before we did and overran the island. That would explain the disarray."

Sam pondered the cat's response. "That's unlikely. We would've heard the commotion." He placed his hand on his chin and rubbed the scruff of

2 Peaks growth. "What if the criminals are still inside their crates? They'll perish if we don't let them out."

"So?"

"What do you mean, 'so?' We can't just let them pass. We should look for them."

Kepler walked toward the railing of the walkway and then used the post at its end to scratch his flanks. "I didn't come to Dragonia to save unwanted beings. I'm here to hunt for a mate."

Sam nodded. "I know. You told me that already." Looking toward the stacks of crates that began over 100 paces away, he added, "Just help me find them. Something tells me that the Merchant Angels won't be returning tonight. Stay with me for a while, and if they don't, I'll travel with you and help you find your woman."

"And when you find these crates filled with the worlds' rejected ... what then?"

"We'll release them. They'll starve to death if we don't."

Kepler's eyes narrowed. He lowered his head level with Sam's. "Truly kind words from the mouth of a king who recently ended an innocent man. Don't toy with me, King of Brandor. Why do you care?"

"I don't know. I just do." Sam reached over his shoulder and retrieved his backpack. Opening the leather flap that kept it shut, he reached in to retrieve the vial that was holding Yaloom's potion. He unsheathed his dagger, uncorked the bottle with his teeth and tilted it. After dipping the end of his blade into the liquid, he lifted it above his mouth and allowed a drop to fall under his tongue.

Kepler watched Sam savor the effects of the potion. The way the king moaned while he licked his lips caused the jaguar to assume the potion was some sort of substance that, over his seasons, he had seen other beings consume. They had all acted in a similar fashion—though their consumption had been in bigger doses. Because of this carelessness, there were many nights where he had hidden in the shadows and waited for those who partook of such toxins to stumble out of the Bloody Trough.

Though curious, Kepler refrained from asking what the substance was and questioned again. "I asked, why do you care?"

When Sam opened his eyes, he reclaimed Kepler's gaze. "I care only because we'll need protection. This world is a violent place. Think about it. We could use the criminals as a first line of defense if we're attacked." Corking the bottle, Sam returned it to his backpack and added, "If I'm right, and I usually am ... the Merchant Angels won't be coming back. You and I are going to need all the help we can get, and expendable help is just as good as any. Wouldn't you agree?"

The jaguar lowered to his haunches and sat in silence as he processed the king's argument. He looked down the docks toward the containers. "Where should we look first?"

Draping his backpack over his right shoulder, Sam sheathed his dagger. "Beats me. Let's just tap on them all until we hear something."

As the pair walked down the dock, the grendle-imp Kepler released from his crate watched from the top of the oak-shingled roof of the dock foreman's office. Pydum crossed his arms and rested them on top of his belly while he whispered, "I wonder who'll be the first to perish." With a pack of his own on his back, the imp vanished.

ANCIENTS SOVEREIGN THAT SAME PEAK
THE HALL OF JUDGMENT
NIGHT APPROACHES

As the gods took their seats around the heavy stone table, Gabriel floated across the hall and stopped near Lasidious and Celestria's chairs. "Has anyone spoken to them lately?" the Book asked. "I'd like to get this meeting over with."

Alistar was quick to respond. "Lasidious has sought solitude after his disagreement with Celestria. He doesn't care about this meeting."

"And Celestria?" Gabriel quizzed.

"She refuses to leave their home. She's waiting for Lasidious to return, and she also doesn't care."

"How wonderful," Mieonus oozed while applauding. "The perfect couple spats. How wickedly delicious is that bit of news."

Alistar looked across the table at the Goddess of Hate. "Yet again, Mieonus, you show no class. Just one more reason for the rest of us to despise your existence."

All the gods laughed as Mieonus' smile vanished. Crossing her arms, she sat back in her chair. "I hate you all!"

Enjoying the goddess' tantrum, Hosseff leaned forward. "Gabriel, as amusing as this meeting has become, why have you summoned us?"

"Yes … why?" Bailem added.

"Because I have recently returned from Dragonia." The Book floated over the center of the table and lowered eye-level with the gods. "The most obliquitous souls within my pages have been delivered to the new Hell."

Lictina spoke up. "How many souls were chosen?"

"More than two billion. They have been given temporary bodies. Most were cast onto the poles and other untamed continents on Dragonia. There, they'll roam in misery amidst the cold and barren lands." The Book paused. "As far as the mainland of Dragonia, the Source has asked for a favor ... one that I honored."

"And what was this so-called favor, Gabriel?" Alistar questioned.

"The dragon asked that I not burden the demon populace with an over-abundance of outcasts."

Calla cut in. "Why would the Ancient One care? He has his new world, as promised. Why would he interfere?"

The Book lowered onto the table before he responded. "The Mighty One said the demons deserved the opportunity to prepare for the tortured's migration onto their lands."

Sharvesa leaned forward. "And you agreed? Why?"

"I did. But why doesn't matter."

The demon-goddess let out a sigh of relief. "Thank you, Gabriel. I'll be forever grateful. My daughter can use this extended series of moments to prepare for their arrival."

"This is good news," Alistar added. "But where did you cast the rest of the souls who were not left on the poles and barren lands?"

"I threw them into the Ocean of Karamoore, south-southwest of Dragon's Backbone. It'll be up to the damned to find their way to the mainland.

For those souls who did not possess the knowledge of how to swim, they sank. They'll experience the sensation of drowning again and again until the moment comes for them to be reborn. Even those who can swim must do so for more than half a season before they reach the backbone. Perhaps this torment will encourage them to live better lives during the next series of moments they're allowed to prove themselves on some other world."

"Half a season," Mieonus giggled. "Even I would not have been so harsh, Gabriel."

Ignoring Mieonus' remark, Alistar questioned, "What of their bodies?"

A look of disgust appeared on the Book's face. "As agreed, their bodies are temporary. Though they'll experience the feeling of passing, they cannot truly die. They'll feel every emotion and sensation, except fulfillment and joy. Dragonia will be a true Hell for the damned to wander until we pluck them from it and give them another opportunity to prove themselves worthy of escaping eternal torment."

Keylom's hooves clapped against the polished marble as he moved to a better position from which to speak. "How many damned souls remain on your pages, Gabriel?"

"Nearly eight billion. Dragonia was not large enough to hold them all."

"Then what will you do with the others?" the centaur questioned.

Gabriel floated back over to the center of the table. "As you know, over 10 billion souls have been given the opportunity to live on the new worlds. Their lives lacked quality and goodness, therefore, they've been damned. Though only two billion were cast onto Dragonia, all of them deserve to be punished."

"Yes, we know this, Gabriel," Hosseff snapped. "But you didn't answer the centaur's question. What did you do with the other eight billion you were forced to leave inside your pages?"

The Book lifted off the table and floated next to Keylom who stood behind Hosseff. Facing the table, he responded. "To compensate for this injustice, the remaining damned have been given a tortured existence within my binding. They'll suffer just as deeply as those on Dragonia will suffer. Their torture will not stop until the moment arrives for their rebirth."

Annoyed by the Book's proximity, Hosseff stood and walked away from his chair. The shade stopped behind Lasidious' empty seat and continued to question. "What of those souls who have not had the opportunity to live on the new worlds? What is to be their existence?"

"Their existence will be the same as it has been for the last 13,000 seasons. They won't suffer, just as the others did not suffer until they failed to live a good life."

Jervaise decided to speak up. "What will you do with the souls who were given life … those who had their chance to live on the new worlds, and in doing so, became worthy of blessing? Will you reward them, Gabriel? Will they experience eternal joy until this collective can find a way to create a Heaven that will rival the Heaven we all once knew?"

A look of sorrow appeared on Gabriel's face. "They'll experience as much joy as I'm capable of remembering, for as we all know, matching the Creator's greatness is impossible."

"'Matching the Creator's greatness is impossible,' he says." Owain removed his hat and set it on the table. "Impossible only for now."

Hearing the God of Water's boldness, Bailem bit his lip and forced himself to remain silent. He stood from the table and walked to the far side of the room and called Gabriel to him. Once the Book was hovering in front of his face, the angel adjusted his robe on his portly belly and whispered, "Why must we let them speak with such arrogance. The Mighty One would not approve. You must speak with him, Gabriel. Tell him to bring down his wrath upon this collective."

The Book smiled and then responded using Bailem's real name. "Be patient, Zerachiel. We knew this path would not be easily traveled when we chose it."

Playing with the point of his hat, Owain shouted across the room. "Are you two quite finished? Using your power to keep us uninformed while you whisper amongst yourselves will solve nothing, Gabriel!"

Putting his hat back on his head, the dwarf stood to stretch his legs. "Perhaps the moment has come to segregate Dragonia and give the planet its own sun. We could increase its size, thus giving you the room to release the other eight billion damned. While we're at it, we should create a number of additional moons to orbit Hell's circumference."

Gabriel looked across the hall at Helmep. "Why additional moons? The moon Dragonia has is sufficient."

Kesdelain broke into the conversation. "It seems to me that Helmep sees an opportunity to use the weres as a means of torture for the damned. Those on Dragonia who change under the full moon and become predators will have plenty to feast upon once the damned migrate onto the mainland."

"Agreed," Helmep added. "Devoured flesh seems a proper fit for Hell."

Alistar slapped the edge of the table. "I also agree. And since Lasidious and Celestria care not what this collective does, there are enough of us present for a majority vote." Alistar paused. "Have the elements necessary to create such an expansion arrived yet?" He looked across the room toward the Book. "Gabriel, have your Salvage Angels returned with the means to create a new star, the additional moons and still add girth to Dragonia?"

The Book floated back to the table and hovered above Hosseff's empty seat. "Yes. My angels returned over a season ago."

"A season?" Mieonus shouted. Standing from her chair, she stomped the lifted heel of her right shoe. "How could you hold back information of this importance from the rest of us?"

Gabriel chuckled. His rosy cheeks bounced as he did. "When last I looked at the laws on my pages, I have free will just as you do, Mieonus. Must I continue with your education, or shall I simply open my binding and show you the laws that this collective ratified."

Mieonus' hateful stare burned into the Book's binding as she lowered to her seat and crossed her arms. "One Peak … I shall see that you suffer, Book. Mark my words."

Rolling his eyes, Gabriel addressed the others. "The mainland of Dragonia must not change. Its landscape must remain the same. If it doesn't, the Source will be displeased. And as we've already discussed, I've agreed to the dragon's wishes."

Hosseff ripped back his hood, stepped around Lasidious' seat and stopped next to the table. As he did, the light within the room caused the nothingness beneath his hood to solidify. With the shade's face now visible, he sneered at the Book's promise and pounded his fist against the table. "The Ancient One agreed to stay clear of our dealings on this plane! He promised free reign! Are we now to be bound by his whims?"

The Book of Immortality became angered. Gabriel vanished and reappeared within a hand of the God of Death's face. The Book shouted, "If it were not for the laws on my pages, I'd strike you down! Do not speak of the Mighty One with such irreverence again! For if you do, I shall sacrifice all that I am, and take you with me!"

Hosseff stepped back from the table. Lifting his hood, his face vanished. His voice became wispy again as he responded. "Forgive me, Gabriel." He bowed to show his submission. "The Ancient One's will be done."

Alistar allowed the tension in the room to dissipate before he interjected. "Gabriel … does the Ancient One truly intend to allow us free reign as he promised?"

Floating back to the center of the table, the Book responded. "Yes. The dragon intends to honor his word, just as he has always honored his word. It was Bassorine who asked the Source to request this of me. The Ancient One would not have done so if this request would not have been initiated by a member of this collective."

Mieonus scoffed, "Why would the Mighty One care about a request made by a destroyed being?"

The Book lowered to a position in front of the goddess' face. "Careful, Mieonus ... I'm not in the mood."

The Goddess of Hate leaned forward. She placed the tip of her nose against Gabriel's. "What will you do, Book? Would you sacrifice all that you are to strike me down?" Leaning back, she taunted, "I'm soooo scared. Get out of my face!"

A long, awkward silence captivated the room. Eventually, the Book of Immortality lifted and took a position at the center of the table. "With the matter necessary to create at our disposal, I see no reason why we cannot send the worlds into stasis. I say we vote on whether to expand the size of Hell, create the new moons, and a new star. We will adjust the minds of every being without godly memories. Those on the new Dragon World, Harvestom, Grayham, Luvelles, and Trollcom will not remember the existence of old Dragonia, while those on the newly reformed Hell, both damned and undamned, will no longer remember the existence of the other worlds. They will only know Hell, but those who are living on Hell, those who are not yet damned, will know that there is something better that awaits them if they choose to live a good life ... but they will not understand what it is ... only that it's better."

The Book looked toward Bailem as he questioned the room, "What say you all?"

The vote was unanimous.

Seeing the hands raised in favor, Gabriel shouted, "Then let it be done!" The Book's voice was heard as thunder throughout all the worlds. A moment later, stasis fell across the solar system.

MEANWHILE, THE NEW HELL
LASIDIOUS, GARRIN AND SAM JR.'S CAMP

Lasidious was lying on his back near the campfire beneath the light of Dragonia's moon when he heard the thunder that was caused by the Book of Immortality's voice. The Mischievous One had just broken through a line of

Garrin's defenses, and as a result, the children were bouncing on the god's belly when stasis fell across the worlds.

The Mischievous One frowned as the boys froze in place. "No, no, no! Not now," he griped. "Garrin was just starting to trust me." Lasidious looked in the direction of the vanishing sun. "Why couldn't they have chosen a better series of moments?"

Lasidious lifted Sam Jr. off his stomach and lowered the prince onto the blanket and then placed Garrin beside him. After covering them both with a second blanket, the Mischievous One jumped to his feet and studied his surroundings.

The flames of the campfire had stopped moving. The clouds, trees, every blade of grass, the birds in the sky and even the light cast by the fire had all stopped moving. Nothing would move again until the gods were finished creating, and there was nothing he could do about it.

As the Mischievous One looked down at the children, he knew they would be safe—but it was not the boys' safety that Lasidious was worried about. "Sam," was all the Mischievous One said as he closed his eyes and pictured the king's face. When he reopened them, he was standing within an invisible veil next to a confused king.

Sam was holding his sword in his left hand. He was walking around a frozen Kepler who was standing next to a tall stack of crates and appeared to be in the middle of taking a step when he froze. Kael's blade was burning, shedding light on the environment while Sam walked around the jaguar and stopped in front of the cat. The king waved his hand. "Kepler! Kepler! What's the matter with you?"

When the jaguar failed to move, Sam reached out and poked him. The cat's fur did not give. Further, Kepler's body was hard and cold—extremely cold—and upon further examination, even the cat's tongue was frozen solid. "What the hell...?"

With Sam not more than three paces away with his back to him, Lasidious stepped out of his invisible veil. "Fret not, King of Brandor. The jaguar will be fine."

Startled, Sam spun around with Kael slicing through the air. The Mischievous One reached up and caught the blade in the palm of his hand and then yanked the weapon away from Sam. The king's eyes widened as Lasidious continued to speak. "Easy, Sam. I haven't come to harm you."

With his eyes still fixated on the way Kael's fire failed to burn the stranger's palm, Sam stuttered. "Wh ... wh ... who are you?"

Lasidious smirked. "Now that hurts. You truly don't remember, do you?" The Mischievous One took a moment to enjoy Sam's confusion before he added, "Think, Sam. Think. You know me."

A long, unaccounted for series of moments passed before Sam responded. "Your voice. I know your voice."

"That's better," Lasidious encouraged. "You're beginning to remember, aren't you? Many moments have passed since last we were together, you and I."

Sam's eyes were filled with a million questions. "How do you know me?"

Lasidious handed Kael back to Sam. "Your mind isn't ready for that answer."

The king reclaimed his sword and rebutted, "If you know me, then you know my mind is capable of anything."

Again, Lasidious smirked. After moving past Sam, the god placed his hand on the jaguar's frozen shoulder. "Then try wrapping your mind around this. Your feline friend stands in stasis. The gods have stopped the worlds' moments. Only those who possess a form of realization of their godly memories remain unaffected."

"That's impossible," Sam argued. "Time cannot be stopped ... nor do I possess any form of godly memories."

Lasidious leaned against Kepler and pulled back his hood to expose his face. After crossing his legs, he placed his hands behind his head and looked to the sky. "Though you may not recognize your realization of your memories, you still stand here unaffected by stasis and remain animated. You know more than your mind is willing to admit."

The Mischievous One's reclaimed Sam's eyes. "You uttered the word 'time.' This word is seldom used anymore. Stopping time *is* possible, King of Brandor. The concept is just simply beyond the realm of your current understanding." After crossing his arms, the god added, "Though it won't be for long."

"Who are you?" Sam demanded. "And don't act like I know you."

Lasidious frowned. "You truly don't remember, do you? You have wounded me deeply, Sam."

The king lifted Kael and placed the blade's point against Lasidious' chest. "Stop screwing with me! I'm not in the mood!"

The flame from the blade lit the smile on Lasidious' face. "I know you have questions, but the answers will have to wait. For now, sheathe your weapon, and take my hands. You're not capable of surviving what's about to happen."

Sam shook his head. "What are you talking about?"

"I'm going to save you. Nothing else matters for the moment."

Sam's eyes narrowed. "Save me from what?"

"The gods are about to create, but what they intend to create, I can only guess. Only those who stand in stasis on this world will survive. Your existence is in danger."

Sam poked his own chest. "To my knowledge, I have no godly memories. If what you say is true, why am I not already standing in stasis?"

Lasidious laughed. "I believe I've answered that already." Closing his eyes, the god vanished and reappeared on top of Kepler's back. He patted the jaguar on the shoulders and admired his new seat for a moment. "He's a powerful beast, is he not? Kepler is one of my best creations."

Sam sneered, "Yet another god who fails to answer questions. I asked you … why am I not standing in stasis?"

Lasidious looked down at Sam. "You may not be able to recall your memories, but you have displayed the realization of these memories on more than one occasion. Have you not had thoughts that certain events, people and languages have felt familiar since your arrival on these worlds?" The Mischievous One pointed at Sam's pack. "You also possess a potion with Yaloom's memories contained within it, though I imagine you cannot recall them yet."

Lasidious crossed his arms again and then continued. "Tell me, Sam … how many drops of his essence have you consumed?"

The king took a step back and pointed Kael at Lasidious. "I won't ask again. Who are you?"

The Mischievous One threw his right leg over Kepler's back and then jumped to the ground. He took a step forward and allowed the tip of Sam's sword to rest against his chest. Reaching out, he snatched Sam's hand and made sure the king could not let go of the blade's handle. Step by step, Lasidious impaled himself onto the end of the sword as he closed the distance, stopping only a hand from the king's face.

Lasidious looked up and spoke over the searing hisses of his flesh. "Do you truly not remember me, brother?"

Sam's face went pale as he looked over Lasidious' left shoulder and stared at the blood that was boiling on Kael's tip. He was unable to respond to the god's question before the shaking began.

Out of spare moments, Lasidious ripped Sam's hand off the blade and pulled the weapon out of his chest. He extended his right hand and commanded, "Take it, Sam. There are not the moments to explain. You'll perish if you don't."

Seeing the king was unable to respond, Lasidious placed the flame-covered blade back in its sheath and then grabbed the king's hands. He extended a barrier of protection that encompassed Kepler, Sam and the crates that sat behind the king.

As the shaking worsened, Dragonia started to drift from its orbit. It was not long before the new Hell and its single moon were traveling through space at speeds beyond the speed of light. The light reflecting off Dragonia's moon faded as they drifted further from the sun the world would no longer orbit.

Watching the light diminish, Sam's face became harder to see. Lasidious shouted from within the protective barrier. "The gods must be moving Dragonia to a new location! To do so, they will need to create a new star!"

Seeing the king's anxiety, Lasidious reached out and grabbed Sam by the shoulders and shook him. "Are you hearing me, Sam? Sam! Sam!"

"Umm..."

"Look at me, brother! Look me in the eyes!"

The king did as he was told.

"You're going to be alright! Ignore the noise! Nothing can hurt you now! My power is protecting you!"

The king's stare was blank. Lasidious shook Sam by the shoulders again. "Pay attention! You would've frozen and perished if it wasn't for me! You're corpse would've been thrown from this world!" He shook Sam again. "Are you hearing me?"

Again, the king did not respond. He was occupied, watching while the last bit of light that reflected off Dragonia's moon dissipated—leaving them standing in what little light that escaped Kael's sheath.

Lasidious retrieved Kael and commanded the blade to burn brighter. He stabbed the tip of the weapon into the ground and allowed Kael to stand on his own.

Lasidious shouted, "Sam, pay attention! I must leave for now!" The god waved his hand across the ground. A banquet of food and water appeared. "You have enough to last until stasis ends! Don't set foot outside the barrier!" Again, Lasidious waved his hand, and the edges of the barrier reflected the sword's glow. "If you step beyond the boundary, you'll freeze! Do you understand?"

After being shaken a bit more, Sam finally nodded.

"Good! When I leave, the barrier will keep you warm! The food is cooked, and the water is clean! Again, don't leave the barrier until Kepler begins to move! You'll know it is safe once he steps out of stasis!" Again, Lasidious shook the king by the shoulders. "Tell me you understand, Sam!"

When Sam did not respond, Lasidious helped the king to the ground. Once seated, Lasidious bent over and gently slapped the king's cheek. "Brother! Do you understand everything I've said?"

Hearing the word 'brother,' Sam looked up. "I … I understand."

"Perfect!" Kneeling, Lasidious placed his forehead against Sam's. "When the proper moment arrives, you shall remember everything! Stay the course, my brother!" Lasidious vanished.

NORTHERN GRAYHAM
THE MOUNTAINS OF TEDFER

When the Mischievous One reappeared, he was standing on Northern Grayham within the Mountains of Tedfer inside another invisible veil.

Not more than 20 paces away, Mosley was sniffing at the frozen figures of Clandestiny and Medolas. The Isorians had stopped moving mid-stride while walking down the same path on which they had set the trap for the snowhounds so many seasons ago. Since Grayham had not moved from its orbit, the night terror wolf was not in danger, but he was confused.

Lasidious stepped out of his veil. "It's good to see you again, Mosley. Ancients Sovereign hasn't been the same without you."

Startled, the wolf crouched and snarled.

"Relax, Mosley. It's me ... Lasidious." The god lifted his hand and commanded the darkness around them to vanish.

With a better look at the god's face, Mosley relaxed. "What do you want?"

The Mischievous One placed his hand over his heart. "I'm touched. You remember me."

"I may not remember everything, but I remember you. What do you want?"

"Must you be like that, Mosley? I've missed you. The god world is witless without you."

"Hmpf!"

"Come now, Mosley. You're breaking my heart."

"I cannot break that which you don't possess!" the wolf sneered.

Lasidious crossed his arms and stared into the wolf's eyes. "I see you still need to work on your hospitality. But no worries, I haven't come for pleasantries." The Mischievous One walked forward and studied the frozen Isorians. "I've always admired their blue skin and the way their feet suckle the ice."

Mosley snapped, "The ice is not a giant teat, Lasidious. What do you want?"

The Mischievous One sighed. "Fine. See things your way." He walked to the edge of the ledge and looked out into the darkness. "I want you to abandon Northern Grayham and keep the promise you gave to Celestria. If you come with me, I'll teach you how to manage the power of the Ancient Mystics and the Swayne Enserad. Then you'll have your vengeance when George falls lifeless at your feet."

Mosley lowered to his haunches. "Why would you help me, Lasidious? Does George no longer serve your purpose?"

"George was useful, but alas, I'm done with him."

"Does George know that?"

Lasidious snickered, "Of course not ... silly wolf. And he won't know it until you deliver the message. You do still desire vengeance, don't you? Don't you also want to return to Ancients Sovereign?"

"At what cost?" Mosley reasoned.

"None that I know of. I simply want you to finish the task you've set out to accomplish. I want George to perish as much as you do."

"Why? What did George do to you?"

Lasidious returned from the ledge and knelt next to Mosley. He reached out and scratched the back of the wolf's ears. "George did nothing to me. He bores me now. Ancients Sovereign isn't the same without you. The others also bore me. I want you back."

"I don't believe you, Lasidious. There's more to this deception."

Lasidious pulled his hand away. "You know me too well. I wasn't going to tell you, but you leave me no choice. The beast who ended your wife no longer travels with George. With my help, not only will you learn to control the power of the Swayne Enserad, you'll be able to avenge Luvera's demise."

Mosley growled. "You would help me hunt Kepler?"

"No. I offer only knowledge. With this knowledge, your hunt will be successful. I also offer a means to reascend."

Mosley lifted from his haunches and started to pace. "Why, Lasidious?"

"Because I want your help."

"My help? Do you mean with something other than ending George?"

"Yes." Lasidious walked to a nearby boulder and sat on top of it. "You have been around children, Mosley. I'm not the father I should be. I find myself lacking." The god paused. "But I desperately want to become one. Celestria and I have given life to a son."

Mosley stopped pacing. "You have a cub?"

Lasidious laughed. "I do."

"How is that possible? I remember the law that states that gods cannot have pups."

Lasidious laughed again. "How matters not. I need your help."

"You want me to raise your cub?"

"No ... not raise him. I want you to teach me how to do it. I want my son to love his father. And you have a way with children."

"How could you possibly know that? You've never seen me rule a pack of my own."

Lasidious laughed. "During all your seasons with Bassorine, do you truly believe that your life went unnoticed? I know you better than you know yourself."

When Mosley did not respond, Lasidious continued. "I offer vengeance for your wife's demise. I offer George and Kepler on platters. I offer reascension. Why would you pass that up?"

Mosley stood in thought for a long series of moments and then looked back at the frozen figures of Clandestiny and Medolas. "What about them? Their territory is in turmoil."

Lasidious walked between the Isorians and then placed a hand on the back of both before he spewed his lie. "Once I release my hold on them, they'll reanimate. Their fate will no longer be your concern, and they won't remember you were here."

Mosley snorted his disapproval. "It figures that you were the one who froze them."

The Mischievous One chuckled and moved closer to Mosley to take a knee. "Would you expect any less of me? I didn't want them to hear our conversation. Besides, this is your best opportunity to avenge Luvera's passing. You could stay behind and fight a war that is not of your making, or you could do something productive."

The wolf started to pace. Every now and then, he looked at Clandestiny and Medolas. Eventually, Mosley stopped. "The girl's power exceeds my own. There isn't much I could do for them anyway." He looked at Lasidious. "I'll go with you."

Smiling, Lasidious walked over and touched Mosley on the head. "Sleep, wolf. Sleep..."

A SHORT WHILE LATER
THE CONTINENT OF EASTERN LUVELLES
THE OCEAN OF AGREGAN

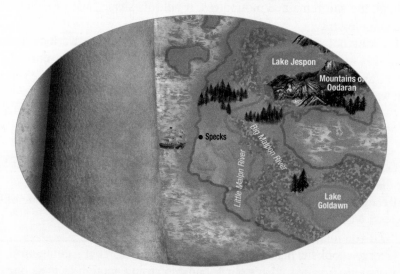

THE SHIP MARKS GEORGE'S LOCATION

After climbing down the rope ladder, George turned his head away from his staff that now hung from the ship's center mast. The gem atop the staff was glowing brightly enough to illuminate the deck of the ship as well as the ocean surrounding the vessel for a short distance.

After using his power to remove the ice, the warlock reached inside his pack and pulled out a piece of bread. Just like the pack, the loaf had been frozen through. Again, he used his magic to restore the loaf to its former form and made it soft enough to consume.

Heading to the stern of the ship, George lowered onto the railing and took a bite as he looked around. The vessel reminded him of an old pirate ship from movies he had seen on Earth.

What the heck is going on around here? he thought. *Why is everything frozen ... and why am I not?*

No matter where the warlock looked, nothing moved. The crew had been like this for many moments, and even the captain was lying in his bunk below deck—just as frozen as they were. The quiet was an eerie feeling, and the ship felt like a floating ghost town.

To his right, a young, male halfling was on his knees. The boy had been scrubbing the deck, and stranger yet, a bead of sweat had fallen from his chin and was suspended just above the planks.

George stood and walked to the edge of the steps leading down. He looked above his staff at the main sail that had been hoisted up the mast. Though the sail remained motionless, it held its shape, just as if the wind was still blowing.

Looking out across what he could see of the ocean, the warlock noticed the waves were just as still. They did not appear to be frozen like normal ice, but the angle of the ship suggested the vessel had been rolling up the surface of a wave before it stopped moving.

I wonder, George thought. He tossed the loaf of bread and watched as it bounced against the wave and slid down its surface. *Yep ... frozen. This has to be the weirdest thing I've ever seen.*

George descended the ladder and walked across the deck to another ladder that led up to the bow. As he ascended, a voice broke the silence.

Recognizing the sound, the warlock turned and took a seat on one of the steps. "I was wondering when I'd see you again."

"Did you miss me?" Lasidious responded.

George shook his head. "'Miss' is a strong word. What's going on?"

Lasidious frowned. "Isn't our friendship strong enough to miss one another yet?"

The warlock rolled his eyes. "Cut the garesh, Lasidious."

The god shrugged. "As you wish. You could've at least asked me how I was doing."

George stood and descended the ladder. "I think we both know I don't care."

"Then why speak to me at all," the god rebutted.

George slapped his own forehead and referred to Lasidious as a character from a movie he loved on Earth. "Hello! McFly! I speak to you because you have something I want. When will I see my Abbie?"

Lasidious laughed at George's antics. "Soon, George, soon. It won't be long before I have the power to release her soul from the Book." The Mischievous One walked to the railing and looked over. "You'll know the warmth of your daughter's touch before night falls 60 Peaks from now."

George clapped his hands. "That's great news, man. Maybe you're not such a prick after all."

Lasidious crossed his arms and turned to take a seat on the railing. "Is your opinion of me truly so low, George?"

"Of course it is. I've done too many terrible things for you for it to be otherwise. Did you really expect me to warm up to you?"

"I suppose not."

"Look, man … it's not like you really care what I think. You want something, and so do I. Let's just finish the job that needs to be done and stop screwing around."

Lasidious nodded. "Agreed."

George looked past the god at the ocean and pointed to a long-necked bird. The bird had been diving for food and its bottom half was sticking out of the water with its head buried beneath it. "What the hell's going on around here anyway? Why is everything frozen?"

The Mischievous One looked around. "The gods are creating."

"Creating what?"

"They've pulled Dragonia out of its orbit and are moving it to a new location. I believe Dragonia has become the new Hell."

George threw up his hands. "Kepler is on Dragonia. How will he get back? Will he be able to teleport home?"

Lasidious shook his head. "Kepler is doomed."

"Doomed? Can't you do something about it?"

"I cannot. Well, not right now anyway. The cat will have to figure out a way to survive until I have the power to control the gods. Once I can, I'll return your friend to you."

George walked to the edge of the ship and placed his hands on the railing.

"Kep is going to be pissed off. I pity the fool that's in front of him when he figures it out."

Lasidious could not stop focusing on the scruff on George's face. He closed the distance between them and touched the warlock on the shoulder. A moment later, the stubble fell to the deck of the ship and left George clean shaven. Satisfied, the Mischievous One continued with the conversation. "The cat isn't alone. The King of Brandor is with him."

George rubbed his hand across his face as he responded. "Why would Sam be on Dragonia?"

"Sam fled to that world after he ended the old man. He fled to escape the consequences of his kingdom's laws."

A look of understanding appeared on George's face. "So that's where he bailed to. I was wondering where he was. I bet Sam will be just as pissed once he realizes he's stuck." The warlock turned to take a seat and then scanned the frozen figures of the crew. "Tell me. Why am I not frozen like they are?"

Lasidious moved to stand next to one of the officers who had been yelling at a member of the crew while he climbed a rope ladder. "I was going to ask you the same thing. I only came to see if my suspicions were correct."

"What the heck are you talking about?"

"Only those with godly memories did not fall into stasis. You know more than you're telling me, George."

The warlock's brow furrowed. "What the hell are you talking about? I know of the gods, sure, but I don't have any of their memories. I know only what I've learned from you since my arrival."

Lasidious scowled. "So you claim."

"And that's the truth!"

The Mischievous One fell silent as George stared him down. A long series of moments passed before Lasidious spoke again. "Perhaps there's more to you than even you know. For now, I'll trust you." He moved to George and placed his hands on the warlock's shoulders. "Whether you can recall your memories or not, they exist. At one point or another, you have employed the use of these memories since you've arrived, or you would be standing in stasis like the others. Perhaps Bassorine knew that I had chosen you. I only wish I knew the depth of his manipulations."

George shook his head. "Dude, you're freaking me out. What the hell are you talking about?"

Lasidious rolled his eyes. "It doesn't matter, George, does it? You want your daughter, right?"

"Damn straight. I've busted my butt for you, because that's all I care about."

Lasidious smiled. "And you've done a fine job. Everything else that needs to be done, I can handle from here on out."

George clapped his hands again. "Great! And I can't wait to hold Abbie."

After a moment of enjoying the warlock's excitement, Lasidious' candor turned serious. "George ... I went to Susanne's home and took Garrin. The boy will be with me and his mother for the next 60 Peaks."

"Why now?" The warlock pointed at his own chest. "Garrin has become a part of my family. You can't just take him."

Lasidious nodded. "I know you love the boy, but you knew this Peak would come. I'm only telling you as a courtesy. I didn't want you to worry."

George's face tightened. "Of course, I'm going to worry. I love Garrin."

The Mischievous One adjusted the hood of his robe. "The boy is safe. I'll return the child to you after I accomplish our goals."

George pointed at the Lasidious. "You'd better ... because if you don't, I'll blow the whistle. I'll make sure the gods know what you're up to."

Lasidious ignored the threat and then reached into the pocket of his robe and removed a small stone. It was black, smooth and perfectly round. He tossed the pebble to George. "When you get home, all you need to do is place this stone into the hands of each member in your family. Once this has been done, peace will fall upon them. They won't feel the loss of Garrin until he's returned."

George threatened again. "Don't think for a moment that I won't sacrifice getting my Abbie back if you don't give Garrin back to me. I'll turn on you so fast it isn't funny."

Lasidious grinned. "As I have said ... Garrin will be returned once our goals are accomplished." The Mischievous One closed the gap between them and placed his hands on the warlock's shoulders. "You'll have both Garrin *and Abbie* within 100 Peaks. I have no desire to lose my immortality because I angered you." Lasidious vanished.

George stared at the spot where Lasidious had been and scoffed. "What an ass."

MEANWHILE, A LOCATION UNKNOWN
THE SHACK OF ANAHITA

When Anahita opened her eyes, she was the only one inside the shack—or so she thought. The part human, part angel rolled to the edge of the cot and placed her feet on the dirt floor. After wiping the sleep out of her eyes, she stretched. Her arms extended to either side, and though she did not realize they were there, the wings on her back spread to stretch as well. It was not until the tip of one of her feathers touched the wall that she jumped to her feet and ran away from the cot.

Spinning around, the confused angel looked toward the bed. As she did, she caught a glimpse of the end of her right wing. For the next series of moments, she looked like a dog chasing its tail, spinning while she peered over her shoulder to get a better look.

Anahita stopped spinning only after she was out of breath and realized that her wings were not a threat. She took another moment to scan her surroundings. Seeing the dressing mirror at the back of the shack, she rushed across the room and stopped in front of it.

"Oh, my goodness-gracious!" she exclaimed while grabbing her face. None of her features were the same. Her eyes were green, her hair was brunette, and her skin was olive.

She caressed her cheeks and her new neckline for a long series of moments before her wings regained her attention. Turning from side to side, she studied them. "They're beautiful," she giggled. Anahita touched her face again. "I'm beautiful."

Spinning around and around, she eventually stopped and faced the mirror. She tried to spread her wings but found that she was unable to do so. Again, she focused, and again, she failed. Anahita sighed. "Well if that don't beat all. What good are they if I can't use them?"

As she continued to study the splendor of her new anatomy, her eyes had no choice but to fall onto the reflection of her gown. Reaching down, she pulled at the fabric. "Figures," she muttered. "Only he would put such beauty in horrible fashion. How can an angel be expected to represent in terrible fabrics?"

Anahita was about to use her power to turn the gown into something far more fashionable when another entity inside her being took control. Her head snapped away from the fabric and turned toward the mirror. Her eyes widened, and then her mouth opened. "Child, Child, Child, Child, Child! What has he done to me?"

Hearing the familiar voice, Anahita tried to answer, but Helga's emotions would not allow Anahita to regain control of the body they now shared. Helga continued to shout as she turned away from the mirror. "Shalee, where are you, Child?"

When Helga paused to wait for an answer, Anahita had the chance to regain control. "I'm right here, Helga. Stop shouting."

Again, Helga's anxiety took over. She spun, looking in every direction. "Where, Child?"

Yet again, Anahita was able to respond. "Would you stop flailing all about? You're fixin' to make me sick. Just turn us around and look into the mirror."

It was a while before Helga's emotions would allow her to comply. Facing the mirror, she stared at their reflection. "Now what?"

Helga watched Anahita take control of their lips. "Something is telling me that Michael messed up. We're stuck in the same body."

"That's impossible," Helga retorted.

Regaining control of their mouth, Shalee frowned. "Don't tell me that's impossible. I've seen some pretty crazy things since I got to these worlds." Anahita stomped her foot. "This really chaps my hide."

"There must be another explanation, Child."

"Is that so? What kind of explanation are you talking about?"

"Perhaps we're dreaming."

Anahita forced their right hand to reach over and pinch their left forearm.

"Ouch! Stop that!" Helga squealed.

"See? Told you. Looks like we're not dreaming after all."

"It's just not possible, Child."

"Really? Then tell me why I'm watching you fuss at me with the same mouth I'm using? Explain that one, why don't you?" Anahita crossed their arms. "And stop calling me, Child."

Anahita's short temper brought an awkward silence to the room. They stood there staring at the mirror for a long series of moments when suddenly, they both lost control of their body. Their eyes narrowed as they dropped toward the reflection of their bosom.

"Aaaahhhh! I have breasts!" BJ screamed in yet another voice that sounded like his. As the old trainer's emotions continued to keep control, he grabbed them. A moment later, his eyes dropped further down their reflection. All three personalities felt their heart fall as BJ reached down between their legs. "No, no, no, no, no! It's gone!"

The emotions of the moment allowed Helga to regain control. "BJ, is that you?"

"Of course, it's him!" Anahita snapped. "It sounds just like him." Able to take control of their free hand, she used it to slap the one that BJ was controlling. "Stop feeling us up, you pervert!"

Admonished, BJ stopped fumbling.

Once again, an awkward series of moments passed before Anahita spoke. "Look, y'all, it's obvious we're all a little tense. We need to take a step back and settle down. Helga, I'm sorry for yelling at you, and BJ, I'm sorry for hitting you … or us … I guess."

Helga's response was soft. "It's okay, Child. I still love you … love us." She took a long, deep breath. "This is so strange."

"I agree. I'm feeling a little crazy," Anahita replied. "BJ, are you okay?"

The weapons trainer did not respond.

"I said, BJ, are you okay?" When he never answered, Anahita barked, "Answer me, doggonit!"

Another silent series of moments passed. Eventually, Helga took control and stepped closer to the mirror. She gazed at the reflection of their eyes and spoke in a soft voice. "BJ, talk to us. We know you're there, honey."

BJ's emotions took control. Their hands lifted and covered their eyes. He started to sob.

Helga and Anahita took pity. They did not try to regain control to stop the trainer from crying. Instead, they allowed him to mourn the loss of his manhood.

Now, fellow soul ... I feel I need to stop the telling of this tale to clear a few things up. If Grayham, Harvestom, Trollcom, Luvelles, and the new Dragon World had not fallen into stasis, it would have been the following morning for those beings who were experiencing night when stasis began. Instead, when stasis lifted, each being continued the rest of their Peak as if nothing ever happened.

Every soul without godly memories now had no recollection of Dragonia's existence. Every book, scroll, letter and map was altered. The leaders of every village, town, and city were given new processes to deal with criminals since they would no longer be sending them to Dragonia, and these changes felt as if they had always existed.

Regarding the new Hell—this world continued to travel through space for a period of moments equal to 4 Peaks before the gods stopped it. Once that happened, the gods created a new star and placed it far enough away from the planet to ensure Hell was capable of supporting life. Next, three additional moons, all various sizes, were created. They were set to rotate around Hell on different orbits at different distances, but not all of the moons triggered the weres' transformations.

Before those who stood in stasis on Hell would be allowed to reanimate, the gods had to set this minor solar system in motion. They had to watch it function for 10 Peaks while they made final adjustments. Because of the increase in size to the planet, Hell's equator split what was once known as the mainland of Dragonia. This world's Peaks became much longer, doubling what they once were. Never again did the beings on Dragonia experience the same length of seasons they once knew.

For Sam, it was good that Lasidious left him with enough food and water to survive. In total, Sam sat for a period of moments equal to 14 Peaks before Kepler stepped out of stasis. But as I move forward with this tale, I must continue during a series of moments that passed while the new Hell was still sitting in stasis.

Fellow soul … allow me to explain the chain of events in order to bring you up to speed. After leaving the frigid lands of Northern Grayham, Lasidious took the sleeping Mosley to Alistar's palace in the Plains of Bounty on Ancients Sovereign. With the Collective busy, Alistar's home was vacant. The Mischievous One laid the unconscious wolf on his brother's bed and then vanished to find George on the Agregan Ocean.

Once stasis lifted from all the worlds, except Hell, the Mischievous One returned to Alistar's home to retrieve the wolf. He scooped the wolf into his arms and then teleported to the priestess' palace on Harvestom.

THE WORLD OF HARVESTOM
THE PRIESTESS' PALACE

ALL PRAISES BE TO HELMEP FOR THROUGH HIS LOVING GRACE THE WRETCHED ARE HEALED.

Lowering the wolf to the floor of the foyer, Lasidious took a moment to look at his reflection in the granite. Smirking, the god stood and admired the many yellow hues present throughout the stone work of the palace. To his right and left, staircases ascended to a second level that followed the length of the corridor before they turned toward one another and met at the far end of the foyer. From this point, two other staircases rose to a third level.

A long, wide, red tapestry with gold trim and black lettering cascaded past the second level and stopped just above an entrance to a great room that had pillars spanning its length. The tapestry read:

ALL PRAISES BE TO HELMEP
FOR THROUGH HIS LOVING GRACE
THE WRETCHED ARE HEALED

"Loving grace, indeed," Lasidious sneered. "How pathetic."

The Mischievous One knew the priestess' palace was grand. With more than 50 bedroom chambers to the west, the east side of the palace was equally as large, housing an enormous kitchen, spacious dining hall and a massive painting room.

The priestess' prayer chamber was unlike any other on the worlds. At the center of the room was a large stone with a flat surface that hovered above a deep shaft that fell more than 300 paces into the darkness below the palace. At the center of the stone was a symbol that had been etched into its surface. Only the priestess and Helmep knew the meaning of the symbol. Lasidious had spent many of his moments trying to pry this information out of both the God of Healing and the priestess, but neither would divulge its meaning.

Lasidious' voice echoed throughout the palace as he announced his arrival. "There are visitors amongst you, Priestess!"

It was not long before a lovely woman with black and red hair walked through a door and stopped at the railing on the third level. Looking down and seeing her visitors, the priestess turned from the railing, snapped her fingers and then called out to an unseen being that had remained in the room from which she had emerged. "See to their studies, Daydoden! Upon my return, I shall administer a test!"

The priestess vanished and reappeared at the center of the foyer. As she approached, the Mischievous One took note of her red dress. The garment had a high collar, laced with gold, and it swayed gracefully as she walked.

Lasidious lowered to one knee and bowed his head. "It has been too long since we last spoke, Priestess. Please, allow me to offer my condolences for your mother's passing. She was a beacon of kindness."

Fosalia Rowaine smiled. "Your words are too true, Barramore. If only my mother could have laid her eyes upon you during her last moments. The face of her truest love would've given her abundant joy."

"You are too kind," Lasidious responded. "But alas, my service to Helmep has kept me detained. I begged Helmep to release me from the burdens that kept me from your mother, but as you know, his will must be done."

"Agreed. A wretch's service leads to a blessed life."

Lasidious nodded and passed his hand across Mosley's unconscious figure.

Intrigued, the priestess knelt next to the wolf and placed her left hand on the fur of his neck. "Barramore, what have you brought me?"

"A full vessel."

Fosalia looked up, her eyes wide with disbelief. A moment later, she looked down and passed her eyes across Mosley's body. "How could this be?"

"There's more," Lasidious urged. "The beast speaks the languages of the Ancient Mystics and the Swayne Enserad. He speaks them fluently."

Fosalia stood and took a few steps back. "That's impossible, Barramore. Never did you bring my mother such a vessel. How could this beast speak that which he knows not how to command?"

Lasidious shrugged, "Perhaps you should ask him." The Mischievous One took a step toward the priestess. "The wolf will wake soon. I did as you asked. Like the others, he knows not the way to your palace."

The priestess stared at Mosley for a brief period of moments before she lifted the hem of her dress and turned to leave. "Wait here."

Before Lasidious could object, Fosalia rushed across the foyer and passed through an archway that led to her herb room. In her absence, the god knelt next to the wolf and whispered in Mosley's ear. "You know not the name Lasidious. You know only the name Bassorine whom you once served." He waved his hand across the top of Mosley's head. "Remember not our past encounters, and remember not your moments on Northern Grayham. May they be forgotten until the moment they are returned to you."

The Mischievous One stood as Fosalia reentered the room. After crossing the foyer, she knelt on the opposing side of Mosley. She reached into a brown, leather pouch and retrieved a pinch of dust.

Scattering the dust across the wolf's body, she chanted, *"Ora gorme sez yalla tafoe."* As soon as the last word was spoken, the fur on Mosley's body began to glow.

Fosalia jumped to her feet and took a step back. She could not pull her eyes off the wolf's coat as she addressed Lasidious. "You're right, Barramore. His vessel is full. What can you tell me about the beast?"

"Nothing other than I found him on Southern Grayham. He was wandering the abandoned lands of a territory known as Neutral. He had walked for many Peaks without food and water when I came upon him. He was babbling in the language of the Swayne Enserad, so I brought him directly to you."

"You did well, Barramore. My mother would have been as pleased as I am." Fosalia paused, and then a look of concern appeared on her face. "No one can know of his presence here."

Though he knew the answer, Lasidious played the part. "Why?"

The priestess sighed, "It has been only 30 Peaks since my mother's passing. This beast is my first vessel. The Dragon Council has already expressed concern. They say my seasons are too few to be capable of executing the duties of High Priestess."

"They'd be wrong," Lasidious rebutted. "Did you tell them that?"

"I did."

"When?"

"The morning before yesterday's Peak. It was then when I met with the Dragon Council."

Lasidious nodded. "Did you demonstrate your power?"

"I did."

"And was it enough?"

"No." Ashamed, Fosalia turned away.

"So what happened?"

Wiping a tear from her cheek, the priestess took a deep breath. "The Dragon Council voted that I be replaced. They said I was unworthy of my post."

"Yet you still stand here. How's that possible?"

"After hearing the council's vote, the Source spoke in my favor. The Ancient One said he saw greatness in me. He said my heart was pure, and that alone made me worthy."

"Is that what it took for the council to change its vote?"

Fosalia sniffled. "No. The council refused to change their vote. I would not be here now, but the Source's vote superseded the others."

"I see." Lasidious walked past the priestess and looked to the ceiling. "I never tire of this place." He put his right hand to his chin and pretended to study the architecture while he thought, *Why would the Mighty One inter-*

fere? Does he do it to toy with the gods? Lasidious turned and watched the priestess kneel next to Mosley. *I suppose it matters not. The Ancient One's whim can be used in my favor.*

Lasidious pulled his hand away from his chin and questioned. "Will the Dragon Council's concern stop you from instructing this vessel? Will they be angry if they find out?"

The priestess did not respond. Instead, she placed both hands on Mosley's chest. She closed her brown eyes and felt the wolf's heartbeat. A long series of moments passed before she reopened them. "He's strong. To deny him tutelage would be unacceptable."

"Then you will deliver instruction?"

Fosalia lifted from the floor and stood in front of Lasidious. "Yes, Barramore, but if word reaches the Dragon Council, they'll ask the Source to reconsider his vote. They already believe I'm incapable of running this school in an efficient manner. The Source would never believe me capable of instructing my students while working to unleash the beast's potential."

Lasidious leaned over and whispered into the priestess' ear, "Then I'll keep my mouth shut. I suggest you do the same."

Fosalia nodded. "Yes, Father."

The Mischievous One frowned. "I asked you never to call me that."

Fosalia's eyes dropped to the floor. "I'm sorry. I simply miss you, and the wolf is asleep and cannot hear me say it."

Reaching forward, Lasidious placed his hand beneath her chin and lifted her head. "I miss you as well. But you must understand why you can't call me that."

The priestess nodded, "I do. I won't slip again."

After a soft kiss on Fosalia's cheek, Lasidious changed the direction of the conversation. "Something tells me the wolf will learn at a rapid pace. I'll return in 30 Peaks to check on his progress." Lasidious vanished.

CHAPTER 10
FRAGILE MORTAL MINDS
NORTHERN GRAYHAM
2 PEAKS LATER

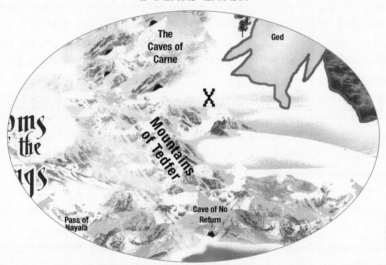

X MARKS CLANNY AND MEDOLAS' LOCATION
NEAR THE MOUNTAINS OF TEDFER

Medolas looked over his shoulder at the daunting peaks that he and Clandestiny had descended the Peak before. He never tired of admiring the treacherous expanse of the Mountains of Tedfer. Their majesty was too awe-inspiring.

Turning back, he smiled at Clandestiny, pushed her long, milky hair behind her ears and then looked northeast toward the city of Hydroth that they knew was waiting more than 50 Peaks from where they stood.

"I wonder what trials lay ahead?" Medolas said as he looked toward the horizon.

Clandestiny did not respond. Her mind was elsewhere.

"Did you hear me, Clanny?" He stroked her cheek.

"My conscience suffers, Meddy," Clandestiny responded after looking up to find Medolas' gray eyes. "I cannot comprehend why the wolf would abandon us. Did we do something ill against him?"

Medolas smiled and then leaned down to kiss her. "Your conscience may sleep well at night. We did nothing wrong."

"But what if something has happened to him? Perhaps we should return to seek his whereabouts."

Medolas' brow furrowed, and then he turned to look at the mountains. "Have you become irrational? The wolf abandoned us. We did nothing against him. We should push forward." He grabbed Clandestiny's hand and started walking. "Besides … where would we look? One moment, the wolf was standing beside us, and the next, he was gone … like vapor."

Clandestiny forced Medolas to stop. She reached up and placed her hands on either side of his face. "Do you think Mosley used his magic to leave us? Do you think he's safe?"

Medolas frowned. "Why must you always ask me questions that I cannot answer? How am I to know such things?"

Annoyed, Clanny pulled her hands away and started walking with her arms crossed. The pysples on the bottom of her feet popped as they released the ice to ensure Medolas could hear her irritation.

"Aww … come now, Clanny. Don't fret over naught. I'm sure the wolf fares well." Medolas closed the gap between them and pulled Clandestiny close. "I didn't mean to cause your mind unnecessary stress."

A few moments of silence passed before Clandestiny softened. "I know. You're forgiven." She lowered her head onto Medolas' shoulder. "I simply don't understand. Mosley enjoyed our association, did he not?"

"Of course, he did."

"Then why abandon us when I was so fond of him?"

Despite his best effort to stop it, a large grin appeared on Medolas' face. He started to chuckle.

Clanny lifted her head from Medolas' shoulder. "What could possibly be funny? This is a crisis, Meddy. Our friend is missing."

Medolas lifted a hand and motioned for the moments necessary to compose himself. "You're right. I apologize."

Eyes glaring, Clandestiny demanded an explanation. "I asked, why do you think Mosley abandoned us? The wolf knew his companionship was desired. How could this be funny?"

Though Medolas tried to fight it, another grin appeared. "Perhaps you smothered him like you did the other sudwals you commanded."

Clanny reached out and slapped Medolas' arm. "How dare you speak such illness to me. The wolf was fond of my affections. He adored the way I stroked his back."

Medolas nodded. "He liked the way you scratched his ears as well." He leaned in and kissed her forehead. "You fret too much."

Clanny grabbed Medolas by the ears and held his head steady in front of hers. "I fret as much as is necessary. Those whom I love recognize my affections are genuine."

Medolas was about to respond when he noticed two figures over Clanny's left shoulder. They were traveling across the ice in the distance. He placed his right hand on the top of Clandestiny's head and forced her to take a knee. "Get down," he ordered.

Confused, the Isorian female did as instructed. Her eyes followed Medolas' finger as he pointed across the ice. The strange beings looked like nothing they had ever seen. "What are they?" Clanny whispered.

Medolas rolled his eyes. *Yet another question I cannot answer,* he thought. A moment later, he responded, "I don't know." He moved his finger and pointed to the south. A large pack of snowhounds was stalking the beings from behind. "They're in danger. They'll need your help."

Clanny gasped. "Meddy, we must hurry, or they'll be devoured."

"We may be too late." Medolas grabbed Clandestiny's hand and began sprinting across the ice toward the strangers.

As Gage and Gallrum made their way across the frozen terrain, the badger tapped his cane against the ice. Despite the layers of clothing they had acquired from the town of Edsmar before they headed north through the Cave of No Return, they had been forced to use their magic to stay warm—and on top of it all, they still had no idea where they were going. Yet something was compelling the badger to push forward. His instincts were fueled by the dream he had on Luvelles, and they were telling him that they were headed in the right direction.

Suddenly, Gallrum commanded Gage to stop. The serwin's wings slowed the pace in which they were fluttering so he could lower to the ice. He turned and looked to the south. Gallrum's ears perked up. "Something is coming. Be prepared."

Gage also looked to the south and listened. "The noise is not far off."

The badger lifted his cane. "I'll shield us from whatever approaches." As soon as Gage saw the pack of snowhounds crest the last of the undulating shelves, the badger used his power to put up a dome of force. "These beasts hunt to fill their bellies," he said while watching the speed in which the hounds covered the terrain.

"What magic do you think they possess?" Gallrum questioned.

"None, let's hope. Though I'd hate to feel the pain of their bite."

Gallrum moved behind Gage for protection. "Me, too."

The badger looked over his shoulder at the serwin. "Really? You would use me as a shield?"

Gallrum shrugged and then gave a halfhearted grin. "Better they eat you first than me."

Gage turned around. "You irritate me."

Seeing Gage and Gallrum standing still, the pack's growls amplified as they drew near. Once they were within striking distance, the pack leader leapt skyward, intending to come down on top of his prey. His jaws opened, but the impact against the invisible barrier slammed them shut.

As the snowhound's lower and upper jaw smashed together, his teeth pierced his tongue. His momentum forced the rest of his body to double over while the other hounds tried to stop, but there was no room. Their claws could not grip the ice fast enough to keep them from colliding into the wall. One behind another, they heaped together until 8 of the 13 hounds were yelping.

Gage and Gallrum grimaced as the pack leader howled in pain. The weight of the other seven had snapped both of his front legs. Though frightened, the badger wanted to lower the dome of force to help, but to do so would only entice the other beasts to attack. He would be forced to use his magic to end them, and the thought of slaying innocent creatures was unthinkable.

As the hounds regrouped, they threw themselves into the invisible barrier. It was not long before they learned that this approach would not work and began to circle the goswigs. Their snarls intensified as they searched for an opening.

Eventually, one of the female hounds started to claw at the ice. She was much smaller than the rest, and she had lowered her nose to a crack in the ice where she could smell Gage and Gallrum's scent.

Gallrum was frantic. "What should we do?"

"I don't know, but we can't hurt them."

"Why?" the serwin shouted.

"Because they haven't wronged us!" Gage replied over the top of the snarls. "They're only doing what comes natural for them!"

Gallrum could not believe his ears. He hollered, "Are you mad?" He pointed at the biggest of the hounds. "It wants to eat us! This may be natural for them ... but it's not natural for me!" He grabbed the hat on his head with both hands. "I don't want to perish!"

The badger jabbed the end of the serwin's tail with his cane.

"Ouch!"

"Be quiet! I need to think!" Gage instructed as he turned his attention to the female hound. She had already dug a sizable hole into the ice, and now her left paw was reaching under the magic of the barrier. *What to do,* he thought. *If I extend the field, her paw will be trapped. She'd be crippled.*

Soon, both of the hound's front legs were reaching under the barrier as the hole grew.

"She's going to crawl under!" Gallrum shouted. "We must strike her down."

"No!" Gage rebutted. "I won't take an innocent life!"

"Then we'll perish!"

Gage thought for a moment. "Perhaps we should teleport away from here and begin our trek again."

Before Gallrum could respond, a deafening sound erupted from more than 100 paces southwest of their position. It was loud—so loud that the goswigs had to cover their ears to stop the pain.

Instantly, the hounds stopped attacking. The 12 who could still run escaped to the north, yelping as they darted across the terrain.

Medolas kept his hands over his ears until Clandestiny finished her roar. She had perfected the call of the gashtion over the last 300 seasons, and Medolas grinned as he watched the snowhounds run away. "Be off with you!" he shouted.

Clandestiny grabbed Medolas' elbow. "There's only one left, Meddy … and it appears wounded."

Reaching down to his ankle, Medolas unsheathed his knife. "I'll handle that one. Your job is complete." He started to run toward the crippled hound.

Clandestiny called after him. "Wait, Meddy! You didn't tell me if I sounded like the real gashtion."

Medolas stopped running and turned around. "Must you always ask me that? Do your eyes not see the result? Are there any hounds here?"

Clanny crossed her arms in a huff. "Well, you don't have to be so ill-mannered about it!"

The Isorian male rolled his eyes and then headed for the hound.

Dropping her arms to her side, Clandestiny barked, "Errrrr, that man!"

Medolas stopped about five paces from the hound. Seeing that the wolf was whimpering and both of the pack leader's legs were snapped, he realized there was no threat. The Isorian took a moment to study the goswigs who had already removed their invisible barrier and took a step back. "What are you?" he questioned. "You wear clothes like men."

Gage knew the blue being was speaking in a different language, but for whatever reason, he understood it. Without responding to Medolas, the badger turned and looked at Gallrum. "Did you also understand it?"

The serwin nodded. "I did, but I don't know how."

Before Gage could respond, Medolas demanded, "I asked, what are you?"

The badger tapped the end of his cane on the ice and then pointed it at Medolas. "Perhaps we should be asking you the same, blue being."

The way the goswig responded caused the Isorian to study the color of his skin. A moment later, he shook off the awkwardness. "The hounds would've ended you if we had not intervened."

Gallrum slapped Gage on his back. "Ha! It thinks it saved us."

Gage looked up and gave the serwin a nasty glare. "Must you always speak before you think?" He redirected his gaze to Medolas. "Thank you for your assistance. Your presence was a blessing. Lasidious be praised."

Medolas scowled. "Helmep is the one who should be praised for sparing your lives."

Gallrum would have argued, but Gage instinctively poked the end of the serwin's tail with his cane. "Not now, Gallrum. Be quiet." Again, the badger looked at Medolas. "If it was, indeed, your god who spared us … then we thank him."

"Ohhh … he's adorable, Meddy!" Clandestiny announced as she walked up from behind Medolas and passed him on her way to Gage. She knelt in front of the badger. "Look at you. Do you speak?"

"Of course, he speaks!" Gallrum snapped.

Hearing the serwin's response, Clanny stood. "And what are you? You appear to be part man, part sea serpent and…" She looked over his shoulder and studied the serwin's wings. "…and part ice bat. Did your mother mate with those creatures?"

The look on the serwin's face caused Gage to laugh. The badger took the opportunity to respond. "No. His mother and father share similar features. Where we're from, his whole race looks that way."

Clandestiny reached out and grabbed the serwin's left claw. She played with the scales on the back of it. "How tragic. Do these hardened flakes itch?"

The conversation was interrupted by a sharp yelp. The group turned to look as Medolas removed his knife from the jugular of the snowhound. The Isorian wiped his blade on the fur of the pack leader's coat and questioned, "Is anyone hungry?"

MEANWHILE, THE CITY OF HYDROTH
THE LEGISLATIVE CHAMBER OF THE ISORIAN COUNCIL

After escaping the throne room of the undercastle, Shiver and Gablysin rode their harugens for 2 Peaks before Shiver stopped their progress. The young king made the decision to return to Hydroth and fight. They would gather the army to end Shiver's grandfather, but upon their return, Shiver learned that his grandfather had left the city.

The young king was standing before the council. "Yes, Ohedri, your point has been acknowledged," Shiver responded. "I'm not Isorian. I was not yester Peak, nor will I be on the morrow. But my loyalty to this kingdom won't be questioned. The crown was bestowed upon me by this council, and there are no laws that would allow you to remove it from my head."

Gablysin stepped forward and pointed at each member of the council. "The Isorian army listens to me. Shiver's grandfather will return. Be assured, his army shall be vast." He looked Ohedri in the eye. "You know me, and you understand the sincerity of my words. Know this: this council shall respect the crown. If you cannot, you'll be replaced."

Arath stood from her chair and leaned forward with her hands flat against the table. The large, wrinkled crease of her bosom temporarily captured the attention of every man in the room. "Who do you think you are? Prophesy or no, you don't command this council." She looked at the others. "We don't have to listen to them."

The ruby eyed man unsheathed his sword and pointed it across the table. "Are those your last words, Arath? If so, I'll end you now. For in my opinion, your words are treasonous." Gablysin studied Arath's seasons. Though still large, her frame was now frail, just as the rest of the council members. "You're not young enough to oppose me." He looked at the others. "None of you are."

Shiver put his hand on Gablysin's shoulder. "Your point has been made, Commander. I can handle it from here."

The ruby eyed man sheathed his sword and turned to bow. "My Lord." He took a seat at the table.

Shiver rolled out a map of the kingdom. "The only way my grandfather can attack is to bring his forces through the Caves of Carne. We'll ready our army for his advance."

Poemas' fat belly rubbed against the table as he stood and spoke through stained teeth. "It'll take the Tormal more than 100 Peaks to travel from Gesper to Hydroth. Why must we activate the full strength of the army now?"

Shiver smiled. "Many a night did my father … my true father, Thoomar, teach me strategies of war. Because of his wisdom, the Frigid Commander and I have been able to devise a plan. Our army shall tunnel west beyond Hydroth for 10 Peaks to this point. He marked an X on the map just west of the city.

"Once this has been done, we shall create a lengthy and massive hollow beneath the ice. East of this hollow is where our army shall make its stand. Many Tormalians will lose their lives as the weight of their army breaks through the ice."

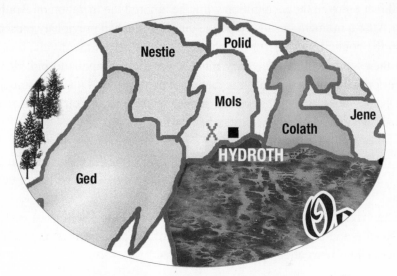

X MARKS THE SPOT FOR THE HOLLOW

"And after the ice breaks?" Arath sneered. "What then? You may be able to create a lengthy crevice that spans a great distance, but you cannot create a hollow wide enough to fit their entire army in such a short period of Peaks. And answer this: what of those Tormalians who fail to fall?"

Gablysin was quick to reply, "We'll flood the cavern."

Again, Arath sneered. "That won't accomplish anything. Our enemy can breathe beneath the water. If they don't perish, that won't stop them. They'd simply cross the divide." She glared at Shiver. "You, of anyone, should know that, Tormalian."

The ruby eyed man stood and unsheathed his sword again, but Shiver was quick to respond. "Relax. You must remember … those are the words of a senile, old woman."

Arath started to rebut, but the young king shouted over her, "Enough, Arath! Sit, or I'll have you removed from this council! I'll see to it that you are shamed amongst your clan."

Crossing her arms, Arath allowed her heft to flop back onto her seat.

Drydeth, leader of the Nestie clan, leaned forward. He was nearing his end. "I never thought that I'd see the Peak that Thoomar's son would govern this council with such authority." He pointed at Arath, though he held Shiver's gaze. "Any man who can shut the gaping hole that woman calls a mouth deserves my respect. The Nestie clan will follow you, Sire."

Shiver enjoyed the recognition while he ignored the irritation on Arath's face. After a moment, he answered the question she had previously presented to the council. "If the Tormal choose to swim across the divide, they'll find themselves vulnerable. They must lower their weapons to pull themselves onto the embankment. It is there that our army will make its stand."

Ohedri spoke up. "What of the tunnel leading to the city? Will it be sealed? We cannot allow the city to be flooded, My King."

Shiver nodded. "It will be sealed."

The leader of the Meslan clan continued. "What of the gashtion? If it attacks, this will leave the army vulnerable. Their only escape will have been sealed."

The Frigid Commander responded. "A second tunnel will exist east of the cavern, and alcoves will be dug. Much of the army will remain below the ice. They'll be called upon only as needed."

THE NEXT MORNING
NORTHERN GRAYHAM
ATOP THE ICE, JUST EAST OF THE CITY OF GESPER

From the back of his harugen, the withered Tormalian, King Meerum Bosand, looked at his Frigid Commander and the 10 Legion Leaders of his army who sat on harugens of their own. All his men were dressed in their finest armor, and they had just finished their inspection of the ranks.

The king nodded his approval of the commander's posture and then passed his eyes across his officers before he scanned the vastness of his army. "We are 36,000 strong, Grandon. You serve me well."

"Thank you, My King. Soon, you shall be the ruler of a united kingdom. Your crusade to conquer the lands of the north shall be realized before your passing." Grandon slung his right arm across his chest and pounded his left shoulder with his fist. All the legion leaders followed suit. "Hail the King!"

A moment later, Meerum doubled over and started to cough.

Grandon dropped his arm and moved his harugen into a better position to shield the king's weakness from the eyes of his men.

Phlegm spewed from Meerum's lungs and covered the palm of his right hand with a dark secretion.

"Can I get you anything, Your Grace?"

It took a moment before Meerum was able to regain his composure. He wiped the phlegm onto the back of his harugen's shoulder and then responded. "No, nothing." The king paused. "On second thought, you can fetch me a victory, Commander. I want to see the look of defeat spread across the faces of the Isor before my sickness claims me." The king forced himself to resume a regal posture. "Make me proud, Grandon. Command the army to march."

The commander lowered his head in reverence. "Yes, My Lord."

MEANWHILE, THE SHACK OF ANAHITA

Anahita took control of the body she shared with BJ and Helga. "I've had enough of this pouting, you two. Y'all are driving me crazy."

Maintaining control of their motor skills, Anahita stood from the cot and stormed across the dirt floor of the shack. She stopped in front of the mirror and pointed at their reflection. "We've been sitting around for Peaks. I can't take it any longer." She poked at the chest of their reflection. "We have a job to do.

"Bassorine …" Anahita paused. "I mean, Michael..." She took a deep breath. "Michael said we need to create a new Heaven." She pointed at the mirror. "Do you know where to start, because I sure don't? And we aren't going to figure it out if y'all keep crying, doggonit! We can't replace the bodies you lost, so you might as well stop pissing and moaning about it."

Again, Anahita paused, but during this series of moments, she refused to release control of their body so the others could reply. "BJ, you're the worst offender. We can't get anything done because of your sniveling. You've got to stop and help us."

Anahita looked at the reflection of their wings and then at the ceiling before she redirected her hostility back to the mirror. "BJ, this is hard on me, too, you know. Don't make me push you to the back of our mind. I know how to do it, and I will if you force me to."

Hearing how harsh she sounded, the part angel, part human sighed and then softened her approach. "Look. I love you both, but you're driving me bonkers."

Anahita released control and waited for BJ to respond, but when he never did, Helga seized the opportunity to speak. "Something's wrong, Child." She placed their right hand over their heart. "Something is terribly wrong."

"What do you mean?" Anahita replied.

Helga surrounded their body with both arms. "Last night while you were sleeping, I felt something strange. The sensation was like a sudden chill and then an enormous loss. It was as if something perished within us." Helga gazed at the reflection of their eyes. "Didn't you feel it?"

Anahita thought for a moment before she responded. "I felt nothing. I slept harder than I've ever slept before."

Again, Helga took control. "I fear that BJ is not with us any longer. He hasn't spoken since we moved from the cot."

"What do you mean? I could've sworn he said somethin'."

Helga took control and faced the mirror. A moment later, she walked toward the table and pulled a chair across the room. Before she could sit, she had to reach behind their body to force their wings apart. Once comfortable, she looked toward the mirror and spoke to their reflection. "Perhaps BJ was incapable of accepting the loss of his manhood. He hated the fact that he was no longer in control of his every action."

Anahita grimaced. "So you think he gave up on us? Where could he have gone?"

"I don't know, Child." Helga's emotions caused their eyes to swell. "Perhaps his love for me was not strong enough to stay with us, or perhaps he couldn't control his departure."

Helga gasped. "What if your anger with him caused him to be imprisoned somewhere within our mind?"

"Why would I do something like that?" Anahita rebutted. "That wouldn't be right."

"Perhaps you couldn't control it, Child."

"I'd never."

Helga reached down with their right hand and fumbled with the fingers on their left. "You said so yourself. You know how to push us to the back of your mind now. What if you pushed him so far back that he can't ever return?"

Anahita captured control. She reached up to wipe the tears from their eyes. "I'd never intentionally hurt either of you. You know that. Please ... tell me you know that. You do know that, right?"

"Of course, Child. You love us like parents. You've said so on many occasions."

Anahita placed their forehead into the palms of their hands. She spoke while sobbing. "If what you're saying is correct, then I'm a horrible person. How could I have been so selfish?"

Helga forced their head to lift. She reclaimed control of their breathing and spoke to their reflection. "You must listen to me, Child. You cannot allow your emotions to control you any longer. If it's your emotions that have done this, then you must find a way to remain calm. Perhaps BJ can return to us if you provide a way for him to do so."

"BJ's return is an impossibility," the Archangel Michael said after appearing near the door of the shack.

Startled by the archangel's sudden appearance, Anahita seized control of their body and stood from the chair. She shouted at Michael. "What have you done to us?" She poked at their chest. "Are we crazy?"

Michael's smile was filled with love. "You're not crazy, my Anahita." He motioned to the chair. "Please, sit."

It took a moment for the ladies to comply. Once they did, the archangel crossed the room and took a knee in front of them. "Anahita ... I only return because you struggle so." Michael stroked her face. "I wanted you to be whole so that, some Peak, you could be mine once again. I've missed you deeply."

Helga rushed to respond. "Oh, my. You're quite the charmer. I know you're not speaking to me, but I must say ... the blood within me is moving to places that it shouldn't. I feel a sweat coming on."

Michael frowned. "Helga ... could you please ... a little privacy?"

Helga sighed. "I'm sorry. I'll go."

Anahita seized control and screamed. "No! You won't go anywhere!" She stood from the chair, stormed across the room, stopped near the door of the shack and looked across the room at their reflection in the mirror. "I can't lose you, Helga! Please don't go anywhere!"

"As you wish, Child."

A moment later, Anahita sighed and then pointed at Michael who was still standing next to the chair at the center of the room. "You lied to me!"

Crossing her arms, Anahita collected her thoughts. "I have a ton of questions for you, buster! You just sit your happy butt in that chair and listen!"

Without saying a word, the archangel did as he was told.

"That's right! You just sit!" she barked. After a moment or two, Anahita started to pace from the door to the mirror and kept at it for a long series of moments while she spoke. "When Sam and I arrived on Grayham, you told us a lot of lies." She stopped next to the mirror. "Tell me ... how could an angel of God ... if you are an angel of God ... lie to us like that? Why would God allow you to do that?"

The archangel shook his head. "Things aren't as simple as they once were."

"What does that mean?" Anahita snapped. "So you can lie whenever it suits you?"

Michael extended his hand and another chair floated across the room and lowered next to the one he was sitting on. "Please ... take a seat. There's much we should discuss. Perhaps you're ready now."

"I don't want to sit!" Anahita argued.

Michael did not respond. Instead, he motioned to the chair and waited.

"Fine! At least tell me how to spread my wings without forcing them open. It'd be a lot easier to sit that way, you know?"

The archangel took the moments necessary to explain. Once Anahita understood, she spread her wings and then lowered onto the chair. "Whatever you're going to say next better be the explanation above all other explanations, or we're done here!"

Michael leaned forward and pulled Anahita's chair closer. "I didn't enjoy lying to you. I despise deception, just as my father does."

"Then why do it? A lot of good it did you." Her eyes narrowed. "Look at me. I'm more than pissed off at you. I'm so mad that I don't even know what to call it."

The archangel frowned. "Are you going to allow me to speak, or shall I return when you're less hostile?"

Anahita's eyes became daggers. "If you leave, don't come back!"

A quiet series of moments passed before Michael decided to continue. "As I was saying ... I despise deception. When you awoke in the temple on Grayham, your mind was not yet prepared to hear the truth. I had to adapt my words to meet what your mind could accept in order to protect you."

Michael stood from his chair and then walked to the door of the shack. Once there, he spread his wings. "Look upon me, my love. This form is glorious, is it not?" He folded his wings and waited for Anahita to respond.

"If you're waiting for me to say something nice, I'm not going to," she sneered.

The archangel sighed. "Still the same old Anahita. Nevertheless, we are unique beings ... blessed beings."

"So what? That doesn't give you the right to lie to me. And what does that have to do with anything?"

"It has everything to do with our current circumstances. The memories we possess within a form such as ours are powerful. When they are ripped from us, along with our souls, they become fragile. They must be treated tenderly."

"Hold on a cotton picking moment. What does that mean?"

Michael crossed his arms. "When our memories and our souls are placed inside a mortal body ... the mind that governs this imperfect form is incapable of handling the transition all at once.

"Because of this, I had to fill your mind with memories that could be accepted as fact. Only now has your mind become capable of handling some more of the truth."

"Some more?" Anahita rebutted. "Why not all the truth?"

Michael smiled. "You always were spirited, but you fail to understand the depth of the power the memories of your former form possessed. If I unleashed them all at once, the human side of you would've been incapable of performing any function at all. Because of this, you would not have been able to finish your transformation, and you would've never been able to reclaim the appearance of your former glory."

"So ... I have the look, but I'm still not complete, am I?"

"You must finish the transformation before your mind is ready to receive all your old memories."

"What do you mean by 'finish the transformation?'"

Michael returned to his seat. "BJ is gone, is he not?"

"Well ... he isn't talking to us anymore, if that's what you mean."

"That's because your mind and soul have absorbed what's left of him. That third of your soul has found its way back to you. An all that is left is for you and Helga to—"

"Don't you dare say it!" Anahita shouted. She extended the palm of her hand and held it in front of Michael's face. "I won't hear that kind of nonsense. Helga isn't going anywhere. She's fine where she's at, aren't you, Helga?"

"Yes, Child. I don't want to leave."

Anahita reclaimed control and glared at Michael. "See? She's happy right where she's at, and don't you dare screw that up."

Michael leaned forward and placed his hands on Anahita's knees. A sense of peace filled her being. "Your third of the soul that you share with BJ and Helga is the dominate third. It's only a matter of moments before Helga becomes a memory. Your body, mind and spirit will be whole once again, and you'll become the angel I once knew."

"I don't want to be that angel!" Anahita snapped. "I want to be the Shalee Helga and BJ knew. I want to live out the rest of my seasons with both of them. I want to be happy, and all of us can live together. I want to be with Sam." She stopped talking. A long pause followed as tears streamed down her face. "I want to live with my baby."

Anahita stood from her chair and walked toward the door. She opened it and looked out into the darkness. "What will happen to Sam Jr.?" She turned away from the door and looked across the room. "Is Sam taking care of him? Does my baby know his mother is missing?" She looked back out the door. "I'm a terrible mother. The baby hasn't even crossed my mind since I woke up in this stupid shack."

Michael vanished from his seat and reappeared next to Anahita. "You're not a terrible mother, nor are you uncaring for misplacing the thoughts of your child." The archangel placed his hand on Anahita's shoulder and then turned her to face him while he closed the door. "Your son is being cared for, but Sam is on a path of destruction."

"What do you mean by that? And who's caring for my baby?"

"Your General Absolute has assumed the throne. He's caring for your son in Sam's absence."

"Explain!" Anahita demanded.

"I'll do my best. I can show you their images, but they will be of the past."

"The past? I want to know what's going on now."

Michael extended his left hand and turned up his palm. A spherical mass appeared above it. "As I said, I can only show you images of the past. It takes a fair number of Peaks for visions from the worlds to find their way to this destination. Events from their Peak will manifest here 3 Peaks from now. Even if I was to teleport to the worlds, it would take 3 Peaks before I arrived. That's how far away from the other worlds are from our location."

Frowning, Anahita grumbled, "So you're saying you brought me to the middle of B.F.E."

A curious look appeared on Michael's face. "I don't know this B.F.E."

"It means, the middle of nowhere!" Anahita snapped.

"Then yes. I brought you here to ensure the others of the Collective could not feel the power of your creations while you mold the new Heaven."

As Anahita pondered Michael's words, an image of Sam appeared inside the sphere above the archangel's palm. She watched as Sam tossed the old cupbearer through the window of the throne room and then rushed to their bedroom chamber. Once Sam had packed, he abandoned the city on his mist mare.

The image went dark and Michael lowered his hand. "That's all I'll show you for now."

"Why?" Anahita snapped. "What are you hiding?"

Michael did not respond.

Annoyed, Anahita kicked at the dirt on the floor. "Can't you at least tell me where he was headed?"

Again, Michael did not respond. Instead, he gave Anahita a look to suggest that she drop the subject.

"Errrrrr!" Anahita grabbed the handle of the door and reopened it. She closed her eyes and tried to teleport, but nothing happened. Eventually, she turned to face Michael and demanded, "At least show me what you can regarding my son!"

The archangel nodded. It was not long before another image appeared above his palm. Michael, the interim King of Brandor, was standing over Sam Jr.'s crib, and he was preparing to tuck a blanket around the prince. Anahita heard Michael whisper as he leaned over, "It appears you'll become a king before you're able to speak, young prince. It also appears your mother and father may never return. But fear not. I'll protect and love you as they would have."

A moment later, the image changed. It looked to Anahita as if the light streaming through Sam Jr.'s nursery window was from the morning sun. What she saw next caused her to cup her hands over her mouth. The prince's caregiver was sitting on a blanket with the young prince at the center of the baby's bedroom chamber. Something captured the woman's attention and caused her to open the door and leave the room. A moment later, a man stepped into the vision and stopped above Sam Jr. The man had a second child with him as he reached down to grab the ends of the prince's blanket to lift the baby off the floor. A moment later, the man and both children vanished just after the caregiver reentered the room. The image went dark and the archangel dropped his hand.

"That's it?" Anahita shouted. "I thought you said my son was being cared for! Where did they go, and who was that guy?"

"The last moment I checked, your son was being cared for." The archangel's eyes dropped to the floor. "That man was Lasidious, but I know nothing regarding their destination or his reason for taking the child. I didn't know of that event."

Anahita stepped forward and got into Michael's face. "Take me to Brandor at once. I need to find my son."

"I can't do that. I don't have the power to take us the distance. The power to return was lost when the Eye of Magic was cracked. When I know more of your son or how the portal was damaged, I'll tell you."

Anahita crossed her arms. "Figures! Only you'd show me images of something you can't do anything about. Did you want me to worry? Are you sick like that?"

Michael nodded. "If worrying will motivate you, then yes, I am sick. With the portal broken, the only way to return to the worlds is if you acquire the power to do so."

"Motivate me?" Anahita barked, "to do what?"

The archangel shook his head. "Must I say it again? You've been brought here to create a new Heaven, Anahita. You are here for that purpose alone."

The depravity of Anahita's stare was enough to cause Michael to feel uneasy. "You're not too bright, are you, buster?" she chastised. "If I can't concentrate ... if I don't know where my son is or if he's okay ... how do you expect me to accomplish anything? You better start searching for some more information."

Michael nodded. "You will know more when I do."

Anahita stared into the darkness beyond the door. A long series of moments passed while she dealt with her emotions. Eventually, she turned around. "Tell me more about Sam, or I won't even bother to create your Heaven."

A look of concern appeared on the archangel's face. "But—"

"Don't even think about avoiding the subject!" she barked. Anahita stormed across the room and pulled one of the chairs back to the table as she did. After spreading her wings, she took a seat and crossed her arms. "I'm waiting." She rolled her hand in a cocky fashion. "Bring up your little ball of images. I want to see Sam's face."

Michael knew it was pointless to argue. As he lifted his hand and turned up his palm, he said, "Your temperament will never change. That's what I loved most about you when we were together."

"Hmpf! Just show me what I want to know!"

It was not long before the images resumed. During this series of moments, the same man who had appeared in Sam Jr.'s nursery was standing with the King of Brandor in darkness. The only light being cast was from Kael, and to the man's right, Kepler was standing motionless like he was frozen.

Anahita looked up from the orb and found the archangel's eyes. "Where are they, and why is Kepler with them?"

Michael walked across the room, placed his hand on top of Anahita's head and then closed his eyes. When he reopened them, he replied, "Your mind is still not ready for the entire truth. What I will divulge is this: Sam and Kepler are on what was once known as Dragonia. Sam abandoned Brandor after he slew an innocent man. It is only by coincidence, or perhaps by the design of someone mischievous, that the two find themselves united. Sam and that other being is a pairing that I had wished to avoid. Sam's soul is in grave danger because of it." Michael stopped talking.

Anahita's brows dropped between her eyes. "Kepler isn't that bad," she defended.

"I'm not referring to Kepler!" Michael snapped.

The shack fell silent as Anahita processed. Eventually, an expression filled with questions appeared on her face. "So that's everything you can tell me, or at least everything you will tell me? Can you at least tell me why Sam would end an innocent man in the first place? And why did Kepler go to Dragonia? And why did you refer to Dragonia as something it was once known as?"

Michael nodded. "I can answer all your questions. Sam ended an innocent man because he has been unable to control the beast that lives inside his mind. It wasn't his fault. Beyond that, I can say nothing further without danger to your mind." The archangel walked across the room and retrieved a drink from the barrel. "Regarding Kepler … the demon-cat went to Dragonia in search of a mate. As for the name 'Dragonia,' this world is now known as Hell. It has been separated from the other worlds and given its own sun. Neither Sam, nor Kepler, will ever see the worlds controlled by the Crystal Moon again unless some sort of divine being comes to their aid."

"Why not just catch a ride with the Merchant Angels? Sam is a king, and he has the power to do so."

The archangel's jaw dropped because of Anahita's ignorance. "Do you really believe the Merchant Angels would serve a world called Hell? Transport home is no longer available. I'm sure you can imagine that Hell is not a destination where anyone will want to go."

"Let me just say that I don't like your sarcasm, mister."

As Anahita walked back to the door and opened it to process, the archangel crossed the room and took a seat at the table. After a fair series of moments, he motioned for Anahita to join him. "Do you have any other questions, my love?"

"Stop calling me that!" Anahita snapped as she returned to the table and dragged the other chair with her. Once seated again, it took a long series of moments before another question surfaced. "Will I ever see my son again?"

"I cannot be certain of that, but I can say this. If you do see your son again, it won't be as the mother he once knew." Michael paused. "Perhaps I can best describe the relationship you will have with the child by calling you his guardian angel. He will know of your love, but not in the same way a child feels his mother's arms about him."

"Well that doesn't make me feel better," Anahita grumbled. "I've been robbed of my chance to be a mom."

Michael did not respond. Instead, he gave Anahita a moment to think.

Eventually, her silence was broken. "What about Sam?" Anahita queried. "I don't want my baby to never know who his father is."

A grave look of concern appeared on the archangel's face. "Perhaps it's best for us to discuss the boy's father during some other series of moments. There is much I cannot divulge regarding Sam right now. This would only aggravate you further."

Michael reached out and caressed Anahita's cheek. "I will say this, however. One Peak, you may be forced to protect your son from his father. Anything else, I cannot divulge."

A dumbfounded look appeared on Anahita's face. "Are you kidding me? And you think that wasn't going to aggravate me further? You're not too bright, are you?"

Suddenly, the archangel looked up. "I'm being summoned." Michael vanished.

Floored at the abruptness of Michael's departure, Anahita stared at his empty chair. An awkward series of moments passed before she whispered, "Helga, can you hear me?"

The older woman took control of their body and turned their seat toward the mirror. "I can hear you, Child. I'm speechless."

That was all Anahita needed to hear. A stream of tears erupted from their eyes.

The Crystal Shard

When you want an update about your favorite characters

NORTHERN GRAYHAM

Medolas, Clandestiny, Gage and **Gallrum**—After meeting up with the Isorians, Gage and Gallrum discovered the reason why Clandestiny and Medolas abandoned Hydroth so many seasons ago. Since the goswigs are still confused as to why Gage's dream brought them to Northern Grayham, they have decided to accompany the Isorians to Hydroth. The badger hopes to meet the boy, now a man, with the ruby eyes. The goswigs are also curious to learn more about the power of the Tear of Gramal and its Kindred Tear.

Shiver and **Gablysin**—The Isorian Army has been gathered. After Gablysin gave the order, they began working throughout every moment of every Peak to tunnel to the spot where their king ordered the hollow created.

Meerum Bosand, King of the Tormal—Meerum left his Frigid Commander with a calling stone. The king is now riding his harugen toward the mountains of the Ko-dess.

THE WORLD OF LUVELLES

Chancellor Boyafed and **King Dowd**—With Kepler's palace finished, Boyafed has returned to the city of Froland. Froland is still undergoing many changes to unify the city after Marcus Id's passing. As for Dowd, he has returned to Lavan. He is working with the city engineers of both Lavan and Inspiration to devise a better way to finish the bridge of glass between the cities. The creation of the bridge has been on hold after the loss of life that happened during its construction over 150 Peaks ago. As initially planned, the bridge will span Lake Lavan to provide a direct route of travel between the two cities.

Susanne and the **Family**—The family is still desperately searching for Garrin. Susanne is a mess, and so is Mary.

George—The ship the warlock is traveling on has made a sudden detour. George has used his power to change the vessel's course. Though the captain cannot understand why the sails blow north, and yet the ship travels east, it is estimated that the ship will see land near the Village of Specks before tomorrow's Peak. George will study his surroundings and then teleport home.

Sharvesa—The demon has watched George's family for the last 3 Peaks and has seen the family suffer because of Garrin's absence. She has also observed the way Athena treats Payne during these moments of crisis. The demon-goddess has made a decision about whether or not she will speak to her fairy-demon son.

Lasidious—Since the Mischievous One cannot return to Ancients Sovereign, he has sought refuge within the Source's old cave on Luvelles. The god cannot risk the others learning of his plans. He must wait for another 10 Peaks before the stasis that covers Hell is lifted. Only then can he progress with the scheming he has yet to set in motion. The Mischievous One will use his moments in the cave to create further plots.

DRAGONIA
THE NEW HELL

Kepler, Sam, Garrin, and **Sam Jr.**—They all sit in stasis. There is nothing further to report here.

THE HIDDEN GOD WORLD
ANCIENTS SOVEREIGN

Celestria—The goddess has abandoned her home. After a discussion with Alistar, she determined that Lasidious does not plan to return in the near future. Alistar has Celestria thinking it is her fault that Lasidious sought solace. In an attempt to replace her sadness, Celestria has joined the others to help with the expansion of the new Hell. In doing so, she will witness the completion of the new star that Hell will orbit with its three additional moons.

Alistar—To keep Celestria from learning about Sam Jr. and baby Garrin's location, the God of the Harvest has helped his brother by concealing the territory where they sit in stasis. Once Hell has been released and the gods realize the solar system is functioning as it should, the need to conceal the babies will no longer be necessary.

The Book of Immortality and the **Archangel Michael**—The Book and Michael plan to meet beneath Gabriel's Hall of Judgment.

A PLACE UNKNOWN

Anahita—After the archangel Michael's departure, Anahita vented to Helga for many, many moments. They are now sitting on a chair at the table. Their eyes are staring at the ancient, leather-bound tome Michael left behind. The cover reads: How to Create a Heaven for a New Plane.

Thank you for reading the Crystal Shard

CHAPTER 11
EMERGING DEMONS
ANCIENTS SOVEREIGN
THE BOOK'S HALL OF JUDGMENT
MORNING, 4 PEAKS LATER

The Book lifted off the table where the gods normally gathered and made his way out of the main hall. After floating down a long corridor, he stopped in front of a door made of black iron. The door was locked—impassable to all, except him and two others. A golden image of the Source sat at its center.

"Con gon onsey," Gabriel whispered. The door opened, revealing a gently arching flight of stairs.

The Book's descent would not be a quick journey. The bottom step had been carved into the core of Ancients Sovereign—a journey of more than 11,000 heartbeats beneath the surface.

Reaching the bottom, the Book stopped in front of another door. Made of pearl, this door's surface remained smooth without markings or symbols.

Again, Gabriel whispered, *"Con gon onsey."* The door opened.

A room with marble walls sat beyond. Emeralds fanned out across the ceiling as it rose to its peak while three jasper chandeliers glistened. The chandeliers had been attached to nothing as they each hovered in front of an arch that shrouded a shelf holding a unique dagger. The arches had been inset with three, large, circular rubies, and they were flanked with an assortment of tourmaline gems.

The floor was made of onyx, and an elevated platform had been placed in the middle of the room. On top of it, a six-pointed star rested at its center, and both the platform and the star had been polished to an unblemished sheen. Their reflective surfaces complemented the light cast by the chandeliers and the glow of six orbs that were attached to the walls beneath sardonyx sconces. Each orb was cradled by three rows of rubies, and they matched those that were inset in the arches.

The Archangel Michael appeared as the Book floated into the room and shut the door. "It's good to see you, brother," he announced.

"As it is to see you, Michael." Gabriel floated to the center of the room. The shape of the Book began to morph into his true form. It was not long before another archangel, equally as glorious, stood atop the carnelian star that had been placed on top of the platform where Michael was standing.

"I see the others have voted to give Dragonia a solar system of its own," Michael said. "How many Peaks will it be before its creation is complete?"

The archangel Gabriel thought for a moment. "Perhaps six, maybe seven. I've lost count. There are many other concerns that weigh heavily on my mind."

Michael crossed his arms and watched as Gabriel spread his wings to stretch. Once folded, he responded. "Speak of these concerns, brother."

Gabriel nodded. "Zerachiel becomes impatient. He grows weary of the others' transgressions. I fear he may take matters into his own hands."

Placing his right hand to his chin, Michael pulled at his skin. "Perhaps I'll visit with Zerachiel. I'll remind him that we cannot force the others to live as we would have them live."

Gabriel groaned as his brows furrowed. "This plane is no better than the other was prior to the tribulation. They'll never get it right. Remind me, brother, why did we choose this path?"

Michael placed his hands on Gabriel's shoulders and squeezed. "Have faith, Gabriel. If but one soul can be salvaged, are not the trials we've faced and continue to face worth it? Would you not be willing to suffer the torment again to retrieve our brethren?"

Gabriel crossed his arms. "Of course, I would. I would do it a thousand times a thousand times for each if I had to. But when will it end? How long must we struggle before they concede?"

Michael placed his forehead to Gabriel's. A single tear rolled from his right eye and fell to the floor. "Dear brother, I'll plow the way for you to follow for an eternity if I must to save them all."

Gabriel took a step back and presented a half-smile. "I feared you would say that. Your dedication is the reason why he chose you to lead his army. I've always admired you because of that."

"Save your admiration, brother, for we still have much to do."

"Agreed," Gabriel responded. "I should tell you, I met with the Mighty One not long ago."

"And what did he command?"

"The Source commanded as you asked him to command. The mainland of Dragonia will remain unchanged. The souls who live in this territory will not be bothered by the damned for many seasons. As we agreed, because they have not failed in life, I cannot make this new Hell resemble the torment of the one we pulled them from."

Michael nodded. "You've done well. They deserve their chance to live a life worthy of the Heaven Anahita will create."

"Then she knows?"

"Yes."

Gabriel turned away from Michael and waved his hand across the floor. A bench made of amethyst appeared. After spreading his wings, he took a seat and then folded them behind the backside of the bench. "How did Anahita take the discovery of her true identity?"

A large grin appeared on Michael's face. "It is safe to say her reaction was as spirited as we once remembered. In fact, it was not long ago that she commanded me to sit."

"What did you do?"

"I sat … as instructed."

Both archangels laughed.

A lengthy conversation about Anahita followed before Gabriel changed the subject. "What will you do now, brother?"

Michael took a seat on the bench next to Gabriel. "I'll continue to do our father's will and work with Anahita to create this plane's Heaven." He reached out with his left hand and patted Gabriel's right knee. "As for you

... you shall continue to work with Zerachiel to maintain the balance the worlds so desperately need."

Gabriel grimaced. "I know I've said this before, but I feel I must say it again. I long for the Peak when I can tell the others my true identity. The laws they live by mean nothing to me."

Michael squeezed Gabriel's knee and then pulled his hand away as he responded. "The laws they have chosen to govern themselves by may mean nothing to you, but it is these laws that allow you to maintain balance without taking their free will. Be patient, Gabriel. One Peak, you will have the satisfaction of revealing your secret. For on that Peak, their laws will no longer be necessary. Our brethren will suffer no more. They will live in a place of joy and peace ... though their existence will be in the shadow of the ultimate reward our father intended."

Gabriel stood from the bench and extended a hand to pull Michael to his feet. "Don't worry. I'll hold the course."

After a short embrace, Michael kissed Gabriel on the forehead. "Until we meet again." Michael vanished.

Before heading back up the stairs, Gabriel reclaimed the form of the Book of Immortality. He opened the door and floated out of the room.

MEANWHILE, ANAHITA'S SHACK

Anahita slammed the ancient, leather-bound tome shut. "I don't understand this stupid thing!" She stood from the table and stormed across the dirt floor toward the front door. Ripping it open, she stepped onto the threshold and looked into the darkness. "Aaahhhhh!" she shouted and then slapped the frame of the door with her left hand. "I hate this place! Damn you, Michael!"

A long silence followed. Despite Helga's desire to take control of their body to comfort her friend, she feared Anahita's rage. She already felt weak and did not want to be pushed to the back of Anahita's mind, only to never return.

Anahita cursed Michael for many more moments before she stopped. She threw up her right hand and extended it toward the darkness. She screamed, "I'm sick of not seeing anything! *Tolamea cun noble ayan!*" A light erupted from the center of her palm.

The unexpected command of the Ancient Mystics caused the darkness to dissipate for a vast area. As a result, what Anahita saw caused her to forget her anger. She gasped, "Goodness-gracious!" Enormous chunks of mass were floating all around the outside of the shack in every direction—much of it nearly hitting the structure.

Helga had to speak. She took control and brought their hands to their forehead. "Child, these are the materials we're expected to use to build the Heaven. Where will we start?"

The question aggravated Anahita. "How in tarnation am I supposed to know? Do I look like some kind of book of knowledge?"

"No, Child. I was—"

"You were what?"

Helga's growing weakness forced her to remain silent.

When no response came, Anahita sighed, "I'm sorry." She turned from the door and walked across the room. Stopping in front of the mirror, she found the reflection of their eyes. "I'm really sorry. I bet you want to hogtie me right now. Would you forgive me?"

No response.

"Look. I know I've been a pill over the last few Peaks."

Helga was still unable to respond.

"Are you there?"

Yet again, no response.

Panic set in. "No, no, no! Helga please! Don't you be leaving me like this. I can't make it without you." Anahita grabbed both sides of the mirror and stepped closer to their reflection. "Please ... tell me you're still with me."

Many moments passed before Anahita's mood calmed to the point where Helga could reply. "I'm here, Child. Though I don't know if I'll be here for long. Your emotions are consuming what's left of me. I've been unable to respond."

Though she struggled to do so, Helga managed to control their right arm. She reached up and patted their chest. "When you're angry, it feels as if I lose a part of me. I'm slipping away."

Tears filled Anahita's eyes as the sadness overwhelmed her portion of their soul. "Are you going to be okay? I can remain calm for you."

Again, Helga had to fight for control. "I don't know, Child. I'm weak."

"Can I do anything for you?"

In order to respond, Helga had to concentrate with all that remained. "Perhaps you could take us to the cot and allow me to sleep. I need rest."

"Yes ... of course." Anahita walked across the room and slowly lowered onto the cot. "How does that feel? Should I close our eyes?"

Helga was unable to respond.

"I'll just close them for now. You go on and take a nap."

Anahita waited for a response, but one did not come. A tear rolled from her left eye and fell to the cot as she whispered, "Don't you worry. Everything will be alright. I love you, Helga."

WESTERN LUVELLES
BEHIND GEORGE AND ATHENA'S HOME
THE PEAK OF BAILEM APPROACHES

Sharvesa waited until Payne was alone to approach the fairy-demon. He was climbing the trees of the forest that surrounded the homes, leaping from branch to branch to keep himself entertained while Athena, Mary and Susanne gathered around George's kitchen table as Brayson worked over the stove.

As per the Head Master's request, Susanne had searched Garrin's crib to find a strand of the boy's hair. Brayson was using it as an ingredient to brew a potion that, when drank, would allow him to locate Garrin and then teleport to his location.

"Do you think this one will work?" Athena questioned.

Brayson shook his head. "I don't know. I thought the last two would. All we can do is hope for the best."

Staring at the pot, the Head Master watched as the purple liquid started to bubble. He desperately wanted to produce a better result than the last series of moments he had tried to find George, but even that potion had failed. Though he did not know it, the magic had been unable to locate the warlock because George's ship had been in constant motion.

Meanwhile, outside the back of the home, Sharvesa stepped out of her invisible veil and looked toward the tree tops where Payne was climbing. "Young one!" she called. "Come down and speak with me!"

Payne stopped his ascent. Once his footing was sure, he turned around to look. Seeing that Sharvesa's skin was the same color as his own, his curiosity was instantly piqued. "You calling to Payne?" he shouted.

The goddess smiled at how the fairy-demon spoke of himself in third person. "Yes, Payne. I'm speaking to you. Come visit with me for a moment."

"How you know Payne's name?"

Again, the goddess smiled. "You just told me."

"Oh." The fairy-demon released the branch he was holding and jumped out of the tree. He fell more than seven paces before he used his wings to stop his descent. Once his feet were planted on the forest floor, he looked up. "You big. What does big, red lady want with Payne?"

Again, Sharvesa smiled. "I only wish to look upon you, young one. You are handsome ... just as I imagined you would be."

"Payne not handsome. That gross." He flexed his biceps. "Payne strong. Dad say Payne is the strongest ever, ever. He say Payne grow to be stronger than Kitty some Peak." He looked up. "What you think?"

"Well ... I think you'll be—"

"Why your horns so big?" the fairy-demon said, interrupting Sharvesa's response. "Payne's horns no big. They small. Payne wishes him's horns were as big as yours." He paused in thought and then pointed at Sharvesa. "You look like Payne. Do you know how to make Payne's horns grow bigger?"

The demon-goddess chuckled. "Have you been eating your vegetables?"

"Vegetables are yuk. Mom makes Payne eat many grossest ones." He reached down and lifted a twig off the ground. "The green ones taste worser than the red ones."

"I'm sure they do. But no matter how awful they taste, they're good for you."

"You speaks like Mom speaks. Are you a mommy, too?"

Sharvesa grinned. Taking a knee, she reached out and placed the palm of her right hand on Payne's left cheek. "What a strange question. Yes ... I am a mother."

"Is your son more stronger than Payne?"

"No. In fact, my son is exactly as strong as you are. You remind me of him."

Payne's face lit up. "I bet him's as gooder to you as Payne is to him's mom."

Sharvesa grabbed the end of her chin. "I don't know about that. You seem like a good child. I bet your mother loves you like no other mother on any world."

The fairy-demon nodded. "Oh, yes. Payne's mom loves Payne so, so much. She tell him every Peak."

"This makes me happy, young one. You deserve to be loved."

Before another word could be said, George's voice was heard from the other side of the home. "Is anyone here?"

Sharvesa patted Payne on the top of his head. "You best run along. I'm sure we'll speak again."

Payne was so excited about George's arrival, he forgot to say goodbye. The fairy-demon lifted off the ground and flew as fast as his wings could carry him toward the front of the house.

The goddess stepped into another invisible veil and followed.

Opening the door, George shouted a phrase from one of his favorite television shows back on Earth, "Lucy ... I'm home!" The warlock closed the door behind him.

Athena pushed open the door leading from the kitchen and rushed across the living room. "I'm happy you're home. But there's no Lucy here."

George rolled his eyes. "Seriously?" He smirked. "Wow. That's all I've got to say."

Sensing her husband's sarcasm, Athena slapped his chest and changed the subject. "Garrin is missing again. We can't find him."

The warlock did not get the chance to reply before Susanne burst into the room. She threw her arms around George and began to sob. "My baby has been missing for Peaks. He's out there all alone. He has no food, no water. What if he's...?" She stopped talking and flopped onto the floor. After burying her face into her hands, she finished her previous sentence. "What if he has perished?"

"Nonsense," George replied. "You worry too much. Get up from there." The warlock reached down and helped Susanne up. He looked at Athena. "Babe, go into the kitchen and get her a mug of water."

As Athena did, Payne barged through the front door and ran across the room. Latching onto George's right leg, he exclaimed. "Payne missed Dad!"

Sharvesa entered the home as the warlock reached down to rub the fairy-demon's back above his wings. "I missed you, too, little guy. Have you been good for Mom?"

The demon-goddess enjoyed the exchange of love as she moved clear of the entryway.

Grinning, the fairy-demon took a step back and used a phrase George had taught him not long ago. "Yeah ... duh. Payne always gooder for Mom."

The warlock laughed. "Is that so?" He lifted Payne into his arms and poked the fairy-demon's belly. "There's never a dull moment with you around, is there? Have I told you I love you on this Peak?"

Sharvesa smiled. *This man is a good father,* she thought.

Between sobs, Susanne chastised, "This isn't a moment for pleasantries, George. My baby is missing. Garrin could perish before we find him."

George lowered Payne to the floor. "Why don't you run into the kitchen, and ask Athena to get you something to eat before she brings me the mug of water I asked for?"

Payne did as he was told.

Admiring George's calm demeanor, Sharvesa strolled across the living room and stopped in the corner. She leaned against the west wall and watched as George pulled the round, smooth, black stone Lasidious had given him from his front, pant pocket. The goddess' eyes narrowed as the warlock placed the pebble in the palm of Susanne's left hand. The effect of the stone was instantaneous. Susanne stopped crying.

A moment later, Susanne handed the stone back to the warlock. She walked toward the front door as if nothing had ever been wrong. "I'll see you soon, George. Love you."

"Love you too, Susanne."

Mary exited the kitchen just after the front door shut. "Where's my daughter?" she queried. "Athena said she had another breakdown."

George pointed to the door. "She just left. You might want to catch her."

As his mother-in-law rushed by, the warlock grabbed Mary's arm. "Hold on a moment. I've got something for you. Give me your hand."

Mary rebutted, "Not now, George. I need to find Susanne."

Reaching down, George grabbed Mary's right hand and forced the pebble into it. "It's good to see you, you know. I've missed you."

Mary's expression changed. It was as if the weight of the world had just fallen from her shoulders. She let out a sigh of relief.

The warlock leaned in and kissed Mary on the cheek. As he did, he retrieved the stone before she realized she was holding it. "Did you miss me, too?"

It took a moment before the cloud that covered Mary's mind moved on. "Of course, I did." Her brows furrowed. "Why do you ask?"

George shrugged. "No reason."

Curious about the stone's power, George questioned. "Tell me something, Mary. Is anything bothering you?"

Mary's face wrinkled as she pondered the question. "Why would you ask me that? Do I look bothered?"

George's smile was pleasant. "No, not really." He changed the subject again. "Weren't you looking for Susanne?" He pointed to the front door. "She went that way."

Mary nodded. "Thank you." When Mary reached the front door, she looked over her shoulder after placing her hand on the door knob. "Why was I looking for Susanne?"

Again, George shrugged. "You said something about talking with her about dinner. I'm sure she remembers. Why don't you go ask her?"

Once the door was shut, the warlock tossed the pebble into the air and snatched it. "Amazing!" He lifted the unmarked rune in front of his face. "You rock, little rock. We might as well get started on the rest of the fam."

From within her invisible veil, Sharvesa tilted her head. *What odd remarks. What are you up to?* The demon-goddess followed as George sauntered into the kitchen.

Athena placed a sandwich on the table and then lifted Payne onto his booster seat as George walked through the door. The warlock crossed the kitchen to greet Brayson. "How are you?" he asked.

Brayson turned from the stove and extended his hand. "Thank Lasidious you're here! I'm anxious. This potion is not easy to brew. I've already failed at two others, and I can't find Garrin."

Since the Head Master's hand was extended, George took the opportunity to place the pebble in it. Like the others, Brayson's worries for Garrin vanished, and then George reclaimed the stone.

As the fog filled the Head Master's eyes, Brayson mindlessly turned back to the stove. A few moments later, a look of confusion appeared on his face. Without saying a word, he lifted the kettle containing the potion he was brewing and took it to the sink.

While Brayson poured it down the drain, George turned to Athena, grabbed her hand and lifted it to his mouth. As he did, he kissed the top of it and pushed the pebble against her palm.

Just like her mother had done, Athena let out a sigh of relief. "Are you okay, babe?" George questioned, placing the pebble in his pocket.

Before Athena could clear her mind to respond, the Head Master set the kettle on the counter. The sound of the iron clanking against the granite captured Athena's attention. A look of forgetfulness consumed her face as she looked past George's shoulder and across the room. "What were you cooking, Brayson? Was it truly so bad you had to discard it?"

Brayson stared for a moment or two at the purple stain the potion left behind on the white porcelain before he responded. "That's odd. I can't remember."

George was quick to react. Though the others could not see the magic work, the warlock used his power to cool the kettle. "He wasn't cooking anything. The kettle's been sitting on the stove since I left. I can't believe no one had thought of washing it until now. Isn't that what you were doing, Brayson?"

The Head Master looked at the kettle and then the sink. "I don't know. It's strange. Why would I not remember why I'm standing here?"

The warlock grabbed the mug of water Athena had left on the table and took a drink. "Maybe you're getting old." He caressed the top of Athena's arm. "Maybe, you're getting old, too, babe."

Seeing the confusion in the room, the demon-goddess froze everyone. She walked over to George and retrieved the stone from his pocket. "What are you?" she wondered as she examined its smooth surface. "You possess great power."

Sharvesa clenched her hand around the stone. She looked at George. "Why would this rune be in your possession?" She moved closer and stared into the warlock's frozen eyes. "Why wield its power in this fashion? What would make you want an outcome such as this? Why would you deceive your family and cause them to forget?"

Again, Sharvesa addressed the stone as she opened her hand and began to rub her thumb across its onyx surface. "You possess the power of the gods. There must be a secret surrounding this missing child." She placed the pebble into the warlock's palm. "You appear to be a good father, but why would you do the bidding of one of the others?"

The goddess crossed her arms. "Who commands you, human? I must know this." The demon-goddess stood in silence and pinched her chin in thought. Eventually, she remembered part of a conversation that happened in the Book's Hall of Judgment. Alistar had addressed Celestria. *"You put too much faith in your pet prophet. George will only be able to spread Lasidious' supposed good word so far."*

Placing her hand on George's head, the demon-goddess tried to summon the warlock's memories. It was not long before she removed her hand and took a step back, frustrated. "Why can I not see your past?" She stared into the warlock's frozen eyes. "You're an intriguing being. There are many secrets within you ... secrets that won't reveal themselves. Your memories must have been protected."

The goddess grabbed the pebble and pinched it between George's thumb and forefinger. Once this had been done, she released her hold on all the mortals.

When George reanimated, the pebble fell from his fingers to the floor. He bent over, snatched it up and placed it in his front, pant pocket. *What the hell?* he thought. *Didn't I already put you in there?*

"What's wrong?" Athena questioned, sensing his anxiety. She looked in the direction of his pocket. "What was that?"

The warlock shook his head. "It's just a rock." He gave his wife a quick kiss and then headed for the front door. Opening it, he shouted, "I'll be back in a little while, babe! I'm going to go check on Susanne and find your mom!" Shutting the front door behind him, he added under his breath, "And everyone else."

Pausing at the top of the porch steps, George reached down under his tunic to make sure the pebble was still in his pant pocket. *I know I put you in there,* he thought. *I just know it.*

On the far side of the porch, the invisible demon-goddess smiled. She thought, *You're not the only being who can mold the minds of others.* The goddess watched George bound down the steps and run across the clearing before she vanished.

Ancients Sovereign
Outside the Book's Hall of Judgment

When Sharvesa reappeared, she was standing on the far side of the lawn, just south of the Book's hall. Seeing the lushness of the grass, she looked down, kicked off her shoes and rummaged her toes through it. A smile appeared on her face as the moisture near the base of every blade cooled her skin.

After plucking a few pieces, she lifted them to her nose and sniffed. *Delightful,* she thought. She sniffed again. *Everything smells so much better on this world.*

A few moments later, Gabriel floated out of the hall. He crossed the distance and stopped only paces away from the goddess. "It's good to see that there is a member of the Collective who still takes moments out of their Peaks to enjoy the simple pleasures of what has been created."

Sharvesa sniffed again. "The others are fools."

Gabriel chuckled. "Perhaps. However ... 'fools' is not a strong enough word to describe their apathy."

The demon smirked and allowed each blade to fall to the ground. "The others should spend a season or two as mortals so they can acquire respect for their handiwork."

"A fine idea!" Gabriel clapped. "Perhaps I'll bring it up when next we convene."

The Book floated closer. "Of all the gods, Sharvesa, you have proven yourself to be the most humble. Again and again, since your arrival on Ancients Sovereign, I have witnessed this. Please ... never allow the depths of your kindness to be filled by senseless manipulations as the others do."

Sharvesa took a moment to ponder the Book's comment. "What actions have I performed that have shown humility?"

The Book smiled. "If I must bear testimony, you have not allowed your vanity to affect your judgment." Gabriel pointed to his hall. "Over many seasons have I seen the members of the Collective sit within those walls and argue. They fight for power, demand respect and seek the prayers of those living on the worlds." He pointed at Sharvesa. "But look at you. I see a humble demon who wants only the best for those she once ruled. You worry not for yourself but more for those who will suffer on the new Hell. Your worry is not limited to demonkind. It encompasses all beings."

Gabriel lifted his hands and opened them. An image of Sharvesa's daughter appeared above his palms. "You think as a mother thinks. You want the best for your child and those who serve her crown."

The Book allowed the demon-goddess a few more moments to enjoy the sight of her offspring before he closed his hands. As the image faded, he continued. "Your love for others is to be commended. This love is the reason you value life." The Book lowered to the grass and then looked up. He motioned to Sharvesa. "Please, sit."

Sharvesa did as requested.

The Book continued. "The others have become hardened to the fate of those living on the worlds."

"Agreed," the demon responded.

After a period of silence, the demon looked to the west and pointed. "Tell me, Gabriel, is that the mountain range Bassorine once occupied?"

"It is. Why?"

"No reason, I suppose." Sharvesa plucked another blade of grass and rolled it between her fingertips. "I have come seeking knowledge … knowledge about Lasidious."

A look of confusion appeared on the Book's face. "Explain."

The demon nodded. "Did Lasidious truly have a hand in the events that led to Bassorine's destruction?"

The Book lifted off the grass. "He did. Lasidious has had his hands in many schemes that have caused the suffering of others. I imagine this trend won't change."

The demon pulled her gaze away from the tallest peak known as Catalyst and found the Book's heavy brows. "Tell me. When the vote was taken to turn Dragonia into Hell, what was Lasidious' vote?

"Why do you ask?"

"I ask only for peace of mind."

Gabriel studied Sharvesa's face. "How can peace be gained through this knowledge?"

"I'm not sure your question is one I can answer. I find my mind often wanders in confusion. For now, I simply want to know if a lie has been told."

The goddess reached out and took hold of Gabriel's binding. She brought up her knees and set Gabriel on top of them. "Do you question me in return to avoid speaking the truth as the others do?"

The Book frowned. "Of course, not. I would never act as they act."

"Then stall no more," Sharvesa demanded. She released the Book and then put her hands behind her back to support her weight. "Speak the answer I seek."

Gabriel lifted from the demon goddess' knees. "I'll tell you what you want to know." The Book's brows sunk between his eyes as a stern look appeared on his face. "Lasidious voted against the others."

"What were his exact words on that Peak, Gabriel? Do you remember them?"

The Book paused in thought. "Lasidious said, *'I vote nay. The demons should not be condemned to suffer with the damned. This Collective should spare their world, and in doing so, create a Hell from the matter that will be salvaged by our Salvage Angels.'*"

"Then Lasidious voted nay as he proclaimed, and the others voted against him."

"He did. He voted against all the others … save one."

"And who was this one?"

"Alistar."

As Sharvesa's eyes widened, Gabriel turned to look toward the northwest. The Book knew Alistar's palace sat in the distance, beyond the mountains, beyond the lakes and the rolling plains. "Alistar was the only other who felt your world should be spared."

This revelation caused Sharvesa to ponder aloud. "Why would Alistar vote nay?"

Gabriel shrugged as a book with arms would shrug. "Perhaps it is because Alistar is a softer being than the others."

"Does he not have a mind of his own?"

"Of course, he does. In fact, Alistar has opposed Lasidious on a great many occasions. But on this particular Peak, he chose to side with Lasidious. But I don't know why."

The Book turned to face the demon and changed the direction of the conversation. "Does this knowledge offer you the peace of mind you were seeking?"

Sharvesa lifted from the grass. "I'll answer once I've finished my investigation." The goddess bowed. "Forgive me, Gabriel, but I must be off."

The Book frowned as Sharvesa vanished.

Moments later, the demon reappeared near the palace of Alistar that sat within the Plains of Bounty. In every direction, fields of exotic flowers stretched before her. The flora was in bloom, and a plethora of sweet, intoxicating scents filled the breeze and consumed her nostrils.

Sharvesa turned toward the south. A beautiful lake and a glorious mountain range sat in the distance. She did not hesitate to lift her nose and take a deep breath. "If I didn't know otherwise," she said, talking to herself, "I would wager I could smell the colors."

Having appeared behind Sharvesa, the God of the Harvest responded, "That is why I chose this spot to create my home."

The demon whirled around. "You startled me."

"I apologize." Alistar bent down to smell the flowers. "There have been many occasions when I felt I was undeserving of the delight these aromas provide. Do you think that's true?"

Sharvesa smiled. "Perhaps. But a more insightful answer could be given once I know you better."

Alistar smiled. "Come with me." The God of the Harvest walked west through the field. He allowed his hands to caress the top of the flowers as he headed toward the steps that ascended to the doors of his palace.

As she followed, the demon professed, "I wasn't sure if you'd be home. I assumed you'd be with the others."

The God of the Harvest reached out and placed his right hand on a large, black, iron hasp. As he pulled the door open, he responded. "I was with the others. I would not be here now, except for the warning I received of your presence."

"Warning?"

Alistar smirked and patted the backside of the door with his left hand. "My palace summoned me. It lives as we live. It told me you were here prior to my arrival."

A look of admiration appeared on Sharvesa's face as she placed her hand flush against the door. "It's warm … like we are."

After a moment of silence, the demon changed the subject. "What of Dragonia? Were you there?"

Alistar nodded. "Yes. The transformation of your old homeworld is nearly complete."

Sharvesa frowned as Alistar motioned for her to step inside. The grandeur within caused her to stand in awe as the sound of the door closing behind them echoed throughout the massive foyer.

Alistar studied Sharvesa's face. "Your appearance suggests that you're pleased."

Sharvesa chuckled.

Indignant, Alistar queried, "I fail to see the humor. Is my structure not appealing to your eyes?"

"Forgive me, Alistar. I mean no disrespect. Your palace is truly a place of wonder."

"Then why laugh?"

The demon stopped. "I laugh only because I chose a home far less grand after my arrival on Ancients Sovereign." She took a step forward and circled. "Seeing all this makes me realize I have chosen poorly. You would not waste admiration on my abode."

Alistar reached out and took the goddess' hands into his. "I'd like to see the existence you've created for yourself. Take me there."

With eyes closed, the demon did as requested. When they reappeared, they were standing in a dark, damp, miserable place.

Alistar used his power to chase away the darkness that consumed the cave. After studying his surroundings, he commented, "I see what you mean. I feel no jealousy."

Again, Sharvesa chuckled. "Then you have given affirmation to my earlier confession. It appears I shall need to seek a new home now that my eyes have been opened to the comforts I can acquire."

Alistar shook his head. "I wouldn't be too quick to give up on the potential this cave offers."

"What do you mean?"

The God of the Harvest extended a hand and motioned for Sharvesa to walk. "I'll show you."

Sharvesa nodded.

Alistar walked deeper into the cave and stopped near a natural column.

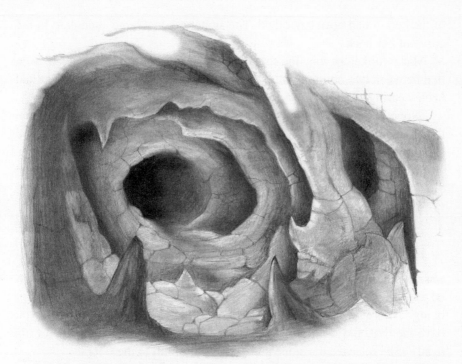

Alistar placed his hands on either side of the column and then closed his eyes. It was not long before his hands started to glow. Thousands of multi-colored crystallizations surfaced, each emanating a shallow light that projected their color. Although it was only a minor change, the feel of the cave improved drastically.

Alistar turned from the column. "Do you approve?"

"Oh, yes, I do."

"Wonderful. Show me where you sleep."

Sharvesa led him into the depths of the cave. Alistar's eyes widened as they fell upon the section of the floor that Sharvesa had taken the moments to smooth over.

Now it was Alistar's turn to laugh. "You must be jesting," he blurted. "This is where you retire each night? How could you possibly sleep on the ground?" He pointed to a fair-sized stone. "And what's that?"

"That is where I lay my head."

Alistar groaned, "You lay your head on a stone?"

"Yes. Don't you?"

"Definitely not."

Sharvesa's pillow was nothing more than a shaped rock, and like the rest of the bed, it had been smoothed. The stone was just large enough to fit the curve of her neck.

Alistar looked beyond the so-called bed. Hanging on a wire that had been tied between two columns were three outfits—all of which the goddess had been wearing over and over since her arrival on Ancients Sovereign.

"None of this will suffice," Alistar admonished. "You deserve better than this devastation. You are the Goddess of War, not a common mortal. No god should live this way."

Sharvesa leaned down and picked up the stone that served as her pillow. "I searched for many, many moments. This was the finest stone I laid my eyes upon."

Alistar sneered, "This is not even a precious gem. How could you settle so?"

"This stone is far better than the one I laid my head upon on Dragonia," Sharvesa defended, slapping the rock. A moment later, she sighed and started to roll the stone in her hands. As she did, a sense of frustration filled her being. "This cave is more pleasant than my old home. Where else would you have me live, and what other object would you have me use to support my head?" She released the stone and allowed it to fall to the floor.

The God of the Harvest shook his head in disgust. "I would not have you lay your head upon a stone at all." Reaching down, he snatched the rock off the floor and crushed it between his hands as if it was an ordinary clod of dirt. He allowed the rubble to fall to the floor. "Stand back," he ordered. "You must think like a god now. You are above discomfort."

Once the demon was out of the way, Alistar closed his eyes and directed his hands toward the floor of the cave. The ground started to quake. A moment later, loud popping sounds echoed throughout as large cracks appeared and turned the floor into rubble as the earth opened. It was not long before the rubble was swallowed by emerging sand that shoved the chunks beneath the surface.

With a large mound of golden sand sitting in front of him, Alistar again used his power. He commanded the sand to melt, just as if it had been placed inside a burning caldron. The sand did as instructed. As the command was modified inside the god's mind, the molten liquid began to move like it had a life of its own.

It was not long before the lava settled into a familiar shape. The God of the Harvest stepped forward and blew. A mighty wind filled the cave and when it dissipated, a bed frame made of glass was left behind. A simple snap of Alistar's fingers was all that was necessary for a mattress and a pillow, filled with the softest of gazalian feathers, to appear.

Turning from his masterpiece, Alistar motioned for the goddess to lie down. He enjoyed the look on the demon's face as her tall frame felt true relaxation for the first moments of her life. "Are you pleased?"

Sharvesa moaned, "More than pleased. Even my wings feel relaxed. How is it possible that my kind never thought to seek such comfort? I must depart immediately to speak with my daughter. I must create a place for her to lie her head."

"A splendid idea," Alistar encouraged. "But Dragonia still sits in stasis. You can meet with her once it has been lifted."

Sharvesa frowned. "In my excitement, I almost forgot about the Hell her world is to become."

Alistar nodded. "For now, you could tell me why you sought me? What can I do for you?"

The demon sat up and allowed her legs to drape over the side of the bed. The yellow of her gown and the back of her calves which were exposed because of the slits on each side, reflected off the glass frame. "I have many questions regarding Lasidious' mind. Perhaps you can enlighten me on a few matters of interest."

"I'd be happy to." Alistar took a seat. "I'll speak on what I can."

"I'd expect nothing less." The demon stood and moved a few paces away to admire her new bed. "Tell me, Alistar … why would Lasidious vote nay when the others gathered to discuss what was to become of Dragonia? Why would he desire to spare my homeworld and save it from the Hell it has become?"

Alistar smiled. "Like the others, Lasidious had his reasons. Perhaps you should ask him that question?"

Sharvesa shook her head. "No. I've chosen to burden you."

"Why me?"

"Because you also voted nay."

Caught off guard, the God of the Harvest stood from the bed. He walked over to the line that held Sharvesa's gowns and then responded. "So … you must have spoken with the Book."

"I did."

"And what did Gabriel say?"

The demon-goddess frowned. "Why do you hesitate to answer? Do you have secrets that you wish to hold dear?"

Alistar sighed. "No. My mind is open to you."

"Good. Then tell me why you chose to vote nay as Lasidious did? What were your reasons for agreeing with him?"

Alistar frowned. "This isn't a short conversation."

Sharvesa crossed her arms. "I have the moments necessary at my disposal."

The God of the Harvest moved beyond the gowns and stopped at the back wall of the cave. "Allow me to make one last improvement while I collect my thoughts."

The demon nodded. "Do as you wish. Your tastes are better than mine."

Alistar smirked. "You could say that on 500 occasions and it would be true on each." Laughing, he lifted his hands and commanded the wall to reform.

Unamused, Sharvesa stood stone-faced as she watched the wall begin to crack and crumble. During this series of moments, no sand emerged. Instead, the rubble that fell to the floor was gathered for later use. Each piece lifted and floated to the far side of the cave and settled into a pile as the wall continued to open. It was not long before an expansive, 15 by 25 pace walk-in-closet was left behind with an opening large enough for the demon-goddess to enter.

With Sharvesa on his heels, Alistar walked through the opening and studied his surroundings. He lifted his hands and placed them against each wall and used his power to command the walls to smooth over. Further, he commanded the crystallizations hidden within the rock to surface, but during this series of moments, he only allowed the soft blue crystals to glow. They began to emanate a peaceful light that added an ambiance to the closet.

Stepping back into the main section of the cave, Alistar turned the pile of rubble into another molten mound of magma. Like before, the liquid began to move. It separated into 90 different piles of various sizes and then took the shape of shelves, rods and supports. Satisfied with their design, the god stepped forward and blew to cool them down. One by one, each piece lifted off the floor and floated past the gods on its way into the closet.

The sounds of the pieces joining could be heard as they echoed throughout the cave. When Sharvesa and Alistar entered, a room fit for the goddess' clothes and more greeted them.

Alistar turned to Sharvesa and studied her figure before he pointed at the rods. He snapped his fingers. Rows of elegant dresses, gowns, blouses, shirts and pants appeared on hangers. Again, he snapped, and now the shelves were filled with 100 pairs of shoes, 7 sets of sheets, 12 blankets, 40 towels, 7 sets of pillow cases and 20 table cloths, all of assorted colors.

Alistar's brows furrowed as he pondered. "Something is missing. This will not suffice."

Sharvesa giggled. "What could possibly be missing? I've never had such comforts."

Without responding, Alistar pointed at the floor at the center of the closet. Like before, the earth opened and allowed sand to emerge. Once a substantial pile existed, the god commanded the sand to melt, reform and settle into an oversized, four-sided dresser before blowing. He filled the 24 drawers, 6 on each side, with seductive undergarments of many colors.

Further, he created seven, large jewelry boxes and placed them across the top of the dresser. Each was filled with various rings, earrings, toe rings, necklaces, head pieces, bracelets and arm cuffs that had been made out of an assortment of gems and precious metals. To put the final touch on the room, Alistar laced the floor with exotic throw rugs to comfort Sharvesa's feet as she dressed.

Without wasting another moment, Alistar looked up and found Sharvesa's eyes. He continued with their earlier conversation just as if there was nothing for the demon to marvel at. "As I was saying, this conversation will take many moments. There is much you don't know. But first … before I utter another word … I'm invoking the Rule of Fromalla."

The demon's demeanor changed. "Fromalla?" she barked.

"Yes. What I have to say must stay between you, Lasidious and myself. I invoke Fromalla only to ensure this happens."

Sharvesa studied Alistar's expression. "Why can't you speak as openly as I can? I have nothing to hide."

Alistar chuckled, "But I do … as does Lasidious. Make no mistake. If you want to learn that which you do not know, you'll profess your understanding of the rule, and agree to enter a conversation that Fromalla protects."

The demon's eyes narrowed. "This feels like trickery."

"Feelings are irrelevant," Alistar rebutted. "You seek knowledge. I seek protection … protection from the others … not from you."

"Why would the others care about our conversation?" the demon-goddess sneered.

"Agree to Fromalla, and you'll find out." Emulating Sharvesa, Alistar crossed his arms and shifted his weight onto his left leg. "I'll say nothing more until the pact is entered."

A long series of moments passed before Sharvesa responded. "Fine! I agree to Fromalla. I'll speak of nothing we discuss with anyone but you and Lasidious."

Alistar walked out of the closet and stopped next to Sharvesa's bed. Once the goddess had followed, he said, "Do you remember the argument you had in Lasidious' home?"

"I do. But what does that have to do with the way you and Lasidious voted?"

The God of the Harvest smiled. His eyes turned red, and his teeth turned to sharp points as he began his transformation. "It has everything to do with it," he chuckled. His laugh was booming, and it echoed throughout the cave as every muscle began to swell.

Sharvesa's eyes widened as she took a step back.

It did not take long for Alistar to finish his transformation into a form the goddess was familiar with. His skin turned burnt red and ivory horns protruded from his head and shot upward.

"You are demon!" Sharvesa exclaimed.

Alistar's voice was deep, and it exuded power. "I am more than demon. I'm your brother … as is Lasidious. This is what we became after being cast from grace."

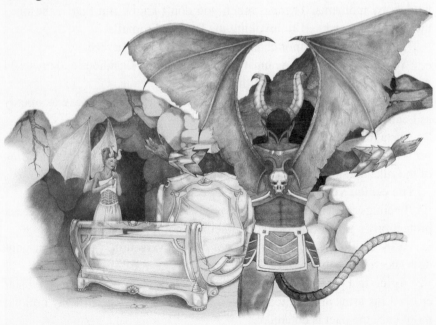

Aghast, Sharvesa lowered to the bed as Alistar allowed her the moments to digest. The demon-goddess' head fell into the palms of her hands. She did not look up when she finally responded. "I remember only pieces of a past once lived. Why is it that I have forgotten and you remember? How can I be sure you're my brother?"

Alistar extended his wings and stretched. After folding them to his back, he responded as he knelt in front of Sharvesa. "What reason would I have to lie? What benefit would be gained by deceiving you?"

Another period of silence passed before Sharvesa responded. "Tell me more."

Nodding, Alistar continued. "After we were cast from Heaven, you became what you are now. Like me, you became an abomination. We had no choice. To survive, we assumed new identities ... as did Lasidious.

"You, sister, took the identity of a goddess who influenced many worlds, not just Earth. On each, a lineage of pharaohs worshipped you throughout many seasons. This cult of beings and the people they ruled knew you by the name Sekhmet. You were depicted as a lion-headed woman ... often being portrayed with a sun disc on your head. You were worshipped as the destroyer, and your followers served you out of fear. Yet you associated with Hathor, your friend and goddess of joy, music, dance, sexual love, pregnancy and birth."

Alistar stopped talking and took a seat on the bed next to Sharvesa. "Do you remember any of this?"

Sharvesa dropped her palms away from her face and looked up. "My mind is broken. I remember only fragments. I cannot fathom being cruel."

"Yet something tells you it's the truth." Alistar did not comment further. Instead, he allowed Sharvesa to think.

The goddess looked up. "Tell me, Alistar ... what identity did you assume after falling?"

Alistar pushed himself back onto the bed and crossed his legs. "I became known by many names. Like you, I created my own history and had followers on many worlds. I allowed these beings to believe I was the all-father of creation. By morning, they knew me as Khepera. By mid Peak, they knew me as Ra. And when the sun was setting, they knew me as Tem or Temu.

"Those who worshipped believed that I was the father of Tefnut and Shu, but in reality, these were alternate identities I assumed only when it pleased me." Alistar chuckled. "I even allowed the people to believe these identities married one another ... despite the fact that I led the masses to believe that

Tefnut and Shu were brother and sister." He grinned and shrugged. "I was bored."

Sharvesa shook her head. "What identity did Lasidious assume?"

The goddess' question caused Alistar to laugh. Once he managed to calm himself, he responded. "Lasidious has always had an affection for mischief. After he fell, he assumed the name Loki, and he ruled a different culture of beings on a great number of worlds.

"Like me ... and like you ... Loki answered to only one. It was our love for this being that caused us to follow him from Heaven. To this Peak, Lasidious and I exist only to serve him."

Sharvesa's face was smothered in confusion. "I don't understand."

"Of course, you don't. How could you? Many of your memories were lost when the war on this plane was fought. This explains why you feel your memory is broken. The truth is ... you weren't strong enough to survive the war. Of those who followed the Morning Star from Heaven, only Lasidious and I managed to live on."

"Are you saying I perished?"

"I am."

"Then ... how am I here now?"

"You were recreated. Lasidious saw to that. His love for you is undying ... as is mine. We wanted to be able to look upon you and know we did what we could. Providing you a peaceful existence is the main reason why we voted nay."

The demon goddess lowered her eyes to the floor. "I understand." Another long series of moments passed before Sharvesa spoke again. "I remember the name Morning Star. I remember loving him and being willing to perish for him. He was so beautiful and glorious to look upon." Sharvesa turned quiet.

"What is it?" Alistar questioned.

Sharvesa stood and stormed away from the bed. Her response was grim. "I remember loving Beelzebub ... up until the moment I was cast into Hell. It was then I realized the error of my ways. After that, I hated him."

With her memories flooding to the forefront of her mind, Sharvesa placed one hand over her mouth and the other across her belly. She returned to the bed and took a seat. "I cannot believe I followed him to my own destruction. How could I be so foolish and abandon the Almighty's love?" She gave

Alistar a solemn look. "How could you continue to serve the Morning Star after what he convinced us to do?"

Alistar pushed himself to the edge of the bed and allowed his legs to drape over the side. "Be careful, Sharvesa. The one you claim to hate is the one who saved you. The Morning Star found a way to escape damnation. And when he did, he took us with him."

Yet another moment of silence passed before Sharvesa responded. "I don't remember his heroics. I only remember the suffering, the torment and the agony."

"How could you not?" Alistar responded.

Reconciling events in her mind, another long series of moments passed before Sharvesa spoke. "If Beelzebub found a way to save us, then why don't I remember?"

Alistar stood from the bed and walked toward the opening of the closet. "Hmmm … something is still missing. A closet isn't complete without a looking glass." A simple wave of his hand was all it took for a full length mirror with an ornate frame to appear on the wall left of the door. Satisfied with its design, the Demon-god of the Harvest spun around. "Do you approve?"

Sharvesa did not take the moments to enjoy Alistar's creation. Instead, she chastised, "I asked you a question."

Disappointed, Alistar walked back to the bed and took a seat. "After the Morning Star saved us from Hell, opposition was waiting for us on this plane. Many of those who were pulled from the torment were powerful and had agendas of their own. Because of this, two sides formed, and a series of wars began. They fought for the right to rule this plane, and the side they fought on was determined by whether or not they believed in free will. In the end, only 14 beings abandoned the foolishness and set aside their differences. We created the Collective and agreed upon rules to live by. We fought side by side against all others until they were vanquished."

Sharvesa cut in. "What of Beelzebub? What happened to him? Is he still alive?"

Alistar's head dropped. "The Morning Star perished. He was defeated by Bassorine after he refused to allow Bassorine to head the Collective."

"Bassorine? How could Bassorine defeat Beelzebub? Wasn't it Lasidious who was able to manipulate Bassorine's destruction? Lasidious is a far weaker being than Beelzebub was … isn't he?"

Though his head remained lowered, a smile appeared on Alistar's face. "Manipulation can be a strong weapon, and if wielded correctly, it can be more powerful than the sword. In the end, Bassorine was unable to swallow his pride. He could not see beyond the manipulation that caused his destruction. It was Lasidious' mind that destroyed him."

Placing his right hand on Sharvesa's back, Alistar continued. "Those of us who survived the wars created the Book. In it, sits the laws we abide by, and as you know, the Book has the power to govern us all. And as you also know, we have been gathering the devastation from the wars and using it to create the worlds that exist on this plane.

"As I have said before, it was our love for you that forced us to vote nay. You're our sister, and I will say it again. It is for this reason that we wanted the best for your world. We did not want you to suffer in Hell again."

Sharvesa leaned over, grabbed Alistar's knee and shook it. "Despite your good intentions, I shall still suffer because my daughter is being forced to live there. What can we do about that?"

Alistar stood from the bed and walked to the center of the cave. He lifted his arms toward the ceiling and spread his wings. "Worry not!" he proclaimed. "Lasidious and I have a plan. Everything we've done has been for the sole purpose of attaining the power to save your world. We will need the power of the demons to stand against the others. We intend to bring Beelzebub back, and when we do, our united army will take control of the Collective and force it to recreate Dragonia."

Alistar pulled his attention away from the roof of the cave and found Sharvesa's eyes. His voice was soft as he spoke. "Your daughter…" he paused, "…my niece … will be spared. You won't have to suffer the worries of a burdened mother."

Alistar smiled. "Because of our actions, peace will fall across the worlds. The souls who live upon them will be given one being to worship. You and I will serve the Morning Star. He will return us to our former glory and allow us to be the illustrious angels we once were."

Sharvesa stood from the bed and concluded. "I suppose this all makes sense. For as many seasons as I can remember, Lasidious has been good to me. On many occasions, he came to me while I lived on Dragonia to help me govern the races of demons. He saw to it that we had a peaceful existence."

The goddess paused. "Tell me, Alistar, why would Lasidious ask us to pray to him if his intent was to eventually glorify the Morning Star? You said you exist to serve him, so I can only assume he has returned. Will not Beelzebub be displeased once he learns of Lasidious' actions?"

Alistar nodded to acknowledge the validity of Sharvesa's question. "Allow me to ask you this: if Lasidious had done otherwise, wouldn't the others in the Collective have become suspicious?"

Sharvesa pondered the question. "Your point has been made. When will I get to lay my eyes upon Beelzebub? I need to speak my mind before I can extend forgiveness."

"Soon. But first ... there are events that must take place. You'll learn of them when the proper moment arrives."

Sharvesa sat in silence for one last moment before she changed the subject. "Lasidious was good to me throughout my seasons as queen. I must remember to thank him."

Alistar held up his hand. "Yes, you must, but Lasidious failed you in one area where I did not." The Demon-god of the Harvest pointed and grinned. "He failed to give you a bed. Perhaps you should thank me first."

Sharvesa smiled as she looked at her reflection in the headboard. "Thank you, Alistar. You've been kind to me."

The goddess' demeanor changed. "I only wish I could remember why I followed Beelzebub out of Heaven. I suppose the memory of loving him will have to suffice until we speak." She looked at Alistar. "My instincts tell me to trust you. If helping you rally demonkind to stand behind your uprising will bring peace to the worlds and spare my daughter the torment of the new Hell, then I shall do what I must."

Alistar walked across the room and extended his hands. After Sharvesa took them, he pulled her into his embrace. "There's much more we need to discuss. We should start with your son, Payne..."

Now, fellow soul ... I need to say one thing. Lasidious and Alistar's manipulations were fathoms upon fathoms deeper than what you've just learned. Just wait until you learn more of what I know.

THE WORLD OF LUVELLES
THE SOURCE'S OLD CAVERNOUS HOME
THE NEXT MORNING

Lasidious was standing next to one of the streams of lava that flowed through the immense cavern when Alistar appeared behind him.

"How are you, brother?" Alistar questioned.

The Mischievous One did not turn around. He kept his eyes fixed on the lava, despite hearing the sound of his brother's voice—the sound of his demon voice. "Your meeting with Sharvesa must have gone well."

"What makes you so sure?"

Lasidious grinned. "You would not have appeared as demon if it had not." The Mischievous One turned and looked up to find Alistar's eyes, which were nearly two paces above his own. "You look powerful." He lifted his hand and balled his fist. "You look ready for battle. Can I count on you to deal with the others when the moment arrives?"

Alistar spit on the floor. "Of course! I'm as ready as you are! Don't patronize me like you patronize the others! I'm with you … just as I have always been!"

Lasidious nodded. "I meant no disrespect." The Mischievous One stepped forward and took hold of Alistar's hands. He admired how the size of Alistar's fingers dwarfed his own. "Soon, we will have everything our hearts desire."

Pulling his hands away, Alistar turned to summon a throne to sit on. The throne was made from the skulls and limbs of his worshipers who had perished throughout the seasons. Once comfortable, the God of Harvest questioned, "Are you confident that you'll be able to acquire the children's trust? If you fail, our hopes for the future we've envisioned will vanish, and you will have sacrificed everything for nothing."

Lasidious responded. His voice grew deeper as he transformed. "You don't need to worry about my ability to perform. Garrin's power will be mine soon enough."

Like his brother, the Mischievous One's skin turned burnt-red. The demon that emerged from the transformation also had horns that protruded from his head, but the size of Lasidious' horns were much larger than Alistar's. They exuded the depth of his power and showed that Lasidious was a far stronger being.

By the moment the transformation was complete, Lasidious stood another three hands taller than Alistar, and his wings extended an additional half-pace in length on either side of his mass. As Lasidious stretched, the glory of his power was revealed, and at 5 paces tall, he weighed more than 700 pounds.

Lasidious' eyes flashed bright red as he looked down. "Make no mistake, brother, this plane will change."

Alistar leaned forward. "Your confidence is comforting, but what about the Morning Star? Once his memory returns, his power will return. Are you as confident in your ability to manipulate him as you are with the children?"

A booming laugh filled the cavern as Lasidious rolled his head back and extended his arms with wings spread. Many moments passed before Lasidious calmed himself to respond. "I shall steal the Morning Star's power as promised." He turned away and walked into the flowing lava. Reaching down, Lasidious cupped a handful and rubbed it onto his skin. "I shall have my revenge. Once I have his power, I'll destroy him and bring change to what has been created. The Collective will grovel at my feet and beg for me to spare their existence."

"What will you do then?" Alistar questioned. "Will you keep your promise to me?"

Lasidious stepped out of the lava and summoned a throne of his own. Like Alistar's, it was made from the bones of past worshipers. After sitting, the Mischievous One leaned forward to match his brother's posture. "I would never abandon my promise to you. I'll leave this plane, and you can do with it as you please."

The Mischievous One leaned back and crossed his right leg over his left. "Besides ... why would I want to stay here when my vengeance will not yet be complete? I have bigger aspirations than to rule a plane with only two stars."

Alistar smiled and leaned back. "You're mad, you know that? Have you forgotten the power he commands? To challenge him will only end in suffering. Perhaps you should stay and rule with me. There's more than enough for us to share."

Lasidious chuckled. "Unlike you, brother, I seek to be the absolute power. This miserable existence won't be enough to pacify my vanity. I must go."

"But it's suicide."

"Not so."

Lasidious stood from his throne and walked back into the lava. "I remember the mistakes Beelzebub made. I'll use this to my advantage. Every being will bow to me."

Alistar stood and waved his hand across his throne. After watching it vanish, he responded. "Let's change the subject."

Lasidious rolled his eyes. "If you must."

The Demon-god of the Harvest grinned. "Sharvesa won't be a problem. She'll help however you see fit."

"I knew it!" Lasidious boasted. "Then the memories I planted into her subconscious are working. Does she believe she's our sister?"

"She does."

"Perfect. And does she want to save her daughter?"

"Of course, she does."

"And does she also believe that she was the former goddess, Sekhmet?"

"Again, she does."

Lasidious clapped his hands. "Ha! Can you believe we tricked someone with a heart as pure as Sharvesa's into believing such nonsense? Sharvesa ... a goddess ... what a farce. If Sekhmet was around to hear what we've done, she'd destroy Sharvesa for having the gall to believe that she could be as glorious." Lasidious grabbed his chin in thought. "I told you Sharvesa's desire to protect her daughter would be strong enough."

Alistar chuckled. "Your head expands too quickly, brother. You didn't step too far out on a limb with that declaration. Protecting their offspring is, after all, what mothers do."

The Mischievous One ignored Alistar's snide comment and reached down to cup another handful of lava. Instead of rubbing it on his skin, he drank it. "Refreshing," the demon sighed. "I've missed that taste." Turning from the flow, Lasidious changed the subject again. "Did you address the situation regarding Payne?"

"I did."

"And what did she say?"

Alistar smirked. "She believes you placed Payne with George to ensure her son's well being."

"Was she irritated that a human was caring for him?"

"Of course, she was ... just as any demon would be. But I explained there was no other option, and Payne was in desperate need of love. Once she heard that, she didn't appreciate the fact that you intend to see George's family perish."

"Did you explain why?"

"Of course, I did."

"And?"

"And she seemed to warm up to the idea of their destruction after I explained George took Payne's power from him and gave it to Kepler. I told her it was only a matter of moments before revenge for this injustice would be served, and it wouldn't be long before Payne could be with her again."

Lasidious grinned and then removed his armor. He tossed it onto the floor of the cave and lowered into the lava to bathe. "Does Sharvesa know Mosley is on a quest to destroy George and Kepler?"

"She does."

"How did she react to that?"

"As expected, she was pacified, and I think she's willing to help Mosley find the power to end George." Alistar also removed his armor and lowered into the lava. "Everything is as it should be. As planned, Shalee has been swallowed by the Eye. She's no longer a threat, and Sam has been trapped on Dragonia where we need him. It will only be a matter of moments before we can move forward with the next part of your plan. Everything we wanted to accomplish has happened, despite the adjustments we've had to make."

Alistar reached into the lava and splashed the flow onto the upper part of his arms. "Is Kael ready to do his part?"

The Mischievous One extended his hand and commanded a nearby boulder to float across the cavern. The stone settled into the lava behind him. After leaning against it, Lasidious responded. "Kael is ready ... just as I said he would be."

"What did you promise the blade for his cooperation?"

The Mischievous One rubbed an additional handful of lava across his right forearm. "I promised to take him with me. I told Kael that he'd feel the blood of the Almighty's angels."

"That is wonderful!" Alistar cheered as he used his wings to scoop the lava and splash it across his chest. "The sword is clearly ready to serve a master without weakness."

"Of course, he is!" Lasidious exclaimed. "Beelzebub failed him just as he failed us! And where he failed, I won't. The blade believes in me. I'll deliver him to his rightful place. Kael will hang from glory's hip for eternity, and everyone will know that he was the weapon responsible for my ascension to absolute power."

Grinning, Alistar splashed Lasidious with lava. "Calm down, or your head will explode." The Demon-god of the Harvest enjoyed Lasidious' frown as he stood and stepped out of the lava. He put on his armor and added, "There's planning that needs to be done. Celestria has joined the others on Dragonia. She has decided to help with the transformation of that world. I was forced to take the moments to hide Garrin and the prince's presence in case her eyes were to fall upon them."

"Did you hide the king as well?"

"No, I didn't. I saw no reason to. There's nothing Sam could say to jeopardize our plans."

Lasidious rebutted. "Yes, there is. He could tell her that I was the one who placed him inside the barrier he sits in."

"So?"

"What do you mean? This would make her angry."

"Who cares?" Alistar reasoned. "Celestria's anger will not help her find your location, nor will it stop the outcome of what we've planned."

The Mischievous One pondered his brother's response. "I suppose you're right. What could she do?"

"Exactly."

"Then we should proceed in earnest."

"Swiftly it is," Alistar nodded and then changed the subject. "When will you approach the Vampire King?"

A wide grin spread across Lasidious' face. "Soon, my dear brother … very soon…"

The Crystal Shard

When you want an update about your favorite characters

NORTHERN GRAYHAM

Medolas, Clandestiny, Gage and **Gallrum**—The party is still making their way back to Hydroth. Gage has learned of Mosley and now knows that the wolf traveled with Medolas and Clandestiny for a brief period of moments. The badger believes the wolf was the reason he came to Northern Grayham, but now that Mosley has vanished, Gage has no idea where to search for him. After speaking with Gallrum about his feelings regarding the wolf's absence, the goswigs have decided to press forward with the Isorians to Hydroth in hopes that they will learn of the wolf's location.

Shiver and **Gablysin**—The Isorian Army is still working throughout every moment of every Peak to tunnel to the spot where King Shiver has ordered the hollow created. Gablysin and the king intend to meet with Hydroth's engineers, and they will determine the best way to flood the hollow once the ice collapses beneath the Tormalian army's feet.

Meerum Bosand—Meerum is now only 2 Peaks from the home of the Ko-dess. After leaving Gesper, the king used his magic to speed up his harugen's ability to skitter across the ice. He travels this way because he isn't familiar enough with the territory to teleport to the Ko-dess' home.

THE WORLD OF LUVELLES

George—After ensuring the family was not going to relapse and remember Garrin's absence, George teleported back to Eastern Luvelles. He is now sitting inside an inn called The Misplaced in a village called Specks. Apparently, the innkeeper's wife is an elderly, fit woman with a short memory. Because of her memory, Jackson, the innkeeper, a chubby halfling, named the inn the way he did. Jackson's wife is always losing her effects, and she is constantly forgetting where Jackson has gone within a few moments of him leaving the establishment.

Lasidious, Sharvesa and **Alistar**—After Alistar and Lasidious finished their conversation in the Source's old cavern, both gods returned to their former appearances. Alistar left Luvelles to meet up with Sharvesa. The demon-goddess has made many more remarkable changes to her cave, and Alistar offered a few other pieces of advice on the design before they rejoined the rest of the Collective on the new Hell.

Alistar plans to keep an eye on Celestria while the Collective puts the final touches on Hell. The gods must set the planet in motion around its new sun and make sure that its moons orbit the planet without affecting the gravitational fields of the others. Everything must be monitored for a number of Peaks before stasis that still lies across Hell can be lifted. This should happen 4 Peaks from now.

DRAGONIA
THE NEW HELL

Kepler, Sam, Garrin, the Prince and the imp, **Pydum**—Sam is getting restless while the others are still in stasis. Other than a few unnecessary outbursts of rage by Sam, there is nothing more to report here.

THE HIDDEN GOD WORLD
ANCIENTS SOVEREIGN

The Book of Immortality and the **Archangel Michael**—The Book and Michael have met again. It has been determined that the Book must go to Anahita and help her with the creation of the new Heaven while Michael attends to other matters that the archangel claims to be the Almighty's bidding.

A PLACE UNKNOWN

Anahita and **Helga**—The duo is fighting to stay together. Helga can feel herself slipping away, and Anahita is unable to focus on the creation of the new Heaven because of the loss she knows she will suffer once Helga vanishes from their shared mind. Anahita can only find comfort when she sits in front of the mirror and allows Helga to control their lips to tell stories of the older woman's childhood.

THE WORLD
OF
HARVESTOM

Mosley—After waking from the deep sleep the wolf was placed into by Lasidious, Mosley has spent the last few Peaks recovering. This is the first Peak that Mosley has felt like exploring the Priestess' palace. But his mind is unsettled.

Thank you for reading the Crystal Shard

Chapter 12
You're Not the Father
The Priestess of Harvestom's Palace
Late Bailem

All Praises Be To Helmep For Through His Loving Grace The Wretched Are Healed.

Mosley strolled through the priestess' palace and stopped beneath the banner praising Helmep. After reading it, he then trotted down the long corridor lined with pillars and entered the herb room. The priestess was inside. "Good evening," the wolf said with a rested voice. "I trust your most recent visit with the Dragon Council went as planned this morning?"

Fosalia Rowaine turned from the stone bowl that she was using to mill herbs she had collected after meeting with the council. "Oh, yes," she verified. "If only I could've taken you with me, Mosley. Everything on Shaymlezman is grand … and massive." Her eyes widened. "Monstrous even!" The priestess giggled. "I feel like I'm a speck of dust whenever I stand before the Source. And though the others on the council pale in comparison to the Ancient One's size, they still tower leagues above me."

Mosley smiled as a wolf would. "I can only imagine. I'm not familiar with the name Shaymlezman. Is this the designation the Source gave to the new dragon world?"

The priestess' brows furrowed. "Yes, it's the name he bestowed, but there is nothing new about that world. It has always been."

Mosley bit his tongue to remind himself that his memories were different than other mortals who occupied the worlds. To them, the dragon world had always existed. The gods had adjusted their memories, and the writings on each world had also been adjusted to document Shaymlezman's history.

To compensate for the awkwardness, Mosley conceded. "Forgive me. I simply misspoke. If only my eyes could've seen what you have."

The wolf's comment caused Fosalia to ponder. "Perhaps they can." She squatted in front of Mosley. "Allow me to put my hands on your head, and I'll show you what I imagine a bird would've seen as it flew over the meeting."

Mosley stepped forward. "I'd like that."

The priestess whispered, "Then close your eyes."

After watching the wolf comply, Fosalia placed her hands on Mosley's head. The command flowed from her mouth like a song. *"Sez yalla tafoe og tomaloyo."* It was not long before the priestess' hands began to glow, and a vision appeared in the wolf's mind.

"I can see the Source," Mosley uttered. "You're right, he's monstrous. I can also see the other dragons, and they tower over you just as you said they did. Ahhhh, and now I see two tiny beings. They're standing near some sort of pillar. I can only assume one of them was you."

"It was," Fosalia responded. "The being standing beside me was Helmep. My Lord set up the meeting so that I could ask the Source for permission to gather the herbs that grow across the valleys of his new world."

"Did the dragon agree?"

"He did. I was milling some of them when you entered." She pulled back her hands and allowed the vision to fade. "Oh, Mosley, I can't express my excitement. The medicines I'll discover because of the plants that grow on Shaymlezman will be far superior to any that I can produce from those that grow on the lower four worlds."

"What about Dragonia? Will the medicines also be better than the ones produced from that world?"

The priestess' eyes filled with confusion. "I don't understand. I've never heard of Dragonia."

✦⊱⊰✦

Now, fellow soul … I should explain something before we go further. Since Lasidious manipulated Mosley's mind and caused the wolf to forget about his journey into Northern Grayham, Mosley had no idea that stasis fell across the worlds. Despite this fact, Mosley still possessed godly memories. The rest of the wolf's mind was unaffected when the gods manipulated the minds of the others who lived throughout the worlds. Because of this, the wolf's memories of Dragonia were still intact, though in Fosalia's mind, Dragonia never existed—or so she allowed the wolf to believe.

Because Mosley did not know about stasis, a confused look appeared on his face. "Of course, you've heard of Dragonia," Mosley insisted. "I was there 10 seasons ago when your mother met with Bassorine and Helmep to discuss a cure for the ailments of a dying forest called Pordrilian."

Fosalia held firm. "You're mistaken. I've never heard of that world, nor did I lay my eyes upon a man named Bassorine."

Mosley growled in frustration. "How could you not remember? Bassorine held you in his arms when he greeted you. Do you not remember how honored you felt to be hugged by a god?"

"I remember nothing of the sort," the priestess defended. "Your mind has clearly been deeply affected by your journey into the neutral lands on Southern Grayham. Perhaps you need further rest."

The wolf took a step back. Instead of arguing, he took the moments to think about previous discussions he had with the priestess when she looked in on him to ensure he had been fed. *Why would she continue to believe I was found on Southern Grayham? I've already claimed that I wasn't there. And if I was, and my memory has failed me, why would I not remember the face of the man she claims brought me here?*

Still unnerved, Mosley spoke. "Perhaps you're right. I'll retire to my den and collect my thoughts. Perhaps we could speak again in the morning?"

Fosalia nodded. "Of course." She knelt in front of the wolf and scratched the bottom of his jaw. "Try to come prepared. I'd like to begin your training. I'll see to it that you're fed well."

Mosley left the herb room and began a walk that would take him through a maze of hallways before he reached his quarters. As the wolf periodically stopped to sniff the corners of various corridors, he continued to struggle with the holes in his memory. *Why can't I remember this Barramore? Who is he, and how could he have found me in the neutral territories. And if he did, how could he have known that I speak the languages of the Ancient Mystics and the Swayne Enserad? And why would he bring me here, and what is his relationship to the priestess?*

The wolf lifted his head from the corner he was sniffing and closed his eyes. He took a deep breath. A long period of moments passed before he opened them. He spoke aloud, though the hallway was empty. "The last thing I remember, I was speaking with Celestria on the banks of the Blood Sea on Southern Grayham."

Rounding the final bend, Mosley used his magic to command the door to his bedroom chamber to open. As the door closed behind him, he thought, *I also remember speaking to Cadromel, but why do I feel as if something is missing from my memory of those moments? Perhaps I should seek the wisp once I possess the ability to teleport between worlds. Perhaps the sphere could enlighten me.*

DRAGONIA
THE NEW HELL

THE OLD MERCHANT ISLAND ON HELL

After 250 push-ups, 500 sit-ups, 250 body-squats, and various other exercises to pass his moments, Sam flopped onto his back. "Aahhhhhhhhhhhhh!" he shouted. "I'm so bored!" He rolled over and looked at Kael.

The sword was still ablaze and shedding light. Their current location was on the far side of the planet that still had not seen Hell's new sun.

"I can't stand this anymore, Kael! If I have to sit in this bubble much longer, I'm going to go insane!"

Sitting up, Sam grabbed one of the apples that Lasidious had left behind and whipped the fruit past Kepler's haunches toward the protective barrier the Mischievous One had established. Sure enough, the fruit passed through the bubble, but it did not fly much farther than a pace before the apple stopped and froze solid, mid-air. It was now trapped in stasis just like the jaguar.

"Dang! Did you see that, Kael?"

Realizing his question was ridiculous, Sam grabbed another apple and chucked it as hard as he could. The fruit made it only a hand or two beyond the first before it, too, froze solid. "Of course you didn't see it!" he grumbled. Punching the ground with his right fist, Sam screamed again, "I'm so bored!"

The blade allowed a moment or two to pass before he responded. "Are you finished complaining? Your tantrum will solve nothing."

"Easy for you to say," Sam rebutted. "You're a piece of metal. You were designed to hang around and pass your moments meaninglessly. I could put you into a corner, and you'd be happy as a lark."

"I wouldn't allow you to place me in a corner."

Sam crossed his arms. "You'd have no choice. I'm the master, not you."

If Kael would have had eyes, the blade would have rolled them. "Your complaining has become tiresome. Why don't you stop?"

Sam snapped, "Don't tell me to stop! Who are you to tell me anything? I own you, not the other way around."

The blade did not offer a response. Instead, Kael's flame intensified. "Allow me to demonstrate who the master truly is in this union."

Sam stood in defiance as the temperature within the bubble began to rise. "Don't speak to me in that tone! Have you forgotten what you are?" The king held up his hands and rolled his fingers. "Without these, you'd be just another sword that collects dust. I wield you ... not you me."

Hearing the insult, Kael lifted from the ground and hovered. His flame pulsated and crackled as the temperature within the barrier elevated. "Is that so, King of Nothing! You've lost everything."

"Really?" Sam sneered. "And what have I lost that I can't reclaim?"

Kael's laugh was devious. "I shall provide you a list. You've lost your home, your wife, the respect of those who bowed to your crown, and you've even lost your self-respect."

"That's it?" Sam jeered. "That's the best you've got?"

"No, King of Nothing. I have more to say."

"Let's hear it then."

"As you wish, Master," Kael responded in a condescending tone, the pulse of his blade matching his mood. "You have also lost your son ... a son that was never yours." The blade's voice turned cold and shallow. "Did you truly believe you were the father? Your seed was not responsible for the fruit that was produced by Shalee's womb."

Sam's eyes narrowed. "Shut the hell up! Just shut up! Don't talk about my kid that way!"

Kael's laugh pierced Sam's soul. "Does the truth hurt, King of Nothing? Your son is a bastard child."

Sam retaliated by grabbing Kael's blade. He wanted to throw the weapon beyond the barrier, but he was forced to let it go since he was no longer protected from the flame. Staring at the boils on his right palm, the king shouted, "Damn you! Who do you think you are?"

The fire enveloping the blade intensified, but Sam remained defiant. "I command you to stop!"

The blade hovered toward Sam and stopped just as the king's backside was about to pass beyond the barrier. "You no longer command me. This Peak will be your last."

Sam tried to stand firm, but the heat emanating from the weapon became too much to bear. The King of Nothing dropped to his knees. "Please," he begged. "Please, stop!"

Kael did not respond. Instead, he waited until Sam fell forward onto his stomach. As the king's eyes shut, Kael allowed his flame to dissipate. He hovered close and then lowered onto his point. The weapon spoke only after he was sure that Sam was unconscious. "You're too valuable to terminate. Perhaps the moment has come for you to consume the rest of Yaloom's potion."

MEANWHILE, EASTERN LUVELLES
THE VILLAGE OF SPECKS
THE MISPLACED INN

George lowered his mug of ale to the bar and placed his hands on top of it. The counter was warm. *The structures here must be alive as well,* he thought.

Like his home, the bar had a pulse, and he could feel the structure's heartbeat as its life's source coursed through the vein that passed beneath his hands.

Looking across the bar, the warlock watched as an elderly, chubby, half-elf male dried a stack of wooden plates and then placed them to the right of an expansive mirror that hung on the back wall. "Didn't you say your name was Jackson?" George questioned.

The innkeeper tossed his rag to the counter and turned around. "Aye, I did." Jackson pointed to George's mug. "Would you be needin' another ale, lad?"

The warlock pushed the mug across the counter. "If you wouldn't mind."

"You just sit tight. I'll be back in two shakes of a nanny's tail." Jackson grabbed the glass and walked toward the far end of the bar.

As he did, George questioned. "What's a nanny?"

Jackson stopped. "Whatdaya mean, lad? Every Shale knows what a nanny is."

George shrugged. "Well, I don't, and I don't know what a Shale is either."

Jackson's expressive brows dropped. "Truly?"

"Yes … truly. I wouldn't lie about that."

"How could a lad like yourself not know such things?"

"I'm not from here." George reached behind his ears and pushed them forward. "See? No point."

Jackson's eyes widened. "Well I'll be," he marveled. He lifted his voice and called, "Grazenna! Grazenna! Come out here and take a look! I have a human settin' in front of my eyes."

Holding his gaze fixated on George, Jackson placed the warlock's mug beneath a silver spigot that had been attached to a large, wooden keg. He slid the mug down the bar after he skimmed the bubbles off the top. "You must be a young one by the looks of you."

"A young what?" George responded.

"Human."

"Oh, yeah, yeah, yeah. I am young, I suppose. Why?"

"No reason. Just an observation. What number of seasons do you claim?"

"Ummm … do you mean how old am I?"

"Of course, he does," a grouchy voice grumbled.

George pulled his eyes off Jackson and directed them to the opposite end of the bar. He said nothing as two, black, swinging doors rocked back and forth after a fit, elderly, half-elf female exited the back room.

"Well, don't sit there, lad. Answer the man!" she commanded. "Do humans not age as halflings do?"

George grinned. "How am I supposed to know? We age similarly, I guess. And to answer the question, I'm 24 seasons."

Grazenna frowned. She grabbed a rag from the counter and threw it at Jackson. "How could you be feedin' this child ale?" She looked at George. "Does your mother know you're traversing the countryside without proper supervision?" Removing George's ale from his hand, she replaced it with a mug of water. "I'd wager my last Helmep that she'd be swimmin' in anger if she knew my husband was poisonin' her child."

"Oh, stop it, Grazenna!" Jackson barked. "He's not a child. Just look at his chin, why don't ya?"

Grazenna motioned for George to lean across the bar. "Come closer, boy." She reached out and felt the warlock's face. "I'll be fit to giggle. This child has stubble."

"Of course, he does!" Jackson snapped. "I can see it from here, and humans don't age as we age. Even I know enough about them to know that."

Grazenna reclaimed George's mug of ale and then returned it to him. "Where do you hail from?"

"Earth," George smirked. "Ever heard of it?"

"Can't say that I have," she responded, "but I've never been much for books and learnin'."

Jackson slapped his hand against the bar. "That right there was the understatement of the season, lad. My wife isn't the most reliable when it comes to knowledge of places beyond the village."

The look Grazenna gave Jackson was enough to make the innkeeper step out from behind the bar. He took a seat next to George. "She can be a tad bit forceful," he whispered.

"I can see that," George whispered back.

Jackson looked away and smiled at Grazenna. "My love ... if memory serves me right, you were about to bake an ospliton pie."

Grazenna grumbled, but did not say a word. She turned and walked back through the swinging doors.

Jackson patted George on the back. "Don't fret none, lad. A moment from now, she won't remember a thing." He lifted his voice and shouted in the direction of the swinging doors. "I'll be back in a moment, love. I'm goin' to show the youngster what a nanny is and introduce him to a fine bunch of Shaloneans."

The innkeeper placed his hand on the back of George's shoulder and led the warlock out of the establishment. As they headed down the road, Jackson pointed to a structure in the distance that reminded George of a high-class, western saloon. "My good friend, Mordain, has an inn of his own. Whatdaya say we make it there and grab an ale or two?"

"What about your wife?" George questioned. "You just told her you'd be right back?"

"Don't fret about her. Her memory is somethin' awful. By now, she's forgotten you were there. You could walk back in and take a seat, and she wouldn't remember your face."

"Must suck to be her," George added.

Unsure of what George meant by "suck," Jackson changed the subject. "What brought you to Specks?"

"I'm looking for someone to guide me to the island of the wood elves."

"Wood elves, you say? A fair trek for a man who's never been to their island." Jackson reached up and played with his beard. "I can't say I personally know of a man who has set foot upon it, so teleporting there might be a bit of a problem."

The innkeeper reached down and grabbed a pebble off the dirt road. "You know, it's been a while since I last spoke in conversation about those devils. Them wood elves are known for their feistiness and evil doin's." He stopped and faced George. "Tell me, why would a youngster such as yourself go lookin' for trouble?"

George grinned. "I'm not looking for trouble. I can't tell you what I'm looking for, but I can say it's not trouble."

"It's your head, lad," Jackson replied. "Whatdaya say I take you to meet the Slave Master in Drandel once we've polished off a few? Perhaps he can get you closer to the island than I can."

"Sounds good to me," the warlock responded. "Let's get going."

Jackson reached out. "Take my hand."

George did as requested. The next thing the warlock knew, he was standing outside the entrance to Mordain's inn, and Jackson was bounding up the steps in front of him to grab an ale.

A PLACE UNKNOWN
ANAHITA'S SHACK

"...Then what happened?" Anahita questioned. "Did she jump?"

Helga struggled to regain control of the lips she shared with Anahita. "She did. Melana always trusted our brother ... just as I did. We looked up to him. She was so brave … much braver than I was. She leapt from the top of the cliff without a second thought."

"Oh my goodness-gracious," Anahita gasped. "Did she float like Drasson said she would? Was the magic strong enough to hold her up?"

"No, Child," Helga sighed. "There was no magic."

"Oh my gosh. Then Drasson lied to you. How far did she fall?"

It took a while for Helga to assume control, but when she did, tears filled their eyes. "She fell for what seemed like forever. Her body tumbled against the cliffs and smashed against the rocks again and again until she met a watery end."

"That's terrible. That's absolutely dreadful."

A depressing silence filled the cabin before Helga was able to speak again. "I was never the same after that. I hated Drasson for making us believe we could fly. To this Peak, I often think about what would've happened if I had been the brave one. I would've been the one to jump first."

"I hate to say it, but I'm glad you weren't. I wouldn't have known you if you had been."

Helga managed to force a smile and then added, "We were so young. I should've known better. I should've protected her."

"You can't blame yourself," Anahita consoled. "As awful as it was, it wasn't your fault." Anahita went to the table and pulled a chair in front of the mirror to take a seat. "I've gotta ask. What did Drasson say after he watched her fall? Did he show any remorse at all?"

"He didn't say anything, Child," Helga sighed. "He just laughed."

Anahita threw her hands across their mouth. "Oh my goodness. What did you do? Did you tell anyone?" She reached out and grabbed the frame of the mirror and stared into the eyes of their reflection. "At least tell me he got what he deserved."

Another quiet period of moments passed while Helga fought for control to answer. "I told no one ... but he did get what he deserved."

"How?"

"I was young, but I was big enough to push him when his back was turned. I shoved him over the edge after he leaned out to see if Melana would surface." Helga struggled to clear their throat. "I didn't look away when I watched him fall."

"Good for you," Anahita affirmed.

Another brief series of moments passed before Helga found the strength to respond. "The sea covered my crime. It consumed Drasson's body just like it devoured Melana's."

Anahita clapped their hands. "That's what I call justice. I love it. You put a foot up his backside." Anahita stood and walked away from the mirror. "Doggonit! I wish I could've been there. I would've helped you hang him by his balls and skin him until he begged to be put out of his misery."

Helga managed to regain control of their lips and then produced a smile. "That would've been a sight to see, Child. If only I had your strength."

"Ha!" Anahita blurted. She walked back to the mirror. "I've looked to you on many occasions for strength since my arrival. Without you, I'd be fit to be tied."

Anahita waited for a response, but one never came.

"Helga. Are you still with me?"

No response.

"Helga! Answer me." Anahita tapped at their reflection. "Come on, old girl. You've gotta answer me."

Anahita kept at it for quite a while before Helga finally responded. "I'm here, Child … though I don't think I can hang on much longer."

"No, no, no, no, no. You can't leave me. I need you."

Near the door of the shack, a voice responded. "You must let her go, Anahita. You're prolonging your recovery by fighting her departure."

Anahita turned from the mirror to face the unfamiliar voice. She would have argued, but what she saw kept her from doing so. "What are you?" she demanded.

"I am the Book of Immortality," Gabriel responded. "I reside on Ancients Sovereign."

Anahita shrugged. "I suppose you think that knowing that would provide me with some sort of peace of mind."

Gabriel sighed. "Allow me to explain the reason for my visit. On my pages rest the laws of the gods, and inside my pages, the souls who have lived good lives. It is these souls who wait for you to create their Heaven. I have come to help you gain an understanding of the writings inside the book Michael left behind so you may begin creating."

It took a few moments for Anahita to accept the fact that a floating book with a face and arms had just claimed it was there to help. Sure, she knew of the Book, but never had she imagined its appearance. Despite her confusion, her thoughts returned to Helga. "I can't spare the moments to speak with you. I need to find a way to save my friend."

"Saving Helga is not what you're here to focus on, Anahita. You must—"

"I must nothing!" Anahita barked. "I don't even know you." She took a step toward the Book. "Don't even try to tell me anything about what I'm supposed to do. If I can't save Helga, then I don't care about creating your Heaven. Find another girl for the job."

"I'm afraid that's not an option," Gabriel rebutted. "There aren't the moments available to us to find a soul with your potential."

"Us? Who's us?"

"I speak of Michael and myself," the Book responded. "We require your cooperation if we're to save the worlds and establish peace on this plane."

"Oh, you require my cooperation, do you? Well it just so happens that I have a bone or two to pick with Mr. Archangel Michael-pants, and I'm not doing anything until two things happen. First: I want the chance to speak my mind. And second: I want you to help me find a way to fix Helga."

Gabriel floated across the room, stopped near Anahita and hovered eye-level as he responded. "It's not possible for you to speak with Michael at the moment. He has left this plane to do our father's bidding."

"Then we have nothing to discuss." She turned her back to the Book. "Get lost."

Gabriel's brows rolled inward. "I may not be able to appease your desire to speak with Michael, but I do have the means to find a solution to your second demand."

"Is that so?" Anahita replied as she looked up at their reflection in the mirror. "We're listening."

"If I give you Helga … would you move forward with the creation of Heaven until I can find a way for you to acquire the moments to solve your issues with my brother?"

Anahita spun around. "Your brother? Are you telling me that Michael is your kin?"

"I am."

"Really now? A book who has an angel for a brother. No shocker there. Perhaps you can answer a few questions?"

"I will do what I can if it creates the desire to move forward with what must be done."

"Alrighty then. You just answer one question, fix Helga, and then you've got yourself a deal."

Gabriel rocked back and forth as a book with a face would in order to nod. "Ask your question. I'd like to expedite our progress."

Anahita grabbed a chair and then pulled it toward the center of the room. As she did, the Book stared at the marks the chair left behind in the dirt until she took a seat.

"I want to know why Michael allowed the folks on this plane to pray to him. Why did he act like a god, and why would he assume a position of authority that is supposed to be reserved for the Almighty? How can I trust someone who says he's an archangel if he has fallen so far from grace?"

"It appears your question has many preceding questions," Gabriel responded, "but I shall answer them all. Michael, or rather, Bassorine, lost his way ... just as I did after we left our father's kingdom to save those who were damned ... those whom we loved."

Gabriel pointed a stern finger at Anahita. "You were the reason Michael chose to suffer in the first place. After you abandoned him for the love of another ... the love of the Morning Star ... you were at Lucifer's side when you were cast into the flames of Hell. Despite your actions, Michael's love for you was undying, and he was unable to abandon his sorrow."

Anahita shook her head. "I don't believe you."

"Your belief isn't necessary for it to be the truth. Perhaps you should try listening instead of speaking. You might learn something."

A deep scowl appeared on Anahita's face. "I'm listening."

"That's the smartest thing you've said since my arrival," the Book jabbed. "As I was about to say, it was because of his love for you that Michael came to me and one other ... one whom I won't name. He asked us to bear the burden of a continual torment to save you. To do so, we had to depart from the joy we knew and enter the flames of Hell. Many seasons passed before we found an escape. When we did, we pulled you onto this plane and gave you a second chance at finding peace. But a problem arose."

"What kind of problem?" Anahita queried.

"After Michael and I emptied the depths of Hell, we found ourselves caught in wars for dominance over the potential this plane offered. It was Lucifer who led the opposition, and by the moment it was over, everything and everyone was destroyed, save 15 beings. This group became known as the Farendrite Collective, and they knew Michael only by his new identity ... Bassorine. Because of Michael's sorrow and his shame, he abandoned his wings and refused to exist in the form of his true self."

"What about you?" Anahita questioned. "What did you do?"

"I went into hiding. But my reasons for this will remain my own."

Anahita frowned. "So then what happened to the others?"

Gabriel's eyes welled-up, and a tear rolled down the Book's right cheek. "Amongst those destroyed were the Morning Star and you. But your destruction came at the hands of the one who loved you most."

"What do you mean?"

"During the battles, you were captured and held as leverage. Since the other members of the Collective were not powerful enough to face the Morning Star, Lucifer challenged Bassorine to a duel for absolute power over this plane and the right to your hand."

Anahita shook her head. "Men. A little testosterone goes a long way."

Anahita's comment caused the Book to smile before he continued. "If Lucifer had not put a dagger to your throat, Bassorine would have declined his challenge, but this wasn't meant to be. You were in danger, and Bassorine's love for you … or rather, Michael's love for you, forced him to accept the challenge. If he had not, the reason we entered Hell would've been lost forever. Lucifer would've hidden your soul, and there would never have been a chance to give you the peace that Michael wanted to bestow upon you."

"What happened next?" Anahita urged.

Again, the Book grinned. "Your enthusiasm pleases me."

"Just get on with it, will ya?"

"As you wish. When the battle commenced, the others of the Collective were bound to stand by and watch, but you were unable to do so."

"What do you mean?"

"I'm getting to that. Allow me to speak."

"By all means, speak," Anahita replied.

"You see, after Lucifer removed his dagger from your throat, he cast you aside, and the battle commenced. The fighting was fierce and two of the last three unpopulated worlds that existed on this plane were destroyed in the mayhem."

A look of sadness appeared on the Book's face. "It was your desire to help Bassorine that caused your own destruction."

"What did I do?"

"You allowed your anger at the Morning Star's threat against your life to affect your judgment. As the fight continued, your anger swelled, and eventually you tried to intervene. You rushed into the battle while Bassorine's sword was in the midst of a whirlwind of strikes."

Anahita reached up and slapped her own forehead. "You've got to be kidding me. You're telling me that I screwed up pretty badly, aren't you? What other stupid things did I do?"

Gabriel chuckled. "I wouldn't be laughing, except for the fact that you are here now. I ask that you to forgive my enjoyment of your candor."

"Yeah, sure, you're forgiven. Keep talking."

Gabriel nodded. "As I was saying, Bassorine's sword was in the midst of a whirlwind of strikes. As I'm sure you've realized, you perished. Your soul was cut into three pieces.

"When this happened, Bassorine became enraged. He overpowered the Morning Star and drove his sword through Lucifer's chest to end the battle. Once our brother fell to the dirt on the last remaining planet … a barren planet that was recreated and is now known as Grayham, Bassorine gathered Lucifer's soul and the pieces of yours. Insanity set in, and he abandoned the Collective to seek segregation, and he did not return for more than 100 seasons."

Anahita leaned forward in her chair. "What did he do while he was gone?"

"After Bassorine regained his sanity, he devised a plan. Invigorated by its design, he returned and spoke only to me. We agreed not to tell the others of my existence, and further, we agreed to place the pieces of your soul into three bodies. Since each was incomplete and possessed a soul that needed to be mended, we decided your pieces would complete the process."

Anahita cut in. "What about the soul of Lucifer? What did Bassorine do with it?"

"In an effort to save our brother and give the Morning Star a second chance, Bassorine was willing to let go of what he cherished most. He made sure the strongest piece of your soul was placed into a new body, and then he offered you to Lucifer, but not in the way you would've expected."

"What do you mean by that?"

"Since our brother also required a new body, he was given one, and it was to this new identity that you were given. After you and the Morning Star were placed inside the Temple of the Gods on Southern Grayham, we decided it was best to alter your memories."

"Why? And when did this happen?"

"As I've said, it happened after you were placed on the altars inside the Temple of the Gods. You see, Anahita, Bassorine and I filled your minds with memories of Earth and lives past lived. It was our hope that you would form a union with our brother's new self, and see to it that he adopted the characteristics that he should've cherished while existing in our father's grace."

Anahita's brows furrowed. "Hold up! Are you saying that Sam is Lucifer?"

Gabriel did not respond. He did not need to since his face clearly showed the answer.

Anahita spoke again only after a long moment of silence. "This is some heavy garesh, but I think I understand what you're getting at. If I'm right, you hoped that I'd keep Sam from remembering who he was, and in reality, who he still is. You wanted your brother to have a good life, but a good life wasn't enough for you, was it? For whatever reason, you just had to make Sam fight his way into becoming a king. I guess I'll never understand a man's mind. You wanted him to be a good guy, yet you asked him to slay his way into power. Is there some sort of archangel badge of honor that made y'all do that?"

Annoyed, the Book floated toward the door of the shack and opened it. He looked into the darkness beyond and responded. "We were forced to make adjustments when we realized Lasidious had the power to take the Crystal Moon from Bassorine without Bassorine releasing his control over it."

Anahita closed the distance. She crossed the room and stopped next to the Book. "Wait a moment. Are you saying that Lasidious has power over the Collective, and he doesn't even know it?"

"Yes. He's had it for a while now."

"Goodness-gracious! Does Lasidious know that Bassorine didn't release his power over the Crystal Moon when he took it from the Temple of the Gods?"

Gabriel reclaimed Anahita's eyes. "No, because Bassorine released his control over the crystal to ensure Lasidious would not find out. We must consider ourselves fortunate that the Mischievous One doesn't realize the power he possesses to control the Collective."

"I'm confused. How could he not know that?" Anahita questioned.

The Book searched for a response. "Self-realization can often be hard to fathom. What I can say is this: Bassorine was the one to discover that Lasidious possessed the power to control the Collective, and this knowledge came before you awoke in the temple. Fear caused Bassorine to release his control over the crystal's pieces to ensure that Lasidious did not come to understand his power. This unexpected course of action was why we sent you and Sam on a journey that caused you to become the pawns we needed to beat Lasidious at his own game."

Anahita grabbed Gabriel's tiny arm. "Hold up! I need to clarify again. Are you telling me that Sam and I were sent on a journey to maintain a necessary deception that was designed to keep Lasidious from learning he had the power to kick your asses? Are you saying the games he plays with the gods are unnecessary, and he could destroy you if he wanted to?"

"Yes, that's exactly what I'm saying, and the laws written on my pages are useless against him. Even if I wanted to, I could not strike Lasidious down. Because of this, Michael and I have been forced to send you on this journey, and we were further forced to put Sam in an environment that we wanted to avoid. We had to ensure that you, Anahita, were on a path to acquire the power that we were lacking to control Lasidious. This power can only be acquired by creating a new Heaven for this plane. The power you must learn to wield throughout its creation will add to your foundation, and upon its completion, you should possess the strength to restore balance within the Collective."

Anahita frowned. "Let's just say for argument's sake that I believe you. How did you know that Lasidious was going to use the Crystal Moon to play a game with the gods?"

A grin appeared on Gabriel's face. "We didn't. We made an assumption."

"You made an assumption?" Anahita snapped. "How could you be sure you made the right call?"

Gabriel's grin widened as he closed the door to the shack. "We were forced to react. We were not sure we made the right decision. We simply reacted to what we felt a mind like Lasidious' would do."

Anahita rolled her eyes and walked to the table. She claimed the other seat and then lowered her head into the palms of her hands. "You're telling me you got lucky. That's all you're saying. I can't believe how crazy this is."

She looked across the room. "At least tell me why Bassorine, or Michael if you will, allowed the beings on this plane to pray to him? Didn't he fear the consequences of the Almighty?"

"No."

"How could he not? That goes against everything the Almighty commands."

Gabriel shrugged. "There is no good answer. By now, Michael and I—"

Anahita cut in. "Who are you ... really? You can't just be a book."

Instead of responding, Gabriel transformed into his true self. As Anahita's eyes witnessed the change, she boasted, "I knew it! I knew you weren't a book. Tell me who you are."

The archangel spread his wings and smiled. "I was known as Gabriel. I possess the same name now only because I influenced the members of the Collective into believing that it was the proper choice over the last 10,000 seasons."

"How in the heck did you influence a group of folks over 10,000 seasons?"

Gabriel smirked, "Subtly, of course."

Anahita could not stop herself from smiling. "But, of course. Whatever was I thinking?"

Once Gabriel stopped laughing, he continued. "You asked why Bassorine allowed the beings on this plane to pray to him. Your answer is simple, I suppose. With you not at his side and our brother, Lucifer, destroyed, Michael changed. For many, many seasons, he fell into a great depression. Over those seasons, his love for you faded, and he sought to appease his ego with the prayers of others."

Clearing his throat, the archangel summoned a mug of water. Once his thirst had been quenched, he continued. "It wasn't until Bassorine learned of Lasidious' desire to betray the Collective that he reclaimed his calling. He feared the freedom he was trying to offer you would be taken from you. He further feared that our brother would not become the man we wanted him to become.

"After much discussion, Michael and I decided a better plan was in order. We would need to make the necessary adjustments if we were to continue with our plan to allow you and the Morning Star to live again."

Anahita stood from her chair. "So how's that plan working for you?"

"Not as well as we would've hoped. It appears Lasidious knew who you were, and if he didn't, he knew enough about you to know you were a threat. But how he knew, we haven't discovered. Our only leverage over Lasidious is that he still believes the Book of Immortality has the power to destroy him."

"Well, do you?" Anahita questioned.

"As I have said, I do not ... nor does Michael, and neither does the rest of the Collective. Lasidious' power has surpassed ours, though the members of the Collective don't know it. The numbers of those who pray to Lasidious' name have increased drastically. It is for this reason he has become so powerful."

"Goodness-gracious! What are you going to do about it?"

The archangel smiled. "We will play the game better than Lasidious."

Anahita rolled her eyes. "Let me guess. Everyone is a chess piece, and it's all about keeping as many pieces on the board as you possibly can. I've heard that before."

Gabriel grinned. "You sound like Michael, but this isn't a simple game of chess. You, Anahita, are the only being who can stand between Lasidious and total domination. If he finds a way to amplify his power, or if he realizes his power before you're finished creating the new Heaven, you won't be able to stand against him. It is for this reason that you must expedite your growth. For only through creation can the power be acquired to win a battle of this magnitude."

A long silence fell across the shack while Anahita digested everything she had learned. Eventually, she walked to the door, opened it, stepped onto the threshold and looked into the darkness. "I need to understand something before I get started." She turned to face Gabriel. "When I learned that Bassorine was really Michael, he said something that stuck with me. You know … something beyond the whole 'you're the love of my life' garbage. He said I'll become more powerful than the mightiest being on Ancients Sovereign."

"And you will," Gabriel added, "if Lasidious doesn't come to understand his power first."

Anahita held up her hand. "Hush for a moment, will you? I'm trying to get out a full thought over here."

"I apologize. Please, continue."

"The problem is … considering what you've just told me about me dying … if Lasidious is already more powerful than both you and Bassorine, how could I possibly become more powerful than Lasidious. I guess what I'm trying to say is … if I wasn't powerful enough to protect myself from Michael's sword, and the Morning Star was not strong enough to defeat Michael, and Lasidious now has the power to defeat Michael … what makes y'all so sure that I'll be able to dominate once I've finished creating a new Heaven. What if you're wrong? What if Lasidious pummels me into the dirt?"

"He won't," the archangel cut in. "Michael and I have seen to that."

Gabriel moved to stand beside Anahita. "When you were lying upon the dais in the temple, Michael surrendered part of his power and filled the staff he intended to bestow upon you with it." The archangel reached down and took Anahita's hands. "Do you remember how it felt when you were learning how to use the staff? Do you remember the surge of Bassorine's power that filled your body?"

Anahita giggled. "That was Bassorine's power? Heck yes, I remember that. How could a girl forget that? Those were the best moments of my life." The part human, part angel walked to the center of the shack. She spread her wings and spun. "I'd give anything to experience that again!"

Gabriel was unsure how to act. "I'm not sure I understand. Perhaps you could explain why it was so amazing?"

Anahita stopped, held up a finger and rocked it back and forth. "You only wish I would explain. That's not going to happen, buster. A woman never talks about something like that." She paused. "Well, not to a man anyway."

"I think I understand," Gabriel responded. He pushed the door closed and returned to the table. "To conclude, you have the ability to become more powerful than the others on Ancients Sovereign because of Michael's sacrifice."

Anahita stopped smiling. "Wait a cotton-pickin' moment. Helga said she experienced similar moments when she trained with her staff. So Michael must have put part of his power into her staff as well." She walked to the table, lifted her wings, flopped into a chair and then crossed her arms in a huff. "I feel like he cheated on me."

Gabriel laughed.

"What's so funny?"

"Michael would not have poured part of his power into Helga's staff. To do so would've weakened him further."

"So how do you explain the fact that she also had amazing moments?"

Gabriel pondered the question. "Michael must have adjusted Helga's memories to believe that she had similar experiences to ensure your training felt as normal as it possibly could."

Anahita arms unfolded. "As weird as that sounds, it makes sense." She leaned forward and placed her hands on the table. "Now that I've had my questions answered, what about Helga? How are we going to fix her?"

THE WORLD OF HARVESTOM
THE PRIESTESS' PALACE
MORNING APPROACHES

Mosley awoke long before the sun rose above the horizon and made his way through the maze of corridors toward the back of the palace. It was there the wolf entered the priestess' library and began his search for any reference that he could find to prove to the priestess that Dragonia existed.

With the sun now cresting, Mosley had come to understand how the library was organized, and he was pawing through the pages of the sixth tome that he had removed from yet another shelf.

There is nothing here, the wolf thought. He used his power to slam the book shut. *How is it possible that there are no references to a planet that has existed for over 10,000 seasons?*

The wolf lowered to the floor and then looked up at the tallest shelf. He commanded two more books with heavy, brown bindings to float toward the table. As each settled, they opened. He reclaimed his former position by placing his front paws on the edge of the table and then stood on his hind legs.

A fair amount of moments passed before these tomes were also slammed shut. "Nothing!" he barked. "This is frustrating. My paws felt the dirt on Dragonia when Bassorine took me there. How is it possible that a...?"

The wolf stopped his rant. *Could it be?* he thought. *If so, the gods have begun the transformation.*

Mosley dropped from the table and rushed up a flight of steps to a section of shelves that stood in the far back of the second level. His eyes had new purpose as they settled onto a large tome with a heavy, red binding.

Like he had done with the others, Mosley used his power to remove the book from the shelf. Its binding opened as it touched the floor. The wolf began to paw through the writings as fast as he could. It was not long before he found a chapter entitled, "Hell."

"Then it has happened," he mumbled. "The gods have removed Dragonia from its orbit and created a home for the damned."

Closing the book, Mosley rushed back down the stairs and reopened one of the tomes he had left on the table. He stopped at a section that discussed the number of pieces the Crystal Moon possessed. "Five pieces," he uttered. "There should have been six after the Dragon World was created."

Mosley closed the book and then reascended the steps to the fifth level of the library. It was there he found a book dedicated to the intricacies of the Crystal Moon. On its pages, he learned the name of each world the crystal's pieces controlled, and Dragonia was not one of them.

He closed the book. "Stasis. It's the only explanation for Fosalia's belief that it never existed. She knows this world as Hell, not what it once was."

The wolf started to pace as he continued to think. "If the priestess' memory is intact, and the gods are responsible for altering her mind, then I can trust in what she proclaims. She must be speaking the truth about this Barramore. Yet how could I have forgotten about my journey into the Neutral Territory on Southern Grayham?"

As Mosley continued to ponder aloud, he left the library to meet the priestess for breakfast.

Chapter 13
For the Love of Your Woman
Ancients Sovereign
The Book's Hall of Judgment
It's a New Peak, the Peak of Bailem

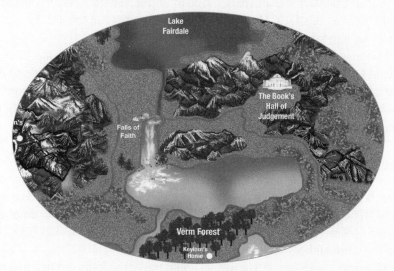

The gods gathered in Gabriel's hall, and Alistar was waiting for Keylom's hooves to stop clapping so he could call the meeting to order.

Since the Book and the Mischievous One were nowhere to be found, those present determined that Gabriel and Lasidious' input was not necessary to move forward to set Hell in motion.

"If you don't mind, Keylom!" Alistar chastised. "I can't hear myself think above the clamoring of your hooves."

The centaur-god stopped fidgeting. "Forgive me. My mind is unsettled. We shouldn't vote without Gabriel and Lasidious."

"The Book does not control how this Collective votes," Alistar responded. "And Lasidious doesn't care about the creation of Hell. He stopped caring seasons ago." The God of the Harvest scanned the faces surrounding the table and stopped on Celestria's. He smiled inside as he watched a tear fall from her eye and run down her cheek. "You know I speak the truth."

Celestria wiped her face with the back of her hand. "Lasidious has made his choice. Let's continue."

Keylom cut in. "But—"

"But nothing, you stupid centaur!" Mieonus sneered. The Goddess of Hate leaned forward in her chair and stomped the lifted heel of her right shoe against the floor. "Must you always be so timid?"

The centaur-god did not respond.

Mieonus leaned back. "I'll take your silence as your approval that this Collective should continue. I despise your weakness."

Alistar shook his head for a moment as the satisfaction smothered the Goddess of Hate's face. He then redirected his attention toward the centaur. "Tell me, Keylom, why are you struggling?"

Mieonus rolled her eyes while Keylom stepped closer to the table and placed his hands on Hosseff's shoulders. "Lasidious felt that this Collective's decision was wrong. I'm beginning to feel the same. I feel sorry for the beings on Dragonia who haven't finished living their first life. They've done nothing to deserve the Hell we've unleashed on them."

The confidence filling Keylom's voice magnified as he continued. "Those who are living their first existence after the creation of the worlds do not deserve to suffer the torment. They shouldn't be forced to bear the wrath of our vote. It isn't their fault that they were born on a world we intended to transform." The centaur clapped his left front hoof against the floor to emphasize his next point. "Hell will be an unjust punishment once stasis has been lifted and the damned begin to migrate."

Sharvesa spoke out. "Perhaps we could move the innocent to some other world?"

"You say that only because of your daughter," Mieonus rebuked.

"Of course, I do!" Sharvesa rebutted. "But my concern extends beyond my daughter. There are many beings on my homeworld that I don't want to see suffer ... not just demonkind."

The Goddess of Hate's eyes rolled again. "This Collective expects you to be the goddess you were chosen to become, not what you want to be."

Sharvesa fought back. "And I suppose you believe you're the example I should follow? You speak as if you're the voice of this Collective."

Mieonus jumped up from her chair. "I should—"

Alistar stepped in. "Ladies! Ladies! Please! There's no need to shout."

After a moment of silence, Mieonus reclaimed her seat.

Alistar continued. "Moving the innocent will be unnecessary. Seasons will pass before the damned manage to migrate that far. Gabriel saw to that." The God of the Harvest captured Sharvesa's eyes. "The Book made sure the mainland wouldn't see suffering for quite a while, and with the additional size this Collective has added to that world, the damned's migration will take even longer than originally anticipated."

Alistar offered a reassuring smile. "The moments are available to us to ensure that your daughter is prepared."

"I second that," Owain added as he removed his pointed hat and tossed it onto the table. "Your daughter can command the races of demons to build walls to keep the damned out of their lands. As queen, she has the resources available to her to prepare for anything."

"And you believe this is a life worth living, dwarf?" Sharvesa snapped. "Would you be so willing to condemn a daughter of your own in this manner?"

Annoyed, Hosseff slapped the table. "This topic is irrelevant! I care nothing for your daughter or the pain she'll experience."

The God of Death jerked his shoulders out of Keylom's grasp. "Get your hands off me, centaur, and stop your sniveling. This Collective's vote has stood for too many seasons to change it, and I don't want to hear another word from a concerned mother."

Hosseff stood and walked around the table. He leaned down to speak into Sharvesa's ear. "As much as it pains you to hear, your daughter is an acceptable sacrifice."

"I totally agree," Mieonus added. "She's just another worthless demon. Her pain will be fun to watch."

Sharvesa rose from her chair and lifted her hands. "Perhaps we should settle this outside?"

Mieonus laughed. "You don't have the power to strike me down." The Goddess of Hate stood, stepped away from her seat and then extended her arms to either side. "But you could try. Strike me so that I may enjoy your suffering once you rejoin your daughter and live out the rest of your Peaks in the Hell you helped create. Nothing would give me greater satisfaction."

All present looked at the Goddess of Hate and shook their heads.

Alistar sighed. "Again, you lack tact, Mieonus. When will you learn to keep your mouth shut?"

"Finally," Hosseff added, "a sentiment I can agree with. Do shut up, Mieonus."

The God of Death returned to his side of the table. His wispy voice continued to emanate from the nothingness beneath his hood as he lowered into his seat. "The Collective's feelings on this matter are irrelevant. The vote was unanimous, and as our laws state, it cannot be changed." He looked again at Sharvesa. "Perhaps I spoke too harshly. Your daughter deserves better than this outcome, but alas, the moments for regret are unavailable to us. I offer my sincerest condolences, but beyond that, I won't give another thought to your daughter's pain."

"Bah! You're as weak as they are, shade," Mieonus admonished.

Though Hosseff's smile was unable to be seen, the Collective experienced the chill of his laugh before he responded. "Are there other matters that should be discussed before we vote?"

Calla, the Goddess of Truth, responded. "I have a topic, though it doesn't pertain to our vote."

"If it's irrelevant, then why should we listen to you babble?" the Goddess of Hate jeered.

Alistar shot Mieonus a nasty look. "Do shut up! The only being babbling at this table is you. If you don't want to hear what Calla has to say, please leave! This Collective will assume that your departure is also your vote to set Hell in motion."

Mieonus leaned forward in her chair. A moment later, a smile spread across her face. "I wouldn't want you to miss me. I think I'll stay." She looked down the table at Calla. "What could you possibly say that I'd find interesting?"

Hosseff's wispy voice pulled the Goddess of Truth's eyes off Mieonus. "Ignore her. Tell us what's on your mind."

Mieonus flopped back into her chair and crossed her arms. "Sometime this season would be acceptable."

It took a moment for Calla to collect her thoughts. "While we were expanding the girth of Hell, I came across something interesting."

Mieonus huffed. "Imagine that! Something interesting on a world called Hell."

All the gods looked in the Goddess of Hate's direction and shouted. "Shut up, Mieonus!" Some of the voices were amplified to the point that the sound caused the hall to shake.

Once the hall was silent, Mieonus sat back in her chair, crossed her arms and smirked. "Fine! Finish your stupid story."

Kesdelain pushed his dreads clear of his face. "Continue."

The Goddess of Truth waited to see if another objection would come from Mieonus, but when one never came, she spoke. "I saw Sam sitting in a protective barrier on Hell. After I saw the King of Brandor, I went to his castle in search of his queen. What I found was unexpected. The castle was in chaos."

Celestria's pointed ears perked up. The halfling-goddess leaned forward and looked down the table. "Calla, I find this most intriguing. Please, go on."

Nodding, Calla continued. "Apparently, the General Absolute has taken the throne. The king and queen have been missing for a fair number of Peaks. But that's not what's most interesting. The Prince of Brandor has been abducted. The army has been secretly searching for the prince for more than 4 Peaks."

Alistar cut in as if he did not know. "Really? The entire house of Brandor has gone missing? How's that possible?"

"I know what happened to the queen," Celestria interjected.

The God of the Harvest gazed down the table at Celestria. His eyes demanded that she stop, but the disheveled Goddess of Beasts ignored the warning and kept talking.

"Since Lasidious has turned his back on me, I shall tell you what has happened to the queen."

Alistar spoke above Celestria. "Perhaps you should think about what you're saying. It's hard to imagine that the depth of your scheming with Lasidious would not fall under the Rule of Fromalla. If Lasidious has turned his back on you as you say, is it truly worth sacrificing all that you are to divulge one of your secrets?"

All eyes surrounding the table stared at Celestria and waited for her response.

Alistar added, "I doubt Lasidious would abandon your love after 10,000 seasons of bliss. Perhaps you're being hasty."

Mieonus leaned forward in her chair. "Why do you care, Alistar? If she wants to sacrifice herself, then allow her to do it."

"Quiet your tongue, Mieonus!" the God of Death hissed. Hosseff stood from his chair and walked around the table. He stopped next to Celestria and then addressed her. "I would receive no pleasure from collecting a soul as beautiful as yours. The table this collective convenes around would not be as enjoyable if you were no longer with us."

"Please!" Mieonus scoffed as she patted the top of the table. "I'm sure the table would survive."

Everyone present ignored the Goddess of Hate except Kesdelain. While the others kept their attention focused on Hosseff and Celestria, the troll reached over and placed his hand on top of Mieonus'. He whispered into her ear, "Well said. Perhaps we should enjoy a cup of Nasha at my place later."

A look of repulsion appeared on the Goddess of Hate's face as she pulled her hand away. "Don't touch me, you nasty troll!"

Everyone turned to look in their direction.

Embarrassed, Kesdelain stood and moved to the end of the table and stopped next to Sharvesa. He looked at Celestria. "You were saying?"

As the Collective redirected their attention toward the Goddess of Beasts, it was easy to see the conflict that was filling her mind. Eventually, Celestria responded. "I shall hold my tongue until I know if Lasidious intends to return to me."

Though it could not be seen, a look of relief appeared on Hosseff's face. "A wise decision," he sighed. The God of Death returned to his seat.

Yet again, Mieonus rolled her eyes. "The sentiment in this room makes me want to vomit."

As the gods turned their heads to give the Goddess of Hate a nasty look, Celestria spoke. "I vote to set Hell in motion." The Goddess of Beasts vanished.

MOMENTS LATER
SOUTHERN GRAYHAM
THE CASTLE OF BRANDOR

When Celestria appeared, she was standing inside an invisible veil at the center of the castle courtyard of Brandor. It was clear the army was still searching for the missing prince.

The interim king, Michael, was sitting on top of his mist mare. He had the crown on his head, and he was addressing the man who was temporarily taking his place as General Absolute. "I don't care how tired the men are, General. If the prince was their charge, they'd leave no stone unturned."

Bouldon, a strong-jawed, dark-haired man responded. "My Lord, they've been awake for over 2 Peaks. They need sleep. They're no good to the search in this condition."

Michael's knuckles turned white as he clenched the reins of his mare. He knew the general was right. He redirected his gaze to his right and stopped on two members of the government. Their robes symbolized the unity of the Senate, and the cloth that hung from their person was elegant. The colors, red, white and gold, reminded those who looked upon them of the bond that every being on Southern Grayham now shared.

The interim king's eyes stopped on the senator who was clearly out of shape. "Tardin, I want the Senate to become more active in the search. Ensure every man in the kingdom starts looking for the prince."

The heft beneath Tardin's chin folded as he bowed his head. "Yes, My King. May I also suggest another course of action?"

Michael's brows furrowed. "I'm listening."

Tardin stepped toward the king's mist mare. "Let's ask Kolton, the voice of the Fourth and Fifth Marks, to call upon the prophet by using Lasidious' Promise. Perhaps the prophet could shorten the search."

Bouldon nodded. "Your Grace, the prophet's assistance would be welcomed. I encourage you to bestow your blessing upon Tardin's request."

Michael dismounted. He handed the reins to one of his officers and then readdressed Tardin. "I want you to call an emergency meeting of the Senate. See to it that Kolton summons the prophet."

From within her invisible veil, Celestria put her hand to her chin. *Calla spoke the truth.*

The Goddess of Beasts closed her eyes and thought of Sam. Now that she knew his general location, her power would be strong enough to find him. She vanished.

When Celestria opened her eyes, she saw the King of Southern Grayham lying face down on the ground with Kael hovering above him, and the empty vial that contained Yaloom's potion was lying next to the king's mouth.

The goddess dispensed with her veil of magic and stepped through the protective barrier that Lasidious had created. After passing Kepler's inanimate form, she addressed Sam's blade. "Kael, what happened? Did he consume the potion all at once?"

The blade rose and stopped eye-level with the goddess. "Yes. I may have forced him to drink too much. He has been unconscious for more than a Peak."

A look of confusion appeared on the goddess' face. "Why would you force your master to do anything? Are you not bound to his service?"

Realizing he had said too much, Kael did not respond. Instead, he lowered to the ground and took his place at Sam's side.

Celestria's look of confusion was replaced with anger. "Don't ignore me, blade."

Again, Kael remained silent.

The goddess adjusted her gown and then knelt. "I said, don't ignore me!" She reached down with her right hand to take hold of the blade, but as soon as she grasped the weapon's handle, a powerful wave of heat erupted from Kael and was followed by a burst of energy.

The goddess was thrown backward with such force that she landed more than five paces outside the barrier that was protecting Sam. Dazed, it took a fair series of moments before Celestria was able to pick herself up. As she stood, she found the blade floating toward her, and it was also outside the barrier.

The pulsating of Kael's blade was intense as he spoke. "I've longed for the Peak when I could end your existence. Did you truly believe that Lasidious loved you?"

Kael's blade turned bright-red, but before the blade could strike down the goddess, the ground started to quake as Hell began to spin on its axis and move along its new orbit.

As the light of Hell's new star peeked above the horizon, its brilliance captured the blade's attention. Celestria seized the opportunity to escape. She vanished.

ANCIENTS SOVEREIGN
BENEATH THE PEAKS OF ANGELS

When Celestria reappeared, she was standing next to the cube-shaped fireplace inside the home she shared with Lasidious. "How dare that blade threaten me!" she shouted. She looked down at the burns that covered her right forearm. "Curse you, Kael!"

Touching one of the boils, the goddess winced. She had to use her magic to mend her skin. Once the pain had subsided, she extended her hand toward the fireplace to summon a blaze. Instead of the green flames she loved so much, the fire that burst into existence was dark-red to match her mood.

A voice from behind Celestria spoke out. "I was wondering how long it would be before you returned. Are you okay?"

Celestria whirled around. To her surprise, the God of the Harvest had made himself at home. He was waiting with his feet up on the table, and a half-full mug of nasha was sitting next to his feet.

Celestria stepped forward and knocked the cup off the table in the direction of Alistar's head. "How dare you show your face here!"

Alistar held up his hands as he ducked. "Whoa! What's wrong?"

The God of the Harvest's apparent ignorance only served to anger Celestria further. "You're what's wrong, traitor! You knew Lasidious' love for me was a farce! How dare you feign a friendship with me!"

Alistar pulled his feet off the table and allowed them to fall to the floor. "I feign no such thing."

"You are a liar and my enemy. Get out of my home!" The goddess waved her hand to revoke the privilege that she and Lasidious had extended to Alistar, but nothing happened. "I said, get out!" She waved her hand again, and again the God of the Harvest was not sent from the home.

Celestria looked at her hands. "How?"

"You don't have the power to banish me. You can't remove me without Lasidious' help."

The goddess lunged toward the table, grabbed the vase at its center and threw it as hard as she could.

Again, Alistar ducked. "Stop that! I haven't feigned anything when it comes to our friendship. You're my brother's love, and his desire for you remains as strong as it ever was."

"Lies! All lies!" Celestria grabbed the chair on her side of the table and used her power to help her throw it.

After ducking yet again, Alistar retaliated. With a flip of his wrist, he used his magic to force the Goddess of Beasts into the seat at the far end of the table and then allowed her to scream and struggle for many, many moments before she finally settled down.

Keeping his hold over her, the God of the Harvest reclaimed his seat at the opposing end of the table. "You do realize your actions would've summoned the Book's wrath if they had not been shielded by the veil of protection you and Lasidious placed on your home, don't you?"

"So?"

"What do you mean, 'so?' Have you lost your mind?"

Celestria snorted and then spit.

Alistar tried to get out of the way before the phlegm flew the length of the table, but he had been unprepared for the crudeness of the act. The lugie hit him on his right cheek as his chair toppled backward to the floor because of the way he pushed off to avoid the impact.

Satisfied with the result, Celestria allowed a shallow grin to appear until Alistar reclaimed his feet.

The God of the Harvest reached into his robe, removed a folded cloth and then wiped his face. "You're making a fool of yourself."

"I'm no longer the fool you hoped I'd be! I'm onto you! You're the fool now!"

Fighting fire with fire, Alistar spit back in her direction.

The goddess was forced to duck below the edge of the table.

With the goddess out of sight, Alistar reclaimed his dignity and took a moment to regain his composure. "The fight between you and Lasidious broke his heart! He has simply sought solitude to determine how to proceed! I know he loves you."

"You lie! He's planning something! I know it!"

"Of course, he is!" Alistar rebutted.

All Alistar could see was from the bottom of Celestria's nose to the top of her head as she peeked above the table. He sighed. "When have you not known Lasidious to plot? I can assure you … his plotting isn't against you."

"I don't believe you! You'd lie for him!"

Alistar's eyes narrowed. "Would you stand up?"

"Why?"

"Because talking to the top of your head is ridiculous." He dropped below the edge of the table to match Celestria's posture. "See? Don't I look ridiculous?"

Celestria had to drop below the table to cover her smile. Alistar did look silly, but she did not want to ruin the seriousness of the conversation by allowing his antics to soften her mood. After putting a distraught look back on her face, she stood. "The two of you are hiding something from me. I know it."

Alistar reclaimed his seat. His tone was soft. "Tell me ... how could you possibly say that about the one being who has loved you for over 10,000 seasons?"

The goddess crossed her arms. "His love was a lie. The sword told me everything."

Alistar's brows furrowed. "The sword?"

"Don't act as if you don't know. I speak of the sword that you and Lasidious commissioned to destroy me."

The God of the Harvest extended his arms away from his body to either side. "How could you possibly expect me to understand what you're talking about?"

A long series of moments passed as both gods held each other's glare.

Eventually, Alistar broke the silence. "Look. I'm sure there's a reasonable explanation for whatever you're angry about."

"No, there's not." Celestria slapped the table with her right hand. "I went to Brandor. Once I saw that Calla spoke the truth about the chaos paralyzing their kingdom, I went to Hell. I saw Brandor's king lying face down with his sword hovering above him."

"Let me guess. The blade threatened your existence."

Celestria was taken aback. "See? You do know."

Alistar smiled. "Only because you were screaming about it when you appeared. I was behind you when you professed as much. I suppose your forgetfulness is understandable, considering your rage. Tell me, why would the sword's threat cause you to believe Lasidious' love isn't genuine?"

A look of pain filled the goddess' eyes. "Because the sword told me as much."

Alistar shook his head and leaned forward. "And you believe the blade spoke the truth?"

"I do."

"Why?"

"Because the sword intended to destroy me. It had no reason to lie. Kael would have succeeded, if it had not been for the Collective setting Hell in motion."

"How did you get away?"

"The world started to shake. The blade became distracted, and in his confusion, I fled."

Alistar exhaled. "Well that's a relief. That blade has the power to destroy most of the Collective. Only Mieonus, Hosseff, Lasidious and I could stand against it."

"All the more reason for you to conspire with the blade to get rid of me," Celestria added.

Alistar rolled his eyes. "Stop that. How could you be so blind?"

"Blind to what?"

The God of the Harvest stood from his chair. He walked to the fireplace and commanded the flame to burn a cooler color. Satisfied with the blue hues, he responded. "The blade sees you and Lasidious as a threat. He wants to rule at Sam's side, and he knows Lasidious is seeking power. Kael doesn't believe that Lasidious intends to serve the Morning Star once Sam remembers his true identity."

Alistar turned around. "Don't you see? The blade will say whatever he must to destroy the union between you and Lasidious. Don't allow your insecurity to destroy everything we've worked for."

The God of the Harvest walked to the end of the table and reclaimed his seat. "Lasidious said there may come a moment when he would need to abandon you in order to protect you. Perhaps there's more to his seclusion than a simple argument between the two of you. He may know something we don't."

Alistar leaned forward and crossed his arms on the table. "After 10,000 seasons, don't you owe it to Lasidious to trust his judgment? You have already threatened your relationship on two occasions on this Peak. Do you really want it to end?"

Celestria stood in silence for a long series of moments before she sat in the chair at the opposite end of the table and buried her head into her palms.

Alistar stood from his seat, walked the length of the table, stopped next to Celestria and then placed a hand on her back. "I know the way Lasidious functions can be frustrating. But I assure you. I believe his love for you remains strong. My love for you also remains strong. You're irreplaceable."

The goddess stood and threw her arms around Alistar's neck. Tears flowed freely as he comforted her. "I'm sorry, Alistar. I should not have doubted you. You're right … 10,000 seasons should be enough to earn my loyalty."

The God of the Harvest rubbed Celestria's back. "Tell you what ... how about I do everything I can to find answers? Why don't you find a place to relax and allow the weight of the worlds to fall off your shoulders?"

Celestria pulled her head away from Alistar's chest and smiled. "I'll do just that. Thank you for putting up with me."

Alistar gave a nod of understanding. He wiped the tears from her eyes and then vanished.

A moment later, Celestria's mood changed. Her theatrical sorrow was replaced with determination. "You're a fool, Alistar. My trust in you is gone, and your attempt to pacify me has failed. The moment has come for me to take vengeance on Lasidious." The Goddess of Beasts vanished.

MEANWHILE, ANAHITA'S SHACK

Sitting at the table, Anahita's right leg bounced as she watched the Archangel Gabriel pace. He had worn a path in the dirt from the door to the mirror near the rear wall of the shack.

"Gabriel, Helga's moments are few," Anahita said impatiently. "I can feel it. Ever since you got back, you've been stalling. You've got to do something now, or she'll be lost forever."

The archangel stopped next to the door and turned around. "I have a way to proceed, but I fear my decision may have been a poor one."

Confusion spread across Anahita's face. "What are you talking about?"

Gabriel took a deep breath and exhaled over an extended period of moments. "When Michael and I discussed the consequences of rejoining the pieces of your soul, we anticipated that you might demand that I restore the part of you that you had come to know as Helga."

Anahita shrugged. "Yeah, so! Is there going to be a problem with that? I thought you said you could do it."

The archangel walked to the mirror, turned around and then made it half way back to the door before he stopped. "I can provide Helga with a body of her own, but there may be side effects."

Frowning, Anahita rebutted, "Whatever they are … they can't be any worse than losing her."

Gabriel shook his head. "You don't understand. What you're asking me to do is no simple task."

"Then explain it to me. What's so daunting about it?"

Again, the archangel began to pace.

After three lengths of the shack, Anahita barked, "Would you stop that already?" She stood and pulled the extra chair to the center of the room. "Sit!" she ordered. Seeing that Gabriel was going to object, she reiterated, "I said, sit!"

Once the archangel complied, Anahita retrieved her chair, placed it in front of Gabriel and then took a seat. "Now look me in the eyes, and tell me everything I need to know."

Gabriel rubbed the stubble of 2 Peaks' growth. "As you know, Helga and BJ were each a third of your soul that were reunited with yours to make you whole again."

Anahita held up her hand. "Skip to the part that I don't know."

The archangel frowned. "Allow me some leeway. What I'm about to describe won't be simple to understand."

Anahita leaned back in her chair and shrugged. "Go on."

Gabriel stood and moved behind his chair. "Now that BJ's third has been consumed, I can no longer separate Helga's third."

Seeing the look on Anahita's face, the archangel lifted his hand to stop her from speaking. "Don't interrupt me. You can ask questions later."

Anahita held her tongue and nodded.

Dropping his hand, Gabriel continued. "Since I cannot separate Helga's third, I was forced to find a soul who was willing to sacrifice their existence in order to allow parts of Helga to exist."

"What do you mean by 'parts?'" Anahita blurted as she leaned forward.

Gabriel frowned. "That was a question."

Leaning back, Anahita bit her lip and motioned for the archangel to continue.

It took a moment for Gabriel to collect his thoughts. "Since I can't separate her third, I'm left with the tedious task of rummaging through your mind. I must separate Helga's thoughts, memories and anything salvageable that makes her who she is and then find a vessel for these elements to control. Further, this vessel, or new mind if you will, must be a willing host. The host must sacrifice themselves and allow me to shove their memories, their thoughts and anything that makes them who they are to the back of their mind. Only then will there be room for Helga to take over."

The archangel rubbed the back of his neck as he continued. "Michael and I discussed this process. We determined that I would need to unite the host-mind with a new body and the soul that once existed inside that body. To do this, I would need to go to the only place where bodies are not burned after they've passed."

Again, Anahita leaned forward and broke her silence. "I thought every body was burned across the worlds."

Gabriel shook his head. "I thought we agreed you would save your questions until later."

"I'm sorry." She leaned back in her chair. "I was just saying."

The archangel took a moment to organize his thoughts. "For the most part, you're correct. The beings throughout the worlds do burn their dead. But there is a race on Trollcom that doesn't believe in ascension by fire. They believe in preserving their loved ones. They bury them in crypts deep within the mountains."

Gabriel turned, walked to the large barrel filled with water and retrieved a mug full. He consumed the entire glass before he reclaimed his position behind his chair. "I had to find a body that was compatible with the host-mind."

Anahita raised her hand and shook it as if she was in school.

Gabriel smiled. "You may speak."

"Why would anyone agree to suppress all that they are so that someone else can control their mind? It doesn't make sense."

The archangel nodded. "I suppose it wouldn't." He took a seat. "Allow me to explain. After you demanded that I fix Helga, I left in search of a host-mind. Because our moments were short, I only spoke with 10 beings who have since passed."

Anahita interrupted. "Let me guess. You're going to tell me that this group of folks had nothing to lose by saying yes since they were about to kick the bucket anyway."

Gabriel returned to the barrel and responded as he refilled his mug. "Yes ... and no."

"What do you mean?"

"I say yes, only because I did speak with beings who thought they had nothing to lose. And no, since they were all unwilling to allow me to manipulate their minds because they didn't fear their passing."

"Okay. So what did you say that caused them to change their minds?"

The archangel grinned. "They feared what awaited them in the afterlife."

"What do you mean by that? I thought the souls of the dead ended up inside the Book of Immortality. I thought…" Anahita paused. An awkward moment passed as she stared at Gabriel.

The archangel questioned, "What is it? Is something bothering you?"

Anahita stepped forward and touched various areas of the archangel's body.

Gabriel grabbed her hand. "What are you doing?"

Walking across the room, Anahita retrieved a mug of her own and filled it with water. She responded after taking a swig. "When you showed up the other Peak, you appeared as the Book. I thought all souls were placed inside its pages after their bodies expire."

"They are."

"Well … if that's the case, then where did all the souls go when you changed into the angel that you are now?"

A look of understanding appeared on Gabriel's face. "Ahhhhh! You want to know what I did with them." The archangel snapped his fingers. An image of a good-sized book with a dark binding appeared on the seat of his chair. It possessed the features the gods gave the Book of Immortality when they were sitting inside the Bloody Trough Inn on Southern Grayham. The Book's arms were folded, its eyes were shut, and it appeared to be sleeping. The hasp that kept its cover closed was secure and locked.

"This is the true Book of Immortality," Gabriel confessed. "When I am in my angelic form, the Book appears as if it's asleep within the Hall of Judgment on the god world, Ancients Sovereign. The Book will remain asleep until I abandon this form and continue my existence within its pages." Gabriel snapped his fingers and the image of the book vanished. "Beyond that, I won't explain further. It would take too long, and there are too many details. For now, we should focus on Helga."

Anahita growled. "You frustrate me."

Laughing, the archangel redirected the conversation. "Needless to say, the 10 beings I approached changed their minds."

"Wait! You've got to tell me what you said that they feared."

"As you wish. They became willing participants because they feared the torment that they would experience once I threw their souls onto the Hell that now exists on this plane."

"Hell? What Hell? What are you talking about?"

The archangel held up his hand. "The moment has returned for you to listen and not speak."

Anahita crossed her arms in a huff. "So, talk already."

Placing his empty mug on the counter, Gabriel returned to his chair at the center of the shack and took a seat. "The gods have separated Dragonia from the rest of the worlds. They have given it a new star and increased its overall size. The minds of the beings who live on the remaining worlds have been recalibrated. They now believe that Hell has always existed, just as they believe the dragon world has always existed. Though they don't know where Hell is, they fear it, and they believe that living a good life is the only way to avoid it."

Anahita had to speak. "Hold on a moment. I haven't created a Heaven yet. So where does everyone believe their soul goes if they live a good life?"

A look of irritation appeared on Gabriel's face. "They believe they'll ascend to be with their god in the heavens."

Anahita shook her head in disgust. "That's terrible. How could the gods allow them to believe there's a Heaven when there isn't one?"

Gabriel shrugged. "Perhaps you should ask the gods once you've ascended."

The part-human, part-angel's brows dropped between her eyes. "So what really happens to the souls of the good after they pass?"

The archangel stood from his chair. "We should change the subject. Speaking of this aggravates me."

"Oh, no! You're not getting off that easy. I want to know what happens to them."

Gabriel closed his eyes and took three, long, deep breaths. "For those souls who serve gods with good natures, they ascend to the Book's pages. They experience a pleasant existence as they wait for a real Heaven to be created. Upon completion, I'll release their souls upon it. It's there they'll stay until the moment arrives for them to be given the opportunity for rebirth."

"Hold up! Why would anyone want to leave Heaven?" Anahita questioned. "Especially the one I'm going to create. It's going to be a marvelous place."

The archangel grinned. "I doubt they'll want to leave, but the opportunity will be provided nevertheless."

"That seems like a waste of energy, but whatever." Anahita extended her wings to stretch. "So what happens to those beings who are good people but serve gods whose natures aren't so good?"

Gabriel reached down with his left hand, grabbed the back of his chair and squeezed. The wood cracked. "Now that Hell exists, their souls will find their way there. During their journey, they'll receive temporary bodies that cannot perish. Upon their arrival, they must pass through the atmosphere that surrounds that world. They will fall from the skies in a tormented blaze until they land in the deepest seas. The salt water shall sting their scorched flesh as they are forced to migrate to land. This will be just the beginning of their suffering."

Anahita's face tightened. "That's downright awful. They serve their god loyally and then get punished for it."

Releasing the back of his chair, Gabriel walked to the door, opened it and then commanded the darkness beyond to vacate a vast area around the shack. "Perhaps we should change the subject since there's nothing I can do about it."

Anahita joined the archangel at the door. She studied the monstrous collections of mass that floated in all directions around the shack. "Then let's talk about the 10 beings who became willing hosts. You're saying they became willing only after they learned of the torture they'd experience on Hell. I'm surprised you told them the truth."

"I had to. If I hadn't, they wouldn't have agreed. But as I said before, I fear my choice may have been a poor one."

"Your choice in what … minds?"

"Yes."

"Why?"

"Because out of those 10 minds, I only found one body capable of merging with one of the 10."

"That's it? Why not just keep the mind in its own body? Why not put Helga's memories into a complete package? Why not just use that person's soul as well?"

Gabriel shook his head. "If only it were that simple. We do not have the moments available to us for an explanation. Helga would be lost by the moment that conversation ended."

"Figures," Anahita grumbled. "So out of all the 10 bodies that were buried, only one will work with the mind from the being who agreed to be sacrificed? Is it really that hard to match up a mind with a body?"

The archangel frowned. "If you can do better, I'd be more than happy to step aside. But don't forget, you'll need to find a soul that can be attached to both. And Helga's elements must be capable of merging with all three."

Anahita elbowed Gabriel. "Nobody likes a smart ass."

The archangel chuckled.

A short silence followed before Anahita spoke again. "So … you could only find one. If I'm guessing correctly, you're worried because this mind is powerful."

"Yes. That's part of it."

"Well, whatever the other part is, I still think it's worth the risk."

"Your confidence is calming."

Anahita squeezed Gabriel's arm. "I have that effect on folks." After poking the archangel in his side, she continued. "Tell me about the body you found. Will Helga be beautiful? Is she going to get a good soul as well?"

The archangel tried to fight back his grin, but he was unable to hide it.

"What's so doggone funny?"

It took a moment before Gabriel was able to stop smiling. "The soul Helga will receive is a good soul, for sure, but whether or not she'll be considered beautiful or not will depend on the being who looks upon her. As I've said, I was only able to find one body."

Anahita's lips pursed. "Spit it out. What are you getting at?"

Gabriel was hesitant to continue.

"Don't be stalling. I said, spit it out."

The archangel walked away from the door to put some distance between him and Anahita. Once he was at the far end of the shack, he turned around.

Anahita had her arms crossed and her foot was thumping against the dirt. "Well?"

Gabriel took another deep breath. "You must remember that this was the only body that I could find that was compatible with the host-mind and the new soul."

"Spit it out!" Anahita demanded.

"Okay! Ummmm … Helga's new body will be that of a dwarf."

"A dwarf?" Anahita shouted. "You chose a dwarf?"

The archangel lifted his hands in front of him in defense. "Hold on. That's not all. The dwarf is also male."

The thumping of Anahita's foot intensified as Gabriel continued. "During this dwarf's last life, he was a bit rugged. He had fiery-red hair, dark brown eyes and a large mole on the right side of his nose."

"Helga would rather die than have a big, old, ugly mole on her nose. Every woman hates moles."

"I can fix the mole," Gabriel rebutted, "but you must remember that this is the only body that was capable of uniting with the host-mind. Helga will just have to adjust to her new anatomy."

Anahita stormed across the shack and stopped in front of the archangel. "You can't put a woman's mind inside of a man's body. Won't that make her gay or something?"

"Perhaps. This would be similar to other beings that you thought you came across in the memories that Michael and I implanted about your life on Earth. In some of those memories, there were individuals who felt like they were trapped inside the wrong body."

Anahita gasped and took a step back. "Oh, my gosh! So some folks really are born gay. That's crazy. And to know it happens only because of the manipulating the gods did with their minds, bodies and souls and such. This whole god thing is about as twisted as you can get."

After many long moments of Anahita pondering her Earthly memories, Gabriel broke the silence. "Perhaps the moment has come for me to begin the transformation. Are you ready?"

Anahita walked to the mirror, grabbed the frame on either side and stared at the reflection of her eyes. "Helga, can you hear me? C'mon old girl. I know you're in there."

When Helga did not respond, Gabriel placed his hands on Anahita's shoulders to rejuvenate Helga's portion of their spirit.

It was barely enough. After a few moments, Helga managed a weak response. "I can hear you, Child, but I fear I may not be able to for long."

Anahita let out a sigh of relief. "I thought I'd lost you. Gabriel said he could help, but you're going to have a penis when you wake up. Are you okay with that?" She grinned at their reflection. "Just think. You'll be able to pee standing up. How lucky are you?"

"Oh, Child ………….. I …"

"Helga. You okay?"

No response.

"Helga. Talk to me, girl."

Still no response.

Gabriel placed his hands on the outside of Anahita's arms. "She's weak. I better hurry. I need you to lie down on the cot."

Anahita did so without question.

ANCIENTS SOVEREIGN
THE BOOK'S HALL OF JUDGMENT
3 PEAKS LATER

When Celestria entered the hall, her chest was heaving. She had spent the last 3 Peaks searching for Lasidious to give the Mischievous One a chance to explain his actions, but she had been unable to find him. Her voice was filled with the anger that overwhelmed her emotions. "Gabriel!" she shouted. "Show yourself! I demand an audience!"

When the Book did not appear, Celestria stormed to the side of the table the gods gathered around. She grabbed the Book's golden stand and then flung it across the room. "I said, show yourself, Book!" The goddess pulled out the chair that Lasidious usually occupied and flopped into it. "Gabriel! Don't you dare make me wait!"

A moment later, the Book appeared, hovering above the center of the table. "What could be so important that you would scream so? I was busy."

Celestria stood from her chair and slapped the top of the table with both hands. "I've come to surrender all that I am, and I want to take Lasidious with me. He'll pay for his abandonment of our love."

The space between the heavy brows above Gabriel's eyes narrowed. "Explain yourself. You've broken no laws. How do you expect to sacrifice your godliness?"

The Goddess of Beasts laughed. "You're so uninformed. The depth of our scheming has broken many laws. Would you like to know which ones?"

The Book rocked back and forth to insinuate a nod. "Why are you doing this, Celestria? You'll regret—"

"I'll regret nothing!" she barked. "His love for me has been a lie for over 10,000 seasons. I intend to see that he pays with the loss of his immortality."

"Even at the cost of your own?" Gabriel questioned.

"Yes. Even at the cost of my own." Celestria paused in thought.

The Book could see the turmoil behind her eyes. "Are you having second thoughts?"

A long moment of silence passed before the goddess responded. "There must be another way for me to have my revenge. Perhaps you and I could come to an arrangement."

"What do you mean?" The Book lowered to the table in front of the goddess. "There are no provisions within the laws that allow me to negotiate when one of them has been broken."

Celestria smiled and stroked the side of the Book's cover. "And yet there are no laws that prevent you from negotiating either. Perhaps you could find a way to spare my being. The information I possess is worth a great deal. It would allow you to stop Lasidious from gaining the power he needs to control you."

Gabriel lifted off the table and floated a few paces away. "I should've let you rant. But alas, I've allowed my caring to get in the way of an objective."

"Aahhhh, come now, Gabriel. Do you really think so ill of me that you would wish to see me destroyed?"

The Book turned to face the goddess. "I happen to be quite fond of you. It's the company you keep that bothers me most."

Celestria stood from her chair and clapped her hands. "Then there is room for negotiation." She closed the distance, plucked the book out of the air and then placed him on the table in front of her as she took a seat at the opposite end. "I want to see Lasidious pay for the lies he's told me, and I want you to avoid being controlled. It's in our best interests to work together ... don't you agree?"

Gabriel frowned. "What do you want for this information?"

Celestria leaned back in her chair. "There are two beings who must be spared. The first is me, and the second I will name when the moment is right. I want to keep my immortality and maintain a peaceful existence away from the others on the unclaimed territories of Ancients Sovereign. The being whom I will name must be allowed to exist with me. No longer will I hold a position on the Collective, nor shall I seek the prayers of those who worship me. You may replace me and give my title to another. I simply want to live and be happy. I'm tired, Gabriel."

The Book's mind was filled with a hundred questions. "I'd like to know if the other being you want me to spare is god or mortal."

Celestria crossed her legs on top of her seat and then leaned forward. "I'll say nothing further until an arrangement has been made."

The Book's eyes narrowed. "You ask for much, yet I have no proof the information you possess is worth a promise of that magnitude. For now, I'll agree to one thing and one thing only. No matter what laws you've broken, I will spare your existence. I won't, however, promise anything else until you've given me something in return."

The goddess smirked. "I figured as much." She stood and prepared to leave. "When you change your mind about that, find me. Your moments are running short. Soon, you won't be able to stop Lasidious. Everything the gods have created will be under his control, and there will be nothing I can do or say to help you stop him."

The goddess vanished before the Book could respond.

Annoyed, Gabriel lifted from the table and floated out of the room toward the corridor that would take him to the black, iron door with the golden image of the Source at its center. He waved his hand and whispered. *"Con gon onsey."* The lock released and the way ahead was revealed. Gabriel began his descent.

Upon finishing his journey into the depths of Ancients Sovereign, Gabriel stopped in front of the final door. *"Con gon onsey,"* he whispered again. The door guarding his private chamber opened. Before he entered, he changed into his angelic form and then stepped inside to address the only other beings who had been given permission to pass beyond the door that bore the Source's image.

Michael and Zerachiel were waiting on the bench made of amethyst that was still sitting on the carnelian star at the center of the room.

"Hello, brothers." Gabriel announced, "It appears Celestria has grown tired of Lasidious' antics. She offers assistance, but I fear her support will come at a high cost."

Michael responded. "We know. We heard her terms."

Zerachiel, otherwise known as Bailem, added, "Why listen to her at all? Destroy her and be done with it."

Gabriel shook his head. "You speak hastily, Zerachiel. To do so would create a disadvantage. Must I remind you that Lasidious already possesses the power to annihilate us? We're fortunate only because he doesn't realize it yet. We can't destroy the only vessel that may contain the knowledge to save us."

"Hmpf!" Zerachiel responded. "I disagree. What could she possibly know that would help us defeat a being that already has the ability to end us? Dispose of her, Gabriel. She's a waste of our moments and can't be trusted."

Michael reached over and placed his right hand on Zerachiel's left knee. "Perhaps we shouldn't focus on what she can tell us, but more on what we can accomplish by allowing her to work with us."

"What do you mean?" Zerachiel questioned.

"Please explain," Gabriel added.

"Let's let Celestria redeem herself. We'll use Lasidious' vanity against him. Allow him to think that Celestria still longs to be in his good graces. Let him believe she'll do anything to be at his side." Michael focused his attention on Gabriel. "Celestria has admitted that they've broken laws on your pages, but until she states how, there's nothing you can hold over her. For now, agree to her terms in exchange for her cooperation. She must help us lead Lasidious into a trap. If she conforms to our demands, she'll receive all that she requests."

"And if she doesn't?" Zerachiel questioned. "What then?"

Michael redirected his gaze. "She will." He then looked back at Gabriel. "But if she doesn't ... destroy her."

Nodding, Gabriel summoned a second bench and took a seat. "Once she agrees, how much of the truth should I tell her?"

Michael leaned forward. "All of it. Call upon her now. Bring her into this room. I want to see her face when she learns that I'm alive."

Zerachiel stood. "Are you mad? What would revealing your ongoing existence accomplish?"

Michael stood to match his brother's posture. "Any belief that Celestria still has in Lasidious would crumble when she looked upon me. When she sees that I've reclaimed much of my former glory, her fear will make her conform."

Zerachiel shook his head. "You give yourself too much credit, brother. Sure, she may fear you ... for now. But this is Celestria we're talking about. She'd seize the first opportunity to salvage her relationship with Lasidious as soon as it presented itself. She won't abandon 10,000 seasons of love over a few Peaks of irritation. Their relationship is too deeply rooted for that. Our best and only chance to get the information we seek was lost when Gabriel failed to let her rant."

"You think this is my fault?" Gabriel rebutted.

Zerachiel shrugged. "Isn't it? She was ready to throw everything away only moments ago, and you stopped her. You admitted as much yourself before you made your way down here."

Gabriel sneered. "You have sat at that table with the rest of the Collective for more than 10,000 seasons, and you have yet to risk anything. You've hidden behind your walls on top of your mountain and cast your judgmental eyes across the valleys! How dare you sit in judgment of me!"

Michael stepped in. "Brothers! Brothers! We'll get nowhere badgering one another. We're united, remember?"

The room fell silent for a long series of moments before Michael spoke again. "Perhaps you're right, Zerachiel. Revealing my existence does seem risky."

"I also agree," Gabriel confirmed.

"At least we agree on something," Zerachiel mocked.

Michael placed his hand on the Angel of the Sun's shoulder, "Must you act that way?"

Another quiet series of moments passed while Zerachiel and Gabriel held each other's gaze. Eventually, Zerachiel dropped his eyes to the floor. "I'm sorry."

Gabriel stepped forward, placed his hand behind Zerachiel's neck and then pulled him forward to kiss the top of his forehead. "We will always be brothers. Your apology is accepted."

Zerachiel nodded. "How should we proceed?"

Michael turned and stepped toward the edge of the star. He studied the orbs that were attached to the wall while he determined a course of action. "Gabriel ... offer Celestria what her heart desires in exchange for her cooperation. If she turns against you—"

"If?" Zerachiel interrupted. "How about when?"

Michael grinned. "As I was saying ... *if* she turns against you, destroy her. Get what you can from her before this happens. That way, Lasidious is none the wiser and has no knowledge of my existence. Meanwhile, Zerachiel can continue to monitor the others while the Source works with Anahita to complete the new Heaven."

Zerachiel nudged Michael and smiled. "So the task was bigger than you after all."

Rather than respond, Michael redirected the conversation. "We're nearly there, brothers. Soon, Anahita will be strong enough to defeat Lasidious with us at her side."

Zerachiel rubbed his hands together. "I long to see the Peak when that smug look is wiped off Lasidious' face." The Angel of the Sun returned to the bench and took a seat. "Do you think our father will allow us to return to his Heaven once we've completed the task we promised to accomplish?"

Gabriel's head dropped. "I don't know. We've fallen so far from grace. We've lied, manipulated and assumed the roles of gods. We know the consequences of our actions. I believe he'll forgive us, but I cannot fathom being extended a key to the gates of the Heaven we once knew. I hate to say it, but I believe our only chance at eternal happiness is to help Anahita create the best Heaven we can imagine. I believe we've sealed our fate."

Zerachiel pulled his eyes off Gabriel and glared at Michael. "And to know we lost it all for the love of your woman…"

NORTHERN GRAYHAM
THE HOME OF THE KO-DESS

THE MOUNTAINS OF THE KO-DESS

The withered king, Meerum Bosand, stood with his frail hand extended. His magic had been invoked, and he had pinned the Ko-dess against the wall of his cave. The king's eyes were cold as he spoke. "It has been too many seasons since last our eyes fell upon each other, Cheval. Your power isn't as strong as it once was. Too bad. I was looking for a duel."

The Ko-dess struggled to free himself from Meerum's magic, but all Cheval managed to do was cut his flanks against the jagged walls of the cave. As the hair from his black and white coat fell to the floor, he fought back the pain in order to respond. "Why doest thou persist in this course of action, Meerum? I've wished thee no ill will."

Meerum released his power over the Ko-dess and allowed Cheval's hooves to touch the ground. "Perhaps not." The king snapped his fingers and two Tormalian slaves rushed across the cave and set a fresh block of ice on the floor. Once Meerum had taken a seat, he looked at Cheval. "My old friend." He paused. "May I call you old friend?"

The Ko-dess did not respond. Instead, his gaze broadcasted his disbelief that Meerum's question had fallen upon his ears.

The king smirked, "I suppose you're right. Friend is a bit presumptuous. Perhaps we should start our conversation over. Allow me to address you in a more civil manner. Please, take a moment to heal yourself."

The Ko-dess stared into Meerum's eyes. When no deception was found, he lowered his head. It did not take long before a shallow glow began to emanate from the center of his being. As the healing light enveloped his flanks, the cuts mended.

Bosand waited patiently until the light faded. "I trust you feel better?"

Cheval nodded.

"You know why I've come."

The Ko-dess did not answer. Instead, he trotted to the far side of the cave and took a drink from a spring of warm water that bubbled to the surface from an underground river that rushed below the mountains.

"Come now, Cheval. Ignoring me won't make me go away. Give me what I'm after, and I'll leave you in peace."

The Ko-dess turned from the spring. "Why doest thou persist to acquire power beyond your seasons? Without the blessing of the High Priestess, the power of the gashtion would surely overcome thee."

Meerum chuckled. "You're wrong, though you wouldn't know it. As I have said … it has been too many seasons since last your eyes fell upon me. They've been absent and unable to bear witness to my growth. I assure you. I'm strong enough."

Cheval shook his head. "If bestowed upon thee, how doest thou intend to wield the Tear's kindred spirit?"

The king's brows furrowed. "I'd wield it like any other. I'd drape it about my neck and use it to help the Isor protect their lands from the gashtion."

The Ko-dess held Meerum's eyes for a long series of moments. "It feels as though deception hideth within thy words. I cannot bestow the Kindred Tear upon thee in good conscience."

Meerum took a step toward the Ko-dess. "Must I give you another demonstration of my power before you concede?"

Cheval shook his head. "No. Thy threat hath fallen upon open ears. But I must warn thee, thou doest, indeed, have the power to take on the form of the gashtion, but thou hast not taken into account the importance of the blessing."

The Tormalian king frowned. "Considering the depth of my power, the priestess' blessing is unnecessary. You underestimate me yet again, Cheval."

A moment later, the Ko-dess dropped his eyes to the floor of the cave. "I hope thou doest not regret thine actions." Cheval regurgitated the Kindred Tear. The gem slid up from the pit of his stomach and fell onto the floor of the cave.

The Tormalian King smiled. "I knew you were wise and would see things my way. Now I shall spare your existence."

The Ko-dess whinnied as he shook his mane. A moment later he lifted his right, front hoof and then brought it down on top of the Tear of Gramal's kindred spirit. The gem smashed into a hundred pieces.

"Noooo!" Meerum screamed. The king hobbled as fast as he could and fell to the floor beside the pieces. As his fingers fumbled through the slivers, the realization of the power that was lost to him fueled his anger.

Cheval's eyes narrowed. "I believevest thou came seeking a duel. Stand, and let us settle this dispute."

The king's rage turned to laughter. "With pleasure, Cheval! With pleasure!"

MEANWHILE, NORTHERN GRAYHAM
THE WILDERNESS 37 PEAKS WEST OF HYDROTH

"Be still, Medolas," Gage ordered as the badger stood next to the Isorian who was sitting on his knees. "I cannot see into your mind's eye unless you're holding still."

"I am still," Medolas argued. "I couldn't be more still if I had passed. Perhaps your power doesn't work."

The badger removed his hands from the top of Medolas' head. "It's useless. Your memories of home have abandoned you. They aren't clear enough to find a place to teleport."

"Well what did you expect?" Clandestiny mumbled. "We fled Hydroth 300 seasons ago."

Gage turned around. "I was hoping for a better outcome is all."

Clandestiny was sitting on the far side of their camp eating the blubber from a carnoth, a beast that looked a lot like Strongbear, but this beast's coat was solid white.

The badger looked away from Clandestiny and found the Gallrum. "I still say Strongbear would be displeased with their choice in nourishment."

The serwin nodded as he studied the carnoth's claws. "Perhaps this beast and Strongbear were related."

The badger grinned. "You jest, but I'm sure Strongbear would think we were against him."

Both goswigs laughed.

"Why do you utter such nonsense?" Clandestiny questioned. "It's impossible to project the feelings of another. I'm hungry, and I'm most certainly not against anyone."

Gallrum hovered over and lowered next to the block of ice that Clanny was sitting on. "We meant nothing by it. It's only a statement from a friend we know from Luvelles."

Clandestiny frowned. "It sounds as if we'll be forced to walk the distance. At least we'll arrive unharmed."

"Agreed," Gage responded. The badger reached forward with his cane and poked the carnoth's carcass in the area where Clandestiny had cut the blubber she was eating from its abdomen. A moment later, an idea popped into Gage's mind. "Perhaps if you were to embrace."

"What for?" Medolas wondered. "Why would she want to embrace a corpse?"

Gallrum shook his head. "He's not speaking about the carnoth. He's speaking about you embracing Clandestiny." The serwin looked at the badger. "These blue beings are not very smart."

"Hey!" Clandestiny chastised. "Don't speak so ill of us!"

Gallrum ignored the Isorian's demeanor and continued to speak to Gage. "You may be onto something. If they were to unite and focus, perhaps their memories of home would be strengthened."

Clandestiny rolled her eyes. "How does embracing strengthen our memories?" she grumbled.

Gage growled. He had had enough of Clandestiny's argumentative attitude. She had seen his magic work on more than one occasion, yet still she challenged its effectiveness. "Perhaps you should speak less of what you don't understand and focus more on what you might remember. Embrace Medolas, close your eyes, and think of home … unless you'd rather walk. I'm tired of your vexatious attitude."

Seeing that Clanny was speechless, Medolas grinned within and then took a seat next to Clandestiny on her block. "Come on, Clanny. Try it. I don't want to walk. I want to see home."

"Fine!" she conceded.

Medolas grinned. "See now, Clanny, that wasn't so hard, was it?"

"Don't, Meddy! I'm not in the mood!" Without further chastisement, Clandestiny stood, pulled Medolas to his feet, and then threw her arms around him. She looked over her shoulder at Gage. "Now what?" she barked.

The badger's cane tapped against the ice as he circled the carcass and stopped next to the Isorians. He touched the skin of their blue legs and looked up. "Close your eyes and focus. And, Gallrum, place your claw on my shoulder."

It was not long before Clandestiny opened her eyes. "Well, is it working?"

Gage growled. "Focus!"

After ensuring Clanny did as she was told, Gage closed his eyes again and searched their memories. Eventually, a smile appeared on the badger's face. The group vanished.

When next Medolas and Clandestiny opened their eyes, they were standing in Clanny's old bedroom, but their arrival was not what they expected. Two Isorian children screamed and ran out of the room, shouting, "Mother! Father! Mishandlers have appeared to abscond our belongings!"

Confusion covered Clanny's face as a large Isorian with a hairy belly, full beard, and a powerful frame entered the room holding a spear that bore the markings of the Frigid Commander of the Isorian army. He pointed its tip in their direction. "Who are you?" he shouted. "You've chosen the wrong home to perform evil doings."

Medolas held up his hands and stepped in front of Clandestiny to shield her from the point of the commander's spear. "My name is Medolas. This is Clandestiny, and these are our friends, Gage and Gallrum. We've returned from our journey to find the Ko-dess. This home used to be the home of Shamand. We had no knowledge that we would be unwelcome."

"Where is Shamand?" Clandestiny queried. With little regard for her safety, Clanny pushed Medolas to her right and then reached out to shove the point of the commander's spear to the side as she stepped forward. "Where's my father, and why are you in his home? Who were those children, and what is your name?"

Seeing the look of bewilderment on the commander's face, Gage motioned for Gallrum to lower to the ice. He whispered into the serwin's ear with his eyes fixed on Clandestiny. "I'm glad the females from our world aren't as demanding as her."

Without adjusting her gaze, Clandestiny crossed her arms and responded. "I heard that, badger." She readdressed the commander. "I asked, what is your name, and why is your family in my house?"

A voice responded from the hallway beyond the room. "Tell her your name, Jeromas."

Jeromas took a step back, lifted his spear, pointed it again at Clandestiny and then addressed his wife who was about half his size. "Hold your tongue, Polesta! I have not yet determined a course of action!"

Irritation spread across Polesta's face. She stepped into the room and moved past her husband. Her hair was long, body petite, and yet she still possessed a strong presence. "There's no action to be taken. If they had been mishandlers, they would've overtaken our abode already." Polesta looked at Clandestiny. "You spoke of Shamand. How could you not know that the Great One perished?"

The life filling Clandestiny's eyes faded as her arms unfolded and dropped to her side. The movement caused the Tear of Gramal to reflect the light being cast by the orb lighting the room.

Upon seeing the shimmer, Polesta gasped. "The Tear! That's the Tear, Jeromas! Thank the gods the Tear has returned to us!" She turned, grabbed her husband's arm and shook it. "Jeromas, you must tell the ruby eyed man that the Tear has returned to Hydroth. We will once again be safe from the gashtion!"

Medolas was quick to add. "Yes, Commander, and tell Gabs that his childhood friends, Clandestiny and Medolas, have also returned."

Jeromas grabbed his wife by the arm and moved her into the hallway. His form filled the doorway as he lifted his spear and pointed it at Medolas. "If you're friends with the ruby eyed man, and if the trinket about your neck is, indeed, the Tear, then you won't fight against me. You'll surrender yourselves into captivity until I can fetch our sovereign and his advisor." The

Frigid Commander looked over his shoulder at his wife. "Fetch my men! I want them bound."

An irritated look spread across Polesta's face. "Why? She has the Tear about her neck."

The commander's voice was strong. "I said, fetch my men and tie them up!"

NORTHERN GRAYHAM
THE HOLLOW BENEATH THE ICE
THE OUTSKIRTS OF HYDROTH, THE PEAK OF BAILEM

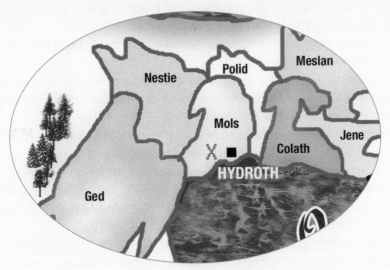

X - MARKS THE HOLLOW

Shiver and Gablysin were standing at the center of the hollow. The pace at which the army had been digging was frantic, and to ensure the hollow would not collapse during construction, large columns had been left behind to hold up the roof. Chains had been attached to the base of each column and stretched the length of the hollow where they ended at a ramp that ascended to the surface.

Shiver looked in the direction of the ramp. "Are you sure the chains will hold, Gabs? When the harugens pull, the pressure will be great."

Gablysin nodded. "These chains were crafted on Trollcom. The dwarves are known as master smiths. I'm confident they'll hold."

Shiver looked down at the chains and pushed against one of the links with his foot. "I don't know, Gabs. I wish I had your confidence." He looked up at the columns. They were nearly 70 paces tall and 6 paces thick. He shook his head. "These links feel feeble considering the task we're asking them to perform."

The ruby eyed man patted Shiver on the back. "You worry for naught."

The king gripped the links with the pysples on the bottom of his foot. As he pulled his foot away, the pysples popped. "I hope you're right."

Gabs shrugged. "And if I'm not?"

"If you're not, this war will consume only a short period of moments before we pass. The Tormal outnumber us two to one. The gashtion has ravaged too many, and we won't stand a chance if the hollow fails to collapse."

Before another word could be said, Jeromas skittered up on the back of his harugen. The commander pulled back on the reins and ordered the beast's undulating body to stop. He looked down. "Sire!"

Shiver stepped over the chain and reached up to pat the harugen on the side of its head. "What is it, Commander?"

"Four beings have been taken into custody. Two of them claim to have previous childhood companionship with you and your advisor."

Gablysin was the one to respond. "What names do they go by, Commander?"

Jeromas reached into his saddlebag to retrieve a parchment. After unfolding the paper, he answered, "One claims to be Medolas and the other, more spirited Isorian, goes by the name Clandestiny. It appears the Tear of Gramal is draped around her neck."

Shiver spun around, his eyes wide and slapped Gabs on the chest. "It can't be!"

Astounded, the ruby eyed man replied, "I cannot fathom their continued existence. It's been 300 seasons."

Shiver ran a few steps away from the harugen. He turned and gave an order. "Commander, take us to them!" The king bounded across the ice, mounted Jeromas' harugen, and then looked down at the ruby eyed man. "Make haste, Gabs. Let's go!"

Once Gabs had secured his straps on the third segment of the harugen's back, the Frigid Commander turned the beast around. As they skittered up and out of the hollow, the points of the harugen's legs tore into the ice at a rapid pace.

The Crystal Shard

When you want an update about your favorite characters

2 PEAKS HAVE PASSED

NORTHERN GRAYHAM

Medolas, Clandestiny, Shiver and **Gablysin**—The reunion between friends was remarkable. Many tears were shed, hugs were exchanged and stories were told. Shiver and the ruby eyed man have brought Medolas and Clandestiny up to speed on the happenings throughout the kingdom. Though Clanny was devastated after learning about the loss of her father and their old friend, Slips, she has been motivated to help the army in the effort to prepare for the upcoming war.

With the Tear draped around Clandestiny's neck, she has been ordered to remain at the king's side. The union ceremony to unite Medolas and Clandestiny will have to wait until after the war is over. Gablysin has agreed to perform their union if everyone survives.

Gage and **Gallrum**—The goswigs have offered to use their magic to help the Isorian army extend the depth and the width of the hollow. What once took the strength of the army 10 Peaks to chisel, only takes the goswigs the majority of a morning. As the expanse of the hollow grows at an exponential rate, Shiver, Gablysin, Medolas and even Clandestiny are finding it difficult to understand how the goswigs summon such power. Further, it frightens Shiver to know that his grandfather wields power of similar intensity.

Gage has also used his magic on the Frigid Commander's cape. The magic will help Jeromas stay cool as the Isorian makes his way to Harvestom to retrieve the High Priestess. Shiver wants to ensure that Fosalia approves of Clandestiny's ability to control the Tear of Gramal before he announces to the Isorian populace that the Tear has found its way back to Hydroth. The clan leaders who sit on the council have already been notified of the Tear's return, but they have been left with orders not to spread word until the priestess visits.

Meerum Bosand— The Tormalian King has returned to his army. After slaying the Ko-dess, Meerum spat on Cheval's corpse and then used his magic to search for the calling stone he had left with his Frigid Commander. The stone acted as a beacon to which Meerum could teleport, and the king is now lying inside his tent in the wilderness west of the Mountains of Tedfer. The power he expelled to end the Ko-dess' life's source was substantial, and it will take 4 Peaks for Meerum to recover.

Once the king's power has returned, Meerum plans to create a portal. The army will use this gate to teleport beyond the Mountains of Tedfer into Isorian territory. From there, they will march east toward Hydroth.

THE WORLD
OF
LUVELLES

Eastern Luvelles—With the family no longer worried about Garrin, George removed all traces of the god-child's existence from the family homes. After ensuring there would be no further complications regarding Garrin's absence, George spent the last few Peaks teleporting back and forth to the Village of Specks.

Getting Jackson, the owner of the Misplaced Inn, off a barstool so that George could complete his journey to the island of the wood elves has proved to be a challenge. The warlock has had to toss down a few ales himself to earn Jackson's trust and solidify their friendship.

Since George's conscience has been bothering him, the warlock has convinced himself that stealing the information he wants from Jackson's mind is unacceptable, and since he doesn't know the lands of Doridelven, he has been forced to

be patient. He has been working to convince Jackson that visiting the wood elves is a necessary evil. He can only hope the innkeeper will stop drinking long enough to take him to the port town of Drandel.

Western Luvelles—The construction of the bridge to connect the cities of Inspiration and Lavan is once again under way. King Dowd and Chancellor Boyafed have pooled their resources. They have also solicited the help of the Ultorians. The addition of the Ultorians' magic has been enough to hold back the water of Lake Lavan while the elves from Inspiration and Froland work with the halflings from Lavan and Hyperia to set the foundations for the pillars that will support the substructure of the bridge.

DRAGONIA
THE NEW HELL

Lasidious and Alistar—The brothers are visiting while they sit around Lasidious' camp in the forest just south of the Mountains of Gannesh. Garrin and Sam Jr. are still in stasis. Alistar has informed Lasidious about the complications the Collective encountered while working to ensure that Hell and its four moons stay in the perfect orbit while they travel around their new star.

The Collective plans to lift stasis in the morning, and all the beings across what was once known as Dragonia will know that they exist on a world called Hell.

Since the beings on the mainland

of Hell will believe that they have always existed on Hell, there will be no change in the way they live their lives—for now. They will not know the size of their world has increased and the damned are migrating. Sharvesa's daughter, the Vampire King and Queen and the criminals who occupy the stronghold south of the Mountains of Gannesh, will all have no idea that the mainland of Hell is about to change. Chaos is coming and all these beings will eventually be affected.

Lasidious and Alistar estimate that it will take the damned over a season to migrate out of the Ocean of Karamoore. The damned will fight one another as they work their way around the Dragon's Backbone. From there, they will need to swim to the mainland. With eternal suffering about to consume the entirety of Hell, the moment has come to implement the next part of the Mischievous One's plan.

Kepler, Sam, and the imp, **Pydum** —Prior to Sam waking up after his disagreement with Kael, Lasidious appeared to the blade. The Mischievous One informed Kael of the Archangel Gabriel's presence. Because of the news Kael divulged to Sam about Shalee's baby not being his son, an opportunity has presented itself. Kael agreed to patch things up with Sam and apologize to the king for his side of their disagreement. After Lasidious' departure, Kael told Sam a lie about who the real father of Shalee's baby was. Since that Peak, Sam has continued

to exist within his protective bubble while stewing about the Archangel Gabriel's liberties with his queen. Though Sam still does not know about his past relationship with the archangel, the King of Brandor has vowed to seek the power to attain vengeance against Gabriel.

Meanwhile, Yaloom's potion has caused Sam's body to feel as if the essence of his being is becoming more powerful somehow. A new kind of power is emerging within the king.

Pydum has watched from a distance. Stasis did not effect the imp, and he has been careful not to allow Kael to learn of his presence. On the Peak Kael forced Yaloom's potion down Sam's throat, the imp shook his head in disgust and then he did it again after Sam learned of Gabriel's supposed misdeeds.

Pydum has decided to create a friendship with the King of Brandor. The imp plans to divulge the truth, but how to do it without Kael interfering is another matter.

THE HIDDEN GOD WORLD ANCIENTS SOVEREIGN

Book of Immortality and **Celestria** —The Book has summoned Celestria to his Hall of Judgment. Gabriel will offer Celestria a deal.

A PLACE UNKNOWN

Anahita and **Helga**—The pair was separated and they no longer share a body. For the past few Peaks, Helga has been spending the majority of her moments in front of the mirror at the back of the shack while Anahita has been studying the ancient book that was left behind by Michael.

Aside from Helga's fiery-red hair that covers the majority of her body, Helga cannot get used to the idea that she can open the door to the shack and pee into the darkness without squatting.

Now that Anahita is full angel, the human need to expel waste no longer exists. She also does not need to consume sustenance to survive. Like Gabriel and Michael, if Anahita decides to partake in the pleasantries of food or drink, it will be solely for the purpose of enjoying the moment.

HARVESTOM

Mosley—With the help of the High Priestess and an unexpected visitor, Mosley has managed to improve his ability to invoke his power. Sharvesa has been working with the High Priestess to expedite the wolf's growth. Though the wolf's knowledge of the languages spoken by the Ancient Mystics and the Swayne Enserad has been helpful, Mosley is still far from powerful.

The wolf can summon magic that equals the power of lesser warlocks on Luvelles. Mosley longs for the Peak that he can slay George and Kepler, and because of what Sharvesa believes to be the truth about her brothers, the demon-goddess intends to avoid the rest of the Collective and see to it that Mosley finds his vengeance. Sharvesa wants George and Kepler slaughtered just as much as Mosley does since George forced Payne to surrender his power to the jaguar.

Thank you for reading the Crystal Shard

CHAPTER 14
DRAGONIA + HELL = SCREWED
STASIS ON HELL HAS LIFTED
THE OLD MERCHANT ISLAND
THE HEIGHT OF THE NEXT PEAK APPROACHES

When Sam woke, he took a moment to stretch. With the sun nearing the peak and two of Hell's four moons passing across the sky, he realized he was no longer waiting for stasis to lift. The barrier Lasidious had placed around the demon-jaguar and the containers was gone, and Kepler was missing. Kael was stuck in the ground, but the blade had gone cold since his flame was no longer necessary to shed light.

"Kael, where's Kepler?"

The sword did not hesitate to respond. "He's gone, Sam. Stasis lifted while you were asleep."

"Okay, okay. But that still doesn't tell me where he went. Did you tell him the bad news?"

"There was no bad news to divulge. Kepler's mind has been altered, just as every being's mind has been who doesn't possess godly memories. Kepler believes he has always existed on this world, and he also believes this world has always been called Hell. Further, he thinks he has traveled with you for many seasons, and you're friends. The jaguar has no knowledge of the other worlds, nor does he remember George and the family he left behind."

The ex-King of Brandor pondered for a moment. "I wonder if he thinks we're nomads since we don't have a place to call home."

The sword's blade pulsated as it responded. "I'm unsure, Sam. I was unable to clarify the demon's mind. Perhaps you'll need to investigate, but he did speak of a stronghold."

"Stronghold? What kind of stronghold?"

"I don't know. You'll need to search for that answer."

"So, where's Kepler now?"

"The jaguar is searching for the containers you said were on the manifest inside the dock foreman's office."

"Jehonas' office? You mean the containers filled with criminals? How did he remember that if his mind has been altered?"

"He didn't. I spoke of it. I told him you wanted the documents found."

"Ahhh. But doesn't Kepler have questions as to why he's suddenly searching for containers filled with criminals on the Merchant Island of Hell?"

"No. In his mind, a logical chain of events have transpired that brought the two of you to the island. Kepler knows the topography of the mainland. He speaks of it as if the two of you have explored every speck of dust."

Sam ran his hands through his hair and then pulled on the beard he had grown while sitting in stasis. "Okay, okay. This has to be the strangest thing that's ever happened to me." He took a moment to look at the mess lying on the ground around him. "Does he also think that I just leave food lying on the ground, and that I sleep anywhere I want to?"

"I don't know, Sam. I do know, he doesn't know stasis has occurred."

Sam took a moment to rub the back of his neck. "So in Kepler's mind, no moments have been lost. He and I have known each other for how long?"

A short period of silence passed before Kael responded. "I don't know. You'll have to figure out a way to explore the length of your relationship without letting the cat know it never existed. Who knows how the demon would react if he were to discover the existence of a different reality."

"Hmmm. Do you think he would become violent?"

"Perhaps. Considering the strength of Kepler's magic, it wouldn't be wise to make him angry or create distrust."

Sam rolled his eyes. "Wow! The gods really love to screw with things, don't they?"

"Indeed. While you slept, I took the moments to instill fear in the jaguar. The cat believes it's wise for you to surround yourselves with an army, no matter how depraved they might be. It is for this reason he searches for the containers."

"Really? What did you say to him that made him feel like that?"

"I told him the truth. I told him that there are beings who are damned, and that they are migrating toward the mainland. I told him that you will need to prepare for their arrival. The demon knows a miserable existence is approaching, but the cat is also searching for the criminals for reasons of his own ... reasons he believes he shares with you."

"What do you mean?"

"That was unclear when we spoke. He said something about adding to the army that protects your stronghold."

"What stronghold?"

"Again, I'm unsure about that. I didn't want to dig for answers. I was concerned about Kepler's state of mind."

"How did Kepler respond to the concept of a bunch of damned souls migrating to the mainland?"

Kael searched for a response. "I suppose he responded just as you did after you awoke from the effects of Yaloom's potion. It took Kepler a moment to accept that change was coming, but he doesn't seem to fear it. He believes his magic, your strength, and the dejected you plan to command will be enough to protect you."

Hearing Yaloom's name, Sam lifted his hand and stared at his palm. "Something inside me is changing. I can feel it. I feel stronger ... like I have energy I've never had before."

"That's good, Sam. You're much easier to talk to on this Peak than you were when last we spoke."

Sam's brow furrowed. "I don't remember much of that conversation. I was out of it. I've never been knocked out like that before."

Kael hesitated as he searched for a response. "Perhaps Yaloom's potion caused your mind to cloud."

Shrugging, Sam changed the subject. "Then Kepler just accepted that, all of a sudden, there's a bunch of damned souls who are going to migrate toward the mainland." The king paused. "Why would Lasidious tell you all of this while I was sleeping and not tell me himself? This sounds even more farfetched than when I showed up on Grayham."

"How am I to know Lasidious' reasons, Sam? Perhaps the gods are busy, and he did not have the moments to wait for you to wake."

Sam stared at the blade. "How can I trust you after what you did to me?"

The pulse of Kael's blade went from a soft white to a shallow red. "I've already apologized for my side of the argument, Sam. I have no desire to alienate you. Lasidious told me about the damned and that you need to prepare for their arrival. He also said to tell you that the moment is nearly upon us for you to know everything."

Sam shook his head. "What does that mean?"

"It means, you will be a powerful being, but I can't say more."

"Hmpf!" the king grumbled. "Isn't it bad enough that I know an archangel knocked my wife up? What else can Lasidious divulge?"

Kael laughed at Sam's candor. The pulse of his blade matched the cadence of his chuckle. "Oh, Sam, as soon as I receive confirmation that your mind is capable of handling what you need to know, the power that's going to fill your being will be enough to fuel this world twice over. I long for the Peak when I'll be able to hang from the hip of your true self."

Sam smirked. "I already am my true self, but you keep saying I'm not. I hate the fact that you won't explain why."

Kael changed the subject. "Kepler went north."

Shaking his head, Sam looked to the sky and frowned. "How did he know which way was north? Do you think the sun…?" The king paused as he looked at one of the two visible moons. Its surface was blood red. "Do you think the sun still rises in the east?"

Kael's blade pulsated as the weapon chuckled again. "I would assume the jaguar's memories of this world are correct since the gods are the ones who molded them." The blade rose in the air and pointed its tip in a direction that matched Kepler's path of travel. "The cat went that way."

Sam looked at the sun and then in the direction the blade was pointing. "Did the sun rise to my right?"

"Yes."

"Then north it is. Let's go find him." Sam reached down and grabbed a few pieces of fruit that Lasidious had left behind when stasis began. After a fair series of moments, Sam found Kepler breaking into an extremely large container that had been stacked on top of three others that matched its size.

"Good afternoon, Kepler!" Sam shouted as he watched the cat reach over the side of the container to swipe at the first lock.

The hasp the lock was attached to broke with ease. "Good afternoon, Sam! Did you sleep well? I didn't want to bother you."

"I did, thank you." Sam studied the length and sheer size of the containers. They were massive. "What's inside them all?"

Kepler placed his back paw on top of four pieces of parchment that he had dropped on top of the container and then slid them over the side. "Take a look for yourself. They are filled with undesirables. We should be able to add to our army."

Sam lifted Kael to his mouth. "How should I respond? I don't know what army he's talking about."

"Just go with it, Sam," the blade responded. "Knowledge will come."

The king reached down and snatched the papers off the ground. In each container, there was a large number of beings comprised of various races. The first container had 23 giant cats, 16 of Seth's serpent subjects, 43 bears, 71 Minotaur, 96 humans, and 1 gray unicorn. Sam smiled. "This container must be from Grayham!" he shouted.

Before Kael could remind Sam to watch his words, Kepler looked over the side of the container. "What's Grayham?"

An awkward period of moments passed before Sam shrugged. "I meant mayhem! This container looks like it's from a place filled with mayhem!"

Kepler sat on his haunches, licked the back of his paw and started to clean his ears. "That's was an odd thing to say!"

Sam returned a nervous grin. "You know me, Mr. Odd!" Walking around the side of the container, he looked up at the final lock that remained secure on the door of the top container. "Before you open it, we should figure out a plan. These other containers are filled with some pretty powerful beings."

Kael lifted from his sheath and hovered to a position not far in front of Sam. The blade was about to give the king a word of warning, but before he could, someone began to pound on the walls inside the top container. The being's shouts were muffled.

A moment later, pounding from the inside of the other containers could be heard. It was not long before all four sounded like a Hell of their own with fists, claws and horns bashing against the walls.

Sam looked down and scanned the manifests of the other containers. The second container had 17 elves, 6 halflings, 1 spirit, 2 sprites, and 11 kedgles. The third container had 86 dwarves, 133 trolls, and 67 lizardians while the fourth container had 72 browncoated centaurs, 63 blackcoated centaurs, 2 humans, 4 elves, 6 wood elves, 1 spirit, and 1 red demon.

Sam's brows furrowed as he whispered to Kael, "Considering the races inside each, I'd wager the second crate came from Luvelles, the third from Trollcom, and the fourth must've come from Harvestom. But why would elves, wood elves, a spirit and a demon be shipped from that world? I wonder if they were students of the High Priestess and committed a crime? I wonder if the demon was returning home."

Kael's response was immediate. "Before you open the containers, you should protect yourself from the elements. Also, the trolls' blood is acidic, and as you know, the snakes' bites are venomous. Some of the beings in the containers wield powerful magic, so you should be ready."

Lifting the blade to his mouth, Sam spoke the words of power necessary to receive these benefits. He further extended their protection to encompass an area 15 paces around him. He then looked up at Kepler. "Are you ready?"

Kepler scratched at the top of the container, his claws sounding as if they were scraping across a chalkboard. "They sound hungry! The container behind you is filled with slaughtered corgans! Perhaps you should scatter the meat across the ground and then let them out! You can establish order as they consume!"

The king pondered Kepler's plan. "What if we can't control them all?"

The demon-jaguar jumped down from the top of the crate. "Then you'll challenge the strongest to a duel as you always do and then slay the being that accepts the challenge. Demonstrate your prowess, and the problem will be solved."

Sam looked down at the manifests and did a quick calculation. "Holy garesh, there are 721 beings inside these containers."

Walking toward the crate filled with corgan meat, Kepler looked over his shoulder. "On how many occasions have we slain more than that? Why are you acting so strangely? We've faced these odds on a thousand occasions."

Without responding, Sam put Kael to his mouth and whispered, "Let me guess, Lasidious was the one who told him that. I must be a mighty being in the cat's mind." Sam smirked. "Just wait until he learns the truth. I'll be screwed when that happens."

The pulsating of Kael's blade matched the weapon's chuckle. "Have faith, Sam. Let the dejected out of their crates and feed them. Take control of your apparent army and dominate this world. Hell is your kingdom now. You're about to go from the King of Nothing to the King of Everything. I admire the strength you'll come to know as your Peaks pass."

Sam grabbed the top of his head and pulled at his hair. "Ugh! The King of Hell. Kael, you make me sound like Lucifer himself. Believe me, I'm no Lucifer."

As soon as Sam finished his declaration, the blade started laughing hysterically.

"What's so funny?"

"Oh ... nothing. Forget that I'm here, and go about your business."

The new King of Hell frowned. "Perhaps you should answer some more of my questions. I think it's best if we're on the same page."

"Yes, it would be best," the blade responded. "But as I've already stated, your mind isn't ready for the truth."

The king returned Kael to his sheath. "That's B.S."

Kepler swiped at the final lock on the crate filled with corgans. The hasp fell to the ground, the doors popped open, and a rush of freezing cold air poured out. "Perhaps you should start a number of fires. Many of the beings are like you. Some of them will want to cook their meat." The cat cringed. "I can't stand the thought of that."

The pounding on the upper three crates continued as Sam created 10 fires, but the container nearest the ground became silent. "They must have tired themselves out," Sam said as he hung the meat above the first fire. Once a side of beef was cooking above every flame, the king set out 10 piles of raw meat for those who would eat like the jaguar.

"Kepler, jump onto the top crate and finish opening it. Let's let them out and establish order."

As the demon leapt skyward, he responded, "With pleasure."

After busting the final lock, Kepler pushed the doors open and peered inside. Each criminal had been placed in separate cells, and most of them were sitting in their own waste.

The giant cats were the closest to the doors. Kepler was about to use his power to break the locks on their cages when a thought occurred. He walked back to the side of the crate and looked down at Sam. "Why would these beings be in captivity? We have roamed the territories of the mainland since you were a baby, and never have we run across anything like this!" The demon looked out across the docks. "Why are these crates here? They feel out of place. None of this makes sense! How can we dominate lands we don't truly know?"

"Don't worry about it," Sam reasoned. "We'll get to know them soon enough! I'm sure there's an explanation for the mess around here!"

Kepler snorted. "How could this be our first encounter with this island?"

Sam shrugged. "I don't know. But as our moments pass, the answer will be revealed, don't you think?"

The king retrieved Kael from his sheath and lifted the blade to his mouth. "I need your help," he whispered. "How should I respond to all these questions. Lasidious must have done some serious tweaking in his mind."

"I don't know what to say, Sam, but you should tread lightly. It appears the gods have failed to account for every question that could arise. Regarding the crates: on the other worlds, Kepler's questions would've been easily answered. However, on Hell, this island shouldn't exist. Nor should the crates be here since the Merchant Angels no longer service this world. Perhaps the gods didn't feel the need to correct this oversight. After all, confusion can be its own version of Hell."

Sam rolled his eyes. "Leave it to the gods to screw with things … morons who torture their creations." Sam shouted back up to Kepler, "Why don't we ask the beings inside why they're in the crates? This whole place seems strange to me as well!"

Seemingly pacified by Sam's response, Kepler returned to the opening, peered back into the container and then addressed the beings inside after he cleared his throat. "May I have your attention? I am the Master of the Hunt…"

Sam put Kael to his mouth. "Well ... at least the gods left Kepler with his self-esteem."

Kepler continued. "…my partner, who is standing on the ground, is your new king. We are your masters. You will do as you're told, or you'll perish. Are there any questions?"

For those beings who chose to challenge Kepler's authority, the demon-jaguar used his magic against them. And since they were from Grayham, they did not possess the power to fight against him. Their bones broke beneath their skin, their bellies ripped open and they folded inside-out while Kepler allowed the others who had remained quiet to watch. As the blood flowed beyond the opening, it poured down the doors of the crates below and pooled at the bottom.

For the remaining 19 cats, 11 serpents, 30 bears, 51 Minotaur, 56 humans, and 1 gray unicorn, Kepler opened their doors and allowed them to make their way out.

In total, the blood of 81 beings had created the pool. It splashed beneath the criminals' feet, coils, paws and hooves as they climbed down and landed on the ground.

Sam lifted Kael, commanded the blade's flame and then pointed Kael's tip toward the food. "Make yourselves at home. Eat until you're full. You will address me as ... My King."

After seeing the display of Kepler's power, no one dared object.

Sam looked down at the manifests. He knew the demon-jaguar commanded power stronger than most every being on Luvelles. "Kepler! Open the second crate! Your power should work on them as well!"

When Kepler responded, he used telepathy to project his thoughts into Sam's mind. *"I've never heard of some of the beings on those manifests before. I look forward to seeing what they look like."*

As Sam stood in silence processing Kepler's form of communication, the jaguar jumped to the ground. "Are you okay, Sam? You look confused."

The king returned a halfhearted grin. "I'm okay. I was just thinking, that's all. Let's just get the locks off the next crate."

Looking up at the second container that sat just below the one he had emptied, the demon-jaguar used his power to rip off the locks. Once the doors were open, the cat jumped into the opening to address these beings just as he had the others. As he did, Sam lifted Kael to his mouth yet again and whispered. "Kael, Kepler just spoke to me without opening his mouth. How does that work? Am I going crazy?"

"No, Sam ... the cat must have the ability to speak telepathically. If you can hear him, you also have the ability to return thoughts, though the process may require you to focus before you can employ the action."

Sam dropped the blade to his side. "No way ... I've got to try that." The king looked up and concentrated on the jaguar. *"Kepler, can you hear me? Kepler. Kepler. KEPLER!"*

The demon-cat stopped his speech to the criminals and turned around. *"What? Of course, I can hear you! Stop shouting! What on Hell is wrong with you?"*

Sam shrugged and focused as he returned another thought. *"I was just making sure."*

The cat's furry face clearly showed his concern. *"Something's wrong with you. Perhaps we should hold off on releasing the dejected until your ability to dominate returns."*

Sam shook his head. *"No. Don't worry about it. I'm fine."*

Rolling his eyes, Kepler turned back around to continue his speech. Only four elves in the second crate were slaughtered after they lifted their voices in protest. As the elves' blood streamed past Kepler's paws, the jaguar took note of the halflings' ears as they worked their way to the ground. He looked down at Sam and sent the king a thought. *"How boring. Their appearance isn't much different than yours. I expected more."* As the spirit floated past, the cat added, *"That's more like it. You can see right through him."*

In total, 13 elves, 6 halflings, 1 spirit, 2 sprites, and 11 kedgles made their way out of the crate to join the others. Sam looked down to study the manifests of the bottom containers. His eyes focused on the red demon that was locked in the silent container sitting on the ground. *"Huh! Kepler, how about—"*

The demon-cat interrupted. *"Call me Kep, Sam! On how many occasions must I tell you that?"*

Sam studied Kepler's face. There was so much to take in. He still could not believe the demon truly felt they had traveled together as he mumbled to himself, "This is insane. I wonder to what end he'll stand at my side. How deep is our relationship supposed to be?"

"Sorry, Kep," Sam finally responded. "You know me and my bad habits!"

The demon yawned and did not respond.

Sam rolled his eyes and then readjusted his gaze back to the manifest of the bottom container. He stepped forward and slapped his hand against the metal. "There's a red demon inside named Orgon. If I'm right, he's the most powerful being in there. We should have a conversation with him."

Before another word could be said, two of the humans started fighting. They had been sitting next to the fire furthest away from where Sam was standing. Without thinking, Sam lifted his hand and shouted, "Shut up!" As he finished his last word, a brutal wave of force erupted from his palm and barreled across the distance. It blasted the two combatants and sent them flying. The newly proclaimed King of Hell watched in awe as the men lifted off the ground and flew more than 18 paces before they landed and tumbled to a stop.

Sam turned his back to the remaining criminals who sat stone-faced looking in his direction. A moment later, he lifted Kael to his mouth, looked down at his free palm and whispered, "I need you to explain what the hell just happened."

A long moment of silence passed as Kael searched for a response. "Perhaps Yaloom's potion has inadvertently helped you release a portion of your old self. Soon, Sam, and I do mean soon, you'll be a powerful being."

Kepler jumped down from the second crate and sniffed Sam's palm. He snorted. "You've never had that smell before. Something large within you is emerging, and it smells magnificent."

The king did not respond. Instead, he lifted his palm in the direction of the bottom crate and shouted the elven word for lock. Both popped open. He turned his back to the criminals and whispered again, "Holy garesh, Kep! Did you see that?"

Kepler nodded. "If you're referring to the simple use of magic that any ordinary imbecile can command, then yes, I saw it. What's wrong with you? You act like you've never commanded magic at all."

Kael was the one to respond. "Kepler, perhaps you could give us a moment. I need to speak with Sam alone."

The jaguar turned to enter the bottom crate. As he opened the door, a wave of heat poured out. The jaguar waited for the temperature to drop and then stepped inside to announce his presence.

With the cat out of earshot, Kael addressed the king. "Sam, you must not react to the changes you're experiencing. To do so will cause Kepler to question his beliefs. Who knows what would happen if he realized a different reality. You must tread lightly. Act like a king … not a simpleton. Be smart."

After pondering the sword's words, Sam turned to face the criminals who were eating. "Is there anyone else who has the desire to piss me off?"

It was unanimous. Everyone shook their heads—even the two criminals who were hobbling back to their meals had no comment.

"Great! Then it's settled. You'll all eat in peace." Sam pointed Kael in the direction of every criminal and commanded the blade's flame. "If any of you run while I'm inside the crate, you will have seen your last Peak. Do I make myself clear?"

Everyone nodded.

Sam turned and walked through the pool of blood. He stepped inside the container and stopped next to Kepler. The stench clubbed the new King of Hell upside the head. Most every being was passed out, except one—the red demon.

"Damn, it's hot in here!" Sam exclaimed as he lifted Kael and commanded the blade to burst into an icy flame. It was not long before the temperature inside the container dropped significantly.

Seeing the condition of the crate's inhabitants, Sam stepped outside and commanded the humans to gather enough meat to feed those who were suffering. Next, Sam commanded the Minotaur to go into the container that held the frozen corgan meat. "Bring me as many blocks of ice as you can. Give them all a chunk. They'll be thirsty when they wake up."

Once his orders were being carried out, the king walked back into the crate and went to the far back. He stopped in front of the cage that held the red demon. "Tell me, Orgon…" He passed his hand across the others in the container. "This is your fault, isn't it?"

The demon smiled.

Sam placed Kael's icy flame against the cage. "Don't be coy. Answer me."

As the demon moved to the far back of the cage to avoid the discomfort of the ice, he responded. "Yes, I'm responsible."

Sam's brows furrowed. Before he uttered another word, the king turned and walked away. He strolled past Kepler, stepped out of the crate and then lifted Kael back to his mouth. "How did I know how to speak Demon just now? I've never studied their language."

Kael's blade pulsated. "Sam, there's much you don't know about yourself. Again, I cannot answer your questions. Your mind isn't ready for the answers. What is, just is. You must accept that for now."

Sam dropped the blade to his side. "You're really pissing me off." The king re-entered the crate and stopped in front of Orgon's cage. "I want to know why you did this to them. What harm did they cause you?"

The demon chuckled. "None. I simply wanted them to be silent. Their clattering was excruciating."

Sam could not help but smile. Not only was he holding a conversation in demon tongue, he could tell the demon was smart. "Seems like a reasonable answer. What do you think, Kep?"

Kepler looked at Orgon and growled. "I suppose if I was locked in a cage, and the beings around me made noise like they did prior to opening their crate, I would also command their silence."

"As would I," Kael added.

The demon's eyes widened as he watched the blade pulsate. "Your weapon speaks. Was it a gift from the gods?"

Sam pondered the demon's question and then thought to himself. *Why would the gods allow the souls on this world to maintain knowledge of their existence? What could be the reason for that?*

Sheathing Kael, Sam redirected the conversation. "Why are you in this crate? What wrong did you do to land you in here?" the king demanded.

It was easy to see that Orgon was searching for an answer.

Sam shook his head. "You don't know why you're here, do you?"

Orgon's response was what Sam thought it would be. The king turned around and walked to the center of the crate. He reached up and grabbed one of the horns of the largest Minotaur who was distributing ice and then forced the beast-man to his knees. "What wrong did you do to land you in your crate?"

As the Minotaur struggled to respond, Sam realized two things. First, he had spoken in the beast-man's tongue as if it was a natural part of his being. And second, he had forced the Minotaur to his knees with ease. He was stronger than before—far stronger than he was after he received the gift of strength from Mosley. He could crush the Minotaur and not even break a sweat.

The king released the Minotaur's horn and took a step back. "What's your name?"

This was a question the beast-man could answer. "I'm known as Poldas, My King."

Sam smiled. "You're a lot smarter than you look. Come with me, Poldas." The king led the Minotaur to the back of the crate and stopped next to the red demon. He grabbed the lock and ripped it off the demon's cage and then allowed Orgon to exit.

With Orgon and Poldas standing speechless in front of him, Sam lifted Kael and commanded the blade to produce a watery flame as he spoke in both languages, consecutively. "This is your lucky Peak." He pointed Kael at Kepler. "This is my advisor." Sam reached out and patted the red demon on his bare chest. "You, Orgon, are my new General Absolute." He then patted Poldas on his hair-covered chest. "And you are Orgon's second in command."

Kepler cleared his throat. "Sam, perhaps we could speak."

The king pointed. "You two stay right there. I'll be back."

Once Kepler and Sam were clear of the crate, the jaguar spoke. "You already have a General Absolute. Why would you create another?"

Sam had to think fast. "I've only got one General Absolute, right?"

The cat confirmed.

364 | Crystal Moon, The Tear of Gramal

"And since he's not with us, he's at the stronghold. Am I right?"

The jaguar shook his head. "No, Sam. She's at the stronghold. What is wrong with you?"

Sam shrugged. "He, she, it doesn't matter. You know what I meant."

Kepler's brows furrowed as a cat's would. "Why promote the demon and the Minotaur when you already have these positions filled. They can't even understand one another."

Sam reached out and patted Kepler on the shoulder. "You didn't give me a chance to finish in there. Their positions are temporary. We've got to get from here to home without incident, don't we? All we've got to do is deal with the language differences for now."

Somewhat pacified by Sam's response, Kepler re-entered the crate. "This seems like a waste of our moments," he said as the end of his tail disappeared.

Sam lifted Kael to his mouth again. "I'm going to have to think fast around here. What a cluster the gods have left me in."

Entering the crate, the new King of Hell stopped in front of Orgon and Poldas and spoke his orders in both languages. "You two open the container just above us and inform its occupants of the order of things. I want them to understand their new chain of command. You'll spend the rest of this Peak interviewing those whom you'll command. In the morning, I want you to choose an officer for each race. This island is about to become our new home. I want shelters built. I want walls constructed that surround the entire island, and I want them to be impenetrable. I want them to be 80 paces high, 30 paces wide, and I want the base of the wall to be submerged in the water that surrounds the island. Anyone or anything that approaches will have to swim up to the wall and climb over it. This should give us the advantage."

Sam looked at Kepler. "We need to form search parties for food. Once the trolls in the container above have conformed, take Orgon onto the mainland and gather the rest of our forces. This island will be our new stronghold. While you're out there, search for reinforcements. I want our army to continue to grow."

Sam reached into his pocket, pulled out a map of the mainland that he had brought with him from Grayham and showed it to Kepler. "Does this map look right to you?"

The jaguar studied the topography. "Of course, it does. Why?"

"I have a reason for asking. Just bear with me." The king lowered the map to the floor of the container. "Put a claw on the location of our current stronghold."

Kepler's response was filled with irritation. "Why? You know where it is."

Sam looked up. "Have you ever known me not to have a reason for doing the things I do?"

The jaguar's response was immediate. "No. You've always employed clear thought."

"Then stop questioning me, and point to the stronghold."

Kepler rolled his eyes and placed the tip of his claw on the location.

Seeing that the Temple of the Gods was to the south beyond the mountains, Sam changed his mind. He pointed his finger at the temple. "Screw this island. The temple is where we're going to go. That building is fit for a king."

"The gods won't approve," Kepler protested. "They won't allow you to claim their temple as your own."

Sam laughed.

"Have I said something funny?" the jaguar queried.

"If you knew what I know about the gods, you wouldn't make that claim. The temple will be my new castle. I don't care how the gods feel about it. We'll surround it with a wall that extends from the mountains into the ocean. The wall will parallel the coast to the south and then follow it east until it rejoins the mountains." Sam used the tip of Kael to poke his finger. He used his blood to mark an X on six different locations and then drew paths between them. He pointed at the first X just west of the temple. "The first wall will start here. It'll follow this line against the coast and end here."

The king looked up at Kepler. "Use your power to make these markings look like fortified walls fit for a kingdom. I want my map to be detailed."

Kepler pondered Sam's words.

Sam could tell the demon was struggling to visualize the concept of a fortified wall.

"Come with me." The king took Kepler out of the container and knelt onto the dirt. He used his finger to draw a wall. "There. Take that idea and put it on my map where my lines of blood are. And get rid of the blood when you're finished."

After spending a few more moments studying Sam's illustration in the dirt, Kepler made the adjustments to the map.

"Perfect," Sam announced. "You're a regular cartographer, Kep. What would I do without you?"

Without waiting for a response, Sam lifted the map and motioned for Orgon and Poldas to come out of the container. As they stepped through the mud the blood had left behind, Sam noticed that many of the occupants inside the container were beginning to stir. He spoke to the demon first and then the Minotaur as he explained the details of the wall that would be built around the Temple of the Gods. Once they understood, he ordered them to empty the final crate and then he walked to the far side of the docks with Kepler while he continued to study the map.

Beyond the spot where Kepler had said the stronghold was located, the mountains failed to provide protection to the north. It would not be acceptable to have this area exposed. "Kep, is the water near the stronghold consumable?"

The demon-cat was astounded. "Of course, it is, Sam. That's why you chose its location."

"Exactly," the king responded to throw the cat off. "So what am I thinking now?"

"How am I supposed to know?" the jaguar growled. "It's as if you've become a stranger to me."

Sam tapped his knuckles against the map. "Relax, Kep. I know what I'm doing."

"Then get to the point," Kepler snarled.

"Okay. Okay. We're going to create a wall to protect the stronghold."

Kepler snorted, "There is a wall already, Sam."

Sam responded without hesitation. "I know, but there isn't a wall like the one we're about to build. With the damned migrating, we will need greater protection. We need a wall that encompasses a vast area of land." Sam marked four more X's on the map. "Walls will extend between these locations. By the moment we are finished, we will have land to cultivate, water to consume, and we will have as much cattle as we—"

"Cattle?" Kepler interrupted. "What is cattle?"

Sam frowned. "I'm talking about corgans, horses and any other kind of animal we can get our hands on. We'll need meat."

The jaguar studied the map. "Sam, the walls you intend to build will encompass a vast territory. It'll take seasons for our army to build them."

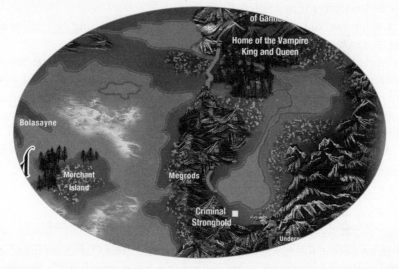

The king rolled up the map. "We're not going to build, Kep. We're going to create. I want you to figure out who wields the strongest magic. Gather them into a group. We're going to make my walls the easy way. We're going to cheat."

"Even if we do use magic, it'll still take the majority of a season."

Sam unsheathed Kael. "How long will it take the damned to migrate?"

The blade began to pulsate. "Lasidious said they're migrating from a location southwest of Dragon's Backbone. You have more than enough moments to build your walls. I also suggest you use the magic in your army to scar the mountains where they remain assailable. You don't want the damned to climb over them."

Sam nodded as he looked up to pat Kepler on the shoulder. "Anyplace you can climb … fix it. If you can't get over it, they won't be able to either. We'll start from the south and work our way north. We will out-create the bastards as they work their way this direction."

Kepler turned and looked at the crates that were scattered about the island. "What would you have me do with the goods inside these?"

"Many of these containers are made of steel. I'd imagine a fair number of them are filled with the magic that keeps food cool. We will use this to our advantage. I want the crates brought to the temple. By the moment we get them there, I want the rest of our army to join us. We're going to take it by force if we have to."

Sam thumped the map with his finger. "With the damned migrating, we don't want to waste any of our moments, so let's get going. Make sure everyone understands my orders."

Kepler smirked. "I'll do as you ask, but I'm not calling you My King." Kepler ran back toward the crates.

With the jaguar out of earshot, Sam pondered the demon's response. A moment later, his anger manifested. His eyes began to glow as if a light had been placed behind them, and though it was only for a short series of moments, they were an intense golden-brown. "You will address me as My King, or you'll perish, Kepler."

Another moment later, Sam grabbed his head. *What the hell is happening to me?* he thought. *I can't go around threatening my allies.*

MEANWHILE, THE FOREST
SOUTH OF THE MOUNTAINS OF GANNESH

In his human form, Alistar reached down and lifted Garrin off the blanket that Lasidious had placed a safe distance from the campfire. "It appears the milk is working. Garrin has dropped his defenses."

The Mischievous One chuckled and then lowered the Prince of Brandor to another blanket that he had spread out not far away. "Don't be so sure about that, brother."

Lasidious stood from the stone he was sitting on and then walked around the fire. As soon as he was within arm's reach of the god-child, Garrin put up a barrier that encompassed both himself and Alistar.

Lasidious smiled and then spoke in his best baby voice. "See? He won't let me near him. Oh no, he won't. But Daddy loves him anyway. Oh yes, he does."

The God of the Harvest smiled. "You should speak baby more often. It suits you."

As Lasidious reclaimed his seat, Garrin lowered the barrier. "Both babies were beginning to trust me before stasis began. Garrin even allowed me to put him on my stomach. Now, I'm not sure why he won't let me touch him."

Alistar spoke in a baby voice of his own as he tickled Garrin under his arms. "Did you decide not to trust your daddy? He only wants to play with you."

The God of the Harvest pretended to eat the fingers off Garrin's hands. The baby giggled as Alistar continued to speak to him. "I'm sure you'll allow your daddy to play with you some Peak, won't you? Did you know your papa can make funny faces? He can make his eyes red, his teeth sharp, and then he gets really, really ugly."

Garrin chuckled as Alistar lifted the child to blow on his belly.

Lasidious lifted the prince onto his lap, retrieved a bottle filled with the Vampire Queen's milk and then placed the nipple into the baby's mouth. "Why don't you feed Garrin? Yolan's milk has got to work, or our plan will fail."

After retrieving a bottle and propping it up in the god-child's mouth, Alistar responded. "Perhaps you need to stop thinking about the plan. Perhaps Garrin can feel the tension. I know I can."

Alistar lowered Garrin back onto his blanket. "We should talk. Did you make sure Kepler's memories were adjusted? Will he protect Sam until his magic manifests?"

"I did," Lasidious responded. "Our brother will come to know his true self shortly."

"Wonderful. I cannot wait to put my arms around him."

The Mischievous One bit down on his lip and then forced a smile. "I also long for that embrace."

"How long will it take before Yaloom's potion has an effect on him?"

"The potion has already had an effect. Sam could hardly keep his eyes open when last I spoke with Kael."

Alistar frowned. "We should stop calling him Sam. We should speak of him by his true name. He would ask as much from us."

Lasidious shook his head. "I say we let him earn it. Though I've missed him dearly, he failed us, remember?"

"I don't know that we agree with you. Perhaps we should change the subject." A fair series of moments passed before Alistar spoke again. "I think

Celestria no longer believes that you will return to her. I tried to defend you, but I don't think she trusts me."

"What do you propose we do about it?" the Mischievous One questioned.

Alistar pondered for a response. "I don't know, but at least Garrin trusts me. Perhaps we should seize this advantage and enter the Vampire King's abode sooner than expected. Strike your accord with Tardon and let's let Yolan help you push our plan along."

Lasidious nodded. "That's a good idea. We'll leave the babies in her care while the Tardon and I finish our negotiations."

"Do you want me to stay while you speak with him?"

"That won't be necessary." Lasidious stood and looked toward the peaks of Gannesh that rose above the tree line. "Tardon won't be a formidable foe to negotiate with. I'd rather you return to Ancients Sovereign and ensure we don't acquire new problems. Find a way to keep Celestria off my trail."

Alistar lifted Garrin from the blanket and then tossed the cover over his shoulder. "I'd feel more comfortable returning to Ancients Sovereign anyway. Shall we get going?"

Lasidious retrieved Sam Jr. and then responded. "Yes, let's get moving." Both gods vanished.

ANCIENTS SOVEREIGN
THE BOOK'S HALL OF JUDGMENT

Celestria appeared inside Gabriel's hall. Gazing at the center of the table, she smiled. The Book was resting on his golden stand with his arms crossed and his eyes closed. *How sweet*, she thought. *A book that sleeps.* The Goddess of Beasts moved to the side of the table and reached out to caress the Book's cover. "Wake up, Gabriel. I'm here as you have requested."

Beyond the door bearing the Source's image, in the depths of Ancients Sovereign beneath the Book's hall, the Archangel Gabriel reached out and placed his hand on Zerachiel's shoulder. "How are you?"

Zerachiel reached out and pulled his brother's forehead to his own. "I fare well. Why did you call me here?"

"I felt uncomfortable after our last meeting. I wanted to..." Gabriel stopped talking and looked toward the ceiling. A moment later, he reclaimed Zerachiel's eyes. "I must go. We'll speak later, brother. I'm being summoned."

Before the Archangel Zerachiel had the chance to object, Gabriel's form began to dematerialize. It was not long before he was standing in the room alone.

Though Celestria was standing above the sleeping Book when Gabriel reassumed his alternate form, the Goddess of Beasts was unable to see the process that allowed Gabriel to possess its pages. When, finally, the Book opened his eyes, Celestria exclaimed, "I thought you were never going to wake! Are you well, Gabriel?"

As the Book lifted off his golden stand and assumed a hovering position in front of Celestria, he responded. "I am well, though I'm tired."

Celestria look puzzled. "I didn't know you needed sleep, Gabriel. All these seasons have passed, and never have I seen you slumber.

The Book feigned an exhausted yawn. "Nor could you have seen me slumber. As you know, I have only recently acquired the features that would allow you to notice.

The goddess nodded. "I've been thinking about our last conversation. My position is this:—"

Gabriel cut Celestria off. "Before you tell me, I also have a position that I want to make known, and my position is non-negotiable. I'll spare your existence and the existence of this one other that you will name as long as this one other isn't Lasidious."

Celestria frowned. "Why would I choose Lasidious? You know I'm angry with him."

The Book lifted his hand to command the goddess to remain silent. "I'm not finished. As I was saying, I shall spare this other being, and in exchange, you will enter into a Promise of the Gods."

Celestria crossed her arms. "Do you distrust me that much, Gabriel, that I must first weaken my position and place my existence in jeopardy?"

"Yes," the Book replied without hesitation. "Though I have acquired a fondness for you, I don't trust you at all. If I am to extend pardons for laws you've broken, then you must extend a promise. If you break this pact, the moment a word of betrayal is uttered, I'll end you."

"You would end me? Why not just strip me of my immortality like you do the others? Isn't that harsh enough, Gabriel?"

Gabriel shook his head. "No, it's not. To simply strip you of your immortality would leave you with the moments at your disposal to accomplish further betrayal. If ever your intent is to betray my confidence, you'll be destroyed, and your soul will not be allowed to see the inside of my pages or the depravity of Hell. You will agree to my terms, because if you don't, I'll begin a search for the proof I need to strip you of your immortality."

Celestria stood in silence as she stared at the Book's firm demeanor. Though she was angry at Lasidious, she desperately wished the Mischievous One was at her side to provide direction. She felt weak without his guidance. "May I have a Peak to think about my response, Gabriel?"

"No!" the Book snapped. "The moments for half-measures and misdirection have passed. You will decide now, or I shall begin my search for wrongdoings against the gods' laws. Don't underestimate me, Celestria. If you leave my hall without protecting your existence, you will see mortality and you'll perish because of it. Make your decision now."

The Goddess of Beasts threw up her hands. "Okay, you win! I choose to enter into a Promise of the Gods with you. I further swear my allegiance. What else would you have me do?"

The Book stared into Celestria's eyes for a fair series of moments. "That was too easy. I expected more of a fight."

Celestria crossed her arms in rebuttal. "You got what you wanted from me, and now it was too easy. Must I choose to end my existence before you realize I'm scared, Gabriel?" Tears filled the goddess' eyes. "The only being that I've ever loved has abandoned me. Our plotting has left me vulnerable to the Collective, and I have no way of protecting myself against those who sit at this table."

Celestria allowed her arms to fall to her side. "I'll do whatever you ask of me. Can you not see my fear, Gabriel? Just look at me. I'm a shell of the woman I was before Lasidious left me. All I ask is that you spare my existence, and allow me to live out my Peaks on Ancients Sovereign with the one I name."

The Book stared at the goddess, but he did not reply.

Fidgeting, Celestria pleaded, "Gabriel, please stop. You're scaring me. I know I have to help you bring Lasidious to his demise. I'll do whatever you ask of me. I swear it. This is my Promise of the Gods. If I fail to show loyalty to you, I shall forfeit my existence."

Hearing the promise, the Book softened. "I accept your pledge. You shall be spared." Gabriel lowered to the table and looked up. "As long as the one you name isn't Lasidious, you may lay claim to any other whom you want to be spared. Asylum shall be granted here on Ancients Sovereign."

"And is that your Promise of the Gods, Gabriel? You'll never hurt us, and we can live freely on Ancients Sovereign?"

The Book confirmed.

Celestria smiled as she pulled out the chair from under the table that was closest to the Book and took a seat. "Thank you, Gabriel. You've taken the worries of a mother and laid them to rest. The one I name is my son, Garrin ... the child I share with Lasidious."

Gabriel rose from the table and moved a fair distance away from the goddess. "What trickery is this?" he shouted. "How could a god-child exist without my knowledge?"

Celestria smiled. "Why do you think Lasidious and I put up the barrier around our home so many seasons ago? You don't truly believe it was because we cared about others in the Collective visiting. We did it to ensure the conception of our baby remained a secret. The fact the others could not enter only ensured our plotting remained undiscovered."

A long period of silence passed while the Book pondered Celestria's revelation. When Gabriel turned to reclaim her eyes, his demeanor was firm. "It appears you've found a way to beat the laws on my pages. Now it is my turn to divulge a secret, but remember, if you betray my trust, you'll be ended."

The goddess leaned forward in her chair. "Must you continue to threaten me? I'm on your side now, Gabriel. I've already promised that much."

Gabriel's heavy, brow-covered eyes narrowed. "It's best you remember that."

Celestria frowned. "Are you going to divulge your secret, or must you find another way to threaten me?"

The Book played with the scruff of 2 Peaks growth on his chin for a moment while he pondered the goddess' demeanor. "I'll say this: the game Lasidious had us play with the Crystal Moon was unnecessary. Lasidious has had the power to seize control of this Collective even before the game with the crystal's pieces began."

Celestria gasped. "That's impossible!"

"No ... it's not impossible ... just improbable. Nevertheless, despite this improbability, Lasidious managed to beat the odds, and he acquired the power ... though he doesn't realize it. Over the last few Peaks, I hoped that I would have the chance to tell you this secret. I've even tried to envision your reaction. But I must say, your eyes speak so much more to me than my Peak dreams ever could."

The goddess' hand dropped to the table. "I cannot believe it. To know our plotting was unnecessary is beyond imagination." Celestria's mind was a whirlwind as she sifted through her thoughts. "Tell me, Gabriel, how could Lasidious not know his power had superseded your own? He should've felt your weakness."

"Yes, he should've, but my weakness was shielded."

"What do you mean?"

The Book smiled. "I asked the Ancient One to help mask my weakness. The dragon ensured it was kept from the others until Bassorine and I could find a way to regain the power to govern the Collective. I had to hide my faults and lead you down a path of deception while I maintained the perception that I could still destroy you at any moment."

Celestria could not stop herself from grinning. "You lie as well as Lasidious, Gabriel. Why would the Source help you in that fashion? He despises deception, and he was the one who agreed to extend free will to those of us who sit around this table. I thought he agreed to stay out of our affairs."

"And the Ancient One has stayed out of our affairs until the Peak I approached him. Other than hiding my weakness as I begged him to, the dragon offered no additional help."

The Goddess of Beasts stood and began walking a continual loop around the table. "The Ancient One has always refused to choose a side. Why would he start now?"

"He hasn't chosen a side," Gabriel responded. "He simply granted the request of a being who sought his help. Beyond that, he said it was up to me to find a way to stop Lasidious and maintain the balance of power."

Celestria stopped pacing and found the Book's eyes. "What am I missing? There's more to this story. I know it."

Gabriel lowered onto the table. With his binding spread to ensure his balance, he responded. "There's much you don't know. As you prove your loyalty, I will continue to share with you." The Book motioned for Celestria to take a seat near him.

"Where do we go from here, Gabriel?"

Gabriel tapped his tiny knuckles against the table as he pondered the direction of the conversation. "What can you tell me that will help us win the fight against Lasidious?"

A wide grin appeared on the goddess' face. "I know so many things, but how can I be expected to divulge the knowledge I possess? Most of what I know was acquired after I entered the Pact of Fromalla."

"Are you saying you can tell me nothing, and everything shared between you and the Mischievous One was under the law of that rule?"

Celestria stood and moved to the far side of the table. After placing her hands on the top of Lasidious' old chair, she responded. "Does one of the gods' laws supersede another, Gabriel, or are they all to be obeyed?"

The Book floated the length of the table and stopped in a hovering position that was eye level with the goddess. "You know your answer. You entered your promise knowing full well that you could not divulge your secrets."

The goddess nodded. "Come now, Gabriel, I didn't enter the promise with malicious intent. I said I'd help, and I will. I just cannot tell you what was discussed under the Pact of Fromalla."

Gabriel rolled his eyes. "It appears you've won again, Celestria. You have protected your baby's existence, and ensured you have a permanent home on Ancients Sovereign. You have even managed to say nothing in the process. What's your true intent?"

"Gabriel, I'm not going to leave you empty handed. I told you I'd help, and I will. When next you see Alistar, I want you to look him in the eye and say this: 'I know everything. You've lied to me for far too long, Alistar, and I no longer trust you.'"

The Book's eyes instantly filled with a thousand questions. "Why would I speak to Alistar in that manner? He's a pillar of this Collective."

"Ha!" Celestria barked. "Fromalla demands that I say nothing other than Alistar isn't who you think he is. I cannot tell you the truth ... only that you question what you believe to be the truth."

The Goddess of Beasts reached out and caressed the side of the Book's cheek. "You must hold steadfast when you accuse Alistar. Simply say the same thing over and over in front of the Collective until he breaks. His pride will take over, and soon you'll be one step closer to defeating Lasidious."

With Gabriel deep in thought, the goddess added, "Now if you will excuse me, I must go get my son. I want to bring him to Ancients Sovereign." Celestria tossed a small, emerald-green, polished stone on the table. "If you need me, you can summon me with that." The goddess vanished.

MOMENTS LATER
ANAHITA'S SHACK

Anahita flung open the door of the shack and stepped onto the threshold. "We need to get some air in here," she grumbled.

From across the room, Helga was standing in front of the mirror. Her fiery-red hair covered her chest and much of her back. Her ponytail dangled to her waist, and she was strong for a dwarf. "I don't see why we have to change my name," she argued.

Rolling her eyes, Anahita extended her hand toward the darkness and called out a command in the language of the Ancient Mystics. As the darkness dissipated, the matter that floated around the outside of the shack was revealed. "Doggonit, Helga, we can't keep calling you a woman's name when you have a penis. It doesn't feel right. We need to think of something that fits your anatomy ... one that folks can relate to."

Helga sighed. As she did, her bushy brows dropped. "I know you're right, Child, but I like my name. I've had it for 248 seasons."

Anahita turned to face the dwarf. "What about Jamus? I like that name. You look like a Jamus to me."

Turning away from the mirror, Helga closed the distance. "I don't like it. Nothing about my hair says Jamus to me."

"What about Jed or Jedediah? Amish people have a lot of hair," Anahita surmised.

The dwarf scowled. "What's Amish?"

"Not what ... who," Anahita replied. She stepped back onto the threshold. "Oh, just forget it. You choose your own name. I need to create."

The angel lifted her hands. "Hold on, this might get a little bumpy." She called out in the language of the Ancient Mystics again, *"Potasa modres en ron molya!"*

As the last word of Anahita's command was uttered, light shot out of her hands and collided with two large pieces of mass that were drifting past the front of the shack. A moment later, they began to move toward the structure and each other. Instead of the collision Helga expected, the pieces merged, almost as if they were made of liquid. It was not long before this new, larger piece of mass attached itself to the small parcel of earth the shack was sitting on.

"Well done, Child!" Helga praised. "Your studies appear to be paying off. Michael would be proud if he was here." The dwarf reached out and playfully poked her friend's side.

For a moment, Anahita's laughter created a lighthearted mood, and it remained lighthearted until Anahita decided to step a few paces out onto her new creation. "Now that's what I'm talking about! We're finally getting somewhere!" she exclaimed. The angel turned and looked beyond the shack. She lifted her hands and commanded the darkness beyond to vacate a sizable area. "Oh my goodness-gracious!" she shouted.

Helga rushed out of the shack. The dwarf stopped at Anahita's side and turned around. Her jaw dropped. "Oh!"

They both wanted to run, but there was nowhere to go. Helga reached out, grabbed Anahita by the arm and squeezed. What happened next left them both speechless.

"Hello, Anahita," the Source said. "I was beginning to think you'd never step out of your refuge. I've come to help."

Neither the angel nor the dwarf could manage a response. The dragon was immense, and he was standing on a piece of land that stretched not much more than 500 paces from their current location. They were all literally standing at the beginning and the end of the world that would soon become the new Heaven.

As they stared at the dragon's size, the Ancient One continued. "Many seasons have passed since last we spoke, Anahita. It's good to see you again." The dragon took note of the dwarf. "It appears Gabriel was successful in finding you a host body. Are you pleased with the outcome?"

Helga remained quiet, but Anahita managed a response. "She's as pleased as one can be considering the circumstances."

The Source chuckled. His booming amusement forced Helga to cover her ears. "As her moments pass, I'm sure she'll eventually adjust to her manhood."

The Ancient One took a moment to study the dwarf's hair and the structure of his body before he continued. "I heard you speaking inside. Perhaps you'd allow me the honor of choosing your name?"

Though Helga was still finding it hard to speak, she did manage to nod.

"Wonderful," the Source mused. "Anahita and I shall call you ... Dorick. I'm sure this name will be pleasing to you." The Ancient One allowed the dwarf the moments to process.

Eventually, Dorick lifted his head, "I don't know why, but I find the name appealing."

"So do I," Anahita added.

The Source lowered his head to a position just above the shack. "You like the name because it's the one that both of you would've chosen if you had been given the moments to discover your fondness for it for yourselves." The dragon focused on Dorick. "I simply looked into the future. Dorick was the name you would've suggested, and it was also the name Anahita would've agreed to without objection."

"I don't know what to say," Dorick responded. "I've never ... never—"

"Yes, I know," the Ancient One interrupted. "You've never spoken to a dragon before. But fear not." He winked. "I promise not to eat you."

Neither Dorick nor Anahita shared the Ancient One's amusement as his booming chuckle forced Dorick to cover his ears again. When his laughter subsided, Anahita questioned, "You said you were here to help. Help with what?"

The Source had to move his head to the side to avoid a large piece of mass as it floated past. Though it missed his horns by a narrow margin, it collided against his back and made a thunderous noise as it broke into many smaller pieces before they continued on a new path toward the darkness that waited beyond the Source's tail.

Anahita covered her mouth. "Oh, my!"

"Are you okay?" Dorick asked. "That sounded painful."

The Ancient One smirked. "I'm fine, little ones." The dragon reached up and flicked a chunk of earth with one of his massive nails. The sound it made as it shattered into thousands of pieces forced Dorick to cover his ears yet again. "When your shack was created in preparation for your visit, I promised Michael that I'd protect the structure from wandering mass after his departure."

The Source waited for Dorick to remove his hands from his ears. "These meager irritations that float about can't hurt me, but I cannot say the same for you."

Anahita responded. "Thank you for protecting us."

"You're most welcome."

"What's your name?" Dorick inquired.

"I am known by many names, but you may call me Mighty One." Seeing the smile that appeared on Anahita's face, the Source added, "No, Anahita. It's not vanity to be addressed by such a name when there's no other on this plane who can stand against me."

Anahita's head dropped. "I'm sorry, Mighty One. I meant no offense by my thoughts."

Dorick's heavy brows furrowed. "I don't know that I like you listening in on my thoughts." The dwarf covered his mouth. "Please forgive me. I don't know what caused my boldness."

The Ancient One grinned. "There are many changes you'll experience because of your new body. Testosterone can be hard to manage, and it makes men say the damndest things. You must also remember that there is another personality buried deep within the back of your mind. I believe leeway should be granted in your case. Should it not?"

Dorick reached up and played with his beard. "Perhaps, considering the circumstances. But still, could you extend me the courtesy of privacy in my head. I'd like my thoughts to remain my own."

The Source nodded. "Your demand is granted." The dragon rose and spread his wings. As he did, nearly 20 pieces of mass smashed into them and burst into thousands. A moment later, the Mighty One commanded everything around them to stop.

"I can only imagine the depth of your magic!" Anahita shouted to ensure the dragon's ears could hear since they were so high up.

A moment went by before the Ancient One folded his wings and then lowered his head back into a position just above the shack. When he spoke, he did not address Anahita's comment. Instead, he ordered, "Go inside, shut the door and lie down. When next you venture out, a new world will exist beneath your feet, and a fresh star will warm its surface. Heaven will be your world to mold. It will be your task to use the book Michael left behind to create the beauty that is to become this plane's most glorious creation."

Anahita and Dorick stepped inside the shack and did as the Source commanded. A moment later, they fell into stasis.

MEANWHILE, EASTERN LUVELLES
THE PORT TOWN OF DRANDEL

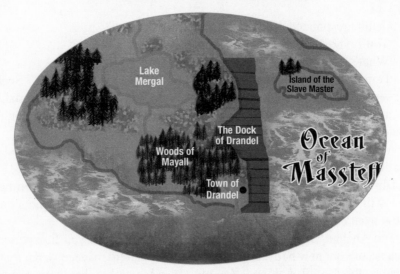

Fellow soul ... the docks west of Drandel spanned a stretch of coastline that equaled a 5 Peak ride on a krape. Though the majority of the town was built near the southern end of the docks, there was a long section that paralleled the distance.

Drandel was a rugged, seafaring community, and many of its structures suffered because of the moisture in the air. Drandel was also the home of the Slave Master, a ruthless man named Grigs.

Much of the wealth the inhabitants of the town possessed was acquired by trafficking weaker beings that had been shipped from most any continent. However, Western Luvelles was off limits to the Slave Master since the kings and the chancellors would not allow Grigs to scout their territories.

With the Peak of Bailem approaching, George and the owner of the Misplaced Inn called their krapes to a halt and then commanded them to lower to the ground.

George patted his krape on the neck. "I still say it would've been more fun to ride the krape lords."

Jackson wrapped his reins around the saddle horn and stretched. "I told you, the Order won't allow it. You must be a member of the army or possess magic strong enough to command a beast of that size."

The warlock lowered to the ground. "The strength of my magic would not be a problem, I assure you." As he pulled the beast's reins over its head and tied them to a pole that had been driven into the earth just outside of the Slave Master's office, he looked up at his krape. "You're not as big as your cousin, but you were fun to ride. It's not your fault you can't fly, is it?" After scratching the krape above its muzzle, George turned around to face the Slave Master's office. "I hope Grigs is in."

"I wouldn't be worryin' none, lad. The lady at The Barnacle said he'd be here for the rest of the Peak." Jackson hopped to the ground and tethered his krape's reins to the same pole. "Grigs and I have ourselves a bond. If he ain't here now, he'll be along soon enough. I know he'll want to see me."

Hearing the name "The Barnacle," George smirked. "I thought you were going to drink that place dry. You know you're a lush, right? I've never seen anyone drink like you."

Jackson had to unbutton his vest. It was stretched so tightly around his chubby belly that he could not reach inside to retrieve his flask. "Every good Shalonean can hold his liquor, lad. You've got yourself a lotta catchin' up to do before you're as accomplished as I." He tilted his flask and poured a hefty sum to the back of his throat.

"You're a freak of nature, Jackson. No wonder I like you."

George turned to study the exterior of the Slave Master's office. Unlike the other structures in town they had passed, the wood of this building was in better shape. *Welcome to Bar Harbor Maine,* the warlock thought. Smirking, he whispered to himself, "Granted, there's no running water, street lights or anything that matches the class of Bar Harbor, but that's all I've got right now."

"What are you mumblin' about?" Jackson inquired.

"Oh nothing. I was just thinking about a place I visited before I ended up on these worlds."

"Whatdaya mean? You speak as if there are other worlds that this old skate doesn't know about."

George smiled. "I simply misspoke, that's all. I should've said, before I ended up on this world. I told you I came here from Grayham."

Nodding, Jackson walked up the steps, across the porch and then pushed through the swinging doors. "I'll be right back, lad!"

"Good! I want to get going as soon as I can!"

The warlock untied the leather straps on his krape's saddle to retrieve his staff. The doors to the Slave Master's office had barely stopped swinging when Jackson came crashing back through them.

"What the hell?" George blurted as Jackson tumbled off the porch and across the back of his kneeling krape before he fell onto the dirt of the road. "Garesh, man! Are you okay?"

Jackson smiled as he stood and wiped the blood from the corner of his mouth. "I think he's still angry with me. I'll be right back, lad. Don't you worry none about me." His belly bounced as he barreled back up the steps and plowed through the doors.

George cringed as the sound of two men's fists and threats filled the evening air. Eventually, Jackson was knocked back through the doors where he landed flat on his back at the top of the steps. "I give!" he hollered. "You win! She's yours!"

A moment later, a man about Jackson's height and build pushed his way through the doors. He was wearing brown leather pants with a belt that barely saved the button of his pants from popping off. His yellow shirt had been torn open and the black hair on his barrel chest was showing.

The Slave Master kicked Jackson's right leg with a heavy-soled boot that matched the color of his pants. "Get up, bugger! She ain't gonna behave for me unless you introduce me properly."

George called up the steps, "Do you need my help, Jackson? I can take care of him for you if you want me to."

Hearing George's voice, the Slave Master moved to the end of the porch and looked down. "You're a brave one, aren't ya?" Grigs turned his head and looked over his shoulder at Jackson who was still crawling to his feet. "Has no one taught your friend to mind his tongue?" He pointed at George. "Is this skate the one you sent word about?"

Jackson spit blood off the side of the porch. "That he is," he groaned. "And as much as I hate to say it, Wendy is yours."

Reaching inside his front pants pocket, Jackson pulled out a piece of dried fruit and then tossed it to Grigs. "Feed her this. She'll love you for it."

Without another word, Grigs bounded down the steps toward Jackson's krape. He placed one hand beneath the beast's chin and then dangled the piece of fruit in front of her nose with the other. It did not take long before the krape scooped the delicacy out of his fingers with her tongue and began chewing.

The Slave Master scratched the bottom of the krape's jaw. "That wasn't so bad, now was it?" He looked back up the steps. "So ... you named her Wendy?"

"Aye. It seemed to suit her."

Shaking his head, George looked up at Jackson. "You're giving him your mount? Why?"

Grigs was the one to respond. "A Shale must pay his debts. I won the beast without bias. That skate should've brought her to me seasons ago." The Slave Master looked at Jackson. "You should thank the gods that I don't claim your teeth as well."

The warlock rolled his eyes and then looked back at Jackson. "Are you really going to let him take your ride?"

Jackson's brows furrowed at the odd way George had phrased his question. "Aye, lad, Wendy is his. Has been since the Peak she was hatched."

George would have responded, but the gem on the end of his staff began to glow. The Senate of Brandor was summoning him with Lasidious' Promise. "Damn it! I'm never going to get to that island," he griped.

Untying his krape, the warlock addressed the Slave Master. "Now that I know where you're located, I'll be back. We have something to discuss when I return."

As the warlock hopped onto the back of his krape, Grigs reached into his pocket and pulled out a pouch that was filled with a substance that looked like tobacco. He grabbed a wad, shoved it in his mouth and packed it into the pocket of his right cheek. "Lad, you must have me confused with a man who cares. I see no reason for your return."

George leaned forward. "The people around these parts might think you're somebody, but to me, you're just another schmuck." The warlock reached out and grabbed the reins of the Slave Master's new krape. "Wendy's coming with me. When I return, you'll tell me everything I want to know, or I'll end you."

To punctuate his message, George flipped his wrist and used his power to knock the Slave Master a few paces backward. Grigs' legs hit the edge of a water trough, and then he toppled into it.

George grinned as he watched the Slave Master flail about. When Grigs finally surfaced, the warlock lowered the tone of his voice and quoted one of his favorite movies from Earth. "I'll be back." He vanished.

MOMENTS LATER, SOUTHERN GRAYHAM
THE CASTLE OF BRANDOR

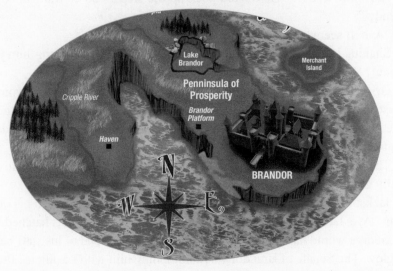

When George reappeared, he was outside the Castle of Brandor in the royal courtyard. The interim General Absolute, Bouldon, and four of his men were entering the side door of the castle with the senators, Tardin and Kolton, on their heels.

From across the courtyard, a woman screamed at the sight of the krapes. Her shriek captured the attention of Bouldon. The general's men were quick to unsheathe their swords and run down the steps.

George quickly wrapped Wendy's reins around the saddle horn of his krape and then held up his hands. "Tell the king, the prophet has responded to the Senate's summons!" he shouted. He then placed his hands on the necks of both krapes and patted them to soothe their anxiety.

Senator Kolton shouted, "Sheathe your swords, and welcome the Prophet with respect!"

Bouldon was quick to add, "And be quick about it!"

George continued to pat the krapes until the change of environment was no longer an issue. Eventually, they settled, and he was able to command his krape to kneel. Sliding to the ground, he handed the reins to the sergeant whose mouth remained opened as he stared at the odd appearance of the prophet's mounts. "What is your name, Sergeant?"

It took a moment before he responded, "I am called Ren, Prophet."

Taking note of Ren's heavily freckled face, George handed the sergeant a Lasidious coin. "Please ensure they're fed and watered."

The sergeant's eyes widened at the sight of the coin. A moment later, he looked up at the krapes. "What do the beasts eat? I've never seen anything like them."

George pointed. "He prefers grain, and she apparently likes fruit."

Seeing the look of disbelief on Ren's face as he stared at the krapes' ferocious jowls, George patted the sergeant on the shoulder. "I know how you feel. I also assumed they ate meat when I first saw them."

The two senators and the interim general stopped a few paces away. Bouldon spoke as Ren led the krapes out of the courtyard. "Your mounts are unique beasts, Prophet. Where did you get them?"

Seeing the faces of the younger soldiers who had remained behind after Ren's departure, George reached into the pocket of his tunic, retrieved three more Lasidious coins and then tossed one to each. "Run along. Buy the members of your family something nice. I want to speak to the general and the senators in private."

With coin in hand, each man instantly looked for approval.

Bouldon shook his head. "Get out of here. You're no use to me when you can't focus."

George watched the three men bolt out of the courtyard before he turned his attention to Kolton. "Why did you summon me?"

"Prophet, we need your help. The prince has gone missing and our search to find him has produced no results. The child's keeper said the boy lifted off the floor and vanished as if he had been absconded by some unseen force."

"Absconded?" The warlock queried. "How long has the baby been missing, and why didn't you call me sooner?"

Tardin pushed back his robe to retrieve a small logbook that he kept tucked inside his sleeve. After rifling through its pages, he pointed to an entry that had been made the morning of the prince's kidnapping and turned the book so George could see it.

From the way it read, the prince had been missing for nearly as long as

Garrin. "So you're saying the baby just vanished. Nobody else was in the room?"

Bouldon was the one to respond. "Yes, Prophet. The child's keeper was playing with the prince. She thought she heard a knock on the chamber door. After she went to investigate, she re-entered the room. One moment the baby was hovering above the floor, and the next, he was gone."

Though the warlock did not vocalize his opinion, he thought to himself, *This can't be a coincidence. Lasidious must have taken him when he took Garrin. But why?*

Tardin closed the book and took a step back. "What should we do? We've searched everywhere for the boy, and no man has come forward to demand a ransom."

George held up his hands. "Give me a moment. I need to think." He turned and walked away from the group as his thoughts filled his mind. *I can understand why Lasidious would want Garrin, but why would he want Sam Jr.?*

A long period of moments passed. *I wonder if it has anything to do with the nasha I used on the baby's corpse?*

The warlock stopped and looked up at the clouds. *Holy hell. I bet it's the nasha. I bet that's why I didn't fall into stasis with the rest of the worlds. The nasha must have left me with memories of the gods that I don't know how to tap into yet. I knew eating that other damn pear was a good idea.*

George pulled his eyes off the clouds and continued to walk away from the group. *Lasidious did say the nasha tree was the gods' version of the Tree of Life and the Tree of Knowledge combined into one. That must be why he demanded that I only take one piece. That must also be why he tried to make me fear the tree. Damn, I'm glad I'm hard-headed.*

The warlock turned and looked in the direction of the group. *But none of that tells me why Lasidious would want the prince. What if...?* He placed his hand to his chin. *What if Lasidious isn't the one who has the kid? What if someone on Grayham does have him? Maybe they'll demand a reward for the prince's safe return.*

No, that's just stupid. With everything that's happened around here, nobody would be dumb enough to take Sam's kid. Everyone fears his damn sword.

Another fair series of moments passed while the warlock continued his thoughtful rant. *Even if Lasidious does have the baby, what the hell can I do about it? It's not like I can make him give him back. What should I say to these clowns to pacify them?*

As George walked back to the group, he searched for a plan. *Something doesn't feel right about this. If Lasidious has the baby, he's no longer being honest with me ... if he's ever been honest at all. Does he need the prince as part of his plan to acquire the power to get my Abbie back, or is this just a set up for something larger?*

He turned around and walked away again. *But how can a baby be a set up for something larger? Could Lasidious have known that Shalee was incapable of carrying the child to term? Could he have done something to make sure she had a miscarriage?*

George looked back up at the clouds. *The more I think about this, the more I feel like there's a snake in the grass. But until I know more, all I can do is play it cool. I need to look like I know what I'm doing. Holy garesh, I hope I know what I'm doing.*

The warlock returned to the group. "Bouldon, I must leave. Since your king isn't here, you will deliver a message. You'll tell him that I've gone to speak with Lasidious. Until I return, Michael is to remain on the throne."

"Where are you going, Prophet?" the general inquired.

"I'm going to find your prince, your queen, and your king. Many Peaks may pass before I return, but until it happens, Michael is to stop looking for the prince. Instead, he needs to focus his efforts on improving the morale of the kingdom. Bouldon, you'll ensure the army helps Michael make this kingdom flourish."

After redirecting his attention to the senators, he reached into his pocket and handed Kolton a hefty bag filled with Lasidious coins. "The Senate will use this currency to create three tournaments, each lasting 10 Peaks. The first tournament will be to determine the strongest human. The second will be to determine the strongest barbarian, and the third will be to determine the strongest beast. The winner of each tournament is to be glorified. They'll be given land and titles. The beings of every territory will come to Brandor to celebrate. These tournaments will inspire the largest celebrations this kingdom has ever seen. This will be the Senate's way of helping Michael and Bouldon get the minds of the people off their problems. Are my orders clear?"

Kolton opened the bag and looked inside. His eyes widened at the wealth. "Yes, Prophet. But why would you have us abandon the search?"

George reached out and secured Kolton's forearm. "If I'm correct, your prince is where no one on Grayham can find him. You must do as I say, and tell your king to get the minds of this kingdom off the royal family's disappearance. Tell Michael the prophet has guaranteed their safe return."

Before Bouldon or the senators could respond, George vanished.

MOMENTS LATER, THE FAMILY HOMES
WESTERN LUVELLES

When George reappeared, he was standing near the pile of boulders above Kepler's old lair. The children who were old enough to play in the woods beyond the community could be heard in the distance.

The warlock walked to the front porch of his home, took a seat and then lowered his head into the palms of his hands. Rubbing his eyes, he muttered, "What the hell's going on? Something's up with Lasidious. I know it."

"You're right, George," a female voice responded. "Something is up."

When George lifted his head, a gorgeous woman with beautiful blonde hair and soft-blue eyes was standing in front of him. She was dressed in an emerald gown, and her smile was warm and inviting. "Who are you?"

"My name is Celestria. You may have heard of me."

George nodded. "You're Garrin's mother."

The goddess smiled. "Indeed, I am Garrin's mother."

"I was wondering if I'd ever meet you. Is Garrin okay? Has something happened to him?" George asked.

Celestria's face showed her confusion. "The baby isn't with you?"

"How could he be? Lasidious took him. If you're his mother, how come you don't know that?"

The confusion on Celestria's face vanished and was replaced with irritation. "When was Lasidious here? I also need to know what he said when he took the child."

George stood and walked down the steps. "All I know is that Lasidious appeared to me when I was on a boat in the middle of the ocean. I was on my way to Eastern Luvelles when stasis fell across the worlds. It was—"

The goddess extended her hand and motioned for the warlock to stop speaking. "How could you possibly know about stasis?"

George shrugged. "Your moment of arrival could not be more perfect. Clearly we're both confused. How about we do it this way? I'll tell you everything I know, but first, I'd like you to answer a few questions."

Celestria crossed her arms. An inquisitive look appeared on her face. Ask away."

George clapped his hands. "Thank you. Not knowing would've driven me insane."

"Not knowing what?" the goddess inquired.

"Where should I start? Did you know Lasidious sent me to find the nasha tree?"

The goddess nodded.

"Good ... then that's one less thing I need to explain."

Celestria extended her hand and rolled her wrist to encourage George to speak faster.

The warlock smirked. "I bet you and Lasidious work well together. He's just as impatient as you are."

The goddess pursed her lips. "George, please! If you wouldn't mind. I don't have all season."

The warlock pondered the goddess' demeanor for a moment before he responded. "Anyway, while I was on Ancients Sovereign, I took an extra piece of nasha off one of the trees in the orchard. When I had a moment to myself, I ate it. This leads me to my next question. Did eating the fruit give me the godly memories that Lasidious said I possessed? Is that why I didn't end up in stasis?"

"You were not supposed to be given the power to pick a second piece from the tree. Lasidious said he would not allow it. Only the gods are to pick the fruit. We saw to that when we created the orchard." Celestria's face clearly showed her aggravation as she took a seat on the steps. "I told him it was not acceptable for you to see the glory of Ancients Sovereign."

George tried to respond, but the goddess silenced him with a wave of her hand. "Why would Lasidious want to end you if he intended to bestow the knowledge of the gods upon you? What would be gained by his actions?" With another wave of her hand, she allowed the warlock to respond.

"Hold on a moment," George barked. "What do you mean, Lasidious wants to end me? I thought we were partners. Sure, the S.O.B can be a little shifty, but he's been going out of his way to help me. Why end me now? That would make the moments he spent molding me a complete waste."

Celestria shook her head. "I was under the impression that your usefulness had run its course, but it appears Lasidious isn't finished with you as he claimed he is. To bestow the knowledge of the gods upon a mortal is risky. He must believe he has found a way to mitigate this risk."

George threw his hands in the air and then placed them on top of his head. "You're creeping me out. When Lasidious spoke to me on the ship, he acted surprised that I wasn't in stasis. If what you're telling me is the truth, then he knew I ate the nasha as soon as he showed up and saw that I wasn't frozen. He must have given me the power to pick the extra piece."

Celestria nodded. "I believe that to be the case."

"Holy garesh," George mumbled. "My brain is so fricking fried right now!" The warlock took a moment to collect himself and then found Celestria's gaze. "I don't know what to think. Lasidious did tell me to pick only one piece ... so is he on my side, or is he my enemy? Perhaps he knows my character well enough to know that I'd take another one anyway. What do you think?"

The goddess played with her bottom lip as she searched for a response. "There was a moment when I would've thought I had the answer to your questions, but now I find that I'm as confused as you are. It wasn't long ago that I thought I'd spend the rest of my Peaks with Lasidious, but as of late, it appears we don't communicate as we used to."

The goddess reached out and took George's hand. "Let's change the subject. You said Lasidious took Garrin. I had no knowledge of this. How did your family react to the loss?"

The warlock reached into his pocket to retrieve the stone Lasidious had given to him while he was on the Ocean of Agregan. He handed it to Celestria. "I placed this stone in everyone's hand. They don't know that Garrin ever existed. They've forgotten everything about him. Hell, that's not all they've forgotten. After stasis, they don't even remember Kepler." Pointing at the goddess, George added, "I know Kepler is in trouble, but I don't know what to do to save him or how to get him back."

Celestria queried. "How do you figure your friend is in trouble?"

George frowned. "Look. I'm not stupid. Kepler went to Dragonia. I haven't forgotten that, but all of a sudden, Dragonia doesn't exist in the minds of my family or anyone else on this world. Even the books in Brayson's office have all been changed. And if that's not bad enough, everybody thinks there's a Hell. Athena told me I was going to go there just the other Peak if I continued to swear as much as I do."

The warlock locked onto the goddess' eyes. "I'm not an idiot. I can put two and two together just like you can. In my mind, it's simple. Dragonia ... plus Hell ... equals screwed. I think Kepler is screwed."

The Goddess of Beasts had to smile after hearing George's equation. "You're right, George. Kepler is in a place where trouble will find him, and the King of Brandor is with him.

"No fricking way! So Sam really is there. But why would he bail to the most undesirable world that everyone feared?"

Celestria stood and returned to the ground. "Sam's choice of worlds makes sense when you consider a god was whispering to his subconscious when he made the decision to flee. The destination he chose would not have been his first choice. In fact, Sam would've chosen to stay in Brandor."

George nibbled on his bottom lip as he pondered what the goddess had revealed. "Let me guess. You're the one who whispered to his subconscious."

"I am ... and he listened."

George shook his head in disbelief. "How do you whisper to someone's subconscious anyway?" The warlock turned his head, looked at the empty space next to him and then leaned forward. He pretended to whisper into an unseen person's ear. "Hey, Sam. Pssst! Sam! Dumbass! Why don't you run to the crappiest planet and hide out? No one will look for you there. It's not like you ended anyone or anything. Don't worry about the criminals, and who knows what else is there?" The warlock reached out and pretended to pat the back of the supposed king. "I'm glad you like that idea, Sam. I hope your subconscious is getting all this."

Celestria had to laugh. "Lasidious spoke of your humor. It pleases me to see it for myself.

George looked down at the stone in Celestria's hand. "So what about the rock? Will it tell you anything?"

The goddess shook her head. "I don't think so. The stone has served its purpose."

"Then what are we going to do? I can't just leave Kepler on Dragonia, and you can't let Lasidious run off with your kid. I want Garrin back just as bad as you do."

Celestria dropped the pebble to the ground and then reached out to place her hand on George's cheek. As she did, Athena opened the front door of their home and stepped out onto the porch. But before Athena could say anything, the goddess extended her arm in Athena's direction and then continued to pass it across the community of homes.

George looked up the steps. Athena was frozen in place. "What did you do to her?"

"She'll be fine. There will be no more interruptions while we speak."

The warlock ascended the steps and stopped next to his wife. He reached out and placed his hand on her forehead. She was frozen solid, just like the crew on the boat had been while they were in stasis. He looked back down the steps. "It can't be good to freeze people like that. Aren't there any side effects?"

Celestria nodded. "Yes, stasis effects the body. Athena's life will be shortened by nearly a season. Every being who has experienced stasis will suffer the same effect."

"So, she's in stasis right now?"

"Yes."

"That makes twice. Is the rest of this world also in stasis?"

"No. The rest of Luvelles continues to live out their Peak. I've segregated this stasis to just the members of your family."

George did the math. "Between the last stasis the gods put on the worlds and this one, you've taken a total of 74 seasons away from the people I love most. That pisses me off. What are you going to do to return their lost moments?"

Celestria shook her head. "There's nothing I can do."

"What do you mean, nothing? You're a god." He took a deep breath to collect his thoughts. "Look ... they're my family. I don't want them to pass sooner than they're supposed to. You wouldn't want Garrin to pass before he was expected to, would you?"

A grin appeared on the goddess' face. "That would be impossible. Garrin is immortal. His life cannot be shortened. It can only be extinguished."

The goddess ascended the steps and stopped on the opposite side of Athena. "I'm not without compassion, however. I shall enter an accord with you."

"What kind of accord?" George grumbled.

The goddess placed her hands on Athena's cheeks. A moment later, she smiled. "Athena is with child. You're going to be a father again."

George took a step back. "Are you sure?"

"I am."

"Hmmm. I wonder why she hasn't told me. How far along is she?"

Celestria closed her eyes and lowered her hand to Athena's belly. "She is nearly 60 Peaks." The goddess' head tilted as if she was searching for more of an answer. "Your baby will see this world in 210 Peaks."

"That makes sense. Her back is covered with acne again. That's what happened during her last pregnancy. But she hasn't been sick like before."

The goddess dropped her hands to her side. "Not all pregnancies are the same, George. It appears you're about to begin another journey. You want your baby to be born on a world without chaos, and I want my son back."

"So tell me about the accord you want to enter."

"It's simple. You help me find my son, and I'll extend the lives of your family."

"How are you going to do that?"

Rather than answer the warlock's question, the goddess placed her hand on George's cheek. "Please, kneel."

"What for?"

"I'm going to rejuvenate your soul."

George remembered what it felt like to have his body rejuvenated. Lasidious had done it once before. He gladly took a knee.

The goddess reached under his chin and lifted George's head so she could see his eyes. "I'm going to do more than just rejuvenate your soul. When I am finished, I will have imparted whatever knowledge I possess of the new Hell into your mind. You will know its lands. This should help you with your search."

Looking up, the warlock protested, "I don't need knowledge of Hell. If anything, I need knowledge of Dragonia. That's where Kepler is, and like I said, I want to save my friend."

Celestria smiled. "Must I remind you of your equation? Dragonia and Hell are now one in the same. The gods have abandoned that world, and soon, the beings who live there will be caught in a neverending nightmare."

George frowned. "Then I definitely need to get Kepler out of there. I can't allow him to suffer. And no matter how much I dislike Sam, I can't let that bastard suffer either."

Rather than respond, Celestria placed her hands on top of George's head. It was instantaneous. The warlock's eyes closed as a soothing energy passed through the goddess' hands and entered his body. It was not long before she took a step back. "How do you feel?"

George jumped to his feet. "I feel like I could take on a Mack truck and win. I've never felt this amazing."

Celestria reached down and took George's hands. A sense of peace entered his being. "If Lasidious has taken my son, it would be in his best interest to hide on Hell."

Nodding, the warlock responded, "That seems like a reasonable assumption. If the gods have abandoned that world, what better place to hide."

Releasing the warlock's hands, Celestria walked down the steps. "You must search for my son while you search for your friends."

"What do you mean, *me*? What about *you*? Aren't you going with me?"

"If Lasidious is on Hell, my presence would be felt if I was to remain on that world for an extended series of moments. He would know something was wrong. If he's on that world, he would abandon it and take Garrin with him. We cannot allow that to happen."

The Goddess of Beasts picked up the pebble off the ground. She enclosed it in her hands. A moment later, she tossed the pebble up the steps.

"What do you want me to do with this?" George queried.

"I'll take you to Hell as soon as you're ready. You will find your friends and search for Garrin. After you find my son, summon me with the stone. As a reward, I'll bring you and Kepler back to Luvelles, and the lives of your family will be extended."

"But I get to choose how long they live," George chided.

"If you wish. I care not about the length of their existence."

The warlock crossed his arms. "I didn't expect you to say yes. What about Sam? Will you extend his life, too?"

Celestria shook her head. "Sam will not want to leave. If I am right, his desire for power will drive him to stay."

George's foot tapped against the top step as his mind created other questions. "Has Kepler's memory been effected because of stasis?"

The goddess nodded. "Kepler will not remember you, nor will he remember your family. You will be faced with the task of recreating your friendship."

"Damn it!" George shouted. "I knew it! How am I going to convince Kepler to return with me if he doesn't remember who I am?"

Celestria motioned for George to toss the pebble back down to her. After catching it, she placed it between her hands. A moment later, her hands began to glow. When the light faded, she tossed the stone back to George. "We will use the stone as Lasidious did, only in reverse. Touch the cat with it, and his memories will return."

George shook his head. "Well that's easier said than done. He's just as powerful as I am. He could rip my head off before I can make that happen."

The Goddess of Beasts smiled. "You will surely need your wits about you."

"Hold on a moment." The warlock tossed the stone back to Celestria. "Can you make the stone work twice more so that I can restore Athena and Brayson's memories as well? If I'm going to be leaving, I need to make sure Athena understands why. I need her to know who Kepler is and how much he meant to this family before I go tromping off to who knows where."

Believing George's logic to be sound, the goddess did as requested and then returned the stone. "I will return in the morning to take you to Hell."

George chuckled. "Ha, and I'm actually looking forward to the trip. I bet you'll never hear me say that twice."

Celestria could only smile. "When I leave, your family will step out of stasis. Do what you must to prepare their minds for your absence. You only have 210 Peaks before your new daughter arrives on this world. Hell is massive, and you won't have a large amount of moments at your disposal. I am sure you won't want to miss your baby's birth."

"You're right, but that's the least of my concerns right now. You and I need to figure out a way to cover up the lie I told my family. Once Athena and Brayson learn that Garrin is yours, they'll have a million questions. I won't be able to help you if my family is falling apart because they've lost faith in me."

The goddess smiled. "I will take the blame for you when the moment arrives. You need not worry about losing their love." Celestria vanished.

As soon as the goddess departed, Athena stepped out of stasis. Confusion filled her eyes since George was no longer standing at the bottom of the steps with a woman's hand on his face.

George smirked. "What's wrong, babe?" Before she could answer, George took Athena's hand and placed the stone in her palm. "We've got a lot to talk about..."

CHAPTER 15
GARESH! GARESH! GARESH!
THE VAMPIRE KINGDOM
BENEATH THE MOUNTAINS OF GANNESH ON HELL

TARDON, THE VAMPIRE KING
AND
YOLAN, THE VAMPIRE QUEEN

Fellow soul ... when Lasidious and Alistar appeared before the Vampire King and Queen with the babies in their arms, Tardon had just finished serenading Yolan. The king's love for Yolan was well known throughout the underworld that existed deep below the peaks of Gannesh, and Tardon's minions worshipped their queen almost as if she was a goddess in her own right. But no matter how much the Vampire King loved his mate, he desired power more.

With the Mischievous One appearing in front of Tardon's throne, the king knew it was only a matter of moments before the final details of their agreement would be worked out, and soon, his eyes would behold what he wanted to see most.

* * *

Tardon pulled his attention off his queen and redirected it toward the gods. "Good evening, Lasidious."

The Mischievous One bowed to show the king respect, despite Tardon knowing full well that he was in the presence of a god. "Your Grace, there's much to discuss." Lasidious looked at Yolan. "You look lovely this evening, Your Highness." He walked up the steps to the throne, stopped next to the queen and then handed Sam Jr. to Yolan. "Alas, we have run out of your milk. I'm sure the children would like to feed."

Before Yolan could respond, Alistar teleported to the top of the steps and placed Garrin in the queen's free arm. "I believe you'll make a fine mother." The God of the Harvest stepped back and enjoyed the look on Yolan's face as Garrin reached out to touch the points on her teeth.

The queen's voice was soft. "Hello, little ones. I'm so happy you're finally here."

Seeing Yolan's reaction to the children, Alistar allowed a smile to spread across his face. "Your milk appears to have lowered the children's defenses. They like you already. Are you prepared for motherhood?"

Yolan kissed Garrin on the cheek and then sniffed the hair of the prince. "I've longed for the beginning of the seasons in which I could show them my love. These children will know true happiness." The queen found Lasidious' eyes. "Thank you for your gift. As promised, I shall stand at your side for the rest of eternity."

Redirecting her gaze, the queen's face turned sad as she spoke to the king. "I know this is your heart's desire, my love. I don't want to hold you back. I shall miss you after you've gone."

To lighten the mood, the Mischievous One added, "I promise to sing better than Tardon if it would make the transition easier. I'll make sure you don't miss him for long, Your Highness."

As the king laughed, Yolan readjusted the babies in her arms while the sadness slowly diminished from her face. "I must feed my darlings."

The queen snapped her fingers. A moment later, two of her female minions, each with long, dark hair and pale skin, entered the throne room. Yolan descended the steps and placed the babies in their arms. "Take the children to the nursery. And don't allow the smell of their blood to tempt you."

Both vampires bowed. "Yes, My Queen."

Yolan turned to face the king. "Please say good-bye before you go. I want to have the memory of one last kiss."

As Yolan turned to leave, Tardon watched the queen until she was out of sight. "I'll miss her."

"How could you not?" Lasidious responded. "But I assure you, where you're going, you won't regret your decision."

Nodding, Tardon clapped his hands and another servant entered the room, but on this occasion, it was a thin male with short, blond hair. "Paramus, bring us three mugs..." The king paused and looked at the gods. "What flavor do you prefer ... red, green or white demon? Or perhaps you would prefer some form of were."

Alistar held up his hand to wave off the offer. "I think I'll pass."

Lasidious smirked at his brother's response. "We have not yet acquired a taste for blood, Your Highness. I shall also have to pass until after the transformation."

Tardon shrugged. "You don't know what you're missing. Since this is my last opportunity, I shall drink the finest blood in my cellar. Paramus, I shall have red demon with a dash of green. Make them both chilled and serve it in a tall mug. I want to savor every drop."

As Paramus turned to go, the king changed the subject. "Lasidious, you've kept your word. You have given my queen that which I could not. For that, I shall remember you once I have ascended. Whenever you need me, I'll be there for you."

The king readjusted his gaze and nodded in Alistar's direction. "How rude of me. I haven't asked your name."

Before Alistar could respond, the Mischievous One reached out and patted him on the back. "This is my brother."

A look of understanding appeared on Tardon's face. "Lasidious has spoken fondly of you over the seasons. Has he informed you of our arrangement?"

"He has, Your Grace. I'm prepared to assist you in any way I can to ensure your arrival on Ancients Sovereign is well-received."

The God of the Harvest reached into his pocket and produced a small flower. The plant had bright red and yellow petals with an orange stigma. He handed the flower to the king. "When the moment comes, you must eat this. It will help you focus and will be key to your success."

The king lifted the flower to his nose. "Thank you."

Alistar turned to face his brother. "Ancients Sovereign won't be the same without you. I'll miss you."

Lasidious grabbed the back of Alistar's neck and then kissed the top of his forehead. "You know where I'll be." The Mischievous One winked and then took a step back. "See to it that Tardon finds the home I've prepared for him. I'm sure the others will want to speak with him first."

With a feigned look of concern, Alistar questioned. "Are you sure this is what you want, brother?"

"It is."

"Are you also sure Tardon will have the power to end him?"

Lasidious pulled his eyes off of Alistar and then placed them on Tardon. He spoke to the king with confidence. "The power you'll possess will be more than enough. You will be untouchable, and everything I've promised will be yours once the task is complete."

Tardon leaned back in his throne. With his hands resting atop the stars at the end of the armrests, he responded. "I don't know that I'll ever understand your reasoning for this arrangement. I can't fathom why a god would wish for an existence that is beneath him."

The Mischievous One smiled. "Perhaps one of these Peaks you will. I look forward to that conversation when it happens. But that is then, and this is now. There is much we need to discuss before we begin the transformation."

Nodding, the Vampire King stood from his throne. "I'll leave you to your goodbyes. Alistar, I look forward to our next meeting."

"As I also do, Your Excellency. I shall return to Ancients Sovereign and call for a meeting with the gods. By the end of the Peak tomorrow, you shall be one of the mightiest gods on Ancients Sovereign, and together we'll rule the heavens."

A large smile spread across the king's face as he left the room.

Alistar smirked. "Poor bastard." He reached out and placed his hands on Lasidious' shoulders. "Are you sure this plan is solid? Are you sure it's even possible?"

"You worry too much. I'm sure of everything."

"I only wish I had your confidence."

Lasidious grinned. "I have enough for both of us."

"There are moments when I forget who I'm speaking with," Alistar replied. "If only I could walk in your shoes for a single season, the lessons I would learn."

Lasidious reached out and patted his brother on the chest. "I often think the same thing about you."

"Really?"

"Of course. You have many admirable traits. I often feel that you're a far better god than I am."

The room fell silent for a moment while Alistar enjoyed Lasidious' compliment.

The Mischievous One pulled the God of the Harvest into his embrace. "You must protect the remains as we discussed. Can I count on you?"

Placing his forehead against Lasidious', Alistar responded. "I won't let you down. Just be careful, brother." The God of the Harvest vanished.

THE WORLD OF HARVESTOM
THE HIGH PRIESTESS' PALACE
THE NEXT MORNING

The room Sharvesa, Mosley and the priestess were standing in was on the third level of the High Priestess' school. The floor and the walls were scorched from the countless number of experiments that had gone wrong during instruction, and the tables that normally sat at the center of the room had been pushed toward the walls.

After another mishap, Sharvesa waved her hands in front of her face to clear the smoke. "No, no, no! You're not teaching him correctly, Fosalia. How could you have attained your position if you can't instruct the wolf with competence?"

The High Priestess did not respond, but Mosley did. "You forget, Sharvesa, your power didn't come to you overnight while you were living on Dragonia."

Hearing Dragonia, Fosalia shook her head. She had already told the wolf on a number occasions that Dragonia was not a real place, but Sharvesa's response suggested that she no longer needed to pretend that world never existed.

"I haven't forgotten the tedious moments of my training," Sharvesa argued, "but I can assure you, my teacher possessed far greater skill than what has been displayed in this room."

Before another word could be said, a voice echoed throughout the palace. "Priestess!" the voice shouted. "Your presence has been requested in Hydroth!"

Fosalia looked up at Sharvesa. "If you'll excuse me."

After the High Priestess stormed out of the room, Mosley sat on his haunches and scratched the back of his neck. "I think you were a bit hard on her. Fosalia's heart is in the right place."

A scowl appeared on Sharvesa's face. "Her heart won't be the one fighting George when the moment comes for you to claim vengeance. I think the moment has come to restore what has been taken from you."

"I don't understand."

Sharvesa adjusted her yellow gown and then knelt next to the wolf. "I want you to relax. I'm going to place my hands over your eyes."

"Why?" Mosley queried.

Sharvesa grinned. "Must you always question me? Have I not been training you for enough Peaks to have earned your trust? Now close your eyes."

The wolf complied.

"Remember," was all Sharvesa said as she placed her large, red hands over the wolf's eyes and restored the memories Lasidious took from him.

As the demon-goddess lowered her arms, Mosley began to laugh. "That explains so much. I knew there was no way I had been found in the Neutral Territory of Southern Grayham." He looked toward the door. "Barramore must also be Lasidious. I wonder if Celestria knows that Lasidious has had a child with another woman. I can only imagine her reaction when she finds out."

Sharvesa shook her head. "I cannot say that I approve of Lasidious' adultery, but I'm sure he has his reasons for sowing his seed."

Mosley walked to the door and looked around the corner to make sure no one could hear their conversation. He had promised the Book of Immortality that he would not speak of his knowledge of the gods unless it was with someone who possessed the same knowledge. Though the wolf's memory was not what it was before the Book had stripped him of his immortality, he still had questions.

The wolf turned to face Sharvesa. "I wonder ... how do you think the Book would feel about Fosalia's existence? I remember you live by the laws on its pages. Was there not a law that states the gods cannot have children?"

Sharvesa shook her head. "No, Mosley. There's nothing within the laws that states Lasidious cannot have a child with a mortal being. The law simply restricts the gods from having children with each other."

Mosley pondered the goddess' response as he returned to take a seat next to her. "You said you despised Lasidious' adultery, yet you're here at his request, are you not? You did say someone sent you. It was him, wasn't it?"

"I am here at Lasidious' request. But I'm also here for reasons of my own. There are many things that you don't know about the gods ... things that have opened my eyes to the truth ... things that have caused me to seek George's destruction just as you seek it."

"Explain," the wolf demanded.

"I cannot tell you all that I know, but now that your memory has been restored, I can explain my reason for choosing to participate in your training."

"I'm listening."

"Like me, you also seek vengeance on a beast named Kepler. I want this demon destroyed."

"Why?"

Sharvesa reached out and placed her hand under the wolf's jaw. "My son is in the care of George's family."

"I know," Mosley responded. "I can't remember his name, but I do know you speak of the fairy-demon."

"His name is Payne. He was a mistake, but I love him."

"How ... how—"

"How did he come to be?" Sharvesa finished.

Mosley nodded. "I'd like to know."

"How is not a story I'd like to tell. The story pains me." The goddess pulled her hand away and then stood to move to the window. The shoreline of the island was not far beyond a lush field that surrounded the palace. "What I will say is that my son was a powerful being before George stripped him of his magic. The demon-cat you hate so much commands what he should never have been given. For this, I want both George and the demon-cat destroyed. I'll do whatever I must to ensure you find the power to send their souls to Hell. Once they arrive, I'll have my daughter torture them further. Their hell will be far worse than any other's."

The demon-goddess turned from the window. "Your power grows at a remarkable rate, Mosley. I would imagine this is because your body remembers what it's like to command the power of the gods."

"I only wish that I could remember more," Mosley added as he lowered his snout to sniff the scorch marks on the floor. "I know there's much that I've forgotten, but the Book said he could not allow me to remember it all."

Sharvesa smiled. "Your memories of Ancients Sovereign are unnecessary to deliver vengeance. If you're successful, I'll do everything I can to ensure you reascend."

A moment of silence passed before Mosley continued. "Tell me, Sharvesa ... why do you trust Lasidious? You must know that he plots against the others of the Collective. I may have forgotten many things, but I haven't forgotten that."

Sharvesa stepped away from the window and reached down to scratch the top of Mosley's head. "My reasons will remain my own. Why don't we see what Fosalia is up to?"

Sensing that he would get no further with the conversation, Mosley agreed. As he and the goddess stepped out of the training room, they looked over the balcony and spotted the priestess standing beneath Helmep's banner. She was speaking with Jeromas, the Isorian Frigid Commander, and the cape the goswigs had given him was wrapped tightly around his body.

With his memories of Northern Grayham now returned, Mosley snorted. "That's impossible. The Isorians don't possess the ability to make such a journey."

Sharvesa closed her eyes. "Magic is protecting that being."

Mosley's face showed his confusion. "How? The Isorians don't possess magic strong enough to protect their skin from the heat he would have to travel through to get here."

The demon-goddess shook her head as she returned her gaze to Jeromas' blue skin. "I don't know who is protecting him, but significant magic encompasses his being."

From below, the High Priestess looked up. "Mosley, I leave you in good hands." Fosalia bowed to show her respect to Sharvesa. "Goddess, I leave the wolf in your care. I must go." The priestess reached out and touched Jeromas on the arm. The pair vanished.

Growling, the wolf looked up at Sharvesa. "As irritated as you were with her ... without Fosalia, my training won't progress as quickly. I was learning from her."

"You're wrong, wolf. Your training won't suffer. I shall return in the morning. Until then, I suggest you get some sleep." Sharvesa vanished.

After dealing with the aggravation of being abandoned without an explanation, Mosley realized he was alone in the palace. It did not take long before he began to notice all the unmarked corners that were calling his name. He walked to the top of the staircase that led down to the second level and sniffed the banister. After looking in every direction to ensure no one was around, he grinned and lifted his leg to deliver a squirt. "Ahhhhhh!"

NORTHERN GRAYHAM
THE NEXT PEAK, EARLY BAILEM IS APPROACHING

Fellow soul ... when Fosalia appeared with the Frigid Commander the previous night, the servants of the undercastle had been quick to explain that the king and the ruby eyed man were with the army at the hollow that was nearing completion.

Jeromas had wasted no moments. He placed the High Priestess on the back of his harugen and then took Fosalia through the tunnel that led out of the city. The tunnel remained beneath the undulating shelves of ice until they reached the hollow. The journey took the night, and when they finally arrived, the sun was just about to peak its head above the horizon.

The priestess was taken to the section of the tunnel that served as the king's camp. It was there where Clandestiny, Medolas, the goswigs, Gablysin and Shiver were sleeping.

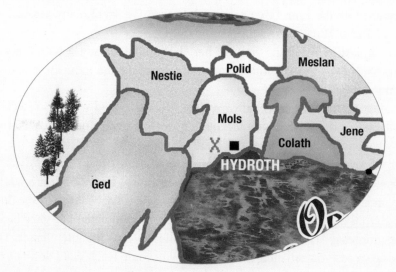

X MARKS THE BATTLEFIELD

Jeromas reached down and shook Shiver gently on the shoulder. "My King ... My King. I've returned."

Shiver rolled over, rubbed the sleep out of his eyes and responded after he yawned. "Your return pleases me, Commander."

Wincing, the king reached down to rub his lower back. "I fear I've become spoiled. The ice here works against me. It doesn't cottle me like the ice of my bed." Shiver sat up. "Where's the priestess?"

The Frigid Commander moved to his right. As he did, Fosalia came into view."

"Excellent, Jeromas. You've done well."

Fosalia bowed. "Your Grace. I came as soon as I received word."

"Your haste is appreciated, Priestess."

"I'm here to serve. Is Clandestiny nearby?"

Nodding, Shiver motioned for the commander to give him a hand. Once he had been pulled to his feet, the king walked across the tunnel to where Clandestiny and Medolas were sleeping and knelt. "Clanny. Get up. You have a visitor."

As Clandestiny made her way to her feet, Fosalia's eyes fixated on the Tear of Gramal. She had heard stories from her mother about the Tear's magnificence, but the tales had not done the gem justice.

The priestess stepped forward to greet Clandestiny, however, her eyes remained on the Tear. "I've been told that you've spent many seasons with the Ko-dess. What was he like?"

Clandestiny lifted the gem off her chest and enclosed it within her fist. "You heard the truth. Perhaps you could spare me the inquisition and visit him yourself."

Hearing the tone in Clanny's voice, Fosalia looked up. "You're clearly bothered. Perhaps when you feel up to it, we can find someplace quiet to see to what end you can control the Tear?"

A frown appeared on Clanny's face. She turned to look at Shiver. "To what end, she says! On how many occasions must I say that this is a waste of my moments before you'll listen. I know the Tear far better than she does."

Before the king could respond, Clandestiny redirected her gaze back to the priestess. "The moments are not available to us for idle chatter. There are no words you can utter or techniques you could teach that I don't already possess. The Tear and I are one. Your moments have been wasted by coming here."

As the last bit of excitement on the priestess' face vanished, Medolas sat up. "Come now, Clanny. Must you be so brash? She's here to help."

"Help with what, Meddy? What could she possibly do or say? She's not her mother, nor has she ever laid her eyes on the Tear prior to this Peak."

Placing the gem back against her chest, Clandestiny reclaimed Fosalia's gaze. "I mean you no ill will, but I've spent 300 seasons with the Ko-dess. How could you possibly help?"

"You won't ever know unless you offer her the chance," Medolas argued.

Shiver stepped forward and placed his hand on Clandestiny's elbow. "This kingdom needs you to be prepared, Clanny. War is coming, and the people need to know you're ready."

"As much as I hate to agree with her, she might be right, Your Grace," the priestess announced. "I cannot argue with Clandestiny's logic. During her absence, we all know the moments were unavailable to me to befriend the Tear prior to my mother's passing. I've never bestowed the blessing as she did on Thoomar."

After refocusing on Clandestiny, Fosalia continued. "I can promise you only this. The knowledge my mother bestowed upon me prior to her passing is yours if you want it. All you need to do is ask."

A long period of silence passed while Clandestiny processed the priestess' pledge. When she looked up from the floor, her milky-gray eyes were filled with confidence. "Go home, Priestess. You're not needed here." Clanny turned and pointed toward Gage and Gallrum who were asleep on a pile of furs on the far side of the tunnel. "What help I need lies over there. My moments are best spent with them to finish the hollow."

Everyone in the group was speechless as Clanny turned to walk across the expanse of the tunnel in the direction of the goswigs. Eventually, Shiver spoke. "I'm sorry, Priestess, but it appears there's nothing I can say. If Clanny's belief in your ability suffers, perhaps it's best if you return to Harvestom."

"Do you want me to speak with her first?" Medolas offered.

Shiver shook his head. "No. We both know Clandestiny. She won't listen."

Medolas looked at the Priestess. "He's right. She has been like that since we were children. She would become angry if I badgered her. You wouldn't like her when she's angry."

The Frigid Commander turned to look down the tunnel. The legs of three harugens pummeled the ice as they approached. The newly appointed Frigid Omayne was on the lead harugen with six of his officers sitting on the saddle behind him.

The omayne stopped his harugen only paces away from the group and then commanded the riders on the harugens that followed to continue on to their destinations. The omayne was completely bald, but still ruggedly handsome, and he was known for adding emotion to the way he spoke through the movement of his hands. After he tethered his harugen's reins to the horn of the saddle to ensure the beast remained steady, he reached up and held his thumb and forefinger close together. "My King, the Tormalians are close."

Shiver's face showed his confusion. "How, Omayne? There's no way for the Tormal to have already passed through the caves."

The omayne's arms created a large circle in the air. "Our scouts returned with reports of the Tormalian army stepping out of a light. They described it as an illumination that appeared in the wilderness." He ducked his face behind his hands. "They remained hidden long enough to watch the entirety of the Tormalian army set up camp."

"He speaks of a portal," the priestess announced. "I didn't know magic of this nature existed on Grayham."

"The portal must be my grandfather's creation," Shiver responded. "How long do we have until they arrive, Omayne?"

Two fingers were extended. "Not much more than 2 Peaks." He turned his hand upside down and walked his fingers up his free arm. "I imagine they've broken camp and are already marching."

Shiver looked at the High Priestess. "Clandestiny was right. The moments are not available for idle chatter." The king looked at the Frigid Commander. "Prepare the army for battle, Jeromas."

Looking up at the Frigid Omayne, Shiver delivered another order. "Gather Clandestiny and the goswigs. I want the hollow finished by morning."

"Yes, My King!"

As the omayne's harugen skittered away, Shiver took a moment to think. "Priestess, if you want to help, stay with Medolas. When the moment arrives, you'll receive the signal. It appears your journey won't be a waste of your moments after all."

Fellow soul ... to keep from boring you with details, allow me to sum a few things up.

Clandestiny, Gage and Gallrum worked through the rest of that Peak and the following night to finish the hollow. And though I'm sure you're dying to know, the moment is not yet right to disclose how Clandestiny contributed. I will say this, however. The rate at which Clanny tore into the ice took 7,000 men and 200 harugens to keep up. Gage had to use his magic to protect the army from wayward ice while Gallrum helped the men load the chunks onto enormous sleds. The sleds were then taken out of the hollow and dumped into the Ocean of Utopia to the south.

Meanwhile, at the southern end of the hollow, Medolas and Fosalia worked together. Medolas brought the priestess up to speed on the tactics that were to be deployed during the battle. With a complete understanding, the priestess extended her hands toward the ice and used her magic to mold the wall that was holding back the ocean. It was a delicate process. The wall needed to be strong enough to hold back the ocean, but feeble enough that it could be torn down when the moment arrived.

Shiver, the Frigid Commander, Gablysin, and 400 Isorian soldiers focused their efforts on attaching chains to the pillars that had been left behind to keep the roof of the hollow from collapsing. In total, the hollow stretched away from the ocean some 100,000 paces and was just over 1,000 paces wide. Seven thousand chains were attached to an equal number of harugens, and it was agreed that these beasts' lives would be forfeited when the moment arrived to collapse the roof of the hollow since it would be impossible to get them out.

When the morning of the war arrived, the Frigid Omayne ordered the men to line up near the edge of the hollow. Behind them, small alcoves had been created in the ice to provide sanctuary if the gashtion was to attack during the battle.

Since the Peak Clandestiny returned to Hydroth, she had to chase the gashtion off on two occasions before the war, but the beast was becoming bolder, and Clandestiny's roar was becoming less effective.

Fellow soul ... the moment has come for a fight.

◆⟨⟨⟨•⟩⟩⟩◆

As Shiver and Gablysin stood side-by-side looking down the expanse of the hollow, they marveled at how quickly Clandestiny and the goswigs were able to complete the cavern.

The king looked up at the top of one of the pillars that had been left behind to hold up the roof. "You know, Gabs, directly above us, the largest war our people have ever seen is about to take place. I've heard the scouts' reports. We're outmatched. If the columns don't break, the battle will be short-lived."

The ruby eyed man gazed down the hollow. "You worry too much. They'll break."

"And if they don't?"

"Then it's simple ... we'll perish."

Smirking, Shiver turned to face the Frigid Commander who was approaching on the back of his harugen. "My King. The Tormal have assumed formations on the far side of the hollow as planned. What are your orders?"

Gablysin was the one to respond. "Are the trumpeters ready?"

"I will check, My Lord."

"Then that's the only command I need to give."

"What of the Tormal?"

Shiver spoke up. "We shall wait for the Tormal to advance. When I give the order, sound the horns."

The ruby eyed man lifted his hands and pointed down the length of the hollow toward the 7,000 harugens that had been chained to the pillars. "Their sacrifice is key to winning this war. Make sure the trumpeters are ready."

Nodding, the commander turned his harugen until its side was parallel to Gabs and the king. "Would you like a ride?"

Once on the surface, Clandestiny, Medolas and the priestess were waiting near the front lines of the Isorian army. As the Frigid Commander's harugen skittered to a stop, Jeromas dropped the reins and then jumped down to join them while Shiver and the ruby eyed man remained on the beast's back.

After Gablysin moved to the front section of the harugen, he grabbed the reins and commanded the beast to skitter out onto the roof of the hollow. As it did, Shiver called out an order. "Jeromas, wait here and ready the army!"

Stopping at the center of the battlefield, Shiver and Gabs waited for Meerum Bosand and the Tormalian Frigid Commander, Grandon, to make their way past their lines. Meerum was the first to call out from the back of his harugen as they stopped some 10 paces away. "This isn't the Peak I want to witness the passing of my grandson!" He teleported onto the ice and commanded Grandon to dismount.

After sending their harugens back behind their lines, Meerum continued. "Let us have a civil conversation." He stepped forward and patted the head of Shiver's harugen. "They are fine beasts, are they not?" He looked up and waited for Shiver's response.

Shiver shook his head. "A friend told me not long ago that the moments for idle chatter have passed. What are your terms?"

Meerum smiled. "You have become curt during your seasons. Please, dismount. This war is pointless. Can we not seek a diplomatic resolution? I am, after all, your grandfather."

The Isorian king sat in silence as he studied Meerum's countenance.

"Please, Shiver. Let us forgive the past and speak as gentlemen. If we're to battle, let us at least enjoy the pleasantries of a final conversation. I want to know my grandson before he meets his end."

Shiver looked over his shoulder at the ruby eyed man. After Gablysin shrugged, the younger king made the decision to dismount to show his bravery.

"Wonderful!" Meerum exclaimed as he watched Shiver drop to the ice. "Despite our differences, it appears you're capable of making wise decisions after all. And to think I had believed you to be hopeless."

Shiver crossed his arms. "It appears you believe slander makes for good compliments. I should've stayed on my harugen, old man. Perhaps my ability to make a proper decision remains flawed after all."

The Tormalian King chuckled as he turned to look at his commander. "My grandson is bold for his seasons."

Grandon nodded. "He's Tormal. What did you expect?"

"Nothing about me is Tormal!" Shiver snapped. "I've lived as Isor, and I will perish as Isor. If only I could strip the gills from my back, I would throw them in your face."

Chuckling, Meerum responded. "That could be arranged." The king looked beyond the back of Shiver's harugen toward the Isorian army. "Your men are no match for mine. They're outnumbered."

Gablysin was the one to respond. "Two to one is fair odds for an Isorian. Our men shall fight like beasts."

"I could end your men myself. They're defenseless against my magic."

Shiver took a step back and stopped within arm's reach of Gablysin. "Your magic will be ineffective on this Peak. You're a feeble, old man, and a fool's army follows you into battle."

Furious at the insult, Meerum lifted his right hand and sent 1,000 needles in Shiver's direction, but the result was not what the Tormalian King expected. Instead of his magic ending Shiver, it bounced off the younger king's skin and fell to the ice as harmless projectiles.

From behind the Isorian lines, Gallrum clapped his claws as the Isorian army cheered for their king. The serwin's wings fluttered as he hovered just high enough to see overtop the ranks. "I knew he'd try something!" he boasted as he looked down at Gage.

Gage uncrossed his furry, little, robe-covered arms as he tried to look between the rows of blue legs in front of him. "What did he do?"

Gallrum grinned. "Well, he didn't hug Shiver, that's for sure. It appears there's no love lost in this family. He just tried to end his own grandson. It's good the priestess decided to protect them from his magic."

As the badger used his power to lift himself off the ground to levitate eye-level with Gallrum, the serwin continued. "Look. You can see the anger on the Tormalian's face from here."

Meerum stared at Shiver.

The Isorian King smiled. "As I have said, Grandfather, your power will be ineffective on this Peak. Go back to your army and make your advance." The young king crossed his arms and glared into Meerum's eyes. "I dare you! Or perhaps you could stay, and I shall slap you around in front of your army."

The Tormalian King did not waste his breath on a response. Instead, he grabbed his Frigid Commander's arm and teleported to the back of his army's lines. When they reappeared, Meerum ordered the Frigid Commander to the top of his harugen and then shouted. "Charge!"

As the Tormalian King teleported onto the back of his own harugen, Grandon reiterated the king's order, shouting, "Well what are you waiting for? Charge!"

As the Tormalian army rushed out onto the roof of the hollow, Gablysin hollered, "Oh, garesh!"

Gabs grabbed Shiver by the arm and pulled him up as he commanded the beast to skitter toward their army.

The pounding of the Tormalians' feet sounded like thunder as they gave chase.

Gablysin and Shiver had not even reached the safety of their side of the hollow before the ruby eyed man called out to Jeromas, "Sound the horns! Sound the horns!"

By the moment the trumpeters received the order, the Tormalian army was within 500 paces of the Isorian lines. Six hundred trumpets were lowered into holes that led down into the hollow and blown. Far beneath the roof of the cavern, the 7,000 harugens reacted. The pitch of the horns hurt their ears and caused them to panic. It did not take more than a few moments before the majority of the pillars had toppled, but the result was not what Shiver and Gablysin expected.

The roof of the hollow held firm. The ice was too thick, and the Tormalian army was still advancing. But now, spears from both armies were filling the sky.

Shiver extended his arm and used a shield to block a Tormalian spear from hitting Clandestiny. He shouted, "If the roof of the cavern doesn't collapse, we can't win! You must roar, Clanny! Roar to buy us the moments to retreat!"

With the Tormal now only 200 paces away, Clandestiny lifted the Tear of Gramal from her neck and commanded, "Move the army back, and have them cover their ears!"

Seeing that the Tormalian army would arrive before her order could be carried out, Clandestiny decided not to wait. The Tear in her hand began to glow as she took a deep breath. After rearing back, she lunged forward and released the mightiest roar she had ever summoned. As her call filled the morning air, both armies were frightened, and the spears from both sides stopped flying as the Tormalian army stopped their advance.

Clandestiny roared again to ensure the enemy would remain at a distance, but during this series of moments her roar had a much greater effect. Not only did the enemy stay back, but the ice beneath their feet weakened, and it was beginning to crack.

From the top of his harugen, Meerum's Frigid Commander lifted his hand. "Stop moving!" he shouted. He now realized his men were standing on a trap. As he looked around, the ice could be heard popping in every direction, and nearly the full strength of his army was in jeopardy.

Shiver placed his hands around his mouth and called across the ice. "No one has to perish on this Peak, Commander! Order your army to yield, or she'll roar again! You don't want your men to fall to their demise! Our people don't need to end one another to find peace! Only your king needs to perish!"

The Tormalian Commander looked over his shoulder in the direction of Meerum. His king was standing on the back of his harugen, and his withered arms were flailing about, imploring the commander to advance.

Shaking his head, Grandon turned to find Clandestiny. Her chest was still heaving, and she was waiting for the order to roar again.

As he turned to pass his gaze across the expanse of his army, Grandon knew that one more roar would carry their ends with it. "We surrender!" he shouted. He turned to find his Frigid Omayne who was on a harugen of his own not more than 15 paces away. "Have the army lower their spears! Do it slowly, and make no sudden movements!"

Far behind the Isorian lines, the real gashtion had heard Clandestiny's roar, and she had made her way to the surface. Though she was still a great distance from the Isorian lines, she released a roar of her own.

As soon as the gashtion's call reached Shiver's ears, the Isorian King looked out across the roof of the hollow. Despite the roar coming from a distance, it was still loud enough that the ice beneath the Tormalians' feet was effected.

As the popping intensified, Shiver shouted an order in Grandon's direction. "Commander, order your army to retreat! I'll consider it an act of peace! They're not safe where they stand!"

Shiver's concern for Grandon's safety made the Tormalian Commander realize he was fighting for the wrong side. He looked over his shoulder in Meerum's direction. The Tormalian King was still screaming profanities, and though Grandon was not able to understand what Meerum was shouting, he knew enough to surmise that his king was threatening to end him if he did not order the Tormalian army into battle.

Grandon spit in frustration, turned to face Shiver and then called out, "Make room! My army shall no longer fight a fool's fight! We'll stand at your side and face the gashtion together!"

Shiver was about to accept the commander's pledge and order his army back from the edge of the hollow when the real gashtion roared again. With her cry being louder than the first, that was all it took. The roof of the hollow gave way.

The look on Grandon's face as he plummeted to his end with more than 27,000 Tormalians was forever burned into Shiver's mind as their screams filled the morning air.

Medolas and the High Priestess were standing at the southern end of the hollow when it collapsed. They were waiting for the order to destroy the wall that was holding back the ocean. But as it turned out, the order would not be necessary. With the weight of the Tormalian army and the roof hitting the floor of the hollow all at once, the wall holding back the ocean cracked, and a moment later, it crumbled. The sound the torrent water made as the ocean rushed in to fill the expanse of the canyon muffled the real gashtion's third roar.

Back on the front lines, the Isorian army was not prepared to fight the gashtion. The beast was too powerful, and their numbers had dwindled throughout the seasons because of the Tear's absence. As planned, most of the men ran for the alcoves of safety while others waited for their king's orders.

Before Shiver could devise a plan, Clandestiny's eyes began to change. Her irises turned to slits, and her voice sounded like a beast's. "Order the army to flee!" she growled. "I'll fight the gashtion!"

As Clandestiny finished speaking, the bones of her shoulders broke and pulled away from their joints as she began to assume the form of the gashtion. Her fingers began to elongate, and her nails turned to claws, and the pain of the transformation was evident as it consumed her face.

Gage and Gallrum sprang into action. They teleported and reappeared a fair distance away beyond the alcoves of safety, between the charging gashtion and the rest of the army who were running toward the beast to get to the alcoves. Seeing the size of the beast, Gage shouted so Gallrum could hear his voice overtop the monster's thunderous footsteps. "Take my paw!" With Gallrum's claw in his grasp, Gage extended his free paw and summoned the power to create a massive, protective wall of force.

Meanwhile, Clanny's transformation continued. The size of her neck expanded as those around her moved away. It was not long before the knotted, leather strap holding the crystal snapped, and the Tear of Gramal fell to the ice.

Gablysin rushed in to retrieve the Tear, but just as the ruby eyed man was about to lean down to pick it up, Clanny fell to the ice. The transformation caused her right leg to extend, and she kicked the ruby eyed man on his left hip.

The force nearly knocked Gablysin off the edge of the cavern and into the raging water.

Shiver was quick to react. He ran to Gabs' side and helped him up off the ice. "We've got to get the men out of here!" he screamed.

As the Isorian King helped the ruby eyed man hobble past Clandestiny toward the alcoves of safety, the real gashtion slammed into the invisible barrier that Gage and Gallrum had summoned. The cry the beast made as it collapsed onto the ice forced the entirety of the army to place their hands over their ears, but the magic the goswigs used to slow the beast's advance was lost. The force of the collision had destroyed the barrier, and the power to summon another wall of that magnitude would not be available to the goswigs for a considerable amount of moments. Gage and Gallrum were left with no choice but to retreat as the gashtion struggled to pick herself up off the ice.

Meanwhile, Clanny was quickly growing and showing no signs of slowing. Not only was her skin changing color, but she was already more than 70 paces from the tip of her tail to the end of her muzzle, and scales were now forming at a rapid rate.

For those men who remained awestruck by the transformation, Shiver shouted another order to capture their attention. "Clear the ice! She's dangerous!"

As the real gashtion continued to shake off the effects of the collision, the goswigs vanished and reappeared near one of the alcoves. A few moments later, the beast began to stumble in the direction of the men who still remained above the ice.

With the alcoves resting a fair distance away, the men who had reacted to Shiver's order rushed across the ice, but not all of the king's men would reach safety before the gashtion was finally able to resume her charge and close the distance.

With the weight of the gashtion causing the ice to quake, Timus and his brother, Amos, both born on the same Peak and only 40 seasons of age, realized they would not make it to their alcove. Their pysples gripped the ice as they slid to a stop to reverse their direction of flight. As they ran back toward the cavern, they looked over their shoulders as the gastion's massive claws tore chunks out of the ice. All Amos could shout as they ran was, "Garesh! Garesh! Garesh! Garesh! Garesh!"

With the gashtion nearly upon them, her mouth lowered in their direction. She was about to chomp when suddenly the weight of Clandestiny's new form flew over the brothers and collided with her enemy.

Both gashtions tumbled across the ice. The sounds of their growls forced the army to cover their ears as they huddled within their alcoves.

With the beasts sliding to a stop, Timus looked at Amos. The brothers shouted, "Holy garesh!" They turned and ran for an alcove.

As Clandestiny reared up, she brought down one of her massive claws and clubbed it against the side of the real gashtion's head. The collision was so loud it forced the men in the alcoves closest to the beast to cover their ears yet again.

With her gigantic mouth, Clandestiny lunged forward in an attempt to bite the real gashtion's neck, but the beast was quicker than she was. Using the back side of one of her wings, the gashtion knocked Clandestiny to the ice and then returned to her feet.

Clandestiny rolled into a readied stance and did not waste a moment. She charged. The collision took both gashtions toward the edge of the hollow that was now completely filled with water. As they landed, a large section of ice broke away from the rest and fell toward the waves that were crashing against the walls—taking the Tear of Gramal with it.

The light of the sun reflected off the Tear's many facets as the gem fell toward the water. Though it was only a brief moment, the reflection caught Meerum Bosand's eye just before it hit. The Tormalian King screamed, "Noooooooo!"

The king grabbed the reins of his harugen and commanded the beast to skitter toward the edge of the chasm. As he looked down, the men who had fallen to their ends could no longer be seen. The rush of the ocean had claimed their bodies, along with the chunks of ice from the roof of the hollow. They had been flushed to the north along with the harugens that had been sacrificed as the water from the ocean rushed past.

This was Meerum's only chance to secure the Tear and accomplish his ultimate goal of knowing the power of the gashtion. Without wasting another moment, the Tormalian King removed his cape and then used his power to protect his feeble bones as he dove from the top of his harugen and fell more than 15 paces before he disappeared beneath the water.

As Meerum began his frantic swim into the depths of the cavern, Clandestiny used her back claws to throw the real gashtion off of her. The beast landed on top of one of the alcoves that was closest to Shiver and Gablysin's. The ice above the Isorians' heads gave way, and over 180 men inside the alcove were crushed.

Shiver turned to face the 200 men who were in his alcove with him. "Clear out!" he shouted. "Run for the tunnel, and flee to Hydroth!"

With the Isorian King's men scurrying across the ice, Shiver and Gabs ran from alcove to alcove and commanded the army to flee while Clandestiny and the gashtion thrashed about. Shiver stopped. One of the gashtions screamed as the other bit a chunk out of its shoulder.

Shiver grabbed Gabs by the arm. "I hope that wasn't her!"

"How do you tell?" Gabs replied. "They look the same to me! Come on! We've got to get the men out of here!"

The ice continued to quake as both men resumed the task. But before the final alcove was cleared, one of the gashtions fell to the ice. The sound its limp corpse made as it collided with the shelf caused Shiver to redirect his gaze. As his eyes passed from the surviving gashtion to the men who were fleeing in the distance, a hopeless feeling encompassed his being.

Clandestiny rose up and roared. She then lowered her eyes to study her surroundings. Her breathing was frantic, and she could see the army fleeing. Though they were on her side, she desperately wanted to end them all. The power that was surging through her had control of her soul, and she craved more. With the sun nearing its peak, Clanny focused her dragon eyes on the men closest to her. Despite the 300 seasons she had spent with the Ko-dess to prepare for a Peak such as this, she began to stalk the ones she had been entrusted to protect.

Seeing the gashtion's intent, Shiver screamed, "Garesh! That's not her! It's going after the army!"

It was easy to see the desperation on the ruby eyed man's face as he responded. "What should we do?"

"Yell! We must make her come this way!"

"Have you gone nordel?" Gabs rebutted.

Shiver shrugged. "Better us than them! Hope you're ready to run, old friend!"

Before Gabs could respond, Shiver began waving his arms and shouting to get the gashtion's attention.

"You are nordel!" Gablysin shouted. A moment later, he lifted his arms and began screaming just as loud. But no matter how much they called out, their efforts would not be enough to get the gashtion's attention—and now Clanny was running toward her next victims.

From a distance, Gage and Gallrum could see the men who were being stalked and knew they had to help. Without wasting another moment, Gage touched Gallrum and teleported both goswigs into the path of the fleeing men. Gallrum used his power to stop the men from running while Gage hobbled in the direction of the gashtion. With the beast nearly upon them, the badger lifted his paws and summoned a blinding light.

Clandestiny was forced to abandon her pursuit. As she slid to a stop, the ice beneath her claws broke apart and tumbled in the direction of the goswigs.

Gallrum reacted. The serwin extended a claw and used his magic to destroy the chunks. Instead of being crushed, the men were showered with a blizzard of shavings.

Lifting her claws in front of her face, Clandestiny used them to shield her eyes from the light as the badger looked over his shoulder and shouted. "Get them out of here, Gallrum! I'll deal with this!"

Nodding, the serwin motioned for the men to form a massive circle. "Touch one another!" he commanded. A few moments later, the group vanished.

Gage kept the light burning bright until the rest of the Isorian army had cleared the ice and were safe inside the tunnel. As his power faded, so did his means of escape. Between the wall and the light, the badger had exhausted too much energy, and he would not be able to teleport to safety.

With the last of the light fading, Clandestiny lowered her claws. The skin of her jowls pulled back, exposing a ferocious set of fangs as she lowered onto all fours.

The badger did not run. His legs were too short. Instead, he looked down at his cane and then lifted it in front of his face. "Well, you're not going to save me, are you? If only you were a sword." He smirked at the ridiculousness of the thought.

Clandestiny lifted her right, front claw.

As Gage watched the gashtion prepare to end him, another roar filled the afternoon air.

Clandestiny turned to face the new threat. The roar had come from the edge of the cavern. Meerum Bosand had used his magic to find the Tear of Gramal. He had teleported to the Isorians' side of the cavern and had begun the transformation.

With Meerum's transformation nearing completion, Clandestiny abandoned her attack on Gage and turned to charge across the ice. As she did,

Gage had to dive to his belly as Clanny's massive tail, spanning a distance of more than 100 paces, passed just above him.

With every step Clanny took, her claws tore apart the ice. By the moment she reached Meerum, his transformation was complete. The collision sent the beasts flying off the edge of the cavern and into the depths of the water. Neither Clandestiny nor Meerum surfaced.

The Crystal Shard

When you want an update about your favorite characters

NORTHERN GRAYHAM

The Battleground Near Hydroth

—With Clandestiny and Meerum failing to resurface after disappearing beneath the water that filled the chasm, the High Priestess gathered Shiver and the ruby eyed man. The trio teleported to the edge while Fosalia studied the body of the fallen gashtion. The priestess delivered the good news, letting the Isorians know that this was not their friend. She further explained that Clandestiny would have changed back into her normal appearance and remained expired.

With Fosalia's ability to teleport, the trio then moved on to where Meerum had transformed. She ensured Shiver that it would be safe to approach the edge of the chasm, and it was crucial that they find the Tear of Gramal and place it about her neck. She would need to stay in Hydroth until a being capable of accepting her blessing could be found.

When Fosalia lifted the Tear off the ice, Shiver looked across the chasm and realized the remainder of the Tormalian army was vulnerable. They had nowhere to go, and though their numbers were still enough to keep smaller predators from attacking, he knew they'd perish if either of the gashtions returned.

To protect these men, the priestess extended her arm toward the water and used her magic to create a bridge of ice that stretched between the two sides of the cavern. As the Tormal crossed, they were directed to the safety of the tunnel that led to Hydroth.

With the estimated series of moments called Midnight approaching, Shiver ordered the Isorian army to accept the Tormal. He further commanded the food that had been left behind on Meerum's side of the cavern be retrieved and brought into the tunnel.

SOUTHERN GRAYHAM

The City of Brandor—The tournament the prophet commanded Michael to hold is being organized with the help of the Senate. The best warriors from every territory will be invited, and many festivals will take place throughout the streets of Brandor during the tournament to get the minds of all beings off the disappearance of the royal family.

Michael has ordered the Senate to ensure that every message board in the kingdom is filled with positive news. Any article that speaks of Sam, Shalee, or the prince is to be removed, and the author is to be spoken to privately and paid for their inconvenience. Further, Michael has ordered that any who oppose the removal of their work be brought to his throne room. If they fail to see reason, they will be thrown in the dungeon until they choose to cooperate.

On an unrelated note, Michael has ordered that the krapes the prophet left behind be taken to the royal stables. With one male and the other female, it is his desire to have them bred just as the army has been breeding the Water Mist Mares. If it works, the krapes will become the new mounts of all those who possess a commission. As the breeding process continues with the mist mares, all non commissioned men will eventually be assigned a mount from their offspring.

HARVESTOM

The Island of the High Priestess —After Sharvesa left Mosley, the demon-goddess went to Ancients Sovereign to retrieve a piece of nasha as Lasidious had suggested. She then returned and fed the fruit to the wolf. The effect was what the goddess was after. Over the past 2 Peaks, Mosley has made many advances in his ability to employ stronger uses of magic, and soon he will be ready to embark on a journey to find a specific member of the Swayne Enserad. It is this soulless immortal on Trollcom who can teach Mosley how to destroy the beings who stripped Sharvesa's son of his power.

ANCIENTS SOVEREIGN

The Hall of Judgment—The Book of Immortality has called for a meeting of the gods. The moment has come to let the others know that Lasidious has the power to assume control of the Collective. The Book also intends to reveal Michael's existence during this meeting.

The Book is looking forward to seeing the faces of the gods once they learn that Bassorine is an archangel, and that he never perished. It is Gabriel and Michael's hope that the Collective will unite to protect all that has been created.

Though their deeds will no longer allow any of them to return to the Heaven the Almighty created prior to them falling, Michael will announce that the Source is creating a new Heaven for this plane.

The gods will need to abandon their petty differences, at least for now, or everything will be lost if they don't prepare for the Peak when the Mischievous One realizes the magnitude of his power.

WESTERN LUVELLES

The Family Homes—As promised, Celestria returned to take George to Hell, but the warlock refused to go. With the return of Athena and Brayson's memories,

George was not comfortable leaving until he was sure that every question they could possibly ask had been answered.

With the help of Celestria, Brayson and Athena were eventually pacified, but their mental state was not the only reason George refused to go. Since Brayson will remain behind to care for the family, George believes he will need to solicit the help of a powerful companion until Kepler can be located and convinced to return to Luvelles.

With a companion in mind, the warlock has asked Celestria to meet him outside the entrance to the Cave of Sorrow on Southern Grayham. It is there a statue of a large ally sits waiting.

Outside the City of Inspiration —The power of the Ultorians has been more than sufficient to hold back the water of the lake while the elves and halflings continue to create the pillars that will support the structure of the bridge. Boyafed and Dowd hope to have the bridge completed before the first white rain of winter.

THE NEW HELL

The Mainland—Sam's army has abandoned the Merchant Island. They have taken every container that they could carry. The new members of his army have some unique abilities, and as it turns out, his choice for a temporary General Absolute in the red demon, Orgon,

has given Sam the ability to control the trolls that were transported from Trollcom.

Many of the trolls are savages, and since abandoning the island, Orgon has had to slaughter three to keep them in line, and Sam has had to slice another four in half.

The new King of Hell has ordered camp to be set up just over 4 Peaks away from the Temple of the Gods. Using the memories that were given to the demon-cat by Lasidious, Sam has asked the demon-jaguar to teleport to the Criminal Stronghold to deliver his orders.

Sam wants his supposed General Absolute, Narasay, an immortal, also Swayne Enserad who was brought to Dragonia seasons ago by the Merchant Angels, to bring the most ruthless of their army to his current location. Sam is anxious and also excited to meet this powerful female who leads his army— an army he has never met—also the same army whose minds have been altered to believe he is their king.

Pydum—Following the members of Sam's army after they abandoned the Merchant Island, Pydum watched Sam from a distance. On two occasions, the grendle-imp made sure the new King of Hell spotted him. Pydum has been searching for the right moment to approach Sam. But to do so could be his end. The king's sword will react when he tries to tell Sam the truth.

426 | Crystal Moon, The Tear of Gramal

The Vampire Underworld—Lasidious has spent the last few Peaks in seclusion with the Vampire King. The Mischievous One's plan appears to be progressing as he estimated it would.

With the Book of Immortality calling for a meeting of the gods, Alistar returned to inform the Mischievous One. The duo agrees that this gathering could not have been called at a better moment.

THE NEW HEAVEN

Anahita's Shack—The Source will release Anahita and Dorick from stasis in the morning.

Thank you for reading the Crystal Shard

CHAPTER 16
A BIG MARBLE OF DIRT
ANAHITA AND DORICK'S SHACK
THE FOLLOWING MORNING

Fellow soul … the Source released Anahita and Dorick from stasis. Though neither the angel nor the dwarf knew it, the dragon was patiently waiting outside the shack for the pair to exit. Since Anahita had been slow to recover after being released from stasis, Dorick made himself breakfast to pass his moments until the angel was ready to explore what the Source had created.

Pushing his bowl away, Dorick grumbled, "I don't like porridge, Child. If you're here to create a heaven, perhaps you should begin with finer dining."

Anahita reached up and rubbed the sleep from her eyes. "I don't know what's wrong with me. I feel weak."

The dwarf reached out and patted the angel on her knee. "Perhaps you should eat something."

"Gabriel said eating wasn't necessary any longer. Besides, it seems like a waste of my moments. I'm sure this feeling will pass."

Bored, Dorick lifted his spoon and allowed it to plop back into his porridge. "I'm not going to eat either, so let's get going. I'm dying to know what the dragon left behind."

Opening the door of the shack, Anahita stepped out onto the barren lands of the new Heaven. There were no trees, plants, mountains or anything that resembled the concept of beauty. "There's nothing here," the angel griped. "I don't understand. He said Heaven would be my world to mold, but there's nothing to work with. It's like we're standing on a big marble of dirt."

A familiar voice responded. Though the sound was not vocalized, they could hear it in their minds. *"There's much more than dirt, little ones. Every resource you need to create exists on this planet."*

As the dwarf and Anahita whirled around, they could see the Source standing in the distance beyond the shack. The Ancient One was so far away that his mass had been significantly reduced. Only the top of his head and the top of his back could be seen above the roof of the shack.

Anahita walked to the side of the structure. With the Source in clear view, she responded. "I don't see any water!"

Again, the Source projected his thoughts into their minds as he looked toward Heaven's new sun to warm his face. *"In this territory, most of it is beneath the surface. It will be up to you to determine where the water flows and how it pools."*

The dwarf began to fidget as he looked in the direction of the corner of the shack while Anahita responded. "Water won't do us any good under the surface, will it? So ... I'll need to get to it and then do something fab with it!"

The Source turned his head in the direction of the shack and projected another thought. *"There's no need to shout, Anahita. All you need to do is think. I can hear every thought you have."*

Dorick released his groin and instantly turned red.

The Ancient One chuckled. *"Yes, dwarf, I know you need to pee. You'll find the earth inviting."*

Anahita grinned as she looked down at Dorick. "Does your tinky-winky need me to turn around so it can have some moments to itself?"

The dwarf frowned. "I assure you, there is nothing tinky-winky about me ... well ... outside my height."

The angel covered her mouth. "Shhhh! Don't be so cocky!" She pointed toward the Source. "He's listening. And yes, the pun was intended."

From across the terrain, the Source could be heard laughing. *"I knew creating with the two of you would be entertaining."*

Undoing the front of his pants, Dorick walked toward the corner of the shack. "The idea of having a penis is starting to grow on me. I'm kind of fond of it." With Anahita's back to him, the dwarf threw his braided ponytail over his shoulder and then took care of business while he changed the subject. "Can you tell us why Anahita is so weak? Is there something wrong with her?"

As the Source turned to walk toward the shack, he projected his thoughts between the placement of each claw since the earth shook with every step. *"An angel's body reacts differently to stasis than other beings."* His right, front foot left an impression, and then he continued. *"She'll feel better soon enough."*

"Stasis?" Anahita snapped once the dragon had finished his next step. "You put us in stasis? Why, and how long—" Another footstep forced her to pause. "How long have we been asleep?"

"Not much more than a few Peaks," the dragon replied.

"What is stasis?" Dorick questioned just before the earth shook again. "What are you talking about?"

With his response requiring a lengthy series of moments, the dragon lowered his claws to gather his balance and stopped moving. *"Stasis was necessary for me to create."* He redirected the conversation. *"If you were not an angel, Anahita, you would not be able to survive on this world as it is now. Many changes will need to take place"*

"Then why can Dorick survive?" the angel rebutted.

"The dwarf survives only because I wish it so."

"What do you mean by that?"

"Do you see vegetation, Anahita?"

"No."

The Source said nothing further. He allowed the angel the moments to think.

Looking over his shoulder at the angel, the dwarf questioned, "Are you as confused as I am, Child?"

Anahita shook her head and responded without turning around. "No. He's referring to oxygen. He's saying there's not enough for you to live."

"Then how did I survive inside the shack prior to the dragon's appearance?"

The Source responded. *"Because Gabriel kept you alive after you were given your new body."*

As the dwarf finished peeing, he grinned and closed his pants. "I don't think I've ever taken this many moments to relieve myself. I believe I've set a new record, Child."

Anahita turned around and rolled her eyes. "The other being's personality that Gabriel pushed to the back of your mind must not have been pushed back far enough. You're disgusting."

The Source laughed. *"The being's persona who was restricted did not influence your friend's last comment."*

The angel touched Dorick on the arm. "Is that so? So, you've been foul all along?"

As both the dwarf and the dragon poked fun at Anahita's demeanor, the angel eventually smiled and then pinched Dorick on the arm. She then placed a hand on the dwarf's shoulder and teleported the distance. When they reappeared, they were within a closer proximity to the dragon.

Anahita looked up. "Despite how crude Helga has become, thank you for keeping her alive."

"'Become,' Child? Have you forgotten our moments in the Royal Garden. Don't you remember our conversation about the statues?"

Anahita elbowed the dwarf. "Will you shut up?"

Dorick looked up at the Source and shrugged.

Anahita extended her wings and stretched while she searched for a way to change the subject. "You said stasis effects angels differently than other beings? How so?"

The Source lowered to his belly, laid his head on the ground and then spoke aloud. "Every being is made of elements. The difference in the way these elements perform is what makes a being mortal or immortal. Take Dorick, for example. If I was to scratch his arm, it would take many Peaks before the cells of his skin closed the wound. Yet you, Anahita, cannot be scratched. Your body functions at a more efficient rate. You heal even before the wound can be inflicted."

"What in tarnation? My brain must still be asleep. How can someone heal before they're hurt?"

The Source lifted his head off the ground. "Allow me to demonstrate. Dorick, will you please stand back from Anahita?"

The dwarf nodded. "Sure. How far?"

"I'll tell you when to stop. You should also cover your ears, and don't let them go."

"Why does he need to cover his ears?" Anahita queried. "And why does he need to move back?"

"You'll see, Anahita. For now, I want you to focus. I'd like you to tell me when you feel like the weakness has left your being."

With Dorick out of range, Anahita eventually announced that she was feeling better.

Without saying a word, the Source's movements were swift. He lifted his claw and brought it down, crushing Anahita beneath it.

With the weight of the dragon's foot causing a vast area to tremble, the dwarf lost his balance. He fell to his backside and watched as Anahita disappeared, but he did manage to keep his hands over his ears.

A few moments passed before the Source pulled back his claw. Anahita was lying flat on her back at the bottom of the crater. She was unharmed, and even her feathers were intact. Her whole body had been smashed into a perfectly shaped alcove that outlined her form.

The Source smiled. "Some lessons are best taught through experience. Don't you agree?"

Anahita did not reply. Instead, she remained flat on her back.

Dorick ran to the side of the crater and looked down. The imprint left behind was so deep that it was nearly twice the height of his body, and Anahita was at the center of the imprint inside her alcove. "Are you okay, Child?"

The angel's eyes looked up at the dwarf and then slowly moved to the Source as she processed her situation. After lifting her hand in front of her face, she made a fist and then slowly peeled back her fingers.

The Source broke the silence. "Should I show you again?"

Lowering her hand onto her stomach, the angel replied. "I bet you think you're funny, don't you? Is stepping on someone some kind of dragon humor?"

The booming laugh of the dragon forced Dorick to cover his ears again as Anahita sat up. Once the laughter subsided, Anahita continued. "As clever as you think you are, stepping on me doesn't tell me why stasis effects angels differently."

"You're right," the Source conceded, "but I never get tired of demonstrating my point."

The Source searched for an analogy to answer Anahita's question. "Let's say Dorick was a dog who could run swiftly. If you were to take the dog and stop his motion, it wouldn't take him long to return to speed after he was released. Now, Anahita, let's say you were also a dog, but you had the ability to run at the speed of light. If your motion was stopped, it would take you longer to return to the speed at which you were previously traveling.

"Everything in an angel's body functions at a much higher rate of efficiency, or speed, if you will. When you're stopped as stasis stopped you, it simply takes longer for you to return to your maximum efficiency."

Dorick was the one to respond. "If Anahita can survive you stepping on her, then she must be one of those immortals you spoke about."

"Yes. She cannot perish, but she can cease to exist."

An inquisitive look appeared on Dorick's face. "What's the difference?"

"To perish, Anahita's body would stop functioning naturally," the dragon explained. "But to cease to exist, a strong enough force could destroy all signs of her existence ... even her soul."

"How can she be destroyed when someone as massive as you isn't able to squash her?"

The dragon lowered his head back to the ground. "That explanation would require a lengthy conversation. For now, I'll say this: if I had wanted to end Anahita, she would've been ended."

The dragon rolled his eyes off the dwarf and focused them on the angel who was now standing in the imprint of her body. "There's much to do. Take the dwarf by the hand and teleport to the top of my snout. I shall lift you up so that you may acquire a better view. The moment for you to reshape this Heaven has arrived..."

MEANWHILE, NORTHERN GRAYHAM
THE TUNNEL LEADING TO HYDROTH

Fellow soul ... once the food from the Tormalian's side of the cavern had been retrieved and brought into the tunnel, Shiver asked the High Priestess to comfort Medolas while he and the ruby eyed man spent the night speaking with the officers of both armies. On the Tormalian side, only two high ranking officers had managed to clear the roof before the hollow collapsed.

When morning finally arrived, it had been determined that the bodies swept away by the ocean as it rushed in to fill the cavern would not be retrieved. Since the perished of both cultures were cast into the water anyway, it would be too costly to recover them all and transport the ended to Gesper, only to turn around and cast them back into the sea.

The Tormalian families would need to find a new way to mourn, and since many of them served a different deity than the Isor, a plan was devised. By the end of the meeting, it was determined that a huge chunk of ice would be harvested from the battlefield near the edge of the cavern and transported back through the Caves of Carne to Gesper. The ice would symbolize the fallen, and the families of those men would be asked to gather in the wilderness above Gesper for the ceremony. The block would be placed above the tallest spire, and the light reflecting off the spire would create an inviting glow as the block was chipped apart. Each family would be given a piece that they could toss into the Sea of Gesper and then pray that their loved one's soul found the comfort of the Tormalians' god, Owain, and his heavenly kingdom.

With the meeting complete, Shiver and Gablysin found Medolas and took him out of the company of the priestess and the goswigs. "I shall order the army back to Hydroth. There is no threat for them to face here now."

"What about Clandestiny? We can't just abandon her."

Gablysin responded. "What would you have the army do, Medolas? You know the outcome. Clanny turned against us. To risk the safety of the men, even for our friend, is unacceptable."

Medolas pointed down the tunnel at a group of men who were nearby. "Their safety? What about Clanny's? If it wasn't for her, they would've been ended, and you would've lost the war."

"Come with me, Medolas," Shiver urged. "We should talk this through."

"Talking will be for naught, unless you intend to find Clanny!" Medolas snapped.

The ruby eyed man reached out and placed his hand on his friend's shoulder. "We're not against you, Medolas. Stop fighting, and converse with us."

Gablysin led the trio to a group of blocks that had been arranged into a circle. With the group sitting on the ice, he continued. "If Shiver commanded the army to stay and seek Clandestiny, how would they know it was her when they came upon her? You saw the gashtions with your own eyes, Medolas. There were two, and one of them was our enemy and wished us ill will during the battle. Would you have Shiver risk the lives of our men to locate a beast that may or may not be the one we cherish?"

Medolas' response was swift. "I would give my life for Clandestiny without needing to ponder for a single moment. Why shouldn't they?"

"They would, if so ordered," Shiver affirmed. "But their lives are more than 18,000. Just look at the men. Would you have them perish before you're satisfied?"

"But—"

"But nothing," Gablysin interrupted. "Eighteen thousand men cannot be sacrificed no matter how much we love Clandestiny. We know you were to unite, but that dream is lost to you now. We can't even be sure that Clandestiny would be the same soul if she was to return."

Medolas stood and shouted, "You can't ask me to abandon her! I can't do that, and I won't return to Hydroth without her!"

Many of the faces throughout the tunnel turned in their direction. Shiver motioned that everything was okay and then responded. "Medolas, sit. Your anger solves nothing."

"You're not my king! You can't command me to sit!"

Shaking his head, Shiver remained calm. "Medolas, sit, or you'll spend your moments in the dungeon. There, you'll find the moments to think, and you'll be unable to search for Clandestiny. Make your choice, Medolas."

A long series of moments passed while Shiver and Medolas held each other's stare. Eventually, Medolas lowered to his block.

"A wise decision," Gablysin encouraged. "I may have an idea that would satisfy us all."

"And that is?" Shiver questioned.

"It best not involve leaving Clandestiny to fend for herself," Medolas warned.

The ruby eyed man grinned. "You're starting to sound like Clanny, Medolas."

Medolas did not respond.

"Anyway, perhaps the High Priestess and the goswigs could assist in the search. With their ability to teleport, they could each lead a small party until she was found."

"We don't know if Clanny survived," Shiver objected. "She may never return."

Medolas was about to respond, but Gablysin was quick to hold up his hand. "Whether she lived or not is irrelevant. Clandestiny is our friend. We owe it to her to do something."

"I have an idea," the High Priestess announced. As she and the goswigs rejoined the group, she pointed. "The men sitting not far down the tunnel, just over there, spoke of a prophecy." Refocusing her attention on the ruby eyed man, she continued. "They say a man with the ruby eyes was prophesied to be the savior of your people. But from what you're to be saved from, they couldn't say."

"They believe in a pretense," Gablysin rebutted. "With their future so uncertain, they seek comfort in fables."

Fosalia extended her arm and used her power to retrieve a hide that was near the wall of the tunnel. After laying it on top of one of the blocks, she took a seat directly opposing the ruby eyed man. "Prior to my mother's passing, she said there would come a Peak when I would need to bestow the blessing on a member of the Isor."

"Ha! What good is a blessing that doesn't work?" Medolas queried.

"Agreed," Gage added. "I was told Clandestiny was blessed as a child, yet she was unable to control the power and turned against us."

"Without Clandestiny, you'd be expired!" Medolas defended.

"She also would've ended us if the other gashtion had not called her away," Gallrum rebutted.

Medolas, Gage and Gallrum would have spent the next few moments arguing, but Shiver cut in. The king's voice was firm. "No man would dispute Clandestiny's contribution, Medolas. The men are appreciative of how Clandestiny saved them. I would, however, dispute your claim that the priestess' blessing was invalid."

"Dispute if you must," Medolas retorted, "but I saw the result."

A few intense moments passed before the king refocused his attention. "Priestess, your mother's blessing was meant to protect Clanny once she assumed the form of the gashtion, was it not?"

Fosalia nodded. "Correct. Clandestiny should not have turned against the army no matter the desperation of her mental state."

"It's not Clanny's fault!" Medolas barked. "She would never hurt her friends in good conscience."

"No one said it was her fault, Medolas," Gablysin refuted.

Medolas crossed his arms. "I can see where this conversation is leading. You need someone to blame." He motioned to the king. "What about your father? How can we be sure that Thoomar would not have lost himself while fighting the gashtion? Perhaps the power is too much for anyone to bear."

Shiver shook his head. "You're wrong."

"How could you know that?"

Gabs spoke up. "Medolas, if you're unable to be productive, perhaps you should leave and allow a more relaxed set of minds to seek a solution to the problem."

"I am relaxed!" Medolas sneered and then reclaimed Shiver's gaze. "Stop avoiding the answer. Is it possible that Thoomar would've lost himself just like Clanny?"

It was easy to see the irritation as it covered Shiver's face. "If you were any other man, Medolas ... any other."

"Well, I'm not! So answer the question."

Shiver shook his head. "If you must know, I was only nine seasons when my father took me into the wilderness to teach me to hunt. On one of our outings, we slew a bearogon, but when we skinned the beast, the gashtion could be heard in the distance. As he often did, my father roared to ward off the beast, but on that Peak, the gashtion didn't flee."

Gallrum leaned forward. His wings stopped flapping, and his eyes were full of anticipation. "What happened next?"

Gage struck his cane against Gallrum's tail. "Hush! Let him speak."

After a brief smile, Shiver did just that. "I watched my father change. I was frightened, and I remember falling to the ice as the weight of his new form made the ice quake."

"Did the other gashtion attack?" Gallrum questioned.

Again, Gage thumped his cane against the serwin's tail, but during this moment, it was much harder. "I said, hush."

The serwin would have responded, but he could see that all eyes in the group were staring him down. He acquiesced, "Continue."

Shiver refocused on Medolas. "As I was saying, I remember falling to the ice. I also remember watching the gashtion flee as my father chased it beyond a berg that protruded from the shelf. Though I was unable to see the battle due to the size of the berg, I could hear the fight."

The king sighed. "Medolas, I believe Clandestiny was not at fault. I believe that her inability to train with Fosalia's mother may be the difference. This lack of training may be why she was unable to control the power that filled her being as she faced both gashtions. Perhaps the priestess' blessing was simply not enough."

The king leaned forward. "I say this for one reason only. After my father returned from chasing the gashtion back to the ocean, he looked down at me and winked before he transformed back into his normal self. I knew he meant me no harm by how he approached, and the expression in his eyes was filled with love ... despite being a beast. Even then, he had the desire to let me know that all was at peace."

Shiver stood from his block and looked at the badger. "When Clandestiny came after you, you said her eyes were filled with rage. You said it was as if she did not care for your well being." The king directed his gaze back to Medolas. "If Clandestiny survived the confrontation with Meerum, she may still be lost to us. There may be nothing the army can do to get her back."

The whole group's eyes focused on Medolas as they waited for his response, but when one never came, Fosalia spoke. "We have no way of knowing the true reason why Clandestiny was unable to control the power. But I do know the Isor believe in a prophecy, and in that prophecy, you, Gablysin, are said to be the savior of them all."

"How would you have me save them?" the ruby eyed man queried. "The color of my eyes doesn't give me the ability to stand against a beast of Clandestiny's size. Even if she survived, what would you have me do?"

"I would have you sing," Fosalia replied. "I could bestow the blessing of the gashtion upon you. You could use the Tear to amplify your gift, and you will sing like you have never sung before."

"What good would that do?" Gabs questioned.

"The Tear possesses many secrets ... secrets my mother would have divulged to Clandestiny if given the chance. I could—"

"These secrets are no good to her now," Medolas grumbled. "You should've made Clanny listen."

Shiver barked, "Medolas, you were the one who informed the priestess that she wouldn't like Clandestiny when she was angry. Do you intend to argue all night, or do I need to have you taken away? I'm not here to satisfy your desire to express your disgust."

"Nor am I," Gablysin confirmed. "Settle your emotions, or leave."

Medolas wanted to argue, but he knew one more ill word would get him sent away. "I'm sorry," was all he said.

Shiver walked across the circle and took a seat next to Medolas. "We all know you love her. We also can't fathom how close the two of you became while living with the Ko-dess. But you must trust us. We'll do our best to find her."

The king redirected his gaze. "Priestess, tell us your idea."

Fosalia cleared her throat. "After your men spoke of the prophecy, they also spoke of the soothing sound of Gablysin's voice. They spoke of his voice as if the weight of the worlds lifted from their shoulders when they heard it. They said you have been singing ever since two beings by the names of Darosen and Blandina passed."

Shiver grinned. "Gabs, the priestess makes you sound like a terrible friend. You began singing again when my parents passed. How awful of you."

Everyone in the group laughed, even Medolas who wanted to avoid it.

When the mood settled, Fosalia continued. "Gablysin, with the Tear's help, you may be able to reach what is left of Clandestiny. If your voice has the effect on her that it does your men, she may choose to reclaim the form of her true self."

"Even if that were true, how would you suggest I get close enough to sing to her?"

Fosalia pondered the ruby eyed man's question and then leaned forward. "Perhaps we should try this..."

As Fosalia continued to explain, deep beneath the surface of the Ocean of Utopia, Clandestiny was being drawn to a massive, underwater cave. It was this cave that would take her into an even larger cavern that had been created by previous gashtions.

With the other gashtions' passing, she was the only one left, and instinct was taking over. Though she did not know why, she felt she had a task to do, but she had no idea what that task was. All she knew was that she had to come this way, and as she entered the cavern, she stopped to study her surroundings.

The slits of her dragon eyes narrowed as she peered through the darkness. It was not long before her gaze found the gathering of eggs that had collected into a pile against the peak of the cavern. Without wasting another moment, she pushed off the floor and swam toward the ceiling. When she stopped, she released a natural secretion that smothered the pile without realizing why she was doing it.

MEANWHILE, SOUTHERN GRAYHAM
THE ENTRANCE TO THE CAVE OF SORROW

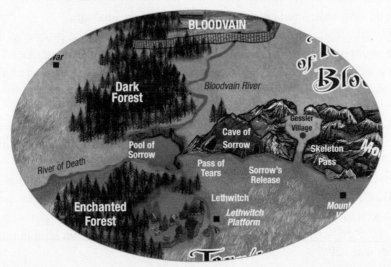

When George appeared with the Brayson outside the Cave of Sorrow, Celestria was sitting on Kroger's gigantic, stone lap. The goddess had cleaned the debris off the ogre that had accumulated over the last season. Her legs were crossed, and she was leaning against the beast-man's belly.

"Good morning, Celestria," George said as he removed his hand from Brayson's shoulder. Taking note of the goddess' black leather pants, red blouse and red leather boots, he added, "You look amazing on this Peak. Lasidious is an idiot for turning his back on you."

"I agree," the Head Master added. "You look stunning."

Celestria leaned forward. "Thank you, but Lasidious is an idiot for betraying us all ... not just me." The goddess teleported off of Kroger's lap and appeared on the ground. "It's up to us to teach Lasidious a lesson."

Nodding, George bent over and picked up the piece of the Staff of Petrifaction that had been jammed under the ogre's fingernail on the Peak the warlock accidentally turned the beast-man to stone. "Brayson is still wrapping his mind around Lasidious being the bad guy. It wasn't long ago that I convinced him to serve Lasidious' lying ass. Hell ... with Brayson's help, I convinced the majority of Western Luvelles and a large portion of Southern Grayham to worship the bastard."

Using the sliver, George tapped its end against the nub of the ogre's broken arm. "I don't know about Brayson, but I'm tired of serving gods who constantly betray my confidence."

Brayson cut in, speaking to George. "What assurances do we have that she won't do the same?" He focused on Celestria. "I mean no disrespect, Goddess, but how do we know you speak the truth? How do we know you won't betray us as Lasidious has?"

The Goddess of Beasts smiled. "There's nothing I could say at this moment to ease your mind. You must do what your heart believes is right." She looked toward the trees that lined the top of the pass. "I don't require the beings on this world or any other to worship me."

"Then what do you require?" Brayson queried.

The goddess dropped her gaze and found the Head Master's eyes. "I require nothing. I'm seeking vengeance for Lasidious' betrayal, and as you know, that is not the only reason I'm here."

Brayson nodded. "Yes. You've claimed that Garrin is your son."

"I claim nothing!" Celestria snapped. "I speak the truth!" She paused to collect herself. "Please forgive me. The boy is of my womb. I wouldn't lie about that."

Brayson frowned. "Even if that's true, the depth of the gods' manipulations has no bounds. I no longer believe in anything the gods teach or say, and I'll never pray again. My faith could never be restored to the point that I could utter a god's name without doubt filling my mind."

Celestria reached forward and placed her right hand on Brayson's left shoulder. "I cannot fault you for your loss of faith. Any man's beliefs would suffer after what you've learned." She paused and then redirected the conversation. "Rest assured, Brayson, none of this is George's fault. Mieonus and Lasidious manipulated him ... just as you've been manipulated. How could he have known the truth that I was Garrin's mother when the child was placed in your family. Even his mind was manipulated."

"I don't know what to say," Brayson responded.

"How could you?" The goddess turned to walk away. After a few paces, she reclaimed Brayson's eyes. "Garrin is my son whether you believe it or not. You may not be able to reclaim your belief in the gods, but you can still find it in your heart to believe in a mother's love, can you not?"

Brayson took a moment to ponder the goddess' question. "I suppose it makes sense that even the gods need love. Knowing what I know now, I believe the gods are just as flawed as I am. The only thing that separates you from us is the extent of your power."

Celestria chuckled. "Oh ... my dearest Brayson, I adore you, and I also adore your ignorance. I wouldn't be so quick to make assumptions if I was you. There's so much more that separates us than my ability to control the arts."

"Here we go," George inserted. "I can sense a lengthy explanation coming."

The goddess nodded. "Indeed." She reclaimed Brayson's eyes. "As a mortal, you employ magic like a tool. You channel it through your being, and over the seasons, you've learned to master the outcome of how you intend to use it."

Brayson crossed his arms. "How's that different from the way you employ the arts? My father taught me that magic is not prejudiced and treats every being the same."

A large smile spread across Celestria's face. "I hate to be the one to disagree, but your father was wrong." With the Head Master waiting for her to continue, the goddess took a moment to search for the best way to explain. "Allow me to say it this way. Throughout your life of more than 700 seasons, you've simply employed the uses of magic, whereas I, throughout my existence of 392,471 seasons, have been, and always will be, the essence of magic. I am a magical being. I do not summon it, nor do I employ its uses.

Magic exists because I and the other gods exist. We are the beginning, but we are not the end."

Brayson shook his head. "I don't understand. If you're not the end, what is?"

"A wonderful question. First, I will say, if the gods were to cease to exist, magic would not perish with us ... despite us being its essence."

"How's that possible?" Brayson urged. "If the gods are the essence of magic, how could the arts continue to exist if the gods were to perish?"

"Not perish, Head Master. I said, cease to exist."

"Explain the difference," Brayson demanded.

Once again, the warlock tapped the broken piece of the Staff of Petrifaction against the nub of Kroger's broken arm. "You guys are killing me!" he barked. "All I'm hearing right now is blah, blah, blah, blah, blah. We don't have the moments at our disposal for this conversation. I'm sure you could spend all Peak explaining this garesh before Brayson would be able to wrap his mind around it. Hell ... I'd even bet the two of you would end up in a big ass debate about the differences between how mortals and gods employ the uses of magic for more Peaks than I could even count."

Grabbing both ends of the broken piece of staff, the warlock placed it behind his neck. "How about we all focus on what we came here for? Celestria, I need you to help me fix this big lug. If I'm going to Hell, I'll be damned if I only take a handbasket with me. Kroger is going to need both of his arms to protect me while I'm there."

Celestria pulled her eyes away from the Head Master. "We'll continue our conversation about this later, Brayson." She looked down at the rubble that was lying on the ground. "Now ... regarding your friend, I can attach the pieces to make his arm whole. I can even restore the ogre's flesh. But as you know, I cannot retrieve his soul from the Book."

"Yeah, yeah, yeah, I know that. That's why I brought Brayson with me. I'm sure you know that his position as Head Master allows him to restore life once per season." The warlock reached out and patted Brayson on the back. "Ain't that right, stud?"

Brayson nodded. "I find it interesting that a mortal, a being who isn't the essence of magic, is able to restore life when a goddess who claims to be magic itself, cannot."

Celestria smiled as she reached down to pick up a chunk of the ogre's arm. "Yet another topic of conversation that will have to wait." She tossed the chunk to Brayson. "As always, it appears George has thought of everything. Shall we stop our debate long enough to work together?"

With the Head Master in agreement, the goddess motioned for them to step aside. She reached out and placed her hands on Kroger's right knee and then closed her eyes. It was not long before the rubble lifted off the ground and turned to dust. The dust floated toward the nub of the ogre's appendage and assumed a shape that matched the proportions of the beast-man's good arm.

George elbowed Brayson and whispered. "I can't wait to see Kroger's expression when he opens his eyes."

The Head Master whispered a response. "I've never restored life to a being of this size before."

"Does size matter?" George queried. "I hope you can still do it. I'm going to need him."

Brayson's sigh filled the morning air. "I suppose we'll know as soon as the goddess has finished."

A moment later, the glow surrounding Celestria's hands intensified. Starting at Kroger's outermost extremities, the grayness of the statue began to fade. First, the end of his fingers and then the tips of his toes softened. With the pace of the change happening so slowly, the Peak of Bailem arrived before the ogre's body eventually slumped over onto the dirt.

As Kroger's head thumped against the ground, George cringed. "Damn! It's a good thing he's still not alive, or that would've hurt."

Brayson shook his head. "You jest, but he may be angry with you when he wakes. I don't believe I'd be in a forgiving mood if the man who turned me to stone was standing over me when I woke."

George smirked. "Like you said, we'll know soon enough. Besides, the last thing he said to me before he passed was that he still considered me a friend. He knew I didn't turn him to stone on purpose. I just hope he remembers that."

With the ogre's transformation complete, Celestria dropped her hand. "It is finished." The goddess took a step back and motioned for Brayson to step forward. "I believe it's your turn."

Brayson closed the gap and placed his hands on the ogre's belly. He looked to the sky, took a deep breath and then closed his eyes. A moment later, he dropped his hands to his side and turned to face Celestria. "I'm lost without my faith. The power to restore life was given to me by my lord. How can I restore breath to the ogre if I no longer believe?"

Celestria had to laugh. "Oh, Head Master, your ignorance is to be cherished. You don't need to pray to Lasidious or even Mieonus to retrieve the ogre's soul. All you need to do is demand its return."

Brayson's brow furrowed. "I don't understand."

"Nor could you, but this is not the moment for explanations. All you need to know is that many, many seasons ago, the gods agreed that the position of Head Master would be allowed the request to restore the life of another. Your god doesn't give you this ability. The Collective gave you the right to restore life. The being responsible for returning the ogre's soul has nothing to do with your beliefs or how you pray."

The goddess pointed to the clouds. "Lift your voice, Head Master. Shout to the heavens and demand that Kroger live..."

ANCIENTS SOVEREIGN
THE BOOK'S HALL OF JUDGMENT
LATE BAILEM

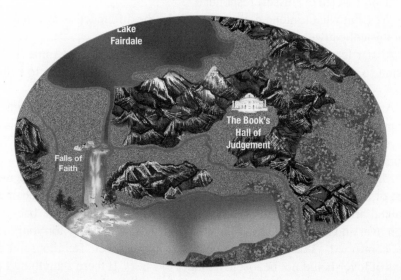

With the gods taking their seats around the heavy, stone table inside the Hall of Judgment, Gabriel floated into the room. He was still in the form of a book, and he had no intention of divulging his true self. But the decision had been made to acknowledge the existence of the archangel Michael before the end of the meeting. Together, they would announce to the rest of the Collective that the Source was creating a new Heaven.

"Good evening, Gabriel," Sharvesa said as she spread her wings and then lowered onto her seat. "I do hope this meeting will be short. My attention is required elsewhere."

"I'm sure Mosley won't pass before you find your way back to Harvestom," the Book grumbled. As Gabriel floated by the demon-goddess, his face was stern. He stopped above the center of the table and then lowered into a hovering position a half-pace above its surface near his golden stand.

"You look vexed, Gabriel," Hosseff remarked. "Are you a bit out of sorts?"

The Book turned to face the shade. "I'm fine!" he snapped.

Kesdelain pushed his dreds clear of his face and nudged Hosseff with his elbow. "That's the kind of fine I am when I want to end someone."

As Hosseff's chuckle emanated from the nothingness beneath his hood, Gabriel realized his tone would not be productive for the meeting. He took a moment to adjust his attitude. "I'm sorry for how I spoke. I simply have many things on my mind and an agenda I hope to accomplish."

"Don't we all?" Hosseff responded.

"Yes, but what I intend to propose may be the difference as to whether or not this collective continues to exist."

Alistar leaned forward, crossed his arms on the table and smiled. "You sound so serious, Gabriel. And I thought this meeting was going to be boring."

As most of the gods chuckled, Celestria was busy staring at Lasidious' empty seat. Her heart still longed for the Mischievous One. Despite his betrayal, her anger was not strong enough to overshadow the pain of how much she missed him.

Mieonus could see the suffering on Celestria's face, but rather than make one of her snide comments, the Goddess of Hate stood from her chair and walked around the table. After placing her hand on Celestria's back, she bent over and kissed the top of the goddess' head. "I'm sorry for your loss," she comforted. "I can only imagine how you must feel. Ten thousand seasons of love should not be lost in a matter of Peaks. If there's anything I can do to help ease your pain, I want you to know I'll be there for you."

The others of the Collective fell silent as they heard the Goddess of Hate's comment.

Celestria stood from her chair to embrace Mieonus. "Thank you. I needed to hear that."

The others were astounded to see that the Goddess of Hate was capable of an actual sentiment of caring.

Mieonus' loving countenance was evident as she held Celestria close. "There, there ... it's okay, dear."

"How could he just leave me like that?" Celestria whimpered. "I gave him every part of me."

Mieonus' response was soothing. "None of this is your fault."

"Then why did he leave?"

"A man's logic is often hard to understand." Mieonus placed her right hand on the back of Celestria's head and gently pulled the Goddess of Beasts closer. "You can't blame yourself for Lasidious' actions. We've all suffered loss, and you know as well as I that love isn't prejudiced and favors no one. Even gods can be victimized by the hand that love wields."

Sniffling, Celestria responded, "I know, but I would've followed him anywhere. I'm lost without him."

Again, Mieonus gently squeezed. "There, there ... let it all out."

As Celestria's crying intensified, the Goddess of Hate kept her nestled in her arms as she rubbed her back.

Right about the moment when the others were beginning to believe the Goddess of Hate's gesture, a sinister smile appeared on Mieonus' face as she placed her chin on top of Celestria's head. "I feel for you, dear. It's not your fault that you weren't enough woman to keep a man of Lasidious' quality from wandering. You had to know it was only a matter of moments before he would abandon you. It had to end."

Appalled, the Goddess of Beasts pushed clear of Mieonus' embrace as her laughter filled the room. "How could I have been so foolish?" Celestria sneered. "I should have known you were up to something and had no real concern for my well-being! I despise you!"

Mieonus' grin cut like a knife. She would have responded, but Lasidious appeared beside her.

As if it had been planned, Lictina, Calla, Owain, Jervaise and Celestria gasped as the tension shrouding the meeting was instantly heightened.

The Goddess of Hate and Celestria parted in opposite directions, each taking a few steps back from the Mischievous One.

"You have a lot of nerve showing your face here!" Mieonus chastised. "But I'm glad you've come. Your harlot can't stop blubbering about how you abandoned her."

Alistar stood from his chair. "Have you no shame, Mieonus? Shut up, and sit down!"

Mieonus shot a nasty glance down the length of the table. "You don't own me! I'll sit when I'm ready!"

As the members of the Collective began to shout curses at the Goddess of Hate, Lasidious did not respond to the mood of the room. Instead, he held Celestria's gaze as he walked past Mieonus and stopped in front of his love. His voice was soft and inviting as he reached out to caress her chin. "Did you truly believe that I would abandon you, my love?"

The Goddess of Beasts was about to respond, but the Book of Immortality cleared his throat to capture her attention. "Choose your words wisely, Celestria. I need not remind you that a promise has been made."

Refocusing her attention, the goddess' voice trembled as she spoke. "Where have you been? And why have you done this to me?"

"I have done nothing that cannot be fixed." Placing his hands on Celestria's shoulders, Lasidious gently stroked the length of her arms. "I have done nothing other than take the moments I needed for myself. You can't truly believe that I'd abandon so many seasons of bliss."

Celestria was unable to respond. The emotion of Lasidious' return was too much. She rushed into the Mischievous One's arms and allowed herself to be held as the intensity of her sobbing filled the room.

Again, Gabriel spoke out. "Why have you come, Lasidious?"

"Yes, why?" Mieonus jeered. "Did you miss your plaything?"

Rather than respond, Lasidious allowed Celestria the moments to collect herself as she kept her head buried in his chest. When finally the goddess pulled back, he gently kissed her lips and then led her to her seat.

"Must we wait all season before you tell us why you're here?" Hosseff questioned. "I have better things to do with my moments than watch your reunion."

Though the Book of Immortality was unnerved, Gabriel could not allow the Mischievous One to see his weakness. He had no idea whether or not Lasidious knew he had the power to destroy the members of the Collective, but he had to find a way to overcome this fear and portray strength. "You have a lot of gall showing your face here, Lasidious. The way you've treated Celestria is inexcusable."

Leaning against the table, Lasidious stroked the back of Celestria's hands and waited for them to stop trembling before he turned to claim his seat at the end of the table.

Mieonus stomped her lifted heel against the floor. "Well? Aren't you going to say anything?"

Again, Lasidious did not respond. He leaned back, lifted his feet up on the table and smiled.

Now, more than ever, Gabriel believed that his greatest fear was beginning to manifest. It took everything in him to sound confident. "Lasidious, this Collective cannot waste its moments on theatrics. We have gathered for a purpose, and I intend to see that it's accomplished."

When the Mischievous One failed to respond yet again, Mieonus surmised, "Something has changed with you. You're more cocky than usual. Stop toying with us, and tell us why you've come."

Lasidious dropped his feet to the floor and leaned forward. "As I look around this room, I'm trying to determine who I'm going to destroy first. I have grown tired of some of the faces that sit around this table." His eyes focused on the Book. "Perhaps I'll start with you, Gabriel."

As the others sat in disbelief, the Mischievous One put his feet back on the table. "It's my opinion that the laws governing this collective are no longer necessary. Gabriel, I'll destroy you if you don't agree to step aside and allow me to rule without opposition?"

The others eagerly waited for the Book to respond. According to the law on Gabriel's pages, a law Lasidious and Alistar initiated more than 10,000 seasons ago, the Book was required to strip any god of their power who threatened to end its existence. Further, Gabriel was to leave the offender's immortality intact and then strip their mouth from their face. The Book was then required to create a place of continual suffering that was worse than any nightmare that could be found on Hell and cast the offender into it. It is there they would exist for the rest of eternity as payment for their threat, and their screams for mercy would forever remain unheard.

With Lasidious threatening to end his existence, the members of the Collective were all shocked as Gabriel just hovered above the table in silence. "What are you waiting for, Gabriel?" Mieonus shouted. "Strip him of his godliness and be done with it. I'd love to witness his suffering."

The Mischievous One pointed a finger in Mieonus' direction. "Perhaps there are two beings I shall need to destroy. Once I'm done with the Book, I may need to focus my attention on you if you're unable to keep your mouth shut." The Mischievous One moved his arm in the direction of Gabriel. As he did, his fingertips began to glow with the power he threatened to evoke. "You'll surrender control of this Collective, or you'll be destroyed. You have 1 Peak to make your decision."

Hosseff stood from his chair. "1 Peak? Have you gone mad, Lasidious? You're in no position to make that demand. The Book would—"

The Book spoke over the shade. "No, Hosseff ... you're wrong!"

"What do you mean?" Calla responded. "How could the shade be wrong?"

Gabriel's eyes dropped. "Because Lasidious knows."

"He knows what?" Jervaise barked. "Speak clearly, Gabriel. You're confusing us."

Bailem was the next to speak. "He isn't confusing all of us. Lasidious has come to realize the magnitude of his power. He now clearly knows he has the power to destroy the members of this collective."

"Ha!" Mieonus rebutted. "As if you would know anything! You're the most witless of us all, Bailem!"

"Agreed," Owain added. "You're a fool if you believe any of us possess the power to destroy the Book!"

"I also agree that none of us has that ability," Calla confirmed.

Returning to her seat, Mieonus stroked the Mischievous One across the back of his shoulders as she past and then plopped into her chair. "We would be fools to believe that this Collective has lost the upper hand. I shall never cower to the likes of you, Lasidious. Perhaps you should return to whatever hole you crawled out of, and take your slut with you."

The Book shook his head. "Careful, Mieonus. This isn't the moment to berate Lasidious. He has realized his potential, and he knows he has nothing to fear. He can destroy us all, and there's nothing I can do to stop him."

The Goddess of Hate would have responded, but she could see the concern in the Book's eyes. She leaned back in her chair and searched for the right thing to say. "It appears I've been a bit hasty with my words. Allow me to apologize, Lasidious. Is there anything I can get for you? Perhaps a tall mug of nasha?"

The God of Water leaned forward. "You can't be serious, Gabriel. Since when has Lasidious had the power to control even you?"

Gabriel lowered onto the table and allowed his binding to open just enough to provide balance. "Since before the game with the Crystal Moon began. There's nothing I can do to protect you now. If it's Lasidious' desire to change the laws, then I must yield or perish just as you must yield or perish."

As Celestria took note of defeat in the Book's eyes, she sat in her chair glancing between Gabriel and the Mischievous One. She was unsure of where her allegiance should be placed. On one hand, if Lasidious was, indeed, more powerful than Gabriel, she no longer had to stay true to her promise to the Book. Yet on the other hand, Lasidious had not offered a real explanation as to why he had abandoned her. Her distrust of the Mischievous One's intentions, no matter how much she still loved him, was dangling at the forefront of her mind. For now, she would remain silent and say nothing that would cause a reaction from either side.

Alistar stood from his chair. "Lasidious, if you are to be the new head of this collective, I have a gift for you to show that my intent is to conform to your rule. I don't want to perish. I shall return in a few moments to bestow your gift upon you." The God of the Harvest vanished.

Kesdelain was quick to stand as well. "I shall also bestow a gift. I have served you before, Lasidious. I'll be happy to serve you again." The troll also vanished.

Mieonus stood, "And I have a home that I could give you. I have seen the way you and your lovely goddess have gazed upon my waterfall. It's yours if you'd like. Meanwhile, allow me to retrieve two mugs of nasha. I shall go and pick the ripest fruit myself."

It was not long before the only beings left in the room were Lasidious, Gabriel and Celestria. The Goddess of Beasts had to smile. "I must admit, I enjoyed the fear on Mieonus' face."

Gabriel lifted from the table and floated closer to Lasidious. "How do you intend to rule...?"

When Alistar appeared, he was standing in the Vampire King's throne room beneath the Mountains of Gannesh on Hell. "Brother!" he shouted. "Show yourself! We have a problem!"

It took a few moments, but eventually, the Vampire King walked into the room holding Yolan's hand. Sam Jr. was in his free arm while Garrin was cradled in the queen's. "How can I help you, brother?" Lasidious replied.

Alistar's exhale was long. "Then the transformation was successful?"

"Of course, it was. It went just as we thought it would. With the king's body not possessing a soul, he was the perfect vessel to occupy. Tell me ... how did the meeting go?"

The God of the Harvest hesitated to respond. He looked at Yolan. "Your Majesty, if you'd allow us the moments to converse. I'm sure there are more important matters for you to attend to than wasting your moments on the senseless babbling of brothers."

The queen reached out and took the Prince of Brandor from Lasidious and gave the Mischievous One a quick kiss on the cheek. "I know when I'm being politely dismissed. Shall we hunt together later this evening? I have a craving for green demon."

Lasidious smiled. "I will look forward to the fear on their faces as you puncture their flesh. I'll find you once our conversation is complete."

Once the Vampire Queen was out of earshot, the Mischievous One was quick to question. "I have to know. Was Tardon stripped of his power? Better yet, what did he look like without a mouth? I can only imagine the fear that must have filled his eyes."

Lasidious could see there was a problem. "What's wrong, brother?"

Alistar's response was immediate. "The words you filled Tardon's mouth with had the opposite effect than we intended. The Book cowered at Tardon's threat."

"What? Explain."

"Tardon demanded that Gabriel relinquish control of the Collective or perish, as you instructed him to do."

"That's good ... isn't it?"

"No, it isn't. The Book did nothing."

Lasidious' brow furrowed. "Nothing?"

"Yes ... the Book did not make a stand against Tardon as you said he would. The Book yielded."

"Gabriel wouldn't yield," Lasidious negated. "The law on his pages wouldn't allow him to once the threat was uttered."

Alistar shook his head. "You don't understand. He yielded because he was unable to enforce the law. Apparently, you've had the power to control the Collective since before your game with the Crystal Moon began. You've given up your godliness for nothing, and now Tardon sits in your seat without opposition. At this very moment, the Collective is coming to the realization that Tardon is their new law."

As the anger built on the new Vampire King's face, Lasidious turned and walked across the room and stopped next to his throne. With his head hung low, his nails dug into the back of the chair.

"What would you have me do, brother?" Alistar questioned. "It's too risky to let the Collective believe that you're the one governing them."

"Aaaaahhhhhhhhhh!" the vampire screamed as he reared back and punched the top of his throne. As the back of the chair broke apart from the rest, he whirled around and continued to shout while the separated piece tumbled across the floor. "How could I not have realized the extent of my own power? The path I've chosen to follow was completely unnecessary!"

Alistar shrugged. "I know, but shouting at me won't get us anywhere. A new plan is in order, and we must act quickly. Tardon won't know what to do with his perception of dominance. He'll say something that gives you away, and Gabriel will learn that he's an imposter."

It took a moment for Lasidious to settle down, but the graveness of the situation demanded that he calm himself. "This is what you'll do. You'll return to Ancients Sovereign and destroy Tardon. Annihilate him before he has the chance to say something we can't fix."

"I cannot destroy him, Lasidious. With you transferring most of your power and your soul into the Vampire King's vessel, you have left your former body as a shell of who you once were. If I were to end Tardon, what soul would Gabriel collect? He would know it wasn't you when he was unable to find your spirit. The Collective would be forced to hunt for it, and I would be unable to keep them in the dark."

"Damn it!" Lasidious whirled around, kicked the bottom half of the throne and watched it tumble down the steps. "Damn, that book! Why can't winning be easy?"

Alistar crossed his arms. "You're wasting your breath with senseless emotions. You need to focus!"

The Mischievous One took a deep breath. "I feel sick to my stomach. This body must be incapable of dealing with these feelings."

"Your new body and mind isn't your problem. We both agreed that Tardon was an acceptable host. Now what would you have me do?"

A fair series of moments passed before the Mischievous One responded. "Okay ... you will..." The conversation continued.

When Alistar finally reappeared next to his seat inside the Book's Hall of Judgment, he was empty handed.

Mieonus looked up from handing the second mug of nasha to Celestria. "What took you so long, and where's your gift? Our new lord has been patiently waiting. He has told us that he intends to spare us all. Isn't he so gracious?"

As the others of the Collective looked in the God of the Harvest's direction, Alistar rolled his eyes. "Mieonus, you're the biggest sheep of them all. Allow me to demonstrate the magnitude of my gift." Alistar scanned the faces around the table and pointed in the direction of the far wall. "I suggest you all move, for my gift is grand and will require space."

The curiosity of the others caused them to comply. Once they were out of the way, the God of the Harvest focused on Celestria. "Please stand beside me. I want you to see Lasidious' face from my perspective as your lover realizes the nature of what I'm about to bestow upon him."

The anticipation of the gift caused Tardon to rub his hands together. "I cannot express my excitement. May I have a hint of what it might be?"

Smirking, Alistar lifted a finger and rocked it back and forth. "Careful, Lasidious, you don't want to appear too anxious. It would spoil the surprise."

"Do hurry. I cannot wait to see it," he responded.

With Celestria at his side, the God of the Harvest turned his back to the others and then stepped in front of her. He whispered in her ear, "No matter what happens, I want you to know there's a reason for what I'm about to do. In your dismay, you must say nothing of my relationship to Lasidious. I will explain my actions when the proper moment arrives. What I'm about to do is going to cause you pain, but I assure you, this pain will be a wasted emotion. For now ... you must feign your despair."

The Goddess of Beasts whispered a response. "What are you talking about? You're scaring me, Alistar."

"I assure you, there's nothing to be scared of. As I have said ... whatever happens next, there's an explanation. That's all I can tell you for now. Do you understand?"

"What would you have me do?"

Mieonus shouted from across the room. "Are you going to give him the gift, or not? Our new lord doesn't have all Peak!"

Alistar extended a hand behind his back and held up a finger, but his eyes remained focused on Celestria's as he continued to whisper, "You must react the way you would've if you had not known there was an explanation. Make sure you say nothing of my relationship to Lasidious. Do you understand?"

With the goddess nodding, Alistar turned in the direction of the Book. "Gabriel, will you please join us? We will need to draw from your power. The gift is of that magnitude."

As the others of the Collective murmured about the possibilities of the gift, the Book floated across the room and stopped next to Alistar.

"Come closer, Gabriel." With the Book floating as close as he possibly could, Alistar continued to whisper. "I believe Lasidious is deceiving us. I'm going to defend you against his threat. You must be ready to act, and enforce the law within your binding once I have proven his weakness."

Celestria grabbed Alistar's arm. "You can't do that. You know the severity of the law. He's your—"

Alistar was quick to put his fingers over Celestria's mouth. "You must trust me. You've been deceived, just as we all have been deceived. I would never hurt you. You must not react to your emotions. I say again ... you must trust me."

Gabriel was the one to respond. "If you're wrong, he will end us. Are you sure you know what you're doing?"

Rather than respond to the Book, Alistar lifted Celestria's chin. He made sure her eyes focused on his. "You must trust me ... okay?"

As soon as Celestria nodded, Alistar turned to face the imposter god and lifted his hands. Before Tardon knew what was happening, his ability to speak had been stripped, and a wave of force was barreling in his direction. A moment later, Tardon lifted from the floor as the power sent him crashing into the wall behind him.

Alistar shouted, "Now, Gabriel!"

The Book's arms extended. From across the room, Gabriel's power seized the imposter and lifted him off the floor. With a whip of his arms, the Book sent Tardon flying into the wall closest to the collection of gods. Lasidious' old body fell to the floor, unconscious, stripped of all its power and without a mouth.

Celestria screamed. "Nooooooo!"

Alistar was quick to react. He turned around, grabbed Celestria and then teleported out of the hall.

Seeing Tardon's mouthless face, Mieonus took a moment to gloat. The Goddess of Hate rushed over to the table, grabbed one of the mugs of nasha and then skipped across the room. After kneeling next to the imposter, she poured what was left on Tardon's head and then waited for who she believed to be Lasidious to open his eyes. Her voice was full of contempt. "Lasidious, before Gabriel throws you into an existence of eternal torment, I need you to know ... I spit in your nasha. And I would've never given you my home."

As the Book floated across the room, the others of the Collective were asking questions, but rather than answer, he shouted, "Silence!"

A long period of moments passed as the Book quietly hovered above Tardon, looking down at the smooth skin that now replaced the fallen's mouth.

True to form, Mieonus' impatience got the best of her. "Well, aren't you going to say something, Gabriel? This is your moment. Enjoy it."

As the Book passed his hand over the top of the imposter's head, Tardon fell into a deep sleep. "He will awaken in torment. Everyone return to your places. I called this meeting for a purpose, and I intend to see it through."

Those who remained returned to their seats without question. With Gabriel hovering above Lasidious' old chair, he pointed to the door of the room and called out, "Michael, the moment has come! Show yourself!"

Every god gasped as the archangel entered the room.

MOMENTS LATER, WESTERN LUVELLES
THE SOURCE'S OLD HOME

When Alistar appeared with Celestria, they were standing in the Mountains of Oraness next to Fisgig's perch.

Celestria was quick to pull away from Alistar's grasp and shout, "How could you betray your own brother? You would expect me to trust you after you sent him to an eternity of suffering?"

Alistar calmly crossed his arms. "That wasn't my brother, nor was it your lover."

The goddess would have responded, but Alistar's claim felt so outlandish she was unable to.

The God of the Harvest leaned against the goswig's perch. "I thought that would capture your attention."

Celestria's stare was so hot it could have burned a hole through Alistar. "You best have an explanation above all other explanations, or I'll return to Ancients Sovereign and tell Gabriel everything you've said."

Alistar nodded. "I'm not a stupid being. I knew this would be hard on you."

"Ha! Other than you sentencing my love to eternal damnation, what could be so hard?"

"The being that was sentenced was not the one who claims to love you. As I told you in the hall, we've all been deceived ... most of all, me."

The God of the Harvest waved his hand across a section of dirt behind the goddess. A throne fit for Celestria's grace appeared near the edge of the water. "Perhaps you should take a seat."

The skin between the Goddess of Beasts' brows wrinkled. "I don't want to sit."

"Once you hear what I have to say, you may."

A confused look appeared on Celestria's face. "You're up to something."

Alistar smiled. "I'm not against you. You need to know that. I know you have many questions, and I promise to answer them. But before I go any further, you need to understand that I feel as betrayed as you will once you learn the truth."

"Stop posturing. Tell me something that will make we want to stay, or I'll leave."

Alistar motioned to the chair. Once Celestria realized it was pointless to argue, she lowered onto it, and then he continued. "Not only has my brother abandoned his love for you, he has also turned his back on me."

"How has he betrayed you?" Celestria snapped.

"His betrayal was made evident when he failed to tell me he took your son out of the care of George's family. He has run off with my nephew."

The goddess was quick to rebut. "How does his secrecy suggest betrayal? The two of you have hidden things from me in the past. Why are you above Lasidious' mischief?"

"It was agreed upon before the God Wars began that we would never hide anything from one another. Lasidious' theft of the baby diverts from our promise. There was no reason for him not to tell me. When he went into seclusion after your argument, I truly believed he needed moments to himself, but now I know otherwise."

Celestria leaned forward in her chair. "I know about Garrin. I know Lasidious took him."

"Good. Then you'll be relieved to know that I've been searching for him ever since I learned of his disappearance."

"I believe Garrin is on Hell," Celestria blurted.

Alistar took a moment to feign his surprise. "Perhaps I should've come to you sooner, but I felt you wouldn't listen. When last we spoke, your words suggested all was well, yet the subtleties in your actions left me with the impression that you believed me a liar."

Celestria nodded. "I believed you were protecting Lasidious. I thought you were plotting against me. I still do."

A long moment of silence passed while Alistar forced a tear to roll down his cheek. "I would never conspire against you. It breaks my heart that you think I would. I've watched you give your love to another for over 10,000 seasons, and during that entire series of moments, I've wanted you for myself. I could never hurt you the way Lasidious has."

Celestria stood from her chair and moved behind it. "I don't know what to say."

Alistar allowed the goddess the moments to process.

Eventually, Celestria refocused. "This feels like a game, yet I can see no logic behind it if it is one."

Alistar maintained his silence.

Another few moments passed before Celestria spoke again. "Even if your affections for me are genuine, they don't explain why Lasidious would betray us." She circled to the front of her throne and reclaimed her seat. "I can almost understand Lasidious betraying me, but you're his kin. Why would he abandon the only relationship he has that is bound by blood?"

The God of the Harvest frowned. "You know Lasidious as well as I. When have you ever known him to seek anything but absolute power?"

"Never, but seeking it at the expense of his own brother is inexcusable."

Alistar pushed clear of the perch. "Careful, Celestria, you sound as if you're starting to take my side."

"I wouldn't find too much comfort in that if I was you," the goddess rebutted.

Grinning, Alistar moved to the edge of the island. "You may be interested to know that I found Garrin, and the real Lasidious is with him."

Celestria reached up and covered her mouth. "Where? Is Garrin not on Hell like I thought he was? I want him with me. I've already made a deal with the Book to ensure he won't hurt Garrin. Gabriel has promised to allow him to stay with me on Ancients Sovereign."

Now it was Alistar's turn to look confused. "Why would Gabriel spare the child's existence? His birth was against the laws of the gods. And why would you tell the Book about his birth in the first place?"

The goddess leaned back in her chair. "I was angry."

"Angry enough to risk the safety of your own son?"

"No! I entered into a Promise of the Gods with Gabriel."

"What kind of promise?"

"In exchange for my help, Gabriel has agreed to spare Garrin and allow me to remain on Ancients Sovereign, but I won't be a member of the Collective any longer."

"What help did you offer?"

"Gabriel believes my relationship with Lasidious will be of use to him. But now it appears the Book will not need my help after all. Garrin is safe, and I don't have to betray Lasidious."

"So you're at the Book's beckoned call?"

The goddess reluctantly nodded. "After Gabriel agreed to spare Garrin, I went to Luvelles to retrieve him. It was then I learned that Lasidious had taken him. As we speak, George is on Hell searching for my baby. In return, I agreed to help George once Garrin was found."

"Why would you send a mortal to perform a task of that magnitude?" Alistar queried.

"Who else was I to send?" Celestria defended. "If I was right, and Lasidious was on Hell, he would've run as soon as he felt my presence. With Gabriel placing the damned on that world, I believed Lasidious was hiding on the mainland. George has the power to defend himself from most any enemy, and with the damned far from the mainland, the warlock has the moments to find Garrin."

Alistar shook his head. "His search is no longer necessary. George may be powerful for a human, but there are still many enemies on Hell that I would consider formidable foes. You may have sent him to his end."

Celestria sighed. "If you know where Garrin is, I can retrieve the warlock and his cat and deliver them to Luvelles. He doesn't need to stay on Hell."

A short period of silence passed before the God of the Harvest responded. "We should leave George where he's at for now. But rather than send him in any direction, we'll send him to the Mountains of Gannesh with his jaguar. That's where Lasidious took Garrin. They're hidden beneath the mountains in Lasidious' new underworld. You were right. They're on the mainland."

"Why send George? Together, we could retrieve my baby," Celestria urged.

"We cannot. Well, not yet anyway."

"Why?"

"Because Lasidious now possesses the body of the Vampire King. He has transferred his soul and the majority of his power into Tardon's old body."

A look of disbelief appeared on Celestria's face. "I don't believe you. Lasidious would never sacrifice his godliness to possess another immortal being."

Alistar reached down and picked up a pebble off the island and sent it skipping across the water. "Your belief isn't necessary for it to be a fact. Lasidious switched bodies with Tardon, but his reasons remain his own."

"How do you know this?"

As Alistar returned to the perch, he responded. "I've been spying on my brother to learn his intentions. After I learned of Garrin's disappearance, you could say I felt uneasy."

To avoid being talked into a corner, Alistar quickly changed the subject. "Garrin is in jeopardy. The baby is addicted to the Vampire Queen's milk. To take Garrin from her bosom would be harmful, and it could drive the baby mad. We're going to need a plan. Since the laws on the Book's pages won't allow us to take Yolan to Ancients Sovereign, Garrin will need to stay where he's at until we can find a way to reverse the effect of the milk."

A look of disgust appeared on Celestria's face. "It sickens me to know that my son has been feeding from her bosom."

"He hasn't been feeding in that manner. The child has been feeding from a bottle, not from her teat."

Celestria sighed.

"You seem relieved. Why?"

"I don't know exactly. I suppose I'm glad that Garrin has not been feeding directly from her breasts. A bottle somehow seems less ... well, less offensive."

Alistar shook his head. "My nephew feeding from a bottle doesn't make what Lasidious has done any less wrong. He's using Yolan's milk to gain the child's trust."

"Why would Garrin distrust him?"

"I'm unsure. The child has been wavering. One moment, he allows Lasidious to touch him, and then another, he won't."

After a breeze passed through the alcove, Celestria had to reach up to push her hair clear of her face. "None of this makes sense. Why would Lasidious give up his godliness to occupy Tardon's body?"

Alistar shrugged. "Because he clearly didn't know he possessed the power to control the Collective."

"But that does not explain why his actions are as rash as this."

"Perhaps he intends to reascend by using Garrin. That would explain the use of the Vampire Queen's milk."

Celestria shook her head. "How could he possibly reascend? With a switch of this magnitude, he can't even summon the power of a Titan. Garrin cannot fix that."

Alistar crossed his arms. "Are you sure about that? He also has Sam's baby, and we both know the child was resurrected using the juice of the nasha. Think about it. What does he intend to do now that you know the full picture?"

A fair series of moments passed while Celestria processed. She gasped. "How could he do that to those innocent, little babies...?"

CHAPTER 17
BAGGES WEED
ANCIENTS SOVEREIGN
ALISTAR'S PALACE
2 PEAKS HAVE PASSED, LATE BAILEM APPROACHES

Fellow soul ... after the events unfolded in the Book's hall, Sharvesa's mind was filled with questions, and without answers, she was unable to focus. The demon-goddess returned to Harvestom to inform Mosley that his training would be temporarily placed on hold, but when the wolf asked why, the goddess did not offer a reason. Instead, she promised to return and then teleported back to Ancients Sovereign.

Since Sharvesa had no idea where Alistar was, she waited at the table beyond the foyer of his palace for the God of the Harvest to return. She knew from her previous visit that Alistar's palace notified him whenever company visited.

When Alistar finally appeared, Sharvesa's legs were bouncing as she sat with her back facing the table.

"I'm sorry for making you wait, but I assure you I had no choice."

The demon stood and moved to the center of the foyer where the God of the Harvest was standing. "It has been 2 Peaks, Alistar."

He nodded. "As I said, I had no choice."

Sharvesa reached up and grabbed her horns. "My mind is filled with questions. How could you attack Lasidious and send our brother to an eternal torment after we agreed it would take the three of us to accomplish our plans? Did he do something against you, or is this a ruse that I should be informed of? He can't truly be gone."

The God of the Harvest smiled. "You're an inquisitive being. Perhaps the moment has come for you to learn the *real* truth. I've longed for the moment when I could see the look on the Collective's faces after they discover my identity. I might as well start with you."

"What are you referring to? You showed me your identity."

Alistar chuckled. "Not really."

"What do you mean? I don't understand."

"It's simple. Lasidious and I claimed you were our sister. That isn't true ... nor am I demon. I'm an imposter ... a master of identities. Only Lasidious is your brother. There's so much more to me than who the Collective believes I am."

"You're confusing me. I thought—"

Alistar spoke above Sharvesa. "Stop thinking! You're clearly unable to employ productive thought." The God of the Harvest took a few steps back. As he did, he continued to speak. "We're all children of a father, are we not? But *my* father is not *your* father. There is not a single drop of blood that is shared between us."

Sharvesa's brows furrowed. "I don't understand."

"You will, I assure you. Just watch." As the identity of the God of the Harvest manifested, Sharvesa's eyes widened. Alistar was right. He was not truly known by the Collective. Sharvesa would be the first to witness his glory. By the moment his transformation was complete, Alistar's overall height had increased two-fold.

Sharvesa's voice trembled. "I know you. I thought you had perished. I thought you all had perished before the Almighty's reign of a thousand seasons. How could you be here?"

"You were told wrong, Sharvesa. So were the others. You should stop wondering how, and start fearing my return." As Alistar spread his wings, a majestic, soft-white glow encompassed his being. He was beautiful, with long, flowing hair, a powerful frame and deep, blue eyes."

Sharvesa dropped to her knees. "Please ... please ... ease my mind, and don't leave me wondering. Are there more of you that survived?"

With his wings folding against unblemished armor, Alistar stepped forward and placed his hand on top of Sharvesa's head. It only took a touch— the softest touch—for a sense of peace to fill her being. "There are many others. It appears your memory is more intact than you led me to believe. I'd love to answer more of your questions, but alas, the moments are not available to me for a conversation of that magnitude."

Sharvesa nodded. "You're right. I don't need to understand. I would abandon my loyalty to the Collective to stand at your side. I'd follow you. Whatever you would have me do, I'd do it without waver."

Alistar reached down to caress Sharvesa's cheek with the backside of his fingers. "As pure as you proclaim your intentions are, you're a liability, and I need to know the extent of my power."

Sharvesa was quick to respond. "I could help you realize your power. Just give me the chance."

A tender smile appeared on Alistar's face. "I know you would try. And you should be rewarded for your loyalty, but the answer I seek demands that you be ended."

"But I could be of use to you," Sharvesa protested. "I don't care for the others. Let me prove myself. I can be everything you need me to be."

The god placed his hand under Sharvesa's chin and lifted her head. He bent down and kissed her softly on the lips. "I'm not strong enough to fight them all. I cannot risk the consequences of loose lips. Good-bye, Sharvesa."

The demon-goddess would have begged, but her ability to speak had been stripped. She would have stood, but her legs would no longer function. As tears welled in the corner of her eyes, she knew her sentence was extinction.

A moment later, Alistar buried his fist into Sharvesa's chest and ripped her soul from her body. Her corpse fell to the floor, and as her horns bounced against the marble, he devoured her spirit.

With the god standing over the demon's corpse, he whispered, "They're all fools. The Book's belief that he has control over me is a pleasant fiction. I so love the games the Collective plays. I'll enjoy the look on their faces once I reclaim enough of my former glory to make a stand with my brethren. Lasidious is a fool to believe that I was his brother, and I was a fool to believe that the Source would remain passive."

Looking down at Sharvesa's corpse, the god opened his mouth and fire erupted from it. The goddess' empty vessel turned to ash as Alistar knelt next to the pile, ingested the dust, licked his lips and then vanished.

MEANWHILE, NORTHERN GRAYHAM

With the water swelling inside the chasm that was left behind by the collapsed hollow, a young Isorian sergeant turned to flee his post. "Sire!" he shouted as he sprinted across the ice. "The gashtion approaches!"

The men of the Isorian and Tormalian armies had collected a massive amount of meat to set the trap. They had worked feverishly to place it in a gigantic pile near the edge of the chasm, and then they returned to the safety of the tunnel that led back to Hydroth.

With the sergeant jumping over the holes that had been torn into the ice by the gashtions' claws during their previous battle, Shiver, Gablysin, Gage, Gallrum, Medolas and the priestess were hiding inside one of the alcoves of safety. The king had chosen the nook just south of the one that had collapsed beneath the gashtions' weight. It was from this spot they intended to stage their offensive.

The king pulled his eyes off the runner and turned to address the ruby eyed man and the goswigs. "You must be bold, yet prudent. If the remainder of the priestess' plan fails, you must teleport to safety."

Gablysin knelt next to Gage. "We shall wait for the gashtion to consume the meat. Once its belly has been filled, teleport us to its location."

As the gashtion crested the cliffs that dropped into the chasm, it tore into the ice, sending chunks falling into the water. Not only did the beast use the claws of its feet, it also used a special claw that protruded from a joint on the front of each wing. With the gashtion's body being so enormous, its tail and hind legs remained in the water as it lowered its snout to sniff the pile of meat.

Gallrum peeked above the edge of the alcove. "It's so big. Are you sure we want to do this? This plan feels like a certain demise."

Medolas was quick to snap a response. "Clandestiny would've given her life's source for you! Would you turn your back on her?"

"Of course, not!" the king snapped back in defense of the goswig. A moment later, Shiver shook his head and sighed. "Must we start this again, Medolas? We all know Clandestiny's mettle and want to help her."

Medolas did not respond. Instead, he turned to watch the gashtion tear into the meat. A few moments later, he looked over his shoulder at the others and grinned. "It eats like Clandestiny."

With the others chuckling, Gallrum raised another question as he flew away from the opening of the alcove. "Priestess, are you sure there's no other way? We'll be so close to it. What if we're unable to teleport fast enough?"

Gage was the one to respond. "Just stay near me, and remember the task you were assigned. Don't take your focus off of the Tear. It is up to us to feed its power if the priestess' plan is to work."

Fosalia reached out and took hold of one of Gallrum's claws. "I'll be protecting you from here. You'll be shielded. The moments will be available for you to flee if needed."

"But what if the beast doesn't respond to Gablysin's song?" the serwin countered. "Are you sure we can focus on the Tear and still realize the moment to flee? What if the gashtion is too quick and breaks through your magic like it broke through our wall during the battle? We'll be squashed."

Shiver looked at the priestess. "The goswig has a point. Are your sure your magic is strong enough to hold the weight?"

"Yes, Your Grace, I'm more than confident. The barrier will hold."

With the pile of meat nearly gone, Medolas had heard enough quibbling. Despite the gashtion's size, he did not believe Clandestiny would hurt him. And if it was not Clandestiny who had survived the battle between the gashtions, he did not want to live without her. With the others debating, Medolas quietly crawled out of the alcove and began running toward the edge of the chasm. He lifted his hand and shouted before the others realized he was gone. "Clandestiny!"

Hearing his friend's insanity, Shiver ran to the opening of the alcove and called for Medolas to stop, but the king's order was discarded.

With the meat still holding the gashtion's attention, Medolas was able to close the distance before Clandestiny finished licking the ice. He waved his arms and shouted again. "Clandestiny, it's me ... your Meddy! You must come back to me and remember who you are! We are to unite!"

"He's a fool!" Gablysin shouted as the gashtion lifted its head skyward and roared. "He's going to become part of the feast."

Shiver placed his hand on Gablysin's shoulder as the ruby eyed man was about to crawl out of the hole. "Wait. Fosalia, place a barrier around Medolas."

Fosalia shook her head. "I can only do it once, Your Grace. Would you have me waste it now? We only have one opportunity for success."

Hearing the priestess' response, Gabs' eyes filled with anger. "Medolas is not a waste. Put up the barrier."

"No!" Shiver rebutted. "She's right. We cannot allow our emotions to control our actions. If that fool wishes to sacrifice his life's source, then there's nothing we shall do to stop him. We stick to the plan."

<hr />

Clandestiny lowered her eyes after she finished her ferocious roar and focused on Medolas' tiny form. She felt he was familiar, but she could not understand what he was shouting. Her instinct was calling for blood, yet something inside was pulling her in another direction. She snorted and then lowered to sniff Medolas' scent.

<hr />

With the gashtion lowering its snout, the ruby eyed man reached out and grasped Shiver's arm. "I hope it's her and that her love for him has remained steadfast." He looked out across the ice and pleaded, "Please, be Clandestiny."

Shiver shook his head. "Medolas is either an imbecile, or the bravest Isorian I know."

Using his magic to hold himself high enough to see above the ledge of the alcove, Gage added, "Perhaps he believes the gashtion will proclaim him a bite not worth taking."

"I vote for imbecile," Gallrum announced with his claws digging into the ice.

Medolas' smell was inviting. The memories of their moments together were fighting their way to the forefront of Clandestiny's mind, yet she was unable to recognize them as thoughts of a life past. All she understood was that this being gave her a sense of comfort, and devouring him, no matter how large her desire to consume, did not feel right.

As her moments passed, the comfort Medolas offered was beginning to be overshadowed by hunger. She sniffed again, but during this moment, she took in a much longer whiff. Another long period followed while the gashtion loomed above Medolas—the drool from her lips plopped onto the ice all around the Isorian as she struggled with the turmoil that was growing in her mind.

"Disgusting," Gallrum groaned as a mound of the gashtion's drool pooled at Medolas' feet.

The badger's nose crinkled. "I second that."

"Do you think he's winning it over?" Shiver queried. A few moments later, the king patted the ruby eyed man on the back. "Gabs, it must be Clandestiny. Look ... her eyes."

"You're right. They're softening. I think she recognizes him."

Fosalia placed her hand on Shiver's shoulder. "But she should be transforming by now. Medolas' love for her must not be enough to trigger her desire to change. Perhaps you should join them. The face of another friend might help."

A look of disbelief appeared on Shiver's face. "You cannot be of sound mind. I'm not going out there."

With Medolas' hand touching the end of Clandestiny's snout, she closed her eyes. His touch was familiar, and she could feel the gentleness of his caress. As he continued to call out her name and profess his love, the language was beginning to make sense. His tone gave her a sense of belonging, and she did not want to leave.

Another long period of moments passed, and still the transformation did not happen.

"Someone needs to intervene before she decides to return to the ocean," Fosalia warned. "The longer Clandestiny stays in this form, the greater the chances are that she'll never return to the being whom you love."

"That would be unacceptable," Gage responded. The badger faced Shiver. "What are your orders? You must make a decision."

The king sighed. "I don't know what to do. I struggle to employ good thought. What do you think, Gabs?"

The ruby eyed man shrugged. "The answer evades me as well. I don't know what to think."

"Well, I do," Gallrum announced. "I'm staying right here. He's doing just fine without us."

Gage struck the serwin on his tail and gave him a look.

"What?" the serwin groaned as he lifted his tail to rub out the sting. "Just look at her fangs."

With Medolas continuing to express his love, Clanny's mind was becoming more in tune with him by the moment. *Oh, Meddy, it's me,* she wanted to express, but her mouth was unable to utter the words. *I love you, too, but this power ... this energy ... the dominance ... it's all so intoxicating. Join me, my love.*

When next Medolas spoke, it felt as if he was responding to her thoughts. "I would join you if I could, Clanny, but I can't. You must return to me. There's nothing to stop us from uniting. After 300 seasons, we can express our love the way we've always desired."

Another fair series of moments passed as Medolas continued to entice Clandestiny into making the change. She was about to surrender and begin the transformation when Shiver's voice insulted the evening air and ruined the peace that was filling her moments.

"Clandestiny! We all love you!" the king called from a distance. "Come back to us!"

Before another word could be uttered, the gashtion lifted her head and let out an angry roar. Clandestiny was able to remember the way Shiver had tried to undermine her relationship with Medolas when they were young. Of all beings to step out of the alcove, the king was the worst choice the priestess could have recommended.

Medolas tried to fix the damage. "It's okay, Clanny!" he shouted. "Look at me! Look down at the one you love! I'm here for you!"

Clanny refused to pull her glare off Shiver.

Medolas turned to find the king. "Go back! We're fine without you!"

As Clandestiny continued to stare at Shiver, her dislike for the king forced what was left of her desire to transform to the back of her mind. Medolas' words became unclear as his expression of love no longer carried meaning. The comfort she had allowed herself to feel was consumed by rage, and once again he became foreign to her.

As her jowls pulled back, her teeth were exposed. A moment later, Clandestiny dropped her mouth to the ice. Her jaw snapped shut as Medolas jumped to avoid the deadly points of her teeth.

"Noooooooo!" Shiver screamed as Clandestiny lifted her head and swallowed Medolas whole, her massive Adam's apple traveling the length of her neck as she did.

Gablysin was quick to react. He grabbed Gallrum's claw with his left hand and touched Gage on the shoulder with his right. "We go now! Take us onto the ice!"

As soon as Gallrum's eyes closed, they vanished and reappeared below the head of the gashtion. The priestess extended her arms and used her power to place a bubble of protection around them.

Clandestiny lifted her massive claw and brought it down on top of the trio, but as promised, the barrier held firm.

Gallrum screamed, "We must flee!"

Gage quickly turned and hit Gallrum on his tail with his cane again. "Focus on the Tear, or we'll perish!"

"But—"

"But nothing!" the badger scolded. "Focus!"

With Gablysin lifting the Tear of Gramal toward the gashtion, Gage and Gallrum set their eyes on the crystal as it began to glow. The ruby eyed man's mouth opened and a song penetrated the air.

Again, Clandestiny's claw smashed against the barrier, but Gablysin and the goswigs stood their ground. The ruby eyed man closed his eyes and put all of his love for Clandestiny into every lyric. As the mood of the song increased, so did the light that emanated from the Tear.

The gashtion's claw pounded against the barrier on four more occasions before Clandestiny was affected by the mood of the ruby eyed man's song. Rather than strike the barrier again, she dug her claws into the ice, lowered her eyes near the bubble and stopped growling.

Many moments passed as what was left of the sun fell below the horizon, and many more moments would pass before the rage that consumed Clandestiny would soften enough so that she could once again understand the Isorian language.

Seeing the shift in Clandestiny's demeanor, Gablysin changed the lyrics to speak of her life with Medolas. The song spoke of their Peaks as children—Peaks when they would hide to enjoy one another's company. The lyrics further spoke of the tales Medolas had told the ruby eyed man upon their return from their journey to find the Ko-dess, and how, through it all, the obstacles they faced only managed to strengthen their love.

By the moment Gablysin had repeated the lyrics for the tenth occasion, Gallrum broke his concentration and whispered to Gage, "Is she ever going to change? We cannot stay here all night."

The break in the goswigs' focus on the Tear effected the power of the ruby eyed man's song. Clandestiny lifted her right front claw and growled as she brought it down on top of the barrier.

With her foot lifting for another strike, Gage barked an order. "Gallrum, focus, damn you! You're going to get us slaughtered!"

The badger no sooner finished his chastisement of the serwin when Clandestiny's claw smashed against the barrier again. She would strike on two more occasions before her mood would soften enough to once again listen to the song.

Back inside the alcove, Shiver had reclaimed his position in the alcove and was remaining out of sight when Fosalia dropped her hands to her sides. "I can do nothing more," she conceded. "If the gashtion strikes again, the barrier will collapse. They'll be forced to flee."

"But if they flee, Clandestiny will be lost to us," Shiver argued.

The priestess looked across the ice. "She may be lost already. She should've transformed by now. There's nothing else I can do."

As Shiver swallowed at the thought, a long strand of drool fell from Clandestiny's jowls. It smothered the bubble and rolled toward the ice as it followed the arc of the barrier's circumference.

The king pulled his eyes off the gashtion. "What about the Tear? Priestess, focus what's left of your energy on the Tear. Perhaps it would help."

Fosalia did not argue. She looked across the ice and concentrated on the light emerging from the ruby eyed man's palm. A moment later, the light intensified.

"It's working!" Shiver exclaimed. "Focus harder, Priestess! Focus!"

With the estimated series of moments of Midnight approaching, Clandestiny finally surrendered. The song brought tears to her dragon eyes as the memories of all that was good about Medolas consumed her mind.

Seeing the change in the gashtion's posture, the ruby eyed man changed the song. He spoke of how Clandestiny needed to release Medolas from her belly and help prepare the celebration of his passing. She would further need to return to her true form so that she could kiss Medolas goodbye.

Gablysin would repeat the lyrics of this subtle demand on 27 more occasions before the dragon finally opened her mouth. She regurgitated Medolas' lifeless form onto the ice, but before Clandestiny surrendered to the transformation, she lowered an eye above his corpse and then used her tears to wash his body clean.

"It worked!" Shiver boasted from inside the alcove. "She's changing!"

Fosalia pulled her eyes off the Tear. They were bloodshot. She had been so focused on the crystal that the news of the gashtion's transformation caught her by surprise. She closed her eyes, and a moment later, the exhaustion from her excessive use of power consumed her being. She collapsed to the ice.

THE NEXT MORNING
THE LANDS OF THE NEW HEAVEN

Anahita shut the ancient tome the Archangel Michael had left behind and leaned back against one of the knuckles on top of the Source's right front claw. "Would you stop that?" she chastised as she lowered the tome onto the dragon's foot.

Dorick smiled as smoke rolled past his eyes. "Why, Child?" The dwarf lowered the pipe the Source had created for him to his lap and then reached down to pat the top of the Ancient One's foot. "If the big guy approves, who am I to argue? This weed is divine."

The angel looked up and found one of the dragon's massive pupils. "I know you said that smoking the leaves of the bagges flower would help a mortal's mind comprehend the words written on the pages of this book, but I fear the plant you taught me to create has spawned an addict. Perhaps you should tell Dorick not to abuse the privilege."

Before the Ancient One could respond, the dwarf smirked. "I'm hungry."

The Source's booming laugh forced Dorick to cover his ears. "You cannot fault him for his enjoyment of the moment. Who is the dwarf harming, and what rule is he breaking here on a world where no beings have yet to establish law? For now, allow the dwarf his amusement. When the moment arrives, I shall cleanse his being before I send him back to the worlds."

Dorick stopped snickering. "Am I to be sent back then? Which world will I be sent to?"

The Source lowered his head to the ground. "The beings who call themselves gods have yet to allow the races to merge. Considering your current form, I don't wish to draw unwanted attention to my plans. I intend to place you on Trollcom."

The dwarf scowled. "When I was on Grayham, I read about Trollcom. I know the trolls on that world enslave the dwarves. I don't want to be a slave, Mighty One."

"Nor do I want him to be a slave," Anahita added. "Why does he have to return to the worlds for heaven's sake? Why can't you let him stay with me?"

The Source took a deep breath of the field filled with flowers that extended as far as his eyes could see. This field was the best of Anahita's creations to date. "I have plans for Dorick. The dwarves on Trollcom must be liberated. They have suffered for far too many seasons, and this shall be his calling."

"That's no small task," Anahita replied. "What can one dwarf do to change the fate of a race?"

The dragon smiled. "And if no dwarf was to ever make a stand, would change occur? Too long have I allowed the failings of the Collective to effect the lives of their creations. There is too much that is perfect with what exists on this plane to continue to do nothing. The moments have come for me to influence the direction of things with a few subtle adjustments."

Dorick lifted his pipe and took a puff. "If liberating a populace is considered a subtle adjustment in your mind, I'd be interested to hear what a monumental adjustment would be." The dwarf hoisted his pipe in the direction of the dragon's mouth. "Perhaps you should be smoking one of these yourself."

As the dragon smirked, Dorick added, "Did I mention, I'm hungry?"

Anahita rolled her eyes. "You're not hungry. You have the munchies."

The Ancient One rose to his feet. When the earth stopped shaking, the dragon spoke. "That is enough talk for now, little ones. The moment has come for Anahita to create my new home. Please don't disappoint."

"No pressure there," Anahita jested. The angel touched the dwarf on the shoulder and then teleported to the top of the dragon's snout. "How would you like a mountain range, a lake and a nice cave that would provide space to expand your wings when you stretch?"

The Source closed one eye so that he would not go cross-eyed when he looked at the angel. "Your suggestions sound wonderful, Anahita. Begin your creations."

Anahita turned to look out across the valley. She lifted her arms and was about to utter the language of the Titans when smoke from Dorick's pipe drifted past her eyes. She looked down at the dwarf. "Must you? I cannot concentrate."

Dorick quickly removed the pipe from his mouth. "My apologies, Child." He tucked the stem of the pipe into the pocket of his pants and left the bowl exposed.

Again, Anahita looked out across the valley and lifted her arms. Her voice was strong as her hands began to circle. *"Faragrosey a men yan, four tuadus diplomas menswallas!"*

The earth began to shake and open as the peaks of mountains erupted from beneath the surface and shot skyward to a height of more than 25,000 paces. At the base of the mountains, a hole opened and fresh water was rushing in to fill the expanse of the crater. By the moment Anahita was finished creating, a valley filled with succulent flora stretched before the trio, and 4,000 head of corgan were roaming from which the Source could feed at his leisure.

Seeing the beauty of the valley, the Source lowered his head and allowed his company to float to the ground before he sniffed the tree tops. "You did well, Anahita. I believe you're getting the hang of creating. Now you shall have a peak to stand upon in my absence."

The angel grinned. "I have often wondered why mountain ranges were so scattered. Now I know it's because the gods needed them to stand on while they sculpted their creations." Anahita found the Source's open eye. "But I don't imagine they had your snout to stand on when the worlds were first created, did they? Something tells me you didn't offer them any help."

"Let us say this: what took the Collective of 'so-called' gods 800 seasons to create, I could have created in 7 Peaks."

Anahita gasped. "You make yourself sound like the Almighty. Are you God?"

"No, no, no, Anahita, but I know him, and he's displeased. Don't allow the power you've been given to change you. You'll never be a real god, nor will the others who claim to be gods. There is only one Almighty. Never forget that, Anahita."

"Goodness-gracious ... a chill just ran up my spine."

"And mine, too, Child," Dorick added, "though I don't know why."

Anahita smirked and then patted the dwarf on the shoulder. "If the Collective is pretending to be gods and the Almighty is displeased," she looked up at the Source, "then why does he allow it? Why was Michael allowed to pretend to be a god when he was known to the Collective as Bassorine? And how could he tell me with a straight face that he was doing his father's will if he has been continuing to play the same game the others are?"

The Source snorted his irritation and then lowered his mass onto the ground. "I've chastised Michael, Gabriel, and Zerachiel on many occasions. They know they'll never see the beauty of the one true Heaven again. They're doomed to spend the rest of eternity on this plane, and they shall never know the Almighty's presence."

"Hold on a moment. When I was in the shack ... this was just before Michael restored my wings, he said his father was calling him. Was he lying?"

The Source closed his eyes and shook his massive head. "Yes, Anahita. I assure you, God has forsaken these worlds. It is I who has been assigned the task of ensuring the archangels never escape this plane. This is their Hell now, and Michael, Gabriel, and Zerachiel know that it'll never be as glorious as the Heaven they abandoned to rescue you from Lucifer."

The dragon frowned. "It pains me to say this, Anahita, but your Heaven will fall short of the beauty that existed beyond the pearly gates, but it will suffice to establish a new order on this plane. Anything more, I care not to discuss. The misdoings of those that call themselves gods is not a topic that I care to expand upon."

The angel put her hand to her chin in thought. "Can you at least answer one other question? I promise to make it quick."

The dragon nodded.

"I suppose my question would be: are there other beings who claim to be gods existing on the worlds? I'm speaking of beings who do not sit at the table of the Collective."

The Source nodded. "Yes, Anahita. The Collective is naive to believe that they're the only beings to survive the wars that happened on this plane. Zeus, Hera and many others exist in hiding beneath the noses of those who claim to be gods. I shall further say that there is one who sits at the table of the Collective that has deceived them all."

"Which one?" Anahita inquired. "And what is his real identity? I must know."

"I also want to know," the dwarf encouraged as he took a drag of his pipe.

The Source chuckled. "Even if I was to tell you, Dorick, you wouldn't remember once I deliver you to Trollcom. Once you are placed on that world, you won't remember Anahita, me, or what your eyes have witnessed of her creations. All you will know when you open your eyes for the first moment inside the home I shall provide is that you'll have a desire to bring about change and free all dwarves from the enslavement of trolls. Not only will you fight for their freedom, you'll fight for the freedom of the lizardians."

Dorick lifted his pipe and started puffing. "And how do you expect me to do all that? What power will I have to force change upon kingdoms?"

"Not force, Dorick ... entice. You'll be given enough magic to protect yourself and the family you'll create. You'll have the charisma to match an ardent wit, and if you remain humble, the masses will follow you."

The dwarf pulled the pipe from his mouth and blew the smoke to the side. "And if I fail to remain humble, what then?"

The dragon lowered his snout. His eyes spoke before he even opened his mouth. "Humility can be a funny thing. It can be stronger than the mightiest blade and crippling to the being who fails to wield it properly. Do you understand my meaning?"

The dwarf nodded. "I understand. You're saying I best not mess up. But if I do this, I get to keep my pipe."

Both Anahita and the Source chuckled as Dorick reached up to cover his ears. Eventually, the dragon stopped laughing and responded. "I will allow you to keep your pipe."

HARVESTOM, THE HIGH PRIESTESS' PALACE
2 MORE PEAKS HAVE PASSED, LATE BAILEM

THE AREA SURROUNDING THE PRIESTESS' PALACE

Mosley lifted his head and looked toward the shoreline to the north. None of the trees on the priestess' island had been marked, and he was enjoying his moments as he trotted between them to claim the territory. After his thirtieth tree and twenty-first stone, he stopped, looked toward the clouds and spoke aloud. "When do you intend to return, Sharvesa? I grow impatient. It has been more than 6 Peaks."

As the wolf continued his exploration of the island, a familiar face appeared near one of the evergreens he intended to mark. "Good evening, Mosley," Celestria greeted. "I trust you're well."

The wolf lowered his hind leg after giving the bark a squirt. "Why have you come, Celestria?"

"I've come to ensure that you don't waste anymore of your moments on Harvestom. Sharvesa won't be returning. She has been detained."

The skin between the wolf's eyes wrinkled. "How has she been detained?"

"I can't say. Alistar was the last being to speak with her. All I know is that you should make your way to this world's Merchant Island and continue your quest for the power you seek. Once you acquire it, I've been advised that it won't be in your best interest to use it as you had originally intended."

"Please explain," the wolf demanded. "I won't abandon my quest to end George and Kepler."

"Your desire to destroy the jaguar is acceptable, but you're going to need George. You may end him however you wish once your task is complete."

"What kind of task?" the wolf sneered. "And why should I spare the human because of it?"

"Because he'll be necessary if you're to succeed in your new mission to destroy Lasidious."

A deeper look of confusion appeared on Mosley's face. "I have no such mission. Lasidious has done me no wrong. Why would I seek his demise?"

The goddess knelt in front of the wolf and reached out to scratch the bottom of his chin. "Lasidious' intent is to bring the worlds under his control. If this happens, darkness will be his main theme. You don't want to live in darkness, do you Mosley?"

The wolf shook his head. "Of course, not." Lowering to his haunches, he inquired, "What could've happened that would cause you to turn against him in this fashion? What are you not telling me?"

Celestria smiled as she stood to walk toward the beach. "Come with me. It's a nice evening for a stroll. Don't you agree?"

As the goddess walked away, Mosley looked back and forth from the base of the next tree to Celestria. No matter how large his curiosity of the goddess' reasons for abandoning her relationship with Lasidious, he desperately did not want to leave the area without claiming as much of it as he could. He dropped his head to the ground and sighed. "It's moments like these when I miss being a god." He lifted his head and addressed the terrain. "I could've marked you all at once."

"Are you coming, Mosley?" Celestria shouted, calling over her shoulder. I don't have all Peak!"

Darting to the next tree, the wolf quickly lifted his leg, gave it a squirt and then ran to catch up.

As they continued to walk toward the beach, the goddess reached down and patted the wolf on the side of his neck.

"I asked ... what are you not telling me?"

"Mosley, there's so much I'm not confessing, but you must know that I do it for your safety. The less you know, the better your chances of success." The goddess reached down and lifted the wolf's snout so she could find his eyes. "You must return to the Wisp of Song on Southern Grayham. He's waiting for you."

"Why would Cadromel be waiting for me?" Mosley suspiciously questioned. "You know that I no longer need his assistance to acquire the power of the Ancient Mystics or the Swayne Enserad. I simply need to learn how to release the power within the words. That's what Sharvesa was teaching me since the priestess was unqualified to do so."

Celestria nodded. "Fosalia has many weaknesses to be allowed to hold the position of High Priestess. I was shocked to learn that the Source objected to her removal."

The wolf shrugged. "How am I to know the dragon's mind? To second guess the Mighty One's decisions would be a waste of our moments." Seeing a bush nearby, Mosley trotted over to it and sniffed at its base. A moment later, he squatted and a look of concentration appeared on his face.

The goddess' tone was filled with disgust. "Must you, Mosley? How can a being as adorable as you be so repulsive during the same moments? It makes me wonder why I chose to help you."

After scratching at the earth with his rear paws, the wolf turned to sniff the pile before he responded. "You're not the only member of the Collective who has been revolted by my actions, yet I fail to comprehend why. Would the gods have me expel waste in any other fashion?"

Celestria crossed her arms. "Of course, I would. I'd have you wait until I had departed. No one wants to see you garesh. It's revolting. How could a being of your intelligence not know to do your business in private?"

The night terror wolf looked at the pile, back at the goddess and then shrugged. "Perhaps you're too sensitive. I see nothing wrong with my actions."

The goddess dropped her arms and groaned. "I suppose you wouldn't. Let's change this subject, shall we?"

Mosley trotted back to Celestria and took a seat. As he spoke, he reached up with his back paw to scratch his neck. "I'm listening. Why must I seek an audience with Cadromel?"

The goddess was about to respond when she noticed a small boat that had been pulled onto the shore not far away. For no reason, she extended her arm and sent the craft floating across the water. "It's against the laws of the gods to tell a mortal how to find the power of the Titans, but Cadromel isn't a god."

"Then you want me to seek Cadromel so he can send me on another hunt?"

"Yes, but this won't be just any hunt. Cadromel is a Titan, and he can—"

"Stop," Mosley interrupted. "I thought the dragons were the only beings to hold the title of Titan."

Celestria frowned at the abruptness of Mosley's interruption. "You're correct, but I've recently learned that the wisp has an alternate form."

"What kind of form?"

Rather than respond right away, Celestria walked to the edge of the water and passed her hand across the top of it. Only a moment or two passed before an image began to form. The image was that of the wisp, and as Mosley stared into the water, Cadromel transformed into a magnificent dragon. His body glowed and a storm of electrical fury raged beneath his scales, almost as if lightning was emerging from the center of his being.

"I had no idea," Mosley confessed. "He's beautiful ... like nothing I've ever seen before. How could I have not known?"

"You're not the only being without this knowledge. There are few who know. Even amongst the Collective, only two share this knowledge."

The wolf did not remove his eyes from the image as the conversation continued. The dragon's beauty required as much. "Then it's Cadromel who is to be my teacher."

Celestria nodded. "The dragon has agreed to impart the knowledge of how to release the power hidden within the language of the Titans once he has completed your training with the languages of the Ancient Mystics and the Swayne Enserad."

A fair series of moments passed while Mosley pondered the goddess' words. "Why would the wisp offer instruction?"

Celestria laughed. "Silly wolf ... he won't simply offer instruction. He'll expect knowledge in return. The wisp is a curious being, and since the Collective has forced him to stay within the mist beneath the falls on Southern Grayham, he desperately wants to know the secrets of the other worlds."

"What world does the wisp want me to retrieve these secrets from?"

"I can't say. That would be yet another secret the wisp chose to keep to himself."

"Don't you mean dragon?"

"Dragon ... wisp ... I care not how he's identified. We're referring to the same being, are we not?"

Mosley pulled his eyes away from the vision in the water. "Why would Cadromel agree to teach me a language that would make me as powerful as he is?"

Celestria shook her head. "I don't know, Mosley. Alistar was the one to speak with the wisp ... the dragon ... the whatever. Perhaps you should ask Cadromel these questions. I'm sure his reasons are epic in nature."

"Epic, indeed," Mosley agreed. "But you have yet to tell me why Lasidious must be destroyed, and why George must be the one I hunt with?"

Celestria chuckled. "You'll never change, Mosley. You're an inquisitive beast. Further questions will need to be asked of Cadromel. I'd take you to the wisp myself, but I cannot."

"What would stop you?" Mosley argued. "Is it against the laws of the gods?"

Rather than answer, the goddess knelt next to the wolf and kissed the end of his nose. "Travel safely, my friend. Know that I wish no harm to befall you." The goddess dropped two Lasidious coins onto the ground. "Your ride with the Merchant Angels will be costly." Celestria vanished.

Mosley looked down at the coins and growled. "Curse the gods! I have so many questions."

ANCIENTS SOVEREIGN
BENEATH THE PEAKS OF ANGELS
THE NEXT MORNING

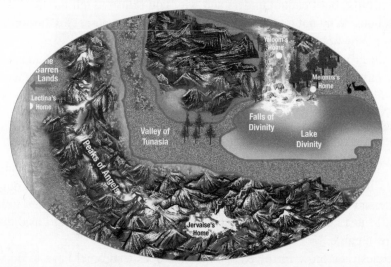

When Celestria returned to her home the following morning, she appeared inside her bedroom chamber. She looked across the room toward the bed and smiled at the being who was lying beneath the covers, waiting. "It is finished."

The God of the Harvest threw back the covers and patted the top of the mattress filled with vestle chick feathers. "Is the wolf on his way to Grayham?"

"He is," the goddess confirmed.

"What about Cadromel? Did you speak with him?"

"It took all night to find him. The mist was thick, and I believe he chose to be elusive ... but I did speak with him. He knows the wolf is coming."

"What about Gabriel? Will the Book fulfill his part?"

Celestria dropped her dress to the floor. "Did I not already say that it was finished when I appeared?"

Alistar grinned. "My apologies. I'm simply being cautious." He patted the mattress again. "Come close, and place your head on my chest. I sense you have more questions."

The goddess refrained. "I'll place my head on your chest only after your answers are to my satisfaction."

"Fair enough," Alistar conceded. "What would you like to know?"

Celestria leaned back against the headboard and brought up her knees to cover her bosom. "I can understand why Garrin must be left in the care of the Vampire Queen until we find a way to wean him from his addiction to her milk, but I cannot understand why you refuse to tell the Book about Lasidious. Why not let Gabriel know that Lasidious possesses Tardon's old body? Why not allow the Book to end the charade?"

Alistar pushed back the sheets and stood from the bed. "Too many seasons have I followed Lasidious, and during that entire series of moments, it was all about him ... his glory ... his power ... his desire to control the Collective. I've had enough of that."

"So, you seek vengeance," Celestria concluded. "You're angry with him."

"Angry doesn't describe my hatred for him. He'll suffer beyond suffering. I'll see that he wallows in misery, and each morning he'll call out my name and beg for mercy before I'm finished with him. But for that to happen, I must keep his identity a secret from the Book and beat Lasidious at his own game."

Celestria's brow furrowed. "What else does Cadromel have to do with your plotting? I know you're not telling me everything. You may want me at your side, but you're not being forthcoming."

Alistar walked around the bed and took a seat next to the goddess. "I'll never keep your mind in darkness the way Lasidious did. All you need to do is ask, and I'll tell you anything you want to know."

"Then tell me of Cadromel."

Alistar reached out and took hold of the goddess' left foot. He then scooted back to the far end of the mattress and began rubbing it. "With the help of Cadromel, I intend to seize control of the worlds ... and the Source. The gods, however, will fall in my wake."

Celestria gasped. "You're insane. You cannot defeat the Source. That's impossible. The Mighty One would summon the Almighty's army, and they would squash us all like bugs."

Alistar laughed. "I knew you'd say that, but you needn't worry. You're the one that I've longed for for more seasons than I can remember. I won't fail you. You'll be the glory that stands at my side for the rest of eternity, and my nephew ... your son ... shall reign with us as a beacon of power on the Heaven that the Source is creating."

Celestria pulled her foot away and moved closer. "You're going to be the end of us. I don't want to perish."

The God of the Harvest leaned forward and gently kissed his new lover's cheek. "There are many things we need to discuss. But first, let us speak of Michael. The Collective is fuming about his return..."

MEANWHILE, NORTHERN GRAYHAM
THE HEALER'S VESTRY INSIDE THE UNDERCASTLE

Fellow soul ... Gage and Gallrum huddled next to the bed of the priestess after they returned from the edge of the chasm. Fosalia's use of power had been tremendous, and it had taken nearly all of her strength to keep the weight of the gashtion from squashing the goswigs. And if that had not been enough, the energy she expended while focusing on the Tear during Clandestiny's transformation had proven to be too much. After her collapse, she remained unconscious, and the healers were unable to assist in her recovery.

With Gablysin's lack of understanding of the Tear, the ruby eyed man reluctantly gave the crystal back to Clandestiny. In exchange, Clanny agreed to allow Gabs to stay at her side. Since that moment, they remained inside a separate room in the healer's vestry where Clandestiny refused to allow the healers to take Medolas' corpse to the morticians to prepare it for his Passing Ceremony. Those Isorians who tried to argue were frightened away as soon as the slits of her dragon eyes appeared to emphasize her control.

It was not until Late Bailem when Fosalia opened her eyes.

"Good evening, Priestess," Gallrum said with a soft voice as he hovered at the foot of the bed, just high enough to peak over the mound of furs and hides the priestess had been sleeping between. "We thought you'd never wake."

With the badger hopping up onto a block of ice that had been placed beside the bed, Fosalia licked her lips as she pulled her arms from under the covers. "I'm thirsty." Her belly growled. It was loud enough it could be heard through the layers. "And hungry!"

Gage smiled as he looked across the room at a healer who was attending to a young boy. The badger tapped his cane against the block. "The priestess is awake. Send for food and water." Seeing the healer was not going to move fast enough, the badger teleported into the royal kitchen and snagged a loaf of bread and a block of ice that had been made of fresh water.

When Gage reappeared next to Fosalia's bed, he placed the ice in a bowl that was sitting on a nightstand carved out of the element. He then used his power to melt the block and then served the water to the priestess.

With Fosalia's belly satisfied, the goswigs led her out of the room into a hallway and stopped outside the next door. Clandestiny and Gablysin were behind it, sitting next to Medolas' corpse.

The badger warned, "Before you enter, Priestess, Clandestiny has refused to allow anyone near the body. She has been unable to let go and cannot accept that Medolas needs to be prepared for his Passing Ceremony. Be careful when you approach, or she won't allow you to remain in the room."

Fosalia looked through a clear piece of ice that served as a window for the door. Clandestiny was sitting in a chair with Medolas' hand placed against her cheek. "Then she remains unstable."

The badger shook his head. "Not entirely, but it doesn't take much to annoy her."

Gallrum chuckled. "You could say that again. Clandestiny has threatened to eat everyone who has tried to take the body away."

Gage smacked Gallrum's tail with his cane. "You're not funny. Her mental state is no laughing matter."

The priestess looked back through the window. Gablysin was on his knees at the foot of the bed that Medolas was lying on, and it appeared the ruby eyed man was praying to Helmep. Fosalia focused on his chest. "Where's the Tear? Why isn't it around his neck?"

"He gave it back to Clandestiny," Gage responded.

"Why would he do such a thing? I already gave him the blessing. The Tear would've been fine where it was until I awoke."

"Clandestiny insisted," Gallrum inserted.

"Whether she insisted or not, the Tear should not have been returned. She has demonstrated that she cannot handle the burden of power."

"I'm afraid it's not that simple," Gage rebutted. "Clandestiny no longer needs the Tear to transform."

"That's impossible," Fosalia argued.

"Apparently it isn't." The badger moved to the far side of the hallway and called the priestess to him. "The ice of the door is thin. We cannot allow her to hear us. It appears the power of the Tear has become a natural part of Clandestiny. Gablysin was forced to give her the crystal because he didn't have an understanding of how to use the Tear to argue against her wishes. He figured it best to keep the peace."

Fosalia looked back toward the door. "Perhaps he was right. If Clandestiny no longer needs the Tear, the power inside the crystal was even beyond my mother's comprehension."

Gallrum looked in the window and then hovered across the hallway to join them. "The Isorians are facing a bigger problem than Clandestiny's refusal to allow Medolas' body to be prepared for his passing. In her grief, she has vowed to return to the ocean as soon as Medolas has been cast into it."

The priestess' heart sank. "This isn't good. She would become the beast the Isorians fear most."

The serwin hovered closer and dropped the level of his voice. "I hate to say it, but Clandestiny needs to be ended. The Isorians cannot afford for her to reassume the form of the gashtion. Who knows what havoc she would wreak on Hydroth if she returns to the ocean without dealing with her grief?"

Gage interjected, "We believe there's no other choice but to have a Passing Ceremony for two."

The hallway fell silent as Fosalia returned to the window. She could see the yellow-blood stain from Clandestiny's tears. They had become a part of the ice that Medolas' bed had been chiseled from. "I don't see the Tear around Clandestiny's neck. Where is it?"

"It is clenched in the palm of her right hand," the badger responded. "It has been there for 5 Peaks."

After taking note of the small piece of the leather strap that protruded from the bottom of Clandestiny's fist, the priestess returned to the far side of the hallway. "Ending Clandestiny's life is unacceptable. The burden of the Tear would need to pass to someone else. It isn't Clandestiny's fault that she was chosen."

The badger looked up. "Fault or not, Clandestiny is a threat to the Isorian people. There's a great possibility that she would not be like the other gashtions. She knows the people live beneath the ice. What if she remembers this after she returns to the ocean? The people would never be safe. There would be no place for them to flee."

"I believe he's right," Gallrum added. "Unless you have a solution, I still say Clandestiny must perish, and only you, Priestess, have the power to end her. You might have to forego your vows to save a race."

Fosalia took a moment to ponder the goswigs' words. "Have you spoken to the king about this?"

Gage nodded. "We have."

"What was his response?"

"As much as it saddens him, His Grace believes we're correct. There may be no other choice but to end Clandestiny's life's source. But his desire was to speak with you once you were awake."

"Where is the king now?"

"He's in the undercastle," Gallrum responded. "He's working with the leaders of the armies to determine how to unite the kingdoms. He waited 2 Peaks for you to wake before he returned to his duties as sovereign."

Fosalia leaned against the wall. "This is an impossible situation. I can't abandon my vows. To do so would bring an end to my own life."

"I don't understand," Gage responded. "How does breaking a vow end your life?"

Fosalia's exhale extended over a long series of moments. "You needn't understand for it to be the truth. For me to murder Clandestiny would carry with it an eternal sentence."

"But to end Clandestiny would save a people," Gallrum insisted. "Clandestiny would return to the ocean, and the Isor would suffer. You must understand that." The serwin looked down at his claws. "I would do the deed myself, but my power has already proven to be ineffective against her ... even with Gage's help."

The priestess shook her head. "For me to take Clandestiny's life needlessly ends two. I'll hear no more of this." Without saying another word, Fosalia walked across the hall, pushed through the door and entered the room.

Gage looked up at Gallrum, shrugged and then followed.

Lowering to her knees on the opposite side of the bed, the priestess bowed her head and said a quick prayer to Helmep before she found Clandestiny's eyes. "I've been told you intend to return to the ocean."

Clandestiny did not respond immediately. Instead, she placed Medolas' hand on his stomach. With the rigor mortis that had set in, the task proved to be a challenge. "Priestess, if you're here to convince me otherwise, you should hold your breath. I will follow my Meddy to the sea. There's nothing for me here now."

"What of your friends? Would you risk their safety to run from your grief?"

Clandestiny closed her eyes. When she reopened them, her beautiful gray irises had been replaced by yellow ones and two elongated, black slits acted like pupils as a darkness appeared on her face. "My decision has been made. Would you challenge it?"

Gablysin spoke out. "Priestess, perhaps it's best to allow Clandestiny her escape. For more seasons than I've existed, our people have fought off the gashtion. I have spoken with Clandestiny, and we've come to a compromise. She has agreed to allow the Isor to relocate to Gesper before she returns to the ocean. She still cares for our well-being. Our people will be safe in the west."

Hearing that Clandestiny would be all alone in frigid waters broke Fosalia's heart. Though her magic was protecting her from the cold, her power did not stop the chill of the air from freezing her tears once they rolled from her eyes and dropped from her cheeks. She had vowed to heal at any cost, and she would be unable to live with herself if she did not do everything within her power to take Clanny's pain from her.

"You should retire to your world, Priestess," Clandestiny said as she stood from the side of the bed. "You should not be near Hydroth once the city has been abandoned. I intend to destroy all memories of the Isor and ensure all traces of my Meddy are buried beneath the ice before I'm finished."

Fosalia brought up the hem of her sleeve and wiped the tears from her eyes. "Your pain must be far greater than I can imagine. If you would allow it, I can take it from you. I can make it go away."

Hearing Fosalia's sentiment, Clandestiny placed the Tear around her neck and then closed her eyes. When she reopened them, a softness had returned, and her gray irises reclaimed the priestess' gaze. "I know what you would suggest. I have seen it done before. I cannot, in good conscience, allow you to sacrifice your life's source for a soul as lost as my own. To do so would be unjust. It's sad enough that one of us must bear the burden of what has transpired."

With Gallrum hovering next to Gablysin and Gage at the foot of the bed, the serwin interrupted. "What am I missing? What are you not allowing her to do? Is there some other solution?"

Gage reached up and struck the serwin on his tail yet again with his cane. "Hush! You never cease to speak at the wrong moment!"

Gallrum lifted his hands and shrugged. "What? I want to know."

Gage growled. "She speaks of giving her life's source for Medolas'. Now hush!"

Because of the interaction between the goswigs, Clandestiny had to chuckle. "I must admit, I hope that when I reclaim the form of the gashtion I don't miss the humor of awkward moments. I hope the memories of my life don't plague me and follow me into the ocean."

Fosalia dropped her head into the palms of her hands. A fair series of moments passed before she was able to stop sobbing. When finally she looked up, Clandestiny was sitting on the edge of the bed next to her, and a smile was on the Isorian's face.

"I misjudged you, Priestess. The willingness to give your life's source for another makes you a good soul. Before we part ways, I do hope that you accept my embrace. I further hope that you would return to your world with a clear conscience. You've done all that you can, and because of you, I'll be given the moments to kiss my Meddy before I fall with him from the cliffs to the ocean. I want you to return to Harvestom knowing that this is the existence I chose."

Fosalia nodded as she once again reached up to use the hem of her sleeve to wipe away her tears. "I shall return knowing just that." She paused to clear her throat. "But there's one issue that I must address before I'm able to return."

Gallrum was about to interject, but Gage poked him with his cane and gave him a look.

"I'm listening," Clandestiny said as she continued to hold Fosalia's gaze.

"If the Isor are to relocate to Gesper, the burden of the Tear shall no longer be necessary. We all know the territory you'll hunt."

"You speak the truth. I'll hunt the wilderness of the eastern kingdom," Clandestiny responded.

"Then you would also agree that there's no longer a need for Gablysin to suffer the burden of the crystal. He should live his life as any other Isorian. I'm sure you would want that ... as would he."

Hearing Fosalia's logic, Clandestiny looked at the ruby eyed man. Though Gablysin did not say anything, he did nod.

"Then it's agreed," Clanny proclaimed. "We'll remove the burden from him." She grinned. "Your blessing doesn't work anyway."

For a moment, though only a brief moment, the mood in the room was light. When Clandestiny stopped smiling, she addressed the priestess. "Will you destroy the Tear? I no longer need it to transform."

"No," Fosalia replied. "I cannot be certain of the consequences that may come with its destruction. It's clear that my mother didn't divulge the full extent of its secrets before she passed. I deeply regret that."

"Then what would you do with it?" Clanny queried.

"I will take it to Harvestom until I can determine the crystal's fate. There, it'll be safe in my possession until I can acquire the understanding of how to deal with it. Would you allow me to do this, Clandestiny?"

A long period of moments passed while Clanny pondered the priestess' offer. Eventually, she reached up, grabbed the leather straps and then removed the Tear from around her neck. "Take it. I care not what you do with it."

Gablysin exhaled with relief as the Tear was placed in the palm of Fosalia's hand.

As the priestess stared into the facets of the gem, she took the moments to admire their beauty before she looked up to reclaim Clanny's eyes. "I'm sorry for my deception, Clandestiny, but I cannot return to Harvestom in good conscience and allow you to flee to a life of solitude."

As Fosalia dropped to her knees and lifted her hands toward the ice of the ceiling, Clandestiny tried to reach out to snatch the Tear as it dangled from the priestess' hand, but she was unable to move her arms or her legs. Her movements had been restricted by Fosalia's power, and she was forced to watch as the Tear began to glow, empowering the priestess' prayer as she called upon the power to restore life.

"You can't do this!" Clandestiny screamed. "I won't allow it!" A moment later, Clandestiny's eyes turned to slits, and her teeth elongated, ending in sharp points.

With the priestess' prayer continuing, Gablysin jumped to his feet and rushed to Clandestiny's side. "Don't do this, Clanny! You're beneath 60 paces of ice. If you transform, the ceiling will collapse, and you'll end us all. Would you end those who love you to stop her prayer?"

Clandestiny's head turned in Gablysin's direction. "Get away from me!" she growled. "Run! Flee the city!"

"I won't!" Gablysin declared. "To flee would be to betray our friendship!" He reached out and placed his hand on Clandestiny's arm. When next he spoke, his voice was soft. "If you're determined to murder on this Peak, then you'll have to murder me as well. My love for you is that great. Medolas was not the only Isorian who cared for you."

Clandestiny's chest heaved as she dissected the ruby eyed man's words. With the intensity of the priestess' prayer matching her growl, she eventually closed her eyes and stopped the transformation. "I won't harm you, Gabs. Please, forgive me."

The ruby eyed man was about to respond, but a blinding light filled the room and forced everyone to shield their eyes. A long series of moments passed before it faded. When it did, the priestess' body laid draped over the edge of the bed.

With Fosalia's life's source expired, Medolas' corpse had been made whole, and his eyes were beginning to move beneath his eyelids.

The power that bound Clandestiny faded. She immediately took a seat on the side of the bed and placed a hand on Medolas' cheek. "Oh, Meddy! Oh, my Meddy!" The emotion of the moment consumed her, and she began to wail.

The Crystal Shard

When you want an update about your favorite characters

NORTHERN GRAYHAM

The Healer's Vestry—With the priestess now lying on a freshly chiseled slab of ice, her body is being prepared to be sent back to Harvestom so that those who loved her can celebrate her passing. Gage and Gallrum have offered to travel with the body.

Upon hearing about the priestess' demise, Shiver ordered Gabs to place the Tear about his neck until the king can find the moments to meet with the council to decide what to do with it.

Clanny has retired with Medolas to the undercastle. Medolas is exhausted and needs sleep. Clandestiny refuses to leave his side.

The ranking officers of the Tormalian army have left Hydroth. Six harugens have been attached to a large sled, and they are pulling the block of ice that was harvested from the battleground near the edge of the chasm. The block will be taken to Gesper so the families of the fallen may celebrate the passing of their loved ones.

SOUTHERN GRAYHAM

The United Kingdom of Southern Grayham—The tournament is un-

derway. The minds of the populace have been successfully diverted. There is no longer word of the royal family's disappearance on any of the message boards throughout the kingdom. More than a million beings roam the streets of Brandor and are enjoying the festivities.

HARVESTOM

The Merchant Island—Mosley's crate has been prepared for transport by the Merchant Angels. He will enter it just after Late Bailem. He is estimated to arrive on Southern Grayham in 2 Peaks.

HELL

Sam—The new King of Hell stormed the Temple of the Gods after his General Absolute arrived with the rest of her legions. To the king's surprise, the temple had been abandoned, but the structure was in pristine condition, and its kitchen was full of food.

When Sam addressed Narasay, his general, to determine why the temple would have been vacated, the Swayne Enserad had no answer, and it was further clear that she had no knowledge of the temple's existence prior to the army seizing it.

Rather than allow Narasay to see his confusion, Sam ordered the army to begin construction of the walls that would fortify the territory surrounding the temple to the west and to the south. The army was further ordered to create a tunnel through the mountains to the north that would end just south of the stronghold. The army was to use the rock that would be pulled out of the tunnel in the construction of the wall.

While Sam has been spending his moments with the army, Kepler has been searching for Pydum at the king's request. The imp's presence has created curiosity in Sam's mind, and the demon-jaguar has been asked to bring the grendle-imp to the temple when he has been captured.

Lasidious—After being informed by Alistar that he had needlessly given up the power he had over the Collective, Lasidious decided to refocus. Though the revelation had been a blow to his ego, sacrificing his godliness had been a part of his plan all along, so it changed nothing.

No one knows the extent of Lasidious' entire plan. The Mischievous One decided long ago that it was important to keep certain things to himself—even from his brother.

Since his arrival on Hell, the Mischievous One has been enjoying his hunts with Yolan, and the moments he has spent with his son to acquire Garrin's and the Prince of Brandor's trust. There have been moments when the boys have allowed Lasidious to play with them, but Garrin has erected a barrier of protection on a number of occasions to keep his father at bay when the Mischievous One's thoughts were not pure. Lasidious is beginning to realize that his own mind has been betraying him.

On another negative note, the Mischievous One has found his duties as Vampire King to be taxing to his nerves. He regrets the switch, but he knows the moment is coming for his reascension. When this happens, he will be stronger than he ever was. Despite this unnecessary detour, the Mischievous One has confidence that he will rule all that has been created on this plane, and he believes he has found a way to get back to the plane of the Almighty where he will beg for forgiveness.

George, Kroger and **Maldwin**—After speaking with the rat, Maldwin chose to travel to Hell with George and the ogre.

The trio is no longer searching for Garrin. After speaking with Alistar, Celestria returned to Hell and informed the warlock that his assistance would no longer be necessary to find her son.

Because George has treated Garrin well while under the care of his family, the goddess agreed to keep her promise and return George to Luvelles after he found Kepler and restored the cat's memories.

Since Lasidious is protected by the laws written on Gabriel's pages, the goddess has asked George for his help. She has pleaded with the warlock to become her assassin.

As expected, George agreed to seek the power to destroy Lasidious once the warlock realized the Mischievous One no longer possessed the power to retrieve his daughter's soul from the Book. Celestria explained how Lasidious foolishly abandoned his seat at the table of the Collective and sent Tardon to his demise in an effort to hide his identity from the Book. The warlock also knows the Mischievous One has plotted to have him murdered. For George, the decision to seek the power to end Lasidious was an easy one.

To help in his search for Kepler, Celestria pointed the warlock in the right direction. The goddess has informed George that Mosley is also searching for the same power that he will be seeking, and George will need to set aside his differences with the wolf and become his ally during the fight against Lasidious.

The goddess also issued a word of warning. After Kepler is found and they are taken to Luvelles, Celestria has deemed it wise for George to leave the jaguar behind. The vengeance Mosley seeks against the cat for the loss of his Luvera will never be set aside, but the wolf's disdain for George can be dismissed.

But before any of this can happen, George must first face the demon-jaguar and keep from being slaughtered before he is able to remind his old friend of their past relationship.

WESTERN LUVELLES

George's Family—To keep Athena's mind off of George's absence, Brayson has taken the entire family to Southern Grayham for the remainder of Michael's tournament.

Mary was excited to go. She could not wait for Brayson to see her old home and her inn in Lethwitch. The family has been staying at Mary's farm while Brayson and Gregory teleport everyone to Brandor each morning so they can enjoy the festivities of the tournament.

At night, after the family returns, Gregory has been using his magic to improve the appearance of Mary's estate and her place of business.

Appreciation has also been extended to her neighbors and trusted employees who took care of her home and inn during her absence. Many of these people have been loyal to Mary for more than 15 seasons.

The family was unable to stop laughing at the reaction of the help after they touched the new walls of the inn and felt the structure's new pulse.

King Henry Dowd and **Chancellor Boyafed Methelborn**—The bridge crossing Lake Lavan is still under construction. With it moving forward as planned, King Dowd and

Chancellor Methelborn have been doing a lot of fishing. Their lives have been peaceful since the unification of the kingdoms.

Upon hearing that his old flame as a younger elf had recently been widowed, Boyafed sought her company. Jennikas is still as beautiful as she ever was, and she has been with Boyafed most everywhere he has traveled since. The possibility of a union could be in their future, and since Boyafed has never wed, the union would be grand.

ANCIENTS SOVEREIGN

The Book—Gabriel has yet to reveal his true self to the rest of the Collective. He had intended to do so at the last meeting of the gods, but just prior to the meeting, Michael appeared to Gabriel and instructed the Book to maintain his secret. Gabriel has also met with Celestria. Garrin's addiction to the Vampire Queen's milk was discussed, but Lasidious' possession of Tardon's body was not.

The Archangel Michael—After making his appearance to those who claim to be gods, Michael informed the Collective of the new Heaven that was being created and the restrictions that would be placed upon its magnificence. The archangel did not, however, speak of Anahita and her role as per the Source's wishes.

As expected, the Collective was outraged by the Source's decision to take an active role in the creation of a world where the Book would release the souls who had managed to live a good life.

When confronted with the question, "Why is the Source breaking his promise to remain out of their affairs?" Michael informed the so-called gods that the dragon was acting upon the Almighty's wishes. He further reminded them that they should consider themselves blessed that they were allowed to escape their eternal torture in the first place.

Because of their failure to heed the Almighty's laws on their old plane, the Heaven on this new plane will not be allowed to rival the glory of the old. The new Heaven will not be allowed to have pearly gates. This was yet another punishment for failing the Almighty.

By the moment Michael was finished speaking, those present after Alistar vanished with Celestria finally realized that their eyes would never again witness the glory they chose to abandon. They also realized that no matter how much power they sought to try and find their way back, their effort would result in failure. At best, their Heaven would be no better than just another beautiful world. There would be no streets of gold, and it would most certainly not be without imperfections.

THE NEW HEAVEN

Anahita and **Dorick**—The angel and the dwarf are no longer enjoying the company of the Source. The Ancient One returned to the dragon world as soon as he felt Fosalia abandon the body the priestess was told to occupy.

The Source will call for a meet-ing of the dragon council. The Titans must determine how to handle the failure of the High Priestess.

Thank you for reading the Crystal Shard

CHAPTER 18
A CHASTISED DRAGON

3 PEAKS OF BAILEM HAVE PASSED
SOUTHERN GRAYHAM
THE HOME OF CADROMEL
BENEATH GRIFFIN FALLS, EARLY BAILEM

Fellow soul ... after speaking with Celestria, Mosley teleported to the Merchant Island of Harvestom, but his departure was delayed since the dock foreman did not have a crate capable of carrying the wolf to Grayham. When one was acquired, it took 2 Peaks to make the journey. As soon as the Merchant Angels set his crate on the ground, Mosley teleported to Cadromel's home inside the mist. When he appeared, he was standing next to the body of water that pooled at the base of Griffin Falls.

With the mist being so thick, the wolf's keen eyes were unable to see the sun as it danced through Early Bailem on its way to the Peak. Instead, all he could see was the large pond that stretched in front of him. Its far side remained hidden, and its familiar, greenish glow that emanated from the water was the only reason the wolf was able to see a fair amount of its surface.

In the distance, the intensity of Griffin Falls could be heard as it crashed against the rocks. The wolf closed his eyes and listened to the force of the water. Though he was anxious to speak with the wisp, this place offered peace of mind, and he smiled as a memory of Luvera filled his thoughts—a memory from just over 400 seasons ago.

"You must promise to love me anyway, Mosley, despite how I appear," Luvera said as she looked up from drinking the water. Her coat had been

saturated by the mist, and she appeared as dreadful as any other wet mutt. Yet her eyes, oh those deep, green, beautiful eyes were intoxicating to look upon no matter how matted her fur was around them. *"I know I look frightful. But you must remember, this was your idea to come here."*

"It wasn't my idea," Mosley had rebutted. *"It was Cadromel's. The wisp has a gift for us. Besides, you could never look frightful to me, my love ... no matter how the mist attacks your coat."*

Luvera had grinned and placed her head against Mosley's. Her mouth had been close to his ear when she whispered, *"Being your mate brings joy to my heart."*

Recalling the smile that appeared on Luvera's face as she pulled away, Mosley remembered the love that filled his heart on that Peak. His Luvera had joined him in howling their vows the night before, and the ceremony had been held inside the Temple of the Gods. Bassorine had attended, and after their union, they had said goodbye. They spent the majority of the night descending the steps inside the cliffs, and then they raced each other toward Cadromel's home.

The song Cadromel sang to them that afternoon had been the perfect gift. It left Luvera in an amorous mood, and that night, their first litter had been conceived inside the den that Bassorine had provided at the base of Griffin Cliffs.

Mosley's memories of the past were interrupted as Cadromel ascended from the depths of the pond. The wolf recognized the wisp's light as he approached. A period of silence passed as Mosley stood with his head bowed while sheets of water cascaded from Cadromel's sphere. The wolf knew not to speak until after the air had been filled with song.

As always, the wisp's sound was beautiful, heavenly, and it spoke of Cadromel's delight in seeing the wolf. "It is good to see you again, Mosley."

"And you as well, Cadromel. I bring good news."

Again, the wisp's song filled the morning air. "I can only hope that you've returned with knowledge of the Tear of Gramal."

Mosley nodded and told Cadromel everything Celestria had divulged about the Tear prior to leading him to the power of the Ancient Mystics and the Swayne Enserad.

The energy that moved inside the wisp's sphere slowed down significantly, almost as if Cadromel was searching for a response. "Then you have returned without need of my help to acquire the power you sought. You are truly a kind being. You did not have to divulge your findings since you've found the power without my assistance. Yet you did it anyway. Why?"

Mosley pondered for a response. "Because I know you are bound to the mist and cannot venture to find out for yourself."

The air filled with a harmonious chuckle. "Indeed. But there is another reason why you've shared the knowledge of the Tear."

Mosley dropped his head and stared at the water beneath the wisp's mass. "I offer the knowledge of the Tear as payment. I need your help."

"Your eyes dropped. You must be seeking something grand."

The wolf nodded, but he did not look up. "I am. I don't feel it's my place to ask for a favor of this magnitude. Yet I have no choice."

Again, the wisp's harmonious melody sounded like a chuckle. "The desire for vengeance often makes the meekest being bolder. I do owe payment for the information provided, do I not?"

Mosley looked up from the water. "The knowledge I seek would require many of your moments to be spent with me. I feel it's an unfair trade. However, I wish to learn the language of the Titans. I ask that you teach me how to release the power of the words once I understand how to utter them."

As the heart that beat at the center of the wisp's core began to race, the energy inside the sphere moved at a rapid pace. "What would make you think that I have this knowledge?"

The wolf lowered his head back to the water and dropped his eyes again. "I know that you're a Titan, Cadromel. You don't need to hide your form from me any longer."

A fair series of moments passed before the wisp responded. When he did, he no longer spoke in song. Instead, his voice was deep and powerful, like a controlled thunder. "When Celestria approached, she didn't divulge the nature of your visit. She simply said she had been sent by Alistar and that you'd be coming. Was it she who told you my identity?"

"Celestria knows your secret is safe with me."

"Yet it was not her secret to reveal. I would not have allowed her to share it."

"Perhaps the goddess should apologize," Mosley responded. "But now that I know, would you prefer that I address you in some other manner? I don't wish to insult you."

All movement inside Cadromel's sphere stopped. "Close your eyes, Mosley. You may want to lower to the ground and shield them with your legs."

Mosley quickly did as instructed.

Satisfied with the wolf's compliance, a soft-white light emerged from the center of the wisp's being as he began his transformation. The mist directly around the pool gravitated toward the light as the sphere's surface cracked. Cadromel's wings, legs, head and neck sprouted from the orb and quickly consumed a vast area.

As the overall size of the dragon's body increased, the majority of his mass submerged beneath the pond. The water that should have been displaced because of his enormous size did not run over the banks. Instead, the moisture was absorbed and used to hydrate his body.

By the moment Cadromel's transformation was complete, the dragon stood at a height of almost 45 paces above the surface of the pool with an additional 60 paces beneath it. As his wings extended, their tips traveled far enough the fog consumed their ends.

As Mosley's eyes gazed upon Cadromel's glory, the energy that had moved inside the wisp now radiated throughout the mass of the dragon's body. It was as if a storm of lightning existed beneath his skin. His scales were thin enough the wolf could see through them, yet Mosley was under no illusion that they were not hard and battle worthy.

"My eyes have never seen such splendor, Cadromel. Your beauty is without equal."

Cadromel's laughter was deep. "Over my seasons, I've grown accustomed to hearing the voices of men profess my beauty when in the form of the wisp. However, I prefer the word aristocratic. Beauty doesn't speak to the stature of my lineage, and it feels a bit sensitive when it comes out of the mouths of men."

Mosley smirked. "I'm sure it does."

For better conversation, Cadromel lowered the rest of his form beneath the surface of the pond. He did it slowly to ensure the displacement of water happened at a pace that would not wash the wolf off the side of the embankment and send Mosley down the hillside as it rushed away from the pool.

With Cadromel's head at a reasonable height, the dragon spoke. "I am a prince amongst gods. Celestria does not know the truth of who I am. She knows I am dragon, but I am so much more than that. Can I trust you, Mosley?"

The wolf nodded. "Of course."

Cadromel smiled as a dragon would. "I believe you. I've watched you live your life, and never have I seen you betray the confidence of those you consider your friends." The dragon focused his gaze on Mosley's. "You do consider me to be your friend, do you not?"

Rather than respond right away, Mosley took the moments to search for the proper words. "There have been moments when I have felt we were friends, Cadromel. But if I was to be honest, your presence on Grayham has always baffled me. I have often felt that there was something more to you. Something inside my gut tells me that you've led many grand packs and have dominated many territories. I've often felt that your glory ... even in the form of the wisp ... felt god-like, though I can't explain why."

As Cadromel responded, he shifted to find a more comfortable position. As he did, a series of shallow waves spilled out over the embankment and rushed down the hillside. "It appears your service to Bassorine and your temporary ascension to Ancients Sovereign will work to our advantage. Your mind has been prepared for a friendship such as ours."

Mosley nodded. "I suppose it has. There's no reason why I shouldn't embrace a friendship of this magnitude."

"Wonderful!" Cadromel exclaimed. "What I'm going to tell you, only 12 others know. I tell you now only because I see an opportunity for mutual advancement, and I see a being who is tired of the lies."

"I'm beyond tired of the lies."

"Perfect. Then I shall extend my help. The information you bestowed upon me regarding the Tear is sufficient as payment. I shall teach you how to speak the language of the Titans and how to release the power hidden inside the words. But I fear the task will not be simple. The language of the Titans can only be learned by those who have had their minds prepared ... and as we've discussed, yours is ... but only to a point. Not even the Collective can comprehend this language."

"This must be why Bassorine never spoke it," Mosley responded. "I didn't know the Titans existed until I ascended." Mosley redirected his thoughts. "There's so much that I remember after eating the nasha, but I can do nothing with these memories since I entered a Promise of the Gods with the Book and swore not to divulge their secrets."

Cadromel grinned. "Whatever the Book's reason for making you promise, I'm sure it would be a lie. Perhaps a better question would be: how do you feel now that you know the Collective's knowledge is limited? How does it feel to know that they cannot speak the language of the Titans?"

It took a moment before Mosley was able to respond. "I don't know how to feel. Why did this never cross my mind when I was living on Ancients Sovereign? I should've wondered about such things. Perhaps my mind was overwhelmed by the games."

"You cannot blame yourself, Mosley. Allow me to tell you the truth of things. The Collective ... the beings who call themselves gods ... are not gods. They fall far short of the right to use the term. There is only one who sits at their table who has this right."

As the wolf's brows dropped between his eyes, Cadromel continued. "My father's name is Odin. You would know him best as Alistar. When the Collective was formed, Odin took on the form of a being who was beloved by yet another whom you know as Lasidious. My father knew the God Wars on this plane would destroy us if he did not create alliances with those who had fallen from the Heaven of a being that the archangels and demonkind alike considered to be their Almighty—the same Almighty they turned their backs on.

"To accomplish the alliances that he wanted to forge, my father pulled Lasidious' brother beyond the dark side of one of the many worlds that we had created on this plane and shredded his soul into a million pieces. Only then did Odin assume the image of Lasidious' brother and approach the Mischievous One to form the Collective."

"I don't understand," Mosley interrupted. "My memory of the gods is intact, and I know that those who occupy this plane were pulled from the Lake of Fire after they failed to heed the Almighty's commands, but somehow, I knew there were holes in my memory. I've always had that feeling."

Cadromel smiled. "Then you were perceptive. You don't know the full truth. Not all beings were pulled from the Lake of Fire. When the being whom the archangels addressed as Father decided to impose his judgment, there were those of us who took our followers and left before the carnage began.

"We came to this plane, created new worlds, new solar systems and new galaxies. Our creations were beautiful, laws were established, kingdoms were forged and lives flourished. More than 1,000 seasons passed before three archangels, Michael, Gabriel and Zerachiel pulled their fallen brothers and sisters from the Lake of Fire. Unfortunately, when they did, they released the most devious of them all. It was this being, known as Lucifer, who had a hand in bringing forth the wars on this plane, destroying all that we had created with his legions of demons."

Mosley's eyes looked more confused than ever. "I know nothing of this devious soul the archangels released. I know the name Gabriel, but I do not know this Michael or Zerachiel. Nor do I know what an archangel is or what one stands for. The Book did not pass this knowledge to me."

"That's because the Book isn't your friend, nor is he your ally, Mosley. You must listen to me. Your mind, and the mind of every being known to the Collective that exists on this plane, has been wiped clean of this knowledge. Normally, the presence of archangels would not be a problem. They were created by their god for noble purposes, but—"

"But if their cause was noble," Mosley interrupted, "then why is their presence a problem?"

"Because when an archangel falls from grace, they can no longer be trusted. They become seekers of power and acquire a fiendish desire to dominate. It is only recently that I've learned that Bassorine and the archangel Michael are one in the same being. To my knowledge, there are only three archangels on this plane."

"I know Bassorine," Mosley defended. "If he's an archangel, then he's a good being."

Cadromel shook his head. "If Bassorine is good, then tell me why he lied to you. Why did he allow you to believe he had perished? Why would he have allowed you to ascend and spend your moments with those who would claim to be gods? And why would he want to destroy the same Collective he made you a part of?"

As the moments passed, Cadromel could see that Mosley would not be able to find an answer, so he continued. "Odin and Zeus expected as much from the archangels. They believed them to be plotters ... plotters far worse than Lasidious and even Lucifer himself. The only reason the Collective still exists is because of the Source's influence over them and our inability to take back what was ours when they arrived."

The dragon stopped talking and allowed the wolf the moments to formulate a question. But the strength of Mosley's question was not what Cadromel had hoped it would be. "You said you came to this plane before the archangels arrived and the Collective was formed. Who else came with you?"

"Only those with the power to do so," the dragon responded. Cadromel stuck out his tongue, cupped its end and then dipped it in the water of the pool to quench his thirst. "In total, 13 of us abandoned our old existence and brought those who worshipped us to this plane. Sixty-seven billion souls were living peaceful lives on many of our masterful creations when Michael, Gabriel and Zerachiel opened the door that led out of their Almighty's Hell. They released those who would later destroy everything we had created on this plane. These battles would later be given the title: The Great Destruction of Everything Known."

"What happened next?" Mosley queried. "I can't imagine what you and the others must have felt like as you watched your creations be destroyed."

Cadromel chuckled. "Let's say that peace was replaced with chaos. Let us also say that my father, Odin, and one other whom I shall call Zeus ... yet another name you're unfamiliar with ... were the only beings in our group who possessed the power to enter the God Wars and fight during the Great Destruction. The rest of us were forced into hiding. We took on new identities and assumed dragon form. We were later introduced to the Collective as Titans by the being whom you know as Alistar ... my father, Odin."

Mosley shook his head as his brain ran wild with thought. "If Odin destroyed Lasidious' brother and assumed a position as a member of the Collective, what did Zeus do?"

Zeus took on the form the Collective fears most. He's known as the Source. Though the Collective does not know his true identity, they fear the Source because they believe he's the being they once knew as the son of the Almighty ... sent to this plane to be the eyes of his father because the Almighty chose to forsake this plane. A clever deception."

"I know of the Source," Mosley interjected. "But the knowledge given to me by the Book of Immortality did not instill fear of the dragon."

"Of course, it didn't. To do so would create questions and require lengthy explanations. Gabriel is no better than the others of the Collective, and he has lost his way."

A fair series of moments passed before Mosley spoke again. "How did this Zeus know what to say to instill fear in the Collective?"

"Zeus knew the Collective's Almighty before we abandoned our old plane. Because of their relationship, Zeus was able to refer to the Almighty as if the Collective's deity was his own. Zeus has deceived the Collective, and they believe the Source has crossed the divide between the planes to ensure that they recreate what has been destroyed and provide the souls who wait to live again with a new Heaven and a new Hell. Zeus knows enough about the Almighty to know that he'll never allow the Collective or those who followed them out of his Heaven to ever see his plane again."

"So ... Zeus uses this to his advantage?" Mosley interjected.

"Yes. He has controlled the Collective this way for a great number of seasons. As the Source, Zeus threatened the Collective, telling them that their Almighty would take this plane away from them as well if they did not recreate what was destroyed. With the Collective believing that Zeus is the son of the Almighty, and that he has the ear of the Almighty, they've been afraid to stand against him. They fear judgment and the full power of the Almighty's army that exists beyond the pearly gates. They believe this army would be sent across the divide to strike them down if they do not recreate."

Mosley sighed. "Yet the Collective does not appear to be frightened enough. They still bid for power over this plane, and I've seen them conspire against one another."

The energy coursing through Cadromel's body slowed as he nodded. "Great power breeds great egos."

"You can say that again," Mosley chuckled. "Please allow me the moments to reiterate my understanding of everything you've said. You have professed that Alistar was, and still is, a mighty god known as Odin, and Zeus is his equal. Zeus has chosen to hide beneath the scales of a dragon that I know as the Source. Together, Odin and Zeus have masterfully forced the Collective to clean up the devastation they caused during the Great Destruction."

Mosley paused as he continued to formulate his thoughts. "It's because the Collective still fears the Almighty that they do not stand against the Source ... a being they believe is the son of this powerful god called the Almighty. They believe this Almighty would send his army across the divide between planes and destroy them all if they oppose the Source who has claimed that it's the will of the Almighty to have what existed on this plane be recreated."

Again the wolf paused. "What kind of an army would this Almighty send across the divide?"

"The mightiest army of angels known to any plane. There is no army that could oppose his will. He's called the Almighty for a reason."

Mosley smirked. "Then it appears I understand."

Cadromel nodded. "But Zeus and Odin also live in fear, though their fear isn't of the Collective's Almighty. Until recently, my father and Zeus have not had the power to oppose the Collective. The power that was expended to create prior to the Great Destruction forced us all to compromise our positions. Because of this, Odin and Zeus chose not to tempt fate. They have ensured the Collective believes that their Almighty has forsaken this plane, and as long as they listen to the Source whenever he speaks, the Collective will be allowed free will. They will further be given the freedom to create however they choose."

Mosley cut in. "Why did it take 10,000 seasons for Zeus and Odin to regain the power they would've had to control the Collective? Does creation take that long to recover from?"

"Yes, and longer for those who are not as powerful as my father and Zeus. The Collective has been wise, and they have chosen to create at a pace that has allowed them to recover over a short series of moments."

"Please explain," the wolf urged.

Cadromel nodded. "You see, when the archangels released the fury of Hell onto this plane, most of us had been depleted of our power. Because of our expeditious creating, we were left unprepared for battle. We were vulnerable and this truth required that we all go into hiding during our period of recuperation. As I have said, only Odin and Zeus were strong enough to enter the fight ... but even they had been weakened and were forced to use caution."

Cadromel stopped talking. He could see the wolf had a question.

"Are Odin, Zeus and the rest of the Titans biding their moments until they're strong enough to destroy the Collective?"

The dragon nodded. "We were, but no longer. Word has reached my father's ears that Zeus has begun to meddle in the affairs of the Collective. Apparently, he has grown tired of waiting and must believe his power has been restored. He has since taken an active role in creating the new Heaven for this plane."

A puzzled look appeared on Mosley's face. "If Zeus is creating and not destroying, why is that a problem?"

The dragon chuckled. "Oh, Mosley, I do enjoy your innocence. My father and Zeus entered a pact many, many seasons ago ... long before we came to this plane ... a pact of peace that was to remain steadfast. After this plane was ravaged by war, Zeus promised my father that he would wait until they both agreed the moment was right to act. As of late, Zeus has made himself unavailable to Odin, and he's begun working on this new Heaven with the most unlikely of beings."

"Which being?" Mosley questioned.

The wolf could feel the anger build as the dragon growled. "My father believes Zeus is conspiring with Michael."

Another baffled look appeared on the wolf's face. "I thought Michael was Zeus' enemy."

Cadromel growled again. "As did I. Odin hopes there's an explanation, but until one is discovered, we must prepare for the worst."

Mosley lowered to his haunches and scratched the back of his neck. "All this is so confusing. Is there any reason why Zeus would pull away from his agreement with your father?"

"None that would make sense," Cadromel responded. "But Zeus was once known as a seducer. This was known throughout the heavens both here and on our old plane. If Zeus intends to break his agreement with my father, I would venture to guess it's for the love of a woman."

"Why would Zeus break his promise to Odin over a woman?" the wolf wondered. "He would be risking regaining control over what has been recreated because of a muse."

A voice from behind Mosley responded. "Zeus wouldn't tempt fate with just any woman."

Mosley whirled around to see who was behind him. A male being was floating above the incline that dropped away from the embankment, and the green glow of the pool was lighting his form. "Alistar," Mosley greeted. "Or perhaps I should say, Odin?"

"Odin will suffice," Alistar responded. The Titan looked past Mosley and smiled. "Hello, Thor. I see you've decided to spread your wings."

MEANWHILE, ON HELL
THE VAMPIRE UNDERWORLD
BENEATH THE MOUNTAINS OF GANNESH

Taransay entered Lasidious' throne room and took a knee at the base of the steps leading up to it. He was known throughout the vampire underworld as the strongest of them all, second only to Tardon, his king and brother. Like Tardon, Taransay's hair was black as his eyes, and yet his face was soft and appealing to the female eye when it was cleanly shaven.

Taransay was known by all vampires for his merciless killing of countless demons throughout his seasons, yet he was also known as the only being who had been able to convince the council of demons to enter into a pact of peace. Taransay had used his charisma to persuade Sharvesa's mother who was queen of the demon council for more than 3,000 seasons to stop the war that plagued Dragonia—a world that all now know as Hell.

"My King," Taransay said as he dropped his eyes to the floor. "The Vampire Council awaits your presence. They're anxious to understand your orders to move the entrances into the underworld to the top of the mountains."

Lasidious stood from his throne and adjusted one of Tardon's old tunics to a better position. He hated the politics of the underworld, but this was the path he had chosen. It would only be a short matter of moments before he would reclaim his position amongst the gods, and after his ascension, he would no longer be bound by rules. With the sacrifice of his godliness came the release of governance. The laws inside the Book's pages would no longer be his laws. He loved loopholes and the way the laws had been written.

Walking down the steps, Lasidious placed his arm across Taransay's shoulders. "I grow tired of the Vampire Council ... don't you, brother? Perhaps an accident should befall them."

Taransay stopped dead in his tracks and leaned in. "I've asked for that for countless seasons, and you've always rejected my proposal. Why now? You've been acting like a new vampire. Something has come over you, I know it."

Lasidious smiled as he reached up to grab the back of Taransay's neck and responded as he placed his forehead against his supposed brother's. "A funny thing happened the other Peak when I took my bath."

"Do tell?"

Lasidious grinned. "I allowed my hands to explore, and I found my courage. I should do something with them, don't you think?"

It took a while for Taransay to stop laughing. "You jest, but I'm glad you found your balls. I'm equally glad your mind has changed. We should rid the underworld of the council and establish two sects ... you the leader of one, and me, the leader of the other."

The Mischievous One pulled back. "I have a better idea. We shall rid ourselves of the council and you can run the entirety of the underworld. I care not for its politics any longer."

Lasidious enjoyed the look of disbelief as it appeared on Taransay's face.

"You're still jesting, aren't you?"

"No, brother. The Peak is fast approaching when I will hand you my crown. It will be yours to do with as you please. But first, there are matters we must discuss. First, did you fly beyond the Dragon's Backbone and see if the rumors were true?"

Taransay nodded. "I did. The seas are filled with tortured beings, and many of them are headed toward the backbone and will eventually find their way to the mainland as you claimed."

Turning to follow his brother out of the throne room toward the chamber of the council, Taransay continued. "I don't know how you knew, but you were right. The mainland won't be the same once they arrive. We must prepare and relocate the entrances. They must be inaccessible."

Lasidious stopped walking. "Our relationship with the demons will be more important to maintain than ever before. We cannot afford to have two enemies. These tortured beings will be mighty enough."

"What else do you know about their migration?" Taransay questioned.

The Mischievous One began walking again. "I know that these beings cannot perish. They're perfect for us to feast upon."

"How do you know? Are you sure you're the same vampire? The Tardon I know would not have been this proactive."

Lasidious chuckled. "The Tardon you know will never return. I've grown tired of him and his passive ways. I vow to be a better leader ... a better vampire ... a better king until the moment comes that you replace me."

The Mischievous One reached out and threw his arm back across Taransay's shoulders as they continued to walk. "We have plans to make. Before we can rid ourselves of the council, we must use their influence to prepare the underworld. A new series of tunnels must be dug."

"Tunnels? For what?"

"With the tortured beings being unable to perish, we'll harvest them like crops. We'll chain them to the walls, and once there, we'll drain them of their blood again and again and again. We'll have a never ending banquet. Hunting will become a sport and no longer be a necessity."

Taransay rubbed his hands together. "A continuous feast that never ends. And to think, I thought these beings would only bring war."

THE NEXT MORNING, THE WORLD OF SHAYMLEZMAN
THE DRAGON COUNCIL HAS CONVENED

With the Dragon Council gathering, Odin appeared near the base of an obelisk that had been erected at the center of a circle the dragons had formed for their meeting. Not far to the south, a lake spanned a vast area as it followed the mountains and stretched to the east. The Mountains of Farramore were steep, but in this spot, the Source had leveled the peaks, and he used the ledges of the cliffs to lie on while the council convened.

The lake acted as home to one of the most esteemed members of the council, yet this body of water remained unnamed. With the lake pressing against the mountains, the dragon did not need to leave the comfort of the water to attend the meeting.

The monument had been given the name, the Obelisk of Planes. The Source had removed it from his old cave on Western Luvelles and had placed it just north of the lake's shoreline. It was this obelisk that Zeus and Odin had used when they brought the rest of the Dragon Council to this plane more than 15,000 seasons ago, but the Farendrite Collective had not been told the truth about the monument. They had been led to believe the obelisk was the Source's way of communicating with their Almighty.

"The perception of Fosalia's passing will be rectified," Zeus announced as he lowered his massive, dragon head to focus on Odin. "She has always had a soft spot for mortals." He turned his head and glared at a dragon who was cowering at the center of the circle. "Fosalia, I grow tired of your poor decisions."

Fosalia cringed at Zeus' tone. "I'm sorry, Father."

A frown appeared on Odin's face as he looked over the priestess' dragon form. "She'll never change, Zeus, you know that. You chastise her for nothing. Perhaps we should speak of your daughter's shortcomings at a later moment. There are other matters I'd like to discuss with this council before we resolve the illusion of the priestess' passing."

Odin spread his angelic wings and flew to the top of the obelisk that sat just shy of 90 paces above the ground. Once his feet were planted firmly on the top of the monument, he spoke again. "Zeus, perhaps we should address your shortcomings. As of late, you've made yourself unavailable to this council. I and the others would like to know why you've broken our pact."

The Source sighed. "Mighty Odin, I haven't broken our agreement, nor do I have shortcomings. I swore my allegiance to you and this council, and my loyalty has not and will not falter."

Fosalia was quick to defend. "Yes, my father is loyal. Zeus would never betray the council."

"Quiet yourself, Hebe," the Source growled. "I don't need to be defended by the likes of you."

Crossing his arms in front of his breastplate, Odin shook his head as he again watched Fosalia, or rather, Hebe, cower. He then directed his gaze. "Tell me, Mighty Zeus, why have you been conspiring with the Archangel Michael to create a Heaven for this plane? Your actions suggest betrayal to the council, and if they don't, why not speak with us first?"

Zeus nodded. "You're right, my friend. I have failed to communicate. There's no excuse for my actions. But I assure you, my allegiance to our cause shall forever remain unwavering."

Odin's face softened a bit. "If this is, indeed, the case, then please explain your dealings with Michael."

The Source took a moment to gather his thoughts. "When the archangel approached and asked for my help, what was I to say? We all knew this

Peak would come. You all remember ... it was the wish of this council that I lead the Collective down a path of deception. Because of me, they believe their Almighty has required that they replace what they destroyed. So when Michael approached for my help, I accepted only because there was no other answer. But the archangel's plea was not the only reason I agreed to help him."

A two-headed, female dragon was standing on top of a massive rock that matched the height of the obelisk. "I'm sure the mouths of this council would wager a woman is involved," she sneered. "It's always a woman ... isn't it? Who is she?"

The Source's booming chuckle caused the water in the lake to ripple. When Zeus stopped laughing, he responded. "You know me too well, Hera. But my eyes haven't found an affection for just any woman. This woman is an angel ... but not just any angel. You may remember her as Anahita."

One of Hera's two heads gasped as the other responded. "Are you referring to the same being that Michael followed out of Heaven and into that eternal Lake of Fire?"

Zeus smirked. "I am."

Hera spit and watched it hit the ground. "That stupid archangel sacrificed his status in his Almighty's Heaven for a woman. And only you would find it wise to conspire with the enemy over a pair of breasts."

With the majority of his serpent-like body still submerged beneath the water of the lake, Poseidon entered the conversation. "Unless you've found a way to manipulate this angel, you should distance yourself from her. You're putting us all in jeopardy."

"Agreed," Odin added. "This council has waited nearly 11,000 seasons for the opportunity to take back what was ours. The full strength of this council has nearly returned. It won't be long before we can reclaim it."

"But Father," Hebe interjected. "My power was expelled when—"

The Source roared and stopped his daughter from continuing. "Yes, we know! You wasted it on the Isorians!"

Odin crossed his arms and shook his head. "It's a good thing we don't consider her a real part of this council, Mighty Zeus. She's useless to us."

Rather than respond right away, the Source transformed. By the moment he was finished, his scales had been replaced with a golden suit of armor that glistened in the sunlight, and a magnificent pair of wings emerged from his back. His overall height and size had reduced to equal Odin's, and his black feathers matched the color of his long, flowing hair.

With a few strong flaps of his wings, Zeus launched skyward to the top of the obelisk. Once his feet were planted and he was within arm's reach of Odin. "Useless or not, she is my daughter. Let us change the subject."

As soon as Odin nodded, Zeus explained, "Anahita is being used to create this plane's new Heaven. An opportunity exists to use the Collective's deceptions against them. The lies they've told shall become our advantage. I've taken this opportunity to gain Anahita's trust."

"Why would we need her trust?" Hera snapped. "And did you have to seduce her to get it?"

The Mighty Zeus grinned. "I did not bed her, Hera. Calm yourself. I believe Michael intends to use Anahita as a weapon against all those who would oppose him and his brothers. I also believe Michael is still angry because of Anahita's betrayal." Zeus found Odin's eyes. "You should've seen it. I've witnessed Anahita's power. She's creating at a remarkable rate."

"How is she doing it?" Odin wondered. "She must have received help."

Zeus reached out and placed a hand on Odin's shoulder. "According to Anahita, Michael surrendered part of his being to her, but I don't understand his reasoning. Why would he create a weapon to use against the others that he would be unable to overcome when the moment came to take his revenge? If he is, indeed, still angry, I'm missing something. And I intend to find out what it is."

The largest dragon, second only to the Source stepped clear of the others. "Your logic is sound, Father," Ares responded. "If there's anything I can do to help, I am ready. My power has nearly returned, and I no longer fear the Collective."

Though Zeus was standing on top of the obelisk, he still had to look up to find Ares' dragon eyes. "Do nothing yet, my son. The moments for action are coming, but until I'm certain that my eyes haven't been blinded by something that exists in front of them, we should wait for a sign."

Zeus passed his eyes across the rest of the council. "None of you will act until Odin and I know more about the Collective's plotting." He turned to face Odin. "Perhaps the moment has come for you and I to be more aggressive."

"I believe you're right," Odin replied.

Hera interrupted. "This council should speak of a new course of action only after Hebe has departed. We cannot afford for her to make another mistake."

It was easy to see the aggravation as it appeared on the Titan's faces when they all agreed.

Zeus looked down at his daughter. "What shall we do with her, Mighty Odin? My daughter keeps choosing the wrong path. She continues to allow her love for the mortals to guide her actions. You may not yet know it, but Hebe has restored the life of a being known as Medolas on Grayham, and then she left the vessel we put her in to rot on the ice. As we speak, the priestess' body is arriving on Harvestom, and it will be taken to her palace by a pair of goswigs known as Gage and Gallrum."

Odin's frown deepened. "I told you we should not have given her the position of High Priestess."

"Yes, we know what you said," Hera growled. "Yet here we are discussing it again."

Odin whirled around and looked in Hera's direction. "Hebe may be your daughter, but that girl is impossible to teach. She's a disgrace to your loins."

Hearing Odin's insult, Hera launched from the top of her rock and landed next to her daughter. "Do you hear how he's talking to me?"

Hebe had to drop to the ground to avoid her mother's claw as Hera took a swing.

"That's right. You duck. I should not have abandoned the post of High Priestess. You're a disgrace." Hera turned, looked up at the top of the obelisk and addressed both Odin and Zeus. "But what other choice did we have? The body I occupied was growing old, and the Collective would've become suspicious if I had not let it perish."

Zeus took a long, deep breath as he pondered the situation. "We will send Hebe back until we can determine a better course of action. For now, I'll speak with the Book." Zeus paused and faced Odin. "Speaking of the Book ... that reminds me of a secret I learned. The Book and the Archangel Gabriel are one in the same being."

Again, one of Hera's two heads gasped as the other responded. "Finally, he resurfaces. I knew he would. I knew there was no way a being with his power could've perished during the wars."

Zeus nodded. "I believe this knowledge gives us an advantage."

"Perhaps ... perhaps not," Odin replied. "We need to know more before we should consider this advantageous. However, I do find it interesting to know that Gabriel has always been this close to the Collective ... and me as I sat at their table. I was a fool to believe that we had placed the souls of the deceased inside a simple book."

"Well said, Odin," Poseidon added. "You do appear foolish. You were the closest to them all. Your position on the Collective should've produced better results."

Zeus smirked. "Odin is no more a fool than you are, Poseidon. If there is one fool amongst us, then we all bear the title. Odin's belief that the Collective placed the souls inside a book is accurate. Even the majority of the Collective doesn't realize that Gabriel uses the appearance of a book as a way to spy on them."

"Then it appears this knowledge of the archangel returning changes nothing for now," Poseidon replied. "We should move forward as planned."

"I agree," Zeus confirmed. "I will go back to Ancients Sovereign and tell Gabriel that it was the wish of the Almighty that I restore Fosalia's soul to her body. I will then tell him that this was why the priestess' soul never entered the Book's pages. We cannot have the members of the Collective learning that her passing was a ruse. They must believe the true power of the Tear of Gramal was invoked."

"What about Helmep?" Hera queried. "He'll know Hebe did not truly invoke the power of the Tear. He'll seek to investigate once he realizes he didn't answer the Tear's call for life."

"I'll take care of Helmep," Odin responded. "My power is strong enough that I can dispense with the weakest members of the Collective without rousing suspicion."

Zeus smiled. "This is good news. If you're strong enough to surpass the rules written on the Book's pages, then Gabriel won't know of our trespasses. How do you know this to be the case?"

Now it was Odin's turn to smile. "You're not the only one who has failed to communicate. I devoured Sharvesa's soul just the other Peak to test my theory. You'll be happy to know that we're ready for battle, old friend."

As both Zeus and Odin laughed, Hera was still anxious. She growled to capture their attention. "Perhaps you laugh prematurely. The rest of us are not ready. What if Gabriel asks why the Almighty would want the priestess' soul returned? What then? What will you tell him to pacify his suspicion?"

Zeus took a moment to search for a response. "I shall say the same thing I always do when I'm questioned."

"Well, go on," Hera jeered. "Tell us what that is."

A conniving smile appeared on Zeus' face. "I will say this: 'Who am I to question the will of the Almighty?' That should shut Gabriel up."

Odin reached out and patted Zeus on the shoulders. "That, my friend, is the one statement that always shuts them up." Odin turned and looked down at Hebe. His eyes were stern. "If your father intends to have you continue your deception as Fosalia, then perhaps you should remind yourself that this council grows tired of your inability to perform the simple duties of priestess in an efficient manner. With the healers of the worlds coming to Harvestom to train under your tutelage, you fail to realize the importance of the position. Anything the Collective tells their followers prior to them coming to Harvestom to begin training will make it to your ears. This should be to our advantage, yet you have continued to fail us. Too many of your moments are spent on foolish emotions. They're your students, not your friends. And the beings who live on Northern Grayham will no longer be visited by you. From now on, you'll stay in your palace until the moment comes for our uprising. Do you understand me?"

"Yes, Mighty Odin," Hebe responded as she lowered her head in reverence. "I won't falter again."

Zeus and Odin dropped from the top of the obelisk and landed in front of Hebe, but Odin was the one to speak. "You may be Zeus' daughter, but I feel it's safe to say that this council won't cover for your mistakes any longer."

"We don't need to," Hera proclaimed. "Her affinity for foolishness is why we allowed Lasidious to believe he is her father. If she fails us again, we will rid ourselves of her and Odin can blame her destruction on the Mischievous One."

"But Mother!" Hebe gasped.

"Don't you Mother me! You're expendable if you cannot make wise decisions. We won't allow you to compromise this council's goals."

"Agreed," Zeus confirmed. "You will leave now and return to Harvestom. Appear to no one until after I've approached Gabriel."

Hebe bowed. "Yes, Father." She vanished.

Zeus turned and placed his hand on Odin's shoulder. "From now on, our communication won't be lacking. Agreed?"

"Agreed."

Before another word could be said, Zeus vanished.

As Odin looked at the empty space, he smirked. "Don't forget to transform."

CHAPTER 19
A SKITTISH SERWIN
THE PRIESTESS OF HARVESTOM'S PALACE
LATE BAILEM

Fellow soul ... after Gage and Gallrum arrived with the priestess' body on the Merchant Island of Harvestom, they had to wait for the dock foreman to check off the manifest before they could leave the island. But as soon as the graphite marked the page, the goswigs met with one of the priestess' groundskeepers who had been sent to wait for them. They touched the side of Fosalia's casket, teleported to her palace and then appeared in the foyer. With school not scheduled to begin for another 12 Peaks, the palace was empty, except for the caretakers that lived there throughout the season.

Gage pointed to a long table that sat beneath a window in the priestess' bedroom chamber and spoke to six other halfling men who were responsible for keeping the grounds outside the palace. "Place the priestess' casket over there," he ordered. The badger opened the door to her changing room and looked up at the rows of gowns. "My friend and I will see to it that her body is prepared for her Passing Ceremony."

The goswig turned from the array of dresses and focused on the halfling who appeared to be the leader of the group. "You may also want to summon the other teachers."

"He's right," Gallrum added. "They can help spread the word of the priestess' demise. Her ceremony should be held before her corpse starts to smell. We can't have a stinky body, or it'll ruin the ceremony. We no longer have a constant source of ice at our disposal to keep her from rotting."

The badger shot the serwin a look to show his distaste for the callousness of his words. "Must you always...?"

Gallrum shrugged his scale covered shoulders. "What did I say?"

The badger just rolled his eyes and refocused on the head halfling. "Perhaps you should get going. Her ceremony will be held at tomorrow's Peak."

With the variety of beings that came to the school to train, the presence of the goswigs did not feel out of place, and their orders were accepted without question. But before the halflings left the room, they chose to pay their respects to the priestess.

As the head groundskeeper approached the casket, a piercing ball of light emerged through another window that existed above the priestess' bed and filled the room with light. The orb hovered in place, almost as if it was sizing up the room. After a fair series of moments, it chose to travel across the room toward the casket.

Everyone took a step back from the table as the orb drew near.

Gallrum reached down with his claw and tugged at the collar of Gage's robe. "What is it?" he queried.

The badger growled and struck the serwin with his cane. "How should I know?"

The serwin frowned. "You don't have to be so mean about it."

"Hush!" the badger snarled.

As the group continued to follow the orb, it was not long before it stopped above the priestess' casket. Another fair series of moments passed while the orb did nothing but hover above the casket.

Gallrum once again reached out and tugged at Gage's collar. "Poke it. Make it do something."

The badger whirled around and poked Gallrum in the stomach. "Perhaps I'll send it after you."

Gallrum would have responded, but a laughing sound erupted from the orb as if the being had understood their words.

Again, Gage smacked his cane against Gallrum's tail. "See what you've done? You've made us look foolish to that ... that ... that thing."

The serwin shrugged again. "What did I say?"

Gage would have struck the serwin yet again, but the orb began to lower toward the casket. As soon as the sphere's form touched the wood, the lid liquefied and allowed the orb to pass through it.

When the last bit of the sphere disappeared, Gallrum blurted, "What's it doing?"

The leader of the halflings was the one to respond. His voice was uneasy and his eyes were filled with concern as he stared at the glow that had found a way to escape through the cracks between the planks. "It's a spirit. I have no desire to meddle with a spirit." He turned to the other halflings. "You can stay if you'd like, but I'm leaving." He ran toward the door.

"Why leave now?" Gallrum called after him. "If it's a spirit, it hasn't harmed us."

"Not yet!" the halfling argued as he barreled through the door and turned the corner.

Another of the halflings with long hair and big eyes began to backpedal. "He's right. Spirits can't be trusted. You can't be sure if it's a peaceful being or not, and I don't care to find out the answer." The remaining four halflings turned and rushed out of the room with him.

Once the priestess' chamber door slammed shut, Gage called out. "Go ahead ... leave, you half-wits! It's in your nature anyway!"

"Yeah, leave!" Gallrum reinforced. "It's in your nature!"

After staring at the door for a few moments, both goswigs turned to face the casket. Nothing was happening, and the glow that was escaping between the cracks faded. Gallrum started to reach down to tug on the badger's robe again, but on this occasion, the badger swatted the serwin's claw with the head of his cane before he could. "Just wait, and stop talking!"

Another long period of moments passed, and still nothing happened.

When the quiet became too much to bear, Gallrum flew over to the casket and placed his ear against it. He took a deep breath, closed his eyes, and a look of concentration appeared on his face. "I don't hear anything," he whispered.

"Well, how could you?" the badger snarled. "You don't shut up."

"But—"

"But nothing. Just listen."

As the serwin placed his ear back against the casket, another long series of moments passed. The serwin was about to pull his head back when all of a sudden a sound erupted from inside.

THUMP, THUMP—was the sound the wood made as the priestess' fist bashed against the side of the casket not far from where the serwin's ear had been placed. The sound frightened Gallrum and caused the serwin to flee.

Gage's eyes widened as the serwin's wings fluttered at a remarkable pace. Gallrum passed over the edge of the priestess' bed, and as he did, his scales caught the corner of Fosalia's blanket. The serwin dragged the bedding through the corridors, out of the palace, and he did not stop flying until he was on the back side of the wall that surrounded the perimeter of the grounds.

Moments later, the nails that had been used to hold the lid on the casket slid out as if they were being removed by an unseen force. The metallic sound they made as each struck the floor caused Gage to cringe.

When Fosalia pushed the lid open, the badger took a few steps back and waited for what was to come next. He wanted to flee, but his curiosity would not allow it. Eventually, the priestess sat up and smiled. "Hello, Gage. Did you miss me?"

The badger's relief was exhaled over a long series of moments as he stared at Fosalia. "How?"

"The Source has chosen to restore my life's source. The dragon still has plans for me. We should rejoice."

The goswig did not respond.

Sensing the badger's anxiety, Fosalia smiled. "It's me. Gage ... you don't need to fear my return. Where's your friend?"

Gage tentatively lifted a claw and pointed toward the door. "He ran."

"I bet he did. He has always been a bit skittish." When the priestess stopped chuckling, she climbed out of the casket and jumped to the floor. "We should find him. Let's hope he's happier to see me than you are."

"No one said I'm unhappy," the badger defended. "I'm just shocked. I expected to prepare a ceremony for your passing, not a celebration of your return. It's a bit unnerving to watch an expired being crawl out of their casket without warning. I can't tell you how many beings have suffered after the news of your passing reached their ears. The beings of Hydroth still suffer."

"But did joy return to Clandestiny's heart when Medolas opened his eyes?" the priestess queried. "Was my sacrifice enough to restore peace to her heart?"

The badger sighed. "It was."

"That's good, is it not?"

"It is good ... and bad. It is good only because Clandestiny now has Medolas, but even that may change. The people of Hydroth are afraid."

"Why? They should be rejoicing."

The badger shook his head. "Your sacrifice failed to account for the bigger truth of their situation. The Isorians know that gashtions lay eggs. They know that somewhere beneath the ice these eggs exist. Clandestiny has even said that she cannot remember where the eggs might be. Clandestiny is afraid to assume the form of the gashtion to search for them, because she fears she may not be able to return to Medolas if she does."

"What of the Tear?" Fosalia was quick to question. "Who has it?"

"After you passed, Gablysin put the Tear around his neck. He has decided to shoulder the burden of its responsibility. But Gablysin believes he won't be able to defend the city against the gashtion's offspring once the eggs hatch. He knows he has not endured the training that's required to control the Tear. It will only be a matter of moments before Clandestiny is once again forced to roar to scare off a young gashtion, and some Peak, her roar won't be enough. She may yet be lost to Medolas when that Peak arrives."

"What about Gesper?" the priestess questioned. "I thought Shiver would order the Isorians to relocate."

"The vast majority of Isorians have refused to relocate. It appears they would rather tempt fate than leave everything they know behind."

A look of sadness appeared on Fosalia's face. "Then I have accomplished nothing. If Clandestiny loses Medolas yet again, her loss would break my heart."

"Then fix it," the badger urged. "Return to Hydroth and teach the ruby eyed man how to control the Tear. He's stronger than Clandestiny, and he'd be able to defend the city. Two roars are far better than one. He may never need to transform."

Fosalia turned to face the casket and looked out the window toward the clouds. The sky was dark, and a chill filled the air. It would not be long before the white rain of winter would return to shower her palace.

Gage could see the distress on the priestess' face. "What's bothering you? You can fix this. You should be happy."

"I cannot," Fosalia responded. "I can't leave the palace."

"Why? There's no law against it."

"I wish it were that simple. There's a higher law that I must conform to."

The fur between the badger's eyes dropped. "I know of no such law."

"Oh, Gage, I wish I could speak of it, but I cannot. Perhaps you could bring Gablysin to me."

Fosalia rushed across the room and walked through the door of her changing room. A moment later, she returned with a red cape that was covered with an array of glitter.

"It's a bit feminine, but we can use it to protect him during his journey. I will place a spell on it, just as you did with the Frigid Commander when he came to take me to Hydroth."

The badger looked at the glitter on the cape. "I don't think he'll agree to wear that. Perhaps a different cape, or even a cloak that would fit Gablysin's stature."

Fosalia lifted the cape in front of her. A moment later, she smiled. "Too bad. The glitter would've complemented the color of his skin. I'll have a new cape made, and I'll create a scroll of teleportation that has the power to take you between worlds. I'll finish his training here in the palace before the eggs hatch."

"That should work," the badger responded. "If only you had a thousand of these capes."

"Why? You only need one."

The badger shook his head. "Only one if you wish to miss the union."

"What union?"

"Medolas and Clandestiny are to unite right away. Clandestiny feels that if she's to lose Medolas again, she doesn't want to suffer the loss without knowing him. Their love is strong and has been for more than 300 seasons. Both Isorians wish to consummate their relationship in case the Peak comes that she is forced to transform."

A look of distress appeared on Fosalia's face. "I cannot miss their union, nor can I expect 1,000 Isorians to make the journey to my palace. That would be unthinkable and an unfair request. I didn't restore Medolas' life's source only to miss an event as grand."

Fosalia walked across the room and took a seat on the bed. A few moments passed before she realized her blanket was missing.

"Gallrum has it," the badger answered before the question was even uttered.

Rather than try to understand why, the priestess' mind began to churn. A long series of moments passed before she stood from the bed and walked into the changing closet. *It's only a union ceremony. How long could it take?* she thought as she shuffled through her gowns. *The council is busy with other matters. I could drop in for the ceremony and then rush right back to my palace. Neither Odin, Zeus or my mother would even know.*

When Fosalia finally exited the closet, she was holding two gowns. One was green with silver lace, and the other was yellow with black lace. "Which do you prefer, Gage? I can't attend a union without looking my best."

The badger grinned. "I'd wear yellow."

"Then it's settled. We'll teleport to Hydroth for the ceremony and return to Harvestom with the ruby eyed man upon its completion."

"Your plan sounds wonderful, Priestess. Perhaps I should teleport ahead and ask the Isorians to prepare the ceremony. They intend to have it near the bridge you created over the chasm. Though the water has begun to freeze and the chasm has narrowed considerably, it is still a poignant spot to speak their vows."

"That would be a wonderful place to hold the ceremony. The battlefield symbolizes so much. Please tell them the ceremony needs to be short. I cannot be gone from my palace for an extended series of moments. There's much riding on my return."

Gage bowed. "I'll leave as soon as you've created the scroll. The Isorians will rejoice upon hearing the news of your continued existence."

THE WORLD OF HELL
THE NEXT MORNING

X MARKS GEORGE'S LOCATION

The mountains on Hell felt as if they shot up into the atmosphere and never stopped. George had seen many mountains since his arrival on the worlds governed by the Crystal Moon, but the thought of these mountains being on a world the gods had renamed Hell, somehow, made the peaks seem more imposing. To his right, the shoreline stretched to the north and to the south, and across the sea, the warlock had left Kroger on the old Merchant Island.

Celestria had dropped them off, and it had been easy to see that the island had been picked clean of its cargo. But George did not bring this to the ogre's attention. Instead, he gave Kroger a task. The ogre was to gather what was left of the crates that remained scattered across the island and use them to make a wall that surrounded the entrance to the dock foreman's old office.

While the ogre was busy, George and Maldwin used the wood from a bunch of piled up wagons to create a raft. Now that they were across the channel, he looked back toward the island and smirked. He did not need Kroger to build a wall. He had only assigned the task to keep the ogre busy while he searched for Kepler. He wanted the big guy to feel important. The last thing the ogre had said before he had left the island was, "George friend to Kroger. Kroger build big wall for George. Wall no break when Kroger done."

George smiled as he thought of the ogre's childlike speech. He was glad that he had been able to rectify a wrong that he had made. No one deserved to be turned to stone, especially a being with a heart as kind as Kroger's.

Celestria had been nice enough to point them in the right direction. She had told George that Kepler was hunting the shoreline and was currently stalking a creature called an grendle-imp. She had said the imp was fleeing north in his direction, and it would only be a matter of moments before their paths would cross.

As the Peak of Bailem approached, Maldwin stuck his head out of George's backpack. The rodent's nose twitched wildly as he spoke. *"Anair asay, Kepler!"*

George quickly dove behind a rock. "I know, buddy," he replied. "I can see him, too." After taking a deep breath, the warlock poked his head above the rock.

Maldwin lowered as much of his body as he could into the pack without losing sight of the jaguar. With his eyes barely peeking over George's shoulder, he whispered, *"Fosay ya molyano."*

The warlock nodded. "I hope this doesn't end up sucking garesh. He knows we're here."

"Besoya na fumar ay."

Though George did not fully understand what the rat said, he knew enough to know Maldwin was scared for their lives. Not far down the shoreline, Kepler was standing with his paws in the water. The demon-jaguar's eyes were glowing burgundy-red, and they were staring in their direction.

"Here goes nothing," the warlock said as he stood to move into the open. "Hey, Kep!" he shouted. "I know you must be looking for me!"

Kepler dropped into a defensive position and growled as Maldwin disappeared from sight.

NORTHERN GRAYHAM
THE WILDERNESS WEST OF HYDROTH
THE NEXT MORNING

With the sun shining bright and the temperature at a brisk 18 below zero, the Isorians whom Medolas and Clandestiny invited to their union ceremony had gathered on the east side of the bridge the priestess had created across the chasm.

The ruby eyed man had been asked to officiate, and Shiver was asked to be their witness. The ceremony was to take place on the west side of the chasm, and as soon as Fosalia appeared with the goswigs, Medolas and Clandestiny gave the priestess a hug and then quickly turned to face Gablysin.

"Let's get this moving," Shiver announced. "The priestess must hurry."

Gablysin lifted a book that held the customary vows that all Isorians spoke on the Peak of their union. "On this Peak, two Isorians vow to pledge their life's sources to one another."

Clandestiny held up her hand. "Gabs, stop."

Medolas pulled his gaze off the ruby eyed man to find Clandestiny's eyes. "Are you okay?"

"I am," she smiled. "I'm more than okay."

"Then why did you stop him?"

Clanny leaned in and kissed Medolas ever so softly on the lips. "Nothing about our relationship has ever been like any other. Why should we start now? I have one question, and one question only to ask."

Medolas liked the tone in her voice. He could not remember the last series of moments when Clandestiny looked this lovely. Her soft, blue skin was flawless, and it complemented the white of her garments and the gems on top of the veil she wore on her head. He decided to play along. "And what would this question be, my love?"

Clandestiny adjusted her body into the sexiest position she could muster. With her head tilted, she used her tongue to wet her lips. "My question is ... do you?"

Medolas' grin spread from ear to ear. "Oh, I do," he declared. "I do until the end of my last breath."

"Then kiss her already," Gablysin encouraged. "What are you waiting for?"

The first kiss of their union was filled with passion.

TO BE CONTINUED

Sneak Peek

Book 4
Crystal Moon
The Liberation of Trollcom
The Vampire Underworld
Early Bailem

With the rest of the vampire underworld hanging from the ceiling amidst the maze of tunnels that existed deep beneath the Mountains of Gannesh, this was the moment the Mischievous One had been waiting for. Everyone was asleep. The claws on their feet were dug into the stone, and if a noise could be heard, it would be that of a vampire snoring.

Lasidious had used his position as king to order the underworld to feast, and a banquet of corgans had been gathered by the minions of his army. With the blood of the beasts being distributed during a celebration of their queen's dedication to motherhood, it would not be until after Late Bailem before anyone would wake.

As the Mischievous One approached the cribs of Garrin and the Prince of Brandor, he took a moment to admire the work Yolan had put into this particular section of the cave. She had turned it into a peaceful place, despite the fact the earth was cool and dark. The children's nursery had been elegantly decorated, and Yolan had used a wonderful array of color to soften the harshness of the walls. She had even used a natural sealant to keep the moisture of the earth from seeping through.

Lasidious smiled as he stood between the cribs and looked at the faces of the boys. Yolan was a good mother. Even the blankets the babies had tucked around them exuded her love. The craftsmanship of their designs had taken the queen many moments to create.

Yolan had waited more than 100 seasons for Lasidious to deliver his promise, and she was not about to give her babies anything but a perfect home. With the children taking to the milk from her bosom, the boys had embraced the Vampire Queen as if she was, indeed, their mother.

Lasidious could only smile as he took a moment to allow himself to think about the joy the children had brought to Yolan's face, but the moments for reminiscing about fond memories were over. It was now or never. Something inside his mind was warning him not to wait. If his feeling was right, judgment could be brought down on him at any moment.

Reaching inside his tunic, the Mischievous One removed a knife. The blade was long and sturdy. He had created it just before he surrendered his position at the table inside the Hall of Judgment on Ancients Sovereign, and a sharper knife could not be found anywhere on this newly created world the gods had renamed Hell.

The handle of the blade was made of nasha wood—which was ironic—since the wood was from the same tree that bore the fruit to restore life. The handle was thicker than most. It had to be. Because on this morning, if it did not hold up under the pressure, the Mischievous One would not achieve his goal, and his sacrifice of godliness would be for nothing.

Taking a deep breath, Lasidious reached into Garrin's crib and pulled back the child's blanket. *I'm glad you've come to trust me, my son,* he thought. *Without it, my reascension would be impossible. This is what you were born for.* He paused and then sighed. *I do wish there was another way.*

Lifting the knife in front of his face, Lasidious took note of his reflection as he watched the mercy he felt for Garrin disappear from his eyes. A moment later, he gently lifted the baby's shirt and placed the blade against the child's sternum.

Books, apparel and other Crystal Moon products:

www.worldsofthecrystalmoon.com

Facebook:

www.facebook.com/worldsofthecrystalmoon

You can email Big Dog at:

Phillip.Jones@hotmail.com